I0760767

VALERIOS

ROAD TO MASTERY

1

aethonbooks.com

ROAD TO MASTERY
©2023 Valerios

Aethon Books
www.aethonbooks.com

Print and eBook formatting by Josh Hayes. Artwork provided by Bad Moon.

Published by Aethon Books LLC.

ALSO IN SERIES

Road to Mastery

Road to Mastery 2

Road to Mastery 3

Road to Mastery 4

CHAPTER ONE
APOCALYPSE DAY

JACK RUST GAZED AT THE MOUTH OF A CAVE, BLACK LIKE THE NIGHT AND BARELY wide enough for a grown man to push through. He clicked a button, and his flashlight burned to life, shooting a wide beam of light into the darkness, dispelling it.

Only rock walls met his sight. This place was a shallow slit in the hillside, but he knew that wasn't entirely the case—another researcher had stumbled upon it and called on Jack to look.

Of course, he thought. By all means, have me explore the dark, dirty cave. I love it.

Jack was an average-built man. His dark-haired head rose six feet from the ground, but he lacked the musculature to intimidate anyone. At least his younger years of sports left him with a slim, athletic build, though he didn't exercise anymore.

His body shape, along with his green eyes and kind smile, made him slightly handsome if you asked most people, or not at all if you asked girls named Maria, of which he had a particularly nasty streak.

It also made him quite suitable to investigate narrow, rocky crevices, which is why he was here instead of a person of lower seniority. He didn't like it, but alas—job called.

Still better than spending the entire day in a cramped lab full of smelly undergraduates.

Grumbling, Jack made sure the pockets of his cargo pants were secured. He surveyed the rocks, mapping out the sharp ones jutting out of the walls, then ventured forth. His body went sideways, eyes glued before him, watching out for errant spider webs or multi-legged annoyances.

Though he could fit pretty easily, the rocks wound tight around him. He felt trapped.

Fortunately, claustrophobia wasn't enough to stop Jack. If not, he wouldn't be here.

He was aware of the precautions. He'd rehearsed them mentally while crossing the nature reserve. If anything felt off, or if the crevice got dangerously narrow, he would go back. He prayed for that, actually; it would make this excursion a paid field trip.

Unfortunately, that didn't happen. A few feet ahead, the crevice opened into a cave fifteen feet across and nine to the side. Jack took out a device from his right pocket and let it inspect the air—it beeped twice; all clear.

Damn, he thought, but smiled. At least he'd make headway. If he discovered even a single female viper caterpillar here, they could mate it with the one they already had and create enough specimens to last. Plus, the cave looked pretty clean, as improbable as that sounded.

He also checked his featureless gray T-shirt. It appeared fine; hadn't been caught in any rocks, thankfully. Though simple, it was his favorite shirt.

Jack then swung his flashlight across the walls. If there were carapaced insects skittering around, he couldn't see them. It didn't matter. He'd only be here for a little while, and poisonous varieties weren't indigenous to this area.

He set his flashlight on a rock, letting it illuminate half the cave. He then removed a pair of gloves from his pocket, put them on, kneeled beside a patch of moss, and stuck his hands into it. As he idly ran his fingers over the rock, sensing nothing through the gloves, he released a sigh.

What am I even doing?

He was shuffling through moss in a tiny, dark cave in the middle of nowhere, trying so hard for something he didn't care too much about. Not that he didn't like his job. Being a biologist could be fun at times, and he even had a PhD—almost. He was financially set for life and with a job more interesting than most.

However, at the end of the day, it was just that—a job—and, if he was being honest, it didn't fill him. Not at all. It wasn't the life he dreamed about.

Jack had followed the yellow brick road. He'd done well at school, done well at university, then proceeded to get a PhD—well, almost. He'd taken all the expected steps and still ended up trapped. It was such a shame.

Maybe it was youth's boiling blood talking—the one he wasted every day. The clock kept ticking and would never go backward.

He shook his head. Unfortunately, the world was what it was. His thoughts were only pipe dreams brought forth by the novelty of exploring a small cave in the Greenway Nature Reserve. He had to survive, somehow, and having a job he didn't dislike was already better than most. There were bright sides. That was reality.

As the professor would say, everybody had to slave away, so why not do it at something interesting?

But he couldn't shake off the fantasy. Was this all life had to offer? Was he doomed to spend forty years of his life doing such tiny things, doomed to constantly suppress his inner desire for... something? Anything?

Jack was just a regular guy, and that brutal reality grained on his soul. It wasn't the rock walls that trapped him—it was everything else.

But there was nothing to be done. He understood that, and at the same time, hated it.

A bump on his fingers brought him back. A little green thing squirmed to escape, and like a hawk, he grabbed it. It was helpless in his hand.

Nice! he mentally exclaimed, raising it to take a better look. *A viper caterpillar!* Going by the color patterns, it was a female one, too. He'd found it.

Whistling in joy, he lowered the caterpillar and dropped it in a small jar he'd been carrying, twisting its lid closed before the little insect could escape. He then wiped his gloved hand on a nearby rock. He smiled. The trip here had taken a while, but it was worth it. At least the searching part had been short.

How long did it take me? Five minutes? Wow. There have to be more of them.

A conscientious worker would keep searching. Jack took one look at the upturned moss and shook his head. Maybe it was due to his previous, morose thoughts, but he didn't feel like doing anything. *We'll just wait a couple days for them to breed.*

He focused on the caterpillar in the jar. It was tiny and trapped. Just like him.

"What am I even doing..." he muttered, sighing. He didn't want to look for caterpillars in dark caves, just to return to his lab. He wanted to feel alive.

It was the millionth time he had that thought, and the millionth time he wasn't going to do anything about it. This time, the universe responded.

Sapience located. Starting Integration...
Branching Immortal System...
Welcome to the New World!

A shiny blue screen snapped into existence in front of Jack's face. He backpedaled—the screen followed—and accidentally stepped on the glass jar, breaking it under his boot. The caterpillar escaped. Jack's elbow met a sharp rock.

"Woah!" he shouted, more surprised than hurt.

A blue screen appeared in the air. That couldn't be right.

Before he could consider the issue further, the world shook. Rocks rumbled and groaned; the earth moaned underfoot. Jack paled. An earthquake was the worst thing to happen in a cave. He dropped to his knees and huddled around them, covering himself under a seemingly sturdy protrusion of the walls. The shaking intensified instead of stopping, and a bright cyan light blinded him again, making him hug his knees, pray for his life, and hope for the best.

A few rocks fell from the ceiling, but fortunately, not on him.

It felt like hours before the shaking stopped, though it couldn't have been more than a minute. When everything stood still again, as caves were supposed to do, Jack opened his eyes and met an impossible sight.

A small pond now lay where the far cave wall used to stand, along with a short waterfall sprouting from the rocks behind it. The water was so cold he could feel it even from a few steps away, but there was no ice on its surface. His flashlight had tumbled into the water—he could see it—but he didn't need it because the pond itself was shining. And had the cave grown larger?

Jack gaped. His mind failed to process the sight. *I'm in a dream*, he concluded. *This is where I wake up.*

But he didn't wake up. Instead, the blue screen kept rolling in his sight, spitting out line after incomprehensible line.

Terraforming complete.
Overseers informed.
Immortal System initiated. Think 'Status' to access your status screen.
Creating dungeons...

Status?

Name: Jack Rust
Species: Human, Earth-387
Faction: -
Grade: F
Level: 1

Physical: 4
Mental: 7
Will: 6

What... the... fuck...

Jack was a smart guy, as were most scientists. Unfortunately, no amount of mental muscle could prepare him for what was currently happening.

He struggled to put things in order.

I am fully aware. If this was a dream, I should have woken up by now, but I haven't. What the hell is happening?

Too many emotions warred inside him. Fear of the unknown, confusion, helplessness, and finally, an inexplicable relief he couldn't deny. He was drifting in a new sea, and, for some odd reason, he suddenly felt alive. He studied the blue screen in his face, the one apparently called 'status.'

This is like a videogame, he realized. Did AI finally conquer us?

He looked at the pond that shouldn't be there, wondering about a bunch of things. The blue screen obliged.

Ice Pond (E-Grade)

A hidden resource of the Forest of the Strong. The piercing cold of the Ice Pond can heal and forge a cultivator's body. The deeper you go, the more painful the cold, and the more effective the forging.

There were so many unknown words, Jack's head spun. The status screen before, the levels, the attributes... Had his world turned into a game?

One thought pushed all others apart. *Am I going to get magic? Fuck yeah!*

Every child dreamed of becoming a wizard. If reality suddenly malfunctioned or was altered by advanced nanobots, why not let him shoot fire too?

Relief and excitement flooded him again, even harder than before. He had no idea what was happening, completely lost in something that didn't make sense, but he didn't reject it. Without even knowing what was going on, Jack instinctively hoped it was true, that the world really had turned into a game and nothing made sense anymore.

Because, if that happened, he would be *free*.

The child inside him awoke. A grin spread on his cheeks, and he neither could, nor wanted, to stop it. Whatever was happening was dangerous, unknown, and something he could thrive in. His escapism fantasies had turned real.

Assuming this *was* real, he needed to rush to understand it. Thankfully, he was good with deciphering complex information. All he needed was time.

The world shook a second time. His vision swam for no reason. Odd smells suffused the space, bringing in mind a clean, strong breeze and fiercely swiping grass. New blue screens sprouted before him, and Jack felt an increasing need for them to fuck off. He'd had enough already.

Unfortunately, they did not fuck off.

1,111 dungeons created.
Monster spawning schema complete.
Integration complete.

Transmitting message from assigned Overlords, the Animal Kingdom (B-Grade):
Welcome to the System world. If your planet did not have magic before, it does now. Monsters and dungeons have spawned everywhere. You have been assigned attributes and Levels, and you have the capability to rise in strength by slaying strong creatures or deeply understanding the world.
We understand you are in a state of shock. Do not worry. Everything will be alright in the end. It is expected that your society will collapse soon, if not already, but you will be fine. We, the Animal Kingdom, will take care of those things.
For now, you should focus on becoming individually stronger. Hunt monsters, conquer dungeons, sink your mind deep into the world, and you will attain power greater than you can dream of. Embrace the new reality.
The first step to that power is the Integration Tournament, which will be held in twenty galaxy days (note: fifteen Earth-387 days) from

now. Comprehend even the tiniest corner of the world by then, and endless possibilities will open up for you.
Good luck, Animal Kingdom

You have entered the Forest of the Strong (F-Grade) Dungeon.
Forest of the Strong (F-Grade): A forest where only the strong survive. There are three monster groups, each holding a unique resource and representing a unique challenge. Slay the leader of a group to despawn them.

This Dungeon is in conquer-or-die mode. Defeat the Dungeon Boss to exit or die trying. We applaud your bravery for entering and wish you the best of luck.

...What? Aliens?

Jack scanned over the screens, barely understanding half of what he read. He was completely lost, so he grabbed onto the few things he knew. He was familiar with games. He knew how dungeons worked—they were special places teeming with monsters, where players could enter at great risk and accordingly great rewards.

Apparently, this new state of the world—the New World, if the blue screens were to be believed—shared many game-like elements, including dungeons. They'd probably spawned around the world.

Except...

We applaud your bravery for entering—Motherfucker! A dungeon spawned around me!

Jack was livid! As if he didn't have enough on his plate. He now had to kill some Dungeon Boss or die trying.

"This is a mistake!" he shouted. "I didn't enter on purpose. Let me out!"

Unfortunately, neither the blue screens nor the walls replied. Jack was left staring at the ice pond.

He crossed his arms. "I don't like this. At least give me magic."

Faint blue light coalesced out of nowhere by the lake. Jack was relieved—he might have been sabotaged, but at least, he was given magic!

As the light expanded and solidified, his hopes were dashed. This wasn't magic—well, it was, but not his. A short, green, humanoid creature with long ears appeared out of nowhere. It barely reached his chest and was fully naked, as well as skinny and bald. Jack thought it looked like a child.

It then turned around, and he almost screamed. This was no child.

Its mouth was unnaturally wide and filled with sharp teeth. Its nose was long like a finger, its hands sported short claws, and its yellow eyes were filled with malice. It grinned, while Jack could only stare.

Goblin, Level 2

Goblins are weak, primal humanoids who move in large groups. They are barely intelligent enough to cook their food, and they often derive pleasure from torturing their victims. Cultivators are advised to kill them on sight.

"Kekeke..." the goblin chuckled in a high-pitched, grating, evil-sounding voice. "Weak, tasty human... I will eat your legs first, kekeke..."

A myriad thoughts ran through Jack's mind. He was terrified of this creature. It wanted to eat him alive. He had to escape.

At the same time, a different part of his brain, the analytical one, couldn't help noticing how this System manipulated him. It spawned a man-eating monster right in his face, made it clear they were enemies, and said it was okay to kill it. Moreover, it gave the monster an ugly, terrifying visage, as well as opening lines that served to squash any doubts in his mind.

Jack had a PhD—almost—in biology. He knew how evolution worked. Nature was brutally efficient, not comically evil.

This creature was not natural. It was engineered. Fake. A target for him to kill or die trying. He didn't know why the System acted like this, but these were unarguable facts, because he'd spent half his life studying nature and the other half playing video games.

These thoughts snapped like firecrackers in his battle-addled brain. It took less than a second for all the connections to be made, and then came the realization that they were worthless.

He could only fight.

Now would be a good time for magic, he thought, but nothing came. He scanned around—no sharp rock for him to use. He carried no knife. His car key was electronic.

There were no weapons. There was also no time.

He got up and clenched his fists. The goblin pounced.

CHAPTER TWO
JACK VS. GOBLIN

THE GOBLIN RUSHED IN, AND JACK RUSHED BACK. IT WAS FASTER.

Claws raked Jack's forearm, which he raised to defend, drawing three thick lines of blood. He groaned—the pain shot fire into his nerves, jolting his entire body. The feeling was immediately subdued. Instincts he didn't even know he had kicked in, dulling the pain, translating it into fuel to push him forward.

He grabbed the goblin's wrist and tossed the entire creature away like a ragdoll, but it only took a few steps before regaining itself. It jumped right back into the fray.

Jack gritted his teeth as he surveyed the space around him. There was nothing he could use, not with a cursory glance. No rock, branch, or even a stick. And his flashlight was buried under the pond.

MAGIC! he screamed to the blue screens. If they could summon a goblin out of thin air, they could certainly give him the ability to shoot fire. Unfortunately, nothing happened.

The goblin was upon him again. Jack panicked, swinging wildly and missing, only clipping its shoulder. The impact was enough to push the little fucker away, but it returned with renewed force, and this time, its claws raked across his upper chest, barely missing his throat.

Jack paled. As the goblin jumped at him, sharp teeth about to tear him apart, time slowed. He was growing weaker. His heart shivered and the world closed in on the goblin—the little green ball of hatred that was going to kill him.

The realization settled in: *I am going to die.*

Suddenly, the world flared. Jack's entire potential as a human was unleashed and directed towards survival. His body surged with power, power he was already using but wasn't conscious of. He'd thrown the goblin many feet aside. He was strong, and it was just a little green ball of claws.

As death approached, something clicked in Jack's mind. His primal instincts stepped in and took the wheel. His thoughts rolled by themselves. He didn't care about injuries. So what if he bled? It was acceptable as long as he killed the goblin and lived to see another day.

The irrelevant disappeared. Jack got serious. He clenched his fist, and the raw power shocked him. His body outputted strength he couldn't even fathom. He felt fast, incredibly strong, and inexhaustibly tenacious. His pupils dilated. His skin tingled. All his muscles buzzed with electricity. The cold terror in his heart became a fuel that drove him. Fear gave way to ecstasy.

He was ready to fight. Jack became a beast.

He didn't know how to punch, but his body did. His fist smashed into the goblin's face, cracking its long nose and throwing it back before it could reach him—he possessed the longer arms, after all.

Jack became intently aware that his fist was in massive pain. Correction: his body didn't know how to punch, either. That didn't matter though.

Just as the goblin got its footing, he pounced. He would kill it.

He fell on it like a wild animal. He didn't care about the scratches he received, the pain, the blood. These all washed away into the back of his mind. He balled his fist and drove it into the goblin's face again, smashing it hard into a wall. It screamed, but the sound only gave Jack hope. He tried to pin the wily beast to the rocks, but it slipped under his grasp and jumped aside. Claws raked him again, cutting his belt—didn't care.

He stared at the retreating goblin, whose eyes were filled with hatred and fear, and charged after it, grinning. He didn't know what he felt, didn't need to. Everything was easy. The violence was rising from inside him, and he was its conduit.

There was something cathartic about violence, about the silence as every fiber of your being focused on a single task. Jack had never felt so complete, so happily monolithic. There were no worries or fears, only a body that brimmed with ecstasy and a cold, calculating mind that inspected everything at impossible speed.

Jack's shoes tilted to perfectly hug the uneven stone, and his body turned with impeccable balance. The goblin threw a feint, but Jack saw through it. As it turned, it didn't find a target, only a fist getting planted hard into its face.

The goblin flew off its feet and into the wall behind, losing its balance, and Jack was there. He pinned it to the ground and pummeled it, channeling the entirety of his newfound strength into repeatedly driving his fist into the goblin's face as hard as he possibly could.

Bones cracked and groaned—some his, some the goblin's. Every punch came in heavy, every strike devastating. The goblin resisted for a while before going still, yet Jack punched a couple more times and only then stopped.

Absentmindedly, he noted he was out of breath, in terrible pain, and several parts of his body felt wrong. His brain calculated everything with cruel precision. It reviewed his situation, then scanned his environment for solutions. His belt and pockets carried nothing of significance. He had to patch up the big wound on his forearm, where blood was flowing, and he had to do it now.

He tore his sleeve—how easy it was—and wrapped the fabric, tightening it so hard it hurt. His shirt was wet with blood at places, so he just removed it. There were more wounds on him, mostly insignificant—the goblin had missed all major arteries.

He was stable, and the enemy was dead. He was fine.

A single fluttering of relief filled Jack's heart, and his battle mode receded as quickly as it'd come. He was left shivering, cold, and breathless. The pain came in warm waves, and kneeling as he was, he failed to stifle a cry.

"FUCK!"

What the hell just happened?

The wretched sight of the goblin corpse entered his vision. He bent to the side and retched on the stone, the hot bile's burn accompanying the ones on his limbs and chest.

He cried.

It took a long time for Jack to regain himself. The pain receded, and the blood stopped flowing. Jack was left sitting on a rock, holding his head between his palms, and trying not to stare at the mangled goblin corpse.

He hated what he'd done. No—he wasn't sure what he felt. Trying to get his thoughts in order was futile.

So many things had happened, and in such a short timeframe. Blue screens had appeared, magic everywhere, a pond formed out of nowhere, a magically-spawned goblin tried to kill him, and he'd punched it to death.

Jack had a steady mind. He could comprehend the blue screens and their magic, or at least accept them. By now, he was aware it wasn't a dream. The world had changed irreparably. Be it aliens, AI, something else, or everything at once, *something* happened, and it had altered the course of his life forever.

He could work with that. He could fit it into the frame, somehow. Could even accept the fact that a dungeon had spawned around him, filled with goblins and who knows what else, and that he had to slay a so-called Dungeon Boss to escape.

Those were all things he could comprehend.

However, the version of himself he saw... That wasn't easy to swallow.

Those feelings saved him, but they'd come from somewhere deep inside him, a place he couldn't even perceive. They flooded him out of nowhere, and he had no control—they were part of him, and at the same time, weren't.

It wasn't a bad thing—he survived, after all—but he never before realized how deep the lightless region inside him was. How much control it could have over him.

Were those things part of him, or dark passengers?

Jack didn't know. His mind had been ravaged by an unknown companion, and its effects were still there. Even as he sat, away from immediate danger, he remained aware that more goblins could show up at any moment.

Whatever was happening, he had no time to lose, and the callousness permeated his mind even now. His eyes were hard as he stood. He had to survive.

He took in everything again. The goblin corpse no longer upset him now, at least to a degree, and he had things to consider.

So, no magic. The world has become a video game, and I'm trapped in a dungeon. OK. What now?

An exclamation mark was blinking in the lower left part of his vision, and he willed it open.

Level Up! You have reached Level 2.

That was it. No acknowledgment of his bitter struggle against the goblin, no words of compassion or comfort, no explanations. Only cold information.

Of course... He shook his head before proceeding.

First Kill Bonus: Fistfighting (I) skill!

That gave Jack pause. Skills were a common element in games, and the System seemed to follow those conventions pretty faithfully so far. Was it a coincidence, or something deeper?

And, at the end of the day, had the world really turned into a game? Had he been drawn into one? It didn't make sense, but it was hard to disagree with the goblin corpse in the corner. He couldn't ask anyone else either—his cellphone didn't have signal in the cave, and he sure as hell wasn't going out there unprepared.

He could only depend on himself.

Fistfighting... Curiosity sprang inside Jack. He reviewed his status screen.

Name: Jack Rust
Species: Human, Earth-387
Faction: -
Grade: F
Level: 2

Physical: 4 (+)
Mental: 7 (+)
Will: 6 (+)
Free points: 2
Skills: Fistfighting (I)

His level was 2, indeed, and it was clear the level up gave him two free points. He could add those in any of his stats, as indicated by the plus marks.

If this really was like video games, adding those points would make him faster or smarter. Taking a step further, he could make himself a better warrior or an... intellectual? Wizard?

Probably wizard.

He refused to believe there wasn't magic—he just didn't have it.

In video games, it was better to focus on one path. Better a master of one rather than a jack of all trades, even though his name was Jack. Given his current stats, coupled with his knowledge of himself, Jack was clearly more gifted in mental endeavors than physical ones. It also worked with his desire—and childhood dream—to one day wield magic.

Unfortunately, the fact remained that he currently possessed no magic or promises of getting it anytime soon. The only thing he had, besides the promise of more goblins, was the ice pond, an E-Grade natural resource, whatever that meant:

Ice Pond (E-Grade)
A hidden resource of the Forest of the Strong. The piercing cold of the Ice Pond can heal and forge a cultivator's body. The deeper you go, the more painful the cold, and the more effective the forging.

Even this pond only spoke about the body.

It was starting to dawn on Jack that he couldn't follow the path of magic. He needed something to defeat the Dungeon Boss and escape, and that something could only be his fists—or, even better, some weapon.

Before committing to anything, he focused on his only skill, Fistfighting. If this really worked like a video game, he could—*Aha!*

Fistfighting (I): Grants basic knowledge of fistfighting. While fistfighting, slightly enhances the user's physical attributes, reflexes, and kinetic vision.

It was promising, also ominous. If this skill's description was true, the System could mess with his entire body and brain... Jack didn't like that, though at this point, it was expected.

At least the skill was good. He clenched his left fist, confidence growing—he understood why he'd almost broken his right one on the goblin's face. He adopted a fighting stance—another gift of the skill—and punched the air, boxing against his shadow in the ice pond's glow.

He felt different. Stronger. Aware. He was like an amateur boxer—not really a master, but familiar with the movements alongside his body. Though it wasn't a stunning difference, if he met the goblin again, he was confident in demolishing it—well, more easily than before.

He chuckled darkly. How quickly I adapted...

There simply was no choice. He needed to adapt. Something was happening, and even if he didn't know what, it could kill him—*would*, if he let it.

I must get stronger.

This new skill was a great boon to his survivability—not just because it increased his attacking power, but mostly because it gave him better control over his body and awareness of the situation. He could avoid injuries, which was essential to his survival.

The only downside was that it required fistfighting, which meant he couldn't use a weapon... He didn't have one, anyway. He would fight with his fists, for now, and reconsider the issue when he found—or made—a knife. Any inferior weapon was incomparable to the fighting experience the skill offered.

That done, Jack returned to the issue of his stat points. Which was a no-brainer.

With a sigh, he allocated both points in Physical and a cold current, like a massive shiver, rose through his body. He tensed up, then realized this was his new normal. He was stronger, faster, and harder than before. He flexed his fist, and it felt steadier than ever.

It was impressive.

Being an expert in biology, Jack didn't have the slightest clue how this could happen. Just made no sense. If this improvement was what it promised—or rather, what his video game knowledge promised—it was a feat completely beyond the reach of modern science.

This System would somehow have to alter both his DNA and body structure, as well as spontaneously create a bunch of extra cells to fill in the gaps. All of these were impossible, and extremely worrying, because it meant the System had complete control over his body and, most probably, his mind.

It was a grim thought—almost grimmer than the goblin in the corner.

CHAPTER THREE
HELLO WORLD

Jack finally managed to process all the information. Not completely, but enough to proceed. He'd also killed a goblin, though he didn't like to think about that.

Gradually, a plan formed in his mind:

Leave the cave; Explore the natural reserve; Find water, shelter, and food, in that order; Survive until someone found him or kill the Dungeon Boss to escape.

A good plan, assuming everything really was game-like. The largest doubt he had was about the environment outside.

Before the Integration, as the blue screens called it, Jack had been in a small, hidden cave in the middle of the Greenway Nature Reserve. The System had called the dungeon Forest of the Strong, and given that the natural reserve was a forest, it was reasonable to assume the entire reserve had been dungeonified.

On one hand, that was good, because Jack had been here many times. On the other, it was a dungeon. Even the best of dungeons sounded worse than, say, his house.

Regardless, Jack now had his bearings, a way to fight, a basic awareness of the situation, and a plan. He was ready to survive harder than anyone ever survived before.

There was just one last thing to do. He set his sights on the ice pond. It promised a forging of his body, which sounded suspiciously nice. If he was going to fight for his life, he couldn't let this opportunity go. Moreover, it mentioned something about healing, and his entire body was still in pain and sore from the goblin fight. His right fist was also bruised and bloated.

Jack reached the pond in two steps. It was nine feet wide and stretched fifteen feet back, by Jack's estimation. A short waterfall was at its end, supplying cold water from a crack between the rocks.

From this distance, the chill was staggering. Jack could've been standing by a glacier. The water was still and extremely clean, letting him easily make out the rock bottom. He could even see his green eyes staring back at him from the surface.

Jack gulped. The smooth incline of its bottom made it inviting, but the cold was forbidding.

What if I get pneumonia? What if this water is full of bacteria?

Many doubts crossed his mind, but at the end, he was in a game-like situation. Mundane things like pneumonia were distant and inconsequential. The goblins were a much more immediate danger, and the pond could help him live through it.

He took a deep breath and removed his clothes, leaving on only his underwear to feel safe. He then stepped into the pond with his right foot.

And instantly thought he lost it. All feeling disappeared, leaving only a numbness and ten thousand frozen needles. His instinct screamed to remove his foot, which he did, and the cave's humid air was heavenly compared to that blitzing cold.

"Holy shit..."

Jack took a few breaths to regain himself, then inspected his foot. It was fine—no, more than fine. It was rejuvenated and sturdy as if brand-new.

Such an odd sensation. One he could only equate to taking a comfortably cold shower, except the rejuvenation was far more intense, and so was the cold. A magical equivalent of a cold shower.

Clearly the System hadn't lied—this was healing and forging—and Jack, having recovered from the cold, decided he had no choice.

"Fuck me."

He decisively stuck one foot into the lake, this time enduring the cold. He waited, and the feeling gradually receded, stabilizing to a level that was cold enough to be painful but not enough to be harmful.

It was safe.

Taking another deep, trembling breath, Jack put his other foot inside. When he got used to the cold again, he kneeled in the water to submerge more of himself. His teeth were clattering. He didn't dare sink any deeper, as he remembered the System's warning that the cold increased the farther he went. There was already a freezing current coming from the depths of the pond. A single step would increase the cold substantially, and he was already at his limit.

Jack's body spasmed. The cold was so piercing it caused him physical pain. His body demanded to get away, but his will resisted, holding himself steady. He could tell it was safe, at least for a little bit, and told himself it wasn't *too* cold.

The frigid temperature spread from his legs to his entire body. He was pale, but he could also sense a new sturdiness seeping in, enhancing him. His skin, flesh, and bones were filled with that cold, all shivering in pain and anticipation.

Finally, the cold settled and he got used to it. Through gritted teeth, he took a deep, deep breath. He couldn't help grinning. This pain was so self-improving it was almost addictive.

Almost. He'd gotten what he ought to.

Save for one thing. He stuck his right palm into the water, the one he'd injured against the goblin's soft bones. He couldn't stifle his scream. The cold assaulted his injured hand as if alive, surrounding it and submerging it in wave after wave of freeze.

Jack instantly lost all feeling, and this time, it felt dangerous. He had to pull away *now*.

He jumped back outside the lake, losing his footing by the drastic change in temperature and fell on his butt. His hand was slightly blue, but the bloating was already receding. It was much better.

Jack let his back meet the ground as he exhaled in relief, closing his eyes. The cave's relative warmth was massaging his entire body, the sensation so euphoric it nearly made up for the pain of the lake.

As he eyed the water, he shivered at the thought of entering again, but he had to. He briefly considered investing in Will at his next opportunity to handle the cold better and decrease the pain, but discarded the notion. How far he could go into a lake like this was dictated by how much cold his body could handle—meaning, his Physical. No matter how strong his willpower got, it wouldn't affect his bodily limits. Plus, he'd already locked his points into Physical—he'd just have to bear through the pain.

When his body grew more resilient, mostly through level-ups, he could go deeper into the lake and reap more benefits... Of course, that's if the lake lived up to its System description.

Ice Pond bonus: +1 Physical

It was a short message of great significance. Jack reviewed his status screen.

Name: Jack Rust
Species: Human, Earth-387
Faction: -
Grade: F
Level: 2

Physical: 7
Mental: 7
Will: 6
Skills: Fistfighting (I)

His Physical had increased by one sixth by simply stepping into a lake. One point didn't seem like much, but Jack had a mathematical mind—it was actually humongous!

Since his initial stats were 4,7,6 for the three stats respectively, he assumed the average was 5. Now, he was as strong as he was smart.

If I put those free points in Mental, would I be smarter than the Professor? he wondered idly, then chuckled and shelved the thought. No way.

Then again, my Physical started at 4, but it couldn't be below average. I'm a healthy young man. Is the average not 5? Or does it include other things besides humans? Is it not built around averages to begin with, and the human average would be 3.689 or something random like that?

Jack shook his head. It didn't really matter.

He then jumped upright, surprising himself. His body was vastly superior to what it used to be, and he even had the Fistfighting skill to augment him. Compared to when he met that goblin, he was a completely new person.

He eyed the tunnel leading upward, toward the surface. The world up there could be filled with monsters, terrors, and nightmares... but Jack was ready. He grinned.

Prepare yourself, world. Here I come!

Jack peeked his head out of the cave. "Gah!" he said, blinded by the sunlight. He rubbed his eyes and tried again.

A rocky surface stretched to his left and right—the hill over the cave. His front was occupied by interspersed trees and bushes, dense enough to be called a forest, but sparse enough for people to walk in between. The trees reached from nine to eighteen feet into the air, their trunks a dark brown and leaves a bright green. The bushes were paler in color, and mostly filled with annoying sticks and spikes.

There was the occasional berry hanging down, maybe the rare fruit, too, but the nature reserve was pretty empty overall.

That is, unless the System had anything to say. Jack hoped it wouldn't.

His current shelter was a crack in the rock, seemingly shallow but actually leading to a hidden cave. Not an easy to find place. Maybe that's why the System put the ice pond inside it. A hidden bonus, of sorts, for those willing to explore—a bonus that would save Jack's life.

With that comfort in the back of his mind, it was time to see the outside world.

The first thing he did was take out his cellphone, an old Samsung model, and give it a shot—there was no signal at all. *Yeah, thought so.*

Like the System would let me call the police. After placing it, his electronic car key, and his wallet in a hidden crevice of the rocks, he looked around.

Seeing no animals or goblins nearby, Jack took a tentative step outside, then another.

The air smelled the same as always—wet grass and crisp breeze. The grass parted easily under his feet, and the tree barks were uneven under his hand. Insects buzzed in the air, animals yelped from afar, and leaves fluttered in the wind—one even flew to his chest. Everything was as he remembered.

Was it all a hallucination? he wondered. Did the earthquake release gasses in the cave?

A blur shot past his line of sight, darting from bush to bush. Jack caught a glimpse of its bushy, orange tail and triangular snout.

Fox, Level 1

Foxes are mostly harmless omnivores that inhabit forest areas.

Not too talkative now, are we?

Compared to the goblin's description, the fox's was tiny. It was clear the System either didn't know or didn't care about them—probably the latter.

Regardless, even this bit taught Jack many things.

His communication with the System was still on. It was aware of the local wildlife. And, most importantly, foxes were level 1—or somewhere around there. This was interesting, because understanding the level classification was crucial to Jack's survival.

The goblin was level 2 and could threaten an adult human. The fox was level 1 and could possibly threaten an adult, but not quite as much as the goblin. Then, were adult humans between levels 2 and 4, with the average at 3?

Sounded elegant. Of course, for every problem, there was a solution that was simple, easy, and wrong.

Jack himself had been level 1 when he beat the goblin, but that couldn't be accurate. He'd been stronger than it—not by much, but stronger nonetheless. It didn't make sense for the goblin to be higher-leveled than him.

Am I on a different scale than everything else? Is it because I can level up while they can't? Or, maybe, everything can.

He shook his head. The more he considered the issue, the more questions came up—which was good, because that's how knowledge was supposed to work. If he could see through the System at a glance, it probably wouldn't be a good System.

Thankfully, he didn't need to know much right now.

After my power-ups, I can fight level 3 creatures and should probably run away from level 4s. I need more samples to understand the power curve, though.

Insects and a squirrel didn't trigger the System's response, giving at least a good estimation about the lower bounds of level 1. Armed with that knowledge, Jack set out to explore.

Well, explore was a generous term. He had to find water, shelter, and food. He already had the second. As for water, the reserve had plenty of creeks to choose from. It wouldn't be too difficult.

First on his agenda was seeking a path to escaping the nature reserve—or, at least, confirm that dungeons were as inescapable as they sounded. If he stayed here for a month and someone came and said, "oh, why didn't you just walk away," Jack would feel like an idiot.

Angling himself south, the closest edge of the nature reserve that probably overlapped with the dungeon, Jack set out. In the process, he kept his eyes open, not only for goblins but also for everything else. The wildlife was abundant in the reserve, letting him make several observations.

First, plants didn't register with the System. The weakest animal he found at level 1 was a big crow, and the strongest a boar he spotted from afar at level 4. He was getting a hang for what levels meant, though it wasn't easy to set in stone.

Thankfully, his forest experience came in handy. It allowed him to cross the terrain stealthily, not raising the ire of any creatures. He knew when and where to hide, which animals were aggressive, and which weren't. There weren't any natural predators in the reserve, at least not for humans, so it was smooth sailing.

Being a biologist had its perks. Jack focused on insects, of course, the testbed of evolution, but he knew a bit about everything.

Excluding goblins.

Luckily, he could get to know them quickly enough, as three were approaching. He could hear them through the bushes.

CHAPTER FOUR

BIG, AGGRESSIVE PRISON MATES

JACK HELD HIS BREATH AND KEPT HIMSELF LOW, HIDING IN A BUSH. THE GRATING voices were approaching—three of them—and he could tell from their wicked cackles they were up to no good.

"Kekeke, me bite."

"Me bite too!"

"The leg is mine!"

"No, mine!"

The goblins weren't just ugly and in bad taste, they were also exceedingly stupid and stealthy like elephants. They were crossing the forest as if they owned it—which they might, for all Jack knew—speaking freely and paying little to no attention to their surroundings. Said attention was reserved for the bloodied fox carcass they carried, from which they occasionally pinched pieces of meat to devour, fur and all.

Their sharp claws tearing through the flesh and sharp teeth chomping with gluttony, his distaste for these goblins only grew. They were repulsive beings, an affront to any possible concept of beauty. His stomach turned, but he held it in until they disappeared, completely oblivious to his presence.

Poor fox... he thought, shaking his head. Nature had its ways, but nobody deserved to die to such distasteful creatures. The fact he'd almost suffered the same fate didn't escape his notice.

The goblins had been levels 2, 2, and 3 respectively. He could probably take each of them individually, just not all at once. Though Jack was coming to understand his plan moving forward—or rather, the rules of the game.

The goblins were weak, stupid, and hateful. They were the perfect grinding stone for a lone human trapped in the dungeon. He could hunt them down for levels relatively easily and without many moral setbacks.

Jack didn't for a moment believe this was a coincidence. Everybody had an agenda, which probably included alien systems or whatever this was—and that's without even mentioning how blatantly engineered these goblins were. They were the perfect mobs.

That left Jack with a question. The dungeon description mentioned three groups of monsters and a Dungeon Boss. If goblins were one group, what about the rest? And what about the Dungeon Boss?

If I really have to fight this dungeon, I should scout the other groups before making a move on the goblins. Information is power.

Right now, the goblins didn't appear to be on to him—how could they? Moreover, going by game patterns, the other two groups would be of similar strength. He should research before committing to something.

Again, information equaled power.

Jack's cave was in the southern part of the Greenway Reserve, slightly to the west. Since the goblins were heading south with their prey, that was probably their headquarters. Therefore, Jack changed his previous plan and headed west instead of south. Reaching the edge of the reserve that way would take a little more time, but it was better than running through a bunch of green-skinned man-eaters.

No other goblins appeared as he made his way through thin trees and wide bushes. The only notable thing was the impossibly wide, impressively futuristic, shimmering blue wall that rose from the ground where the reserve ended, stretching to the sky and fading after some point. It extended as far to the right and left as Jack could see at an almost imperceptible curve, presumably enclosing the entire reserve.

"Fuck me..." The blue thing was opaque too, so he couldn't see outside. "I really am trapped... unless I can go through."

He grabbed a stone and tossed it at the blue wall. It bounced off. He threw another stone, harder, and it was catapulted backward with such force, Jack barely managed to pull his head out of the way. The stone zoomed past and buried itself in an unlucky bush.

"No escape, got it."

His gaze traveled up again, to where the blue wall faded away and only air remained. It must have been at least sixty feet high.

Can planes go through, then? he wondered. Can birds? Can Superman?

He did his best to throw another stone that high up. He succeeded on the third try, then watched the stone bounce against a patch of blue that solidified out of thin air. It fell back down with a small thud, and when Jack grabbed it, the stone was hot to the touch.

"Only looking, no touching... No way out, then."

He considered touching the wall, but the System had already informed him he was stuck here until he got the Dungeon Boss. Calling its bluff sounded like a terrible idea.

I'm trapped. Suddenly, his chest tightened, and panic welled up inside him. He forced it down. Deep breaths, he repeated several times to himself. I'm trapped. I have to fight and level up until I can beat the boss, no matter what it is. Either that or die trying. So, fight now, existential crisis later.

Jack steeled his resolve and forced himself to focus on the here and now. What were his next steps?

Right. Scout out the other monster groups. Maybe they'll be easier than the goblins.

With the goblin headquarters likely in the south, the other monster groups would be to the north and... east? Unless they were all jumbled up, of course, but Jack doubted that. It didn't mesh with the game mechanics he was familiar with.

I'll be on guard, in any case.

Therefore, Jack turned his back to the wall of his new prison and moved deeper inside the reserve, where he'd come from. He could have followed the wall, of course, but its sight upset him greatly. He wanted nothing to do with it.

After the blue wall disappeared in the tree branches, he turned north, keeping his eyes and ears open for any change. Crossing the entire reserve would take hours on foot, and there were monsters out there trying to kill him. He would be damned if he let them.

While traveling, he wondered how he'd adapted so quickly, how he'd accepted magic, goblins, and reality becoming a game. Had the System messed with his mind?

He didn't think so, though it'd already proved to clearly possess the power. Something inside him just latched on to the change, a part of him desperately hoping for his smothering reality to crumble. Maybe due to how trapped he'd felt in his life; or, maybe, because of how many times he'd fantasized about similar scenarios as a teenager. The world had just gone to shit, everything he knew was thrown out the window, and though there possibly were dull, realistic explanations refuting magic, deep in his heart, Jack wished this was all real.

He didn't fear the danger. He simply felt alive. Like this was how things were supposed to be.

He didn't have much to lose, anyway. His friends could probably handle themselves, and he had little family. He was only worried about the professor, but... she would manage. She was smart. If anybody could find a way to survive in a new world, it would be her, even despite her old age.

As for himself, there was nothing holding him back. If everything returned to normal, he only had a dull life to look forward to. He would get his PhD, work his ass off as a researcher for thirty-five, forty years, then retire. At least he liked biology, but it didn't fill him. It wasn't enough.

This was. Stalking goblins through a forest.

Life is so weird... He shook his head, refocusing. He wasn't safe here. He couldn't afford daydreams.

It was only a moment later that a faint growling reached his ears. Jack froze. Nothing in this forest was supposed to growl. His mind went through all possible animals before settling on one.

Slowly, as quietly as he could, he got on the ground and crawled inside a bush. It scratched him, but he couldn't care less. Inwardly, he prayed the creature would move away. He'd made a mistake. The other monster groups weren't as weak as the goblins. The System had cheated.

An animal made its way into his field of vision. He could barely make it out through the branches—a brown behemoth, putting tremendous weight on the ground with each step. He also caught sight of yellow flashes on its fur, but he was too far away to discern them. Not that it mattered—a bear didn't need magical enhancements to maul him.

Earth Bear, Level 15

Bears are omnivorous creatures that stand at the apex of most food chains. Earth Bears, in particular, are a stronger, highly territorial variant. They can use very limited earth magic, and the rocky parts of their fur can be used to craft F-Grade weapons and armor.

Earth Bears are most commonly found in the Ursus Forests of planet Ursi.

It wasn't heading directly toward Jack at least, but the mere sight of a bear froze him solid. He couldn't even shiver or breathe.

If it sees me, I'm dead.

That would be the end of it. There was almost no way to escape a bear in the forest. The wise song came to mind:

If it's brown, lie down. If it's black, fight back. If it's white, goodnight.

Well, this one is brown, but also magical. I guess if it's magic, fucking fantastic.

Jack's thoughts screeched to a halt when the bear stopped and raised its snout to sniff the air. He panicked.

I'm sweaty; can it smell me? Did the bush scratch me? Can it smell my blood? It probably can. Oh, God, I'm so dead.

He considered bolting, but again, he couldn't escape a bear in the forest. They could even climb trees—at least, the non-magical variant could, and he wasn't willing to test this unless he had to.

His mind worked at great speed developing plan after plan to somehow survive. His entire body trembled with tension.

Eventually, the bear lowered its head and kept going. Jack couldn't believe his luck. When it disappeared and the sounds of its growling faded, Jack was left panting and terrified.

I'm trapped in a forest with bears.

This brought everything under a new perspective. Not only was there great danger, the bear wasn't even the Dungeon Boss. The level range of this dungeon had just risen precipitously. There had to be level 20 creatures at the very least, and that's assuming this particular bear was the leader of its group, which didn't seem too likely.

Plus, there was still a third monster group, which could be even stronger than the bears. That seemed unlikely, but so what? For all Jack knew, the System could have spawned kung-fu tigers in the north-eastern part of the reserve. Even risking a glance at the third group felt idiotic.

Sweat pooled out of him until he drenched the soil. Escaping this dungeon now seemed impossible, and even surviving until someone rescued him was unlikely. His arrogance was stomped to the ground and shit on.

I have to survive.

Jack headed back. In this game-like environment, there was a clear path forward. He no longer cared about how premeditated these goblins were, or what the System's agenda was for guiding his actions.

There was only one way to survive, and it was called "kill a shit-ton of goblins."

CHAPTER FIVE

BEATING THE SHIT OUT OF STUFF

Jack Rust sat on a branch, waiting. Strips of fabric were wrapped around his fists and knuckles, courtesy of his now-ruined shirt, so they wouldn't break or bleed.

He'd considered making a weapon, but the Fistfighting skill's enhancements were too good to pass up. A spear was only nice until you tripped and impaled yourself. Plus, his fists were more than enough for the task.

Below, his victims approached, unaware of the human predator eyeing them.

They were green, ugly, and wickedly stupid. The three goblins were arguing over a piece of wood—a club, probably, though it looked like a fallen branch.

They had no idea what was coming.

As they passed nine feet below Jack's perch, he took a deep breath and fell on them.

The sight of the earth bear and the ramifications it implied sharpened Jack's resolve. He was on fire now, in a race against time. He couldn't afford to hesitate.

The nine-foot fall was long, but Jack broke it on the back of an unsuspecting goblin. His fists were clenched, and his Fistfighting skill helped him make the landing, though he had to roll once—that wasn't the skill, he could always do it.

Jack and the goblin collided with a heavy thud, and the poor greenskin was driven into the ground hard enough to break its neck. Jack rolled, stood, and grinned.

One down, two to go.

The other two goblins were surprisingly quick on the uptake. Before their comrade had even stopped moving, they were already screaming and pouncing at Jack, claws extended.

Goblin, Level 2
Goblin, Level 3

He grimaced. The goblin he'd just killed had also been level 3. Unfortunately, he didn't have time to observe them fight beforehand. He assumed the level 3 goblin would be faster than its brethren, which was true, but he completely underestimated the world of difference.

The fucker was *fast.*

The attack was almost instant, claws blitzing to tear him apart. Jack defended by punching back. His reach was significantly longer, given that the goblins were child-sized, so he should win this exchange.

Unfortunately, the goblin was slippery. His Fistfighting skill only provided basic familiarity with the movements, and the goblin slipped under his punch to enter his guard. Jack panicked. His battle mode activated in full throttle. His veins were filled with steel, and his entire body felt on fire while his mind turned ice-cold. His eyes widened to take in everything. The world slowed down.

The goblin remained fast.

A set of claws raked his chest, while another went for his eyes, only narrowly missing. The chest attack hit dead-on, but no blood came out. With a grin, Jack's knee rose to meet the goblin's face and catapulted it backward.

This time, he was prepared to fight—and, though he couldn't use a weapon without sacrificing the skill's bonuses, he could wear armor. A layer of bark decorated the inside of his half-torn shirt, protecting against the goblins' short claws. They could have seen it if they weren't stupid.

The second goblin arrived as soon as the first went flying. It screeched, grabbing his leg before he could knock it away. Its claws pierced skin and drew blood, and it refused to let go when Jack pulled his leg back, intent on maiming him. It opened its jaws wide and lunged in for a bite.

That wasn't a very good idea.

Jack's fist bashed onto the goblin's head like a meteor, smashing its mouth shut. It stumbled, still weakly holding onto Jack's leg right under the thigh, but a brutal punch to the face threw it back, forcing it to let go. Thin bones bent under Jack's fist. The goblin didn't stand back up.

Thankfully, it had missed the major artery in his thigh.

He turned around with an elbow already striking out, trying to hit the other goblin before it surprised him, but it wasn't there. A hard strike to the back of Jack's head brought stars to his eyes. He fell forward, instinctively rolling to the side and avoiding a second attack.

Motherfucker...

The level 3 goblin, bleeding from where its long nose had been broken, was now wielding the branch-turned-club. It lunged at him again, shouting a grating "Kekekeke!"

Jack, still on the ground, blocked with his forearm and it cracked under the impact. He growled, seeing red. The world was swimming, he was in pain and deadly danger, yet his heart was filled with rage. He gave in to the beast, letting violence take over.

The goblin smashed its club down again, and Jack defended with the same arm, sensing it crack further. He lunged at the goblin before it could retract its heavy weapon and grabbed the top part of its face. Twisting around with the goblin in hand, he put a leg behind its knees and smashed its head into the ground. Hard.

The club left its hand as the goblin screamed, and Jack screamed back, right in its face. Sharp jaws bit his palm, ripping a piece of flesh—he didn't care. When the goblin tried to rise, he drove a left punch into its face. Its head bounced off the ground, but its level wasn't for show.

Despite the heavy hits, it was still kicking and clawing. Crimson lines appeared on Jack's arms, along with a thin one on his cheek, right below his eye. Jack remained relentless. If he stopped now, the goblin would stand back up.

He braced through the claws and kept pummeling. He roared like an animal. His fists rained on the goblin's face, each punch jolting its head to the left and right. The goblin's throes weakened—and then, with a tremendous burst of strength, it rolled under his feet and jumped upright beside him.

It tried to run away, but Jack couldn't let it. If even one goblin escaped, the entire tribe would learn about him, and he would die.

Even as it tried to run, Jack grabbed its ankle and pulled it back—the beast was light. With a massive roar, he raised the entire goblin over his head like a club and smashed it head-first against the ground.

The head exploded, painting the dirt red and decorating it with brain matter.

Jack plopped to the ground, staring at the dead goblin with horror. As the battle fever died down, he realized what he'd done. It was necessary but so madly brutal...

I did this.

He puked. *I did this*, he kept thinking, spiraling into guilt and disbelief. *I did this...*

It wasn't about killing the goblin. It wasn't even about the brutal way of doing so. These were all necessary, and Jack had already come to terms with it before attacking.

No, what terrified him was the mad rush of satisfaction he felt while doing it. Fighting these goblins, he was *alive*. When he let go of everything, the increased brain activity and awareness, as well as the feeling of omnipotence his body gave, were almost ecstatic. When he smashed the goblin like an octopus, he wanted to roar in triumph.

These were the same feelings he'd experienced against that first goblin in the cave. Only, back then, they'd been overshadowed by the fact he'd killed something and all the new information he received. Now, these feelings were laid bare, and he had to face them.

At least his injuries weren't too deep, and his enhanced body was quick to stop bleeding.

Jack stayed there for a while, struggling to get his thoughts in order. An increasing panic and a desire to run away threatened to spill over, but he forced himself to calm down. Eventually, he succeeded, at least to the extent where he could think and operate as normal.

He stumbled away and back to his cave, then sat near the entrance. He took a few deep breaths.

Transitioning from a researcher to a forest killer wasn't easy.

Jack was in control though. The emotions were too many to comb through quickly, but he wasn't overwhelmed after the initial onslaught. The same drive that pushed him to survive no matter what, now helped him put himself in order.

He'd known this was coming. He could handle it. He just needed a bit of time.

The minutes ticked by for Jack, turning into hours. In his mental self-healing state, time had lost its meaning as recovery took priority. His entire being was focused on digesting the brutal reality that the modern world didn't let people experience.

Now, Jack was speed-running it. The experience was harrowing but necessary—and, thankfully, he could handle it.

No, not just handle it. He would *thrive* in it. He could feel it in his bones. This was where he belonged. This was him.

Transitioning wasn't easy, but he would get there.

Jack kept comforting himself until the sun hung low in the sky. He was better, and all at once, terribly thirsty. The back of his head hurt like hell, and his stomach was empty enough to burn.

Shit! I forgot to find water!

He had shelter—his cave—but water was the single most important resource. Without food, he could survive for weeks. Without water, not even a couple days. It just hadn't crossed his mind before.

There was a creek nearby. The water wasn't too potable, but it would do—stomach and intestine problems were better than dehydration. He would even drink his own piss if he had to.

The only thing he wouldn't drink—besides saltwater, the only fluid that doesn't help dehydration—was the ice pond. He suspected it was something more than simple water—something magical—and that its freezing cold would persist inside his stomach, destroying him from the inside out.

At least, he wouldn't take the risk unless he had no choice.

He could always capture a small animal and experiment, but... Jack had his bottom lines. Killing man-eating goblins was fine. Torturing innocent animals was not. At least while he could help it.

He stood up to head to the creek, but before that...

Level Up! You have reached Level 3.

Another cold announcement, product of an unfeeling System that pitted living creatures against each other. Jack shook his head, then opened his status screen and put both free points into Physical, raising it to 9. He intended to invest in Mental as well—it should help with everything, including his unstable mental state—but not yet. Not when he almost died every time he battled.

The familiar surge of power passed over his body. He was stronger, faster, healthier. By now, he was already at the level of a professional athlete, if not past that, and all it took was four goblins...

His status screen reminded him of how many things he didn't know yet. What were factions? Grades? He'd seen F before in the dungeon description, and the ice pond was an E-Grade resource, but what exactly did that mean?

More importantly, his species was referred to as *Human, Earth-387.* This clearly implied the existence of multiple Earths, possibly multiple intelligent species.

Was the System really alien? Did it refer to a galactic empire or an inter-dimensional one, where many variations of Earth existed? Maybe that Animal Kingdom? Then again, if intelligent species existed on other planets, why wouldn't they name their planet Earth? It literally meant dirt. It could be the most common planet name in the galaxy.

But yes. Water. Then, Jack would revisit the ice pond to try and get extra bonuses—after his level up, he might be able to take an extra step—and then, goblin-hunting.

By the end of it, he would be a superhuman killing machine. The thought should have been terrifying.

Why did he feel excitement instead?

CHAPTER SIX
THE HIGH GOBLINS

THE GOBLIN TRIBE WAS A BUNDLE OF MISSHAPEN WOODEN HUTS, UGLY GREEN forms, and burnt animal carcasses. Just placing it in a forest was an affront to nature.

Jack squinted from the bush he hid in. After reaching level 3, healing himself, and satiating his thirst, he'd decided to gather more information before launching his anti-goblin campaign. There was some time before nightfall, anyway.

He'd located a goblin squad—it wasn't difficult—and followed it to the tribe. After cresting a hill, the ugly visage greeted his sight, and there were many things to notice.

First, there were many dozens of goblins. These guys had a full-on village going.

Second, there weren't just goblins. Jack spotted a few off-green forms, paler and larger than their goblin brethren. These were the size of short humans, had dark hair—goblins were bald—and walked with a sharpness that belied intelligence.

Hobgoblin, Level 6

Stronger, meaner, and smarter than normal goblins, hobgoblins are

an evolved version of the same ugly monster. It is advised to kill them on sight, but they should not be underestimated.

The System's description was short as always, filled with details Jack could already discern. The only real information was their level. After scanning all hobgoblins within sight, Jack determined them to be level 6 or 7. Normal goblins ranged from level 1 to 5.

In Jack's most recent estimation, he could fight a level 4 goblin head-on, maybe even a level 5 if he was lucky. Hobgoblins should be outside his reach, so he was glad they weren't participating in the hunter squads.

In short, Jack was incredibly weaker than the goblin tribe.

Moreover, the largest problem wasn't the hobgoblins, but their leader.

Goblin Shaman, Level 9

Goblins aren't always stupid. Some of them are born intelligent, and when that happens, they often develop shamanic powers. Goblin Shamans can lead small tribes of goblins and hobgoblins, though they're usually seen as elite soldiers in larger tribes.

This Goblin Shaman is the group boss.

The leader of the tribe wasn't a hobgoblin, but a goblin dressed in ruined robes. It cackled like the rest of them, but even the arrogant hobgoblins made way for it—the flames that danced on its fingers brewed respect.

Moreover, its eyes carried a cunning glint that was hard to miss.

Jack admitted that fire-slinging enemies challenged his current experience. Goblins were fine. Hobgoblins would also be fine, eventually. However, this shaman would prove to be a pain in the ass; he just knew it.

"Fire in the forest?" he whispered with a tsk. "So much for an omniscient, omnipotent, intergalactic System. Can I get a refund, please?"

No reply came his way. The System wasn't the most talkative of partners.

However, there was one thing that was even more impressive than the shaman. The goblins were high. Not tall—*high*.

A wide, short bush stood in the middle of the tribe, sporting long, thin leaves. Some goblins were gathered around it, chatting and cackling without making much sense, while occasionally snapping off a leaf to chew on. They weren't eating it, just licking it before dropping the remainder on a big pile.

The eyes of these goblins were completely red, they toppled over whenever they tried to stand, and wouldn't stop laughing. On closer inspection, many goblins were carrying a few of those leaves or munching on them, just measuredly. The ones falling all over themselves were probably on their day off.

High Speed Bush (F-Grade)
A resource guarded by the goblins of the Forest of the Strong. Commonly found in the wet jungles of planet Peruvian, the leaves of this bush can enhance a person's reflexes, dexterity, and agility. They can also make you high as a kite.
The stat increase is a one-time bonus.

I just knew things couldn't be simple... Damn you, System. Can't you at least destroy my planet with decency? Did you need to drag weed-licking goblins into this?

The System, again, didn't reply, and Jack could only keep observing the goblin camp. There wasn't much else to see—he already had more than enough.

He slowly made his way back, keeping an eye out for guards—which were non-existent, as the goblins apparently felt safe. On the way, he processed all the new information, as he often did lately.

The goblins aren't just strong, they have intelligent leaders... Which means if I keep picking them off, they'll catch on. Therefore, I must get as many of them as possible before they're on to me. I can't afford to take it slow.

However, when they do catch on, will I be strong enough to face them? Probably, if it comes to guerilla tactics. If I can reach level 6 or so, I should be able to handle hobgoblins, especially if I set up an ambush... but they'll eventually get me.

This sounded like a pickle, but Jack recalled the dungeon description—any previous blue screen could be willed into reappearing, apparently.

Forest of the Strong (F-Grade): A forest where only the strong survive. There are three monster groups, each holding a unique resource and representing a unique challenge. Slay the leader of a group to despawn them.

This dungeon is in conquer-or-die mode. Defeat the Dungeon Boss to exit or die trying. We applaud your bravery for entering and wish you the best of luck.

The last paragraph's sarcasm aside, there was one important clue hidden in there.

Slay the leader of a group to despawn them... So, if I kill the shaman, all the goblins will simply go poof. That's almost too good to be true.

On second thought, it wasn't. It was a double-edged knife. Monsters—in this case, goblins—were dangerous, but they were also walking bags of levels. An equilibrium was shaping in Jack's mind: the later he assassinated the shaman, the more danger he would face, but the more goblins he would be able to kill before they disappeared.

After all, there was no way the System would reward him for the creatures he despawned. It wasn't that kind.

Jack needed the levels. There were level 15 magical bears in the forest, along with their group leader and a third group of monsters which could, potentially, be even stronger than the bears. There was also the Dungeon Boss, an existence undoubtedly stronger than anything else.

If Jack wanted any chance against them, he needed levels, he needed wits, information, and battle experience—the only thing he had so far was pants. The goblins could provide most of those. He couldn't afford to take it easy. He had to gamble.

Jack would try to drag on the conflict as long as possible, and when things got insufferable, he would assassinate the goblin shaman. Certainly risky, perhaps too risky, but it was the only long-term plan he could come up with.

He could also just hide and hope for someone to save him, but he somehow doubted the System would let him escape that easily.

Therefore, Jack made his decision. He would wage war on the goblins—possibly a genocide, too. Was he evil for thinking that way? Maybe. Was he justified? Probably, since they clearly wanted to eat him too. Was it necessary? Absolutely fucking yes.

Jack Rust refused to die.

But, before waging his war, he needed to find food.

Jack held the rabbit carcass tenderly. It pained him to kill an animal like this, but he had to eat something...

At least he'd killed it painlessly. He'd found a den under a tree soon after night fell, then dug behind it to scare the occupants. As soon as the rabbits rushed outside, he grabbed one, and before it could understand what was happening, snapped its neck. It was easy, like snapping a twig, and Jack grew forlorn at his new power and the way he used it.

When he killed the goblins in heated battle, he felt triumphant. This time, he was empty... Still, hunting was a part of nature, and it was more ancient than compassion.

Jack shook his head to clear it. This new reality was grim, but he had to accept it.

He was currently standing over the ice pond, holding the carcass. He was going to light a fire and roast it, but he thought that maybe the lake's body forging properties could be transmitted through food. It was a theory he needed to test, as he couldn't afford to let anything go to waste.

Besides, the freezing cold might have a purging effect on harmful microorganisms. It was magical, after all, so why not? The cold didn't stick to his body when he left the lake, so it probably wouldn't stick to the rabbit's, either. If it did, he'd just have to go hungry.

He gently dipped the rabbit into the water, feeling the numbness on his fingers. Nothing happened, except for its fur turning slightly whiter, and that was it. When he withdrew it, the rabbit was cold to the touch, but no other difference could be seen.

He let it sit for a while and confirmed that the cold was seeping out. That was good, because it meant he wouldn't freeze to death, and bad, because it meant his body wouldn't be forged. He shrugged.

Well, good to know.

He went outside, a ways off the cave entrance, and lit a fire under the moon—he'd prepared tinder beforehand. He wasn't particularly familiar with cooking rabbits on campfires, but he had cooked a lot in his life, so he had some ideas. If he messed up, his 9 Physical would hopefully pull him through.

In the night, the fire's smoke couldn't be seen, so he only worried about the firelight itself attracting unwanted visitors. The goblins were already gathered at their tribe when night fell, and bears weren't nocturnal—and, even if they were because of magic, they had no reason to be in this area.

That left the final monster group, but Jack didn't believe they would turn out to be nocturnal wanderers. Nocturnal, maybe, but not wanderers—and, if they were, he'd just face them. He had to cook at some point. Doing it now was certainly better than doing it mid-day when the goblins could easily spot his smoke and come knocking.

Jack cooked for a while, enjoying the night sky in silence. It was beautiful. Maybe the System had magically removed all air pollution and shut down the lights, but Jack could see the sky as his ancestors did. Stars shone everywhere, ten thousand sparkling dots, and a long river of light stretched between them—the galaxy—farther and larger than the mind could comprehend.

It wasn't just beautiful, Jack corrected himself. It was breathtaking. He was sitting under the infinite cosmos.

Is this what the ancients saw every night... he wondered, and its beauty was so striking that, for a moment, Jack wondered whether the System's arrival was a good thing.

He idly realized that, against such a night sky, his smoke was visible, as it hid the starlight behind it. He shrugged. If the goblins made the connection and came over, let them.

Time passed with only the crackling of fire and the sizzling of juices on the burning logs keeping him company. The forest was quiet, most nocturnal animals still shivering in fear from the arrival of the monsters, and only some birds dared squawk, undoubtedly in confusion from everything that was happening.

The smell of cooking meat flooded Jack's nostrils like a delicacy from another dream.

He may as well be the last person in the entire world, and for a moment, he was crushed by heavy loneliness and despair. He felt primal. In his element. Also alone, scared, and in pain.

Was he having fun?

Jack gazed at the stars, the same ones he always saw and a million more, and found no answer. Of course he didn't. He was alone.

He closed his eyes and endured the heavy emotions that darkness bred. It wasn't his first tough night, not even close, and it certainly wouldn't be the last—unless he died.

That was a sobering thought, and he chuckled as he pulled the skewer of rabbit meat off the flames. *The last man in the world... Take that, Maria. Heh.*

He then bit on the rabbit, savoring the taste. It was disgusting. And, at the same time, it was the most heavenly meal he'd ever had.

CHAPTER SEVEN
CHALLENGING THE ICE POND

The Integration happened on the 19th of September, 2024. A day later, on the 20th, the world was nowhere near adapting. Millions had died and the rest were busy organizing into small communities that could protect their members. The bravest had already defeated a monster or two.

On the morning of that day, Jack Rust waged war on a goblin tribe.

The goblins didn't know it, of course. He didn't walk in with a war declaration and his head on a silver plate. All they saw was an increased number of hunters failing to return.

Jack stalked them from the high branches, hid in bushes, sprang from under the dirt. His fists dealt swift death, and where he passed, only broken goblin corpses remained.

Each kill made him stronger, his fists harder, and his battle experience greater. His Fistfighting skill let him fight above his level, and Jack gradually began to internalize the knowledge. When the margin between success and failure was razor-thin, he understood why his skill made him move in exactly the way it did.

He knew what did and didn't work, to an extent, but he gradually understood why. At the same time, his increased Physical attribute gave him better awareness and control over his body.

His fighting skill kept rising. Unbeknownst to Jack, this constant life-or-death pressure was the perfect grinding stone.

A goblin squad passed by a bush, yapping about something. The bush exploded, and a human jumped out, wearing a pair of tattered shorts and nothing else. His shirt had long been torn apart or cut into bandage-like strips, and after a point, he didn't need shoes.

In their eyes, *he* was the monster. Caked blood and filth covered his skin, he smelled, but his eyes were the hardest, sharpest things they'd ever seen.

The three goblins screamed. Before they could react, a fist smashed into one's head and burst it apart. Another fist buried itself in a goblin sternum, breaking bones and sending its entire body flying backward. The last goblin recovered in time and made a mad dash for safety. Before it could take two steps or shout for help, a hand firmly grasped its throat.

Jack squeezed and the neck snapped. He let go, and the goblin's body collapsed to the forest floor. He stared at his hands.

I am a killer...

For the past two days, he'd been hunting and annihilating the goblins. They couldn't offer resistance anymore, only stand there and die. The only thing restraining his carnage was the time needed to locate new goblin squads—there weren't too many left.

Am I a monster? he wondered idly. Or am I justified?

The gruesome sight didn't bother him anymore. He'd gotten used to corpses, to death, to blood and brutal violence. He'd gotten used to the way his soul fluctuated when he went in for the kill, sparking crimson, to the feeling of breaking bones with his bare hands.

He'd come to peace with his path. This was reality. In this dungeon, it was him or the monsters—the goblins, in this case—and they would gladly devour any humans they found, they would wreck nature and rampage on innocent people.

He would kill them first. Between himself and monsters, he chose himself, even if it meant becoming a cold-blooded killer—which, in all honesty, wasn't the worst of things. When the initial social conditioning wore off, he managed to acclimate. It wasn't easy or pleasant—but not too terrible either.

Jack looked aside, where the notification waited.

Level Up! You have reached Level 5.

The leveling difficulty didn't scale too much. It took him one goblin to reach level 2, three for level 3, nine for level 4, and another nine for level 5. Of course, these last ones were higher-leveled—either the goblins had gotten scared, or they were leveling up as well.

He'd tried to keep his numbers low to delay the inevitable. So far, he was okay—the squads were still made up of three goblins each, and he hadn't seen a hobgoblin outside the tribe. That was bound to change, eventually, but by then, Jack planned to be strong enough.

Another factor that kept his number of kills low were injuries. He was steamrolling them now, but at the start, every fight hung at the edge of a knife. Each ambush was a hard-fought battle that left him with heavy injuries. One time, he even almost died.

Forced to crawl back to his cave after each battle, enter the ice pond and endure the torturous cold that assaulted his injuries. As he grew stronger, he had to go deeper for the healing powers to take effect, and the cold only grew worse, but at least, so did his stat bonuses. The lake had given him another three points in Physical, the equivalent of a level and a half.

Jack's life had become a cycle of looking for goblins, killing them, healing at the lake, and repeating. It was a fine life.

He assigned the free points from his most recent level up to Physical, then took a look at his current status.

Name: Jack Rust
Species: Human, Earth-387
Faction: -
Grade: F
Level: 5

Physical: 16
Mental: 7
Will: 6

Skills: Fistfighting (I)

By now, his physical prowess was approaching superhuman levels. He possessed three times the strength of a normal pre-System human—or maybe more—along with a vastly sturdier body, lightning-fast reflexes, crystal-clear kinetic vision, and agility that would put cats to shame—not that he had any to check.

He was possibly exaggerating, but the ease with which he dispatched the goblins confirmed his hypotheses. He was like a martial arts champion.

The gradual enhancements of level-ups intrigued him. Just how high could they go? Would he eventually become strong enough to break mountains or run faster than cars? Was there an upper limit?

The F-Grade part of his status screen, along with the E-Grade ice pond, implied the existence of D, C, B, and A Grades, but even the earth bear had only been level 15, and it was in an F-Grade dungeon. The Dungeon Boss, which could be level 25, was also F-Grade, unless Jack had misunderstood something.

Just how far away were those other grades? What was the limit? Was there one?

A sense of progression infiltrated Jack's psyche and took over. Constantly improving yourself by such tremendous amounts was addictive—and familiar, too. He'd been addicted to video games once, and this felt similar, though a hundred times better.

He clenched his fists. He wanted to grow stronger, as strong as he could. Then, he could finally take control of his life and be free.

Power was the foundation of everything.

And, luckily, Jack had more than one way to get it.

The sun was setting, so he walked back to his cave. He had explored the surrounding territory well by now and knew exactly where he was.

The crack in the rocks was still there, untouched, as was the cramped passage that led deeper in. Jack took the familiar steps, weaved around the rocks and into the small cavern he'd come to call home.

He was welcomed by the ice pond's familiar glow, a soft white light that now accompanied his sleep. The cold was condensed, thankfully, so he could rest comfortably on the other side, where he'd taken to sleeping on a patch of flat rock.

However, Jack didn't plan on being comfortable tonight. He'd met his goblin quota early. Now, he planned to once again challenge the pond.

He'd already done that a few times, and understood how things worked.

From the shore to the small waterfall at the back, the pond was only fifteen feet across. Fifteen short steps. For every step he took, the cold would augment his body by a single point of Physical.

One point wasn't much for the current Jack, but, if his calculations were correct, the pond had the potential of fifteen points, which was massive. Moreover, he suspected the waterfall hid something more.

Unfortunately, the pond wasn't a free lunch. Each step was harder than the last, and even now, Jack had only managed to take four steps. Today, he would go farther. He was determined to test his limits.

He took off his clothes and stepped in the lake with resolve. The cold assaulted him, traveling up his legs and around his body, but he was familiar with the feeling now, and his body was stronger than it used to be. This cold couldn't faze him.

He stepped forth. The temperature dropped further, sending long, sharp pins through his calves, but he persevered. Another step. The freezing current licked his legs. He shivered and clenched his teeth—he still had a ways to go. If he let the third step stop him, how could he defeat the Dungeon Boss?

The fourth step. The water level reached his knees, and his legs felt encased in ice. It was clearly water, but it was hard, requiring effort to move. By now, the cold was downright painful, and this was his current record. Jack was resolved to keep going. He had to take at least the fifth step.

That was easier said than done. His body was stronger than the last time he'd been here, but the crippling fear still ate at him at the thought of the next step. He took a few moments to get used to the cold before proceeding. He had to be careful.

Finally, he was ready—as ready as could be. He took a step.

He instantly lost feeling in his legs. They were completely numb, and the cold that reached his chest was so painfully piercing, it felt like someone was knitting with his bones. For a moment, he was paralyzed from the waist down. Jack was in terrible pain. His skin was turning blue.

Ice Pond bonus: +1 Physical

The bonus came as the cold finished permeating him. It was a slight respite, but nowhere near enough. Jack's body screamed at him to turn back, but through the cold and crippling pain, his eyes were fierce. He only stared at the waterfall, so close yet so prohibitively far.

It mocked him. The waterfall was *mocking* him. A fire burned in Jack's heart, fighting against the ice, and his mind was taken over by an unbreakable resolve. Moving farther would be dangerous, something bad could happen to his body or he could really lose control of his legs and collapse in the pond forever, but in that moment, he refused to retreat. He would make it. Never again back.

He took a step.

He was in a frozen hell. His entire body was encased in ice now, not just his legs. He lost feeling everywhere. His pale skin was truly blue now. His legs spasmed, and it took all his concentration to stay standing despite not feeling them.

His head hurt so bad it was about to break, and his heart struggled to keep beating, almost stopping. Jack's pain tolerance was swiftly expiring, and he released a muffled roar as he was unable to open his mouth, eyes bulging out as if someone were squeezing him to death.

Jack's entire body screamed to return to shore. This time, he didn't dare say no. If he stayed here any longer, he would die. He'd gone too far.

Except his legs weren't moving. They were as solid as rocks. Trying to move them was as plausible as trying to fly.

Jack panicked.

Is this how I die?

Suddenly, a blue exclamation mark flashed in the lower part of his vision, and the cold got a tiny bit easier to withstand. Jack's eyes bulged again with effort. His entire mental capacity was squeezed into making *his fucking legs move.* They shivered.

Jack fell backward. His back splashed into the water that swiftly moved to embrace him. Despite its freezing cold, it was also warm compared to the freezing hell he'd just endured.

He still couldn't move. He lay completely still under the water, gazing at the clean surface just above his eyes.

Am I going to drown? he wondered. Fear, panic, bitterness, spite—it all threatened to overwhelm him. His body caught on fire. With a tremendous pull of will, Jack used his hands to turn around, then crawled forward through the water. Every moment was torturous. The end was near, both literally and metaphorically.

He'd only taken six steps into the pond. As he fell back, his head was very close to the edge. He just had to crawl a tiny bit before his breath ran out. His lungs burned. So did his arms. He kept pushing.

With a final tug of will, his head broke the surface of the water and rested on the cold rock, which felt heavenly. He could breathe—and, as he'd pulled himself away from the center of the pond, the cold was receding. He managed to crawl out completely and lay on the stone, shivering, panting, and thanking every god he knew for making it out alive.

FUCK! he would have screamed, if not for his incessantly clattering teeth.

Ice Pond bonus: +1 Physical
Feat of Will performed: +1 Will

He wished he could chuckle.

He'd almost fucked up real bad... but at least he'd made it. He'd gotten the extra stat point, another one, too, and even proved to himself what he was capable of. He could push himself to the very limit. He could make it out of this fucking dungeon.

He was Jack Rust. And no matter what the world threw at him, he would survive.

He would thrive.

CHAPTER EIGHT
THE LAST MONSTER GROUP

The goblin tribe originally had seventy-two members, including the one that spawned in Jack's cave. Five were hobgoblins, and one was their leader, the goblin shaman. On the first night, seven hunters failed to return—three had been killed by Jack. On the second day, the goblin squads went out as usual, but a whopping thirteen goblins never returned.

On the third day, nine more went missing—the goblins had learned to avoid the other monsters. They couldn't have lost nine goblins naturally. Something was hunting them.

Of the seventy-two goblins, only forty-two remained, and that alarmed their leader greatly. He didn't know what they were facing, but something was after them—something that didn't dare attack the tribe, choosing to pick off hunter squads.

That night, the goblin tribe echoed with whispers of the Hunter.

When morning came, seven squads left the tribe. Each was led by a hobgoblin or a level 5 goblin, and each numbered five goblins instead of three. The leader would have liked to further condense his forces, but they still had to procure food for the entire tribe. This would have to be enough.

———

Crap... Jack stayed in his bush and let them pass by. This squad had five members, one of which was an evolved version, a hobgoblin. *They're onto me.*

It was bound to happen. He'd already killed a total of twenty-two goblins, including the one in the cave, so if they hadn't caught on yet, they would be extremely stupid.

It's okay. All good things must come to an end.

Jack let this squad go, wagering he probably couldn't take them yet. However, since they were bound to reach this stage, he already had a plan.

The first order of business was to scout out the last monster group. Now at level 5 and with multiple bonuses from the pond, he was confident he could either beat, escape, or hide from most things. If the System gave him kung-fu tigers, well... that would just be playing dirty.

He had to take the risk at some point, and since the goblin squads had just gotten dangerous, now was a good time. Depending on what he met, he would just brave the risks to keep attacking goblins or switch to the new group.

Jack receded into the shadows. His destination was northeast, approximately where the final monster group would lie, according to his calculations.

He also hadn't met the Dungeon Boss yet, having no idea where it could be. His best assumption was the big rocky hill at the center of the reserve, because why not, so he took a roundabout route. His cave was in the southern part and just a bit to the west, so he circled around the center to the northeast. No other goblins crossed his path—there were too few squads now.

Jack was careful, the journey taking two hours.

As he approached the northeastern part of the Greenway Reserve, his suspicions proved correct. The forest was different here. Wilder. Silent.

The trees rose higher, reaching up to thirty feet at places, and their foliage was thicker. The System clearly messed with this part of the forest, as such vegetation had certainly not been here before. Moreover, despite the forest's silence, its floor was strewn with shit as if suffused with wildlife.

His previous thought about tigers crossed his mind. It had been a joke then, but now...

Could it be true?

Jack hesitated. If there really was a strong, fast enemy here, proceeding might be a mistake. He'd already spent two hours to reach this area—four, including the return trip. Was it such an ugly risk?

He decided to keep going. His pace slowed to a crawl, and his eyes constantly surveyed the overgrowth. As he snuck from hiding place to hiding place, the distant caws of birds made him jump. He bit his lip and steadied his heart—he shouldn't be nervous.

He continued for another hour. Gradually, he relaxed, not meeting any enemies. Only some random forest critters got in his way, but they all disappeared quickly enough. Jack's eyes never left the overgrowth, and that's why he saw it.

A small dark shape left the higher branches of a tree and flew his way. It was a projectile of sorts, but that's all Jack had time to see. He moved his head so fast his neck cracked and barely dodged it, rushing behind a tree.

At the same time, the forest around him came alive. Screams and bangs filled the air, and the creaking of branches was clearly audible. Jack counted many voices, and as soon as he recognized the animal they belonged to, he peeked from behind his tree in shock.

He barely had time to scan the creature before a dry, brown thing smacked him right in the nose.

Gymonkey, Level 7

A primate variant from planet Green. Gymonkeys inhabit all forest biomes and move in packs, defending their territory with flying poop and great muscles. Their unique name comes from their habit of lifting heavy things to increase their strength.

While not particularly aggressive, they are highly territorial.

The poop smacked Jack's nose and fell to the ground with a plop. His brows shivered in irritation.

Did they really throw poop at me?

A pack of monkeys screamed at him from the branches—but these weren't any normal monkeys. They had short, off-brown fur, and were bulky, way bulkier than monkeys had any right to be. It was a miracle the branches even supported them.

Their saliva-filled jaws were intimidating, but nowhere near as much as their stunning pecs. These monkeys had thick biceps, low body fat, even six-packs! They could probably snap a human in two with one hand. It was like the System got a bunch of body builders and turned them into monkeys.

There were five altogether, and they were using their humongous muscles to hurl poop at Jack. One was already reloading, its face covered in an evil grin.

The analytical part of Jack's brain, the one dedicated to biology, wondered just how these monkeys managed to evolve like this. What kind of ecosystem could push them toward strength? Maybe predators that were fast but weak? Was it a mating thing? And did the conscious act of exercising hint at intelligence, or was it just completely ingrained into their DNA?

Every other part of his brain was just pissed they threw poop at him.

However, Jack's annoyance switched to fear when their levels registered. His surprise and disbelief evaporated. These were five level 7 creatures. He couldn't handle them.

At that moment, a deep roar came from farther inside the monkey territory, making Jack blanche. He knew about monkeys.

They have a gorilla!

He wasn't going to sit around and wait for the monkey-daddy to arrive. He entered flight mode, and his entire body erupted with power as he ran for his life. His bare feet thundered on dirt and roots even as a rain of poop whistled around him. A few even hit his back, some more recent—and wetter—than others.

Jack didn't know whether to curse or scream in fear.

THIS IS UNFAIR, SYSTEM!

He ran with all he had, and the monkeys chased him for a while, content to pelt him with their poop from a distance. They were strong, but luckily, they were also slow. Jack could outrun them.

Coming this deep had taken him an hour, but it took less than three minutes for him to fly out of their area, still zigzagging amidst flying poop. They didn't harm him, but they were annoying, and the force of the impact was enough to make him trip a couple of times.

Even when the poop stopped coming, Jack kept running for another minute before he dared look around. Then, he stopped. The monkeys watched him from the far-off trees, threat in their eyes and fresh poop in their hands. He wasn't welcome there.

Jack also glared at them. He'd been pooped! The dishonor! The humiliation!

"I will remember this, monkeys..." he said through gritted teeth. He couldn't defeat them now—but soon, he might, and then he'd get revenge. He'd make them eat their damn poop.

Ridiculous! Goblins and magic bears, and then poop-hurling monkeys? He fumed on his way back to familiar ground. It took you this long to show your true face, System? Fuck you! You will not make a joke of my death!

He spent the entire trip hurling insults—mental poop—at the System before he could calm down enough to think. He'd been so high-strung lately that seeing something even remotely funny had completely riled him up.

In the end, he was lucky. Maybe the monkeys were annoying, but they hadn't tried to harm him, only kicked him out. That was a good thing—and, at the same time, a bad one.

He couldn't afford good monsters. They had to be evil, like the goblins, to justify killing them and turning them into level material. Those gymonkeys—what an awful name—didn't want to harm him, just to be left alone. They were animals, not monsters.

Had the System lied? Weren't all monsters evil? Or had he only assumed that?

Jack didn't enjoy that train of thought.

Whatever, he concluded. For now, I'll keep fighting the goblins—I can't handle the monkeys or bears, anyway. When the time comes, I'll revisit the issue.

He used to hate how manipulative the System was for engineering the goblins and making them such easy to kill creatures. They were weak, ugly, clearly evil, and exceedingly hostile—the perfect humanoid enemies for someone unused to violence.

Now, he understood their utility. If the System wanted him—and all humans—to dive head-first into a world of violence, goblins were, indeed, a good solution. He was thankful for that. Because if he had to kill a more peaceful species while dealing with this change, he might have been in such harrowing confusion, that he'd end up dead.

He still hated the System with a passion, but he acknowledged it was good at its job.

What's the end goal, though... he wondered, walking through shrubberies and undergrowth. Are they training us to fight a war? Are they broadcasting our struggles as a tv show? Is this simply a form of torture? Since the System can clearly enhance us, why demand we level up instead of simply augmenting us to the point of superheroes?

These were difficult questions, and unfortunately, he didn't have the information to answer them.

Maybe the goblin shaman will know more. If possible, I will capture it, he resolved grimly. He hadn't captured a goblin yet or even exchanged words with them, fearing it would make him soft. He acclimated to this new world and its law of the jungle, but he didn't want to give himself the opportunity to regress.

The forest around him became familiar. He'd reached his area, his territory, and that meant he was ready. He had scouted out all monster groups and could determine a plan of action.

Kill the goblins. Kill the bears. Kill the monkeys. Dodge the Dungeon Boss for as long as possible.

It was simple and clean. The bears came before the monkeys because they were solitary, according to his earthen knowledge. Even if they were strong, he could ambush them and hopefully deliver a blow strong enough to swiftly take them out. He could start from the weakest bears and slay them one by one.

The monkeys wouldn't be as easy. When—if—he did attack them, he would need to be a one-man army.

"Oh!" he exclaimed, the pattern now obvious. The goblins are many but weak. The bears are strong but few and solitary. And the monkeys are something in between.

It was only a hypothesis, but it checked out—and, even if it wasn't done on purpose by the System, it still held.

Now, Jack was ready to continue his war against the goblins, and he would do so by killing his first hobgoblin.

He cracked his knuckles as he slid into the shadows. He was the hunter. And he was coming.

CHAPTER NINE
FIGHTING A HOBGOBLIN

THE GOBLINS RESTED IN A CLEARING.

There were five in total, including the hobgoblin, arrayed in a loose circle so that all angles were covered. The corpses of a boar family rested between them, while only one goblin appeared lightly injured.

The hobgoblin was clearly much more skilled in warfare than its lesser brethren. The scene Jack currently saw was a far cry from the distracted, disorganized, inefficient hunting squads he'd fought before.

That made things difficult. Half his success was based on goblin stupidity, and that weakness was now covered. It only enhanced his decision to start with the hobgoblin—which was level 6. He'd met another squad but ignored it as their hobgoblin was at level 7.

The hobgoblin had to fall first, or it might rally the other goblins into an organized attack, which would end badly for Jack. Moreover, there was no visible tell about its strengths and weaknesses. If it was fast, as goblins tended to be, he couldn't escape unless he killed it.

As he watched from a distant bush, while they rested before returning to the tribe, he focused on the hobgoblin. It was a male of average stature, with long dark hair done in a ponytail. Its body was slightly taut, and its seemingly empty eyes took in everything calmly.

Jack had no doubt the hobgoblin was on guard. He only dared inspect it from the side.

Moreover, it carried a weapon. A shortsword. And that was really bad news because Jack had no idea how to deal with a shortsword. His basic Fistfighting skill didn't cover that.

At least it was unarmored.

I must kill it before it draws that weapon, he concluded.

The goblins were in a solid formation, so there was no way to lay an ambush. He did know which forest path led to their tribe, so he lay in wait on a branch they would have to pass under. The leaves hid him well, so even if the hobgoblin looked up, it was unlikely he would be spotted.

Time went by. Soon, far-off cries resounded—the goblins were ready to return. He couldn't see them, as any glance risked his stealth. He could only watch under his branch and wait for the hobgoblin.

Footsteps and hushed yapping drew closer. Jack's body was almost shivering from the tension, but he kept it in check. His eyes sharpened. His breath grew deeper. His fists were clenched and ready to draw blood.

As his tension reached its climax, a green form passed below him. He almost lashed out on instinct and barely held himself back. One goblin walked past, carrying a little boar in each arm, followed by another. The hobgoblin was third in line so it couldn't be easily attacked.

A smart plan. Unfortunately, it hadn't accounted for Jack's tree-climbing genius.

The moment Jack saw the hobgoblin, he rolled around the branch and fell on its head. At the same time, likely having heard a rustle of leaves, it looked up and only saw a fist.

Jack channeled his entire falling momentum and Fistfighting skill into this single punch. He turned his body and ignored the landing. His punch smashed right into the hobgoblin's raised face like a meteor from the sky, with enough force to almost break Jack's hand and completely break the hobgoblin's face.

The sound was sickening, and its neck released a crack, barely holding. Jack fell to the ground and rolled amidst the goblins, which were too slow to react. The hobgoblin, blinded by pain and shock, similarly didn't react in time.

He jumped up and nailed a punch into its sternum, then another into its falling throat. The hobgoblin was already stumbling, but it possessed admirable tenacity. Despite taking the hits head-on, it still stood.

Jack grimaced. The weakness of Fistfighting was that it couldn't easily deliver critical strikes—or, at least, he didn't know how.

The hobgoblin's hand was already grasping for its shortsword, so Jack had no choice. He pounced on it like an animal, pelting it with bone-cracking punches. It screamed.

The other goblins came to their senses. Seeing their strong leader helpless and injured, their first reaction was to shout, "THE HUNTER!" and run away. That saved Jack's life.

He kneeled on the hobgoblin's body and punched with every fiber of his being. Each hit was strong enough to reverberate through its bones, and his knuckles bled through the fabric strips—the goblin's body was hard. Level 6 wasn't a joke.

Deep in its pain, it reacted instinctively. It kicked out and punched at Jack, slamming him with the full power of an evolved goblin, and his eyes swam for a second. That was enough.

The hobgoblin drove a fist into his ribs and rolled with it, escaping under Jack's legs and turning to face him. Its face was a mask of blood. One hand grabbed its shortsword handle. The other reached for its eyes to wipe them.

Jack wasn't an idiot to let it.

Ignoring his burning ribs, he fell on the hobgoblin again with all the force of a desperate, cornered man, not letting it wield the shortsword properly.

He was in deep shit. This fucker had prodigious defense, and the other goblins would catch on eventually. If he couldn't finish this off quickly, he might be finished himself.

The shortsword handle dug into Jack's belly and he released all air, but had escaped the blade. The two rolled on the ground, each struggling to come out on top. Jack held its wrist firmly.

This close, he could tell the hobgoblin was struggling to stay conscious. It just needed a little push to go over the edge.

That push came in the form of its ponytail. Jack stepped on it with a knee and the hobgoblin's head jolted sideways, letting Jack have the upper hand. He positioned himself, then drove a devastating jab into the back of its neck while still holding the ponytail down.

The hobgoblin's neck finally snapped with a sickening crunch, and its lifeless body crumpled.

Jack didn't stay to watch. He turned to find the goblins, some of which were about to group up against him. When they saw him kill their leader, they froze, then scattered and ran for their lives.

Level Up! You have reached Level 6.

Through the pain, Jack's eyes remained sharp. He'd known some would escape. His goal was to kill the hobgoblin and as many others as he could. So what if they ran? Any goblin he let go now would become another grunt to face in the future. Mercy at the enemy was cruelty at oneself.

Jack wouldn't make that mistake. He put both points in Physical in the blink of an eye.

He pounced, landing one punch at the back of a low-level goblin's head and killing it instantly before turning to another—

—and then he stilled. Completely.

There was no goblin there. What met his gaze was a dark-furred wolf larger than any he'd seen before. Its snout was only three feet away from him, chewing on a just-slain goblin. Its teeth crumpled the body like paper.

The wolf was completely calm. Jack met its eyes and felt true despair. This wasn't the panic of an ambush going awry. This was the hopelessness of a predator he could never, ever escape. If this wolf wanted him dead, he was dead. Simple as that.

Black Wolf, Level 49 (Elite) (Dungeon Boss)

Black wolves are mostly solitary creatures. They are also territorial, proud, aggressive, and infamous for being a scourge at the peak of F-

Grade. If a Black Wolf is spotted, experienced hunter squads should be dispatched quickly, or all big game of the surrounding area will disappear.

Jack averted his eyes, not daring to move a muscle, so as not to be seen as a challenger.

The black wolf chomped down hard three times, then swallowed, and the goblin was gone. It then turned to survey Jack.

His mind raced. His newfound confidence disappeared, replaced with fear. It wasn't just the level. He could *feel* the difference between him and the wolf. He was helpless, hopeless, thoroughly and utterly fucked.

Left without options, Jack fell to the ground and bowed to the wolf. It was all he could do. The System description said the wolf was proud—perhaps, if he showed subservience, it would spare him.

The goblin beside him—not the dead one—followed suit in a moment of genius. It fell to the ground next to Jack, its butt quivering. The other goblin, the more distant one, chose to run.

Jack didn't even see how the wolf moved. A blur crossed his eyes as fast as a blink, and the wolf was no longer there. It was now chomping on the goblin that tried to run. It screamed once, then the wolf's jaws closed around its head, killing it without any resistance whatsoever.

For the goblin beside Jack, that was the straw to break the camel's back. Its entire lifetime of smartness spent on its previous decision, it now stood and ran like the stupid shit it was.

Jack held his breath and lowered his head even farther. Unexpectedly, the sound of the goblin's footsteps didn't stop. He could still hear them, tapping against the ground and slowly getting farther and farther away.

He dared raise his eyes. The wolf was still devouring the previous goblin. Then, without turning around, it simply walked away.

We are insects to it... Though this thought should have been terrifying, it lit a howling bonfire inside him. The wolf didn't know this, but it was Jack's designated enemy. He had to kill it to escape. There was a target on its back, and though Jack was currently too weak to even stand in its presence, that would change eventually.

Then, it wouldn't ignore him.

As the wolf walked away, Jack didn't dare move just yet. It was only after the sound of its unsuitably light footsteps had disappeared that he raised his head, gazing in the distance.

He'd survived. And, where there's life, there is hope. He quickly brought his thoughts in order.

A goblin had escaped, but that wasn't too important. He'd expected it. The tribe would know of him, but he would handle whatever they threw at him. In Jack's mind, the goblins were only stepping-stones to reach that wolf.

level 49... He shuddered. The highest level he'd seen so far was the earth bear at level 15, but the wolf was so much higher than that. It didn't make sense. How would he get that high? With the goblin weed bush?

Are you trying to kill me, System...

He chuckled. Of course it was, and that was okay. The odds might have been against him, but so what? Jack would find a way—or gather food, block the entrance to his cave, and hide in there until more people came from outside the dungeon. Such a scenario was bound to happen. He couldn't be the strongest person on Earth.

For now, his hope was that the System would form a level ladder for him to follow. The goblins could maybe take his level to the tens, then maybe the bears and monkeys would be hiding a soft incline of levels deeper in their territory. Maybe there were a bunch of gorillas at level 30—how would he know?

If yes, he could take things slow, or at least slower than jumping from level 15 to 45.

Jack refocused. The wolf's seemingly unreachable level hadn't just terrified him, it also fueled his resolve to go higher. Night was falling. He would sleep, and come morning, he would keep hunting goblins. They had to eat, so they would send out squads, and now that he knew what hobgoblins were capable of, he could craft a better plan against them.

It would all work out.

His fingers tightened around the hobgoblin's shortsword—a half-way-decent shiv—and stuck it under his belt. He wouldn't use it as a weapon—he had no idea how to wield it, and his fists were effective enough—but it could help with skinning the rabbits or other practical tasks.

Plus, after using his fists to fight for so long, using a weapon now would feel hollow. Muted. Distancing himself from the thrill of the fight. *What the fuck is wrong with me...* he wondered, though he didn't stop grinning. *Is the constant fighting turning me insane? Is my brain adapting to cope? Or am I simply unearthing what was always there?*

Why do I feel so alive?

That night, he dreamt of dark wolf jaws tearing him apart, over and over. He didn't sleep well.

CHAPTER TEN
SERIAL BONKER

UNFORTUNATELY, THE GOBLIN LEADER WAS NOT AN IDIOT. WHEN HE LEARNED about Jack, he stopped sending goblins out to be killed. The next day, only one hunting squad left the tribe, and it was made up of three hobgoblins.

They weren't only hunting prey, but Jack too, and he scrambled to avoid them. He didn't even dare come close. The hobs were brutally efficient, constantly wary, and fiercely intelligent. Even beating one was difficult, let alone three. Moreover, the three hobs were so good at hunting, they secured enough food for the entire tribe—what was left of it, anyway.

In light of those facts, Jack decided the goblin shaman had outplayed him. He couldn't fight these goblins, and he was far from able to storm the tribe itself. That left only one option.

And that was how Jack Rust found himself stalking a bear.

Man, I've come a long way... he thought, shaking his head. Four days ago, I was looking for slightly brighter caterpillars. Now, I'm trying to kill a bear with my bare hands. That's life for you.

What happened to that caterpillar, I wonder? Wait—I don't care. Hah.

Jack's mind returned to bear hunting.

His fighting style was set in stone by now. He fought with his fists like a boxer on hard drugs. He didn't have time to learn something else from scratch.

However, his almost-failed ambush on the hobgoblin had taught him that fists, for all their power and versatility, couldn't easily assassinate someone. Therefore, Jack now carried a big-ass stone hammer, which he planned to smash into a bear head with all his power.

Fisting time would come after that.

He'd channeled all his inventiveness to create that hammer. He'd found a young tree and hacked it into two pieces with a big, sharp rock. Then, he made the lower part into the hammer's handle, and the top part into twine. Another unlucky tree fell at this point, as the twine wasn't enough. He got a rock bigger than his head and used the twine to tie it to the handle. It wasn't too steady, but that was okay. He only needed it to hold for one strike. Then, he could easily remake it.

Armed with resolve and what made humans the planet's apex predators, Jack set to the hunt.

The majestic beast prowled through the undergrowth. Sticks snapped under its heavy paws, and branches bent where they met its head. Its fur was riddled with yellow patches that glinted in the afternoon sun, indicating their rock-like hardness.

Earth Bear, Level 13

Bears are omnivorous creatures that stand at the apex of most food chains. Earth Bears, in particular, are a stronger, highly territorial variant. They can use very limited earth magic, and the rocky parts of their fur can be used to craft F-Grade weapons and armor.

Earth Bears are most commonly found in the Ursus Forests of planet Ursi.

Jack had spent the morning scouting the bears from a distance and managed to spot a few. Based on his observations, they ranged from level 13 to 17, though there could be stronger specimens or variants deeper in their territory.

For now, he'd singled out the weakest bear he could find, extrapolated its path through the forest, and hid on a branch it would pass under. It was a tried and tested method which minimized the risk of missing its mark—except bears didn't follow predictable paths. This was his fourth attempt at ambushing the bear.

And it remained the best plan Jack could think of, so he stubbornly clung to it. He'd already invested all afternoon. He might consider retreating and trying something else if this attempt failed too, but he was in luck.

The bear ambled below him, not looking up. Strangely, Jack noticed that the bears were constantly wary of their surroundings, scanning left and right for danger, which made his task harder. He didn't know what they had to be afraid of assuming that the wolf boss liked to hunt in this area. That would explain why he hadn't met it so far.

Unfortunately for the bear, though it constantly scanned the distance, it didn't expect a predator from above. Jack fell from a high branch, swinging his stone hammer that he struggled to carry despite his 20 Physical. The bear sniffed the air and looked up, a tendency that, apparently, most things shared when ambushed from above.

The heavy stone hammer, the twelve-foot fall, and Jack's entire physical strength combined to smash the bear's head so hard it broke open on the spot.

Level Up! You have reached Level 7.
Level Up! You have reached Level 8.

Just like that, a level 13 earth bear had been slain.

Jack had rolled and sprung up ready for a fight, only to realize what had happened. He stared at the headless corpse, unable to believe himself, then broke into frenzied laughter. The System thought it was being funny with poop-throwing gymonkeys, but *this* was funny.

For once, things were going well! His struggles were paying off!

"Hooray for human intelligence!" He laughed, scaring a pair of birds on a nearby branch. "Who needs goblins? Bears are so fucking easy!"

Succeeding so effortlessly on a task that seemed herculean was surreal.

Of course, it hadn't actually been easy. Jack had gathered information, prepared carefully, and spent a lot of time to set up the perfect ambush. That was the main reason he succeeded, along with his great strength, which allowed him to use the hammer, and his agility, which let him swing accurately from such a difficult position. Moreover, if he failed in the original strike, the risk was tremendous.

But he'd prevailed. Water under the bridge.

Now, Jack had four free points to allocate, and he considered the issue. Physical had been his go-to stat for a while now, and would likely continue being so, but this last battle reminded him of humanity's greatest weapon, the one that allowed them to rise above animals and become the rulers of the world—their intelligence.

He already felt pretty smart, but now that he had points to spare, maybe it was time to test what Mental would do. More brains never hurt anybody, and at this point, one or two points in Physical hardly made a difference. He allocated two points in Mental.

The world brightened before his eyes. Patterns of movement emerged in the floating leaves, Fibonacci sequences everywhere. For a moment, he felt like the God of Math—or maybe Albert Einstein.

At the same time, his grasp over the world's workings solidified a bit. He was more aware of himself and others, could decipher and use the patterns that his heightened intelligence unearthed.

In short, he'd become smarter and wiser—but, while the difference was clear, it felt a bit useless.

Jack was a smart person to begin with—his starting Mental was 7. He'd also spent a lifetime studying and polishing his mind. He already had the foundation to navigate this dungeon situation and come up with plans that were close to optimal.

The Mental increase was welcome, of course, but it would only be useful if he returned to his lab. It was unnecessary to the current him, in the same way that extra Physical would be unnecessary to a scientist—how much strength did it take to turn doorknobs and open jars?

The only useful thing was his increased insight into himself, which helped him deal with this ongoing modern-to-primal transition, but mental health paled in importance when compared to not being eaten by wolves.

In the end, Jack had done his experiment, as he should, and concluded he should focus on Physical for now. As he liked to say, better a master of one than a jack of all trades—even though his name was Jack.

He allocated the remaining two points in Physical and inspected his status screen.

Name: Jack Rust
Species: Human, Earth-387
Faction: -
Grade: F
Level: 8

Physical: 22
Mental: 9
Will: 7
Skills: Fistfighting (I)

Not bad, not bad at all.

He'd stopped looking for a normal-world equivalent of himself. He was at least four and a half times more fit than a pre-System normal person across the table. He was roughly as strong as a professional weight lifter and as fast as a professional sprinter, while also having the endurance of a professional marathon runner and the durability of... Well, he wasn't sure there was an equivalent for that. A brick wall, maybe?

In any case, Jack was pretty sure that, if the current him was in the pre-System world, he could steamroll any decathlon competition to ever exist.

Presently, he was using his power to steamroll bears and goblins, but to each their own.

The takeaway was that Jack was a total badass, and that felt damn good after twenty-seven years of barely making ends meet in a life he didn't like much. Even his appearance was improving—muscles were beginning to bulge under his bare chest and arms, and he had hints of a six-pack.

Physical was great.

Snapping back to the present, Jack looked at the bear corpse, then at the sky. Hunting monster bears was his new shortcut to levels—unfortunately, it was a time-consuming hobby, and the sun was already setting.

Though he was uninjured, he had to retreat and come back tomorrow—but, on the bright side, he was uninjured. With his recent level-ups, it was time to get an extra stat point or two from the ice pond. So what if there was hellish pain?

Could it be worse than death or losing the one opportunity he ever had to shine?

Night came and went. Jack managed to go one step farther into the pond. The difficulty wasn't linear, it rose exponentially the deeper he went. The waterfall was less than ten steps away now, and he estimated he'd need to reach the twenties in level before getting there, maybe more.

Not that he could complain. The pond had already granted him the equivalent of three levels in points and a little more, and it wouldn't stop anytime soon. It was the gift that kept on giving. Jack's lucky star.

Come morning, the hobgoblins were scouring their territory again, and Jack considered attacking them but didn't. He might have, if there were only two, but there were three. The goblin shaman was proving its intelligence. It would rather go hungry for a bit than lose more of its people. It had ramped up the difficulty too much at once, and Jack's leveling speed couldn't cope—for now.

Fortunately, the bears weren't as smart. They probably hadn't even noticed yesterday's assassination. Therefore, Jack, in his endless generosity, would give them more opportunities to notice.

Morning found him hiding in branches and hoping for his target bear, at level 14 this time, as he hadn't found a weaker one, to pass under him. It didn't. And after four such failures, Jack got irritated.

He kept himself in check. Arrogance could get him killed. He didn't have the strength to fight bears head-on yet, so he could only take things slow.

After five hours of stalking the same bear, he finally managed to pull off his ambush.

Bonk!

Level Up! You have reached Level 9.
Level Up! You have reached Level 10.

Jack smiled. He put all four points into Physical, raising it to twenty-seven, and kept on with his merry hunting. His progression was so fast these days, he'd almost gotten addicted to the dings that accompanied level-ups.

He carried his bloody hammer through the forest until he spotted another bear, this one at level 14, too. He then employed his signature move, hiding in branches and waiting for the unsuspecting bear to cross underneath.

However, the moment it appeared under him, the bear sniffed the air. Its head whipped up, eyes meeting Jack, who was only starting his fall. He froze in midair. Panic took him over. He hadn't realized this, but he was looking a fucking bear in the face.

What gave me away? he thought, and instantly, he knew. The hammer! I never cleaned the blood!

Far too late for regrets. At this point, Jack had to go all-in. He swung and gloriously missed as the bear moved its head.

Its yellow eyes now glared at Jack from only a few feet away, and its entire body tensed up to attack. It growled, spitting on him and exposing large, sharp teeth. The yellow patches on its fur glowed.

Jack paled. *Shit!*

CHAPTER ELEVEN
RACING A BEAR

Jack stared at the bear. The bear stared at him. It growled. He jumped.

"Shit!"

The bear wasn't one to waste time. It lunged at Jack, swiping a large paw, and he narrowly dodged the strike. The claws dug thick lines on the tree behind him.

Jack caught on fire. The now familiar fight or flight instincts kicked in, taking control and giving him greater power than his body could wield. A thousand synapses fired in his brain all at once.

Fight or flight?

As if in slow motion, he considered the issue. One hit from the bear could incapacitate him. At the same time, it wasn't particularly agile. He could dodge everything. Maybe he could make it.

The bear swiped again. Jack ducked under the blow, letting his stone hammer fall as he clenched his fists. His Fistfighting skill kicked in, further heightening his fighting awareness. As he dodged the claw, he rotated his body and shot a hard hook into the bear's belly, throwing all his weight behind it.

His fist met rock-hard fur. The impact was so strong that, despite his augmented body, his knuckle bled and almost cracked. The bear, on the other hand, only bent its body a bit—a yellow glow had appeared on the point of impact and absorbed most of the damage.

Jack remembered its description. *Limited earth magic. Fuck.*

He jumped back—avoiding a set of sharp jaws so close the heat of its maw curled against his skin—and turned around in midair. He was faster than the bear, but the damage he dealt was minimal. It would catch him, eventually. He couldn't afford this fight.

Flee.

Decision made, Jack's entire body lightened as his legs hummed with power. They smashed into the forest floor, throwing dirt and stones all around, shooting him forth at tremendous speed. A patch of bushes practically zoomed past his vision.

A roar and four heavy thuds indicated the bear would give chase. Of course it would.

And so began Jack's first race.

Humans cannot outrun bears. However, that only concerns pre-System humans. At 27 Physical, Jack had already outgrown that entire civilization—but had he outgrown a bear?

There was only one way to find out.

His bare feet smashed the ground hard enough to break it. His body was slanted forward, riding the air resistance to stay upright, and his hands frantically moved back and forth. The bear's roar was approaching. Jack accelerated.

Running for your life was a unique feeling. Everything disappeared, all thoughts went silent, letting the running become your entire life.

Jack was one with the air, one with the forest. He wasn't a human, but a movement, a gale crossing through bushes and over roots. His high Physical made the forest's terrain easy to traverse. He zoomed left and right, purposefully passing through narrow parts to slow down the bear. In a straight line, he couldn't match its speed, but this was a forest.

Where he only had to duck, the bear had to plow through fallen branches and hollow logs. It wasn't only the roars that indicated its position, but also the breaking of wood and uprooted vegetation.

Despite all that, it was still gaining ground. A claw fell only inches behind his back. Jack's eyes sharpened as he went all-out.

He jumped over logs, swung from branches, and stepped on trees to make his turns sharper. The terrain became his ally, not an enemy. Though he'd only tried parkour once or twice before, he imagined this was how pros felt.

The bear was close. He spared a glance its way just as it emerged from an exploding bunch of logs, splinters flying everywhere but unable to penetrate its fur. It galloped at full speed, heedless of any obstacles in its way. Only trees could slow it down, but those, too, were snapped in half occasionally.

Jack gritted his teeth. The speed he was moving at was superhuman. He'd run before, of course he had, but he only possessed 4 Physical then —before the System. Now, he'd claimed 27. The difference was stunning. Trees and bushes momentarily snapped into his vision before disappearing. His body reacted beyond what his conscious processes could pick up.

He was sprinting at the top of the world, and the bear slowly, slowly began to fall behind. Its roars became hollower, the sound of its crashes duller.

And sprinting like this was beginning to take its toll on Jack. He was growing tired. His lungs burned, his legs were made of lead. He caught himself panting.

He hadn't tried out his running abilities, except when escaping the monkeys, but he was focused on them, then. Now, he could take in the changes of his body, and they were majestic.

His surroundings were changing. He began to recognize things. That crooked tree, this malformed bush, the perfectly round clearing. He'd left the bear's territory and entered his own, where the hobgoblins prowled, but he had a big-ass bear on his back. Stealth be damned.

As he jumped over a fallen log, he saw them. Three hobgoblins, each standing slightly apart from each other as they gaped with surprise that quickly turned into fear when the log behind him exploded and an enraged bear flew through, galloping wildly.

Jack didn't dare lead it at them. He was only barely outrunning the beast as it was. The slightest complication would doom him.

He kept running, filled with the mad desire to flee, and as he did, a wondrous feeling took over. His exhaustion disappeared. His strength grew. His senses sharpened. His feet now hammered even harder against the ground, pushing him forward so fast the air screamed in his ears.

Exhaustion turned into fuel, into ecstasy. Jack now loved running. He could go on forever, and as he thought that, he accelerated, surpassing his previous limit.

The bear didn't. Its tired panting was evident through the growls, the creature was slowing down, and he grinned. In the animal kingdom, humans weren't sprinters, they were endurance runners. Since the bear hadn't caught up yet, victory would be his.

Confidence swelled inside him, enhanced by the euphoria of being one with himself. He felt fast, strong, invincible, that he could take on everything the world threw at him. He controlled this entire forest. He could grab the ground and stop Earth's rotation, then spin it in reverse.

He almost stopped and turned to face the bear before catching himself. That unmatched arrogance disappeared as quickly as it had come, but the euphoric confidence remained.

He kept running, savoring the feeling. At some point, the thuds and growls had disappeared. The bear had given up.

Jack stopped, too, taking a look at the empty forest behind him. How long had he been running alone? It didn't matter. He was still full of energy, full of vigor and strength, and though he didn't dare face the bear yet, there was another enemy in the forest.

His forest.

Jack ran in the opposite direction. They couldn't have gone far. The trees zoomed past him, he ducked under branches and jumped over bushes like an Olympic athlete. He wasn't going at full throttle now, just enough to stay fast. And he was being silent.

He flew into a forest path, and through a patch of bushes, he spotted them. The hobgoblins were huddled in a circle, discussing something, possibly him. He shot right at them like a barbaric missile.

He'd struggled against one hobgoblin when he was level 5, but he'd now reached level 10, plus the increased bonuses from the ice pond. He was massively stronger than before, and most importantly, he was fully warmed-up. So what if they had shortswords? They couldn't touch him.

The hobgoblins turned to look, and one of them caught a punch in the face, sending it flying into a tree and cracking the bark. A trembling groan escaped the hobgoblin's lips before it stumbled, still upright but barely. Its fuzzy eyes met Jack, and it drew its sword.

Jack didn't go after it. As soon as he landed the first punch, he stepped into the ground with enough force to extinguish his momentum. The dirt exploded. His entire body creaked, but he didn't mind. Before the hobgoblins could escape their surprise, he elbowed a second one in the chest, cracking ribs and sending it kneeling on the ground.

He then punched ahead, but the third hobgoblin jumped back in time and drew its sword. It adopted a well-trained stance, and despite Jack's overwhelming ambush, the hobgoblin's eyes didn't falter.

The first hobgoblin, the one he'd punched in the face, stepped behind him. It still hadn't recovered from the strike—it might even have suffered a minor concussion—but it was ready to fight.

Hobgoblins were nothing like goblins. They were disciplined, trained warriors. They were hardened veterans. Tricks and ambushes wouldn't be enough to take them down.

And Jack knew that. He wasn't counting on an ambush. He wanted to fight them head-on, test himself against their blades. He was flooded with battle lust, eager to try out his skills at the edge of danger.

He banged his fists together, eyeing the two hobgoblins that were trying to surround him. "Come!" he shouted.

The two of them looked at each other and nodded.

Jack, still in their encirclement, watched them intently. Besides the two standing hobgoblins, the one that had been elbowed before still struggled to stand due to its broken ribcage, but Jack didn't discard it entirely. It could still throw out its shortsword, trip him, or do other nasty things if he wasn't careful.

But he would be.

The two goblins rushed him at the same time, one in front and the other from behind. Their movements were sharp, their stances solid. Jack didn't see an easy way to attack or dodge.

Despite that... they were slow.

Jack's stats had already jumped beyond theirs. Training and expertise could only achieve so much in the face of absolute power.

As they fell on him, blades swinging, Jack's body came alive. He twisted, dodging attacks at the last moment even when they seemed unavoidable. His speed was such that their weapons couldn't follow, and their carefully devised stances weren't designed against overwhelming opponents. Hobgoblins were used to fighting other hobgoblins, not superheroes.

Jack was like a dancer. His reflexes were so fast he moved at the same time they did, and his speed was such that he'd dodged before they even finished their attack. Two shortswords fell from different directions, and Jack weaved between them masterfully, passing through gaps the naked eye could only barely catch.

This wasn't just his stats, of course. His Fistfighting skill was running at full throttle, and as he dodged and weaved, he grew more and more familiar with his body at a stunning rate.

Dodging like this wasn't easy. Jack was dancing on the razor's edge, and yet, he kept going. When he had the opportunity to counter-attack, he didn't. This feeling of harmony was beyond wondrous, and he felt if he stopped now, this opportunity wouldn't reappear easily. He had to grasp at straws to survive this dungeon, to dig out even the last dregs of his potential. A little danger was nothing.

His movements sharpened. His thoughts accelerated. He leaned from one movement to the next, using skill to dodge instead of pure speed. His body became one with his will, and he felt in complete control of his every limb and muscle.

The hobgoblins didn't know he was holding back, of course, so they remained careful, not daring to attack too wildly in case he struck back. Unbeknownst to them, they were spelling the doom of their tribe.

Finally, in one movement, everything came together in Jack's mind. He, his body, and his enemies became one.

Ding!

Skill upgraded. Fistfighting (I) → Fistfighting (II)

Through the battle haze, he grinned.

CHAPTER TWELVE
THE JACK-GOBLIN WAR

EVERYTHING SUDDENLY BECAME SO MUCH EASIER. THE TRAJECTORIES OF THE shortswords were clearly telegraphed before his eyes, and he could tell where the next attack would come from before the hobs even moved to enact it.

These weren't veteran fighters, they were merely familiar with fighting. Their stances weren't refined, just decent. They had holes he could see and punch through.

And he did.

Through the maelstrom of attacks, a fist jumped out and fell on a hobgoblin's face like a meteor from the side. It stumbled, and Jack rounded on the other hobgoblin, dodged an attack to get into its guard, and stared it down.

Its face was hideous, but in its eyes, there bloomed fear. He was a head taller to begin with. Right now, he felt incomparably grander.

The hobgoblin froze in fear as a fist shot into its gut, then the same fist slammed its falling face into an uppercut. The impact was so strong that the hobgoblin's feet left the ground, and it flew a couple of feet before it landed on its back, unmoving and very dead. This was the same hobgoblin he'd punched at the start—the amount of punishment it could take was limited.

Jack then turned to face the other hobgoblin, dodged the strike heading for his head, grabbed it hard by the throat, and pummeled its face into mush with his other hand.

A second later, the hobgoblin was dead.

He turned to the third goblin, the one that couldn't stand due to its broken ribcage. He frowned as he looked it over. Its eyes were still fearless and full of fire, but he couldn't just execute a fallen enemy.

"What should I do with you?" he asked.

"Kill me," the hobgoblin spat out in a rough, calloused, yet slightly high-pitched voice, "or I will kill you."

Jack shook his head. "No. I think I'll—"

Whatever he was going to say, it disappeared. A stick snapping behind him was the only warning Jack got. He jumped aside and barely dodged the earth bear's charge, which barreled through his previous position and into the kneeling hobgoblin.

It hadn't been more than two minutes since it stopped chasing Jack, so it was still nearby. Hearing the sounds of combat, it'd come to investigate.

Jack rolled upright and eyed the beast, already moving backward. "You can't catch me," he said. "Just get the fuck out."

The bear met his steady gaze, and this time, it didn't chase. It was still exhausted from the previous run. So was Jack, actually, but the bear didn't know that. It only knew it'd lost once.

Jack had already retreated a couple dozen feet, more than enough to escape any surprise attack and run away.

The bear growled once, clearly dissatisfied, then turned to the hobgoblin, which lay by its feet. It tried to grin heroically. "I—" A claw easily snapped its neck. The bear threw a last glance at Jack before leaning in for its meal, and he only grimaced before turning away.

Despite his skill upgrade, he still didn't feel confident against an earth bear—not without an ambush.

That was fine with Jack. He was confident in his strength, having finally graduated from prey to hunter.

He even had choices on what to hunt. The bears were doable. He'd be in huge trouble if he failed the ambush, but he liked his chances. He'd succeeded twice, after all. However, the risk of death was still there, even if not high.

The only problem was that Jack was reluctant to kill too many bears. There had to be bigger, meaner variants deeper in their territory, along with a group boss, and that mystery filled him with a sense of dread he'd rather not provoke.

The other option was the goblins, who also had the promising High Speed Bush. They'd holed up in their tribe, leaving Jack helpless before, but now, he was forced to reconsider. His current power was enough to steamroll hobgoblins, of which there were only two left. There were dozens of regular goblins, but he could face those in his sleep.

They could only be a problem if they utilized ranged weapons, large numbers, as well as...

The shaman.

The goblin shaman was at level 9, close to Jack. Plus, his powers remained a mystery.

Finally, there were the monkeys, but Jack still felt somewhat apprehensive. Not only were they dangerous, with the only group he'd seen sporting the equivalent of five hobgoblins, but they were also monkeys, which implied a level of intelligence that could doom him if he wasn't careful. The System could have installed a Monkey Sage as their leader, or something equally ridiculous, and he didn't want a bunch of gorilla bouncers scouring the forest for him.

Plus, they hadn't tried to kill him. That was a major concern for Jack.

In the end, the High Speed Bush of the goblins won him over.

Alright. I'll take one more bear to level up, then try the ice pond again, and then... I will destroy the goblins once and for all.

Night had fallen in the Greenway Natural Reserve. The moon was hidden, but the stars shone bright, lending their light to the night like fireflies stuck on ceiling glue.

For the first time, Jack was out and about in the dark. He'd only used the night to cook before, but now, he was using it to skulk. To prowl through the undergrowth unseen and hunt his enemies.

The goblin tribe was arrayed before him, an amalgamation of little green things, rough huts, and random squealing from said huts. There were more than thirty huts, each housing two goblins, indicating their original number to be around sixty or seventy. Jack estimated there were around forty left, including the goblin shaman and the two hobgoblins—as well as any hobgoblins he'd missed the first time.

It wasn't a fight he could take. The shaman was an unknown variant, the hobs needed time to neutralize, and the goblins were so many they could swarm him.

Fortunately, he didn't need to fight them head-on. Hence the night.

Killing the leader would despawn the entire monster group, according to the System. All Jack had to do was infiltrate, reach the shaman's hut—the largest one, obviously—and slit its throat. Then, goodbye, goblins.

Despawning them would lose him some experience, but at this point, goblins just weren't worth it. They were too low-level. Even if he manually took out the entire tribe, he'd only get two levels at most, and half of that would come from the leader himself.

Risking himself for a smidgeon of extra EXP—to speak in game terms—just wasn't worth it. He would assassinate the leader, benefit from their High Speed Bush, then go fight bears and monkeys to level up.

High Speed Bush (F-Grade)

A resource guarded by the goblins of the Forest of the Strong.

Commonly found in the wet jungles of planet Peruvian, the leaves of this bush can enhance a person's reflexes, speed, dexterity, and agility.

They can also make you high as a kite.

The stat increase is a one-time bonus.

According to Jack's estimate, this bush was exactly what he needed. The bonuses could help him consistently outrun the earth bears, at least the low-level ones, significantly decreasing the risk of his ambushes. It could also help him escape the monkeys, when he decided to head that way.

Plan determined, Jack inspected himself a final time before jumping into action.

Name: Jack Rust
Species: Human, Earth-387
Faction: -
Grade: F
Level: 11

Physical: 30
Mental: 9
Will: 7
Skills: Fistfighting (II)

He'd killed an extra bear for a level up, and also managed to take an extra step into the ice pond—the seventh one—almost reaching its halfway point. Thanks to his Physical stat, he overflowed with power.

He also checked out his upgraded skill.

Fistfighting (II): Grants expert knowledge of fistfighting. While fistfighting, enhances the user's physical attributes, reflexes, and kinetic vision.

It wasn't a large change from the previous version, just a few of the adjectives had changed.

Still, Jack wasn't going to complain. The difference between basic and expert was massive, as he'd experienced when fighting the hobgoblins. He clenched his fists, and was filled with the confidence that comes from skill.

He prepared himself for the coming action against the goblin tribe. His eyes sharpened. His bare feet—given his high Physical, shoes slowed him down tremendously—were tickled by the moist grass below. The night breeze swept around his bare chest, hugging it, and his nape-length hair fluttered.

He smelled blood in the air. There wasn't any yet, but there would be.

Jack slid into the bush and down the hill. He was quiet. His bare feet made no sound on the grass and soil, while his breath was deep and steady. He was used to high adrenaline now.

He darted from bush to bush like a rabbit, easily hiding from the sentries' sights. Though their leader had devised an excellent patrol pattern, the goblins were too dumb to understand it, and they ended up looking the wrong way. Jack snuck through the gaps, a human-shaped wolf entering the sheep pen.

There were many guards tonight, but that was expected. The three hobgoblins hadn't returned. The goblins were undoubtedly on high alert.

The tribe was situated in a large clearing—System-made, as Jack didn't remember it being here before—and he reached its edge without being noticed. Then, things got tough.

There was a thirty-foot gap between the last bush and the first tent, a gap he couldn't easily cross. The goblins had no torches—they could see in the dark—but the starlight was enough for Jack. The problem was that the lack of torches meant a lack of shadows for him to sneak through.

But, well, Jack was Jack. If there weren't holes in their defense, he'd make one.

The moon swung overhead as time passed. The ten goblin guards were split into groups of two, patrolling in and around the tribe. There weren't walls or palisades, only these ten little goblins.

As a duo of goblins circled the clearing, arguing about something in low voices, two hands sneaked out of a bush, grabbed their mouths, and pulled them in. Then, silence.

The other goblins didn't realize a patrol had gone missing. The gap was enough for Jack to go through.

He slithered across the clearing as quickly as he could manage while remaining stealthy. He reached the first hut and dove in its base, making himself one with what little shadow it cast. Low squeals came from inside, but he didn't pay any mind. These goblins had been at it for a while.

He circled around the hut to avoid a passing patrol, then headed deeper inside. Stalking in the dark, Jack felt like a primal, nocturnal beast seeking prey. The feeling was wildly exciting, and his body adapted to the hunt.

He followed the hut walls deeper into enemy territory. There were patrols even inside the tribe, so he had to be careful, not to mention the entire camp was so small he could be seen by pretty much anywhere.

As Jack skulked by a wall, a door opened right in front of him.

CHAPTER THIRTEEN
PUNCHING A BOSS

Jack froze for a fraction of a second before darting behind the wall he'd been skulking by and held his breath. Inwardly, he cursed. He didn't just have to watch out for patrols, but also random goblins that needed to pee!

The door sandwiched him against the wall, and he was forced to put out a hand and gently stop it. He cursed again. In the silence of the night, and with his senses heightened from all the stalking, the door's creaks came to his ears as loud as lovemaking pigs. Admittedly, they *were* pretty loud—goblins weren't the best of builders, even though these huts had obviously been spawned by the System.

Through a crack in the door, Jack could see a naked goblin on the other side. It rubbed its eyes to send the drowsiness away, then, with a, "Hmm?" it gazed at the door, which didn't make the normal *bang* of hitting the wall.

Jack prepared to attack.

The goblin then shrugged and went about its business. Taking two steps to reach the corner of its hut, it started pissing at it. Jack's brows spasmed. He stifled a groan.

Ugh. Disgusting...

When the goblin was done, it went back to the door, grabbed it from

Jack's gentle hands, and shut it. Jack was left plastered on the wall, not knowing whether to be relieved or irritated that he had to hide from such beings.

He settled on resolve.

His feet slid across the dirt, carrying him across another gap and next to the wall of the largest hut. He looked around; nobody had spotted him. Good.

Jack put his ear against the wall, and hearing nothing, raised his head a bit. There was a window here, like most huts, and he peeked through.

Before him lay a despondently empty space. There was a rough table and chair, the pinnacle of goblin furnishings, as well as a shamanic staff leaning against the wall. A large pile of stones waited behind the closed door—an alarm system that Jack would bypass—while the fur of some unknown animal served as bedding on the ground—unprocessed, of course.

On the beddings, covered with another fur, lay the sleeping form of a goblin. Jack grinned. He stuck his head a bit deeper inside, inspecting all corners where a guard might lay in wait, then raised himself through the window. Now inside the goblin master hut, he got a better view.

He wasn't an idiot. Something was fishy here. This was too easy.

Yet, there was nothing besides the alarm stones by the door. He even wondered if this was another goblin serving as bait, but the shamanic staff was here—a crooked piece of wood adorned with colorful feathers and animalistic tokens—and the sleeping goblin wore the same face paint as the last time he'd seen it.

Either the goblin shaman was incredibly smart, or it wasn't. Given its goblin nature, Jack was inclined to believe the latter.

He paced to the sleeping goblin and snapped its neck. Then, he waited. Nothing happened. No notifications, no warning bells, no fuss. Jack frowned. He looked outside the window and saw a goblin patrol at the edge of the clearing. He looked back at the dead goblin. He frowned deeper.

Well, shit.

And *then* came the warning bells. Shouts rose from the edge of the tribe, rousing all goblins within earshot—that is, every single goblin.

"Fuck!" Jack cursed. He didn't know how they'd discovered him, but they clearly had. And worst of all... he'd been outsmarted by a goblin.

That left a sour taste in his mouth. Thankfully, he was determined to kill said goblin, and killing washed all sour tastes away.

As the tribe burst into activity, Jack jumped outside the window and landed on an unfortunate goblin passerby. He turned its head to mush before looking around, only to find at least a dozen pairs of eyes on him. Both hobgoblins stared him down, surrounding a goblin thinner than most, with creepy painted lines on its body and sparks dancing on its fingers.

"Kekeke," it chuckled. "Stupid intruder. We will eat your fingers one by one as punishment, and I'll wear your hair as mine."

"Oh, yeah? Give it a shot, little man."

Jack wasn't going to play around. As forty goblins screamed and pounced at him, he clenched his fists. His body caught on fire. His eyes sharpened, and his breath deepened. He became a fighter—an expert fistfighter.

It was time to crack some skulls. Jack roared.

Screams came from all sides as the goblins swarmed him.

Jack became a force of nature. A storm made of fists.

One punch took a goblin's head clean off. Another landed on a chest and broke it apart, while a third uppercut a goblin hard enough to send it flying. His hands turned into blurs, but there was a limit to his power.

A swarm could not be stopped by single-target attacks.

Though some goblins died, many more landed on him. They were fearless, ignoring the death of their comrades to attack him frenziedly, and they succeeded in harming him. Claws ripped into his skin, teeth tried to dig his eyes out. Jack grabbed goblins and tossed them off his body like cats, but they were too many.

No matter how many he killed, more arrived to take their place. The wounds were shallow—his body was extremely durable—and his critical places were well-protected, but the sheer weight and violence of the goblins dragged him down. Something had to be done, or he would fall.

Through the bodies that covered him, Jack could see the two pale forms of the hobgoblins approaching. Their swords glinted in the moonlight, and their yellow eyes shone like embers.

His every instinct kicked in at once, inciting the familiar state of all-encompassing resolve. His muscles pulsed and groaned as they pulled beyond their limit, and his primal urges took to the forefront. Gone was the man, leaving only the warrior. Cold heart and burning body.

It was intoxicating.

Jack roared again. He dug his heels into the ground, stuck to the wall behind him, and spun around, smashing all goblins into the wood. The large hut creaked. The goblins' claws drew bloody lines on his skin as they were torn away. He succeeded; he was free, if only for a moment.

Jack didn't waste any time pummeling them. Already, goblins watched him from the nearby rooftops, and they jumped down like little green suicidal bombers—but when they landed, Jack wasn't there.

His soles smashed into the ground, raising hell under a dark sky as he darted through the village at speeds the goblins couldn't follow. He danced between walls and huts. He jumped on roofs and broke through them. Goblins flew around him, some attacking and some tossed away by brutal punches.

Jack was a hurricane that tore the goblin tribe apart, huts, bodies, everything, and only the rock that made up the huts' foundations could withstand his fury. The goblins shrieked, only seeing a blur before getting punched to oblivion.

Jack was a moving storm, and the tribe could not take him.

But the shaman could.

His body suddenly slowed. Red ethereal snakes wrapped around his limbs, dragging him down, impervious to his touch. They were ghosts. At the same time, frigid cold assaulted his soul. Fear and despair threatened to overtake him, and his heart was shackled, trapped in cold iron.

Jack lost his footing and fell from the rooftops, landing on the soil a few feet below. A hobgoblin was there. A shortsword stabbed unerringly at his throat while his eyes were cloudy.

The shortsword missed its mark, and a punch landed on the hobgoblin's sternum so hard it spat blood and flew back amidst the sound of breaking bones. Jack was there, squatting and panting, his eyes redder than the snakes binding him.

The chill to his soul had been tremendous, but Jack had withstood the ice pond. How could a mere goblin shaman stop him?

The goblins reached him as he struggled. The little fuckers still didn't care for their lives, and they fell on him in waves.

Jack was a menace.

He grabbed one by the head and crashed it into another. He punched a goblin so hard that three flew back, like pins in a bowling court. He ducked under a goblin's assault, grabbed its leg, and used it as a weapon to send more of them flying.

Yet, there were many, and he could not face them all. He was bleeding from a hundred little wounds, and the losses were beginning to accumulate. He had to do something.

His gaze cut through the swarm of goblins, through the remaining hobgoblin, and into the eyes of the goblin shaman. It grinned as it met his stare, and Jack grinned back.

He flew backward. Some goblins missed him and fell to the ground, only to be stomped by their companions as they chased him. Jack ran around the village, letting the mindless goblins gnaw at his heels as he changed directions. The red snakes still bound him, but his soul could handle them, for now.

A moment later, he emerged at the center of the tribe, where the huts formed a small opening, and where the goblin shaman waited. A hobgoblin stepped in Jack's path, shrouded in pure resolve. Its entire body shone black as phantasmal lines covered it, and Jack thought he saw a ghost.

He didn't care.

He fell onto the hobgoblin without slowing in the slightest. It backpedaled to keep him within range, its shortsword weaving clean lines through the air. Jack struggled to dodge. With the red snakes around his limbs, moving was difficult, but he was still faster and better than a mere hobgoblin.

His face morphed into a mask of utter focus. His fists dove through the gaps, smashing into the hobgoblin. The shortsword cut him deep, but he didn't stop—because if he did, the goblin swarm would catch up.

One punch broke the hobgoblin's jaw, another cracked its ribs, a third tossed the shortsword away. Jack caught a swing with his shoulder, letting the sword carve his outer arm as he punched the hobgoblin right in the face, sending it reeling and barely missing the shaman, who only cackled devilishly.

"Foolish human!" it shrieked. "You're almost dead!"

Jack barely heard it. Not only was he bleeding profusely, the hobgoblin had also scraped the surface of his arm so deep that the bone showed. He was in terrible pain, surrounded, and with an army at his heels. Moreover, the red snakes still tried to infiltrate his soul, and the more exhausted he got, the weaker his resistance.

He no longer had the strength to escape the tribe. All he could do now was kill the shaman.

Everything else disappeared. Only that hateful little creature was left, with its evil laughter and gloating eyes. It was within range. Jack pounced. His punches dug into the goblin's body and tore it apart, destroying it so hard it turned into smoke. Jack roared in triumph.

But goblins didn't turn into smoke.

"Kekeke, silly human."

He turned around, and the shaman was there, on the large hut's rooftop. This time, it held its staff, too. Jack was sure this was the real body—but through his pain and haze, he looked deeper.

As soon as he did, the goblin shaman turned transparent, and a new body appeared, watching him from behind a flood of goblins that poured right at Jack. "Not so silly," the shaman gloated. "But tasty, anyway. I will eat your brain. Kekeke!"

Jack grunted. The sound was barely human, more like a bull's, and so he acted. Bringing both arms before his face, he ducked deep and ran at the horde, aiming to blast right through it. The shaman laughed. "You're crazy!"

And maybe he was—but it worked.

Faced with Jack's unstoppable charge and their own momentum, the goblin army was broken. Some flew away, others were stomped, and yet more were simply pushed aside as Jack plowed through.

Some goblins grabbed on to him, trying to carve his skin even further. He paid them no mind. Only one thought remained: the goblin shaman had to die.

"Fool!" it shouted. Its staff shone red, and a wall of flames rose from nothing to block Jack's path. He faced an open oven, a wildfire in the middle of the forest. Whether he turned left or right, more goblins awaited to tear him apart.

Jack didn't turn left or right. He didn't break pace, either. He just kept running.

He dove into the flames. The goblins on him screamed as they were scorched, and Jack screamed too. These weren't normal flames. Every spark was like molten iron on his skin, every ember striving to burn through his bones. Even the red snakes were extinguished.

But Jack was strong, too. He screamed through the pain and kept running, channeling the resolve he'd built in the ice pond.

It was only a second, but it felt like eternity.

Everything was worth it when he burst out of the flames and met the goblin's shocked, fearful gaze. He stood before it, bleeding, injured, burned—*triumphant.*

"What?" it muttered, stepping back. "That's impossible!"

"Nothing is impossible."

Jack reared his right fist, gathering as much strength as he could. The goblin waved its staff, trying to cast something, but it was far too late. His fist dug deep into its face, smashing the goblin against the ground so hard it bounced off higher than his head. It was dead before it landed.

At the same time, a wave of euphoria flooded Jack. He'd won.

The flames disappeared, but behind them, the remaining goblins jumped at him once again. His eyes snapped back to reality. *What! But I—*

Level Up! You have reached Level 12.
Level Up! You have reached Level 13.
Level Up! You have reached Level 14.
Level Up! You have reached Level 15.

Goblin Boss defeated! Would you like to despawn the group? Y/N

Wh—Yes! Yes! Fucking yes!

The blue screens disappeared, revealing a claw heading right for his face. Jack closed his eyes.

And the claw never arrived. When he opened his eyes again, the goblins had disappeared, soundlessly dissolving into thin air. Despite his pain, he looked around incredulously. Not the slightest hint of their presence was left. Their weapons, their bodies, their clothes, even their huts were gone. Jack was left alone and bleeding in an empty forest clearing, where only the High Speed Bush remained.

He invested all eight stat points from the level-ups into Physical, and his skin squirmed as mortal wounds shut themselves. The bleeding slowed down, then stopped. He still felt dizzy and weak, but at least he was alive and would continue being so.

Those four levels saved his life. For once, the System had been kind to him.

Jack fell to his knees. His strength left him. So did the battle haze, and the pain of all his wounds shone through, but it was welcome. It only showed he was still alive.

That he'd won.

And, at the end of it all, a new blue screen shone before his eyes.

Level 15 reached. Congratulations! Class System unlocked. Please choose your Class:

CHAPTER FOURTEEN
CLASS TIME

After the goblin tribe was defeated, Jack lay on the grass, struggling to take in his rewards. He couldn't sleep here. He needed to move.

Four levels at once was a massive bonus, and it indicated there was something else at play besides the experience from individual monsters. Maybe the monster group counted as a big monster itself?

He'd also gotten the High Speed Bush, the resource guarded by the goblin tribe. Finally, the System had informed him he could now choose a class—and, knowing video games, this should be a bonus even greater than those levels.

Jack lay on the grass for a while, letting his tension die down before he dragged himself up and made his way to the High Speed Bush.

From up-close, the bush looked pretty natural. It was short, wide, with a multitude of branches extending from a barely-visible trunk in its center. The leaves were laid on thick, and were long, thin, and appeared soft. When he reached to touch one, it bent easily under his fingers and graced them with a thin, slippery coating.

This coating was the bush's excrement, which apparently made the goblins high. Jack looked at his finger, then licked it.

It didn't taste like much, similar to thin oil. He waited, but nothing happened. This quantity obviously wasn't enough for someone of his size—and stats.

Sighing in resignation, Jack plucked a few leaves off the bush and licked them one by one. It was a weird thing to do, but he couldn't just sit around. His battle against the tribe hadn't been discreet, and there was no telling what manner of creature was already galloping this way.

Just as Jack considered that maybe he'd misunderstood something, a blue screen appeared with a ding.

High Speed Bush bonus acquired!

Well, what is it?

He opened his status screen but saw no changes besides those he already knew.

His Physical was still climbing to the heavens, but that was just the points from the four level-ups. Where did the bush's bonus go?

He considered it, chewing on a leaf.

Maybe the bonus was too small to count as a full point? Like, 0.4 Physical or something? But that's so little... It can't be right. All this for a quarter of a level's worth? The ice pond has given me seven points already, and it can provide at least double overall. I know it's E-Grade, while the bush is F-Grade, but I refuse to believe the difference is that large.

Maybe it compounds as I consume more leaves? I'm not the slightest bit high yet.

He licked a couple more leaves, then sucked on a few more. No more status screens came, but he didn't mind that much. Points were just numbers; he had a fist, and the fist was always stronger than math. The professor might disagree, but if so, she should go fight a goblin tribe.

Jack giggled at the thought of the elderly lady lecturing the goblins.

Right. It's okay, my bushy friend. You can keep your extra points. Maybe you need them more than I do. I mean, licking any more leaves would be inappropriate, right?

Giggling again, Jack decided to explore his class choices. He'd planned to retreat and do this at the cave, but why? If there was a reason, he couldn't remember it, so it didn't matter.

Jack took in the wall of text and giggled. He liked reading. He squinted as he approached the screens, his nose almost touching them, and he tried to make out the letters.

He struggled to focus for some reason, but it didn't matter. Why hurry?

Goblin Fighter: Goblins are genetically engineered lifeforms that make for great first enemies. They are usually slain by the native species during a planet's Integration, but when they aren't, they proliferate rapidly. If left unattended, goblins can span planet-wide empires, with peak specimens even reaching the D-Grade in power. Goblin fighters rove the cosmos while destroying goblin infestations, as well as any of the many variants. They are perfectly equipped to locate, investigate, and exterminate them, and they are rewarded handsomely for their services.

Goblin fighter sounded cool! But also dumb. He didn't want to spend his life hunting stupid, annoying goblins.

Survivor (Elite): Survivors specialize in withstanding extreme environments. They usually act by themselves, exploring desolate planets, infiltrating monster-infested biomes, and expertly treading the razor-sharp edge between life and death. Survivors don't always succeed in their endeavors, but they almost always escape with their lives. Adapting is their second nature.
"Where there is life, there is opportunity."

Elite. That was a new word. Well, not quite—it's new for the System. In video games, which the System was proving similar, elite meant strong. One plus one equals two.

The first paragraph excited Jack tremendously. He almost chose it on the spot before reading the next one, too. He scowled.

I don't want to be a turtle. I want to fight!

He remembered the burning of his body as steel flooded his veins, the razor-sharp awareness that came with life-or-death battles, the sweet release of violence when he was at the good end of it. The exuberance of being completely one with himself, in his element, vibing.

He giggled. Just thinking about it got him fired up again.

Escaping from the bear had been fun too, just not as fun as punching the shit out of things.

Then again, Jack didn't want to die, either. His entire reason for trying so hard was to survive—and, taking things one step further, did he want to become a punching monster? Or was he, at heart, a survivor? Maybe most survivors were weak and failed often, but he could be strong!

Pugilist (Elite): Pugilists are one of the few F-Grade combat Classes ranked as Elite. This adjustment was made to reflect their tiny proportion compared to other Classes, as well as the difficulty of reaching Level 15 as an unarmed, non-magical combatant.

Pugilists are devastating in close combat, an advantage counterweighted by their lacking survivability. Their battles are simple, straightforward, and barbaric. When a Pugilist enters the fray, there are no half-measures; it is victory or death.

"Fist means power."

This was exciting. The Pugilist's description sounded underwhelming compared to the others, but Jack's blood boiled as he read it. He needed no fanfare, no flowery words; simple meant strong. The straightforwardness drew him in, the hidden resolve behind these seemingly simple words.

Fist means power. He savored the phrase. He liked it.

A corner of his mind whispered that the Pugilist was suicidal, and Jack's main drive was survival. Punching was fun, but it wasn't the main goal.

Everything else in his mind resisted that thought. Punching *was* the goal. In a moment of clarity, he realized that survival had been the starting point and a handy excuse, but at the core of his being, he just loved to fight.

Jack Rust willed himself into a Pugilist.

Congratulations! You are now a Pugilist (Elite).

Yay!

Physical subcategories unlocked: Strength, Dexterity, Constitution. Stats distributed.
Class Skill unlocked: Drill (I). More Class Skills will be unlocked at regular Level intervals.
Drill (I): Passive Skill. Your punches now carry a hint of drilling power, letting them penetrate hard defenses.

Woo! New stats! New skills! Armored magic bears, here I come!

If the System still followed video games, Strength represented his muscle mass, Dexterity his fine control over said muscle mass, and Constitution his ability to withstand damage.

However, just as Jack willed the blue screens away, his world changed.

He was no longer in a forest. He wasn't on Earth, either. An endless expanse stretched before him, a desert of tremendous proportions. Purple sand reached the horizon, and the sun burned so hot he questioned how he wasn't on fire yet.

Looking down, Jack understood the answer. He had no body.

A loud growl drew his attention, a sound loud enough to burst his eardrums, if he still had any. His gaze met a colossal serpent, a form resembling a bipedal, spiked crocodile. His eyes widened.

Godzilla!

Lizard Titan, Level ??? (C-Grade)

C-Grade!

Jack couldn't even see its level, but C-Grade now felt so far beyond him. Just how wide were the gulfs between grades?

The massive beast was tall like a mountain, and—why was it growling? Jack squinted, and there, before its feet, stood a human. He was tiny—normal-sized, but tiny compared to the beast.

Jack quickly scanned him as well.

Human (Earth-4), Level ??? (C-Grade)

Faction: Exploding Sun
Title: Eighth Ring Conqueror

Exploding Sun? Eighth Ring Conqueror?

Jack didn't understand anything.

This man was bald with plain features, donned elegant yellow clothes, and wore a red cape. However, his simple face was practically chiseled from stone. Facing the full brunt of the beast's fury, he only clenched his fist. He opened his mouth, and his words fell on Jack's ears like thunder.

"Fist means power."

He jumped hundreds of feet into the air. Sand and rock crumbled below his feet, and from the distance, Jack could only stare.

The man reached the height of the beast's chest and punched. It was just a simple punch. Yet, the moment his arm completed its motion, a storm of violence erupted. The sky shook and the earth rumbled from the momentum of this one punch, and as it met the beast's colossal, scaly chest, both exploded.

One punch drilled through the beast, mincing scales, flesh, and bones alike. It wasn't merely a fist, but an irresistible force of nature.

This is a real punch.

The scene replayed itself in Jack's mind, ten times, a hundred times. This ideal punch stabbed through the air and drilled into the beast's body, and he soaked in how everything worked. It wasn't just a punch. There was something more, something so much more.

At some indeterminate point, it clicked.

Jack had a sudden realization. Understanding dawned on him, and the next moment, it receded, as if he wasn't able to utilize it yet. It retreated into the depths of his mind and locked itself there, waiting, slumbering.

The essence of what a fist was and what it could be. An insight greater than anything he'd ever comprehended. An understanding so gigantic and world-breaking it should have been impossible. He couldn't fathom it yet, but when he could, it would already be inside him, shining like a beacon.

When he exited his own mind and returned to the purple desert, time seemed frozen still.

A large hole had been punched clean through the beast's chest, wide enough to fit a house, perfectly round, and completely empty. As the large body began to collapse, the man looked at his fist and shook his head.

"Still not enough," he muttered.

The vision disappeared. Jack was back in the forest, but all vestiges of highness had evaporated from his system. He was covered in cold sweat, shivering, and his eyes were wide as saucers.

"What the fuck was that..." he whispered.

C-Grade... Holy hell, those guys are gods.

It was nothing like the movies. He'd felt the man's power in his *soul*, comprehended the seeming invincibility of the giant beast. Seeing superheroes on-screen was completely different than experiencing their power first-hand.

Jack sat on his butt, then looked at his own fist. He managed to clench it.

"Is that... a Pugilist?" The shock in his voice turned to awe. "Such power... If I can have it too, how amazing would that be?"

His feelings wavered. He was overtaken by childish excitement and equally childish fear. He had no doubt that the vision he'd seen was real. Those things existed. The monsters in the dark were part of his world now, and he had the strength to fight them—no, he didn't have it yet, but he could earn it.

The class hadn't given him extra muscles but something so much better.

Now shivering from excitement, Jack regained his bearings. He stared at the bush accusingly.

I must be careful... Even with 38 Physical, I still lost my mind a bit. Oh, right! My Physical was broken into Strength, Dexterity, and Constitution. I wonder how much I have.

He opened his status screen and immediately gasped.

What? That high? This is impossible!

CHAPTER FIFTEEN
BEARY STRONG

Name: Jack Rust
Species: Human, Earth-387
Faction: -
Grade: F
Class: Pugilist (Elite)
Level: 15

Strength: 38
Dexterity: 48
Constitution: 38
Mental: 9
Will: 7

Skills: Fistfighting (II), Drill (I)

There were so many high numbers. When his Physical broke into three sub-stats, he expected his 38 points to be divided, not tripled.

What does this mean? Did I become three times stronger? And this Dexterity...

He didn't feel three times stronger than before. A bit, sure, but not to such a degree. *What does this mean?*

Thankfully, Jack was a scientist—he did almost have a PhD.

Maybe a point in Physical always meant a point in each of the stats. It's the same thing. Nothing changed. I just saw a simplified version so far.

This hypothesis was based on little, but it made sense. The System wouldn't just triple his power for no reason.

Still, why is Dexterity so much higher? Is it because of the High Speed Bush?

Unlike his other stats, he *did* feel faster than before, more flexible, more in command of his body. It had to have been the bush, unless the ice pond's bonuses were skewed toward Dexterity, which shouldn't be the case. He hadn't noticed an imbalance before, but he could feel it now.

Huh. Then why did my Physical remain at 38 after the bush bonus? Maybe it's not the average, but the minimum? Or some other, more complicated function?

In any case, he could see the utility of breaking down the stats. Keeping things simple at first was nice, but a stat imbalance would be hard to depict in a single number. Plus, if Jack's suspicions were correct, this would allow for greater customization of himself.

There was a question mark on how exactly his points would be distributed from here on. Would he still get two per level, or six? And if it was six, did that mean he could put six into Mental, for example?

I probably still get two points as I did before, but if I want to put one point into the Physical sub-stats, it becomes three subpoints to allocate however I want.

Only that made sense, so it had to be true.

In the end, he didn't intend to scrutinize the System's choices. It was seemingly omniscient and omnipotent. It should have its reasons for everything. Still, he wouldn't be surprised if the professor had already released a peer-reviewed publication criticizing the System's procedures by the time he returned to civilization.

He chuckled.

She can handle herself... probably.

It was a grim thought. Not all people were as equipped as him to handle a global overhaul... Then again, neither was he. The professor was a genius. She'd pull through.

Jack snapped out of his thoughts. The clearing was as quiet and empty as ever. That was lucky. He'd overstayed his welcome while high. He didn't know how long the vision took in real time, but he must have been idling here for at least twenty minutes.

Minutes...

Another sobering realization. He hadn't considered time in minutes for... a while. The sun's position had been enough.

Done reminiscing, Jack decided it was time to get going. He'd already taken everything he could from the bush, and there was nothing else in the clearing.

His feet took him into the bushes and up a hill, heading in the familiar direction of his cave. He still had to go into the pond again to see if he could take any extra steps—or rather, how many.

Midway to the cave, he stopped. Yes, he had to try the ice pond... but he really wanted to see the effects of Drill. He was far enough from the clearing now. Nothing was following him.

Clenching his fist, he shot it at a random tree trunk.

The moment it made impact, he sensed the change. His punch was so straight and controlled that no energy escaped the point of impact. Instead, its entire momentum bypassed the tree's surface and exploded deeper, not mitigated at all by the hard bark.

The entire tree shook—leaves fell from its branches, and the trunk itself groaned and cracked from the inside.

Jack stared at his fist in surprise, then grinned. Its next target would be an earth bear and its stupidly hard magic fur.

There were a few more things to settle, but they all went by quickly.

The ice pond was the first. After submerging his entire body into it for the first time and withstanding the ensuing agony, the cold closed his wounds, healing him completely in the span of a few minutes. For the zillionth time, Jack thanked his lucky stars for spawning this gift of the gods beside him.

Due to his increased stats, he also managed to take another two steps into the ice pond. It was great progress! He was now at two thirds of the way to the waterfall. As he'd approached, he could now better estimate it would take him thirteen steps, and he'd made nine.

One last thing was left, and that was to test his strength.

I hope all that pain bears fruit... he thought, walking outside his cave and surveying the poor rocks and trees.

He had earned four levels for beating the goblins. He'd also taken two steps into the ice pond, each giving him a point in Physical—well, to be more precise, in each of his new physical stats—so his stats had risen by the equivalent of five levels. Moreover, he hadn't really measured himself in a human scale in... a long time.

He itched to know how strong he was.

With a stupid grin, he stood before a boulder that reached up to his waist. There was no way a pre-System human could lift this thing. Jack bent his knees, grabbed it by the edges, and lifted.

"Heave-ho!"

The boulder shot up.

"Wha—"

He let it fall, and it did with a massive thud that shook the night forest. "What the..." he repeated, looking at his own two hands. "Did I do that?"

Knowing he was strong was one thing. Actually comparing himself to the pre-System him was a different matter altogether. More real.

He flexed his fists, sensing the raw power that lay within, just waiting for him to direct it. Without thinking, he turned and punched a tree. Its entire trunk shook, leaves fell from above, and a few birds that perched on its branches hurried to fly away.

Jack's hand was unhurt.

He jumped on the tree. Each leap could easily reach the lower branches, and his agility was such that he was certain he would never fall, even if he didn't have the terrible gripping power that he currently possessed.

Letting himself drop, he somersaulted once midair before landing on his feet. It was easy.

"Wow..." he exclaimed breathlessly.

He thought back to the pain, the panic, the anguish he forced himself through to survive. Every fight brought him close to death, starting from that very first goblin, but he always survived. The goblin shaman had almost destroyed him, but he'd prevailed.

It had been hell, and still was—but not for nothing. With danger came power.

Now, he was no longer weak, no longer helpless. He wasn't a pest that had to hide from little goblins. He was a strong player in this dungeon. He'd earned it.

Jack clenched his fist tight, and the relief that flooded him was enough to almost bring tears to his eyes. He tightened his lips and nodded.

This wouldn't be the end. There were the bears to fight, and the monkeys, and the damn wolf that saw him as a bug. Outside this dungeon, there was a wide world, too. Gone were the days of endlessly toiling away at a lab table.

Jack always yearned to feel alive. His wish had been granted. An entire planet waited for him after he conquered this dungeon, an entire galaxy, even, full of mystery and power for him to grasp, and he had a head start. He was so excited he got goosebumps.

The bald man had been at the C-Grade. The Animal Kingdom, the power that now apparently controlled Earth, was B-Grade. Jack didn't know what those meant exactly, but he would reach that level of power, and then, even higher. There was so much to learn, so much to discover, so much to experience. He would go all-out in a world that finally fit him. He would thrive. He would *live.*

He could see the path. F, E, D, C, B... and A. Sleep with the lights on, world. Jack Rust is coming.

However, long dreams would have to wait. First came the bears, the dungeon, and then the world.

Jack chuckled and shook his head as he walked back to his cave.

How far I've come, and how far there is to go.

Satisfied from a day and night full of rewards, and filled with dreams for the future, Jack went to sleep. The night was still young, and he deserved to rest well for once. A few hours after the sun rose, Jack was already crossing the forest toward the bear territory. They would have the honor of being his next opponents—or prey.

His fists itched to face a bear head-on, but he kept himself in check. Even the weakest earth bear was at level 13, and though he could probably take it, every close battle carried a substantial risk of death. There was no need to throw his life away.

Stronger, faster, and harder than ever, Jack fell into a routine he knew well. He crafted a trusty stone hammer—heavier than the previous one—and snuck around the edges of bear territory, aiming for weaker specimens.

The worst part about traveling this area of the forest were the carcasses. Not the eaten ones—bears left little behind—but the ones that had been broken for sport. Earth bears were quite sadistic, apparently. That was bad for the nearby wildlife and good for Jack, because it meant he could keep killing them without moral remorse.

He averted his sight and kept going. Unfortunately, the bears had a slim population, so it took him a long time to finally find one. When he did, it was level 15.

Normally, he would have let this go and looked for another bear. However, he'd already spent a good chunk of time looking.

Jack was a biologist that focused on evolution. He knew about bears. The normal kind—the non-magical ones—weren't territorial, unlike what the System suggested. However, he could adapt his knowledge.

Since these bears were territorial, and given the places at which he'd located them, he assumed they'd split their wider territory into chunks, and each bear got one chunk. That was why he'd spent so long looking for one; he'd been searching the chunks where he'd already killed a bear.

Due to his job, Jack had visited this reserve many times, enough to know its general layout by heart. He understood the size of the bear area. Assuming all chunks were similar in size, he estimated there were thirteen to sixteen earth bears. That wasn't much. It also meant he'd probably run out of low-level bears and have to dive deeper soon.

He still hadn't seen the bear boss or any stronger variant than the earth bear—all in due time. Jack was finally ahead of the curve, and he'd take full advantage of it.

The clock was still running. He wasn't going to search the entire area for a slightly weaker bear. Level 15 would do.

He climbed a tree and held his stone hammer at the ready. The bear didn't come by, and Jack scowled as he rushed to another branch, keeping tabs on the bear's location by its growls and other sounds.

Two hours later, after failing yet another branch ambush, his patience was growing thin.

Why wait for hours when I can just kick its ass?

Because I might lose, he replied, regaining himself. He wasn't rash or stupid. Even if on the clock, rushing things would bring ugly consequences. He was nowhere near the king of the forest.

Another hour later, as the sun reached its peak, Jack heard the bear approach. He tensed up in joy. *It's happening!*

A brown shape with yellow splotches came under his branch, its wide ass swerving from side to side as it walked. Jack descended.

Bonk!

He stood over its headless corpse, frowning. This was quite anticlimactic...

Not even a level up... Fine. I'll find a level 14 or less and try to fight it.

Since he now understood how their territories worked, he could start from the ones at the edge of the bear area, which, according to game logic, would have the weakest bears.

And it worked! Only half an hour later, Jack parted the leaves of a bush to spy on a level 14 behemoth. It was busy stomping a bunny's corpse to death.

At least eat it, you fat prick.

Coincidentally, this was the same bear that chased him down before —he would recognize it everywhere. Jack's spirit burned at the thought of finally taking revenge.

He set the stone hammer aside and cracked his neck, then his knuckles as he prepared himself for a good fight. Ambushes were easy but time-consuming, and he didn't want to waste hours on each bear. With some luck, he could take one down without major injuries—and, if not, he was confident in escaping. He'd done it with half the stats.

Now ready, Jack bumped his fists together one more time, then calmly walked toward the bear. When he stepped on dry wood, it turned to look, yellow eyes easily spotting him. It growled. Jack held its gaze and grinned.

The bear was confused now. It recognized this creature, but last time, it had run away. Everything tried to escape when it growled. What was this?

Jack stepped between the trees and approached the bear. They weren't in any sort of clearing, so the terrain would only help him.

The bear growled again and charged. Jack charged right back, releasing a roar of his own.

An enraged behemoth was charging right at him, fangs wide and claws racing to tear him apart. For a moment, he reconsidered all his life choices; then, he realized the bear was slow. Too slow.

It lunged, but he jumped to its side. The bear rose on two feet to rip him apart.

He ducked under a hairy arm, then another. Jaws snapped shut before his face but couldn't touch him. He swerved aside, dodging a blow before stabbing two quick jabs into the bear's fur. Like last time, a yellow patch rose to meet him.

This time, however, the yellow patch was ineffective. Jack felt the difference. His fist slammed into protected fur and sent the impact through it, directly onto the bear's skin. He couldn't go deeper yet, unfortunately, but this was already a massive improvement.

The bear growled as it stepped back, falling on all fours. It eyed him warily. The impact had clearly hurt it.

Jack didn't eye anything warily—he only attacked harder.

He was on the offensive. Blow after blow rained on the bear. Each of his attacks couldn't hurt it too much, but when they stockpiled, the weight became unbearable.

The bear frothed at the mouth. Claws, jaws, even the back of paws and body slams came his way, but Jack dodged it all. After consuming the High Speed Bush, speed was his specialty, and it was also this bear's weakness.

He grinned at what was happening.

In game terminology, this bear was a slow tank, and he had both the speed to dodge everything and the skills to gradually decimate it.

Thanks to Drill and the High Speed Bush, he countered the bear completely.

That's not to say it was easy. Each of the bear's strikes were cataclysmic, and though they were slow to Jack's eyes, a pre-System human couldn't even see them coming. For Jack, dodging one attack was easy, but the more the bear attacked, the higher his chances were of making a mistake.

He kept his cool. Danced around the bear, gracefully weaving between attacks as he landed his own. His brain was honed and at maximum capacity the entire time.

The fight took place at great speed but still lasted more than three minutes. Jack didn't make a single mistake.

Eventually, the bear slowed down. Jack's punches increased in strength and volume, and the large beast was taken down. Its head slammed against the ground, leaving Jack panting, sweaty, and victorious.

He raised a fist into the air and roared his triumph.

"Fuck yeah!"

He'd finally defeated an earth bear, these devils, for the first time!

No level up yet, but they would come. Now that he knew he could handle it, Jack's hunting speed would increase by many times. The fight required his full focus, but it wasn't too difficult. He hadn't even come close to getting hit. He could easily be consistent for that long.

Grinning and leaving his stone hammer in that random bush, Jack went on with his hunting. The earth bears of the Greenway Natural Reserve were quickly whittled down, from the weakest to the strongest. Over the next twenty-four hours, eight more monster bears lost their lives to the forest's rising star.

Until, on the ninth bear, the rising star met the king.

CHAPTER SIXTEEN
A SUMMIT OF KINGS

IT HAPPENED AS JACK WAS STALKING HIS NINTH EARTH BEAR IN A ROW, A prowling beast at level 18. In the past day, he'd already cut down their population by more than half, meaning only the high-level ones were left. He'd even seen one at level 20 but avoided it.

He'd also gotten two levels for his hunt, bringing him to 17. By willing the free points into his Physical, all stat points were distributed evenly between Strength, Dexterity, and Constitution. He could always choose a different ratio, such as putting all points into Strength, but the balanced approach had worked well so far, so he stuck with it.

Name: Jack Rust
Species: Human, Earth-387
Faction: –
Rank: F
Class: Pugilist (Elite)
Level: 17

Strength: 44
Dexterity: 54

Constitution: 44
Mental: 9

Will: 7

Skills: Fistfighting (II), Drill (I)

As Jack stalked this bear, debating whether to attack it or not, a low growl hummed through the trees.

Jack knew this growl. He instantly froze. He didn't dare to even look around.

The earth bear also recognized the growl. It looked around in sudden agitation, the fear clear in its yellow gaze. A dark shadow shot out of the bushes straight for it. So fast, even Jack's enhanced kinetic vision only saw a blur.

The bear panicked. The sound it made wasn't a growl, closer to whining. Jack didn't know bears could make that sound. Yet, the dark blur showed no signs of stopping, and the bear could only try to fight back.

Its claws sliced, but the blur ducked under them and smashed hard into brown fur. The bear flew back—Jack could at most make it stumble—and made a desperate attempt to bite down on its assailant. It missed, and at the same moment, another set of jaws found its way around its neck. With a deep crack, the earth bear was dead.

Jack was still frozen.

A dark wolf now stood atop the bear's corpse, holding it by the throat. The two bodies were similar in size, but the wolf's power was far, far higher. The bear Jack would need several minutes to dismantle, if he didn't die first, had fallen in two attacks.

Black Wolf, Level 49 (Elite) (Dungeon Boss)

It was the second time he'd met this king of the forest. He had grown a lot since that first crossing, but the difference between them hadn't closed by much... and Jack's only way to escape this dungeon was to defeat it.

He did, however, notice a scar on its snout. It wasn't there last time, he was sure. Was there something that could rival the king in this forest, or did an earth bear get lucky before its death?

The wolf glanced at Jack, and he quickly looked at the ground, all thoughts forgotten. He didn't dare challenge it—not yet. However, before averting his sight, he'd managed to catch a glimpse of its eyes.

One would expect the Dungeon Boss to be a regal, proud, sage-like existence. It wasn't. In its eyes, Jack only saw a fierce animal, a killer. Cold sweat drenched his back, and his legs began to shake a bit. His fight or flight instincts didn't even activate. What level 17? If this wolf wanted to kill him, he could do nothing to resist.

Still feeling its gaze on him, as if deliberating its next move, Jack repeated his trick from last time. He fell on his knees and bowed to the wolf, acknowledging its strength and status as the king.

The wolf still didn't look away. Jack stayed like that, perfectly still, trying to calm his breathing. Time slowed. Was it a second, a minute, or an hour?

Finally, the sound of fur dragging on dirt came. The wolf darted away, easily carrying the massive earth bear in its mouth and disappearing between the trees, headed toward the center of the reserve.

Jack remained kneeling. Only after another minute did he dare stand. He looked at the ground ahead of him, where the bear's blood had dyed the dirt red.

"Fuck me..." he whispered.

He'd thought himself ahead of the curve, and in a way, he was. He could finally choose his prey instead of settling for what was not prohibitively difficult. However, strength brought a price.

Last time, the wolf hadn't even glanced at him. He'd been an ant to its eyes. This time he had clearly received its interest. Had it recognized his increase in strength and considered him a future threat? Or was his current power a source of worry anyway?

In any case, Jack could clearly see the pattern. The wolf would spare an ant, but not an elephant.

The next time it met Jack, it wouldn't let him go. He had to hurry and get the strength to protect himself... or hide in his cave until someone rescued him. But Jack hadn't come all this way to cower. He clenched his fists as sparks jumped in his eyes.

I must get stronger, and fast.

He was still very much on the clock—a clock he'd helped accelerate.

Thanks to Jack's hunting, the wolf's prey was dwindling. Both of them hunted the same big game. The fewer the bears became, the higher the chances of Jack and the wolf meeting, and it would eventually realize the implications. It might even come directly after him.

This threw a wrench into Jack's plans. He'd been an idiot. He could no longer hunt bears, as they were needed to satiate the big wolf's appetite. He had to start hunting monkeys, level up fast, then defeat both the monkey and bear boss. Then, maybe he'd be strong enough to match the wolf if he used his human intelligence to its maximum extent.

The moment he'd had that thought, Jack's face went hard as a rock. His chances were grim, but he had to try.

A second growl cut through the forest. Jack became rigid, thinking the wolf had returned, but this growl was different. He dove back inside his bush.

From deeper inside the bear area, a massive form slowly made its way through the trees. A giant of a bear, a walking tank. Its body was at least nine feet in length, probably more, and it was taller than Jack while on all fours. Its fur wasn't just covered in yellow splashes, it was riddled with yellow, rock-like surfaces that served as shields, and its claws were so long and sharp, they cut grooves through the dirt.

Jack raised his brows.

Rock Bear, Level 30

When Earth Bears mate, they have a small chance of producing Rock Bear offspring. This variant is bigger, stronger, and more closely attuned to earth than a normal Earth Bear. Rock Bears command the innate respect of Earth Bears, allowing them to form and control packs that share a single, large territory.

In the Ursus Forests of planet Ursi, Rock Bears are regional overlords,

only under the Tyrant Bears in strength. Their power usually reaches the E-Grade.
This particular Rock Bear is the group boss of the bear monsters of the Forest of the Strong.

That was an extensive description that did Jack little good besides providing context. From the earth bear description, there was a planet called Ursi that probably had a lot of bears—ursus meant bear in latin, and ursi was the plural of that, though what did latin have to do with the System? Now, he also knew earth bears were weaker than rock bears, which were, in turn, weaker than the so-called tyrant bears.

He could even understand how their ecosystem worked, and how they formed pack hierarchies that stretched through a large number of smaller sub-packs. Unfortunately, all that interesting knowledge couldn't help Jack in the slightest.

The rock bear approached the spot where the previous bear's blood still smeared the ground. It hadn't noticed Jack yet—thankfully he'd been hiding somewhat farther away.

It sniffed the ground, then raised its large head in the direction the wolf had taken. Jack could see its eyes from where he was hidden. The bear was angry, bloodthirsty, but also hesitant. There was a grudge in the way it looked toward the center of the reserve, one it could not fulfill.

Jack held his breath. Would the bear boss fight the wolf? That would be such a waste of levels for him...

In the end, the bear didn't give chase. After staring, it stood on its hind legs—God, was it tall—and smashed a paw into a nearby tree, easily breaking it into pieces. Jack blinked in surprise.

The bear then released a massive, earth-shaking roar, the likes of which Jack had never heard. It would obviously reach the wolf's ears—though it wasn't a challenge. It was just a venting of the rock bear's impotent rage.

There was just nothing it could do.

But the wolf is proud, thought Jack. Will it come after the bear boss next?

It was a worthy consideration, unless there was some rule that forbade bosses from fighting each other, but that just sounded stupid.

There had to be some eco balance. A bear boss without its pack wouldn't be much of a boss, and Jack assumed the System had the ability to craft circumstances that would favor the creation of a balanced monster ecosystem.

Maybe it did, and I was the one who broke the balance, somehow. Maybe the goblins served as a food source for the other monsters, including the wolf, and me killing them forces everything to fight each other.

Is the dungeon going to implode on itself? Am I the pest here?

It was an amusing thought. Then again, if the System cared about its delicate ecosystem, it shouldn't have placed him in the fucking middle of everything.

These were Jack's thoughts as he watched the rock bear steam in rage. However, when it turned around to leave with heavy steps, new ideas sprung in his mind.

If the wolf hunts down this bear, as it probably will, I will lose a bunch of levels. I need those levels. Unless... I kill the bear first.

This sent his mind spinning in a wholly new direction. *Can I take it right now?* he asked himself, not believing his own thoughts.

It's just a bigger bear. It's stronger and more durable, but not much faster than the earth bears. I can ambush it just like the others, and if worse comes to worst, I can probably run away. Plus, its increased defense can do nothing against my Drill punches.

A plan was taking form in Jack's mind, and as more and more ideas sprung up to support it, he was overtaken by equal parts anticipation and disbelief.

Our level difference is large, but each individual level matters less and less the more I climb. It's not about the raw number, it's about percentages. This bear is a bit over one and a half times my level. When I killed a level 13 bear at level 7, wasn't the difference even greater? And it still died to a single, well-timed strike from my stone hammer.

I no longer have the hammer, and making a new one would take too long, but my punches shouldn't be that far off. Its head can't be made of rock. If I can pull off an ambush, I can probably kill this bear and shower in levels.

Oh, God... I can't believe I'm considering this.

But he *was* considering it. And the more he thought, the more reasons he found to reaffirm this crazy course of action.

If I delay until I'm certain of victory, the wolf might kill the bear first, and I'll lose all those levels I desperately need. No. I can't let this opportunity go to waste. It's already near impossible to kill the wolf and escape this dungeon. If I don't take some risks, I'll never make it.

Slowly, everything came to a point. Jack's body moved by itself, stealthily following the level 30 titan of a bear. His eyes sharpened.

I must hunt this bear. Right now.

CHAPTER SEVENTEEN
JACK RUST VS. BEAR KING

THE ROCK BEAR'S STEPS WERE SLOW AND HEAVY AS IT TRUDGED THROUGH THE forest, heading for the depths of its territory. This entire bear area belonged to it; the earth bears were only renting small parts.

As they dove deeper into the forest, bear first and Jack second, the scenery didn't change much. The trees remained normal, pre-System varieties, the chirping of birds filled the air, and uneaten corpses still littered the ground, proof of these bears' monstrosity.

Their path crossed another bear, a stunning level 20, but it reverently made way for the rock bear, which didn't even look at it. An hour later, the rock bear reached a small lake in the middle of a clearing, where a stream branched off to head for the northwestern end of the reserve.

This lake hadn't been here before the System, Jack was certain.

A rock outcropping stretched over the lake, and the bear stopped there. Its enormous body—it must have weighed at least a ton—splayed fully on the rock, which held without a problem. It rested, but Jack could still see the clouds in its mind. It was clearly distraught. The black wolf was killing its kin, and there was nothing the rock bear could do about it besides assisted suicide.

Of course, the fact they'd walked an hour to get here sent chills down Jack's spine. The rock bear arrived at the site of battle less than a minute after it was over. It had clearly been in the area already, looking for whomever was killing its kind like flies. This beast had been on his trail.

If the wolf hadn't shown up, and Jack had been the one to attack the level 18 bear, it was very probable the rock bear would have caught up before the battle was over. Jack would be pincer-attacked, and there was no way he was getting out of that alive.

The black wolf accidentally saved him. Jack, unfortunately, would have to do the exact opposite.

For now, he stayed hidden in a distant bush, observing the rock bear's lair. The small lake—more a pond than a lake—was spawned in a clearing where the only notable feature was the rock outcropping that stretched over one quarter of the pond's area like a pier.

This area was beautiful. Jack could see why the bear had taken it as a lair.

Fortunately, it was also pretty handy for an ambush. The bear was currently resting on its rock outcropping, so, when it left, it would probably head for the nearby edge where the first trees stood. One of those trees had thick enough foliage for Jack to hide in. There, he would have a good shot at success.

Without leaving himself more time to consider his actions, he made a big circle around the clearing to arrive at its back side. He then moved slowly to his chosen tree, less than fifty feet away from the bear. It wasn't a short distance, but Jack knew better than to underestimate an animal's senses—especially a magical one's.

His high stats made it easy to quietly climb the tree, and before long, Jack lay on a branch ten feet off the ground, completely still and with his ears stretched. A bug climbed on his back, and he let it. Another paraded before his nose, and he gently blew it away.

The ridiculousness of it all was blatant. He, Jack Rust, was trying to ambush a van-sized magical bear and kill it with his bare hands. He'd been in a laboratory only a week ago, doing boring things for boring people, and he was excited to catch a rare caterpillar six days ago, when the System descended.

No, not descended—integrated. That was the proper terminology, according to the blue screens.

What was the world like right now? How did people react when they weren't trapped by themselves in a deadly dungeon? What happened to society and politics? Was there resistance? People had guns and nuclear weapons, there was bound to be resistance. Then again, the System seemed quite omnipotent so far. Nuclear weapons might only be a tickle to an alien starcraft.

He remembered the announcement from the B-Grade Animal Kingdom, whatever that was. B-Grade sounded strong.

And the announcement warning them about an Integration Tournament in fifteen days, which sounded extremely important. Jack didn't know what it was, but if it included punching stuff, could he maybe join? This dungeon was bound to put him way ahead of the curve if he could survive.

Of course, killing the wolf came first, and he doubted his chances of success...

Jack let his mind travel to forget his tension. He envisioned scenarios of revolutions around the world, of white-collar tyranny and uprisings of battle-hardy nations. He pictured some people like the orcs in movies, ready to go to war and give everything for strength and honor. He saw dozens getting classes as he had, probably in a streamlined way of human ingenuity, and new, strength-based hierarchies springing up from the ground.

What level would it take to catch a bullet? How strong were wizards?

All these beautiful thoughts dispersed like smoke when a tired growl echoed from the clearing. Jack dared peek through the leaves—the rock bear was standing. It made its way from the pond with slow steps befitting its stature, approaching Jack's hiding spot.

His ambush just might work! He panicked. He'd started hoping the bear would choose another way.

What am I doing? Maybe I should just stay hidden. The strongest creature I've killed so far was level 17, and this bear is 30. Who knows what hidden weapons it has? What hidden abilities and magic? I don't even have my stone hammer. This is suicide.

The bear inched closer, mockingly slow.

No, this is the right way. The chances are with me, and I must risk to survive. I can and will kill this bear.

The bear's form kept growing in his eyes.

I'll stay hidden. There's no way I can take it.

It disappeared, too close to his branch to see through the leaves.

I will fight.

A muzzle entered his field of vision, parading below him as if daring him to attack. It was a large muzzle on a long body. Like watching a train go by.

I will stay.

The bear fully entered his sight. It hadn't noticed him, and its head came right below his branch, completely exposed from above. He could even see the individual hairs on its fur. It was the perfect opportunity. Jack steeled his heart.

I will fight.

He let himself fall, using everything he had to strike the bear's head with enough strength to pulverize it. The bear, like all of its kind, looked up just in time to meet his punch with its nose.

The moment Jack crossed eyes with the rock bear, from only a couple feet away, he suspected he'd fucked up.

His punch met the bear's nose so hard, so violently, that a bell-like sound echoed alongside the crack of bones—the inside of its head was rock-hard. Jack's body almost stopped in midair from the recoil.

The bear's eyes flickered, almost passing out. Blood dripped from its ears, and its nose was nearly entirely broken. Its brain threatened to turn into mush, or it partially did. The bear wobbled and almost fell—but *almost* was the key word here.

It was the perfect ambush, but it wasn't enough. And so began Jack's punching marathon against the rock bear. On one side stood a tall, bare-chested man with finely chiseled muscles. On the other, the king of bears.

The rock bear was a tremendous creature. Seeing it from up-close, with nothing between you and a gruesome death, was quite the experience. When Jack rolled on the ground and stood across from it, he gulped. He'd gotten used to earth bears, but this was no earth bear. It was far bigger, stronger, and nastier.

The bear's face was the size of his torso. Stone plates slid on its brown fur as bulging muscles swam underneath, and its sharp jaws released a stench so visceral, he struggled not to gag.

This was a majestic, fearsome beast—and one that was currently injured. Blood dripped from its orifices, and its furious gaze hid clear pain. Its movements were slow, not much faster than an earth bear's.

I can take it, Jack thought and raised his fists. The very next moment, he felt like an idiot. He was tiny.

The bear roared and attacked. Clawed paws whooshed through the air, each strong enough to uproot a tree. Jaws snapped shut before him, and they could easily crush his entire skeleton to paste. The bear's humongous body lumbered after Jack, and getting caught by that thing, even in the slightest, would spell his doom.

Fight or flight? asked his mind.

Fight, Jack responded, and his entire being complied.

All thoughts left his mind. There was no hesitation, no fear. His body was fire and his mind ice. The world slowed as his mind raced at incredible speeds, calculating and telegraphing everything. Facing the primordial fear of a bear, his mind was faster than at any other time, so fast he could glimpse at the million little calculations and adjustments that always happened in the background.

He could feel how his muscles contracted to step back, sense the trajectories his fingers followed to form a fist. When his eyes took in the bear's incoming paw, Jack saw the options his mind instinctively discarded before dodging to the right.

It was a unique sensation, and one that could not be understood until one has felt it.

The bear's attacks came like an avalanche, and its body plowed across the ground like a truck. Jack weaved between them. At this moment, he wasn't a human, but a fly, and he dodged all attacks heading his way. No matter how fast the bear struck, or how many times, it couldn't catch him.

A fist met the bear's hind leg, buckling it. Jack's power could penetrate its defenses but not quite harm it. The damage was minimal. Jack wasn't a fly, but a wasp, darting around the bear and pelting it with annoying stings.

So what if his strikes were weak? They were getting through. The damage was there, just not immediately visible. And, since the bear couldn't catch him, he refused to believe he'd fall from exhaustion before it.

Roar came after roar, strike after strike. As Jack and the bear danced around each other. Their battle moved through the clearing's edges, tearing trees and bushes apart. Jack had to dodge these obstacles too, making things a bit harder, but the bear also took some time to uproot or break them.

Jack bobbed, and weaved, a veritable leaf in a storm, that wasp stubbornly facing an enemy much larger than itself. Yet, he persisted.

One minute turned into many, and the moments dragged on. Jack's body was growing heavier, his mind imperceptibly slower, but his strikes were accumulating. After the first five minutes, he'd struck the bear at least a hundred times, if not more.

His knuckles were flayed from striking stone and hard fur. There was no skin there anymore, only bone that held strong. The pain was great, but his adrenaline-filled brain shut it out.

Sensing the damage, and with its fury continuously mounting, the bear redoubled its efforts. It roared and hit harder, abandoning all defense to catch this vicious little creature. Jack accelerated in response. His body turned into a blur, his punches faster than a blink.

Jack and the rock bear were a maelstrom of violence ripping the forest apart. Where they passed, only destruction followed. Animals scattered in all directions, the birds having long left the area. In the back of his mind, Jack worried that more bears might arrive, but there was nothing he could do about that.

He ducked under a flying bush and took a branch to the chest, ignoring it. It could only scratch his skin. Another bush flew into the bear's face, blinding it. It raised a claw to rip it away, and as it did, Jack found the opportunity to nail a hard straight into its belly, shaking its insides. Something within that stone body gave way.

The bear growled deeply and pounced again. Jack dodged around it, moving to the back and punching again. A leg flew back to meet him, but he was no longer there. The bear jumped to the side, and he barely avoided it, darting back.

Jack was undoubtedly much weaker than the bear. He shouldn't be able to take it in a straight fight, regardless of the ice pond bonuses or his class.

However, he countered it perfectly. His speed was enough to evade everything so long as he made no mistakes. His skills perfectly countered the bear's hard defenses—all that enormous strength was useless if it couldn't catch him.

Plus, the ambush he'd landed at the start had clearly been effective. Even now, the bear still bled from its muzzle, its eyes were bleary, and it occasionally stumbled for no reason. It had internal injuries, not just dizziness. Jack was glad for that.

The only question was, could he last long enough without making a single mistake?

CHAPTER EIGHTEEN
KING OF THE RING

JACK AND THE ROCK BEAR KEPT DANCING THROUGH THE FOREST, TEARING IT apart. Trees, bushes, and rocks flew. So did a fox.

After ten minutes, Jack's arms were heavy. The ecstasy violence brought was dying down. His dodges were sloppy, his strikes missed. More than once, he only escaped a swiped claw by a hair's breadth. He was dizzy, exhausted, and the world swam in his eyes.

The bear was equally troubled. It had slowed down considerably, forcing strikes with clear intervals between them. It was also panting, and one time, it even lost footing and collapsed, rising back up that much more whittled down. Its rage hadn't abated, but there was a limit to how much its body could endure, especially after being pummeled by a man with 44 Strength for ten minutes straight.

Jack, too, had his limits.

The human body placed many limiters on itself. The muscles could only operate at 30 percent efficiency, and the brain kept its processes low. Under extraordinary circumstances, these limiters were removed. That was how women lifted cars to save their babies, or how grown men could fight wolves.

If pushed to its limit, the human body was strong, even before the System's arrival. Humans were one of the strongest animals in their weight category, even stronger than most monkey species, and they could only decisively lose to gorillas or big wolves.

When push came to shove, they could release incredible strength and feel no exhaustion. Humans could punch fast, hard, and inexhaustibly.

However, these limiters existed for a reason. To unleash such power, the human body destroyed itself, and it could only last for a small amount of time. Ten minutes was already beyond such capacity.

Jack's entire body burned, and not in the good way. His muscles were in pain, ready to snap. His mind was muddled, overheated, and overworked. He could sense his conscious control over himself slipping away, diving into slumber, and he only acted on instinct now.

Punch, dodge, weave, punch. Duck, slide, punch. Punch. Duck.

The bear was in pain with every step it took. Jack had felt many of its bones breaking under his fists, and many of its organs faltering, but it still stood, refusing to stay down. It was slow but relentless.

Jack, too, kept going, but he was running dry. He'd thrown everything he had at the bear, and his soul was bleeding as he forced himself to draw even more energy.

Retreat was impossible. One of them would kill the other.

Over the next five minutes, Jack wasn't sure what was happening. The bear still stood, that much he knew. It swiped at him occasionally, threw its body over. He dodged by the skin of his teeth, mustered all his energy to throw himself aside. He could only keep going because the bear had slowed down tremendously.

He even fell down thrice, tripping in his attempt to dodge. Every time, the sweet release of sleep almost took him, and every time, he forced his eyes open, forced his body to stand through the pain and keep going. Jack refused to die. He refused to lose.

Injuries peppered his body. Scratches ran over his bare chest and back, and three long gashes covered the right side of his ribs. He didn't remember if he'd been hit. His gums were bleeding from all the gritting, and he'd lost all feeling in his hands. He didn't even know how they remained clenched; they were probably stuck.

There was no pain in Jack's mind, only limitless exhaustion, and it was worse than any pain he'd felt throughout his life. Only the goblin shaman's fire came close to this, but that only lasted for a moment, while Jack's present torment stretched to infinity.

They weren't even moving anymore. Both enemies were stationary, striking each other whenever they found the strength.

The bear growled low, bleeding internally, from many places, and its bones were cracked. Now it no longer stood. Only its arms moved, and it threw them out like stones to hit the human before it, its greatest enemy. It tried its best.

In a flash of lucidity, Jack's eyes met the bear's. There was anger there, hatred, exhaustion. The bear wanted to lay down and sleep, and so did he, but neither did. In the bear's eyes, Jack found understanding and recognition, and so did the bear in his. They acknowledged each other's pain and resolve.

They silently agreed to give it their all until one died, not knowing who would win.

Jack's mind became a haze. His movements were so slight they weren't proper dodges, but the bear missed by itself. It could no longer aim, and after another punch in its face, it couldn't see either.

Move. Duck. Punch. Dodge. Punch. Punch.

Jack couldn't see either. His vision was muddled. When he dodged, he followed the patterns engraved in his body, not reacting to any of the bear's attacks.

Punch. Punch. Punch. Move. Duck. Mo—

Jack slipped, fell, and stayed there. He no longer had the strength to stand. He didn't have the will, either. Every part of his being had bled dry already.

He could only wait there, laying face-down on the ground, for death to come. As his consciousness dissipated, Jack didn't blame himself, nor did he regret anything. He'd tried his best. It simply wasn't enough.

Jack woke up to an oink in his ear.

"Ohh..." he groaned. The little boar next to him, scared, ran away.

With strained, pained movements, Jack forced himself to roll over.

He opened his eyes and found the rock bear's muzzle over him, staring, debating which part of him to eat first.

"Cra—" He tried to roll away, but his body refused to obey. He belatedly realized he was in massive pain and released another groan, this one louder. He balled up on the ground and hoped for this to end fast. A whisper from the back of his head said that bears started with the legs or entrails—a gruesome death, in any case. Jack hoped magic bears were more efficient.

However, though he waited, no jaws closed around his body. He looked back again.

The bear was there, but it wasn't moving. It was dead, sprawled on the ground and bleeding from many places. The stones on its fur had been broken, though its menacing yellow eyes were still open.

Did I... kill it?

Jack heaved a massive sigh of relief, then grimaced as his chest rose in pain. When he'd fallen, the bear had already been dead. Maybe it had died a long time ago. Who knows how long he'd spent fighting alone?

A blue exclamation mark blinked in the corner of his vision, and Jack willed it open.

Level Up! You have reached Level 18.
Level Up! You have reached Level 19.
Level Up! You have reached Level 20.
Level Up! You have reached Level 21.
Level Up! You have reached Level 22.

Earth Bear Boss defeated! Would you like to despawn the group?
Y/N

There was one more screen, but Jack willed it away for now. He sighed again. This was a lot to take in.

First, he split all extra points—there were *a lot* of them—equally among his Physical stats, as he'd been doing so far. For the first time in a while, the increase was noticeable. He could feel his muscles repairing themselves and growing tougher like iron strings. His limbs became lighter, bending easily to his will. His entire body hardened, his skin tightening—a quite chilling sensation.

Finally, he noticed the skin regrowing on his rubbed-off knuckles, and this time, they felt as if made of metal. Despite the pain, he grinned. This was nice.

Without thinking, he turned and punched a nearby tree. The bark exploded at the point of impact, and the softer tissue behind it erupted out by the power of Drill.

Jack's grin widened even further, then he winced. That foolhardy move aggravated his injuries. He was just too excited to *not* try out his power. It was amazing how he kept growing beyond what his mind indicated was the limit.

Now, he was *strong.*

The extra points hadn't healed him magically, they'd helped recover his energy a bit. With energy came thought, and with thought, Jack realized he needed to get the hell out of here. Bears were attracted to the smell of blood. Given his luck, so were Dungeon Bosses who liked to snack on Jacks.

Actually, that was rather unfair on his part. Jack had many things to complain about, but luck wasn't one of them.

He forced his body to stand before inspecting the status screen.

Earth Bear Boss defeated! Would you like to despawn the group? Y/N

He almost replied yes on reflex. Then, almost replied no on reflex, before finally willing the screen away again.

He didn't want to despawn the bears, as the wolf boss needed something to feed on while he got stronger. However, saying no right now wasn't good, either. What if he met a bear on the way back? He couldn't possibly fight in his current condition. He needed to get to the ice pond as soon as possible.

Since the System gave him no time limit, he simply ignored the screen. If a bear came after him, he'd have to despawn them.

However, why weren't any bears here already?

The sun was falling toward the horizon, meaning Jack had slept for an hour at most. Maybe the bears hadn't dared approach the leader's den yet, but they would. He needed to get out of here.

There was one last blue screen to check. It was the greatest reward he received from the fight, probably, but Jack decided it could wait. He had already delayed long enough.

Amidst groans and panting, Jack dragged himself away. His left hand held his right ribs, where the bear had grazed him with its claws. Every step was painful. There was probably something cracked in there, if not broken.

The trip back wasn't quite agony, as the fight itself had been, but painful nonetheless. He had to stop several times to rest, always fearing a wolf, bear, or even monkey would assault him out of nowhere. His battle with the rock bear hadn't been discreet. Who knew what was heading his way.

Eventually, he made it to his cave without incident. He forced himself through the narrow passage, gritting his teeth to avoid screaming, then dove into the ice pond.

The pond offered healing, but everything had its price. In this case, the price was excruciating pain. Jack's ribs went so cold he thought his soul would freeze over. It felt like needles were sewing his bones together, as if his skin was burnt away and a new one grew in its place.

Ten minutes later, Jack crawled out of the pond and lay on the hard rock, more grateful than ever for its even temperature. He almost drifted asleep before remembering he had one last thing to do—for good measure.

He opened the last status screen, the one he'd put away for later. His greatest reward from the battle.

Congratulations! Level 20 reached. New Class Skill acquired.

CHAPTER NINETEEN
CROSSING THE POND

Congratulations! Level 20 reached. New Class Skill acquired. Pugilist Body (I): Your body is a vessel of your fighting style. You gain extra flexibility, reflexes, and durability, as well as increased hardness on your knuckles.

Ohh! Jack's eyes flashed as he read through the skill. *A harder body... and finally, hard knuckles.*

While he'd gotten the skill right after defeating the rock bear, it seemed that reading about it acted as the activation trigger. As soon as Jack finished reading, his body squirmed.

It was a disturbing, unnatural feeling. His skin tightened, then somehow stayed there and felt normal. His insides were clenched, but more like he'd been way too lax until now, and this was his normal state. Moreover, his knuckles momentarily burned, and when he tapped them, the skin felt hard like iron.

He grinned. *Finally.*

With all changes completed, Jack reviewed his status screen before falling asleep.

Name: Jack Rust
Species: Human, Earth-387
Faction: -
Grade: F
Class: Pugilist (Elite)
Level: 22

Strength: 54
Dexterity: 64
Constitution: 54
Mental: 9
Will: 7

Skills: Fistfighting (II), Drill (I), Pugilist Body (I)

Come morning, Jack awoke to the glowing darkness he was used to. The sunlight didn't reach his cave, meaning it was always illuminated by the ice pond's white glow. Nothing changed here. An entirely isolated world.

Jack rubbed his eyes and stood, noting the ease with which he pulled up his body. He felt light as a feather and strong as an ox.

After taking a moment to go over yesterday's events, making sure he wasn't forgetting anything, he directed his gaze to the ice pond. He calculated.

With his five new levels—seven, actually, because he hadn't attempted the pond in a while—he could probably go fairly deeper than he used to. When he last entered, he'd reached the ninth out of thirteen steps. If his predictions were correct... he could now touch the waterfall.

He looked over. A stream of ice-cold, glowing water fell from a crack in the cave wall, dropping three meters to the pond's surface. Despite the pond's small size, the waterfall was substantial. As it fell, it fanned out and came crashing down into the waters.

This ice pond had saved Jack's life many times, both with its healing and the extra stats it provided. It was his lucky star.

However, he feared it. Its freezing cold could reach the soul, and he'd almost died inside it once. Moreover, it was full of mysteries. Where did the water come from? Where did it go? There had to be a tunnel feeding the waterfall's output into an underwater current, but how exactly did this work?

And, finally, what would happen when Jack reached the waterfall? His instinct told him it hid great rewards, along with great danger. The moment he touched it, the cold could skyrocket, and if he was already at his limit, he'd be frozen solid.

He'd still go for it, of course. Jack didn't have the luxury of waiting. Except it required him being at his best, and that made Jack turn away from the pond for now.

"In a few hours," he declared behind his back, "I'll return to defeat you."

He then left his cave.

As he went over yesterday's events, he realized something, and he even brought up the dungeon description to be sure.

Forest of the Strong (F-Grade)

A forest where only the strong survive. There are three monster groups, each holding a unique resource and representing a unique challenge. Slay the leader of a group to despawn them.
This dungeon is in conquer-or-die mode. Defeat the Dungeon Boss to exit or die trying. We applaud your bravery for entering and wish you the best of luck.

Three monster groups, each holding a unique resource. Then, where was the bear's resource?

The goblins had the High Speed Bush. Meaning the bears had to have something similar, he'd just missed it due to the heated battle. Now, he would search.

Jack crossed the forest at a brisk pace. He didn't care much about stealth anymore. He didn't need to. With his all-around upgrades, he was confident the only creatures that could threaten him now were the black wolf, which was stealthier than him anyway, and the monkey boss, which shouldn't leave its area.

Even the level 20 earth bear would barely be a serious opponent.

It was a touching thought. The Greenway Natural Reserve—the Forest of the Strong—once held terrifying monsters at every turn, and even the weakest link could eat Jack alive. Now, he was almost the apex predator, and only the strongest were his opponents. How far he'd come.

Less than an hour later, he stood by the rock bear's corpse. It had been eaten in places, probably by other bears, and it looked like shit, but Jack still paused.

This bear had been his greatest opponent so far, the one who'd brought him closest to death. They'd fought with their lives on the line. There was a camaraderie born of that, an acknowledgment—even if it was a man-eating monster.

Jack nodded deeply at the bear, then carried on.

The clearing opened before him soon after. This was his destination, the rock bear's den. Any secret resource had the highest chance of hiding here.

This clearing had a clean pond in its midst, larger than Jack's and without the frigid cold, with a rock outcropping over it. An earth bear currently sat on that rock outcropping, having already assumed the pack's leadership.

Earth Bear, Level 20

Jack didn't give a flying fuck. He walked out of the bushes and met the bear's surprised stare with his own calm one. This earth bear was the largest he'd seen, but so what? He could take it if need be.

The bear stared him down and growled, revealing its teeth. Jack smashed his fists together, producing an almost metallic sound from his knuckles. "Fuck off," he commanded. His intention was clear: he wanted this clearing.

Surprisingly, the bear hesitated. It could have been his confidence, or they may have had a way to sense when they were facing higher-leveled beings. Maybe the bear even smelled the rock bear on him or had spied on the battle from afar and knew he'd been the one to kill it.

Whatever the case, facing Jack's steely stare, the earth bear retreated. Under warning growls, it became one with the overgrowth, then disappeared.

Jack, meanwhile, raised a brow. He hadn't expected that to work.

Huh. Well, better for me.

A single bear wouldn't give him a level now. It was more useful as a wolf meal.

He turned his gaze to the clearing and the pond in its center. This scenery was too striking to be coincidental. He suspected the resource had something to do with the pond, maybe a plant at its bottom or even a cave under the rock outcropping.

As he thought that, and his gaze lingered on the pond inquisitively, Jack barked out a laugh. *I should have known!*

Clear Pond (F-Grade)

Clear Ponds are naturally-occurring formations spread around the universe and often used as parts of resorts. Anyone who relaxes in these waters will find serenity, their body will loosen completely, and their potential will emerge, making the entire body sturdier. The stat increase is a one-time bonus

Jack grinned at the screen, then at the pond. Some relaxation was exactly what he needed. Without removing his clothes—he only wore pants—he dipped his toes into the pond and was floored.

The temperature was ideal, the water so soft it hugged his pores. This was completely unlike the ice pond's brutal test. This was heaven.

Jack quickly entered the waters, submerging his entire body. The pond was shaped like a shallow bowl with a diameter of twenty feet. At its center, the water was barely over Jack's head, and its shore was smooth and easy to rest on.

It was this shore that Jack leaned against, letting his head fall back and closing his eyes. A week of incessant fighting poured off his body like grime, dissolving in the waters. He was as free as a baby. The next moment, he slipped deeper into the pond, relaxed to the point his body might just dissipate entirely, or maybe his limbs would float away without him noticing.

The feeling was beyond euphoric. It was the single best thing Jack had experienced in his life, and he unconsciously released a long, drawn-out, heartfelt groan of ultimate serenity.

Everything was worth it for this moment.

Despite its extraordinary effects, the pond had no addictive properties, not a hint of mind control. It was just damn good.

Jack couldn't help himself, he deserved it, and stayed in the pond for an hour before finally pulling himself away, rising as a new man. His mind was calm, his spirit steady, and his body elastic without losing any of its hardness.

Clear Pond bonus acquired!

Strength: 54
Dexterity: 64
Constitution: 64

He smiled. His Constitution had increased by ten.

Going by this pattern, the monkeys should have a strength-boosting resource... That would explain why they're so buff.

Jack's path was clear. He would go to the monkeys, gather a few levels off them, defeat their boss, then use the strength-boosting resource. Then... he'd find a way to deal with the wolf.

What could go wrong?

Before that, there was something else he ought to do. After serenity came endless torment. He'd enjoyed the clear pond. Now, it was time to see the end of the ice pond.

Jack faced the ice pond, staring it down like a warrior. The pond ignored him, as ponds ought to do.

He took a deep breath, then stepped in. The first step was refreshing now. The next few were only somewhat chilling.

Jack recalled the times when just dipping his toes into this pond was harrowing. He shook his head and kept going. The fifth step, the sixth. The familiar cold bit into his body but found no purchase. The seventh, the eight. His legs were shivering now, reminding him of swimming in March.

The ninth. This was his previous limit. The pond was deepening too. By this point, it reached his waist, and the cold held his lower body like a vice. It was hard, yes, but he could go on. This was nowhere near his limit.

The tenth step. His legs went numb.

Ice Pond bonus: +1 Physical

The eleventh step. The temperature dropped exponentially as he approached the waterfall. There was no way this was anywhere close to the freezing point—far below it—but the water here didn't seem to care.

Ice Pond bonus: +1 Physical

The twelfth step. The cold raced through his body and into his head, trying to freeze his thoughts. The waterfall was close now, and drops of liquid ice splashed him occasionally, speaking of temperatures far below the current one. Moving was difficult, but Jack could still go on.

Ice Pond bonus: +1 Physical

The thirteenth step was the hardest. Jack sensed himself turning into ice. His legs were cranky, his body hard to move. The waterfall splashed right before him, showering him in icy droplets. Even breathing was difficult, but Jack persisted.

Ice Pond bonus: +1 Physical

Finally! Jack had crossed the entire ice pond! Only the waterfall was left, but he was already very close to his limit. If he went any farther and the difficulty spiked, as he imagined, he might be in danger...

Except he'd already come this far. He couldn't retreat now. He put a hand through the waterfall and gasped. It was so terrifyingly cold... but he could stand it, for a bit. Probably.

Jack took a deep breath and plunged into the waterfall.

CHAPTER TWENTY
WORLD OF THE WATERFALL

Jack's arms were outstretched as he dove into the waterfall.

He instantly lost his vision and all his senses. The world disappeared. There was only him and endless cold, so piercing and biting it encompassed everything. He couldn't even feel pain, regret, or fear. All he felt was cold.

Jack's body froze. Not metaphorically—it literally froze into an ice statue. His blood barely kept circulating, and his heart and brain slowed to such a degree, he might as well have been dead.

In his own little world, Jack was alone. Everything had been lost, even his own thoughts were solid ice. He could only stand there, in a blue, empty world.

However, even though his body and part of his mind had frozen, a vestige of his consciousness remained. In that moment, as everything else faded away, Jack experienced absolute clarity. He felt like a god. His mental reserves were limitless, and he had no needs. He could devote everything to any path he desired, and could travel endless miles in a second.

His mind was unfettered, lost in endless tranquility. He was acting on instinct. A scene appeared before him, the scene of a man punching through a mountain-sized beast. The vision he'd only glimpsed before was magnified, analyzed, slowed down, and replayed from multiple angles.

Jack barely had any awareness of himself. He was an empty shell, and that shell was freely flooded with the essence of that fist. He became the fist and the bald man who wielded it. He became the punch that tore through the beast. Became the beast itself, sensing everything as his body was torn apart.

He felt everything. There were so many things that didn't make sense, so many things to learn.

That scene had been carved in his soul with all its details, but his mind hadn't been capable of comprehending them. Now, it was, and though he only understood the tiniest part, his world was growing. Jack was on the cusp of a realization so massive it dwarfed every thought he'd ever had.

It was the same realization that came to him with the original vision, the one that had slipped out of his grasp.

However, just as he was on the verge of understanding, something tugged at him. An annoying feeling rose from his legs, slowly spreading to the rest of his body, as if he were losing control. He frowned in annoyance, unwilling to lose focus over something so small, but the feeling persisted.

A voice in his mind whispered that he should leave. That he was in danger.

Danger? he finally wondered. *Why?*

And the moment he did, the whisper turned into a thundering shout. The vision dispersed as his own voice thundered across the little realm he stood in.

"LEAVE!"

Jack opened his eyes and fell back. He could barely feel his body. The cold had invaded his every nook and cranny, from the wrinkles of his brain to the marrow of his bones. Only the System's magic—his Constitution—saved him. Terror blanketed him.

I almost died, he thought.

Everything was fast. When he fell back, his body practically teleported to the lake's bottom. His lungs were swiftly losing their oxygen, and the water danced over him like crazy.

No, it wasn't that the world was fast. He was slow. Frozen. The only reason his lungs still held was that his bodily functions underperformed so greatly they didn't draw much oxygen.

I will die.

He'd had nightmares like this before. He was slow, much slower than everything. In those dreams, he'd try to rise from his bed, only to fall on the floor, unable to coordinate his body at such painfully slow motion. He'd try to speak, to call for help, but he could only make deep, unintelligible sounds.

His current situation was similar, but it wasn't a dream. He couldn't control his body. He could barely sense his thoughts. And the more he waited, the greater the pain became—everywhere.

Jack was drowning in more than one way. He struggled to stand, it was simply impossible. In the end, he turned around on the pond floor and crawled forward, his arms uncoordinated but enough for such a simple task.

The pain kept growing. His head was about to burst. His eyes were frozen. His lungs burned. His focus narrowed on the simple motions of reaching out, dragging himself forward, and repeating.

Jack was sure he'd die, but for some reason, he pressed forth. He didn't want to go quietly into the night. He would charge ahead, break through everything with overwhelming power, or die trying.

He was a fist.

Time passed. Jack didn't know how he found himself on the shore, but he did. Next thing he knew, he was heaving and panting, his body surrounded by a little pond of his own. Time had returned to normal—*he'd* returned to normal.

He was shivering, and not just because of the cold.

What the hell was that? he thought, still shaken to the core. What had happened? Just how freezing was that damn waterfall? And how had he survived?

He didn't know. His memory was a jumbled mess. All he remembered was the empty blue world, the crawling through ice water, as well as a giant, world-encompassing fist...

What the hell just happened? he repeated the question, then turned to the one entity that might know. The System.

Ice Pond bonus: +5 Physical

Ice Pond bonus acquired!

That was all. Jack was left staring at the first screen. *+5!*

An insane amount! He'd finally gotten all stat benefits of the ice pond, according to the second screen, and they were a total of 18 points in Physical—or 18 in each of his physical stats. That was the equivalent of nine levels!

However, he'd paid dearly for such a boon. He didn't even know how close he'd come to death, but it couldn't have been more than a hair away. If he hadn't retreated at that final moment...

He spared a glance for the waterfall, which still poured down calmly, as if harmless. Only Jack knew the incredible danger that hid below its surface, and he gulped. He swore not to approach it again unless he got significantly stronger. No matter how dire his situation, that was a risk he couldn't afford.

But how dire was his situation, really? With all the ice pond bonuses and the other resources, Jack secured a gain of over ten levels worth of points. Given that he was level 22, his current fighting prowess should be in the mid-thirties. In this forest, besides the wolf boss, who could stand up to him?

Only the monkey boss held a chance, but not for long.

Jack saw a glimmer of hope. If the monkey monsters gave him enough of a boost... maybe fighting the wolf wasn't that far-fetched of an idea.

Jack lay there for a long time, putting his thoughts in order and letting his body readapt to the environment. He shivered, and water kept rolling off him, escaping his body from wherever it had entered.

Eventually, he felt ready. There was a battle to fight. No more distractions, no more bonuses, no more side-quests. Monkeys, then wolf. That was all.

Jack stood, testing his body and finding it in perfect condition. He clenched his fists and prepared himself for battle.

Before he left the cave, Jack spared a final look for the waterfall.

That blue world wasn't a dream... What did it mean? What was it? What secrets does the ice pond hide? And that fist...

He clenched his own. He hadn't forgotten his insights while in the blue world. The fist was a weapon, a path forward. It was relentless, brutal, visceral, and primal. It represented strictness and discipline, the law of the strong, and how everything came down to killing and harming each other.

The fist was *not* a pretty thing. it was necessary and natural, representing the conviction that, in life, there was only the path. Ever forward.

Fist meant power.

These were pretty thoughts, if useless. And yet, he was on the cusp of... something. These ideas and concepts, if properly understood, hid special meaning. The bald man's fist in his vision wasn't merely a fist. It was a world of its own. A way of life. A path.

If only he could comprehend it, he had the feeling his entire existence would ascend to a completely new level.

Jack shook his head. There was something there, he was sure, something vital and fundamental. Something titanic. His instinct screamed it was there, only a paper's width out of his grasp.

Yet, as great as fist magic sounded, he still lacked something, a focus to complete his understanding, fill in the holes and turn thoughts into reality—into magic. And the thing he missed wasn't something he'd discover through thinking. He'd find it through punching.

As it should be.

Jack's eyes shone as he exited his cave with steady steps. The steps of a warrior. His bare feet crunched leaves and snapped sticks. He arrived in the monkey area and stared deep into it.

Red eyes gazed back from its depths. They didn't attack, only waited. And then, Jack hesitated.

The truth was, Jack wasn't a murderer. A killer, maybe, but not a cold-blooded one. The goblins had made it easy by trying to kill him first and being disgusting little fuckers. The bears had eased his doubts by being bloodthirsty, aggressive, and sadistic enough to torture the little animals in their territory even without eating them.

But these monkeys had done nothing wrong. If he massacred them, it would be cold-blooded, undeserved genocide.

Jack followed the law of the jungle. He would do it if he had to... maybe. But he didn't want to become that person. If there could be another way, he wanted to at least give it a shot.

When he'd invaded the monkey territory, they'd only thrown poop at him and chased him out despite having the strength to kill him. They'd let him go. Couldn't he do the same?

Such mercy might doom him.

These were Jack's thoughts as he hesitated, debating what to do. The monkeys still stared from their trees. In fact, they'd approached enough that he could make out their brown, beefy forms.

Gymonkey, Level 9

A monkey variant from planet Green. Gymonkeys inhabit all forest biomes and move in packs, defending their territory with flying poop and great muscles. Their unique name comes from their habit of lifting heavy things to increase their strength.

While not particularly aggressive, they are highly territorial.

The one he scanned was of medium beefiness. The pack that approached contained seven monkeys ranging from levels 5 to 12, from normal monkeys to bodybuilders-turned-primate. He wasn't afraid of them, of course.

They stared at him, and he stared back. *What should I do?*

A deep growl came from deeper in the monkey area. Jack supposed it belonged to a gorilla—though, with how stupid the name gymonkeys was, he assumed the gorilla would have an equally silly one.

A thought struck Jack. They were watching him, and they were magical monkeys. Could they be... intelligent?

The moment he thought that, he sighed. He knew where this would lead, and he felt stupid for even thinking about it. Yet, what choice did he have? Between suicidal, psychotic, and stupid, he'd always choose the latter.

"Hello," he said, surprised at the sound of his own voice. He hadn't spoken to anyone in days, barring crude battle taunts. "I'm Jack."

The monkeys glanced to each other. One of them exclaimed what sounded like *ooh-ah-ah* to him, which he obviously couldn't understand. They made sounds at each other, seemingly conversing about something.

Jack's suspicions were further reinforced. These monkeys clearly understood him, or at least understood he was trying to communicate. They had some degree of intelligence. Moreover, they weren't hostile.

The biologist inside him was intrigued. The survivalist, annoyed—but fuck that guy.

One of the monkeys turned around and motioned for him to follow. Jack, grinning, complied.

He had no idea where this would go, but he really wanted to find out.

CHAPTER TWENTY-ONE
THE STRONGEST MONKEYS

JACK FOLLOWED THE GYMONKEYS INTO THEIR TERRITORY.

They jumped from branch to branch, and trunk to trunk. They didn't have the patience to walk, apparently, and Jack jogged to keep up. The branches above creaked from the weight of those beefy bodies.

As they dove deeper, more monkeys appeared. Some stared at Jack warily, dry poop ready to throw. Others made faces at him or approached to inspect him. One lifted his arm and sniffed his armpit.

Jack laughed. He wasn't afraid of these little guys, of course.

A gorilla appeared from behind a tree. Its entire body was covered in dark fur, unlike the monkeys' brown, and its yellow eyes stared Jack down from below a wide, wrinkled forehead.

Of course, the gorilla was full of muscle. Even its fingers had biceps. Jack was certain that below its fur hid a perfect six-pack.

The monkeys guiding Jack stopped, beginning a series of *uu-uu-aah.* The gorilla ignored them. Walking on its knuckles, it approached Jack. From this close, it reminded him of a grumpy old man. It could have been funny if it wasn't vaguely threatening.

Brorilla, Level 16

A gorilla variant from planet Green. Brorillas live with Gymonkeys

and train them in the ways of working out. It is due to the Brorillas' unmatched pecks that Gymonkeys use poop to fight—they consider themselves too weak for anything else.

Brorillas are usually calm, measured animals. However, if anyone harms their little cousins or invades their territory, they go bananas.

Hmm... Not the boss, then.

"Hello, I'm Jack," he said.

The gorilla looked him in the eye, then turned to the rest of the monkeys. Their conversation comprised of various monkey sounds Jack couldn't bother to decode, as well as very expressive jumps and body language. One monkey mimed that Jack was strong by flexing its biceps, and another smashed its fists together, conveying a message Jack didn't understand.

The rest of them got it, though. After a series of wondrous exclamations, they began walking again, heading deeper into the forest. The gorilla led, Jack followed, and about ten monkeys trailed behind.

Jack began to suspect this was not a good idea.

However, he was a biologist at heart. As they walked, his previous questions about the gymonkey evolutionary traits resurfaced. Why did they work out? Natural predators? Mating preferences?

Looking around, he spotted something alarming. All the gymonkeys around him were female. The brorilla was—of course—male.

Oh, hell no.

His brows spasmed. If all brorillas were male, as he suspected from their name, and all gymonkeys female, that was ridiculous from an evolutionary standpoint. They seemed too different to mate. Sure, cows and bulls had their differences, but they were the same species. Were these ones, too?

Is that why the System called them cousins in the brorilla description? Oh, come on. This is just ridiculous.

Jack began to suspect their habit of working out was based on mating competition, but he wasn't in the mood to care anymore.

At least their antics were cute. It wasn't every day he saw flexing monkeys and gorillas. His non-scientist self was having fun.

The forest became sparser. More monkeys arrived to take in their weird visitor—all female—making the thick trees groan under their collective weight. One more brorilla showed up, joining its bro after a few questioning growls. When the two brorillas met, they flexed their muscles at each other in greeting, while the surrounding gymonkeys stared in awe.

Jack held back a chuckle. The more ridiculous these monkeys became, the less danger he felt, and the smaller his desire to harm them was.

Eventually, the forest gave way to a clearing, and Jack could only stare.

A massive gap in the trees was occupied by a series of equipment. There were sticks with heavy rocks on both their ends, inclined wooden surfaces, benches with rows of weights above them, as well as a primitive machine that allowed one to pull weights with their legs.

You have got to be kidding me.

It was a forest gym, and a dozen monkeys were currently working out on the various equipment. Sweat dripped down their bodies, and their muscles shivered as they completed one repetition after another. A brorilla was also working out, raising multiple stone dumbbells with one arm, and a few gymonkeys surrounded him, possibly admiring his gains.

Another brorilla stood in the middle of everything, watching the gymonkeys with a sharp eye and barking out corrections when they messed up their stance. Occasionally, its gaze would flick to its bro, and it would nod in manly acknowledgment.

When Jack entered the clearing, everything went silent. The brorillas both struck him with stony gazes, and the various gymonkeys all rushed to equip themselves with poop—there was a reserve pile at a side, as many were already pretty clenched from working out.

The brorillas leading Jack initiated the greeting ritual with the other brorillas. Each of them nodded at every other brorilla individually. Then, all together, they assumed various bodybuilder poses and flexed their muscles, while the armed gymonkeys forgot all about Jack, now blinded by this demonstration of gains.

Done with their greeting, Jack's brorillas explained to their bros what the situation was—unfortunately, Jack couldn't understand them, but he was fine enjoying the show.

A brorilla motioned at Jack and indicated his lack of muscle. Another shrugged, while Jack's brorillas looked at him questioningly. One threw him a dumbbell, which he caught easily—or tried to, as the blasted thing must have weighed more than the average man. He settled for gritting his teeth and raising it above his head a couple of times.

The brorillas nodded approvingly. To be precise, they all nodded at him, and he returned a nod to each individually. When in gorilla-land, do as gorillas do.

A low, commanding growl cut through the clamor. Jack turned toward the edge of the clearing. A banana tree stood there, looking completely out of place in the forest, but he hadn't noticed it behind the monkeys' homemade forest gym.

From behind that tree, munching on two bananas at once, came the largest gorilla Jack had ever seen.

Big Brorilla, Level 25

A gorilla variant from planet Green. Brorillas usually live with Gymonkeys and train them in the ways of working out. It is due to the Brorillas' unmatched pecs that Gymonkeys use poop to fight—they consider themselves too weak for anything else.

Brorillas are usually calm, measured animals. However, if anyone harms their little cousins or invades their territory, they go bananas. This particular Brorilla is larger and stronger than most, righteously becoming their Big Bro. It is the group boss of the ape monsters of the Forest of the Strong.

Big bro stood a head taller than Jack even on its knuckles. All over its body, muscles bulged underneath its fur, and it walked with the confidence of a multiple-times Mr. Olympia winner. Its large hands, easily able to squeeze a human head dry, now held a banana in each, and it chomped down on them alternatively while its yellow eyes took in Jack.

Through all the chaos, Jack's mind insisted that banana trees had no place in this forest. Moreover, these bananas bulged oddly, as if they were flexed biceps instead of fruit.

Bananarm Plant (F-Grade)

A resource guarded by the apes of the Forest of the Strong. Commonly found in the plains of planet Green, the bananas produced by this plant are so rich in nutrients they can instantly develop one's muscles. They are also said to be a rare delicacy.

The stat increase is a one-time bonus.

Of course it would be bananas. Why the hell not? We already have a gym forest and gorilla bros.

The big brorilla casually made its way to the center of the clearing and stopped. The four brorillas nodded in respect, and the big brorilla only returned a single nod at all of them. It was clearly the big bro, eyes solemn. He didn't look very friendly.

Jack nodded, then tried to be polite.

"Hello, big bro. I'm Jack. Wanna team up against the wolf? I'm sure it will start eating you guys soon, if it hasn't already."

The brorilla stared, not moving a muscle—of which it had many. Jack wondered if it could understand him. The monkeys could—why not their big bro?

The brorilla finally replied. It let out a series of noises that Jack couldn't make heads or tails of. It flexed its gigantic pecs, pointed its thumb at itself, followed by a thumbs-up.

"Are you saying you'll handle it yourself?"

The brorilla shook its head, then spread its arms to indicate the entire pack.

"All of you are going to handle it?"

A nod.

"Oh. Is that why you're training so hard?"

A brief pause, a shrug, then another nod.

"Okay. Can I help, too? I'm strong."

The big brorilla clearly had its doubts. Jack lifted the dumbbell above his head again, but the big brorilla wasn't impressed. It picked an entire benchpress off the ground and tossed it at him.

"What the—"

Jack barely jumped aside as the massive gym instrument crashed into the ground. He rolled back up.

"Bro! That wasn't nice! I can't catch a fucking benchpress!"

Every single gymonkey and brorilla gasped. The big brorilla frowned in dissatisfaction.

"What?" asked Jack, looking around. "Was it something I said?"

He grew worried. He was strong, sure, but he wasn't confident in taking on every monkey in this clearing and their big bro, especially when said big bro threw gym instruments around for breakfast. Maybe coming here was unwise.

The big brorilla stood on its hind legs, reaching nine feet in height. It pointed a finger at itself and another at Jack. The two fingers then came together, and when they did, one was clearly higher than the other.

"Ohh, it's because I called you bro before. You're the big bro and I'm the little one, right? That's what you're saying," he tried. The big brorilla stared. "I don't mind. Still, though, can I help against the wolf? I don't know if you guys can see levels, but it's pretty strong... I don't think you can handle it just by yourselves."

The big brorilla's frown deepened. When it didn't reply, Jack continued, "Okay, maybe you can do it, but it will be easier if you let me help. I'm about as strong as you. With me here, imagine how many of your little bros will be saved."

A second collective gasp. The big brorilla's body shivered, flexing every muscle it had at once. It stared Jack deep in the eyes, then beat its chest and unleashed a loud, deep roar.

The monkeys went bananas. They started throwing poop into the air, pushing each other, and jumping in place. Jack was lost. He had no idea what was happening, but he didn't like it.

Calming down slightly, the gymonkeys and brorillas ran around and formed a large circle around an empty part of the clearing, then kept hollering at the top of their lungs like monkeys often did. The big brorilla jumped over them to land in the circle. It pointed a finger at Jack, then himself, then smashed its two large fists together.

"Oh, no, I didn't mean to challenge you. I'm just saying—"

The brorillas behind Jack pushed him, sending him stumbling into the circle, which then closed behind him. "Hey!"

The big brorilla growled, then assumed a boxing stance and hopped in place. Its large fists rotated around each other like a mill.

"Will you guys *listen* to me? I'm not a monkey!"

They did not listen. He snorted.

"Fine. Fine! You think I'm afraid? If you guys don't want to play nice, I'll show you who's the boss around here."

More frenzied hollering and wild cheers. The big brorilla leveled its stare at Jack, who also adopted a boxing stance.

Jack could take this gorilla. It was at level 25, while he'd calculated his current battle prowess to be in the mid-thirties thanks to all the stat bonuses. If this big bro wanted to be taught a lesson, he would oblige. Becoming the monkey leader would make things easier in the long run, anyway.

Can I become a group boss? he mused, eyeing the gorilla from between his fists.

For a moment, he wondered what they saw. His muscles had developed as he got stronger, eventually covering his entire body in fine, symmetrical lines. He was like a perfect barbarian facing down a massive gorilla. He was a warrior.

The image lit a fire in his heart. Something drew him in. Maybe it was the incessant hollering that filled his ears; maybe it was the battle lust around him, or the allure of winning a public fight; maybe it was the excitement of boxing a fucking gorilla.

Whichever the case, Jack dropped into a state of mind he didn't often reach. All his battles so far had been desperate life-or-death struggles. There was no room for anything else.

Here, where he was called to prove his might against a worthy opponent, things were different. Honestly, even if he lost, he felt that the monkeys wouldn't kill him. His primal instincts didn't completely take over, as they always did. There was room for other things.

He felt the stress of the coming battle. The anticipation. The fear. The anxiety. He was more aware of himself, and thanks to that, he saw a side of battle that normally stayed hidden.

For the first time, he wasn't fighting for his life, but for himself. To prove his worth. To achieve things. To become great.

And, as Jack explored this aspect of battle, a wall in his mind cracked a little. He'd experienced the bald man's world-ending fist in the waterfall world. He'd seen it from many angles, pondered on its secrets, and from the sight of a single punch, he'd drawn so much inspiration about what it truly meant to fight.

He was on the cusp of something great, something titanic, but there was still a thin barrier stopping him—something was missing. Now, that barrier was cracking, and the big brorilla would help him open it up completely.

The gorilla attacked. So did Jack, and they began to box.

CHAPTER TWENTY-TWO
BOXING A GORILLA

THE MONKEY HOLLERING WAS INTOXICATING. THE RUSH, THE HAZE, THE SPIKE OF adrenaline as Jack faced a gorilla with his bare hands. He grinned. He didn't burst into action. Action burst out of him.

Jack and the big brorilla crashed into each another like trains and began boxing. Despite his small physique, Jack was strong. Very strong. He wasn't instantly annihilated like a pre-System human—he stood his ground and met the gorilla's big fists with his own small but hard ones.

Jack had adopted a boxing stance as dictated by his Fistfighting skill, which was completely in its element. He weaved and bobbed, dodged and jabbed where he found an opening. Jack's punches flew straight and true, impacting the big brorilla's body with strong thuds, making it grimace.

The brorilla's punches were like homing missiles. Its muscular arms carried such power, a single punch could undoubtedly rip a normal human's head clean off. But Jack was no normal human, not anymore. He couldn't just dodge, he could block, too!

The gorilla was stronger, as it was a strength-oriented creature, but Jack was much faster and, surprisingly, more durable. He could take those massive fists, while the gorilla buckled every time Jack sneaked in a strike. His little punches fell like hammers, bypassing the gorilla's thick fur to strike the skin underneath.

The big brorilla's eyes widened. Its mouth opened, revealing a pair of sharp teeth. It couldn't use the System to inspect Jack, but it could vaguely sense the level difference between itself and another creature. Most animals and monsters could.

That was why the monkeys invited Jack in. That was why the brorillas and even the big brorilla spoke with him. That was why, when Jack was disrespectful, the big brorilla challenged him. It could sense they were roughly on the same level, but it should have been slightly stronger.

However, that didn't appear to be the case. Its little mind was puzzled. Here it was, boxing with all its tremendous strength, driving punch after punch into the body of this small creature, but it took everything like a champ. Instead, when the little creature's punches struck the gorilla, they felt like swinging logs!

The big brorilla growled and struck faster, harder. He howled and became a flurry of blows on Jack, who still fought skillfully. He dodged one strike, blocked another, parried a third, and dug his fist into the gorilla's belly. The gorilla bent, and it spat saliva on Jack's head from above. Its eyes shook.

How could this little creature be so strong!

All around them, the monkeys were going bananas. They jumped up and down, climbed on branches to see better, and generally raised a ruckus that would make any sports fan go green with envy. The smart ones even snacked on bananarms. Some were even smarter, and distributed bananarms to other monkeys in return for favors or kisses.

The gymonkeys had invented stadium snacks.

More monkeys appeared from the trees as the battle raged on. Even three brorillas rushed over, bringing the total up to seven. All the brorillas then spent a minute greeting each other like proper bros.

Jack didn't miss all this. Though the fight was hectic, he was in control. It wasn't that difficult. He hadn't lost himself like usual.

He could sense the crowd's burning gazes. They landed on his body as intensely as the big brorilla's punches. Their excitement, surprise, fervent joy at such a spectacle was palpable. Even their respect for his strength was obvious to him, a creature who could match their big bro.

He felt like a champion.

It wasn't only good. There was undeniable pressure, a great amount, and there was hostility from some of the monkeys. He was under scrutiny, like his every movement was judged. He felt a veil stretching over his fists and dampening their blows.

The big brorilla sensed his weakness. It smacked him harder, abandoning defense except for its most vulnerable parts. Its punches rained down like meteors, and its monkey cries filled Jack's ears. He was forced on the defensive. The monkeys cheered, watching their big bro recover the upper hand, and some even booed Jack.

Jack grew frustrated. Why was this happening? He didn't understand. He had the higher stats, the finer skills... Why was he losing? Why were his movements weak and his reactions slow? Why did he make bad calls and expose his weaknesses?

This was the reverse of his vision. The bald man had exhibited strength that his body couldn't possibly contain. Jack was failing to use the strength that his body definitely possessed.

Why?

He knew why.

The tension was getting to him. He could fight with his life on the line, except now, he hesitated. The booing drew him away. The myriad movements at the edges of his vision sapped his attention. The pressure fell on his punches like fabric, making him slow and clumsy.

The big brorilla, on the other hand, was used to fighting like this. It kept the upper hand and pushed.

Jack was back to the basics. Facing elementary weaknesses he never had to deal with against the goblins or bears. His body knew the way, but his mind and soul couldn't follow.

He was incomplete. His foundation was lacking—and then an epiphany washed over him. He'd been trying to grasp the bald man's secrets, but those were so high up the ladder he didn't even deserve to reach for them. He didn't even have the first step.

Slow and steady. Wait a moment. This is like academic research!

A punch to his jaw made him spin in midair and snapped him out of irrelevant thoughts. Jack landed on his feet and ducked under another punch, then delivered a devastating uppercut on the gorilla's chest—height difference. The poor animal almost left the ground but quickly replied with a deft jab that Jack dodged.

Basics, he repeated to himself, trying not to lose focus. I must work my way up. To become a good fighter, I must first become a fighter. I must be able to stand on stage and fight. I must develop the mental resilience to perform under any circumstances. I must not allow myself stupid, gaping flaws.

He looked at the big brorilla with gratitude. This was such a great opportunity. He'd found his missing piece. He needed the heart of a fighter—the eye of the tiger.

A punch whistled by his ear, and another smashed into the gorilla's belly.

Jack returned to the fray with renewed resolve. He opened his mind to the surrounding tension, letting it flow over him without affecting him. He'd spoken on stage before, had even given lectures. He could handle it.

Only, this wasn't the same. The eyes of dozens of monkeys and a few brorillas were all on him, and the pressure wasn't something his razor-sharp battle brain could handle. Resolve alone wasn't enough.

With growing terror, Jack realized he couldn't ignore them. He couldn't tune it off. It worked great in theory, but not in practice.

Crap!

This was bad. He was lost and confused. His brain refused to act at normal speed. On the other hand, the big brorilla had gathered so much momentum and confidence it was about to steamroll Jack. This was now a fight he could lose, and he would, if he didn't find a way to recover his footing.

This must be how athletes feel... But I don't know how to handle the pressure! How do they do it?

Wait. I don't need to handle it, he realized. I have fists. I can simply break it.

He grinned. That's right. So far, he remained a scientist at heart. The fighter only emerged automatically while fighting. Jack now had to summon him at will.

A scientist would ignore the pressure. A fighter would muster his stubbornness and smash right through it.

His fists clenched harder. These monkeys wanted to boo him? Their burning gazes would make him cower? Hah!

He stood straighter. His gaze, that had been trapped at the gorilla's chest-level, reached its eyes and stared defiantly. The big brorilla noticed the change. So did the brorillas and gymonkeys. Their sounds changed. Their boos hesitant.

The big brorilla tried to smash a fist into those defiant eyes, but Jack was no longer there. So far, he'd been pummeling the gorilla's torso, whittling its endurance down. He couldn't reach any higher due to the height difference—the big brorilla was nine feet tall.

However, Jack now realized he shouldn't care. If he dared, his Fist-fighting skill knew the way.

The crowd's pressure was still wrapped around Jack's fists, obstructing them, but so what? He ignored it, pushed harder, and ripped right through it. He was the king of the ring, and he fucking loved it.

The brorilla's fist met empty air. In the next moment, Jack rose from the ground, jumping up and reaching the brorilla's head. Its eyes widened. Jack pulled his hand back. The brorilla tried to recover, to dodge, but there was no time. It saw death.

Jack's punch drilled straight into the big brorilla's face, stopping a few centimeters before its nose and turning it into mush.

The gorilla flew back and collapsed to the ground. Jack landed on his feet, a wild grin on his face. He hadn't lost himself. He was still in complete control. He simply enjoyed this fight enough to smile, and he didn't see a reason to hide it. He would do whatever he wanted. Fuck them all.

The brorilla growled as it stood. It faced Jack, and he stared deep into its eyes. There was anger there, shame... and helplessness. Resignation.

The big brorilla gave a sad growl as it fell to both knees and bowed toward him.

In that last strike, Jack had stopped his punch before it struck the gorilla's face. Otherwise, his Drill skill would have sent the momentum deep enough to break several delicate bones, and he might have even killed the gorilla on the spot.

He wasn't sure if his actions had been noticed, but apparently, they had. These apes were smart animals.

As soon as the big brorilla bowed, the rest of the monkeys followed suit. Seven brorillas and around thirty gymonkeys bowed to Jack, who accepted his victory.

Due to his science, he knew how monkey society worked. As ridiculous as it seemed, he'd challenged the alpha male and won. He was their leader now.

Jack looked at the various monkeys, all of them buff as fuck. He had a monkey pack under his command, valuable allies against the black wolf. Moreover, the fight with the big brorilla helped him discover a major flaw and fix it. He now had the heart of a fighter—or at least the beginnings of one.

This difference might sound small, but Jack could feel it resonating with the vision inside him. The bald man approved. Now that Jack had the heart, he understood that the bald man was similar. He was a fighter through and through, pushing forward until nothing remained.

Maybe that's what made his punch so magically unstoppable.

Jack was on to something. A light bulb shone in his mind as all his insights started to come together. A vague form began taking shape—

—and then a ding came out of nowhere, breaking his concentration. The idea retreated back to the very edge of his mind, right outside his reach.

Motherfu—He stopped himself. No meaning in insulting an omnipotent entity that could read your thoughts.

Stifling his frustration as best as he could, he turned to look at the status screen that interrupted him.

Primate Boss subjugated! Would you like to despawn the group?
Y/N

Level Up! You have reached Level 23.
Level Up! You have reached Level 24.
Level Up! You have reached Level 25.

Forcing a boss to surrender clearly counted as a victory. It didn't matter much to Jack. *No*, he replied. He wasn't going to despawn his new allies.

However, it seemed his assumption of each monster group counting as a killable entity was true. By defeating the group, he'd gotten the respective experience, even though he didn't kill a single monkey.

And these levels mattered. He allocated all bonus points equally among his physical stats, of course. The difference between him and the black wolf was closing by the day. His battle prowess now had to be around level 40.

Not too far away... Unless that Elite tag means what I think it does. Dammit.

In video games, Elite enemies were stronger than their levels would indicate. Jack really hoped that wasn't the case... Even if it was, he had an Elite class of his own, plus a monkey army that would help him pull through, especially if he trained it a little.

Finally, there was one extra benefit from all these level-ups. Jack grinned as he looked at the last status screen. It was almost enough to make him forgive the System for distracting him—almost.

Congratulations! Level 25 reached. New Class Skill acquired: Calamitous Punch (I).

CHAPTER TWENTY-THREE
CALAMITOUS PUNCH

Congratulations! Level 25 reached. New Class Skill acquired. Calamitous Punch (I): All warriors have a finishing strike. At the cost of exhaustion, overdraw your body's potential to unleash a devastating attack.

UNLIKE HIS PREVIOUS SKILLS, THIS ONE WAS ACTIVE, NOT PASSIVE. SUDDENLY, something appeared inside him. Like a switch or a big red button.

There wasn't an actual red button in his head, obviously, but that's what it resembled. Jack got the sense that, just by willing it, this skill would tug at all his muscles and unleash every scrap of strength in his body at once. The result would undoubtedly be catastrophic—both for the enemy and himself.

But not so catastrophic that he couldn't test it.

He turned to the monkeys, whose reverent eyes watched him. He raised a clenched fist.

"My friends!" he began, hoping they could understand him. "Don't call me big brother—your big bro is right there. Call me Jack. I am not here to conquer you, but to help you and be helped in turn. We share a common enemy. The hateful black wolf that wants to snack on your brothers and sisters, rip your muscles apart, and feast on your bananarms."

Jack was gambling a bit here, but it worked. The gymonkeys and brorillas were riled up, unable to believe the size of this wolf's audacity. Not their bananarms!

"But don't be afraid!" his voice thundered, cutting through the clamor. The monkeys shut up. "I am like you! We will fight *together*! We will put our lives on the line and kill that arrogant canine. We will be *free*!"

They cheered, even the big brorilla. Jack ramped up for his finale.

"For victory! For alliance! Apes together"—he clenched his fist and drove it toward the ground, activating Calamitous Punch—"STRONG!"

It was a nice finale. Simple, direct, and targeted. Perfect for riling up a monkey pack. The only problem was that Jack had no idea how strong his new skill was. The effects of Drill and Pugilist Body had been useful, but nothing too pronounced.

He wanted a simple bang. That's all.

When he activated Calamitous Punch, his clenched fist already heading for the soil, the world went dark. His punch accelerated so hard it pulled him completely off-balance. Yet, his movement remained perfect, as if his body knew what to do.

Every unnecessary muscle went lax as all strength left him. It gathered on his torquing waist, his turning shoulder, his clenched fist. Jack sensed the power of this one fist and was overcome with terror, and he couldn't stop it. It reached the ground almost instantly.

Color returned to the world with an explosion. Jack flew back. The ground erupted under his feet, showering the nearby gymonkeys with gravel, and the impact's booming sound echoed over the entire forest.

"Fuck..." Jack gritted his teeth. His right hand lay limp at his side, many bones broken—only his 79 Constitution saved it from shattering completely. The monkeys alternated their incredulous stares between him and the point of impact, unable to believe their eyes.

Where Jack used to stand, there was now a half-foot-deep crater as if a meteorite had fallen. The soil was upturned in its perimeter, the center scorched black, and Jack could even see an underground rock that his fist had torn through like paper.

Calamitous Punch sure packed a punch. Only a full-power strike from the rock bear could come close to this level of destruction. It was a real calamity.

Of course, the price was heavy. Jack's entire body was sore and exhausted as if he'd just run a marathon. He was starving, and his hand was broken. He'd underestimated the strength of his new skill, but that was okay. Now, he knew its strength. It was a last resort, a hidden ace in his sleeve.

It was the weapon that would kill the black wolf.

His new friends recovered from their stupor. The monkeys gathered around the crater to inspect it, while the big brorilla and two of its gorilla bros approached Jack to make sure he was okay. He assured them he was fine and thanked them for caring.

Another brorilla approached a minute later. It had apparently gone behind the bananarm plant, where they kept some of their gym equipment, and fetched a roll of processed leaves that could serve as bandages. Jack thanked this brorilla, too, wrapping the leaves around his broken hand, grimacing in pain—or rather, in expectation of the pain.

The broken hand itself was nothing compared to the ice pond and the agony it would demand while fixing it.

Somehow, the gymonkeys had come to the conclusion that they should fill the hole with poop. The big brorilla sent the brorillas to enforce order and awaited by Jack's side.

Jack looked at the gorilla. Just a few minutes ago, they'd been fighting frenziedly, and now they were bros. He chuckled and shook his head.

This world keeps getting crazier and crazier...

The gorilla extended a hand to help Jack up—he'd been sitting against a tree till now. It pointed one finger at Jack and one at itself, then brought the two fingers close together, and again, one finger was clearly higher than the other.

Jack laughed. "Nah, bro." He grabbed the lower finger and raised it. "Both of us are big brothers. In fact, you know what? There's no big brother between us. I'm just Jack, and you are..." He considered it for a moment. "Harambe. Yes, I think that's suitable. It's from another gorilla, an honorable one. Do you like this name?"

The big brorilla thought for a moment, then nodded. Suddenly, its eyes were filled with manly tears. It extended a hand and gave Jack a firm, earnest handshake that would make any father proud.

"The honor's mine, Harambe. Now, let's go kick some wolf ass, shall we?"

The gorilla cheered. The monkeys and brorillas, not knowing what was happening, cheered too, and the clearing was filled with hollering that quickly turned into war cries.

Jack raised his voice again. "But before that, follow me." An evil grin appeared on his face. "I will make you guys even stronger."

The monkeys cheered again. They had no idea what was waiting for them.

They were on the clock. He'd despawned the goblins, killed the bear boss and most of the bears, and took over the entire monkey pack. He had basically turned the dungeon on its head, and the boss was sure to know.

In fact, it *could* already be after him. They had to hurry.

Under Jack's instructions, the monkey pack abandoned their gym equipment for now, took some bananarms for the way, and headed for the bear area. This all took them ten minutes, and most of those were spent trying to make the monkeys understand what he was saying. Thankfully, they were fairly intelligent. He was glad he didn't treat them as monsters.

While the big brorilla was organizing things, Jack had also tried a few bananarms. He was stunned. They were delicious!

Flavor overflowed from inside them. Their juices were thick enough to fill his mouth and thin enough that they weren't sticky. Jack had eaten at many good restaurants in his time traveling the world for conferences, but nothing came close to the taste of these forest bananarms.

In fact, the bananarms were so thick in nutrients, that the taste resembled meat a little, but in such a way that it meshed perfectly with their natural fruity flavor. There was sugar, too, along with a bit of spice, though Jack had no idea how it had gotten there.

This heavenly taste was like the love product of bananas and the finest beef.

Which was a tiny bit suspicious, too, given that earth's bananas had been selectively bred to reach their current state, but Jack didn't want to be too paranoid.

The first bananarm also gave him ten points in Strength. Along with his recent level-ups, Jack's status screen was quickly becoming a sight that would entrench any proper number junkie.

Name: Jack Rust
Species: Human, Earth-387
Faction: -
Grade: F
Class: Pugilist (Elite)
Level: 25

Strength: 79
Dexterity: 79
Constitution: 79
Mental: 9
Will: 7

Skills: Fistfighting (II), Drill (I), Pugilist Body (I), Calamitous Punch (I)

Things were looking up. He was now a real superman.

The big brorilla growled something to get Jack's attention, and turning, he saw everyone ready to go. Thirty gymonkeys and seven brorillas, led by their big bro, all awaited Jack's commands. It brought a tear to his eyes.

"Let's go," he said, closing his status screen. "A battle's waiting."

Their first stop would be the former bear territory. As the monkeys left their area of the forest, they looked around in wonder and behind in hesitation. They briefly warred with some instinct that told them to stay put—the System's mind control, probably—before following Jack out.

Their eyes were instantly filled with new life, and their enthusiasm rocked the world before Jack shushed them. They had to be stealthy, or the black wolf might come and slaughter them. They weren't ready yet.

Stealthy like that, they crossed into the bear territory and headed deep inside. Jack wasn't worried about the remaining earth bears. Even if they spotted his group, he and the big brorilla could make quick work of any bear unlucky enough to cross their path.

They reached the clear pond without any accidents, and Jack sent all monkeys and gorillas to relax in its waters. It was a bit crampy, but they fit. He stood guard outside.

Clear Pond (F-Grade)

Clear Ponds are naturally-occurring formations spread around the universe. They are often used as parts of resorts. Anyone who relaxes in these waters will find tranquility, their body will loosen completely, and their potential will emerge, making the entire body sturdier. The stat increase is a one-time bonus

The monkeys' reaction was priceless. They first tested the water with their toes, afraid of entering it, but soon, they lounged inside, full of euphoria. Their sighs and moans of relaxation were so pronounced, Jack grew uncomfortable.

He let them relax for ten minutes before pulling them back out—literally. All monkeys and brorillas now had eyes full of serenity, and their gazes at him were filled with gratitude. Clearly, they loved the clear pond. Jack grinned. Each one of them, from the weakest gymonkey to the big brorilla, had increased by a level.

Jack then turned sharply to the left and led them south, to the goblin area. Thanks to the clear pond, they were even quieter than before, and no wolf crossed their path. In fact, the pond's relaxation powers were so intense, that some monkeys even fell asleep and had to be carried by others.

Eventually, they reached the large clearing where the goblin tribe used to be located. It remained empty; almost. A lone boar walked in circles around the High Speed Bush. Its eyes were red like traffic lights and it could barely stand. Jack grabbed it and unceremoniously placed it back into the forest.

"Be careful," he instructed the monkeys. "This stuff is strong. As soon as you feel yourselves getting stronger, stop *immediately*."

They nodded.

High Speed Bush (F-Grade)

A resource formerly guarded by the goblins of the Forest of the Strong. Commonly found in the wet jungles of planet Peruvian, the leaves of this bush can enhance a person's reflexes, dexterity, and agility. They can also make you high as a kite.

The stat increase is a one-time bonus.

Ten minutes later, Jack cursed loudly. How could the monkeys know about the delay between licking a leaf and its effect kicking in?

The brorillas were fine, thanks to their high stats, but most of the monkeys were rolling on the ground and laughing like crazy. A few had even formed a gang and tossed poop at the big brorilla from across the clearing, heedless of its growls, and giggling like human children that had rang a doorbell and ran away.

True to its description, the bush made them high as a kite.

It took a few minutes for Jack to round them all up and make sure they'd gotten the Dexterity bonus. This time, their power had increased by two levels, not one—Jack assumed this was a rounding error from before.

By now, gymonkeys ranged between levels 8 and 16, brorillas between 17 and 20, and the big brorilla stood proudly at level 28. They were a force to be reckoned—or they would be, when the bush's effect wore off.

Monkeys weren't the most disciplined creatures. High monkeys, of course, were completely uncontrollable. It took massive effort from Jack and the gorillas to guide them, and any concepts of stealth were thrown out the window.

It didn't matter. From the goblin clearing to Jack's cave was a short way.

Laugh while you can, thought Jack, staring at the high monkeys. An evil grin reappeared on his face. *Soon, you'll get your lesson.*

Jack had visited the clear pond first, hoping the increased Constitution would help the monkeys resist the High Speed Bush better. Maybe it worked, maybe it didn't. They reached his cave, and he ushered them through the narrow opening. The big brorilla couldn't fit, but they broke some sharp rocks at the sides, and then it barely managed to get through.

The cave was crampy with so many creatures inside. Jack held his nose, too. However, as soon as the monkeys laid eyes on the ice pond, they froze, and their eyes became filled with wonder.

Jack's evil grin widened. The pond was extraordinarily beautiful, but the pain it hid was equally extraordinary. At least it was the good kind of pain.

For the first time, someone else would have to suffer this too. The monkeys had to get stronger—he couldn't wait to see their reactions.

CHAPTER TWENTY-FOUR
MONKEY SEE, MONKEY DO

JACK STEPPED INTO THE ICE POND FIRST. HE WANTED TO ACT LIKE A PROPER leader. Unfortunately, the moment his broken hand touched the water, he screamed like a little girl.

The pain was the worst he'd felt so far. Someone may as well have been using pliers to readjust his bones, except these pliers were ice-cold and everywhere at the same time.

The monkeys watched from outside the lake, torn between trying to help and watching the water with fear. A moment ago, it had looked beautiful. Now, they no longer felt like swimming.

"It's fine!" Jack gritted his teeth and spoke through the pain. "This is only because I'm injured. Fuck! Just come in."

They looked at each other. They did not want to go in.

The big brorilla, Harambe, stepped forth. With a snort at his fellow monkeys, he stepped into the water and frowned. The cold had reached him, and though it couldn't harm him, it was a unique sensation.

The monkeys watched with bated breath as their big bro took a step forward, then another. Soon, the gorilla was halfway across the lake and still going, but now, his steps were slow. Measured. Careful.

The pauses between each step got longer. Harambe was shivering now. Ice glinted on his fur, shining like little stars. The monkeys cheered him on, ignoring Jack, whose screams of pain had died down.

The gorilla took another step, then stopped. Jack had needed thirteen steps to reach the waterfall, but Harambe, being larger, had only taken nine. The pond was thirteen feet long, anyway, and Jack resolved to measure it as such from now on. Confusion would help no one.

"Don't go any farther," said Jack. Harambe turned to look, and his face was pale below his fur. His eyes were shaking but still full of passion. "The waterfall is dangerous. Stay there for a while, get used to the cold, and I'll help you touch it safely."

He nodded. Jack turned back to the monkeys.

"All of you. In," he commanded.

The brorillas were first. They all frowned when they touched the water, but their brohood was too strong to fear a little bit of cold. Walking side-by-side in two rows—they could barely fit—they crossed the first half of the pond before slowing down. Eventually, each brorilla made it between the seventh and tenth foot, all of them pushed to their limits.

It was a brave attempt.

Finally came the gymonkeys, who weren't nearly as stoic as the gorillas. The moment they touched the water, they began screaming, jumping on top of each other and making faces. The fact that most were still high didn't help.

It took both Jack and Harambe to convince them to enter the pond. The monkeys weren't happy, but they complied, still letting out the intermittent cry. At least the cold washed away the High Speed Bush's effects.

In the end, the gymonkeys reached anywhere from the second to the fifth foot of the lake, with only one of them barely stopping at the sixth.

Their efforts weren't for naught. According to Jack's inspection, each gymonkey gained one to three levels, the brorillas got three to five, while the big brorilla, Harambe himself, increased in power by a whooping six levels, reaching level 34—and, if he could enter the waterfall, he'd get another few.

Everyone felt the change in themselves and were overjoyed. The monkeys hollered and did their best to advance farther, while the brorillas grinned and nodded at each other as they flexed their muscles. The big brorilla, intoxicated by power, stared at Jack, debating whether to challenge him again.

A moment later, he shelved the thought. He was smart enough to appreciate that this increase in his power was only thanks to Jack.

However, it remained that, while all the monkeys had ventured into the pond—whose power seemed inexhaustible—Jack himself was only at the shallows, nursing his wounds. The gymonkeys didn't care much, but all gorillas stared at him in question. Would he not surpass them? Was his mind too weak to traverse the pond?

Jack raised his eyes from the crystal-clear waters. He took in the gazes of the gorillas, the challenge in Harambe's stare. He grinned.

Watch and marvel. I'm healed already.

With slow, purposeful steps, he crossed the lake. He went past the gymonkeys. He reached the gorillas, whose eyes were transitioning from doubt to respect, and stepped past them without missing a beat. His speed was steady, his pace fluid.

The gorillas entered the ice pond for the first time, but Jack was a virtuoso.

He reached the big brorilla and stopped beside him. He met his stare with pride: *If you want to challenge me, I'm right here.*

Harambe growled but didn't act. Jack nodded.

"Come, Harambe. Since you could stay here this long, you're ready to touch the waterfall, but be prepared. The cold in there is incomparable to here. You might die. Are you ready to risk your life for power?"

Harambe didn't even consider it. He nodded.

"Good. Then go in. I'll spot you—to speak in gym terms. If you freeze, I'll try to pull you out... but I might fail."

Jack had grown stronger since last time, but not by too much. He had zero confidence against this waterfall.

Every single monkey watched with faith and curiosity. Harambe turned to stare at the falling water. On his grumpy face, yellow eyes shone with resolve. Despite the cold, he balled his fists, released a monkey cry, and dived right in.

Then, silence.

Through the hazy waters, everyone saw Harambe's body freeze before his voice was abruptly cut short.

The gymonkeys wreaked havoc with their howls, and even the brorillas growled. Jack ignored them. He kept his eyes glued on Harambe, watching him intently.

Freezing over wouldn't kill you—he'd tested that himself. The gamble was to pull Harambe out after he got the stat bonuses just before he froze to death.

Unfortunately, Jack didn't know how long he'd spent frozen himself, nor did he know when the bonuses would come. Therefore, he simply kept scanning Harambe over and over, hoping for his level to suddenly spike.

Nothing happened for a while. Harambe's fur took on a paler shade as time went by. The monkeys were going insane from worry. Jack remained still as a rock, ignoring the cold that slithered up his spine. He fired off one System inspection after another. Nothing changed.

Maybe I won't see it, he thought. Maybe the System won't let me cheat like this. Maybe it's already too late.

He steeled his resolve. Better a weaker Harambe than a dead one. He was a good gorilla and didn't deserve to die.

Jack took a deep breath. All of a sudden, he burst from immobility. His arms snaked into the waterfall to grab Harambe to pull him out. At that moment, he fired off an inspection.

Big Brorilla, Level 37

The bonus was there.

Jack would have smiled if he could move his face. His arms in the waterfall were assaulted by relentless waves of soul-freezing cold. He couldn't feel them anymore. His mind was slowing down. His body was growing heavier. His fingers refused to close around Harambe's arm.

But he had to save his bro.

Jack gritted his teeth and screamed through the freeze. Veins popped in his forehead as if snapping through solid ice, and with a burst of will, he caught Harambe's ice-cold body and pulled.

The two fell backward into the pond. Jack struggled to recover and get back up—thankfully, he'd only barely entered the waterfall or he'd be frozen solid already. On the bright side, Harambe had frozen in an upright position—as upright as a gorilla on his knuckles could be—and he was big enough for his head to stay above the surface even when he fell back.

After Jack recovered, he pushed Harambe a bit toward the brorillas waiting close behind. They were fine. They grabbed Harambe and pulled him out, showering him with their worry. All the gymonkeys had already exited the pond, and were crowded over Harambe, pushing each other for the right to stand beside him.

Jack smiled. These monkeys really adored their big bro. Harambe would be fine—he was already defrosting.

Jack then turned back to the waterfall. It cascaded as calmly as ever, unconcerned with the mortal affairs around it. In its endless cold, a gorilla and a human were nothing.

But, in Jack's eyes, the waterfall was many things. It was a mystery, a challenge, and a blessing.

In that endless cold lay the hidden world he'd entered, a world in his own mind he could only unlock through this waterfall. Last time, he'd inspected the bald man's punch from all angles—the scene was carved in his mind with crystal-clear precision, but it was only in that frozen state that he could freely inspect it.

Jack had spent an unknown amount of time pondering on that vision, watching it again and again, trying to discern its secrets. How had that bald man unleashed such power? What did Jack lack?

Unknowingly, the vision had become an obsession. When he slept, he dreamed of the bald man's punch. When he rested, his mind kept jumping back there, analyzing every tiny movement.

There was something there. Something gargantuan hid just beyond his sight, he was certain. He could sense it, almost touch it, but every time he tried, epiphany escaped like a slippery fish. He wanted to know. He *needed* to know. It was extremely important.

Unfortunately, his progress was slow outside the waterfall. In there, he'd analyzed everything, and despite that, something was still missing. He was trying to solve a puzzle with a few important pieces still in the box, and no matter how he tried, whether in or out of the waterfall, he came up empty.

During his fight with Harambe, he'd discovered something, a clue in a direction he hadn't considered before. The bald man's punch was clearly magical, in some way. Why, then, would its origins be strictly physical?

This might have been the missing piece of the puzzle, and Jack yearned to enter the waterfall to find out. He needed that frozen state to progress fast.

The waterfall was dangerous, sure, but he'd survived it before when he was three levels weaker. Plus, he now had a bro to spot him. He would be fine. It was a risk worth taking.

But not hastily.

Jack turned around and followed the monkeys outside. Harambe woke up, and impressed everyone with his new power. He even considered challenging Jack again, but not only were the circumstances less than ideal, Jack was also busy.

He sat on a rock and stared at infinity, lost in thoughts so deep that even the monkeys' incessant howling didn't budge him. Harambe left him alone for now. Even stood beside him, making sure nobody disturbed his bro for any reason. Jack was clearly busy with something important.

An hour later, Jack stood. All cold had left his system, and his body was back in pristine condition. His eyes were sharp, his breathing steady, and he radiated an aura of no chill.

"Harambe," he said, making the gorilla turn around. "I will go in the waterfall. Spot me."

Harambe nodded. As the rest of the monkeys watched, the two of them headed deep into the pond—thanks to Harambe's stat bonuses from the waterfall, it was now easier.

They reached the waterfall at the back and stopped before it.

"Don't pull me out too early," said Jack. "I can probably get out by myself, so act only if you think I'm dying. I trust you, Harambe. Okay?"

The big brorilla met Jack's eyes and nodded. He wouldn't let his bro die, but he'd do his best to delay the saving.

"Good."

Jack dived into the waterfall and let the cold consume him. The next moment, he opened his eyes in the plain cyan world of tranquility, where his mind belonged entirely to him.

It was time to solve the riddle.

CHAPTER TWENTY-FIVE
BREAKING THROUGH

JACK STOOD ALONE IN THE EMPTY BLUE WORLD. THERE WAS NOTHING HERE, NOT even a chair to rest on. Only an endless cyan expanse, where the sky stretched from the horizon to beneath his feet.

He didn't remember many things. His mind had been frozen on entering, and only his innermost reality had carried through.

As he stood puzzled in this empty world, without any distractions whatsoever, a desire sprung forth from the deepest parts of his being. He wanted to be like that man.

A vision appeared. A bald man clad in yellow, punching through a beast taller than skyscrapers. He seemed tiny, and his movements inconsequential. However, the world shook the moment he moved, the air screamed, and the phantom of a fist crossed the air like a meteor to smash into and through the beast's scaly chest.

"Still not enough..." he muttered, looking at his fist, and the vision disappeared.

Jack made it replay. It was engraved deep in his soul—he could review it at will.

He didn't know how many times he saw the same vision. Setting, punch, destruction, finale. He reviewed it in slow motion and from multiple angles. He observed every tiny change in the man's body and the surrounding environment. He saw everything, but he was missing something.

How *infuriating*! All the information was there, right in front of him, letting him review it at will, and he still couldn't figure out the secret. The destruction wasn't caused simply by the man's bodily strength. Where had it come from? And why did it feel so... natural?

It was like watching someone else play a game they were good at. It seemed easy, but when you tried, you couldn't even take two steps without falling.

Jack was determined to succeed.

Think... a voice whispered in his head. It was his voice, coming from far away. *Remember...*

Jack frowned. The vision disappeared, replaced by other images.

He saw himself screaming as he mauled a goblin before the ice pond. That was the first real battle in his entire life. He'd discovered despair and the power it could give. He'd realized how much power humans kept in reserve, the part of themselves that never saw the light.

The images shifted to when he ambushed a goblin squad in the woods. He'd come to terms with violence, with survival of the strongest, with killing.

He ran away from an earth bear, barely escaping with his life. It was only proper. If he wasn't strong, he couldn't fight, and he had to run.

He ambushed three hobgoblins. He was unarmed, while they brandished shortswords but didn't know how to use them. Power mattered little without the skill to apply it.

He warred against the goblin tribe. He snuck through, then massacred. He faced great pain and despair but broke through everything with sheer stubbornness. And he won.

Jack stopped. He'd felt something in this last memory. A part of that battle, as he said, 'fuck it,' and ran through the burning flames, resonated with something deep inside him. At that moment, he'd felt complete, but was that all?

He sensed there was something more and followed the feeling to another scene.

Jack faced off against the rock bear. After his partially successful ambush, the two had fought fiercely for a long time. During that battle, and especially during the end, what drove him? How did he feel?

Despair. Fear. Rage. Bitterness. Frustration. The rock bear was forcing him to dance on a razor's edge. He had to dodge every single attack, hundreds of them, or he would die. He was on the weaker end. The world was suppressing him, trying to take him down, but he stubbornly refused. He stood his ground over and over, gritting his teeth and beating at the problem until he won or died.

There it was, again. The resonance inside him. This stubbornness, this undying will to make it, the headstrong approach to life that refused to take a single step back. It expressed him. Defined him.

Jack fought the big brorilla. His power was enough, and so were his skills. Yet, he'd almost lost. Why?

Because he was pressured, and he'd been trying to fight the problem as a scholar, like the pre-System Jack. Which didn't work. He couldn't let the problem wash over him without affecting him. That wasn't him. He wanted to face the obstacles head-on, set his jaw, and break through it. Punch through it.

Like a fist.

"Oh."

Jack blinked. Something inside him finally clicked, and then, he was whole. He saw it.

The Fist.

This was his path to life, the path he would walk to the end of time. He would face the world with strength, like a thrown punch, until either he or any obstacle broke. Never defeat. Only victory. Fist meant power and nothing else. This was his innermost truth, the way he was meant to be. This made him feel whole. This was him.

And not just him.

Riding the wave of realizations, Jack's mind expanded. That's what was missing before. This state, breaking through everything like a clenched fist, didn't just resonate inside him.

It reminded him of the bald man.

He'd seen the vision so many times that he felt intimate with him. He understood it. Suddenly, he realized he'd never once considered the bald man a person, only a punching machine. But that wasn't so.

He knew every tiny movement of the bald man's body as he threw the punch. Now, he understood that his state of mind mattered as well. If he could combine those, if he could reach the apex in both will and technique, if he could touch that absolute peak, even just once...

Only a faint gauze of mist separated Jack from something truly world-shaking. Only a last, tiny step remained.

Jack put himself in the shoes of the bald man and imagined what he might be feeling, facing down a titan by himself. Fear. Helplessness. Stubbornness. Resolve. When he punched out, he must have felt ridiculous, punching something so large with such a tiny fist. Yet, he persisted.

What drove him?

In the vision, the man's attack left no way out. He didn't hold anything back. He only punched, supremely confident that he could break through. It was a confidence fueled by his undeniable strength, and the more Jack considered it, the more he felt there was something deeper.

It wasn't just confidence. Even if the bald man hadn't been certain of success, he'd still punched out in the same unyielding way. There was a fire shimmering inside him that commanded him to act as such. He was a man that faced everything like a clenched fist. A man that could break but never bend. A man that went ever forward, laughing until he died. That was him.

And that was Jack.

Everything clicked. The thin gauze separating Jack from the truth wasn't lifted—it was broken through. He understood. For a moment, even the blue world disappeared, and Jack found himself facing a titanic fist, a Truth, a natural law. The majesty stunned him.

He only withstood its presence for a single moment, and it was enough to know with absolute certainty that this was his Path. The Path of the Fist. The massive fist saw him as well, not even an ant in its eyes, but acknowledged him.

Jack returned to the blue world, but he wasn't the same. He was a new man. Something shimmered inside him, burned like the bald man's heroic heart. The path of the fist was part of him, and he a part of it. He could borrow its strength. He could *understand.*

Jack closed his eyes. He found himself hovering over a purple desert, facing a titanic scaly beast. The heat caressed his skin, the fear and excitement, and the fast beating of his heart were all at the forefront. His resolve hardened so much it filled him completely. He could do this. He would never take a step back. He would break through this enemy. Absolutely.

Jack clenched his fist and shot it forward with the absolute belief that it would succeed. He'd seen the vision so many times that his movements unknowingly copied the bald man's to the last muscle. His soul did, too. They shared a vision.

The fist traveled forth, crossing the sky like a meteor, and smashed into and through the beast's chest. Of course it did.

He'd succeeded.

But he also realized just how far there was to go. His fist had pierced through a massive beast, but true meteors could destroy planets. The potential excited him. He sighed as he looked at his fist.

"Still not enough..."

Jack opened his eyes and found the blue world broken. He'd punched it. A large hole lay open before him, revealing stones and clean water tumbling over them. And he was so terribly cold.

Two large hands grabbed his shoulders and pulled him back. A wail entered his ears as, like a mirror, the blue world broke into tiny pieces that dissolved into nothingness. Jack could barely move, but he could sense Harambe pulling him through the ice pond. His body was almost failing. He must have stayed in the waterfall for far longer than last time... but he'd made it.

He grinned wildly. He was different. An aura shimmered around him like a clenched fist. He'd found his path in life. All was well.

Celebratory blue screens flooded his vision.

Congratulations! You have developed the Dao Root of the Fist.
The world is endless, but your path is your own. Stride forth with vigor. Fist means power.

Congratulations! For being one of the first ten people on your planet to develop a Dao Root, you are awarded the Title: Planetary Frontrunner (10).

Jack was overwhelmed by cold and information. While he would need some time to put everything in order, for now, he knew one thing: He'd found his path. He would tread it to the very end.

And the first enemy to know his true strength would be the Dungeon Boss. The black wolf.

Harambe took Jack to the shore and collapsed beside him, while the gymonkeys and brorillas rushed to help. Not that they could do much. Time would take away the cold.

Jack managed to turn his head toward Harambe. "Thank you..." he muttered, barely able to move his lips. "You really waited... until the last moment..."

By his side, Harambe's monkey lips were drawn into a weak grin. He managed to form a thumbs-up.

Jack smiled. And then, he fell asleep.

It took some hours for Jack to wake up. The combined exhaustion from fighting Harambe, touring the forest, healing at the pond, and entering the waterfall had gotten to him.

Thankfully, the monkeys were good people, and they let him rest. They even stayed slightly quieter than usual.

It was morning, and Jack was finally putting things in order. He had a lot of information to go through, so he started with the easy ones.

CHAPTER TWENTY-SIX
EXPLORING THE DAO

SYSTEM, JACK THOUGHT CURIOUSLY, WHAT IS A PLANETARY FRONTRUNNER?

Planetary Frontrunner (10): A Title awarded to the first ten sapients to develop a Dao Root in an Integrated planet. A sign of great potential, marking the owner as a person worthy of the Immortal System's assistance.
Efficacy of all stats +10%

System, what's a Title?

Titles: A complementary system meant to award those who achieve extraordinary deeds. Titles are rare and can offer various benefits.

The System had an integrated FAQ. How handy. If only he knew earlier.

Two monkeys were bickering in front of Jack's flat stone, arguing about the ownership of a bananarm, but he didn't pay attention. Harambe appeared, grabbed the bananarm in his large hands, and broke it into two. He then gave each gymonkey one half and a glare.

Okay. So, I'm one of the first ten people on the entire planet to get a so-called Dao Root... That's so special. One-in-a-billion special. Can it be real?

Thinking back, there were a ton of coincidences that helped Jack. He'd been trapped in a dungeon and forced to go above and beyond to survive. That dug out his potential. He also had the ice pond spawn right next to him. Without it, he would have never survived this ordeal.

The ice pond also had the waterfall that granted him his epiphany, putting him in a frozen meditative state.

Moreover, everything he'd experienced up to now guided him toward the Dao of the Fist, where he was also personally inclined. This last reason wasn't necessarily a coincidence—after all, everyone saw things through their own eyes. Still, Jack had to admit that his experience so far seemed almost entirely optimized for getting a Dao Root.

Of course, none of this would have happened without his sweat, tears, and blood. Many people had opportunities, but very few could utilize them. This achievement belonged entirely to Jack.

So, if I make it out, I'll be super strong... Wow.

The vision blinded him for a moment. How would it feel? He'd be like a superman among mortals. People would form rows to watch his punches. He could guide them, lead them, protect them... and, most of all, he'd have freedom.

However, all of that would only happen if he defeated the black wolf. Jack snapped back to the present and focused on the more practical part of the Title.

+10% in the efficacy of all stats... God, that sounds huge.

Ten percent didn't sound like a large increase, except when it happened across the table, it compounded. Moreover, it scaled. If he previously had the stats of a normal level 40 person, he now had the stats of a level 44. This stat increase would stay with him forever, no matter how strong he got. He would always have a leg up over everyone else. And, if he could get more titles like this...

He almost salivated.

In a few words, it was an incredible bonus. Jack was a man of science. He knew how important even the tiniest of percentages were.

The black wolf thought it was the boss—Jack would show it.

Finally, he turned his attention to the most precious benefit: the Dao

Root. He had no idea what that meant. Fortunately, he had someone willing to answer all his questions.

System, what's a Dao Root?

Dao: The Dao represents the world. It is the natural laws that govern everything, from the tiniest atoms to the largest stars. A deep enough understanding of the Dao can translate into real-world applications. For example, people who pursue the Dao of Fire can often breathe fire.

The Immortal System has streamlined the Dao. It is recommended that cultivators progress simultaneously in Levels and the Dao for maximum benefits.

Right. So, magic. Got it.

He was aware of the word "Dao." It was used in eastern philosophy, though he always found it too abstract to take seriously—it literally meant path. The System description had given some interesting tidbits of information, but it wasn't what he'd asked.

System. What's a DAO ROOT? He thought the words slow and intensely, hoping it would help.

Dao: The Dao represents the world. It is the natural laws...

It was the same screen. The System obviously knew what a Dao Root was, so why wasn't it telling him?

Maybe it will only reveal the most basic stuff, and I have to discover the rest...

It was common practice in videogames, if annoying. Thankfully, Jack was smart enough to have his own hypotheses. He remembered the infinite vastness of that gigantic fist, having only touched its tiniest corner.

The Dao Root should be the first step toward mastering a Dao. The starting point, so to say. There are probably other classifications as one goes deeper... but it's suspicious. Everything else in the System is classified as numbers or letters. Even "Elite" is self-explanatory. So far, the Dao is the only thing with a more flowery hierarchy. Hmm...

It was an interesting mystery for later. Utilizing this Dao took priority.

He considered sparring with Harambe, who was also itching to test his power, but that wouldn't work. This cave was too cramped, and if they fought outside, the black wolf could jump on them at any time. They were the only creatures in the entire reserve, save for the natural animals and maybe a couple earth bears.

Thankfully, he didn't *need* to spar with anyone. The Dao of the Fist —as the System liked to call it—was a part of him. It was instinctive. He clenched his fist, and all sorts of notions began to unravel.

He was much more in tune with it than ever before. He even felt certain that this connection would help him in combat. His fists were decisively more absolute, be it in offense or defense, though it made no sense.

Had he finally attained magic?

Fist magic. He chuckled. Could be worse. I'm only an '-ing' away from getting censored.

He jabbed the air a few times. His fists shot true. He was aware of what they signified. Now, they weren't just powered by his body, but by his heart as well. He even thought he saw the air shimmer around them.

Nah. Must have been my imagination.

Lost in his musings, he didn't realize that the monkeys had quieted down. When he finally noticed, they were gathered around him, watching his practice intently like he was a piece of art. Even Harambe stared, and his eyes narrowed as if trying to comprehend something. There was reverence in those eyes.

Jack understood why. His Dao Root wasn't limited to his punches. It was a superior existence inside him, and it leaked into his every motion. When he walked, talked, or even turned to look at someone, he was very faintly exuding the aura of a clenched fist.

It wasn't noticeable unless someone paid close attention, or unless he was consciously channeling it into his fists. But it was there.

Facing the gazes of the monkeys, Jack raised his head higher. He sensed their desire for the power he bore. They were primal creatures of strength. Of course, they yearned for the power of the fist.

"The power I have," he said slowly, the monkeys maintaining absolute silence, "is called the Dao, and it is something you can all obtain. Work hard. Be true to your heart. And it will come."

They looked at him as if he'd given the greatest of sermons—which, in a way, he had. Harambe was the most touched of all. His eyes carried great admiration for Jack. He clenched his big fists and looked at them, still frowning.

"Don't stress, Harambe," Jack's voice floated over. The gorilla looked up. "There are many Daos. Maybe yours will be the fist, like mine, or maybe it will be something else. Don't try to copy me. Work hard, be true to *your* heart, and it will come."

Harambe looked deeply at Jack. Then, his eyes widened, and he nodded. He'd understood.

"Good." Jack clapped, snapping the monkeys out of their stupor. "We're going to hunt a wolf. It should be doable with our new powers, but many of us might die. However, for those who make it, danger hides opportunities. Be brave. Are you ready?"

It was a simple speech, yet the monkeys erupted in cheers and cries to the point where Jack suspected they'd gone to fetch some High Speed Bush leaves while he was asleep.

It wasn't that, though. They'd just gotten fired up by his demonstration of a Dao Root. It was a power that spoke to the hearts of all living beings, including Jack, which was why he'd been so obsessed with the bald man's vision.

Having given his rousing speech, Jack nodded with pride. These were brave monkeys.

There were thirty gymonkeys ranging between levels 9 and 19; seven brorillas, from level 20 to 25; and Harambe, who was at a whopping level 37.

The entire monkey army was vastly stronger than before, as was Jack, whose current battle prowess reached into the early forties—not including the Dao Root, whose precise strength was still unclear.

All in all, they were a brave group, and Jack was proud of them. In fact, he realized he'd neglected some things. He'd only treated them as allies so far, not as people, not as friends. Maybe he'd paid some extra attention to Harambe, but it wasn't enough.

Jack was all at once overcome with guilt, and he rushed to fix his wrongs.

"Brorillas," he said, stepping forth, and the seven of them hurried to do the same. "Do you have names?"

The brorillas glanced at each other and shook their heads. "Very well. From now on, you will be Oz, Herom, Amoh, Loha, Raza, Brodul, and Ehamba."

They were random names, but he felt they matched the brorillas' nature. He also named them in order of highest to lowest level.

"I am Jack. It is a pleasure to meet you all."

He shook hands with the seven brorillas, then joined them in flexing their muscles. Though his were admittedly smaller, nobody made fun of him or looked weird. His strength was all the proof they needed.

The monkeys cheered at this impromptu bodybuilding demonstration, and the brorillas nodded to each other with pride. They nodded deeply at Jack, then at Harambe, who'd also joined the flexing.

Jack then turned to the big brorilla. "Harambe, you will name the gymonkeys. Remember, as you are now people, you all need names!"

Harambe nodded. He then turned to the monkeys, pointed at them one by one, and uttered names that Jack's ears couldn't quite catch. Regardless, the gymonkeys seemed satisfied. Tears were in their eyes, proud to finally have proper names. Then, in an unspoken accord, they rushed toward Jack.

"Hey—"

They buried him in a big group hug that nailed him to the wall. Thankfully, he had high stats, or he might have been squashed.

"It's fine, it's fine." He laughed as he pushed them off. "We're friends now. We should help each other. Just a few names are nothing."

It was a touching moment. So touching, in fact, that Jack realized he'd made a mistake. Many of them might die against the wolf. Maybe he should have held back on the whole bonding thing...

What's done is done. Jack followed the Dao of the Fist. He was all or nothing, no half-measures.

"We've delayed enough," he spoke up, drawing everyone's attention. "Let's go. We have a wolf to kill."

They cheered again. Then, they streamed out of Jack's hidden cave like an army of ants, crossing the reserve and heading for its center, where Harambe knew the wolf had its den.

Jack was touched. He'd only been in the Forest of the Strong for a few days, but it felt like an entire lifetime. His time here was so full of tension, action, danger... and he'd grown so massively, too.

Now, things were coming to an end. He would escape and return to civilization. He would finally see what the world looked like, and he could live without fear for his life—hopefully.

Everything had converged to its final point: the black wolf. The Dungeon Boss.

CHAPTER TWENTY-SEVEN
WOLF HUNTING

Jack and the monkey army prowled through the morning forest. The pleasant chattering of birds, the last drops of moisture rolling off leaves, the vivid colors, these all formed a joyful mood that contrasted the soberness of the situation.

They'd chosen the morning because wolves enjoyed hunting at night. Also, because Jack was getting tired of all the monkey business in his cave.

A howl cut through the forest. Their bones rocked; their eyes narrowed. This howl hid fury and determination. The wolf was no longer playing around. It was out to get them.

Unless they got it first. It didn't sound like the wolf was sleeping, as they'd hoped, but maybe it was still in its cave—placing the howl's origin was difficult. With any luck, they could enact an ambush. If not, they would just wait for it to return.

The dungeon's final battle was arriving, swiftly and unavoidably.

Harambe led them through the trees until they reached a rocky hill in the middle of the forest. It stood only a few dozen feet tall and many dozen wide, and its back hid a shallow cave.

Fun fact: When the System arrived, Jack was on a tour to inspect two caves. If the coin had just flipped the other way, it wouldn't have been a level 2 goblin spawning beside him, but an Elite level 49 black wolf.

Jack and Harambe walked ahead. They found a hidden alcove in the rock and crouched to watch.

"Wait, Harambe," Jack whispered. "The wind is blowing toward the cave. It may smell us. Let's circle around the hill and approach the other way."

Harambe growled. They retreated with the monkeys and approached from the northeast, where the wind wouldn't betray their presence. Again, Jack and Harambe went ahead to scout. They hid behind a large rock.

The wolf's cave was a gaping maw in the side of the hill. It was pitch-black inside, as the towering rocks blocked the sun rays, giving the impression that the cave was endless. It could lead anywhere from two feet deep to China.

That they couldn't see inside was a bummer.

"It's probably empty," said Jack. "Why would the wolf howl from inside its cave? Let's see if this hill can hide forty monkeys, Harambe."

However, the big brorilla shook his head. His nose twitched, and he mimed jaws as he pointed in the cave.

"It's inside?" Jack raised a brow. Harambe nodded. "Very well. Then, we go with the original plan. We can't ambush it, but we can smother it. Let's fill the cave with gorillas."

They retreated to prepare. Two minutes later, the entire monkey army stood arrayed with the gorillas at the front, watching the cave's opening from just where they couldn't be seen.

"Get ready, everyone," Jack commanded. "We go quietly, and when I give the signal, we run. Got it?"

The monkeys nodded. He took a deep breath. Memories of his struggles passed through his mind: the goblins, the bears, the wolf that insta-killed anything it wanted...

"Let's go."

A gentle, rocky incline led up to the cave's mouth. The monkey army crawled over it, trying to stay silent so as not to spook the wolf. They wanted to reach the cave before it noticed them. In the open space outside, the advantage would belong to the wolf. In the narrow cave, to them.

Jack was first, with the big brorilla farther behind due to his large size. He leaned on a rock and peeked over it. He was only fifty feet away from the cave. Close enough to notice the two yellow eyes glaring at him from the darkness.

Black Wolf, Level 49 (Elite) (Dungeon Boss)
Black wolves are mostly solitary creatures. They are also territorial, proud, aggressive, and infamous for being a scourge at the peak of F-Grade. If a Black Wolf is spotted, experienced hunter squads should be dispatched quickly, or all big game of the surrounding area will disappear.

Jack froze for a single moment, then jumped forward like a spring. "Charge!" he shouted, initiating the battle, and waves of monkeys flooded the open ground behind him.

The wolf didn't expect the monkeys. It released a low growl and stepped outside its cave, making to escape.

Unfortunately for the wolf, the cave mouth was preceded by a short corridor of rock. Under normal circumstances, a few feet were nothing. But right now, Jack was bounding forth with long steps, jumping over the rock at speeds that would make any Olympic athlete jealous.

The wolf wouldn't make it in time. Its gaze landed deep inside Jack's eyes, who stared back. They'd met twice in the past—this was the third and last.

Yesterday, Jack might have been scared. He was charging at a superior opponent by himself. Today, however, he was a fist. This charge was his nature.

He slowed slightly, keeping himself close to the ground so he could react quickly. The wolf, realizing it couldn't escape, threw its head back and released a loud, drawn-out howl.

Hearing it from up-close was an experience. His ears rung and his vision swam. The sound penetrated his soul and shook it, but something fought back. The Dao Root of the Fist reacted as if it had met a worthy opponent, and it extinguished the wolf's attack.

Jack regained himself only to find the wolf's claws inches away from his face. He ducked on instinct, letting himself slide on the rock and gaining a long, bloody gash on the top of his head. He'd survived.

It has a Dao Root! he realized, paling. Shit!

He rolled upright and pivoted to face the wolf, which hadn't stopped running. It was charging the monkeys, who were still dazed, like a dark arrow.

"HARAMBE!" Jack roared.

A massive form stepped in the wolf's charge. A large fist shot at its face with the power of an elephant, forcing the wolf to slow and side-step before lunging for Harambe's throat. A day ago, the big brorilla couldn't have dodged this, but the High Speed Bush and the ice pond had raised his speed tremendously.

He leaned back, barely dodging the wolf's jaws, then slammed a heavy uppercut into its lower jaw, sending it flying.

The wolf wasn't injured. It somersaulted in midair and fell claws-first right where Jack was waiting. He danced away and the rock under his feet was sliced into pieces. The wolf's claws weren't joking.

It landed on all fours and shot at Jack, chasing him down. Jack's eyes widened. It was too fast. He managed to dodge the claws, taking only a small graze on his forearm, but the wolf smashed bodily into him and sent him flying into a tall rock. He slammed into it, cracking the stone, then slid to the ground.

The wolf stared him down from ten feet away, its eyes colored by nothing except hatred, menace, fear, and animalistic fury. Jack stared straight back.

This wolf was stronger and faster than him. More durable, too, since Harambe's uppercut had seemingly dealt no damage. But Jack wasn't alone.

Monkey cries echoed over the hill. Thirty brown shapes surrounded the wolf from a distance, holding stones at the ready—Jack had convinced them that poop was mostly harmless. Jack faced the wolf from the front, Harambe from the back, and the seven brorillas had formed a loose circle around them, ready to intervene or slow down the wolf with their lives.

The wolf looked around—it was surrounded—and growled. Jack

grinned and cracked his knuckles. "Come. I'll show you who's the boss around here."

It lunged sideways. Apparently, it still sought to escape, solidifying its relative weakness in Jack's mind.

The wolf charged between Jack and Harambe, trying to escape the encirclement from the side. However, there was a brorilla there. His name was Herom.

Herom opened his mouth and screamed at the approaching wolf. He stood on his legs and balled his fists, ready to box. His heavy eyes scowled under that wide forehead.

The wolf fell on him like a wrecking ball. Claws flashed and jaws snapped shut. Herom was sent flying in two pieces, but he'd achieved his goal. To kill him, the wolf had slowed down. And that was enough for a massive hand to wrap around its tail, jerking it still. The wolf looked back and shivered.

Harambe had arrived, and he was fucking pissed.

With a massive roar of rage, he swung the wolf from its tail and smashed it into the ground, showering the approaching Jack with gravel. He raised the wolf, then slammed it down again. And again. And again. Harambe had just seen one of his bros get killed. His rage could not be put into words.

He howled as he planted the wolf deep into the ground with each strike, making its bones groan. It couldn't do anything to keep from getting swung around by its tail. Finally, Harambe reached a boiling point. He smashed the wolf into the ground a final time and let go of its tail to beat it up with his bare hands.

A rain of punches and kicks landed on the wolf amidst gorilla growls. Harambe had turned into a beast. Jack didn't dare approach.

In the end, the wolf was stronger. Despite getting smashed like an octopus, it could still fight, claws glinting in the sunlight. It bared its fangs, and growled. Harambe was sliced by the right, then a pair of jaws wrapped around his left leg and broke it.

He screamed, letting the wolf squirm out of his grasp. It was bloodied, panting, injured, and with multiple broken or cracked bones, but it could still fight. In fact, being cornered and near death, this wolf was currently at its most dangerous.

However, it still tried to escape. It charged to the side, smashing head-first into Raza, a brorilla, and sending him flying, thankfully without other injuries. It then headed for the group of gymonkeys, who fearlessly showered it with stones.

Stones thrown by gymonkeys were nothing to scoff at. They were heavy, fast, and precisely aimed. The wolf received two in each of its eyes and many more all over its body, aggravating its wounds, but it didn't stop. It barreled into the monkey army and started ripping them apart, clawing blindly at all sides.

A few monkeys were bisected and many more were injured. The rest ran away with screams, letting the wolf claw away at nothing. Just as it was about to escape, a heavy fist slammed into its side. Its hard fur was useless against this fist. Its skin shook, and the broken ribs underneath sent burning pulses all over its body.

The wolf howled in pain as it flew sideways to land on a heap of rubble, and Jack was already upon it.

He'd seen what it did to Harambe, Herom, and the monkeys. His rage was boiling, but he wouldn't repeat Harambe's mistake. He wouldn't give the wolf a chance to fight back.

As it lay in pain and defenseless, Jack clenched his right fist. He reared it back, gritted his teeth, and as he was falling from the sky, smashed it into the wolf's face. It recovered from its pain just in time to see the fist landing.

"Calamitous Punch!"

There was an explosion. Rubble flew everywhere, along with blood and pieces of fur. The wolf's head was mangled, its body unmoving. It was dead.

Jack stood beside it, panting like he'd just run a marathon, and his fist was shivering. It wasn't broken like last time, when he'd Calamitous-Punched solid ground, just slightly injured.

But he'd done it. The wolf was dead. They'd won.

"We won!" he roared. Some monkeys cheered. Others, not so much. It was a pyrrhic victory. Harambe was out of commission, Herom had died, Raza was injured, many monkeys were killed or wounded, and the army was disorganized. Ironically, Jack was almost fine.

But they'd won.

Level Up! You have reached Level 26.
Level Up! You have reached Level 27.
Level Up! You have reached Level 28.
Level Up! You have reached Level 29.

Jack roared again.

A terrible, soul-stirring, wolf's howl answered him. His eyes widened as he looked down—the wolf's corpse was still unmoving. He looked up.

Beyond the injured gymonkeys, beyond the mourning brorillas and Harambe who was nursing his wounds, beyond the other half of the gymonkey army, stood another wolf. It looked identical to the first one, with two key differences: it was completely uninjured and absolutely furious. And its yellow eyes were trained only on Jack.

Black Wolf, Level 49 (Elite) (Dungeon Boss)
Black wolves are mostly solitary creatures. They are also territorial, proud, aggressive, and infamous for being a scourge at the peak of F-Grade. If a Black Wolf is spotted, experienced hunter squads should be dispatched quickly, or all big game of the surrounding area will disappear.

There wasn't one Dungeon Boss. There were two. And Jack's army wasn't ready to deal with the second one.

Oh, fuck me.

CHAPTER TWENTY-EIGHT

BETWEEN LIFE AND DEATH

JACK QUICKLY ALLOCATED ALL HIS BONUS POINTS EQUALLY.

The wolf stared at him with boundless rage. Time seemed to freeze. Slowly, Jack understood what happened. He remembered the wolf's description.

Black wolves are mostly solitary creatures.

Mostly.

Well, these ones lived in pairs. They just looked the same. *Fuck you, System! Why do you do this to me?*

Unfortunately, the System didn't give favors. Sometimes, luck was on the table, and sometimes, there was misfortune.

Then it occurred to him—the last time he saw a black wolf in the forest, it had a scar above its snout. The one lying at his feet didn't. He stifled a dry croak. He should have known. This was so unfair.

Fuck you, System, he repeated, this time with heavy bile.

The wolf didn't give him time to think any further. It charged. The back half of the gymonkey army was only just noticing the wolf. It ripped into them with ease.

Monkeys were sent flying. Blood and body parts littered the ground. The wolf had seen Jack deal the final blow on its partner, but it understood that the monkeys were involved. It would give them no quarter.

Almost a dozen monkeys were slaughtered in the span of a few seconds. The rest were either injured or running away in fear. A growl came from the middle of everything as Harambe tried to stand and failed. His leg was thoroughly broken. After getting bitten like that, it was a miracle it was even still in place.

The wolf saw Harambe and pounced at him.

The five remaining brorillas saw blood. They formed a line before their big bro, determined to defend him with their lives. They flexed their muscles in unison to intimidate the enemy.

"No!" Jack screamed, already sprinting, but the wolf was faster. It fell on the brorillas like a piano from the fifth floor, ripping into them as easily as it had into the monkeys.

Amoh's leg went flying. His head followed soon after. The wolf ripped out a chunk of Brodul's shoulder as it broke through the brorillas, reaching Harambe. This was its goal.

Unfortunately, Harambe was in no shape to defend himself. He could only stare defiantly at the claw that came to behead him.

A hard fist smashed into the side of that claw, sending it off-course. A bare-chested human form stood between the wolf and the gorilla, tiny but full of resolve.

"Leave my bro alone," he commanded.

Seeing Jack, the wolf's eyes flashed with something between revenge and ridicule. He should have run, but he charged into death's maw instead. The wolf would oblige.

Claws slashed and jaws snapped shut. Jack dashed back, desperately dodging the blows. This wolf was as strong as the rock bear, but its speed was worlds apart. It deserved to be the Dungeon Boss. Jack could barely dodge, and not for long.

He danced left and right to distract the wolf, but those yellow eyes, full of rage and blood, followed him unerringly. He ducked under the jaws and tried to throw an uppercut, but a claw smashed into his side out of nowhere, sending him flying. He barely had time to defend. Three long gashes now adorned his forearm.

Jack smashed hard into a rock. All air shot out of his lungs.

The five remaining brorillas made gorilla noises as they threw themselves at the wolf. The gymonkeys joined the fray, throwing a hail of stones and hoping to hit something sensitive. However, the black wolf wasn't an opponent they could beat. It was simply on another level.

Its body became a maelstrom of sharpness. Claws were everywhere, jaws snapped beside their ears. The wolf's dark fur filled everyone's vision, infesting it with images of gruesome death. The world became dark—magically so.

The gymonkeys screamed and ran away. The brorillas clenched their fists, and their faces spasmed as they struggled to resist.

Jack rose from the rubble, darkness flooding his world. The sun was replaced by a bloody moon, and the stars winked out one by one. The breeze smelled of blood and iron as terror slithered down his spine.

Something inside him rebelled. The Dao Root shook in outrage. Jack roared and punched, and the illusion broke like a mirror.

The wolf stared at him, its gaze filled with bloodlust. It had lost its mind to rage and lived only to devour Jack, whose body was covered in the blood of its partner. Jack looked around. The gymonkeys were running away, and the brorillas had fallen on their butts. Harambe's wide forehead was wrinkled as he tried to shake off the illusion, but even if he succeeded, he was too injured to help.

Jack was left alone. He gritted his teeth and stared the wolf down. There was no retreat. He would live or die. His mind raced, his heart beat like a drum, blood shot through his veins and filled his body with power.

Primal instincts returned at full force, with Jack steady at the helm. He'd earned that right. His mind was ice and his body fire. Deep inside him, the Dao Root shimmered with the power to annihilate everything.

The wolf wasn't intimidated.

By using its Dao Root, Jack thought. *It can create illusions. Can I do the same?*

His instinct told him he couldn't. He could punch hard and that was it.

The wolves have different Dao Roots, he analyzed through this moment of slowed time. *The first one was less developed, something to do with sound or fear. This is about illusions, maybe darkness, but I broke through. Can it be used again?*

The wolf wasn't inclined to answer. It charged Jack, who stood his ground. Every single scrap of skill he'd accumulated was poured into this fight. This was the culmination of everything. He'd fought so hard to reach the end. He couldn't fall here.

Claws, jaws. Red lines on white skin, yellow eyes with black irises that never lost him. A body of darkness that fell on Jack like a freight train.

He resisted. The wolf's patterns weren't much different than the rock bear's, it was just incomparably faster. Jack understood these patterns well. He'd faced them for what seemed like eternity.

He dodged on instinct, knowing where to weave and where to duck, he predicted the next hit's trajectory. His Fistfighting skill, his greatest ally, shored up his weaknesses. For the first time since the skill reached the second tier, it became strained.

The wolf tried to bite him and missed. A claw came for his face. Jack had already turned, nailing a hard straight into the wolf's ribs. They creaked but held. The Dao of the Fist was making his strikes harder, and Drill helped him bypass the wolf's thick fur. Unfortunately, its skin was equally thick, and a large part of the damage dissipated before doing any harm.

Another claw. He weaved to the left, ducked, then spun to narrowly avoid a strike. He smashed a fist into the wolf's snout right as the top of its head slammed into his belly, sending him flying into the hill. He jumped back up just in time to dodge the wolf's claw, which buried itself into the rubble.

Jack and the wolf danced under the bloody morning sunlight, while the monkeys and gorillas could only watch. Harambe had escaped the illusion, but could only bite his lips. His eyes were filled with concern, hope... and faith in his bro.

Jack had no time to feel anything. The wolf's speed pushed him to the absolute limit. Surviving by the skin of his teeth was an achievement. Each strike he received bloodied him or cracked his bones, and each punch he dealt had little effect. He had no advantage. The battle was losing.

The Calamitous Punch was his only hope, but he could only use it once more, maybe twice. He had to time it perfectly.

The wolf pounced, a whirlwind of death, and Jack danced between its claws like a leaf in the wind. One punch after another flew out, but they could only push the wolf back. Jack was losing ground. His retreat sped up, but that only increased his disadvantage.

The wolf went in for a bite.

There! His eyes widened. Calamitous Punch!

His fist shot out like an arrow, faster and stronger than before, smashing hard into the wolf's snout. The impact was as calamitous as the name indicated, shaking Jack's entire body and the gravel he stood on. The wolf was sent flying, then rolled on the ground and recovered. Its nose was bloody, but not much else happened.

It had taken a Calamitous Punch in the face and easily survived.

Jack fell on his knees, panting. His secret weapon had failed. There was nothing else in him. Despair threatened to cloud his mind, and as the wolf pounced again, he almost stayed still and let himself die.

But at the last moment, his Dao Root pulsed like a second heart. The fear washed away, evaporating the despair. Jack jumped aside, dodging the strike. So what if he was going to die? So what if he couldn't win? He would just punch until the end and go out as a warrior.

He laughed in the face of the wolf, which looked at him like he was crazy. Its attacks intensified, menace growing, and Jack simply did his best. He'd abandoned all hope. Merely living to fight a little longer.

If anyone saw Jack right now, they would be terrified. They would see a bare-chested barbarian dancing chaotically between a black wolf's strikes. He survived on the edge of the razor. His eyes were red, as were the wolf's, and he was grinning. He looked like he was having fun, a madman with zero respect for his life. A terrifying man.

Jack's world was clear. He was going to die, that was certain. He couldn't beat this wolf. He barely had enough energy to fire off another Calamitous Punch, but even when timed perfectly, it couldn't harm the wolf. His normal punches didn't cut it. He could not escape. There were no tricks.

Therefore, he would simply fight and express himself in the purest way he could: by going down punching.

The monkeys disappeared from his mind, and so did the stakes. None of that mattered. Only the wolf's attacks remained, and though Jack was growing tired, things became slightly easier. In the nick of death, he'd unknowingly achieved a mental state perfect for battle, where he could act at his absolute peak. His world was this battle. Nothing else remained.

He entered the zone.

He read the wolf's moves before they happened. He bobbed, weaved, and punched—if ineffectively. He let some strikes land on him, perfectly aware of what he could handle and what he could not. He assumed complete control of his body, clenching muscles he didn't even know he had, to move better. His skin turned into a substance he controlled, and he willed it to become harder, stronger, more suitable for someone who used his fists. His Dao of the Fist told him how.

Congratulations! Pugilist Body (I) → Pugilist Body (II)

He didn't see the screen. Only felt himself become sturdier and took full advantage of that. Jack accepted some strikes in order to retaliate. He let the wolf's momentum bleed into his own attacks. He became a menace. If the wolf was a beast, then Jack would be a warrior.

At some point, he abandoned defense. He let it run on autopilot. What did it matter?

Instead, he focused on offense. Amidst the howling and growling, and clawing and jaw-snapping, Jack swam like a fish, taking two light hits to land one. His fists smashed into the wolf's body with greater and greater force. Which proved useless. He could feel the skin's resistance nullifying his strength.

On instinct, his attacks turned sharper. His arm was straighter and steadier, almost longer. No energy escaped. The Dao of the Fist whispered how to punch, and Jack listened.

Punch after punch, he got stronger. His attacks hurt more. They were so direct that their energy didn't dissipate easily, penetrating both fur and skin to impact the soft tissue underneath. For the first time after the Calamitous Punch, the wolf growled in pain. Jack hammered another punch in the same spot and the wolf jumped back, wariness in its eyes.

Congratulations! Drill (I) → Drill (II)

In the eve of death, Jack's full potential was unlocked. He'd only achieved such clear-headedness in the ice waterfall. His skills were advancing at a breakneck pace being forced to his limit. His Dao Root flooded him with meaning that he absorbed like a dry lake sucking in the rain.

Exhaustion didn't matter. Jack had shelved it away in some hidden part of his mind. He'd fight like mad and just collapse when he ran out of steam.

He was growing stronger by the minute, but would it be enough? The wolf attacked again—attacks flying in every direction.

Jack was a worthy opponent now. He wasn't winning, but he wasn't losing either. The wolf also accumulated injuries. Punch after punch, he was getting through, but his body was on the brink of collapse.

Suddenly, something changed. The wolf slashed, but Jack saw its entire leg get covered in darkness. He couldn't tell the claw's exact position. In such a high-speed, razor-sharp battle, one mistake could be fatal.

This wasn't normal. It was magic. A Dao Root at work.

The bloody bastard had been holding back. It'd been toying with him, humiliating and mocking him out of spite. It wanted to drive him to despair, give him hope, and take it away again.

Hot rage bubbled in Jack's gut.

CHAPTER TWENTY-NINE
METEOR PUNCH

He didn't know where to dodge. Was it early or late? How far should he lean?

Jack would later swear that, at that moment, the wolf grinned. Its claw came at him, and there was nothing he could do except gamble. It possessed the Dao Root of Shadow but hadn't used it until now, except for that small illusion it activated at the very start.

The claw came for his head, its position vague. Jack had to make a decision. What was best?

His brain practically exploded. Every single synapse fired off at once. Time didn't slow, but he saw a thousand thoughts go through his mind at the same time, like he was watching a hundred bright minds work together inside his.

He had perfect awareness of his body. Could sense every muscle, every injury, the exact millimeter at which he could lean and how much time it would cost him to recover.

Even the wolf's stance. Every tiny thing was taken into account. He remembered all patterns he'd witnessed and contrasted them with the current one. His brain, trained by years of study as a biologist, was now fully devoted to battle.

A hundred simulations—the claw's most probable patterns on full display, three of them, and the different scenarios they would lead to. He included the inevitable feint. He considered every possible way to dodge and saw two moves into the future. He contrasted his options and the wolf's, pruning the scenarios with unbelievable speed.

For a single moment, he had perfect awareness.

Congratulations! Fistfighting (II) → Fistfighting (III)

He dodged. His movement was accurate to the millimeter. He'd taken into account his momentum, his injuries, even the strain on his muscles. He knew how fast and where the wolf could move.

The claw sailed two fingers over his head. He leaned to the side with mathematical accuracy, letting the next strike pass just under him as he used his momentum to turn and jump back. The maneuver was perfect. Jack was safe.

In the next moment, his head squeezed with a terrible headache that assaulted him as if his brain were cramping. Under normal circumstances, he might have fainted on the spot. Except he didn't have that luxury.

But his reflexes dropped. The previous perfect awareness gave its place to lethargy, confusion, and dizziness. Everything was fuzzy. Jack's mind was spent, and so was his body.

That bastard... he thought, watching the wolf pounce with jaws wide open. He hid until the last moment... There was nothing I could do... I'd lost before the battle even began.

Jack was determined to fight until the very end. He scrounged up his last dregs of energy and prepared a Calamitous Punch. With the upgrade in Drill, perhaps it would work this time.

The wolf's head blurred in darkness. Jack chuckled. It didn't matter, anyway. His fist sailed forth unerringly. The two were about to meet. Jack would die, but at least, he'd go down with a bang.

At that final moment before his death, a tiny candle burned in his mind. Something called at him from deep within. He let it, curious where the thought would lead. He let himself become distracted because it really didn't matter.

Then, Jack saw the wolf's previous attack in replay. He saw how it'd fused its Dao Root into the attack.

He saw the bald man's punch. He felt the Dao of the Fist at work, operating at a level he couldn't fathom. And, for the first time, under the veil of death, he realized that Dao and fist didn't move separately. The bald man didn't envelop one in the other, as Jack assumed. They were one and the same. The Dao and the fist could become one—no, they always had been.

Jack snapped back to the present. His fist inches away from the wolf's open maw and felt himself activating Calamitous Punch.

Why stop there?

His Dao Root flowed into the fist as well, majestic and undeniable. Then, something magical happened. His Dao was absorbed by the System's skill, tamed, and released in a way far more effective than his own crude use.

Just before impact, the sun went dark. The world turned black and white. Every eye was drawn to Jack's fist as if the world were ending. In the colorless void, his arm left a meteor trail behind it. The fist shone purple. It sped up and attained such momentum that Jack couldn't control it anymore. Its power far belied his fist's size.

The punch exploded on the wolf's snout like a sun was born. Color returned to the world abruptly, along with a thunderous sound wave as an actual explosion enveloped the site of Jack and the wolf's clash.

Congratulations! Skill Calamitous Punch (I) upgraded into Dao Skill, Meteor Punch (I).

Meteor Punch (I): When meteors fall from space, they cause exponentially more damage than their size would indicate. Your punches can carry the same effect. Overdraw your body's potential and combine it with your Dao of the Fist to unleash a devastating attack.

Jack flew back and smashed into a rock, unable to move an inch. He moaned in pain. His hand wasn't just broken, it was completely disfigured.

But it was worth it.

Near the site of impact, the wolf lay still, bloodied, and headless. It was like a small meteor had fallen from orbit and smashed straight into its head.

Jack had won. *No*, he corrected himself, meeting Harambe's incredulous stare. *We won.*

Level Up! You have reached Level 30.
Level Up! You have reached Level 31.
Level Up! You have reached Level 32.
Level Up! You have reached Level 33.
Level Up! You have reached Level 34.

He tried to shout in triumph but couldn't even move his mouth. Only the bonus points from the level-ups, which could be allocated by simply willing it, kept him conscious.

With a shallow sigh of relief, Jack quickly invested some points in Mental and Will, bringing them both to 10. The ensuing lucidity would help him stay awake, hopefully. It wasn't time to sleep yet.

His mind was expanding, his willpower doubling down over his body, the world unraveling in slightly clearer patterns than before. It was like a spiritual awakening—and, at the same time, Jack understood this wasn't his path. He'd grown, but the power of the fist inside him remained stagnant. He quickly invested the rest of the points into Physical, enhancing his body to limit the effect of his injuries, and shuddered as he sensed his muscles compacting further.

At least he'd brought both Mental and Will to a nice, round number, something he'd been itching to do for a long time. He used the mental enhancement to read the next few blue screens faster.

Congratulations! You have conquered the Forest of the Strong! If you belong to a Faction, you can choose to assimilate the Dungeon into your territory. Calculating rewards...
1 F-Grade Faction-Forming Permit.
1 Trial Planet Token.
1 F-Grade Dao Fruit of the Fist.

A few trinkets materialized before his feet.

...*What?* Jack was thoroughly exhausted and in tremendous pain. He was in no mood to deal the System's shenanigans. He also had no idea what any of those things were, but at least the screens confirmed this was the last black wolf. If there was a third one, Jack wouldn't know who to curse.

However, the screens still weren't over.

Dungeon border lifting on hold. Total monster despawning on hold. Faction territory assignment on hold. Would you like to assimilate the Dungeon into your Faction's territory and assume control or proceed with the automated parameters? This decision has a time limit of 1 minute.

...*What?*

Jack still had no idea what was happening. He was at one of the most exhausted points of his life, and the System thought he was in the mood to play with interfaces. He almost willed the screen away before his addled mind caught up to one important piece of information.

Wait. Total monster despawning? Will it despawn the monkeys?

He gazed at Harambe. The big brorilla was giving him a thumbs-up, his grumpy face curved into a big smile. The gymonkeys were hesitantly celebrating from afar, while the brorillas were only now recovering from their shock. Four of them went to take care of their injured bros, while Oz, the strongest brorilla, rushed over to Jack and tried to mime something.

Jack ignored him. Moans and screams of pain littered the air—the cries of his allies, who'd risked themselves to grant him victory. There were also many others that would never make a sound again.

They will all be despawned? Jack's eyes widened. *No!*

He forced his mind to parse the information. Due to his exhaustion, he had to read through the screens thrice to understand.

No, he told the System. *Do not proceed with the automated parameters. Let me choose.*

It ignored him.

30 seconds left before automated dungeon recovery.

Jack gritted his teeth. He couldn't take control of the dungeon himself—he needed a faction.

Unfortunately, he didn't have one.

20 seconds left before automated dungeon recovery.

The reward! His eyes shone. The System had given him 1 F-Grade Faction-Forming Permit for conquering the dungeon. It was self-explanatory.

He gazed at the trinkets by his feet. One was a tablet made of blue crystal with a green F engraved on it. Going by instinct, he grabbed it.

Form faction! he shouted in his mind. Form faction. Please!

The tablet turned into dust.

F-Grade Faction founding activated. Please choose the name of your faction:

I… uh…

10 seconds left before automated dungeon recovery.

He looked at his fist. *Bare Fist Brotherhood!*

You have chosen the name 'Bare Fist Brotherhood.' Please confirm.

Confirm, dammit, confirm.

5 seconds left before automated dungeon recovery.

Faction registered. Please think 'Faction' to—

He ignored the last screen.

Assimilate the dungeon into my faction, he thought.

2 seconds left before automated dungeon recovery.

Come on! Please!

Forest of the Strong has been assimilated into the Bare Fist Brotherhood's territory. Automated dungeon recovery canceled. Please handle everything manually.

Jack felt more relief than when his first date said yes.

Oh, thank God...

He slid back to the ground. Oz the brorilla was still miming his congratulations and asking if Jack needed any help, which he very much did. He was bleeding from multiple places, had lost much blood already, and his hand was ruined. If nothing was done, he would die.

Unfortunately, he'd already used even his last dregs of energy. There was simply nothing left.

"Please help me..." he croaked out before his world turned black.

CHAPTER THIRTY
REAPING THE REWARDS

JACK WAS DRAGGED OUT OF HIS BLISSFUL SLEEP BY BURNING AGONY. HE WOKE UP screaming.

The last thing he remembered was the black wolf coming for him. He was still in battle. Hell, his entire body burned everywhere the wolf injured him. The pain was immeasurable.

He jumped up with a splash, still screaming at the top of his lungs. Two gorillas were before him, trying to calm him down—or kill him. Rocky walls surrounded him like a coffin, his body was filled with the cold of death, and everything was illuminated by a pale, white light.

Looking down, his feet were dipped in cold, clear water.

Oh.

It was the ice pond. He was in the ice pond. In his cave. He was safe.

Jack unclenched his left fist, which had almost taken off Oz's head. "Sorry," he tried to say, but found himself exhausted. The next moment, the pain returned at full force. "FU—" Jack bit his lips not to scream.

This agony. The pain of healing. He had to take it.

Still unsure of what was going on, Jack gritted his teeth and sat back in the pond, letting the purifying cold burn his body. He couldn't stifle a few screams, especially when his right fist touched the water. It was completely ruined, with bones sticking out in various locations. How did that happen?

The memories came in flashes, synchronized with the pain. A second black wolf had appeared, determined to kill him. It was strong, very strong. He'd resisted. The battle was fuzzy, but at the end, he'd fused his Dao into the Calamitous Punch skill to create a new skill—a Dao skill—called Meteor Punch that destroyed both his hand and the wolf's head.

He remembered that impact clearly. There was a blinding flash and the roar of thunder, and the wolf was gone.

Despite the pain—which he tried to avoid by thinking—he shivered.

A Dao skill... Is that a skill based on my Dao? Is that why it's so strong? I didn't even know skills could upgrade like that.

It was too much to piece apart right now.

Wait. There was more.

He'd gotten some rewards, then founded a faction, or something like that... That part was unclear.

Thankfully, the two brorillas had also brought his other rewards along. A golden coin and a pear-shaped fruit that exuded violence. Jack didn't know how violent fruit could be, but this particular one was definitely at the top of the charts.

He'd deal with those later.

The pain flared once more before receding, and Jack growled as he stood. He was fine, though terribly exhausted. In fact, he felt something odd, as if his body was still fixing itself even without the pond's assistance.

His thoughts were still slipping through his mind, so he decided to ground them by reviewing some blue screens. He had a bunch.

Congratulations! Pugilist Body (I) → Pugilist Body (II)
Pugilist Body (II): Your body has adapted to your fighting style. You gain significant flexibility, reflexes, and durability, as well as increased hardness on your knuckles. *You have heightened control over your body, including its natural limiters, and slight regenerative powers.*

Congratulations! Drill (I) → Drill (II)

Drill (II): Passive Skill. By punching straight and true, you carry significant drilling power, letting your strikes penetrate hard defenses. *You can bypass most kinds of armor, including thick ones.*

Congratulations! Fistfighting (II) → Fistfighting (III)

Fistfighting (III): Grants expert knowledge of fistfighting. While fistfighting, enhances your physical attributes, reflexes, and kinetic vision. *Moreover, your brain's wiring is better suited for combat, especially fistfighting.*

Huh.

Besides some adjectives becoming stronger, the System was helpful enough to highlight the main improvements.

He didn't get a new skill at level 30—looks like three was all the class could give him for now—but these improvements were nothing to scoff at.

Pugilist Body looked great. It offered increased control over his body, which was the equivalent of removing his training wheels. And the difference was apparent. Everything felt slightly more complicated, even simple movements like raising his arm. At the same time, it was all done more consciously, granting him far greater control and awareness.

In other words, he had manual control of processes that had so far been automatic.

This skill could be a double-edged sword for most, but for Jack, it was a godsend. He could make up for the complexity by practicing hard, and the benefits would be reaped forever.

Plus, he could now do all sorts of funky things. With amusement, he flexed his intestines—almost getting a cramp—and moved his ears. *Take that, Professor*. She could always do that and used to mock him for being unable to.

He clenched his fist. It was amazing how many little muscles coordinated to achieve such a simple thing. There was still a lot of underlying assistance, but Jack was in conscious control of the movement. Living the rest of his life like that was daunting, and at the same time, massively intriguing. If he could get over the steep learning curve, the sky was the ceiling.

Besides this massive increase in bodily control, he now had regenerative powers, which was excellent. He wouldn't always have the ice pond handy to heal him. Granted, this regeneration wasn't anything great—he could feel it at work, slow as a snail—but it would hopefully get stronger as the skill advanced.

Drill, on the other hand, was a bit underwhelming. Bypassing armor was great, sure, and it had saved his life, but it wasn't anything world-breaking.

Jack shrugged. Maybe that was a good thing. Too much change at once could be overwhelming.

Finally, there was Fistfighting, which claimed to have changed his brain's wiring. Jack couldn't feel anything different. Though being a biologist—and a scholar—he understood how impactful this change was.

Rewiring the brain usually took years of concentrated practice, and it was the hallmark difference between a novice and a master. As you worked on the same field for years on end, your brain adapted to make the most common patterns more accessible. All relative connections were strengthened to achieve superhuman performance in a particular field.

This was the reason why chess masters could analyze a position and calculate three moves ahead in the blink of an eye. To a layman, that was unimaginable. It wasn't because they were geniuses. Their brains were just appropriately rewired after years of concentrated effort.

To be frank, most chess masters *were* geniuses, but that wasn't the sole reason for their superhuman performance.

Jack was shocked that such a feat could be performed by the System. Years of hard work were replaced by a single *ding!* and a blue screen. He wasn't sure how he felt about that.

Plus, his brain had already been wired for something: research. He had a PhD in biology—almost. Were those skills still in place, or had the System wiped them away in favor of combat without asking?

And, if it had, was that a bad thing?

Jack shook his head. There were many things to consider, but now wasn't the time. He moved on to the next screen.

Congratulations! Skill Calamitous Punch (I) upgraded into Dao Skill Meteor Punch (I).
Meteor Punch (I): When meteors fall from space, they cause exponentially more damage than their size would indicate. Your punches can carry the same effect. Overdraw your body's potential and combine it with your Dao of the Fist to unleash a devastating attack.

This skill was insane. Devastating was an understatement. If his hand was hard enough, he was confident in demolishing houses with a single punch.

Are skills split into ranks? he couldn't help but wonder. His other skills couldn't compare to Meteor Punch, at least not in their first tier. Was a Dao skill stronger because of his Dao, or was it just a better skill to begin with?

Regardless, Jack now had a tremendous weapon at his disposal. Based on what he'd seen so far, few things in the F-Grade could take a Meteor Punch head-on—or, at least, few things below level 50. For all he knew, F-Grade extended to level 9000.

He'd also gotten nine level-ups in the fight against the wolves. Done reviewing himself, Jack opened his status screen to take in the spectacle.

Name: Jack Rust
Species: Human, Earth-387
Faction: Bare Fist Brotherhood (F-Grade)
Grade: F
Class: Pugilist (Elite)
Level: 34

Strength: 93
Dexterity: 93
Constitution: 93
Mental: 10

Will: 10

Skills: Fistfighting (III), Drill (II), Pugilist Body (II)
Dao Skills: Meteor Punch (I)
Titles: Planetary Frontrunner (10)

It was shaping up. He'd almost reached 100 points in all his physical stats, which made him giddy. In fact, he was already there, if he included Planetary Frontrunner's 10 percent bonus.

Right now, he could probably match a black wolf head-on, even without Meteor Punch.

Jack spent the next few minutes experimenting with various things. He tried fusing his Dao Root with his other skills, but nothing happened. He wondered why he'd succeeded on Calamitous Punch. Was it due to the skill itself and its connection with the bald man's vision, or was it due to the life-or-death state he'd reached at the time?

Jack had no idea.

He also experimented with his stats a bit. He approached a massive boulder, taller than him, and picked it up.

It must have weighed a ton. Lifting the boulder was strenuous, but nothing too serious. Jack was impressed with himself, and he let it fall back down with a massive bang that rocked the cave and made dust fall from the ceiling.

"Sorry," he told the frightened brorillas.

He then approached his other two rewards—besides the faction-forming permit—and took a good look at them. And, by good look, he asked the System to do it.

Trial Planet Token
Can allow one person into Trial Planet.

Not much to see here. Jack shrugged and pocketed it. He'd find out later.

Dao Fruit of the Fist (F-Grade)
Allows the user to enter a meditative nirvana state, where the speed of

Dao cultivation is greatly increased. Breakthroughs are greatly assisted. This particular fruit is oriented toward the Dao Root of the Fist. Effects are reduced as the user's Dao gets further away from the fist. Effects are reduced as the user's Dao ascends beyond the Dao Root stage.

Only one Dao Fruit can be used per Grade.

Well, he had his confirmation that the Dao was split into stages, and Dao Root was just one of them.

This reward looked like a great thing for him. He assumed he could advance his Dao, though he was unsure how. Maybe this fruit would hold the clue. Moreover, his eyes lingered on the 'breakthrough' part. That smelled important. Like his Dao would advance from Dao Root to the next stage, which sounded like a crucial and difficult process.

Should he save the fruit until then?

He had no idea. Therefore, he decided to keep it for now. For the first time since the System arrived, he didn't feel the need to get immediately stronger. He could take his time. Now that he could exit the dungeon, he could even ask people. The professor would know for sure.

Speaking of people...

He sat back down. There was one more thing to check before leaving. *Faction.*

Faction: Bare Fist Brotherhood (F-Grade)
Leader: Jack Rust
Members: 1
Capital: Milky Way galaxy, Milky Way sector, Animal Kingdom constellation, Earth-387 planet, Forest of the Strong dungeon area.

Jack hurriedly closed the blue screen. It contained entries for a hundred little things, from resource management to monster status, alignment, a topographical description of the territory, hierarchical structure, buildings, to...

Most of those were null, of course, but Jack was allergic to large-scale management. It didn't matter, anyway. He already had a bunch of things on his plate. He'd deal with the rest later.

The one thing he kept was his faction's capital.

Milky Way galaxy, Milky Way sector, Animal Kingdom constellation, Earth-387 planet, Forest of the Strong dungeon area... Wow. Those are a lot of specifications.

Did it imply that the System stretched over multiple galaxies? That was insane! And how many stages of division were there? Earth—his Earth—apparently belonged to the Animal Kingdom constellation, which belonged to the Milky Way sector, which was a part of the galaxy.

What the hell was the Animal Kingdom constellation!

And just what kind of intergalactic empire had the System shoved them into?

Suddenly, Jack was leery of leaving his little dungeon, where things were nice and simple. He sighed. *Well. If anything confuses me, I guess I can just punch right through it.*

The social equivalent to punching was asking stuff, so he'd do just that. The time to leave the dungeon was nigh. Since the world was so big, he shouldn't linger in a tiny corner for too long.

However, before that, there were two things he needed to do. The first was take care of Harambe and the monkeys. Would they join him? Would they stay here? Could they protect themselves against whatever was out there?

That would be up to them. Monkeys or not, they could make their own decisions. Jack would just let Harambe know of the situation.

The next thing to do...

Then it hit him. He'd conquered the dungeon. He'd escaped. He could return to civilization. He would see humans again.

The relief was so strong he almost fainted again.

Prepare yourself, world, he thought, grinning. I'm coming!

CHAPTER THIRTY-ONE
BROCK THE MONKEY

Jack stood in silence. Yesterday morning had been full of tension. Today, grief.

Two brorillas and eleven gymonkeys had given their lives against the black wolves. They were brave. They could have chosen cowardice or half-measures, but every single one of them went forth to fight knowing their lives might be forfeit.

There were many injured, but the ice pond healed them. That wasn't a pretty sight either. Oz had been forced to keep some monkeys in the pond, as their mental fortitude wasn't enough to handle the searing pain.

At the end of the day, they were alive, and that's what mattered. All injured gymonkeys thanked Oz for helping them, while he only nodded stoically. His wide forehead was wrinkled further, and his grumpy eyes were filled with sadness.

Monkeys didn't do much with their fallen brothers and sisters, only dumped them somewhere far away for the parasites and fungi to do their job. Jack wasn't having that. After the injured were healed, he organized a funeral and taught the monkeys how to handle death.

In the process, he'd also taught them the concept of death, which they didn't understand too well.

The morning sun illuminated a forest wet from the night's moisture. Droplets hung from leaves like teardrops, and the light refracted through them to reveal all colors of the rainbow. The birds and critters were quiet today, as if sensing the heavy mood, and the wind didn't dare blow too hard.

Jack stood in a peaceful glade, surrounded by twenty-five monkeys: nineteen gymonkeys, five brorillas, and Harambe. This glade was situated behind the monkey forest gym, close to the edge of the nature reserve. Jack had chosen it for its scenery. There was something about the sparsity of trees and the harmony of foliage that gave this place a serene, holy sensation.

It was also close enough to the monkeys' residences that they could visit whenever they wanted, and far enough that it wouldn't be a bother.

Thirteen graves had been dug and refilled. They didn't have coffins, but they didn't need them, either. The monkeys were part of nature in life and death. Jack stood to the side, facing both the graves and the downcast monkeys.

"We are now brothers and sisters," he declared somberly, the weight of goodbye falling on him. "You are all brave. I'm proud of you. And I am most proud of those who fell, because they were perfect. They gave their lives to protect the rest of us. That is an achievement we, who are still alive, cannot claim. We owe our lives to the fallen."

Nobody dared speak or even breathe loudly. Their gazes alternated between Jack and the graves.

"We will not let their lives go to waste," he continued. "This is a rough, unknown world, and we will carve out a home. We will protect ourselves and our children and create a future. We will be united like the fingers of a fist, and we will defend each other as they defended us."

A monkey shivered. Another sniffed. A few tears rolled.

Jack turned to the graves and bowed. "You have given everything. You are worthy. Now, rest in peace... and we will handle the rest. In the name of the strong primates, Jack Rust, and the Bare Fist Brotherhood, we will lead lives that will make you proud. This, I swear."

As his speech finished, the monkeys erupted into mourning. They cried without fear of where their voices carried, shedding fat tears.

Some fell to the ground and punched it, while others tore off tufts of their fur and threw it on the graves. The brorillas left a bunch of banan-arms before each grave, then flexed their muscles as tears rolled down their hardened faces.

Harambe, the big bro of the monkeys, stepped before the graves after the brorillas were done. He flexed his large muscles hard enough for his eyes to pop out, then bowed deeply and spread some soil on his face while crying. All monkeys followed.

This was their form of tribute. Jack didn't understand everything, but he let them do their thing. He put some soil on his face, too, to honor their customs. No tears left his eyes, though his heart was filled with sadness. They'd fought together, and they died because he couldn't protect them. Had he been stronger, everyone would still be here.

He vowed to remember this.

It took half an hour before things calmed down a little. During that time, Jack remained still as a rock. When the monkeys began dispersing, he stepped beside the big brorilla.

"Harambe," he said, "walk with me."

Harambe nodded at the brorillas, who nodded back, then he followed Jack deeper into the forest, heading back toward the forest gym.

"What are you planning to do, Harambe?" Jack asked. "The world is large, and there are many things we don't know, many dangers we cannot fathom. I feel that the only way to survive and be free is to get stronger. I plan to leave this place, enter the human world, and see how everything has changed. What do you think?"

The gorilla remained silent for a long time. His thoughts weren't the fastest, but that was okay. Jack waited. They crossed glades and forest paths, stepped over rocks and roots. Finally, Harambe turned to Jack and shook his head. His big knuckles tapped the ground.

"You'll stay here?" Jack asked. "Are you sure? There could be others like you in the wide world, maybe even on this planet. Don't you want to meet them?"

Harambe shook his head again. He pointed at himself, made a scary face, then flexed his muscles.

Jack's eyes mellowed. "You want to get stronger, too..."

The System didn't consider the monkeys sapient, like him. They couldn't level-up or do anything like that. They were simply classified as monsters. To get stronger, they had to toil away at their forest gym, lifting weights and sparring each other.

"You have it right, my friend... but you are *not* monsters. I don't care what the System says. It's wrong. And I swear to you that, when I'm strong enough, I will force it to reconsider. I'll find a way to let you in."

Harambe nodded, then tapped his knuckles on the ground again.

"You'll stay here until then... Yeah. I'm sorry for doubting you. That's a sensible choice. On my part, I'll make sure all nearby areas know not to mess with you—though, from what I imagine, they can't, even if they wanted to. The System won't let you in my faction, but this area is marked as mine. I need you to be the guardians of this place, and in return, everything here will belong to you. Even if more people come, you'll still be the owners of the forest. What do you think? Is that a good offer?"

Harambe nodded, bringing a hand to his chest. Then, he stretched a hand out to Jack.

He looked at the hand, then chuckled. He grabbed and shook it. "You have a deal, my friend. Take good care of your little bros while I'm gone. I'm counting on you."

For the first time since they'd met, Harambe grinned. Jack grinned back. The monkeys were in good hands.

"Then, this is goodbye for now. I'll be back as soon as I settle things out there, whatever they are. Try not to kill humans, if you can, but I'll handle the fallout if they force your hand. Oh, and if you see anyone bearing a"—he looked around, then picked up a jagged stone of peculiar shape—"bearing this stone, know they were sent by me. They'll give you my name, anyway."

Harambe nodded. Then, unlike his usual stoic self, he pulled Jack into a big hug.

"Oof! Dude! This would have killed most people!" Jack laughed as he hugged the gorilla. After bathing in the ice pond, everyone was clean, and the waters remained as crystalline as ever.

Jack had checked the wolf cave for rewards but found nothing. *Fair, I guess. I already got plenty.* He'd also entered the waterfall again but received little benefit. He could sense he'd already reaped all he could from there. To advance his Dao, he needed to experience more things. That was another reason why he was in such a rush to leave. The first was that the System's hints about intergalactic empires had instilled a sense of urgency inside him. Plus, he needed to find out if the professor was okay.

"See you, big bro," Jack said, waving, and made to leave. However, Harambe suddenly shook his head. "Hmm? What is it?"

Harambe pointed somewhere, and Jack turned to look. They'd reached the forest gym, and Harambe was pointing toward its far end, where the bananarm tree stood.

"What is it, Harambe? Do you want to show me something?"

The brorilla nodded and started walking over, slowly. Jack was suddenly curious. Why did Harambe say goodbye before showing him whatever this was? It was clearly deliberate but made no sense.

"Where are you taking me, Harambe?" Jack muttered as he followed Harambe behind the bananarm tree, where he always liked to rest. The vegetation was denser here. Moist bushes with long leaves and vines hanging from the trees above. It looked more and more like a jungle, which had no business being here, in biology's humble opinion.

The analytical part of his mind whispered that this was ridiculous. Everything else reminded him that, after everything the System had done, a little change in topography was nothing.

Harambe led Jack through thick bushes and foliage until they were a couple minutes away from the clearing. Jack got more and more curious. What could Harambe be hiding?

Another E-Grade resource? His heart sped up.

Harambe approached the base of a large tree. Its roots formed an alcove over the soil, and nestled inside them was a gymonkey that eyed Jack warily. What was it doing here? They were all supposed to be at the funeral—but come to think of it, he did notice one missing.

Harambe said something to the gymonkey, in a tone Jack hadn't heard from him before. It was soft, almost caring, not the sound of a big bro, but of a partner.

Then, the monkey moved, and Jack was left staring at the smaller monkey hiding behind. It was as tall as his forearm was long, had short brown fur, big ears, a long, flexible tail, and looked at him with wide eyes. It resembled a child gymonkey.

A moment later, it snarled and jumped at him. Jack raised his arms in surprise.

Harambe growled. He grabbed the little one by the top of the head midair and growled something in its face. The small monkey flailed ineffectively—it was still airborne—then crossed its arms and glared at Harambe.

Jack looked between the two of them, observing the dynamic, before finally managing to say, "Is that your son, Harambe?"

Harambe nodded. Then he presented the little monkey—still holding it from the top of the head—which stared at Jack as defiantly as it had at its father.

Brorilla, Level 2

A gorilla variant from planet Green. Brorillas usually live with Gymonkeys and train them in the ways of working out. It is due to the Brorillas' unmatched pecs that Gymonkeys use poop to fight—they consider themselves too weak for anything else.

Brorillas are usually calm, measured animals. However, if anyone harms their little cousins or invades their territory, they go bananas.

This particular Brorilla is a variant that visually resembles a Gymonkey. Though not weaker than other Brorillas, the members of this variant are often shunned due to their lack of bulging muscles.

"He's cute." Jack leaned in. The little monkey tried to claw at him, infuriated at the name. He pulled back. "And feisty."

Harambe nodded with pride. He was so much bigger than his son that it looked ridiculous. The little one could sit on Jack's shoulder, and Jack could probably sit on Harambe's.

"Why didn't you tell me before?" he asked.

Harambe growled, making animated descriptions with his arms. The little monkey flew around, as he still held on to its head, and tried to grab his forearm but failed, making it even more pissed.

"He'd want to join the fight?" Jack tried deciphering Harambe's meaning.

Harambe nodded.

"I see. Congrats, man. And who's this lucky lady?"

He approached the gymonkey, who shook his hand gracefully. Her pecs were more pronounced than most of the gymonkeys—probably why Harambe liked her.

"I'm happy to have met your family, bro," Jack told Harambe. "That makes us real bros. Next time, let's drink together."

Harambe chuckled, then shook his head.

"You don't want to drink?"

More shaking.

"No... it's something else? What are you trying to tell me, Harambe?"

Harambe looked at his partner. Something was exchanged between them that was only too human. Jack saw pain, resolve, and deep longing in those eyes. Then, Harambe brought his son before his face and growled harshly. The little one tried to glare but succumbed under his father's hard stare.

Harambe held his gaze at the little one for a while. Then, he simply turned it around and placed it in front of Jack's feet. Jack blinked in surprise. "What?"

The little monkey glanced at Jack, considering attacking him, then remembered its father's warning and calmed down.

"What are you trying to say, Harambe?" Jack asked hesitantly.

Harambe pushed the little one toward Jack with his knuckles. Then, he took a step back and passed an arm around his partner, who looked at their son with sadness.

"Wait," Jack said. "Are you entrusting your son to me?"

Harambe nodded. The little monkey's eyes widened. Suddenly, it wasn't so wild anymore. It rushed at its parents so hard it tripped. When it got there, Harambe grabbed it and unceremoniously tossed it at Jack, who had to grab it in a hug. He thought it would go wild, but it didn't. The little guy rushed out of his arms without hurting him, then jumped at Harambe who tossed it back again.

"Wait. What is happening?"

Harambe grabbed his child by the head, placed it in front of Jack, and growled sternly. He pointed at it, then at Jack. The little monkey tried to complain, but a second growl, even sterner, cut it short.

"Harambe," Jack said, putting a little bit of force into his voice, and Harambe looked up. "What is happening?"

Harambe then proceeded to mime a long series of things.

"You are entrusting me with your son?" Jack deciphered. "You want him to adventure alongside me? You think I can protect him and make him into a proper brorilla? Let him see the world?"

Harambe nodded.

"Harambe! That's..." Jack was lost for words. He looked down at the little one, taking it in carefully. It had understood its father's words. It was gazing at its parents with longing, but when it looked at Jack, he saw a hidden desire there. The same one he'd felt before the System's arrival. The call of adventure.

"That's such a responsibility..." he managed to say. "You're putting a lot of faith into me..."

Harambe growled in question. He seemed anxious, hoping Jack would say yes.

"It's not about me accepting or not. You have to know that my life will be dangerous," he said. "I don't know what's out there. I might die tomorrow and take this little one with me. I might make enemies."

Harambe's eyes were resolute.

"My adventures could be painful, Harambe, and they might not end well. Are you absolutely certain you want to entrust your son's life to me, knowing you might not see him again soon or ever?"

Harambe nodded. By his side, the gymonkey whimpered, two salty tears appearing in her eyes before she blinked them away. She made sounds of agreement, taking Harambe's hand in hers.

Jack's heart was heavy. "Why would you do that?" he forced out, unable to comprehend.

He wasn't planning on anyone tagging along. He would take the monkeys if they asked him, but a child? What did he know about them? Could he protect it? Raise it?

Should he?

He stared deep into Harambe's eyes and saw the truth. The gorilla wanted his son to become something better than him, to surpass him.

At the same time, he couldn't offer that, and not just because this child was doomed to remain less muscular than other brorillas.

Harambe understood the futility of his existence, the hard limits set on him by the System. He'd been created—spawned—as an adult. Even if he was never despawned, there was only so far he could progress. But his son was more fortunate. He was still a child. If life treated him well, he could ascend to heights that Harambe himself had no hope of reaching.

And only Jack had access to the System to offer such potential.

Harambe didn't want to part with his son, give it for another man to raise. Who would? But he steeled his heart and did what was best for it. And he trusted Jack.

Jack had never felt like this before. His heart was filled with equal parts pride, warmth, and weight. He didn't know if he was ready.

But if Harambe could part with his own son, Jack could at least accept it.

"My bro..." Jack kept his voice even as he held out a hand. Harambe grabbed it in a firm handshake, then pulled Jack in for a hug. The two men—one human and one brorilla—held each other tight for a long moment. Then, Harambe turned to the side and pulled his wife into a hug, who grabbed the little one, too.

Their family hug was tighter than Jack's, and it lasted longer. It was a very touching moment. So touching, in fact, that Jack felt guilty, and salt threatened to roll down his cheeks.

Sometime later, the magic was broken. The family slowly withdrew, Harambe pushing the little one into Jack's hands while his partner buried her face in his fur. Harambe's eyes were resolute—and, surprisingly, so were the little one's.

Jack stared at it in wonder, giving a smile whose emotions even he wasn't certain of. "What's his name?"

Harambe made a sound, slowly and purposely.

"Brock?" Jack asked, just to be sure, and Harambe nodded. His partner held on tighter.

"Brock..." he repeated, turning to look at the little one. "What do you think, Brock? Would you like to explore the galaxy with me?" It was a brave one. Not only had it tried to attack Jack when he first appeared, despite the size difference, but when it met his gaze now, it wasn't as grief-struck as a human child's would be.

Maybe it was because animals were less attached to their parents. Or, maybe, this one had a strong soul. In any case, it stared deep into Jack's eyes, pouted its lips to keep them from trembling, and nodded despite the tears rolling freely down its face.

"You are a very brave monkey, Brock," Jack said, petting it on the head. It let him. "I would love to have you along."

Harambe made an odd sound, and his cheeks tightened. It was time to leave.

"We'll go, then," Jack said, holding a fist to his heart. "I promise to come visit you again soon—as soon as I can. And I vow on my very soul that I will keep your son safe, even if it kills me. No matter what."

Harambe nodded, his face spasming with effort to stay still. The gymonkey looked at her son, eyes dripping, then at Jack, with a depth of emotions he never expected from an animal. But, then again, that was an outdated thought. These were people.

"See you both," Jack said. He took Brock by the hand and walked away. Brock kept looking back, but Jack didn't. The sobbing sounds made him think his bro wouldn't want to be seen like that.

And so, a human and a monkey that barely reached his knee walked into the bushes and faded away, each leading the other by the hand.

CHAPTER THIRTY-TWO
ENTERING CIVILIZATION WITH A BANG

Jack crossed the woods, feeling like Christopher Colombus discovering America. Everything he saw was the same as he remembered, and also different. Being outside the nature reserve—the Forest of the Strong dungeon—was like a dream.

What changed? How had the System impacted humanity? What was the world like?

Was it all real?

Everything was exactly as he remembered. The trees, the broken branches, that fat bush he'd stepped over once upon a time... It made him doubt whether this was all a hallucination induced by some gas in the cave.

He grabbed a thick branch from the ground and easily snapped it in two. Shrugging, he threw it away.

"What do you think, Brock?" he asked the monkey on his shoulder—its short legs made walking side-by-side annoying. "Will we like what we find?"

Brock made monkey sounds. There was undeniable excitement there, though he clearly missed his home, too. He'd looked back multiple times on the way and almost ran away once but stopped himself. He was a brave little monkey.

"Yeah, I think so too," Jack said with a smile.

The System's arrival breathed life into his world. He was strong. Whatever happened, he could take it.

He was just worried about the state of his loved ones, especially the professor, whose old age wasn't suitable for punching monsters.

Jack stepped out of the trees and onto a dirt trail. For the first time, it occurred to him what he looked like: a wild, dirty, bare-chested dude. He was ripped, too. He must have seemed like a savage.

He shrugged and went on his way.

The dirt trail snaked through the forest before ending at a wider trail, where a gray jeep was parked. Seeing a car was completely disorienting. It made such a hard contrast against last week's primal lifestyle that Jack had to stop and stare, unable to reconcile the two worlds.

With a low chuckle, he fished the keys from his pocket—he'd retrieved them from their hiding place in the cave before leaving—unlocked the door and sat in the vehicle. It groaned under his weight. Constitution made him heavier, not too much, but noticeably.

Brock jumped in the co-driver's seat like the experienced monkey he wasn't. He then realized he couldn't see anything from there, so he jumped behind the steering wheel. The windshield was a shock—the poor thing hadn't seen glass before. Thankfully, it was dirty, or he would have headbutted it for sure. It took three swipes of the wipers to make out the road beyond through a green-brown smudge.

Jack revved up the engine, welcoming the familiar rumbling of the car below him. The seat was soft on his back and a bit scratchy, while the wheel felt like a toy in his hands.

The car jumped a bit as it started, then rolled on slowly. Jack lowered the windows and let his arm hang outside, while Brock was quick to stick out his head and enjoy the faint breeze. He even occasionally put his hand out and tried to resist the breeze. It was nice.

The dirt trail ended on a snaking asphalt road that crossed the forest, and Jack could finally pick up some speed. He stepped on the pedal, eager to feel the acceleration, and the wind buffeted his face. Trees zoomed past him, the occasional stone crunched under the wheels, his body leaned on the turns.

A brief moment of fun. Then, the acceleration stopped, and boredom claimed Jack. He could run faster than this.

Poor car companies...

At least it was comfortable.

The snaking road gave way to a larger one, where the speed still wasn't up to Jack's standards, until small houses began to pepper the countryside. It was Jack's first contact with civilization in over a week. He kept his eyes wide.

By the side, Brock had climbed on the co-driver's seat and couldn't pull his eyes from the forest behind them. His tail curled up in sadness. The forest drifted out of sight, and the little monkey fell on the seat defeated, staring at the empty road ahead.

Theirs was the only car on the road.

The houses were mostly abandoned. The few people Jack saw stared hard at him until he made some distance. They held guns, bread knives, anything dangerous they could get their hands on to protect their homes. Many were injured. Some wore armor, though he couldn't make out any details.

He also saw a few monsters. There were small packs of goblins roaming the countryside, along with feral wolves, oversized wild dogs, small scaly people, walking mushrooms, and all sorts of nasty things. There were even large maneater plants in the middle of nowhere, where it would take tremendous amounts of idiocy to fall for them.

Right on cue, a goblin stumbled into one of the plants and was summarily swallowed. He chuckled, turning back to the road.

The wind curled around his arm outside the window, making the little hairs wave. His right hand gripped the hard leather of the wheel, while his bare foot stepped on the pedal. Brock screamed in joy as they accelerated, maneuvering around the occasional goblin that littered the road. The poor little fuckers were dumb enough to simply stare at his car as it approached, and a few even dared each other to jump in front of it. One tried, but thankfully chickened out.

Jack only scanned a few of those monsters—they all seemed weak. Only a distant stag with vines on its antlers was somewhat threatening, and that's because everything else avoided it. The monsters were sparse overall, not really grouping together, letting the few farmhouses survive.

With the notable exception of the goblins, they also had the good idea of keeping their distance from the road, which let Jack simply drive through.

Soon, the houses grew denser and the monsters thinner. Neighborhoods appeared, which soon gave way to wide streets and infrastructure. There was an upturned bus by the side of the street, along with a few burned or violently ruined houses. Most cars were just sitting there.

The System's coming hadn't been easy. At the very least, the scenery reaffirmed that Jack wasn't hallucinating.

There were more people, too. Jack spotted them roving in large bands, upwards of ten members each, and attacking any monsters that came within sight. A twelve-person group armed with bread knives fell on a pack of five goblins. After a fierce fight where three of them were injured, they managed to take the goblins down.

Jack shook his head. Their weakness would have been funny if it wasn't sad—or even expected. The leveling speed of such large groups would be atrocious. But who in their right mind would go against the odds to hunt alone?

He didn't stop the car.

As he rode deeper, the people had been growing denser, too. There were guards where the town began, holding handguns. They flagged him down.

"Halt," said one of them, a woman with sharp eyes and a ponytail. "You are approaching Valville, the territory of Henry's Fang. Please enter on foot and surrender any firearms you're carrying."

Brock narrowed his eyes and clenched his little fists. Jack was already getting a headache. Maybe that's why Harambe dumped the little menace on him like that.

"No attacking," he told Brock strictly. "Everyone here is a friend by default. You won't touch anybody unless I say so. Understood?"

Brock released a small holler of protest, only to buckle under Jack's gaze. He was in an unknown place, surrounded by unknown people, and his only connection to his home was this weird big bro. He would listen.

Jack parked at the side of the road and got out of the jeep. Their eyes widened. Whether that was due to Brock on his shoulder or his barbaric appearance, he didn't know.

"I have no firearms, as you can see," he said, approaching carefully. "And I don't mind leaving my car here."

He didn't intend to cause trouble, though he was pretty sure he could survive gunshots. His close to 100 Constitution wasn't for show. As he approached, he scanned them.

Human (Earth-387), Level 5
Faction: Henry's Fang (F-Grade)

The System wasn't too talkative about sapients. Still, Jack got a bunch of information.

The head guard here, on a major road artery, was only level 5. The other four were even lower. Moreover, what kind of stupid name was Henry's Fang? Jack felt better for naming his faction Bare Fist Brotherhood.

As he willed the screens away, he noticed the five guards looking at him like they saw a ghost—they'd obviously scanned him back.

"Welcome to Valville, sir," the head guard said, suddenly way politer. "If I may ask, what is the purpose of your visit? Are you here as a representative of the Bare Fist Brotherhood?"

"Not sure yet. For now, I'm just making sure my family is okay."

"Would you like to arrange an audience with Henry's Fang?"

"Not yet."

"Very well. Please go on, sir."

"Thank you."

For the first time, Jack felt like a VIP. Life was easy when you were strong.

He didn't spare the guards another glance as he entered the town, walking through streets he knew.

Valville wasn't large. With a population of only twenty thousand, its area was even smaller than the Greenway Nature Reserve. Its only notable quality was the nearby town of Tahlequah, which housed the Northeastern State University's Department of Natural Science. That's where Jack studied, and where his foster parents used to teach before retiring.

Valville itself was a dot that didn't even appear on most maps. It was a nice place. The scenery from above the mountain was beautiful, and the streets well-maintained.

Jack liked it here. It was peaceful and pretty—at least, it used to be.

Now, rubble and trash were everywhere. No monster corpses, but he did spot some human bodies haphazardly thrown in alleys. There was no sign of the police.

At the same time, there was new energy suffusing the town. Muscular men and fit women walked around with intensity, doing this or shouting that. The weather was still good, so everyone wore short sleeves—or makeshift armor.

It had only been a week since he'd last seen Valville, and it had changed drastically. Many shops were closed and new ones were springing up like mushrooms. Jack saw a smithy next to a torn-down McDonald's, manned by an older man with a yellow mustache that wouldn't stop grinning through his sweat. He found a tannery on the very edge of the town, where three men worked on the skin of what looked like a deer. He spotted people pulling carts through the streets, as well as merchants loudly proclaiming their wares in a way that wasn't common before the apocalypse.

Jack had to stop and do a double take. *Is this really Valville?*

The buildings were similar, but the town was a mixture between reality and fantasy. Like someone planted a medieval society in the ruins of modern civilization. With their lives on the line and monsters to hunt, people were regressing so fast it was mind-blowing.

Jack got drowned by laughter, cries, shouts, the loud clang of the smith's hammer, the shouting peddlers, children wielding sticks and playing humans versus goblins, the fragrance of food carts, and the heavy odor of blood. The entire street stank of sweat and death—nobody seemed to care. In fact, Jack caught people smiling all around.

That's odd. Are they all like me?

Taking a closer look, he observed a clear dichotomy. On one side, there were people huddling behind windows and shivering, as well as some darting from pedestrian to pedestrian and begging with tears in their eyes. There were crazies shouting incoherently in alleys.

On the other side of the dichotomy were the warriors. Armed with bread knives and armored in pans, they moved with energy and sported clear, smiling eyes. For the first time in his life, Jack realized that people didn't smile on the street before the apocalypse. They were just rushing from place to place full of stress, like zombies. But not anymore.

Jack doubted they all shared his love for battle. However, level-ups and getting stronger had a way to bring euphoria, and life-or-death struggles had a way to make people feel alive.

Jack was stunned. He stood in the middle of street, gawking at everything. The world had turned upside down. It felt like home. He loved this.

A moment later, he shook himself awake. His feet moved by themselves as he approached the smithy; a wide wooden shack with a heavy anvil and a burning oven in the middle, which looked like an electric kitchen adapted to work with wood or coal. The walls were decorated with shitty-looking, uneven swords, as everything better had no doubt been taken already.

Though, to be fair, perhaps proper swords were too much for a week-old blacksmith. Said man was currently hammering away at a glowing lump of metal on his anvil, so focused on the task he didn't notice Jack's approach.

"Hey," Jack said, scanning the man.

Human (Earth-387), Level 7
Faction: -

The blacksmith frowned, then raised his gaze and scanned him top to bottom. His eyes shuddered as he took in Jack's level.

"How can I help you?" he said, abandoning the rapidly cooling metal on his anvil.

Jack raised a brow. "You don't need to do that. I can wait."

The blacksmith smiled under his thick blond mustache, then started hammering again, the metal bending under his System-augmented strength. The clangs were loud enough to be annoying, and the heat of the open oven could be felt all the way to where Jack stood, but he wasn't annoyed. He simply admired the work.

"I can speak while hammering," the blacksmith said, eliciting Jack's chuckle.

"You seem pretty good at this."

"Been doing it for years. Never imagined my hobby would come in handy, but here we are."

He used a pair of long pliers to pick up the lump of metal—it resembled a sword—and stuck it in a water barrel nearby. Steam filled his hut. Brock screamed at the hissing sounds.

"You are enjoying this, aren't you?" Jack shouted over the hissing.

"As much as everyone," the blacksmith replied, wiping his brow. His gaze remained with the blade, weighing it. "I didn't enjoy seeing my best friend murdered before my eyes, but the apocalypse has its bright sides. This is one of them."

He took out the blade, inspecting it through the steam. Jack did, too. This thing was an actual sword. There was an iron handle and a long, straight blade. Tiny bumps riddled its surface, but it at least looked serviceable.

"That's pretty good!" Jack said.

"A piece of shit," the blacksmith replied. "Don't judge by the garbage on my walls, friend. That's just decor."

"Oh," Jack said, looking around. "Don't you think your decor is bad marketing?"

"Doesn't matter. All my blades are bought instantly. The ones I've hung up are unusable, but they were my first efforts. Helps me remember where I came from."

Jack nodded. "Why the iron handle, though?" He pointed at the newly-made sword.

"It just came out of the oven. I'll wrap the leather later."

He left the newborn sword on a counter and turned to Jack, removing his gloves. He stretched a hand.

"George," he said.

"Jack."

His hand was sweaty and hard, but Jack didn't mind. They smiled at each other.

"So?" George the blacksmith asked, wiping some sweat off his forehead again. "How can I help you?"

"I'm just looking, if you don't mind."

George gave him an odd look. "Not with your level, I don't."

"What happened to Valville?"

Another odd look. George grabbed a chair and took a seat. "You weren't in town?"

"Forest."

"Lucky you. Things went to shit at first. Many died before the strong banded together to drive the monsters out. Goblins, mostly, so easy opponents, but it still took four days. Then, we rebuilt with monsters in mind. Most people are warriors or losers now, so we don't need accounting and all that shit. We have plenty of food and water, thankfully, what with many dying and the town's food storage. We also have the farms."

"Losers?" Jack raised a brow. "That's a bit harsh, don't you think?"

"Everything is harsh now." George shook his head.

Jack didn't quite agree, but he could see where the sentiment was coming from.

"And Henry's Fang?" he asked.

At this, the blacksmith raised his eyes. He was clearly deliberating his next words. "They're okay." In a way, that implied the opposite. After all, Jack could have been an ally of Henry's Fang.

A bad omen, Jack thought, nodding again. I hope the professor is okay.

Realizing he had nothing else to offer and was just taking up the man's time, he made to leave. "Thank you, George. Happy smithing."

"Anytime, Jack. Come find me if you ever need a new weapon." He eyed Jack's empty hands. "I reckon it will be soon."

Jack only smiled. He walked away to the metallic clangs of Geroge's smithing. At least he wasn't the only one enjoying the apocalypse. *Enjoying? When did I become like that...* He shook his head. *Enough sightseeing. Now, the professor.* He ventured deeper into Valville.

Stares fell on him. He stood out, what with his bare-chested musculature and monkey on his shoulder, so it was natural. He even felt kind of proud when a wave of whispers followed his path as people noticed his level.

He was quite an outlier. Jack scanned dozens of people and only saw one person above level 7; everyone else ranged between 1 and 5. The members of Henry's Fang were rare—most people were factionless—but when he found one, they usually walked around with a swag that resembled his. Others kept their distance from them, looking over with a mixture of fear and disgust.

All members of Henry's Fang glared at Jack before noticing his level, at which point they became subservient. He shook his head and ignored them.

Brock was clearly excited. He tried to jump off once or twice and explore or play with something, but Jack held him back—any random accident could get him sliced to pieces. He was just a monster monkey, after all, and the people of Valville were now warriors. A clear edge shone under their joviality. Jack had no doubt they would have cut Brock to pieces if he came here alone.

Warriors... He focused on that feeling, looking at individual people rather than the general image.

They were different than he remembered. Hardened. Hushed whispers and commanding voices were everywhere under the clamor. When he crossed gazes with someone, most held his gaze for a moment. Groups of people were either going out to hunt monsters or returning, carrying their wounded and seemingly random monster parts—from goblin eyes to brown hearts. The former had clenched fists and set jaws; the latter, empty eyes and palpable relief that they were still whole.

They'd also tried to armor themselves. There were those who wore several thick coats, with pans and pots tied in front of their vulnerable parts as armor, or even holding thin iron plates with jagged sides like shields—maybe that's why most cars lacked a roof. When it rained, they would quickly begin to stink of rot.

Overall, the weapons and armor of these monster hunters were makeshift, and their tactics ineffective, but they were doing their best. Jack could respect them.

The exception to that was the members of Henry's Fang. They held actual swords or handguns as they went out hunting in groups of three to five people, and they wore what looked like real leather armor. They must have had leatherworkers and blacksmiths—like George—working for them.

Moreover, they were relaxed, even cracking jokes as they strutted through the town, shooting mocking glances and pointed comments at those who weren't as well-equipped. Despite their overt mockery of others' misfortune, nobody dared retort. No doubt there would be consequences. This disharmony really ruined Jack's image of the new Valville.

The people of Henry's Fang he'd seen so far were dickheads, but he didn't want to judge too quickly.

After all, he stood out himself. His steps carried confidence, and his gait was wide. His level sent everyone out of his way, including the members of Henry's Fang.

It felt good.

Jack made a beeline for the town's west side. His first priority was making sure the professor was okay—most of his friends were in other towns, and telecommunications were down, so he couldn't contact them. Then, he'd speak to Henry of Henry's Fang. If they were good guys, Jack could work with them to ensure the town's safety. He had much to offer. If not...

His walk through the town took the better part of an hour. He didn't hurry, taking the time to observe the situation.

The areas near the town entrances and close to downtown were as lively as he'd seen them. Everywhere else was abandoned, highlighting the previous dichotomy. There were destroyed buildings and injured people everywhere. Many were obviously sick, too, probably from the dust and grime they carried. Nobody was cleaning or working for the benefit of the town, only hustling from place to place to hunt monsters or procure necessities. There were no ambulances or electricity, either, though the hospital would certainly be filled to the brim.

Seemed like nobody cared for the townspeople. But again, Jack didn't want to judge too quickly. This was a ton of work, and it was the apocalypse. Maybe Henry's Fang was just doing their best—though their many hunting groups indicated otherwise.

At least the town seemed safe from monsters.

A small white house entered Jack's vision as the sun reached its peak. It had a single story and a pink chimney rising from its tiled roof, and the windows were clean. It would have been a picturesque image if not for the patches of blood where the walls met the floor.

Jack's worry mounted. A stubborn knot was in his throat, like when he'd been about to fight the rock bear. There were no sounds coming from the house.

Jack reached the door, mustered his resolve, and knocked.

"Coming!"

His worry deflated instantly. "Oh, thank God," he whispered.

The door opened to reveal a woman in casual clothing. She was short and slim, while her brown eyes remained sharp despite their wrinkles. Jack used to joke that her mind was filled with firecrackers. She kept her white hair short, above shoulder-length, and always spoke and moved around with an energy that belied her old age.

When her gaze met Jack's barbaric form and monkey, she gasped in fear. Then, she scoured his face and recognized the lines. She shivered.

"Jack!" she exclaimed in joyful disbelief.

"Professor!" Jack shouted back, rushing in to hug her—carefully. Besides a suspicious swelling on her cheek, she wasn't injured. Everything was okay.

Except for the unknown burly man standing with crossed arms behind her. That one was not okay.

CHAPTER THIRTY-THREE
SEEKING REVENGE

JACK RAISED HIS GAZE TO THE MAN BEHIND THE PROFESSOR. HIS EYES DARKENED. "Who are you?" he asked.

"This is Hugo," the professor hurried to respond. "He's with Henry's Fang."

"And?"

"I'm here on orders, sir," Hugo said in a deep voice. "We have an agreement with Professor Rust. I make sure everyone honors it."

Jack narrowed his eyes. Hugo was a big man of Slavic descent, with a flat nose and a thick neck. His ears resembled cauliflowers, and his face betrayed a man of stark resolve. Moreover, he wore an overcoat. Before the System, he could have been mafia muscle—they had some in town. Now...

Human (Earth-387), Level 11
Faction: Henry's Fang (F-Grade)

"Here's what we'll do, Hugo. I will catch up with my mother. You will go take a long walk and return when we call you."

Jack didn't see a threat in this Hugo, and he had zero intentions of letting a nightman linger in his mother's home. Just Hugo's presence was enough to alert Jack that something was very wrong, and he would get to the bottom of it immediately.

When did I become like this? part of him wondered. Maybe it's the Dao of the Fist... I don't dislike it.

Hugo frowned. He'd scanned Jack, hence his respect. "That is difficult, sir. My orders are strict. I am to accompany Professor Rust at all times."

He let his dark overcoat flutter as he moved his hands, not accidentally revealing a gun handle. Jack saw that and nodded.

"Listen, Hugo. I understand you have your orders, okay? I really do. The thing is, I don't give a shit. So take a walk before I make you."

"Jack!" The professor jumped. "What are you saying?"

Hugo's frown deepened. A set of dangerous eyes met Jack's. Jack didn't budge.

Hugo's glare was hard and professional. Coupled with his gun and large body, this was an edge that could intimidate even the staunchest of bar fighters. Unfortunately, he was facing Jack Rust, a man who'd conquered a dungeon by himself.

Jack clenched a fist. A savage aura erupted from his body, burying the room in almost palpable violence. The professor gasped and stepped back, leaning against a wall to stay upright. Then Hugo's edge cracked. His eyes trembled. He looked around, then focused on Jack. Jack's eyes remained calm.

After a moment of tense silence, Hugo ceded. "Yes, sir."

Jack stepped aside, and the Slavic man walked over. Their bodies were very close to each other, and the tension was so explosive it seemed to form sparks. Hugo kept going and left the house, not looking back. Jack closed the door behind him.

"Jack!" the professor shook awake. "What—Do you understand what you did?"

"It's okay. If anybody wants to mistreat you, they have to get past me. How strong is Henry of Henry's Fang?"

Her eyes narrowed. She was catching up. Jack could see all the pieces of the puzzle coming together behind her eyes. "Level 22. A swordsman. He once sliced a bullet in two. What happened to you, Jack? I thought you were dead."

Jack nodded. Level 22 was pretty low.

"So did I," he admitted. "Can we sit? Hugo won't be back for a while."

"Yes, of course. Bring your... monkey... too. It's an unconventional pet, but then again, many things are unconventional lately. I like it."

"His name is Brock." He smiled. "The son of a friend." Brock agreed, reaching out to shake her hand like he'd seen his parents do. The professor smiled, and obliged, scanning him at the same time.

"A brorilla? Son of a friend? You have so many things to tell me, Jack..."

"And I will. Can we go in, first?"

"Of course."

The professor led Jack through a simple, minimalistic house filled with only the necessities—and books, lots of books. There were also a few electronics scattered around the house—a tablet, a laptop, a computer, and various gadgets, all turned off.

They crossed the corridor and entered the living room, where the picture of a smiling old man with a wide mustache stood atop the empty fireplace. The professor sat on a fluffy cushion chair, while Jack chose a simple couch. He looked around as if lost. Brock climbed on the couch next to him and stayed there, watching the professor with crossed arms as if ready to participate in the conversation.

"I can't believe it's all here," Jack said. "Coming back is so surreal... It feels like a dream."

"A nightmare, you mean."

"Depends on how you see it," he replied, eliciting a chuckle.

"No doubt. Many think the same... I'm just tired, that's all. I thought I was over learning new technologies when I retired. Well, guess again, Margaret."

Margaret Rust was a researcher and professor of informatics at Northeastern University, specializing in cybersecurity. When she retired two years ago, she and her late husband moved to Valville, where they could spend their twilight years in peace. Too bad the world had other plans.

"So many numbers, though," Jack said. "Dad would be happy."

"Or distraught."

"Maybe."

Margaret waited but was unable to let her questions go unheard. "What happened to you, Jack?"

"I was in the Greenway Nature Reserve when the System came, which got transformed into a dungeon. I couldn't leave until I beat the biggest, baddest monster around. Long story short, I did, then befriended the native monkey pack, and now I'm back with little Brock here."

"I thought you were dead..." Her eyes watered. "Was it hard?"

"Hardest thing I've ever done. But I made it. Now, I'm strong. Strong enough to protect my mother from criminal idiots with terrible naming sense."

Despite her tears, she chuckled. "They're dangerous people, Jack. They won't let us get away with this."

"Leave that up to me. How was your Integration?"

"Easy. Two goblins appeared outside the house, but a neighbor—you remember Mike—beat them up with a shovel. I just waited inside until things calmed down."

"I see. I'm happy you're alright. Where's Mike? I want to thank him."

"You'll struggle. He died to a wild dog two days later."

"Oh..." Jack digested the information, then nodded. "Keep speaking, Professor. I sense there's much to tell."

"Of course. Three days after the Integration, Henry White's gang formed a System faction and established order. They declared this town their territory. They became the bosses around here. After that, things happened. An alien arrived in the town square; an information merchant. I sold him knowledge on cyber security and got System knowledge in return. I also got an experience ball, which is how I made it to my current level."

She was level 6. Not bad at all, compared to the general population. Jack chuckled. Knowing her, she'd probably invested everything in Mental.

"So, you know things," he said. "About what's happening."

"I thought it was a safe bet. There isn't much an old lady like me can do, even if I learned to slingshot fire at goblins. Information, on the other hand, is my territory. I could help us get a step ahead of the monsters."

He sensed a 'but' there. "But?"

She sighed. "*But*, I miscalculated. Henry White came looking for the information. I don't like that man."

"Who is he?"

"He ran a shady organization downtown, extorting shops for "security" fees. I don't know how he got so lucky during the Integration, but he ended up a few steps ahead of everyone else."

"I see. And then?"

"Then, I miscalculated again." The professor's face turned into a scowl. "I couldn't tell them no, but I tried to hide some things. Unfortunately, the alien merchant traded in information; Henry bought a list with the contents of my transactions. They knew what I had."

"The merchant sold you off."

"Not really. It was my fault. Anyway, Henry's Fang knew what I had."

Jack raised a brow. "You told them everything."

"Kind of. The merchant had given me an information crystal—a wondrous invention, by the way. They store information in the crystal's molecular structure, then read it through the System."

"You gave them the crystal." Jack brought her back on track. "What was it about?"

"Ah, yes. It wasn't much. The merchant didn't deem my lifetime of expertise particularly expensive." She chuckled bitterly. "Then again, they do have a futuristic AI. Perhaps it could replicate our technology in milliseconds. The crystal was mostly about how to progress through the System. Listen well."

She instantly launched into lecture mode.

"Most people around think stats and levels are the important part; they're wrong. Apparently, the most crucial aspect of progression is something called the Dao. Unfortunately, the crystal didn't mention much besides the name, only some intentionally cryptic things. Then come skills. Those are split into many grades and degrees of proficiency, and they are the bridge between Dao and stats.

"A skill can be enhanced, upgraded, or fused with others. The first option just makes it slightly stronger—it's what usually happens. The other two create skills of a higher-grade, which are exponentially more effective than skills of lower grades. Higher-grade skills channel your Dao better—whatever that is—increase your battle strength, and let you progress further on the path of cultivation—as the System calls its progression."

Jack considered the information. "I think I did that once. Upgrading a skill. It became a Dao skill."

Margaret grinned. "Very game-like, isn't it? Makes you wonder... However, upgrading a skill is tremendous, Jack! Congratulations!"

"Thank you," he replied somberly. "Is there anything else before I get to the important stuff?"

"The System is the most important thing in our lives now, Jack. By far." Margaret's smile turned sad. "There is a lot more information, but... it can wait. Oh! Except one thing. Do you remember what the System said on Integration? About a tournament?"

"No, but I can look it up."

Jack made the first blue screens reappear. Soon, he found the one he was looking for—a part of the Animal Kingdom's message.

The first step to that power is the Integration Tournament, which will be held in twenty galaxy days (note: fifteen Earth-387 days) from now. Comprehend even the tiniest corner of the world by then, and endless possibilities will open up for you.

"I see. What of it?"

"That tournament is extremely important, Jack. You must get in no matter what. Pardon me for asking, but... do you have a Dao Root?"

He nodded and her eyes lit up like a Christmas tree.

"Excellent! That's wonderful! A Dao Root is the requirement to enter the Integration Tournament. You are in, my boy! You're in!"

"What's so special about that tournament, anyway?"

"There are incredible rewards, even for participation. It will put you on the fast track forever—it's like getting a Harvard scholarship. And, if you do well there... Well, that's unlikely. The strongest people from all over Earth-387 will be competing."

"You mean Earth."

"We are part of the galaxy now, Jack. Don't cling to old notions."

He considered it for a moment, then agreed. "Fine. I'll join that tournament and do my best. I'm plenty strong. Which brings us to the main point; what happened to your cheek?"

She looked deep into his eyes. "Jack..." she began, but he raised a hand to cut her off.

"You fought no monsters. Your cheek is swollen. A strongman was in your house. What's up?"

She hesitated. The cogs turning behind her eyes. He even saw her briefly consider lying before she looked straight at him. Jack was inwardly proud.

If there was one thing that stood out about Margaret Rust, it was the speed at which she adapted to new information.

"Henry's Fang left Hugo here to make sure I didn't disseminate the information freely. As for the swelling... Well, they slapped me when I tried to lie. It's not a big deal. The world is far more violent than it used to be. People die all the time."

Jack had stopped listening. "They slapped you."

"It's fine. It was light."

"But they did slap you," he replied calmly. "Who was it?"

She looked into his eyes. "How strong are you, Jack?"

"Plenty."

"It was Henry White."

"Got it. And I assume those guys are bad people?"

"They've been taxing everyone at the gates, and they've been terrorizing the town since they formed. They're tyrants."

"Good."

"Will you be careful? Please. I don't want to lose you again."

"Don't worry about me, Professor. Worry about *them*."

He grabbed Brock and stood. The couch's wooden handlebar was bent out of shape where he'd grabbed it.

"Stay here, little guy," he told the monkey. "I'll be back soon."

Brock, who'd been quiet so far, suddenly protested. His cute little eyes stared fearlessly at Jack. He bared his little fangs. He wanted to come along.

Jack placed him on the table and got on eye level. “Listen. I am *trusting you* with my own mother, okay? You must protect her while I’m away. This is an extremely important mission that only you can complete. Do you understand?”

Brock hesitated. Inwardly, Jack was impressed. Could the monkey actually understand him? However, on the outside, he was stern and earnest, looking at Brock as he would a brother.

“Do you understand?” he repeated, and Brock finally agreed. Glancing at the professor, he jumped at her feet and stood there as tall as he could—which wasn’t much—beating his chest and generally doing his best to look threatening. He screamed assertively.

Jack smiled. “Thank you.”

“He’s cute,” said Margaret, sitting back down to pet Brock. He scowled in disgruntlement, as if saying, “I’m a warrior! Do not pet me!”

She laughed.

“Hide in the bunker, Professor. I’ll be back.”

“Take care, Jack.”

They exchanged a hug. Jack watched her climb down to the basement before turning around and heading for the door, which was white and surrounded by flower-painted glass. He turned the doorknob. The door swung open. Three gun barrels were pointed at him.

Jack grinned and cracked his fists. “Hello, Hugo. I see your walk’s been productive.”

CHAPTER THIRTY-FOUR
AR'TAZUL THE MERCHANT

Three men stood at the edge of the yard fifteen feet away, pointing handguns at Jack. Two looked like hoodlums. The third was Hugo, the Slavic mafia man charged with watching the professor.

Jack stared down the gun barrel and didn't flinch. "You found a few more dogs, too."

Hugo's face was still as if cut from stone. "I never got your name."

"See those guns, Hugo? That's called deadly force. If you use deadly force against me, I will use it against you, and you will die. I want that to be very clear."

Jack's fist was clenched, and an invisible, savage aura rolled out of him in waves. The goons by Hugo's side—levels 3 and 4, both members of Henry's Fang—shivered. Their eyes flickered toward Hugo in hesitation, but he remained still as a rock.

"Only one thing is absolute in this world," Hugo said. "Bullets. Goodbye."

His gun spewed fire. The goons yelped—one dropped his gun from the sound, the other emptied his magazine in Jack's general direction.

At the same moment Hugo's finger clenched the trigger, Jack moved. His body flickered with speed, dashing sideways faster than the gunmen could react. Bullets flew left and right, passing by but not touching him.

He wasn't faster than bullets—yet—but he could calculate their trajectories from watching the guns.

The second goon managed to pick up his gun and start firing, trying to catch the blur that headed his way. He failed. Jack reached him, and a terrible slap almost emptied his mouth of teeth. He was unconscious before he even hit the floor.

Hugo was now behind the other goon. Jack didn't care. He grabbed the goon's gun, snapped it in half, and slapped the man hard enough to send him flying like a ballerina. He then stared at Hugo, who stared back.

Only the two of them were left. Hugo had three bullets remaining. He hadn't panicked and wasted them all like his goons.

Excitement glittered in Hugo's eyes. The gun danced in his hand as it spat death. The bullets dug into Jack's chest from almost point-blank, barely penetrating the skin before falling to the ground with a series of plinks.

Jack let himself be shot on purpose, of course. He was confident he could take the bullets, but how much damage would they deal?

Not much, was the answer. They felt like strong finger pokes.

Man... I'm Superman.

Hugo's elation morphed into terror. His clean-shaven face went pale. He looked at Jack in askance and raised his hands, letting the gun hang from his finger. His lips shivered as he tried to speak.

"Sorry, Hugo."

Jack's fist smashed into his face like a sledgehammer. Hugo's head exploded, and his body hit the ground a beat later, covered by its own trench coat.

Jack gazed at his fist. He'd just murdered a man. He could have shown mercy, but he didn't. Was that... bad?

The thing is, he felt nothing. No remorse, no regret, no doubts. His Dao had reinforced his resolve, and so had his multiple life-or-death experiences in the dungeon. Hugo was threatening Jack's mother and tried to kill him. Jack killed him back. It was natural. That was the law of strength, which apparently ruled the world now.

So what if he tried to surrender at the last moment? That shit was fake. He would plant a bullet in my eye the second he got the chance.

Jack looked around. There were people watching from the distance. A few were puking, some looked the other way, and a few were running away. A woman stared at him like he was a monster. Jack only snorted.

If they can try to kill me in broad daylight, with more people and guns, I can at least punch them back.

He shook his fist to get the blood away. *Next stop, Henry's Fang.*

There were definitely safer, more diplomatic options than simply storming in. However, like in the dungeon, Jack had enough of being smart. Now, he wanted to be strong—simple and direct—and he possessed the power to do it. He wanted to strike ahead like a fist and make the world adapt to him instead of the opposite.

That was his life now. And if he died at some point, so be it. At least he had fun.

Heh. Fun. He chuckled, baring his teeth. I could get used to this.

After breaking the other guns as well, Jack stepped over the two unconscious thugs and left the professor's front yard. *I should get that cleaned at some point...* he mused. He hadn't considered the issue before, but well, nothing he could do about it now. He was busy.

But where's Henry's Fang? Well, shit. He didn't know. Thankfully, there were people nearby he could ask.

Jack paced to the group watching from afar, keeping his hands high to avoid scaring them. Most ran anyway, but a few remained.

"Hello," he asked politely. "I'm looking for Henry's Fang. Can you tell me where they are?"

"Across the town. They've commandeered the hotel behind the town square. Valville Hotel, it was called."

"Thanks."

The man who replied was in his fifties, with eyes that struggled between respect, hope, and disbelief. His lips were clenched as he watched Jack go. "Hey!" he shouted. "Will you get them?"

Jack looked over his shoulder and cracked a smile. "You bet."

The man shivered, and his lips trembled for a moment. "Thank you! Thank you!"

Jack didn't look back, only gave a thumbs-up.

Let's see now... Valville hotel. It was a nice place. I hope they haven't ruined it. Since I'm going by the town square, I should check that alien out as well. The information merchant.

The streets were rowdy as he passed. The rumors had time to spread, and everyone looked at him with mixed feelings. Some held hope, others, pity, and a few, even hostility.

Jack ignored them all. He walked to the town square neither slow nor fast, letting the town know of his coming. His mind was rolling. Supposing he dismantled Henry's Fang, someone would need to run the town. In other words, he needed reliable people, and thankfully, he already had a plan to find them.

Valville's town square was a large square area surrounded by wide streets. There was a dry fountain in its center and not much else, creating a large empty space where children used to ride their bicycles or run around like the little monkeys they were.

Now, the town square was a far colder place. It was mostly empty, save for a few merchant stands around the square selling knives or makeshift armor, and the alien at its center. Jack's gaze focused there.

This was an alien. *An alien*. Right there in the middle of Valville Square. Just standing around.

The alien was a blue-skinned little man. He sported a short brown beard, wore a turban, and colorful, lax clothes, and generally resembled someone from the merchant cities of Africa or the Middle East if they were painted blue and were only four feet in height.

He was also pudgy, with a healthy belly and a satisfied smile as he lounged on the fountain's edge and whistled a little tune. He seemed to be having a blast.

Jack shook his head, pulling his gaze away. There was nobody trying to shoot him. Henry's Fang probably knew he was coming and waited for him in their hotel, gathering their forces.

A crowd was already forming, but it still wasn't enough for his plan. Jack wanted to get two birds with one stone. He had some time to waste.

As he approached the little blue merchant, he made out more details. A crate was by his feet, which were covered in pointy shoes. His facial features were pronounced. He wore only a light jacket despite the autumn chill, and he seemed completely relaxed in this planet of strangers.

Djinn, Level ?? (E-Grade)
Faction: Merchant Union (C-Grade)

Oh.

There were many new things there. This guy was a djinn; was there a relation to Earth's mythical creatures? His level was question marks, but it was in the E-Grade. Besides the Dao Vision, this was the first creature Jack saw that wasn't F-Grade.

This merchant could probably kick Jack's ass easily. No wonder he was so relaxed.

Moreover, he belonged to a C-Grade faction. That grade was so beyond Jack's current infantile understanding, he couldn't even fathom what it meant. The bald man in his vision and the skyscraper-like beast had both been in the C-Grade as well.

He gulped.

When Jack approached the merchant, he was still lying on the fountain edge, enjoying the afternoon sun without a care in the world.

"Hello," Jack said, making the merchant open an eye.

"Hello to you, my little friend," he said in an eastern accent. "How can I—Oh. You're pretty strong, aren't you?"

"I do my best. I hear you sold information on Professor Rust's transactions. Is that true?"

Though the professor had said it wasn't the merchant's fault, Jack didn't fully trust that. He still felt like blaming the merchant.

However, he was brave, not suicidal. He'd just express his dissatisfaction and begone. After all, this guy was E-Grade. Taunting him would be no good.

"Hmm?" The merchant's eyes twinkled with amusement as he jumped upright. He stood at his full height, barely reaching Jack's chest, and crossed his arms. He smiled brightly. "I did, but she was fully aware of that possibility. The contents of all transactions with me are sellable information. If you want confidentiality, just pay for the confidentiality bonus. It's in the terms."

"The terms?"

"The terms and agreement of the Merchant Union. All transactions are public knowledge unless indicated otherwise. It's even written in the condensed version for non-legally versed sapients."

He whipped out a yellow brochure. It didn't look more than a few pages long, and it was written in big letters. "I gave a copy to the human woman you mentioned; she read it end-to-end, understood it, and when I specifically asked about this, refused to pay for the confidentiality bonus. Here, have one too."

The merchant stuffed the brochure into Jack's hands, who was left trying to process this information. "Okay... Thanks."

If the professor knew about the confidentiality term and explicitly refused to pay it... Hmm. Guess she wasn't lying, after all. It wasn't the merchant's fault.

"No problem. Happy to get that out of the way," the merchant said. "Is there anything else I can do to help?"

"Well..." Jack looked around. Still not enough people. He turned back to the merchant, his previous grudge dissolving as he let excitement tinge his voice. This was an alien. "What *are* you? And how can you speak English?"

"A djinn of planet Bing." The merchant laughed, his voice sonorous. "I don't usually give my name to customers, but I'll make an exception for you: I'm Ar'Tazul, at your service. I know *aliens* seem like a big deal right now, but you'll start seeing a lot more of us soon. Don't get too excited. As for the language barrier you mentioned, the System takes care of that."

"I'm Jack." Jack mechanically shook the djinn's outstretched hand.

"A pleasure. Would you like to browse my stock? I have some things you might be interested in."

"Information?"

"That, too, but I have more. Experience balls, skills, empty crystals, advanced weapons, even Dao Fruits... I suspected there would be high-end customers on this planet, so I brought high-end goods—and you get them at Integration discount, mind you."

Ar'Tazul winked, then retrieved a crystal from his robes. It was rhombus-shaped and pink, and it could barely fit in his small palm. Jack took the crystal. *Now what?* he thought, looking at it. The moment he had the question, a blue screen appeared before his face.

Ar'Tazul's Store

Basic Information Package – 500 credits
Advanced Information Package – 3,000 credits
Simple Weapons – 10 credits
Small Firearms – 20 credits
Experience Ball (tiny) – 100 credits
Experience Ball (small) – 300 credits
Experience Ball (medium) – 1,000 credits
Experience Ball (large) – 10,000 credits
Empty Crystal – 20 credits
Dao Weapon (F-Grade) (made on demand, delivery times vary) – 5,000 credits
Dao Fruit (F-Grade) – 10,000 credits

There was also a large assortment of trinkets, electronic devices, medieval weapons, and names Jack didn't recognize. There was even a section about skills, and it included a bunch of stuff ranging anywhere from knitting, to advanced cybersecurity, to swordsmanship. There was the Fistfighting skill, too, but it belonged to the top echelon price-wise, as did most melee combat skills. Skills were expensive overall, starting at a thousand credits and going up to five-digit numbers.

There were no Dao skills, however.

Jack skimmed through the list before returning the crystal to Ar'Tazul.

"Did anything catch your eye, my friend?" asked the merchant, his eyes gleaming.

"I'm just in a hurry. Also, I have none of these... credits."

"Not a problem."

Without batting an eye, Ar'Tazul handed Jack a small plaque made of green, transparent jade. The number 0 shone on its surface in clean white letters. Jack took it and turned it over. It looked pretty.

"Here's a credit card." Ar'Tazul smiled. "It's free of charge; Integration benefits."

"A credit card?"

"Exactly."

"I see... In any case, I still have zero credits. How do I gather them?"

"You sell things for credits, obviously. It's the System currency used in most places throughout the galaxy. For example, we take a selection of monster parts—I have a brochure on that. Additionally, if you have any interesting items or premium information, I could give you a good deal..."

He looked on leadingly. Jack considered it. He did have a few things to sell—expensive ones, too. The Dao Fruit he had was listed in Ar'Tazul's catalog as worth 10,000 credits, which, given the context, was a lot. He remembered the description.

Dao Fruit of the Fist (F-Grade)

Allows the user to enter a meditative nirvana state, where the speed of Dao cultivation is greatly increased. Breakthroughs are greatly assisted. This particular fruit is oriented towards the Dao Root of the Fist. Effects are reduced as the user's Dao gets further away from the fist. Effects are reduced as the user's Dao ascends beyond the Dao Root stage.

Only one Dao Fruit can be used per Grade.

Unfortunately, it sounded pretty damn useful and tailored *specifically* for him. Plus, Ar'Tazul mentioned that the prices he saw were after the Integration discount was applied, whatever that was. In any case, selling the fruit sounded like a waste.

Which left the other reward he'd gotten from the dungeon.

Trial Planet Token

Can allow one person into Trial Planet.

Hmm...

CHAPTER THIRTY-FIVE
CHALLENGING AN ENTIRE FACTION

Trial Planet Token…

He had no idea what that was. Sounded like a random trinket he couldn't use. Maybe he'd get cheated if he sold it now. Then again, he could at least appraise it and ask what it was. He took it out of his pocket—seemed like an old gold coin.

"I have this. What do you think it's worth?"

"Hmm?"

Ar'Tazul inspected the coin in Jack's hand, then froze. His eyes widened, his professional smile falling, and he released a gasp.

"That's a Trial Planet Token!" he shouted. "How did you get that? Can I see?"

"That's my business, and no." Jack got defensive, stuffing the token back in his pocket. "What is it?"

"Extremely precious, that's what it is."

Ar'Tazul regained his bearing, coughing into his blue hand once and rubbing his beard. He finally took Jack seriously. "I can give you 10,000 credits for that one. It's a useless item to you, but invaluable to many people throughout the galaxy."

"I see. Well, I'll hold onto it for now. Let's discuss it again later."

Jack wasn't a fool. He was absolutely sure Ar'Tazul was trying to cheat him, even though the price *sounded* high.

Ar'Tazul hesitated, then moved a little closer.

"Listen, my friend—Jack. Listen, Jack. I understand you think I'm cheating you; and okay, it's not entirely false. I'm a merchant. I have to make a living, and 10,000 is a good price for me, but we can discuss it. That's not the issue. The issue is that, if people find out that an F-Grade cultivator has a Trial Planet Token, they won't hesitate to kill you for it. Let's try to work out a good deal and everyone will be happy. I'll get my profit, and you'll get a decent profit plus your personal safety, which is priceless. Otherwise, when news spreads..."

Jack's face became hard. "Oh, yeah? And how would *news spread*?"

"Well, I might have accidentally raised my voice before."

Jack blinked, then looked around. A large crowd had already formed, only a few dozen feet away from him. When Ar'Tazul had shouted "that's a Trial Planet Token!" everyone must have heard him.

Blood went straight to Jack's head. He pointed at the merchant.

"You tricked me," he said grimly.

"It was an honest accident. Could happen to anyone." Ar'Tazul shrugged apologetically. "By the way, acting violently against merchants is prohibited by the Merchant Union, a C-Grade faction."

Jack stared with severe irritation. Showing that coin had been a big mistake. He missed his dungeon, where he could punch things with no regard for merchants or unions. Civilization sucked. "Who will they even tell? I'm about to kick the town boss's ass, anyway."

"They won't. But, well..." Ar'Tazul looked to the side. "I am an information merchant, so..."

Jack's eyes narrowed. "You wouldn't dare."

"Hey, it's my job. I told you before, everything I learn is public knowledge unless we agree on a confidentiality term."

Jack was speechless. This guy was trying to con him. Maybe the coin meant nothing at all! But could he take the risk?

If only he could punch this guy... Except he was an E-Grade alien with unknown abilities and a C-Grade organization as his backing. At this point, Jack could only grit his teeth and admit he'd been conned. "How much?"

"How much for what?"

"The confidentiality term."

"Oh, that? Only a thousand credits."

Jack almost exploded. He really was about to punch the merchant, and damned be the consequences. "You know I don't have that much!"

"Sorry, kid. I really want that coin."

"Well, fuck you. I'm not giving you shit."

His raging, bare-chested, muscular form towered over the little merchant, but he didn't seem to mind.

"That's a dangerous call," Ar'Tazul replied.

"I don't fucking care. You can take that confidentiality term and shove it up your blue ass."

"Okay, I understand we got off on the wrong foot here." Ar'Tazul took a step back. "Tell you what. Keep the coin, and I'll keep my mouth shut for a week. Until then, you can buy the thousand-credit confidentiality term whenever you like."

"That's bullshit. Why should I trust you?"

"Because I'm not asking for anything. This is called customer loyalty, kid. That coin is very, very precious, but I see you're determined to keep it. That's fine. Even if I got it, I'd only get a tiny cut of its true value myself. Instead, I'd rather foster a good relationship with you. You're way ahead of the power curve. If you continue like this, you might even do well in the Integration Tournament, and I'm your resident merchant. A good relationship will benefit us both. Maybe even more than a single Trial Planet Token."

Jack peered all the way to the merchant's soul, and saw nothing. "You're lying."

"I can't do much to convince you," Ar'Tazul said, completely calm in the face of Jack's outrage. "But my promise stands. I'll keep my mouth shut for a week—unless you die, of course—but you better hurry. Everyone here heard me, so you never know who the news might reach."

Jack took a deep breath, calming down a bit. This situation was potentially dangerous. He had to handle it well.

When his eyes reopened, they were sharp. "Give me information on the token," he said.

"What?"

"Information on the token. Free of charge. You said you want to forge a good relationship, right? Start by helping me understand the deal you're offering."

Now, it was Ar'Tazul's turn to think. He relented. "Fine." He reached into the crate by his feet and retrieved another information crystal. "Here. This is yours. A gift."

Jack snatched it and put it in his pocket. "Good. I'll consider things again later and come back to you, Ar'Tazul."

"Tazul."

"What?"

The merchant's smile widened, revealing a perfect set of teeth. "Friends and good customers can call me Tazul. No need to be formal, Jack."

"I am not your friend."

"But you *are* a good customer."

"Whatever."

Jack was in no mood to talk. He first wanted to vent his frustration, and coincidentally, the perfect targets waited just around the corner.

Before that, he turned around to survey the crowd. News of him killing Hugo and marching at Henry's Fang had spread already, and throngs of people congregated to watch from a distance. They knew shit was going down. Some supported him, some hated him. He only cared for the former.

"People of Valville," he roared, quieting all murmurs. He wasn't used to such big crowds—he'd only lectured small groups of university students a few times—but the anger helped him overcome social anxiety. "Henry's Fang is a gang of hoodlums. They dared touch my mother. I *will* destroy them, disband their faction, and punish their leaders. I can do it by myself, but I'm aware they've been suppressing and terrorizing you. If you want to get revenge, now is the time. Is there anyone brave enough to join me?"

His speech was short, direct, and shocking. The first rows stared at him with wide eyes—so did the back rows, probably, but he couldn't see them. Behind him, Ar'Tazul had an amused smile.

Jack didn't need help to defeat the gang. However, when the dust settled, he would need people at his side, people who were both capable and trustworthy. People who would join his faction, the Bare Fist Brotherhood, and help him protect both Valville and the Forest of the Strong.

In short, he needed allies. This was a perfect opportunity. Whoever stepped forth now and fought by his side would be both capable and trustworthy.

Jack had hatched this plan on the way, and he was quite proud of it.

However, even after waiting for half a minute, nobody stepped up. Nobody took Jack's offer. Did they not believe him? Even if they didn't, wasn't there anyone willing to risk his or her life for revenge?

Jack waited another half minute. Then, he shook his head, sighed in disappointment, and turned to leave.

"Wait!"

A single man squeezed through the crowd and stepped into the square. He was slim, young, bespectacled, and average in every respect. His messy dark hair and brown eyes would never stand out in a crowd, and his slightly hunched posture didn't scream 'special' either.

He was just your average joe—but his heart was in the right place. He, alone, had accepted Jack's offer.

"Who are you?"

"I'm Edgar!" the man replied, panting slightly. "A wizard."

Jack's smile widened. He inspected the guy.

Human (Earth-387), Level 11
Faction: -

That level was enough to pique Jack's curiosity. "A wizard?"

"Yeah. I can shoot fire and stuff."

Edgar whispered something under his breath, then aimed a hand at the sky. A fireball burst out of his palm and flew two dozen feet before dissolving.

Jack's eyes widened. He'd seen System stuff before, but this was real, honest-to-God fantasy magic!

"Damn, man," he said. "You're in!"

Edgar approached and reached out for a handshake. "Cool."

"I'm Jack, by the way. Jack Rust. Why do you hate these guys?"

"They killed my parents."

"Oh..."

"It's not as bad as it sounds. We were on terrible terms." Edgar shrugged. "But they were still my parents, so I have to take revenge. Even if they sucked most of the time."

"Yeah... Okay, hold it. How about we go through the battle first, and you can tell me your personal issues afterward if we both survive?"

"Sure."

"Alright. I'll go on ahead. When I start bashing heads, you come in finger guns blazing and handle the stragglers."

"Works for me." Edgar smiled. Jack smiled back, having forgotten his previous anger.

What an easygoing guy...

"See you there," Jack said, then turned to the merchant. "And I hope I don't see you ever again, Ar'Tazul."

"I'm your resident merchant, friend. I'm the only one here. You're going to see lots and lots of me if you survive." Ar'Tazul waved goodbye. "Take care."

Jack cursed under his breath and took off. He ran to the edge of the square. Then, under the shocked gazes of everyone present, he jumped on a second-story rooftop. Valville Hotel was only a street away. Hopping from rooftop to rooftop, Jack got there in no time, then jumped on the hotel. It had three stories, meaning he stood dozens of feet high.

A wide wooden courtyard stretched below him. It was clean, simple, and filled with roughly thirty people. Most were armed goons, but a few wore trench coats and held themselves straighter. Everyone was busy lounging by a pool, talking to each other, drinking, or playing poker.

In the center of everything, a dark-skinned man in a white suit sat at a poker table, gambling away an obscene amount of chips. Beside him rested a Japanese sword—a katana.

They hadn't noticed Jack yet. In fact, as he watched them from above, they seemed too relaxed. They probably thought he was still in the square—maybe, they didn't even know he was coming. Hugo had done them dirty by not warning them.

It mattered little. He inspected his status screen, taking in all those pretty, pretty numbers.

Jack grinned, bumped his fists together to ramp himself up, then roared, “Henry White! Get your ass out here!”

CHAPTER THIRTY-SIX
TRIUMPH

"Henry White! Get the fuck out here!" Jack roared from the hotel roof, sending his voice throughout the town. Thanks to his enhanced body, his shout was even louder than usual.

The people below froze. Looked around, then up, to find a menacing figure standing over them. Some whispered. Others averted their gaze—the afternoon sun shone behind Jack, hiding his form.

The dark-skinned man at the center of the yard stood up. "I am Henry White," he declared evenly. "Who might you be?"

"Vengeance."

Henry smirked. "You are not a scion."

"A scion of what?"

"Hah!" Henry laughed, hard and loud. "Fuck off, vigilante, before my men fill you with lead. I'll give you a ten second head start."

"Sure." Jack smiled. "How about you start the countdown?"

"Ten—"

Jack leaned forward and fell from the roof. Everyone gasped. No gun fired. Jack landed on the soil of a garden, and before anyone could take in his form, he'd disappeared.

"Fire!" Henry yelled, but his men couldn't react fast enough.

Jack roared like a bull. He smashed a fist into a man's chest and sent him flying. He elbowed another, breaking his ribs. Before they knew it, this crowd of armed mafians had a red-eyed madman in their midst.

Guns rattled. Bangs filled the air, stealing everyone's hearing. Their world turned mute. People screamed.

A barbarian was going berserk on them. He was tall, bare-chested, and lined with muscles, and his hair fluttered by his sheer speed. His eyes shone like twin stars, and his body moved at speeds they couldn't even follow. His every punch was enough to break people, walls, trees, anything that got in his way. People flew away with soundless screams.

He opened his mouth and gave a silent roar, letting bullets graze his hair. Many missed, their wild shots piercing into other gunmen. However, nobody here was too low a level, and their bodies could take a couple bullets.

What they couldn't take, were the punches. Jack smashed a fist into a stomach, holding back to ensure the other man's body didn't explode. He grabbed a man by the head, and tossed him at another, sending them both rolling on the ground and through a wooden column. His bare feet dragged against the gravel as he shot forward, landing between three cloistered together. His fists shot out, sending them flying away like ragdolls.

More guns turned on him in slow motion, and he easily leaned away from the bullets. Most missed due to his speed.

It wasn't just the guns. These people were clumsy, their bodies reacting so pathetically slow it made him feel bad. He held back on purpose, not wanting to slaughter them, but even that was difficult against such frail opponents.

If any die, it's on them. They have guns.

Jack felt vindicated. His ordeal in the dungeon was finally paying off. He was strong! Mid-battle, he clenched his fists, letting the thrill of battle wash over him and show on his grinning lips. For the first time in a long while, *he* was the hunter.

This was like fighting the goblin tribe back in the day, except even easier. His love for fighting shone brighter than ever. The world had gone silent around him from the many bangs, giving the battle a surreal feeling.

His Dao Root of the Fist was a revving engine in his chest. Every punch flew true, his every step carrying him away from danger. It was trivial.

A bullet flew hard into his ribs. Jack stumbled and lost all air inside him. He turned to the side. A man in an overcoat stood behind a knee-high white fence and held an honest-to-God rifle. Jack hadn't expected that, having only seen handguns. He gritted his teeth.

Human (Earth-387), Level 16
Faction: Henry's Fang (F-Grade)

Fuck.

Jack ignored the goons and moved in dodging patterns. The rifle bullets screamed by his ears, barely missing him every time. A hint of worry appeared in his heart. Not only were these bullets stronger than the others, able to injure or kill him if they struck at the wrong spot, but the man's marksmanship was superb. He must have had a relevant skill, possibly many.

Jack weaved between the goons like a snake, changing directions and zigzagging as unpredictably as he could. The rifle barrel followed him closely, seeming to have a never-ending magazine. A bullet grazed Jack's ear; another struck his thigh and almost made him fall.

At least his hearing was recovering.

Right then, a loud shout came from a corner of the courtyard. "Yeetus fierus!"

It was followed by screams as balls of fire flew between the goons, hitting some and distracting the others. Some turned to fire on the source.

"Shieldus!"

A blue hemisphere appeared to face the goons, blocking some of the bullets. Behind the shield stood Edgar, hands and eyes blazing with sparkling cyan flames. "Fierus Whipus!" The flames morphed into a long whip that he snapped the air. Any goon it met fell to the ground screaming. "I'm here, Jack!" Edgar shouted over the screams. "I'll handle the little guys. Go get them!"

"What kind of idiot spell names are those!"

Jack's voice came distorted as he still danced around, desperately dodging the rifle bullets.

"They're from Har—Shieldus!" His shield sprang up again, barely blocking a new hail of bullets. "Hurry up! I can't do this for long!"

Jack gritted his teeth. The rifle was persistently on him, eager to reap his life. One bullet in the wrong place would be enough to end him.

Fortunately, there were plenty of human shields around. Jack grabbed one and rushed at the rifle man, still zigzagging at speeds that these low-level hitmen couldn't match.

He leaped over the comically short fence—clearly decorative—and got within a few feet.

The marksman was a short, stocky man with heavy features. He had a scar running from his right wrist to deep inside his trench coat's sleeves, and his eyes were so cold that Jack had goosebumps. This man was a killer—probably before the System.

However, now that Jack was so close, he could—

A sweet smell reached his nostrils, making him stumble. He was violently pulled out of his battle state as more instincts awoke inside him. The smell wasn't exactly sweet, it was also a little sour. Not the bad kind, but like a juicy, mellow lemon. The moment he smelled it, various images sprang uninvited in his mind, and a fire burned his body, starting from his groin. He lost focus.

He looked to the side, where a ravishing woman in underwear stared at him. An urge to drop everything and be with her overcame him—he couldn't afford to miss this chance. A bullet ripped the human shield from his hands, but he didn't care.

His Dao Root roared. A mental fist struck the illusion and broke it like a mirror, snapping Jack free. She was just a woman in underwear.

Human (Earth-387), Level 18
Faction: Henry's Fang

Jack growled, finding the rifle barrel staring at him from inches before his face. He ducked. The bullet grazed the top of his head, no doubt burning some hair. But now, he was too close.

Jack planted a foot firmly into the ground and smashed a fist into the rifle man's abdomen with all his strength, making his back explode into a shower of blood and bones. The rifle went flying. Jack pivoted toward the woman, who was frenziedly backing away, but she was too slow.

His fist crushed her beautiful face into paste. She was too dangerous to spare. She'd almost developed a Dao Root.

A sudden sense of danger assaulted Jack, screaming out of nowhere. He leaned back, letting a naked blade whistle inches over his nose. He tumbled back. The blade pursued him until he managed to escape beyond its reach.

"Fire, you fools! We almost got him!" Henry White jumped after Jack. He'd let his subordinates scout out Jack, but now, he entered into the fray himself.

From up-close, he was an impressive man. His dark skin cut a clear contrast against his white suit, and his Japanese sword glinted in the afternoon light. His green eyes were incredibly piercing, like he could see through your soul, while his concentration was honed like a blade. He was clean-shaven and exuding an air of transience.

"Surrender!" Henry shouted between swings. "I work for Lord Gan Salin, one of the five scions! Even if you kill me, you'll die too!"

Jack had no idea what that meant, but he sure as hell wasn't going to surrender. He laughed.

"Then, die!" Henry roared.

The blade sang before Jack. For the first time in this fight, he couldn't just waltz in. Henry's strikes were fast and vicious. Skillful. If he just rushed in, even his close to 100 Constitution wouldn't save him.

Fortunately, Jack was faster on his feet. He retreated, observing Henry's patterns. Bullets were still flying, but not nearly as many as before. Many goons had been incapacitated, some were fighting Edgar, and most of the others had run.

Jack's back met a wall. Henry's eyes glinted with excitement as he rushed in for the kill. Jack punched back. Both men aimed for the other, but Henry's sword would reach there first.

Jack's eyes flashed. *Meteor Punch.*

His fist accelerated like a missile, flying so fast that all the bones in his arm creaked. He was pulled forward by the fist's momentum, escaping the sword's trajectory, but it was unnecessary. His punch met Henry's chest and exploded in an incredible display of blinding, ear-rattling force. A fist-shaped meteor had fallen right there.

The world went white for a moment. The katana flew away.

When everyone's vision recovered, they saw a pair of legs flopping to the ground. Henry's entire upper body had disappeared. Some of it incinerated into dust, and some sent flying over the hotel's walls.

Jack's hand remained whole this time, thanks to the level-ups and meeting Henry's soft body instead of the black wolf's fur, but a few bones had cracked. He couldn't control Meteor Punch perfectly yet.

He didn't show that. Instead, he looked at the remaining goons and grinned. "Who's next?"

In hindsight, they couldn't hear him thanks to the multiple gunshots and the meteor's explosion. Even Jack could barely hear himself. But his words had the expected result.

The goons fell on their butts, guns dropped. With their leader dead, what could they do against the natural disaster that went by the name of Jack Rust?

"Fuck off, then," he said. "And Edgar... good job."

"Thanks, man." Edgar adjusted his glasses, nonplussed by the copious amounts of blood and gore around him. He gave Jack a thumbs-up. "You did pretty well yourself."

Jack nodded, ignoring the escaping goons, and jumped on the hotel roof, where he wouldn't be disturbed.

The territory of Valville is now unoccupied. Would you like to add it to Bare Fist Brotherhood?

It didn't take much thought.

Yes.

"People of Valville," he roared, sending his voice over the entire town. "Henry's Fang has been disbanded. From now on, this town is part of the Bare Fist Brotherhood, and under the protection of me, Jack Rust. We will handle things. You can sleep easy."

Of course, he didn't mention that he was the only member of the Brotherhood. *Whoops.*

He then had another thought. System, how long until the Integration Tournament?

Seven Earth-387 days

Got it.

Jack had many things to do, but first, he had to take care of the aftermath. Even better, find someone else to do it for him. He knew just the person.

He also wanted to go through the headquarters of Henry's Fang for any useful items like his Dao Fruit or the Trial Planet Token. He had to find things to sell so he could buy useful skills and items from the merchant, Ar'Tazul. He also needed a lot of information. For example, what exactly was the Integration Tournament? What were those scions Henry had mentioned?

And, most importantly, who the fuck was Gan Salin?

CHAPTER THIRTY-SEVEN
SHOPPING THERAPY

After making sure everything was fine, the first thing Jack did was take the rifle and sling it across his back for safekeeping, then he entered Valville Hotel to find the secret stash of Henry's Fang. They'd been taking items from the townspeople as "tax," so they were bound to have some good stuff. By conqueror's right, everything now belonged to Jack—though he would return anything he didn't need to the town.

The gang had taken over the entire hotel. There were no signs of employees or other guests. The only person inside was a shivering goon by the counter.

Jack smiled. "Show us everything."

The goon hadn't bowed deeper in his entire life.

After exploring for some time—with the help of Edgar and the random goon—they found two interesting places. One was the cellar, and the other was Henry White's room. Both were equipped with several security and alarm measures that blared. Of course, they were now useless. Jack tore both places apart to find anything hidden.

The cellar held an assortment of guns, ammunition, and medieval weapons. There was no other rifle or heavy weaponry, but Jack did find a grenade, which made him go pale. He pocketed it quickly, then resealed the room. These guns would go to the Bare Fist Brotherhood's future members, though he suspected firearms were of limited utility in the System world.

Henry White's room held more surprises. The first was a System credit card with a nice, round 3,000 shining on its surface. Jack's eyes turned golden—this was 3,000 more than he had! After quick negotiations with Edgar, they would split any loot 70-30, with the lion's share going to Jack. He could have gotten even more, but he wanted to invest in his future faction members.

The other surprise was a Dao Fruit. It resembled a cabbage, but each of its leaves was sharp like a razor.

"Holy shit," said Jack.

"Holy shit," said Edgar. "I have no idea what that is."

"It's a Dao Fruit worth 10,000 credits."

"What!"

Dao Fruit of the Blade (F-Grade)

Allows the user to enter a meditative nirvana state, where the speed of Dao cultivation is greatly increased. Breakthroughs are greatly assisted. This particular fruit is oriented toward the Dao Root of the Blade. Effects are reduced as the user's Dao gets further away from the blade. Effects are reduced as the user's Dao ascends beyond the Dao Root stage.

Only one Dao Fruit can be used per Grade.

Edgar pieced apart the fruit's description, and his eyes were instantly filled with desire.

"Jack! I know this is a lot to ask, but can I have this fruit? I leveled up twice during the fight, reaching level 13. After I get to level 15 and choose my class, I might be able to develop a Dao Root and join the Integration Tournament. It's an opportunity that could change my life."

When Jack didn't speak right away, Edgar's shoulders drooped.

"It's fine. I understand." Edgar shook his head. "I went too far. This fruit belongs to you, after all. I'm sorry if I crossed any limits."

Jack still didn't speak. Edgar waited. A moment later, Jack said,

"Give me your share of everything else, join my faction, and owe me a favor. Then, you can have it."

Edgar perked up. "For real?"

"For real."

"Shit, man... I've known you for half an hour and you're already my best friend. You want one? I'll owe you *two*!"

"One's enough," Jack laughed. "I already have a fruit, and it's one perfectly suited for me. However, are you *sure* you want a Blade fruit? It's not well-suited for you, so maybe selling it would be better."

Edgar cupped his chin. "Hmm... I wonder if the merchant would be willing to exchange this fruit for another. What do you think, random goon?" He turned to the shivering hoodlum beside them, who stuttered.

"I—The boss exchanged another fruit for this one. I think he paid extra, but I don't know how much. I'm sorry!"

"That's fine. We'll just ask." Edgar eyed the fruit with hope, while Jack shrugged.

"I have some leverage with that smurf. Maybe I can get him to waive the premium."

"Nah, man. You've already helped me plenty. I'll handle it."

"Suit yourself."

After picking up the fruit and making sure there was nothing else to discover, Jack and Edgar exited the building. They also ruffled through all the bodies in the courtyard for credit cards, picking up an extra few thousand. Jack discovered he could transfer funds by touching the cards to each other. The System gave him something like a bank interface when that happened. He regretted not looting Hugo's body, too—and who knows how many credits he carried on his person before Jack blew him up.

Are credit cards fragile? he wondered. He tested that on a random one from the corpses. It took a full-force blow and cracked. When that happened, the number on its surface disappeared. Presumably, all credits would be lost if it contained any.

Keep it somewhere safe, then. Got it.

Ironically, they also found some Earth credit and debit cards, for banks, which were probably useless now. Jack kept them anyway.

Their gains were massive. Jack ended up with 6,000 credits on his card, while Edgar procured a Dao Fruit. It wasn't the lion's share Jack intended to get, but he believed this investment would pay off in the near future.

"Let's go to the merchant together," he said.

The crowd was still waiting in the square, though most had dispersed after the sounds of gunfire and Meteor Punch's explosion. Besides those gazing fearfully from the windows, only a couple dozen people remained, standing proudly with their fists clenched. When Jack arrived, they looked at him with tears of gratitude and helplessness.

These were the people that hated Henry's Fang, many likely had family members killed by them. They were too weak to do anything, so they could only look at Jack's back as he handled things for them.

More people emerged from the surrounding streets and buildings, where they'd been hiding, but Jack shooed them away. "Fuck off," he said, then turned to those that had already been in the square. "You guys, come here."

Hesitantly, they approached. "Thank you," a man said from the depths of his heart, speaking for everyone.

"You're welcome, but words are useless. If you really want to thank me, join my faction and protect this city."

Their eyes shone. "Really?" a woman couldn't help but ask. "We are weak..."

"It doesn't matter. I am plenty strong myself. What I need now is loyalty, and I believe you can offer that."

He'd seen the intensity of their gazes, their resolve, their respect and admiration for him. Those were pure eyes. Or so he thought, at least. He planned to take responsibility for disbanding Henry's Fang, the administrators of Valville, and he needed loyal people for that. Without them and a capable leader at the helm, the town would probably plunge into chaos.

Jack wasn't necessarily a capable leader, but he knew someone who was.

"System," he said aloud, "invite these people to my faction."

Everyone looked at the empty space before their faces and made sounds of affirmation, including Edgar.

Nineteen members have been added to Bare Fist Brotherhood (F-Grade). You can review their details at the Members tab.

I can? Members tab, he thought.

Jack Rust (leader), Human (Earth-387), Level 34, Pugilist, Planetary Frontrunner (10)
Edgar Allano, Human (Earth-387), Level 13
Mary Gander, Human (Earth-387), Level 5
John Li, Human (Earth-387), Level 4
...
Natasha Russon, Human (Earth-387), Level 1

That's handy.

The people he'd recruited ranged from level 1 to 5, with a gaunt woman being the strongest. Perhaps the steady knife in her hand was the reason.

"I'll give you all guns," Jack said, retrieving the rifle from his back and handing it to the level 5 woman. "You shouldn't rely on them, but they'll be helpful in the short run."

Everyone nodded. Jack continued, "I'll go fetch another member. You guys go into the hotel, arm yourselves, and don't let anyone else in. Spread the word that the Bare Fist Brotherhood rules this place now."

Even as he said that, he felt tired. He had no intention of ruling anything, but it wasn't hard to imagine how things would play out over the following months. Having a steady base would be good for him, and his name could protect the townspeople.

"See you, Jack," Edgar said with a smile.

"I'm not going yet. You and I must speak to the blue man."

"Now? Sweet!"

They headed for Ar'Tazul, who still lounged in the middle of the square as if oblivious to everything. When they approached, he rose from the fountain edge. "Nice to see you back, Jack," he said with a smile. "Or should I say, new regional overlord."

"I told you before, Ar'Tazul. I am not your friend. Give me the catalog, please."

"Sure."

The blue merchant didn't seem to mind. Jack took the information crystal and perused through it, more purposely this time, while Edgar approached the merchant to ask about a Dao Fruit exchange.

Jack's eyes shone as he scrolled. There were information packages, experience balls, firearms, even something called a Dao weapon. This last one sounded intriguing. Jack assumed it would be a weapon suited to his Dao, like Henry White's suspicious katana—why the hell would Valville have a katana? He had to remember to secure that weapon for his faction.

Unfortunately, his own weapons were his fists, and even iron knuckles would only distance him from the core of his Dao.

After a few moments of scrolling, Jack narrowed his options down to a few things:

Advanced Information Package – 3,000 credits
Earth-387's Major Factions – 1,000 credits
Dungeon Locations (small) – 2,000 credits
Experience Ball (medium) – 1,000 credits
Stomp Dance Footwork Skill – 4,000 credits

The information package's utility came without question. Depending on what it contained, he could understand how the System worked, how the galaxy was partitioned, what the Dao was, how to progress faster... Its utility was likely the highest out of everything here.

The powerful factions of Earth would be useful for context. He was stronger than Henry White, sure, but Valville was barely a dot on the map. There were bound to be stronger people than him on the planet, and he would like to know by how much.

Had anyone reached the E-Grade yet? Was there a strong enemy in their immediate vicinity? Who would be his opponents in the Integration Tournament?

The dungeon locations usefulness was also irrefutable. According to game knowledge, dungeons had strong enemies, and they could greatly help Jack with leveling up before the Tournament—as could the medium experience ball, which he also considered.

"Ar'Tazul, how many levels would a medium experience ball give me?"

The merchant replied instantly. "One, maybe two."

"Oh."

It wasn't much. Jack mentally crossed it out.

"What about me?" Edgar asked from the side, and Ar'Tazul gave him an appraising look.

"Around seven."

"Oh!" Edgar almost smiled before remembering he was poor.

"You could always sell the fruit," Jack said, but Edgar shook his head.

"Even if it wasn't for the Tournament, I get the feeling that a Dao Root is more important than a few levels. Plus, experience balls seem to defeat the purpose. Leveling up is supposed to be a sharpening stone to forge yourself, not a technicality to get over quickly."

Jack agreed. His suggestion had only been a test.

"How much would it cost to exchange fruits, by the way?" Jack asked.

"Ten percent over the base price."

"Do you have that much?"

"No... but I have a few hundred. I'll gather the rest before the Tournament. You've already helped me enough."

Jack nodded in appreciation again. He liked Edgar more and more.

"Very well."

He then returned to his own options. The last thing he considered buying was the Stomp Dance Footwork skill, for multiple reasons. The professor had told him about the importance of skills. This one was the only suitable-sounding footwork skill in his price range, and he'd discovered that he lacked maneuverability in combat.

He wasn't exactly slow, but he suspected that his high stats were underutilized when moving around. Maybe it was because his Dao let him punch too well, or because his Fistfighting skill was geared toward mostly stationary combat. Either way, his movement abilities were lacking.

He wanted to be faster, and Dance Stomp Footwork seemed perfect.

Stomp Dance Footwork: Use precise stomps to explosively move around the battlefield. Well-suited for strength-oriented builds.

All in all, after removing the experience ball from his list, he ended up with the following:

Advanced Information Package – 3,000 credits
Earth-387's Major Factions – 1,000 credits
Dungeon Locations (small) – 2,000 credits
Stomp Dance Footwork Skill – 4,000 credits

Together, they came up to ten thousand credits. He only had six.

"Hey, Ar'Tazul," he said. "Give me a discount."

"Impossible," Ar'Tazul declined outright.

"Come on. You said the two of us will have to work together in the future, right? If you do me this favor, I'll forgive you for selling out the professor."

"I didn't sell out anyone. It was only business—as it will be when I spread information about your item, if you don't buy the thousand-credit confidentiality term. That is already a favor to you. Some people would pay in the high five-digits for that information, even on *this* planet."

"Then, why don't you sell it to them?"

"Because I can't reach the D-Grade without taking risks." Ar'Tazul shrugged. "Regardless... show me the items you want. Maybe I can help you work things out."

Jack narrowed his eyes, then told the merchant what he wanted to buy. All of them were important, so any discount would go a long way. Plus, he'd forgotten about the confidentiality term, so that was an extra thousand he lacked.

"Hmm." Ar'Tazul mulled it over. "Given your budget, I'd recommend the advanced information package first. Your older friend—"

"Mother."

"—your mother bought the basic one, but that's not enough to run a faction or follow the right path to power. The information inside will help you and your followers avoid many pitfalls when cultivating."

"I see." Ar'Tazul's assessment sounded reasonable.

"I'd also recommend skipping the dungeon locations. The small variant covers only a few hundred square miles around us, and dungeons are quite rare overall. Since you conquered the Forest of the Strong, the surrounding area is probably empty."

Jack narrowed his eyes. "How do you know about that?"

"I'm an information merchant. I know many things. Plus, you don't need dungeons to level in the F-Grade. There are many dangerous beasts roaming the land. If you set your mind to it, you could get three, maybe four levels by the Integration Tournament."

At his current power, three of four levels wouldn't make much of a difference. "Go on."

"You can also skip the information on Earth's powerful factions for now. These things only depict the situation the moment you buy it. It's better to wait a week and get it shortly before the Integration Tournament. Unless you're afraid of strong enemies nearby, of course, but there aren't any. You can relax for now."

Jack raised his brows. Ar'Tazul didn't have to give him that information. Suddenly, the little blue merchant seemed slightly more pleasant to the eye—unless he was lying, of course.

"Removing the dungeon locations and the faction guide, that drops your total to seven thousand. You're still one short."

"And that's where the discount comes in?"

"No." Ar'Tazul smiled. "But, let's see... What made you choose the Stomp Dance Footwork skill?"

"It's cheap, shores up one of my weaknesses, and sounds suitable for me."

"That skill focuses on explosive movement based on stomping the ground. It is suited for you, as you said, but it's mostly an offensive movement skill. It lets you move fast and explosively in straight, predictable lines. *That's* why it's cheap. It can play to your strengths, but if you're looking to be more versatile, it's not for you."

"Oh..." Jack replied. "So, I shouldn't get it."

"Depends, of course, but probably not. However, I have another skill in that price range to recommend."

"Really? I didn't see any."

"That's because it's not in the catalog."

Ar'Tazul smirked, then looked into space. A blue screen popped up in front of Jack. Jack looked at it, then at Ar'Tazul's grinning face, then back at the screen. His eyes widened.

"You have got to be kidding me."

CHAPTER THIRTY-EIGHT
PARKOUR!

A BLUE SCREEN APPEARED IN JACK'S FACE—THE SKILL RECOMMENDED BY Ar'Tazul, the one that wasn't even in the catalog.

Parkour Skill – 3,000 credits

Parkour: A mix of finesse and bodily strength can allow you to navigate obstacles efficiently, have better control of your body, and move unpredictably.

"It's a skill formed from information we found on this planet," Ar'Tazul replied. "It's not properly tested yet, so there might be *some* deficiencies, but it should last you through the F-Grade. The lack of testing makes it cheap. I can let you have it for three thousand."

"But it's parkour."

"I am not aware of the name's cultural implications. I just know it's a movement skill and your current best bet. You might be able to gather a couple thousand credits before the Tournament if you work hard, but you won't be able to get a good movement skill."

"I guess..." Jack considered it. Parkour's description sounded simple, even suitable, and Ar'Tazul recommended it. After all the free information he'd just given, Jack was inclined to trust him on this, though his general motives remained doubtful. After all, he wouldn't get anything if he lied to Jack here.

"Okay. Then, let's leave Earth's powerful factions for later. I'll gather some cash till then. I'll buy the advanced information package and the Parkour skill. This brings us to six thousand, right?"

"Seven, including the confidentiality term for the coin." Ar'Tazul grinned. "And *that's* where the discount comes in."

Jack couldn't help but laugh. "You sneaky bastard. Fine. Deal."

Ar'Tazul smiled widely and shook his hand. "Always a pleasure, Jack. Come back for more!"

After watching his credits drain away to 0, Jack got two information crystals. One of them was filled with a ton of information he didn't want to go through at the moment. The other held nothing—but the moment he asked about it, the crystal broke into pieces.

"Wha—"

Something entered his head, grabbed his synapses, and moved them around, then carved information into his muscle memory. It was the most invasive, violating thing he'd ever felt. And then it was over.

From one moment to the next, Jack knew how to parkour.

Congratulations! New Skill unlocked:
Parkour (I): A mix of finesse and bodily strength can allow you to navigate obstacles efficiently, have better control of your body, and move unpredictably.

He shook his head. No matter how many times he experienced it, this feeling remained disorienting.

"Have fun, Jack!" Ar'Tazul waved him off cheerfully.

Jack looked at his hands, then a nearby rooftop. He turned to Edgar. "I'll be back soon. Take care of the others."

"Will do."

Jack burst into a sprint. The crowd parted amidst shouts, but he ignored them. When he approached the street, he pushed hard against the ground and shot up with more force than any pre-System human had ever achieved.

He grabbed the ledge of a rooftop and let himself roll on it, then burst into a sprint without breaking pace. He jumped over gaps. He stepped against vertical walls and flew around columns. The wind buffeted his face, and the finesse required only accentuated the joy of speed.

Pre-System, he'd seen some Red Cow events where people parkoured on the rooftops of Greek islands, but it was nothing like this. Those athletes were much better than Jack, but they were limited by their pre-System bodies. How much strength could they have had? Ten? Twenty? Jack had close to a hundred.

Under his sure feet and smart hands, the town became a playground. He jumped, rolled, twisted, and jumped again. He even performed tricks. All the while, he grinned. This was great fun.

The people below stared at him as he passed overhead. Their mouths hung open. His speed was such that they weren't even sure what they were seeing.

"Is that a bird?" asked a man.

"Is it a plane?" asked a woman.

"No!" replied another man. "It's—"

His response was lost to the wind as Jack sped past. He laughed. Children looked at him starstruck, and he even saw teenagers mutter breathless *wows*.

As he got used to the movement, he sped up. The skill became more and more integrated into him until they became a seamless existence. Jack was in control.

In truth, the first tier of Parkour wasn't enough to control his current strength. He misstepped at times and landed awkwardly at others. He could barely react as he practically flew over the rooftops, but even that was orders of magnitude better than simply running like normal.

Moreover, as time passed, Jack realized with glee that Parkour was helping him deal with another problem: his increased control over his body.

The last upgrade of his Fistfighting skill had expanded his conscious control of his body. He could now perceive and control an extra layer of mental processes, allowing him to finetune his bodily responses to any given situation. On one hand, it was great.

On the other, there was a reason humans didn't have conscious control over their entire bodies. It brought a sharp spike in difficulty, even when it came to simple things like throwing a punch. He'd lost a degree of automation. The only reason he could fight now was that he'd spent an entire day practicing in the forest, and even then, his performance was lacking. That was why he'd struggled a bit against Henry White, who should have been an easy opponent.

This difficulty was a big part of why he felt his stats were underutilized. Because they were.

Parkour required fine control over the user's body. Therefore, on acquiring the skill, Jack had gained a tool to help him master this new body of his. He was slowly getting used to it. With practice, he could regain his previous level of control, and then...

Then, he would become a beast.

Rooftops flew under him as he approached the western part of Valville. Seeing the town like this was a unique experience. He noticed things he never had before, though he'd walked these streets a hundred times. Broken crates in dark alleys; a tavern's backdoor; a dead-end he'd never followed; a house yard connecting two streets that anyone could cross; a closed yard between two apartment buildings.

All those tidbits of neighborhood knowledge would have come in handy as a kid. Not now, of course, but it was nice to fill up his gaps, even late.

The cramped houses gave way to spacious yards. Parkouring became more difficult, and Jack almost jumped on an overhead electricity wire before remembering he wasn't stupid.

Eventually, the professor's house came into view. Jack leaped from his current rooftop, landed on the side of a telephone pole, pushed hard against it to shoot away, then landed with a perfect roll on her lawn. Belatedly, he realized his roll put him close to the corpse of Hugo, that Slavic hitman who didn't know his own good. At least he didn't land *on* the corpse.

People had searched it, of course. Any credits there were gone.

Even more belatedly, Jack realized he was covered in blood and grime. That may have been why the crowd in the square had kept their distance, but he'd grown so used to being like this that he hadn't noticed.

I can't enter the house like I was just born.

He went to the green hose by the corner and washed himself clean —halfway decent. Realizing how bad he probably stank, though he couldn't smell himself, Jack decided to only have a quick chat with the professor before visiting his own house and giving himself the hard-scrubbing shower he desperately needed.

Letting himself dry a bit, he went inside and straight down to the basement. When he rang the doorbell by the heavy metal door, nothing happened—power was out. He hadn't seen a single electrical device operating since he entered Valville, except for the hotel, where Henry's alarms had gone off when searching his room.

Really. Was I blind on the way in?

Unfortunately, the bunker's backup power generator wasn't connected to the doorbell—an oversight his father always brought up but never got fixed.

Out of options, he simply used his fist to knock on the bunker door.

"Who is it?" a voice came from the other side, muffled by many inches of metal.

"It's Jack!" he shouted back. "You can come out now! I beat Henry's Fang!"

"What's Eric's favorite book?" asked the voice.

Jack chuckled. The professor was as sharp as ever. "Highly Probable: An Introduction to Statistics!" he shouted back. "By himself!"

Creaking noises came from behind the door. Hydraulic levers groaned as the metal opened to reveal a dark, candle-lit room, and a monkey that was already flying toward Jack.

"Oof!" he exclaimed, catching Brock in the chest. "Easy, boy. I'm here."

"Thank God you're back," Professor Margaret Rust said as she walked out of the vault. "Your little friend wouldn't stop running around and doing push-ups. He almost drove me crazy."

"Yeah, Brock is full of energy. You should have seen him trying to attack me when we first met." Jack smiled, scratching the little brorilla's head. Brock enjoyed it for a moment, then shook his head to dislodge Jack's hand.

"What happened, Jack?" the professor asked.

"Nothing much. I just annihilated Henry White and his two classed allies, then had some dealings with that merchant."

"The alien one?"

"Yes. He didn't sell you out, by the way, did he?"

The professor shook her head. "He didn't help me, either, but it was my fault for getting greedy and neglecting the confidentiality term."

"He helped me out with some financial stuff. He isn't necessarily a nice guy, but he's smart enough to get on my good side for now. Unless he betrays us, of course, but you know how those things work."

"Of course. Did you really beat them all yourself?" Her gaze was filled with doubt. "I thought you'd die."

Jack flinched. Now that he took a closer look, there were wet grooves on her wrinkled cheeks. Putting Brock on his shoulder, he drew her into a hug.

"I'm fine," he assured her. "Just a bit—Oh, crap!"

He quickly let go and stepped back, remembering that he was still filthy. She laughed.

"It's alright, Jack."

He scratched his head. "I beat Henry's Fang, anyway. Not quite alone. There was an Edgar fellow helping me out. Good guy. A wizard. Then, I declared this town the territory of my guild, recruited some trustworthy-looking people, and came here to let you out."

"I see," she replied with an amused smile. "Does that make you our new mayor?"

"No. That's you."

"Excuse me?"

"I said, *you* are the mayor. I have no desire to manage a town or a faction. How about I make you the vice-leader? You'll have authority over everything, and you'll be able to use that bright head of yours to help the people of Valville. I think you're the best person for the job."

"You want to make me the general manager?"

"Yes."

Her eyes narrowed, and she stayed impeccably still. Jack knew this stance. This was her reaction when receiving a lot of information at once. Right now, her mind was pulling everything apart at incredible speeds, analyzing and understanding the situation.

It took her only a few seconds to consider her options.

"Fine," she replied. "I can do that. You go fight monsters without a care in the world. I'll handle everything else."

"That's gre—"

"But!" she cut him off. "Under one condition."

"What?"

"You must do what I say. I have decades of experience leading complex research teams, so if I'm running an entire town, I don't want a novice doctor of biology at my feet."

"Almost doctor," Jack muttered. "But yeah, that's fine. I trust you."

"Good. Then, we have a deal."

Jack smiled. "System, invite the professor to my faction, and give her the rank of faction vice-leader."

She accepted the invite, but the role he tried to give her apparently didn't exist. "Well, what ranks are there?" he asked in irritation.

Available ranks:
Leader: Jack Rust
Supervisor: -

"Just leader and supervisor? Nothing else? Seems terribly inconvenient."

"Not really," the professor disagreed. "The System generally takes a hands-off approach. Most things are arranged by people. For example, you can just name someone your vice-leader, you don't need System approval. The supervisor role is probably there to let people access some faction-related System screens."

"I see. Then, System, appoint Margaret Rust as faction supervisor."

The moment he said it, it was done.

"Very well. I will explore the available screens and handle everything. Can you also tell me what exactly happened with Henry's Fang?"

Jack's exhaustion was starting to creep up on him. Too many things had happened in too short a time span.

"Yes... Just, give me a moment, please."

He walked back to the living room and took a seat on the floor—no sense in ruining the furniture with his lingering filth. With that amused smile still on her face, the professor followed.

After a moment of rest, Jack spent the next few minutes filling her in with the specifics of his town adventure. In the end, Professor Margaret had all the information she needed to get to work.

"I think I get the idea," she said. "You can leave everything to me."

"Great! Have this, too," he said, handing her the crystal containing the advanced information package. "You can read it first. I'll take it after you're done. You'll be faster than me, anyway."

"Okay."

"Plus, I need to take a shower. I'll get going now. I think that's all."

"Yes. And Jack..." the professor hesitated. "I know you're strong, but you really should be more careful. Valville is just one small town. There are many strong people on Earth, like Gan Salin that Henry White mentioned. I haven't heard of him before, but he's undoubtably fearsome."

"Don't worry. I know my limits. I'll be careful," Jack reassured her. "And if Gan Salin holds a grudge against me when we meet, either now or in the Integration Tournament... I will gladly kick his ass."

She cracked a smile. "You've changed."

"We all have. Let's go, Brock. See you around, Professor."

CHAPTER THIRTY-NINE
ROOFTOP BEER

JACK LAY AGAINST THE COOL ROOF TILES, HANDS CROSSED BEHIND HIS HEAD. Brock rested by his side, his little chest rising and falling as he took gentle breaths. He was copying Jack's posture.

Jack's gaze was lost above.

The sky had been different since the System arrived. The pollution had been cleared, revealing an expanse full of stars. Twinkling dots of all sizes filled the dark dome, a masterpiece of unprecedented beauty. Some stars were condensed in a long, snaking river that reached from one end of the sky to another—the galaxy.

Is this what the people of old saw? he wondered, letting himself be lost in the breathtaking beauty. *Wow...*

He imagined going to sleep every night under this sight. How had modern humans managed to lose such beauty?

In a way, the System had turned back time for Earth. The sky was clear again. People were walking around with swords and primal hearts. All satellites had been disabled, according to the professor, returning the planet to an age where communication and transportation were difficult. Monsters roamed the countryside, bringing back the risk in venturing outside town walls—Valville's were already in construction.

The world was full of mysteries, and an entire new frontier—space—was open for exploration.

Despite the danger and death this new world provided, Jack loved it. It was like a dystopian illusion had been pulled off his eyes, revealing a world as it was meant to be, and it was *beautiful.*

He took a deep breath, enjoying the clean air.

"God," he whispered with stars reflected in his eyes, "thank you..." He wasn't religious, but seeing the sky like this, he could understand why people were.

His thoughts wandered, and they were only interrupted when a beer can floated shakily over the rooftop. Jack looked at it, then did a double take. It was just floating there, before his hand, as if begging him to reach out.

He did. The can was cool to the touch. Magic.

"Edgar, is that you?"

"No," came Edgar's voice.

"Okay."

He waited a few moments, enjoying the silence.

"Can you help me up?" the wizard called out from below. "I can't fly yet."

Jack chuckled at the last word. Letting his beer rest at the side—Brock grabbed and shook it curiously, then tossed it two streets away and laughed in monkey. Jack fell off the rooftop, grabbed Edgar in a princess-carry, and jumped back up.

"There," he said, dropping him on the roof tiles. "Also, Brock, don't do that. You could hurt someone."

"Woah! Thanks."

Edgar's laughter contained excitement. He wore loose cyan clothes—wizard robes, Jack noted—but, instead of a wand, he held another beer can.

Jack motioned at it, saying, "Can you at least open that yourself or should I do it for you?"

"Of course. I'm a wizard, not a baby."

"Don't say that. If you eat your nails, opening cans can be a struggle." He chuckled. "Thanks for the beer, man."

"No problem."

Brock inspected Edgar closely, reached as if to poke his glasses, then huddled closer to Jack and stared at the wizard suspiciously. Both men laughed.

Jack lay back down on the roof tiles, and Edgar lay beside him, fishing another beer from inside his robe and giving it to Jack. Both men opened their beers at the same time, then cheered as they took the first cool sip.

"That's Brock, right? He's cute," Edgar said.

Brock protested fiercely. He was a *warrior*, not cute!

"He is a cute warrior," Jack corrected. "How did you find me?"

"It's a rooftop, Jack. People can see you from the surrounding streets. It's just that nobody else dares approach you."

"Am I that scary?"

"Yeah. There are also members of the Brotherhood keeping everyone at bay."

Jack chuckled. "I'll be more discreet next time. Didn't want to burden you guys."

"Nah. Just do whatever you want."

They took another sip, then rested in silence. It was odd. Jack had known this guy for, what, a few hours? He knew absolutely nothing about him. Yet, drinking beside him was nice, like they were old friends.

It prompted Jack to think about what his friends were doing. Though he'd grown up in Valville, he'd met all his current friends at the university, so none of them lived here. They used to meet at least twice a week in Tahlequah.

They were probably fine. Those guys were smart. They could handle themselves—especially Maria.

He refocused on the present.

"What's your Dao Root, Edgar?" he asked.

"I don't have one yet. But check this out."

Edgar reached inside his robes and retrieved a Dao Fruit, but it wasn't the one they'd found in Henry White's room. This fruit was cyan, sparkling, and almost transparent, giving off a translucent, ethereal feel. As Edgar held it in his palm, Jack found it as mesmerizing as the starry night sky.

"Magic," he whispered.

"Exactly," Edgar gushed. "The Dao Fruit of Magic. Interesting, isn't it? That there's a Dao Fruit for that. I thought I'd have to get one for imagination, or maybe willpower."

"I thought Ar'Tazul wouldn't let you exchange for free."

"Heh. He changed his tune after you left. Let me borrow the missing thousand credits if I promised to pay him back before the Tournament."

"Oh no," Jack paled. "At what interest rate?"

"Ten percent."

"Oh. That's decent."

"It shoots up to 100 percent if I can't deliver it in time." Edgar laughed. "Merchants are not fun folks, Jack."

"Ar'Tazul is into that business too, huh?" he responded, eyes darkening a bit. "I'll have a chat with him tomorrow."

"They all are. Just don't pay back my debt. I can handle it."

"I know."

"I think Ar'Tazul is okay, though. Slightly more cutthroat than I would like, but a decent person overall."

Jack shrugged, not taking a stance yet.

"So yeah, I hope to get the Dao Root of Magic." Edgar's eyes lowered to the fruit, lost in its etherealness. "It's amazing, man. That magic is real. It was never fake. The owl just came for our entire planet at once."

"Owl?"

"You know, the owl. The one that brings kids letters saying they've been accepted into a magic school and can leave their shitty lives behind."

"Ohhh, that owl." Jack cupped his chin. "I noticed your skills were named weirdly. Yeetus Fierus, Shieldus, Fierus Whippus..."

"Those aren't skill names. I made them up. Just sounds like magic, you know?"

Jack laughed. "Not to me, but what can I say? I'm no wizard."

"That's for sure."

"Do you know I've always wanted to learn magic, too?" Jack said, and Edgar's eyes opened wide.

"I see," he responded. "That's why you became a boxer."

"That was necessity. I didn't have much choice when a goblin spawned in my face. Then, things just sort of rolled to their current state."

"The first kill bonus?"

"Yeah. But I like my path. It's... completely unlike anything I imagined. The violence is so releasing, so cathartic. I spent half my life mocking the people who weren't intellectuals, but guess what: they had a point."

"Everyone does."

"What about you? Did you always dream of becoming a wizard?"

"Every single day of my life." Edgar drew a deep gulp, then looked at the sky as he struggled to swallow. "You know those books? The ones with the owl letter magic school?"

"Duh."

"Of course. Everyone does. Do you know why? Do you know what part of that book sells? It's exactly that: the owl."

Jack frowned. "I'm not following."

"It's a dream." Edgar sighed. "Deep in their hearts, every child and teenager wishes an owl would come and magically change their lives without any effort. That they could get rid of bad parents, boring school, shitty friends, insecurities, a scary future, everything, and go become wizards with nice friends at a cool school."

Jack considered it. "I guess you're right. I've fantasized about that before."

"Everyone has. All children more or less identified. Me too... more than most... My uh, my parents were bad people. My school sucked. I only had half a friend. I was bullied a bit—childish things, thinking back, but they were a big deal then. And I couldn't escape. I was trapped in hell. Can you imagine how hard I hoped for my magic owl to come? That my letter had been lost on the way, and they'd eventually discover it?"

Jack thought back to his own life. It hadn't been lain with roses, but not bad, either.

"No," he replied honestly.

"Maybe that's for the best. I dreamt about it every night." Edgar shrugged. "Anyway, I escaped hell, eventually. I cut ties with my parents the moment I got my first job and never saw them again until Henry's Fang paraded their heads in Valville Square."

"That's, wow..."

"Yeah. I mean, I didn't like them, but it was still rough." He shrugged again. Jack noticed that his beak-like nose didn't fit a reminiscing man. "Anyway, I don't remember where I was going with all this. The point is, I had a sharp imagination and hard discipline. When a goblin appeared in my basement apartment, I used deodorant and a lighter to set it on fire, getting my first kill bonus in the form of the fireball skill. I *finally* had the chance to live out my fantasies. But, how funny that the owl came ten years too late. I'd already put in the effort to escape, goddammit. What a waste."

"No wonder people use e-mail nowadays."

Edgar looked over in surprise, then chuckled. "I suppose so... Anyway, that's the story of how I became a wizard. Then I figured that, oh well, since I'm here, might as well go all the way and become a *strong* wizard. The strongest. Then, I'll create a magic academy for children with bad families. Maybe I'll name myself Dumblewindow, too."

"That's a nice dream."

"Yeah. Childhood me is finally happy inside."

"Is he really?"

"I think so."

"Then, that's good."

"What about you, Jack? What are you going to do with all this power?"

"Punch stuff, I guess." Jack laughed. "To be precise, I will punch progressively stronger stuff progressively harder. Sounds like a fun occupation."

"Ah, yes. Very noble."

"They'll be bad stuff, too. I'm a good guy."

"Then, that's something I can get behind." Edgar smiled. "You could make a boxing academy."

"I'm a Pugilist, not a boxer."

"Is there a difference?"

"Yeah. Fewer rules."

"Neat."

Jack drew a large gulp from his can, tilting it higher up and realizing it was empty in the process. “Shit,” he said. Edgar laughed. Drinking the last of his beer, too, he raised a hand, and two more beer cans floated up from the streets below.

Jack was puzzled. “What?” He looked over the edge, finding a crate of beer below. He turned to Edgar. “That wasn’t there before.”

The wizard shrugged. “Magic.”

Both men laughed, then grabbed their cans and kept drinking.

“By the way,” asked Edgar, “did you climb this house on purpose, or was it random?”

“Completely random. Why?”

“There was a very confused old lady looking at me through the window before. I waved at her, then someone dropped from the roof, picked me up, and flew away.”

“Of course. That’s regular stuff now. Maybe we should invite her for a beer, too.”

“I don’t think old ladies like rooftops, Jack.”

“How do you know?”

As if on cue, the sound of a broomstick hitting the roof from below reached their ears. “Go sit on another house!” the old lady shouted. Both men laughed. She probably wouldn’t join, but oh well. Her loss.

CHAPTER FORTY

ALIEN OVERLORDS ARE NOT VERY FUN

The next morning found Jack refreshed. He'd been high-strung for a long time, and desperately needed some time to unwind. With any luck, the next few days would hide no surprises... and then would come the Integration Tournament.

Jack's eyes sharpened in anticipation. Until then, he would try to level up, understand more things about the System's world, work on his Dao, and train with his new body. The Pugilist Body (II) upgrade had given him increased control over everything, which would be good in the long run, but made everything a bitch right now. It would take practice.

For today, his first order of business was to visit the professor. He'd entrusted her with combing the faction screens for information and generally organizing the faction, and he was curious to see what she'd achieved.

He exited his house—a simple first-story apartment in downtown Valville that had luckily escaped the apocalypse—wondering at how foreign it now seemed. Like it wasn't his. Sure, he knew where the cutlery was and how to properly close the leaking window, but everything now felt like a washed-out memory.

The white walls, the cozy desk, the single bed, and narrow balcony where only a single chair could fit... It was his house, sure, but it'd become a reminder of a previous world. His problems had gone from a leaking window to fighting bears bare-handed.

Perhaps it was a remnant of the past. Perhaps it reminded him of a life he now knew he hated—though it wasn't as clear back then. Complacency was an insidious killer.

Whatever the case, Jack didn't feel like staying home any longer. He would only return to sleep, if even that.

He took a deep breath of the clean air that made him feel alive, then headed west.

This time, he chose to walk through the town instead of fly over it, curious as to what people's reaction would be. Most looked at him with awe, but they made way before him and didn't dare meet his eye. Jack felt like a conqueror—a nice though disturbing feeling.

"No, wait, I'm one of you," he said, to no avail. Sometime later, he got annoyed, changed his mind, and parkoured over rooftops. Brock was holding on tight to his shoulders, screaming in joy and enjoying the high-speed ride that resembled an amusement park's. Jack smiled at the thought.

There were still groups heading in and out of town—monster hunters—but at least they seemed better organized now. Each group was smaller, three to five people, and had a single handgun just in case. The professor was already at work.

Marveling at her efficiency, Jack reached her house, let Brock down —the poor monkey wanted to go another round—and knocked.

"Come in!" came a voice. Jack opened the door and found himself facing a small group of wide-eyed people.

"Hello. I'm Jack."

"We know," a middle-aged woman in a ponytail replied. "We're part of your faction."

"Oh. Okay. I suppose you're the professor's assistants."

"That's right."

"Can you take me to her?"

"Of course. Follow me," replied the same woman, smiling at Brock before turning away. "My name is Emilia Rogers, by the way. A pleasure to make your acquaintance."

"Likewise. Are you from the university?"

"All of us have worked with Professor Rust at one point or another, and we also happened to live in Valville—recruiting from other towns is still difficult."

"I see. So she brought all her nearby associates onboard?"

"Not everyone. Some didn't make it through the Integration, some were away on business, and others..." She shook her head. "They just weren't invited."

Bad apples. She took the opportunity to clean house, Jack thought, approving of the decision.

While chatting, Emilia led Jack through familiar rooms and into the living room, where the professor lounged on her armchair, staring into space. Her hands were busy scribbling on a piece of paper. Brock ran to her feet and held out a hand.

"Professor," Emilia said respectfully. "Jack Rust is here to see you."

"Jack?" Joy lit up in her face. "One moment, please."

Half a minute later, her eyes refocused. She shook Brock's hand with a smirk, and hugged Jack. "Hello, Jack."

"Hello, Mom." Before he could say anything else, Professor Margaret pulled away and entered business mode.

"Come with me. I have discovered some incredible things. You have to see this. Thank you, Emilia."

The woman bowed lightly and left the room.

"Well, I'm here," said Jack, taking a seat on the sofa. "What do you got?"

"First, open your faction screen."

Jack obliged. *Faction.*

Faction: Bare Fist Brotherhood (F-Grade)
Leader: Jack Rust
Members: 25
Capital: Milky Way galaxy, Milky Way sector, Animal Kingdom constellation, Earth-387 planet, Forest of the Strong dungeon area.

...

And then came a bunch of things Jack tuned off.

"No," the professor said, "read those too."

He grumbled, then kept reading.

Resource Management
Contracted Monsters
Alignment
Topographical Description
Hierarchy
Buildings
Portals
Relations
Members

He'd seen these things before, having promptly ignored them. Each was split into a dozen sub-menus, and he always had better things to do.

"You know I dislike management, Professor."

"I do know, unfortunately. You don't need to go deeper. I've kept notes on the important parts. Pay attention."

With a sigh of relief, Jack focused. Professor Margaret detailed her findings, occasionally looking over her notebook for directions. Jack noticed it was titled 'Faction Management for Dummies.' He scowled.

"First, I've noticed an interesting segregation of power," the professor began. "The System handles some things: it knows our members, any areas under our control, contracted monsters, and specific types of buildings. However, most of a faction's running falls to us. The System won't streamline our hierarchy, rewards for contribution, job assignment, menial work, border surveillance, justice system, and other things. Maybe it's different for higher-ranked factions, but at least for us, the approach it takes is very hands-off."

"But I see a hierarchy tab right there," Jack noted.

"Open it up."

He did.

Leader: Jack Rust (F-Grade), Pugilist – Planetary Frontrunner (10)
Supervisor: Margaret Rust (F-Grade)

That was all. "Okay. No streamlined hierarchy."

"Exactly. I assume more roles will open up as we advance, but for now, we definitely need more divisions than that, and we'll have to do it the old-fashioned way. Not that I mind. Old people like me love the old-fashioned way."

"Right."

"However, there is one thing you should know. See the Buildings tab? And the Portals one?"

"I do."

"Those are science-fiction. Literally. From what I discovered, we can spend credits to make the System spawn buildings out of thin air."

Jack raised a brow. "What kind of buildings?"

"Not too many. As I said, it's generally hands-off. From what I understand, the purpose of this functionality is to eliminate barriers that might be caused by an Integrated planet's low technological level or otherwise difficult conditions. It keeps the ground at least somewhat even."

Not too many, was all Jack heard. He opened the menu, groaned, and closed it again.

"There's *hundreds* of them," he said.

"Try filtering by price. See everything under or at a hundred thousand credits."

"I can filter? How?"

"Just think of it."

He frowned, then tried again. Indeed, the System now gave him only three options.

Energy Wall: 10,000 credits per mile. Creates a shimmering, transparent, incorporeal wall that releases a flare and loud noise on touch. Upkeep: 10 credits per hour, 1 credit per touch.
100-mile Portal: 100,000 credits. A teleportation portal that can connect up to 100 miles away.
Personal Starship: 100,000 credits. A vehicle that uses the Dao to propel itself. It can fit up to three people and can freely traverse space at 3000 miles/hour. Upkeep: 10 credits per hour.

"Wow."

"That's what I said," she agreed. "Teleportation and space travel at the tips of our fingers. I can see why the merchant only gave me five hundred credits for my knowledge in cyber security: it's useless."

"Yeah... So, should we build any of these?"

"Not immediately. First of all, we lack the funds. Second, let's not invite trouble on our heads. Anything could pop out of a teleportation portal—I don't know how they work. And what would we even do with a starship?"

"Go to space?"

"Of course. Tourism is more important than the Integration Tournament."

Jack's eyes widened. "Did you call going to space tourism?"

"We're part of an intergalactic network now, Jack. Space is to the System what the sea was to our planet. Not to mention we might be under critical danger."

"What kind of danger?"

"I have no idea!" She threw her hands in the air. "Even the advanced information package you gave me says nothing concrete. However, there are two critical events in a newly-Integrated planet's life. The first is the Integration Tournament, where the best of the best are given a massive extra push. It's what creates the future elites. The second critical event is the end of our grace period."

"Which you're about to explain."

"Yes, if you'd stop interrupting. Every planet is given a grace period which lasts about five hundred galactic days—that's around a year in Earth time. 370.5 days, to be precise. Before that time, aliens cannot enter Earth. We do not have to pay taxes, follow their laws, or submit ourselves to anything. We basically get free rein so we can adapt and grow reasonably strong. The only exceptions to that are merchants, non-combative administrative personnel for the Integration Tournament, and a single C-Grade Planetary Overseer."

Jack's eyes snapped to focus. "C-Grade?"

"Yes. They aren't allowed to intervene in anything except events that threaten the integrity of our planet or population. They basically make sure nothing terrible happens while we're alone, like a widespread plague, a full-blown monster outbreak, or space pirates invading us."

Jack's eyes widened further. "Space pirates!"

"That's beside the point. The issue is that, after the one year is over, things go south fast in a bad way. We have to pay heavy taxes, surrender our freedom, and be submitted to the whims of our alien overlords with minimal self-governing. The information package says the Animal Kingdom are generous overlords, but... I don't trust that one bit. Even the wording is awful: *generous overlords*."

"Yeah. That sucks."

"It does."

"What can we do about it?"

"Nothing, basically. Your best bet is to get strong enough to be accepted into the Animal Kingdom faction, the overlords of our constellation, as a disciple. That should make Earth's situation better, especially for our faction."

"I see... So, aliens are bad news."

"Aliens are bad news," she agreed with a nod.

"I don't know, Professor... This all sounds a bit negative to me."

"Did you expect an alien invasion to be fun?"

"I expected the System to be fair. So far, danger has coexisted with opportunity. If overpowered alien overlords just show up after a year and suppress us, there isn't much we can do, is there?"

"No, there isn't. There's little to no chance of anyone reaching the D-Grade in a year, let alone the C-Grade, as the Planet Kings usually are. We'll be doomed to subservience until one of our natives reaches the C-Grade and chooses to take over our planet, but... that is also a form of balance. We won't be slaves, just temporarily shoved to a lower position. It isn't ideal, obviously, but it isn't entirely unfair either."

Jack opened his mouth to say something, then thought better about it. The professor always knew what she was speaking about. Hastily arguing against her was foolish.

"It is fair, I guess. It just doesn't work well for us."

"It will for our children—well, yours—who will be the old ones at another new planet's Integration." The professor smiled. "Cheer up,

Jack. It's not that bad—and, most importantly, there's nothing we can do about it."

"Yeah..."

Jack scoffed. That someone would come rule them sounded ugly after all the newfound liberty he experienced. Yet it made sense, no matter how he turned it. It was natural. They would destroy the freedom he so enjoyed, though he understood the need for order, and the stronger and more experienced would naturally rule. So, why did he feel unsatisfied?

Because a fist is ruled by no one. The thought came unbridled to his mind, rising from its deepest depths. Jack enjoyed the thought but didn't entertain it. He was a warrior, not a fool—and if his path was a bit extreme, he wasn't obligated to follow it.

His Dao Root protested, and he scolded it. Even the strongest warrior must know when to yield. Especially when I can do nothing about it. Maybe the Animal Kingdom, or whatever they're called, are nice people.

No matter how he pushed, he still disliked the idea. *What if you* could *do something about it?* his Dao insisted, excited at the prospect. He frowned deeper.

Whatever.

"Jack?" the professor said. "Are you okay?"

"Yeah. I'm fine. Just considering things, that's all."

"Hmm."

"So, is that all?"

"For now. I'm still looking at things, but—Oh, yes. What are these" —she squinted—"gymonkeys and brorillas I see in the Contracted Monsters section? Brock's pack, I assume, but I need more details. And who's Harambe?"

"Just a friend," Jack said, his mood instantly taking a turn for the better. *That's right. I should visit them before the Tournament.*

The professor cocked a brow. "I understand you like sounding cool, Jack, but I cannot work with 'a friend.'"

Jack laughed. "They were monsters spawned in the Forest of the Strong, the dungeon I conquered. You can probably see it in the territory tab, or whatever it's called. I became friends with them. They're the reason why I made a faction, actually; the System would just despawn them otherwise."

"Hmm." The professor's eyes glinted. "I see here that they're very strong."

"Yeah. There's twenty of them. The weakest is level 9, and the strongest, Harambe, could easily turn Henry White into mush."

"That's interesting."

"The dungeon had several useful resources, actually. We should move our faction there. It can *significantly* increase the physical stats of our members. Plus, you get the protection of the monkeys if anything happens."

"I see." Her eyes narrowed. "Is there a reason why you neglected to mention this before?"

"I didn't want to overwhelm you, Professor. Information works best bite-sized." Her eye-narrowing intensified, but Jack paid her no mind as he stood. "Anyway, got to go. I suddenly feel like training. If you want, we can grab Edgar and go visit the forest tomorrow. The monkeys will want to meet you, too."

"Alright, let's meet here at dawn."

"Sure. By the way, did you have any news about that Gan Salin? The one Henry White mentioned?"

She shook her head. "Nothing. I asked around, but nobody's heard of him—and Ar'Tazul asked for more credits than I could spare."

"I see... Well, no big deal. I guess I'll meet him in the Tournament. See you at dawn, Professor."

"See you, Jack."

He turned to leave.

"And Jack?" she said. He turned around. Her gaze was mellow. "Be careful, please."

Jack smiled widely. "I will. Let's go, Brock."

Brock, however, stayed to play with the professor—they'd developed a good relationship. He struggled and managed to lift a short table despite being short himself, then smiled smugly. The professor exclaimed in surprise.

"What a strong boy!" she said. "Can I give him some treats, Jack? I have salami in the cupboard."

"Knock yourself out," he replied with a laugh. "I'll be outside."

He headed for the door. It was still surrounded by clean glass with flowers drawn on it. Jack opened it and found a young man standing outside with his hand ready to knock.

"Oh, hello," he said politely. "Are you Jack Rust?"

Jack's eyes narrowed. This person was short, with brown eyes and hair, as well as a wiry body that seemed full of energy. He wasn't the least bit intimidated by Jack's bare-chested, barbaric appearance, and despite his relaxed attitude, something in his eyes put Jack on edge. He knew that glint. Behind those eyes hid deep-seated insanity.

"I am. Who are you?"

"Gan Salin. And I hear you took some initiative in my town."

CHAPTER FORTY-ONE
GAN SALIN

Gan Salin's gentle appearance contrasted the threat carried by his name, but only until someone noticed the mad glint in his eyes.

"It's my town, not yours," Jack said. "So, you're the famous Gan Salin. The same one who let loose Henry's Fang in Valville?"

"You know what? I like you," he said. His teeth showed more than they should, and, surprisingly, he seemed to salivate a little. He quickly scooped that up with his tongue. "Yes, Henry's Fang was one of my satellite factions, but that's not important. They were pretty weak. You, on the other hand, are strong. We could use an ally like you in the Tournament."

Belatedly, Jack realized he'd forgotten to inspect this person.

Canine (Earth-387), Level 30
Faction: -
Title: Planetary Frontrunner (10)

Oh, shit.

He reviewed his own status to make sure he wasn't misremembering his title. Sure enough, he hadn't.

What luck. There were only ten people on the entire planet with that title, and Jack managed to stumble upon one of them. Though that did make Jack wonder... Could everyone see Jack's title?

On the other hand, he should have known. The bald man in his Dao Vision also had a visible title.

And what the hell was a canine? This guy looked like a human, just with messy facial hair—like a hairy boy entering his teens. Now that Jack took a closer look, his canines were slightly longer and sharper too, making them easily noticeable when Gan Salin opened his mouth.

"We?" Jack asked, putting titles and species aside for now. "Who's we, and why do you need allies?"

"The five scions," Gan Salin replied. "We come from the Animal Kingdom, the B-Grade faction that rules this constellation. In the Integration Tournament, we are each tasked with finding the most suitable candidates and pitting them against each other. The winner gets extra rewards. So, what do you say? Wanna fight for me?"

"Not particularly. I fight for myself. What Animal Kingdom, anyway? The System says you're from Earth. And I thought aliens weren't allowed here in the first year after the Integration."

"Technicalities." Gan Salin waved it away. "Anyway, being chosen by one of the scions is a blessing. The first benefit is that you can avoid getting killed by another scion to eliminate competition!"

He grinned nonchalantly. This was a threat, and both men knew it.

"The second benefit is that I'll help you," Gan Salin continued. "I have many resources at my disposal. Where do you think that White person found his Dao Fruit?—which I'll be taking, by the way. There are other things I can offer, too. A Dao Fruit is only the dog's tail."

The expression rolled naturally off his tongue, like it was real.

"Why should I give you the Dao Fruit?" Jack said. "You gave it to Henry White. I took it from him. It belongs to me."

"Nonsense. Come on, just say yes."

He reached for a handshake, entering Jack's personal space. Jack slapped his hand away and stared him down.

"Keep your hands to yourself," he replied coldly. "And stop ignoring me. I'm not giving you the fruit. I'm not fighting for you. You're lucky I don't kick your ass right now for unleashing a gang on my town."

Jack's words were biting. Gan Salin didn't seem to mind. His nonchalance remained.

"That's pretty bold. You understand that I'm going to kill you if you refuse, right?"

"Is that so?"

"But of course! I thought I made that clear earlier. Sorry."

"Mr. Rust!" Emilia's voice came from behind. "Is someone there?"

"Stay in the house," he barked back.

"You should be careful," Gan Salin said. Jack noticed he was salivating again. No, it wasn't saliva; it was foam. *What the fuck?* "Our levels might seem close, but a native could never match a scion. I have *decades* of experience on you. Just lay down and show me your belly, or whatever you guys do here."

Jack didn't budge.

"I see you're resolved," Gan Salin continued with a mock sigh. "Very well. It's a shame, but whatever you want. I'll give you three moves so you don't—"

Jack's fist met his face before he even finished talking. Gan Salin flew backward, then flipped midair and landed on his feet. He took Jack's blow easily.

"Wait," he said. "I'm not done posturing."

"Too bad."

Jack punched out again, closing the distance in two steps. This time, the attack wasn't hasty. It smashed into Gan Salin's crossed arms and catapulted him backward with tremendous force, sending him across the street and into an already-ruined house—probably from monster attacks.

The scion stood back up.

"You pack a punch," he said, grinning despite his pained expression. "Come on. I said three attacks. Do your worst."

Jack raised a brow. This guy had been sent flying and still insisted on keeping his word. It was rather commendable.

However, Jack didn't attack right away. He looked at his fist. That had been an all-out attack. It should have dealt more damage. No. Jack had felt the impact. It *had* dealt damage. Was Gan Salin pretending? Or was he simply enduring it?

"Fuck your three attacks," he said, looking up from his fist. "I'm not weaker than you. Fight me straight."

"Are you sure?"

"Yes."

"Very well."

"Jack?" a voice came from behind him, the professor's head poking out of the door frame. "What's going on?"

"Well, a douche—"

Gan Salin rammed into Jack with enough force to send him flying. He ripped through a wall of the house, then another, creating a see-through hole, then skipped across the street to imprint himself on another house's wall.

Jack extracted himself and leaned against the wall, spitting a bit of blood. "Motherfucker, that hurt. I thought you were honorable."

"Hey, you're the one who looked the other way," came Salin's reply as he stepped through the hole in the wall. He stood across the street from Jack, opening and closing his fists as if in warm-up. For the first time, Jack noticed his long fingernails. He also noticed five shallow, bleeding holes on his chest.

"Did you try to grab my *heart*?"

"You have strong skin." Salin nodded. "Is it a skill, or do you focus on Constitution?"

"Like I'd tell you."

"Yeah. Thank the immortals I don't really care."

Jack dusted himself off. He wasn't really hurt. "Prepare to die, dipshit."

"*Finally*, some good posturing. I'm sure we'll work together just fine after I beat you to the ground."

Jack moved sideways, repositioning himself. This way, whoever was sent flying would only sail over the street, not through houses. He pounced, rearing his fists back and preparing to pound Gan Salin like fine dough.

His opponent smirked. Darting forth to meet Jack, he drew his hand back wide, sharp fingernails gleaming. "Five-Star Grasp!" he yelled. Jack raised a brow.

Punch met nails in a heavy collision. Salin's hand was pushed back, while small holes appeared on Jack's knuckles. He struck again, nailing two jabs into Salin and following them up with a fierce straight to his face. Gan Salin didn't retreat, either. He dodged the attacks, blocked, and dealt his own.

It was peculiar. His strength was nowhere near enough to harm Jack, but every time he clawed, the strike felt unstoppable. Jack almost hesitated to meet those strikes, imbued as they were with a sense of absolute confidence. It was a sensation that reached inside Jack's soul. A Dao Root. But which one?

Gan Salin mirrored the question. "What's your Dao Root?" he asked between strikes.

"Shut up!"

"Is it Strength? Anger? Stubbornness? Or Resolve, like me?"

Jack's eyes flashed. *So that's what.*

His Dao Root and Salin's were close in meaning. His fist contained resolve. They had significant overlap, but in the end, they differed. Jack's fighting spirit flared. This wasn't only a battle of men, but also of their Daos—and he would be damned if he let himself lose.

Fine. Show me a similar Dao, and I'll pulverize it with my fists.

Gan Salin's eyes exhibited a similar resolve.

Jack punched and punched and punched. Salin dodged and slashed. The two were practically standing still, fighting at close quarters.

Heavy strikes rang out. Two steel-like bodies clashed. Arms struck like hammers. Nails whistled like blades. The street had gone silent, with only the sound of their strikes echoing.

Jack was impressed. The speed of his opponent was extraordinary. His strikes were light and cut like sharp blades, and when Jack landed the occasional punch, Gan Salin took it like a champ. Moreover, his fighting skill was nothing to scoff at. If not for Jack's great Constitution, he would have been helpless.

But he wasn't.

In fact, as they fought, Jack steadily gained the upper hand. He didn't bother dodging, so he could attack harder, and their brawl fell in his favor.

Suddenly, Gan Salin disappeared.

"Canine Dash!" came a voice from behind Jack. He barely had time to turn before Gan Salin was onto him, slashing like a wild animal. He disappeared again, running circles around Jack. He was so fast, Jack struggled to follow the movement with his eyes.

Salin zigzagged wildly, pouncing and retreating at random intervals. These attacks carried momentum, so Jack couldn't ignore them, and he was forced on the defensive. Salin circled like a demon, rendering it almost impossible for Jack to seize the initiative.

Shit! he thought, defending against an onslaught of nails. *I feel like an earth bear!*

His body was bleeding from many places, though he was still mostly fine. His regeneration closed the shallow holes almost as quickly as Gan Salin opened them. Moreover, with his clearly higher Constitution, Jack was confident he could outlast his opponent. The problem lay elsewhere.

Why the hell is he running on all fours!

"Five-Star Grasp!" Salin shouted again, turning sharply and pouncing at Jack. Jack was ready. He let the strike land and grabbed tightly onto Salin's hand, pulling him along as he sailed over the street and skipped on broken asphalt. His back slammed against a car, loosening his grip and letting Salin squirm out.

Jack groaned but recovered quickly. He pounced on Salin, raining his own blows and not letting him drop on all fours again.

"Five-Star Grasp!" Salin tried, but this time, he missed. Jack's punch met his jaw.

"Why the hell are you shouting out the names of your moves?" Jack roared as he attacked.

"That's what we're supposed to do!"

"It's fucking ridiculous!"

"Tail Swipe!" Salin's foot slithered under Jack's, knocking his feet out from below him. Jack was having none of that. Anger started to burn in his chest. Not only was this guy fighting in such an annoying fashion, he was also *mocking him*.

Even as his legs gave way, he grabbed Salin's hair and slammed him to the ground. Salin jumped back but Jack was on him again.

"And why are the names stupid as shit?"

"That's—what—they—are—called!" Salin called out between dodges, no longer able to take the hits in stride. Jack was pushing now, advancing a step every time he punched, while Gan Salin was running backward and panting. "Why aren't you shouting yours, you imbecile?"

"I—Because I'm not an idiot!"

Jack's momentum kept rising, his punches getting heavier. Despite fighting for so long, Gan Salin refused to tire. He was only panting a bit. And Jack was flying into a rage. This guy was making fun of him.

"You fucking bastard, I can shout my moves too! Punch that Breaks your Jaw! Fist that Cracks your Ribs! Jab to your Teeth!"

"Those are fak—Ugh!"

A good strike finally landed, sending Gan Salin flying into a large, upturned dumpster. Jack kicked the lid closed, lifted the dumpster, smashed it with the lid on the street, and began striking its wall. The other side of the dumpster burst open as Salin jumped out.

Jack pursued. He wasn't playing around now. The banter died down as Jack's momentum increased. He punched and punched harder, not giving Gan Salin a single moment of respite. When he tried using Canine Dash to fall on all fours and escape, Jack grabbed him by the leg and slammed him into the ground. When he tried to run away, Jack pulled his hair back and bitch-slapped the shit out of him.

Gan Salin yelped in pain. Jack was completely wiping the floor with him, not letting go of his initiative for a single moment, and Salin could only stand there and take a beating.

Finally, Salin let a punch meet his nose head-on, breaking it with a crunch and sending him flying.

"Fine!" he screamed out. "I wanted to let you live, but fuck it!" He took another punch to the gut, and this time, he didn't try to defend. "Hit harder, you fuck. Come on. Hurry the fuck up."

Something was wrong. He stared into Salin's eyes and saw the madness intensify, his irises taken over by a burning red. Reason disappeared as Gan Salin's eyes turned into an animal's.

At the same time, the Dao aura Jack had been sensing shifted. This wasn't resolve anymore. It was something else. Something wild.

Jack's eyes widened. The fuck! He has two?

He jumped back, taking in his opponent again, for real this time. The previous Dao Root of Resolve had given way to a new one, but what was it? Jack got a confusing read.

Gentle appearance, ill-timed jokes, thinly-veiled madness. Foam at the edges of his mouth. Violence only barely held at bay.

Gan Salin reminded Jack of a crazed dog.

CHAPTER FORTY-TWO

DAO OF THE WILD DOG

Jack gazed at Gan Salin, who'd just switched to using a different Dao Root than before—and, from the looks of it, this was his best one. But it came with side-effects. His reason was dwindling as madness emanated from the center of his being, filling him up to the brink.

Jack recognized the feeling, as it wasn't the first time he saw it. *Insanity... This madman has the Dao Root of Insanity!*

"You're taking too fucking long!" Gan Salin barked. The more Jack looked, the more he resembled a wild dog. "Fine! If you're not coming, I am!"

Shit.

Gan Salin shot forth at tremendous speed. Jack could barely react. Salin was upon him in an instant, clawing and biting like an animal. He had long nails and sharp teeth. The foam from his mouth was flowing like crazy, splattering on the street below them. His eyes were a deep red, and he released wild screams as he attacked.

He was a terrifying opponent.

Jack fell on the defensive. These attacks were faster and harder than the black wolf's. He didn't even have time to think, let alone fight back.

He dodged and wove between the strikes. He took a few scratches as he retreated to the side, dodging a house and breaking through a meticulously arranged garden instead, then into another house. The entire time, he moved backward.

He broke through a wall. A woman's screams reached his ears from the right. *Shit!* Jack turned to the left, taking a good blow from Salin, who fought like an absolute madman. He wasn't defending, only attacking over and over, as fast and as hard as he could.

Jack's durability was great, and Salin's attacks still weren't that strong, but they were relentless. He was a storm. The damage piled up. Jack's forearms were covered in bloody scratches. At least he was dodging those humanoid fangs.

They broke through another wall and back into the street. Jack was still retreating at top speed, barely keeping Gan Salin at bay. He needed to do something!

His primal instincts were revving up. His body was filled with strength, his mind sharpened by the fear of death. Unfortunately, these instincts were muted now. Jack was the warrior; he was the one in control of his body. He could no longer rely on the mad fervor of battle unless he created it himself.

And that's what he did.

"Enough!" he roared. He planted his feet firmly against the asphalt and let Gan Salin bite down on his left forearm, teeth tearing through muscle, to smash a fist into his abdomen with all his strength. Salin went flying over the rooftops, his teeth ripping Jack's flesh apart as he was torn away.

Jack roared again and pursued. Stomping hard on the ground, he jumped after his opponent, planting a punch midair and tossing him even higher. A couple teeth went flying, covered in foam. Salin didn't even register the damage, he just tried and failed to bite Jack's hand.

Jack was midair, waiting to land. Many people had noticed the fight, filling up the area. Screams came from everywhere, fingers were pointed his way, and people hesitated over whether to run or watch. Jack didn't care what they did. That was their problem, and the insane juggernaut was his.

His feet touched a rooftop and he instantly shot back out. Salin landed a second later, rolling once before regaining his footing, and lashed out at Jack. The two jumped over rooftops like it was nothing and crashed over a tall building, punches interweaved with scratches and bites.

One, three, ten. The strikes were coming and going, both fighters refusing to give ground.

Gan Salin was taking Jack's punches like a champ. Each attack could bring down a house, but he barely even flinched on impact. With the Dao Root of Insanity fueling him, his ability to take punishment was off the charts, and so were his speed and unpredictability. However, his claws weren't sharp enough. He lacked Strength, which let Jack endure his blows and strike back.

At the same time, Jack grimaced. As much as Gan Salin was crazy, he knew how to fight—even better than before, in fact. This was Gan Salin at his best. His strikes were tight. His defense—which he seldom used—was solid. He alternated between slow and fast attacks, straight and curved, bites and scratches, keeping Jack on his toes.

This was practiced, expert-level insanity. His body flowed from one frantic movement to the next, leaving only tiny gaps for Jack to take advantage of. Almost like he was up against a high-tier skill.

In turn, Jack let Salin's strikes land, then plugged the gaps between them with a series of fierce punches. They hit hard and true. Flesh was mangled under them, organs shaken. He was dealing damage, and the fact that Salin ignored it infuriated him.

Jack was a man of the fist. If Gan Salin wanted a battle of attrition, he would get a battle of attrition.

Jack abandoned defense and went all-out in attack. He let most strikes land to strike back, only guarding his vitals. The System gave both of them extraordinary durability. Their battle dragged on. Gan Salin was the one pushed back, and not because he was losing, but because Jack's strikes carried more momentum and often sent him flying.

They traveled over rooftops, occasionally landing on walls or the streets. One time, they found themselves in a screaming crowd, and it was only by a miracle that no one got hurt.

They were fighting at speeds the naked eye couldn't process. Most only saw a bloody blur flying past them, and the few that could understand what was happening didn't dare intervene. Jack and Gan Salin were in a league of their own.

Jack was aware of their surroundings despite his battle fervor. His mind raced. As time went on, his movements grew sharper, his strikes deadlier. He wasted less time and energy. He got optimized on the anvil that was Gan Salin.

Pugilist Body (II) had given him finer control over his body, but that was a double-edged sword. It wasn't easy to control. New aspects were added to every simple movement, temporarily working against Jack. When he adapted, it would be a great boon, but that would take time.

This battle greatly reduced said time.

Jack hadn't been in a real battle since getting the skill. Henry White's power had been fairly one-dimensional, and the fight ended very quickly. Gan Salin was a different beast. He fought hard. A real opponent.

This wasn't an easy battle. One misstep, one claw to his eye, could spell disaster. The constant threat of death hung over Jack's neck like a guillotine, serving to sharpen his mind. It dragged him further and deeper into battle, forced him to push himself to the very limit.

He forced his body to adapt. When his muscles mis-coordinated, his iron vise of a will grabbed them and forced them to obey. The right patterns were burned into his brain. Jack's battle prowess returned and kept rising, surpassing his previous limit.

Gan Salin lunged in for a bite, but stumbled just the tiniest bit. For an instant, he was defenseless.

Finally!

All color disappeared. All sound was buried. The sky went dark as a single purple meteor hung midair, followed by a majestic tail of stars. Everyone froze. The meteor struck Gan Salin's face, and everything exploded into existence as one.

The impact was deafening. Gan Salin was tossed like a broken kite, sailing over a dozen houses before crashing into one and reducing it to rubble. Jack hoped it was empty. He also hoped that the madman was dead, because his hand wasn't usable anymore.

A Meteor Punch against Henry White's fragile body was okay.

Against Salin's Constitution, Jack's bones were broken. *Oh, well. At least I'm getting better.*

Against the black wolf, his entire hand had almost disappeared. He was making strides.

He leaped from rooftop to rooftop until he reached the site of Gan Salin's landing. The wild dog was plastered on the wall of the next building after the one he'd demolished. His clothes were ripped in several places, letting the contents of his pockets fall to the ground. As he clutched his face, blood dripped between his fingers.

"Had enough?" Jack asked, bloodied himself. "I can do this all day."

"Fuck you," Salin responded. He sounded hurt, both physically and mentally. "I will see you at the Tournament, bitch. You challenged the scions. We'll kill you for it."

"I really don't think you will. You won't even reach the Tournament if you keep spouting shit like that."

Like lightning, Gan Salin reached for one of the items on the ground, a frail-looking wooden doll. Jack tensed. Salin crushed the doll. The next moment, a blue flare blinded Jack, and when he could see again, Salin's body had just disappeared.

What?

He looked around and found nothing. No blood trail, no marks, no suspicious amounts of screaming in any direction. He jumped on a rooftop and then as high up as he could to survey the town. From this height, he could see all the way to Valville's edges, and he almost lost himself to the ecstasy of flying before refocusing on Gan Salin, of whom he found no signs.

Weird... Jack thought. Was it not a flashbang? Did he teleport away?

He let himself fall back down, where Gan Salin had disappeared. A couple items were still strewn on the ground there. Jack's Meteor Punch had ruined his pockets, and he hadn't had time to collect them.

Chief among them was a face-down credit card. Turning it around, Jack saw the number 20,000 written on its surface. He grinned wildly.

Well, well. You're my lucky star.

Gan Salin had escaped, but at least the battle hadn't been fruitless. That's without even mentioning the invaluable battle experience Jack had gotten.

He then looked over himself, noticing the many scratches. His regeneration could handle those—probably. He hadn't lost too much blood, but he recalled the foam on Salin's lips.

Whoops.

Pocketing the credit card and ignoring the other items—Earth money and a half-eaten Tony's chocolate bar—Jack made his way to the professor's house, Parkouring over roofs and telephone poles. Fortunately, everything was safe when he got there. Brock was waiting by the door, jumping and hollering at Jack in protest for fighting without him, and the professor was also there, inspecting him with a worried look in her eyes.

"Was that..." she asked.

"Yeah."

"Did you..."

"No. He escaped, I think. There was a blue flash, and then he disappeared."

"That's an item. Escape Talisman. It sends the user to a predetermined location within a hundred miles."

"Really? That's awfully useful."

"And extremely expensive, too. Our blue merchant sells them for three hundred thousand credits each."

Jack whistled. "Wow. Some people have money. By the way, guess how much was left in his credit card. Twenty thousand. And guess how I know."

The professor smiled. "At least we got something out of the whole thing. Selling goblin eyes for a credit apiece would never make us a fortune."

"Yeah. Speaking of that, I suspect that merchants only buy monster parts to help pour credits into our economy. I can't imagine why someone would want a million goblin eyes."

"I suspect the same thing." The professor's smile widened, then grew sentimental. "You've gotten strong, Jack... but my heart aches seeing you like this. You're bleeding, yet you act like it's nothing. Can you tend to your wounds, please?"

"That's why I'm here. My regeneration can handle it, but I suspect that guy had rabies. Any idea where I can get a shot for that?"

She cocked a brow. "The pharmacy, Jack... They're still in operation."

"Right. I knew that."

Jack had defeated one of the five scions. This news did not go unnoticed.

"Elena," said a suited man, currently residing in the deep north. "Update, please. Is there any change in the faction rankings?"

"No, sir... but the leader of the Bare Fist Brotherhood appeared. And he defeated Gan Salin of the five scions."

The man's eyes flashed a cold blue. "Is that so? Get me all missives on this man. Spare no expense. I want to know everything."

"Yes, sir."

A dark-skinned woman stood in an empty savannah. "Someone beat a scion? Heh. What a guy."

A man lounged on a rock, sleeping, when his eyes fluttered open. "Salin?" As he stood, his golden mane of hair fell over his back. He seemed to be speaking to himself. "Interesting. Who? And who is he under?"

His eyes narrowed as he listened to the response. "Interesting... Well, no sense in moving now. The Tournament is approaching. If he doesn't come, he's as good as dead, anyway."

He then lay back down to sleep. The level 49 tiger behind him didn't dare interrupt.

CHAPTER FORTY-THREE
MEET THE APES

COME MORNING OF THE NEXT DAY, EDGAR AND PROFESSOR MARGARET RUST stepped into the forest with suspicion in their eyes. Their hearts were filled with excitement, but fear for the unknown weighed heavily on them, their feet shuffling warily through the undergrowth.

Behind them, Jack trailed with a wide grin. He'd experienced so many things in this forest. It had only been a few days, but he remembered every tree and bush. It smelled like home.

Edgar looked at the trees around him. Nothing had changed from a few steps back, where Jack assured them was the dungeon's border. "So, this is a dungeon," he said. "Looks... okay?"

"A conquered dungeon," Jack corrected.

"I assume there are changes deeper inside," the professor noted, inspecting everything with a sharp eye.

"And you said there are monkeys?" Edgar asked. "Like Brock?"

"In a sense."

"What?"

"You'll see."

Jack took the lead, crossing the foliage at his normal speed. The others lagged behind—whether due to stats, experience, or old age, in the professor's case, he couldn't tell. To help them, Jack set to gently pulling the bushes aside and choosing easier paths. He didn't harm the forest; it felt so dear to him now.

Birds chirped overhead, and small animals darted from branch to branch. Now that the monsters were gone, the forest was repopulating, and the entire fauna heaved a collective sigh of relief.

Life was returning.

Jack spared a look for two little birds on a branch. They weren't bothered by the System's arrival. No blue screen was shoved in their faces, no life-or-death calamities, no alien overlords looming in the horizon. They were just birds.

He smiled.

The wind ruffled some leaves above, letting a ray of sunlight, dotted by leafy shadows, fall on the birds, scaring them and making them take off. One followed the other as they zigzagged through branches and out of sight.

Jack followed them with his eyes. As soon as he lost track, he noticed another shape silently watching from the overgrowth, melding with the shadows, hoisting a piece of poop.

"Hold!" he shouted, raising a hand. "Wait!"

The monkey stopped just short of launching its projectile. It made sounds of surprise as it noticed it was him, then of joy as it fell from the tree and gave him a bear hug.

The professor screamed and Edgar readied a fireball.

"No fire in the forest, idiot!" Jack berated him.

"Sorry!"

"*Uu-uu-aha*!" the monkey yelled, hugging Jack by the waist and lifting him up with enough strength to break a pre-System human twice over. Brock rushed at the monkey and hugged its leg, happy to be finally seeing one of his kind again. The monkey froze, then petted his head—he let it.

"Easy, easy." Jack laughed. He patted its shoulder and it dropped him back down. "Professor and Edgar, this is one of the gymonkeys I was telling you about."

The professor was already squinting. "Fascinating..."

"Oh, wow. I didn't know the System had a sense of humor." Edgar looked the monkey up and down, adjusting his glasses as he scanned it.

Gymonkey, Level 13

•••

"Not the System, my friend, evolution! From what I understand, these monkeys appeared naturally on planet Green."

"It says here they're territorial, Jack," the professor noted. "Aren't we intruding?"

"Nah, it's okay. I'm bros with their big bro, so I can bring friends over."

"Excuse me?"

"You'll see. Come on, little one. Take us to Harambe."

Edgar's ears propped up. "To whom?"

Jack only laughed. The monkey excitedly led them through the forest, heading to the northeast near their forest gym. Jack saw the hill that hid his cave from afar, gazing at it with nostalgia. They also crossed the rocky terrain where the wolves used to live—it was clean of blood and battle remains—then made their way to a wave of vegetation that seemed out of place.

The trees were taller here, and the air moister. Edgar's clothes stuck to his torso, while the professor's shoulder-length gray hair clung to her nape.

"This is a jungle!" she exclaimed. "What's a jungle doing here?"

Jack grinned. "When the System spawns a monster group, it also spawns part of their environment. The goblins, for example, came with an entire village. However, I think the System isn't actively maintaining this mini-biome now that the dungeon is over. It will go back to normal eventually, but I believe our new friends will adjust just fine."

"A goblin village, you say. Did they have more subspecies?"

"Just goblins, hobgoblins, and a goblin shaman. They were pretty low-level."

"As they should be. Have you noticed they seem to be genetically engineered?"

"Not just noticed, I've confirmed it." He puffed his chest in pride. "One of my candidate classes was called Goblin Fighter, and it said goblins were an experiment gone wrong. I don't know if it was an accident or not, but I won't complain. If they weren't such perfect enemies to start with, I would have had a lot more trouble."

"That is akin to mind control," the professor said, her hands clasped behind her back. "Doesn't it trouble you?"

"Everything is mind control. I don't mind goblins—I mind the System."

But he didn't. Not really. The System had given him a new lease in life. As much as he opposed it morally, its arrival was the best thing that ever happened to him. The professor stared deep into his eyes, gave a nod that implied disbelief, then looked away. Jack frowned.

"I don't mind the System," Edgar said, not quite reading the room. Two amused glances landed on him, but before anyone could respond, a massive gorilla fell from the tall branches and landed before them.

The professor screamed and jumped back, while Edgar summoned another fireball.

"Goddammit, Edgar!" Jack said. "What did I tell you? No fire in the forest!"

The wizardling looked between Jack and the gorilla, who was flexing its muscles at Jack like a bodybuilder. His fireball winked off. "It's a jungle, not a forest," he muttered. At the same time, both he and the professor scanned the gorilla.

Brorilla, Level 22

...

Brock rushed to the gorilla and excitedly shook his hand, then flexed a pair of small biceps. The gorilla flexed back, at which point Brock realized he was losing. The brorilla gave a deep, low chuckle.

"Hmm," the professor hummed, unsure what to comment on first. Her mind seemed to instantly pierce through ten layers of information as she asked, "Is there something off about their genders?"

"Yeah," Jack replied, looking at her with surprise. "They're all the same species. Brorillas are male and gymonkeys are female, like bulls and cows."

At this, the professor's expression scrunched up. "That's not right. Are you sure?"

"I've seen all brorillas and gymonkeys. It's either that or a massive, unfortunate coincidence."

Her face warped further into a scowl. "I'll ask Ar'Tazul to be sure," was all she said, dropping the matter.

Meanwhile, Edgar eyed the gorilla warily. Flexing or not, seeing a live gorilla from up-close was quite the experience. "We're sure it's friendly, right?"

"*He*, not it," Jack replied. "And yes, he's friendly. His name is Brodul."

The professor raised a brow. "Did you name him that?"

"Yeah."

"It shows."

"What? Oh! I was just going for gorilla-like syllables. The rest don't have *bro* in their name." He considered it for a moment, then added, "I think."

While the three humans were talking, the gymonkey informed Brodul of the situation. With a nod of acknowledgment, the brorilla lead them deeper into the jungle-forest.

More gymonkeys and another brorilla appeared on the way. Brock greeted them excitedly. Though it had only been a few days, he was beyond happy to be back, even walking ahead of the others and tapping his foot in annoyance when they were slow.

Edgar and the professor stared at the primates with wonder. When they reached the forest gym, their wonder turned into astonishment.

"You have got to be kidding me," said Edgar.

"This is fascinating!" the professor said, watching everything wide-eyed. "I can't wait to study them."

"Let's leave the studying for later, Professor—and be polite, please."

A third brorilla—Oz—stood in the center of the forest gym, inspecting the exercising gymonkeys. Harambe himself appeared from behind the bananarm plant, where he liked to lounge mid-workout. The professor and Edgar gasped.

"That's a big gorilla," said Edgar.

"Of course! It's their big bro," Jack said.

A brown blur flew through the clearing and smashed into Harambe, who laughed deeply as he hugged his son. It was a touching reunion.

When Brock finally let go and fell to the ground, Jack exchanged a handshake with Harambe. He'd quit flexing back at the gorillas, since his comparatively tiny muscles only drew their nods of sympathy.

Meanwhile, Brock had rushed over behind the bananarm tree, to the place where his mother usually rested.

Harambe took his time studying Edgar and the professor. Then, slowly, he nodded and moved in for a handshake.

"Easy, Harambe," Jack said quickly. "Be very gentle or you'll break their hands."

He listened. Despite his hands looking gigantic compared to theirs, his handshake was soft like a baby's. The professor nodded in approval. "What a well-behaved young man."

"It's nice to meet you, Harambe," Edgar said, eyes sparkling. "Nice name."

Harambe smirked. The rest of the apes had also congregated around them, eyes gleaming with curiosity. The two of them felt nervous, of course, though they tried not to show it.

Meanwhile, the professor was staring at the groins of the gymonkeys and brorillas with obvious disappointment, which made the brorillas extremely uncomfortable. Three of the five started working out on the spot just to feel better.

She shook her head. "I have only seen such idiocy in undergraduate exam answers... I have to say, Jack—" A gymonkey reached out for her hair and smelled it. She continued. "Your friends here are very strong. Any of the brorillas could take on Henry White, and Harambe is level 37. With them as the faction's contracted monsters, I dare say we're one of the strongest factions on Earth."

The monkeys and gorillas, hearing that they were very strong, cheered and flexed at once. The professor, Edgar, and even Jack watched with mild amusement.

"They're plenty strong, yeah," Jack agreed. "They don't like leaving their forest, but if we move our headquarters here, they'll help protect everyone. Maybe work them out, too. That's one reason why I said we should move."

"Hmm. And the other reason?" the professor asked.

"Check this out."

After asking permission from Harambe, Jack took two bananarms—Brock had already eaten one, of course. "Try these." He handed them over.

Edgar peeled the bananarm and took tentative bites, while the professor studied its shape and coloration. "Earth bananas have been selectively bred for centuries," she said.

"I know, Professor, I know. It's suspicious. Just eat it."

After hesitating another moment, she slowly peeled it and nibbled a bite. Jack and the primates watched, making Edgar so nervous he struggled to swallow. He managed, and then his eyes widened at the notification.

"Wow," he said. "I got a bonus!" Then, after perusing his status screen, his excitement morphed into puzzlement. "Where is it, though?"

"Physical consists of Strength, Dexterity, and Constitution," Jack explained. "The bananarm increases your Strength by ten points, but that isn't immediately visible in the Physical stat. I suspect it shows the minimum of the three sub-stats or something like that—not the average."

"Ten points!" His eyes widened. "Wait. I do feel stronger. Can I have that?"

A monkey handed him a dumbbell, which he struggled to lift. "Look at that!" he exclaimed when he got it above his head, then let it drop to the ground with a thud. He flexed his biceps. "I'm strong!"

Every primate smiled, nodded, and gave him encouraging pats on the back. Oz slung an arm over his shoulder and tried to lead him to a bench press but was stopped by Jack.

"Later, please," he said. "I have more things to show them."

"There's *more*?"

"Of course! The bananarm was just the start."

CHAPTER FORTY-FOUR
A FOUNDATION OF GREATNESS

Waving goodbye to the apes, the three of them—four, as Harambe followed—took off for the northwestern part of the reserve, where the clear pond lay. They met no earth bears on the way. Harambe had cleared them all out.

They also picked up Brock, who returned ten minutes later looking all clean and happy.

Jack, the professor, and Harambe waited by the trees while Edgar and Brock lounged in the clear pond. They returned ten minutes later, Edgar's clothes dripping from head to toe—they hadn't brought towels —but exuding vitality. His eyes were the clearest Jack had ever seen them.

"That was nice. My Physical went up by 5, by the way," he commented. Brock nodded excitedly in agreement—he couldn't use the System, but he felt the difference.

The professor went after them, and she had the same comments when she returned, all dried up. She'd brought a backpack which, for whatever reason, included a towel. Jack, who was carrying the backpack for her, could only shake his head in wonder.

They then moved to the High Speed Bush.

"You're saying there was a goblin tribe here," the professor said, looking around. "And that the System made everything vanish into thin air instantly."

"Either that or teleported them elsewhere," he replied. "It's so weird. Even the burnt logs from their campfire are gone, as well as every out-of-place rock and hole in the ground. How did the System decide what to take away and what to let be?"

Edgar cupped his chin. "Maybe the System kept a copy of this glade from before it spawned the goblins. Then, when you despawned them, it simply replaced the real thing with its previous copy while not harming the lifeforms in the radius—at least, not the sapient lifeform called Jack Rust."

"That's time displacement with extra steps," the professor retorted. "Sounds easier to manipulate mass into nothingness, remove what looks out of place, and fill in the holes in the ground."

Edgar shrugged. "Maybe."

Harambe growled, annoyed by all this complicated stuff.

"In any case, this is the High Speed Bush," said Jack, pointing at the bush, which simply stood there like it wasn't illegal.

They gazed at it, then raised their brows at the exact same time.

"High as a kite?" Edgar said.

"The System keeps surprising me," the professor said. "Here I thought it was just a cold-blooded alien machine of doom. Turns out, it's not cold-hearted."

Jack chuckled, but before he could say anything, the professor narrowed her eyes and kept speaking.

"Actually, I suspect this information is not produced directly by the System. It has access to our brains. Why brave its own descriptions when it can crowdsource the task to the trillions of sapient creatures under its influence?"

"What?"

"I mean, these descriptions weren't necessarily written by the System itself. Maybe an expert provided them for a price, or it simply aggregated all the information and opinions people had on the bush. After all, the System is spread to at least an entire galaxy. It needs to be scalable, and the way to achieve that is using local resources to solve local problems."

Jack and Edgar stared at her. She met their gazes and shook her hands from side to side as if swatting flies. "It doesn't matter. Let's just get this bonus."

"Be careful though," Jack warned. "This is strong. I'm not joking."

Both nodded, then grabbed a leaf each and licked it as Jack suggested. Brock tried to follow soon after, but Harambe grabbed his leaf, cracked just the tip, and gave it to his disgruntled son. Brock looked at the leaf tip, then at the bush, then his father's glare, and finally chewed on the leaf tip while pouting.

"That I'd end up doing drugs..." The professor shook her head. "Oh, the woes of alien invasions. Thank God Eric isn't here to see me. Right, Jack?"

"I think Dad would rather get punched by Harambe than use this bush." Jack chuckled ruefully. His smile turned sad, and the professor put her last leaf aside before consuming it.

"This is enough," she said with a frown. "I got the bonus. What about you, Edgar?"

"Mm?"

Edgar looked over, still sucking on his last leaf. He gazed into space. "Oh yeah, me too."

Jack sighed. "Great. A high Edgar sounds fun."

"I'm not high. And I'm no kite either." He chuckled. Jack honestly couldn't tell whether the bush got to him or not. Maybe he was always high.

The next moment, Edgar's eyes widened. "Oh! Guys! This is amazing!"

Jack sighed. "Well, here we go. What is it, Edgar?"

"This bush! It helped me! My magic is based on imagination, and now I feel like my mind is totally free! I got a skill upgrade—Look!"

He extended a hand, and a blue bird appeared over it. It was rough around the edges and flapped its wings in jagged, not particularly lifelike patterns, but it was clearly a bird. Jack raised his brows. He hadn't seen this trick before.

"I thought you could only make fireballs and levitate beer cans," he said.

"I also have a skill for visualization. But look! I made a bird! I couldn't do this before!"

"Be careful, Edgar," the professor cautioned. "If you base your powers on drugs, I can guarantee you'll have a terrible time."

"I know, I know. But look!" He waved his hand, and the bird took off, flying for a couple feet before dispersing. He grinned widely. "I made a bird."

Jack wondered whether the bush was addicting. He didn't feel any inclination to try again, so that was good.

"Let's keep going," he said. "There's one last thing to see, and it's massive. I left the best for last."

The professor looked at her wrinkled hands. She wasn't getting any younger, but life was returning to her due to all the stat-ups. She turned her gaze to Jack. "My Physical just increased by another 5. I am stronger than young men used to be, Jack... Just what could be better?"

He only grinned. "You'll see. But I have to warn you... It isn't pleasant."

Cocking a brow, she stood straighter, a new spring in her step. "Then, let's go! We want to be back before nightfall."

Edgar was still manifesting little blue animals on his hands. They quickly got more recognizable as he practiced, until he could even have a little dog walk beside him. Dispersing it, he formed a bird and sent it flying to a branch, perching right next to a similar bird, except alive.

The living bird took one glance at its blue counterpart and flew away.

"Look at that!" Edgar laughed wildly. "I'm a real wizard! I'll call this spell... Formus Fakus."

"Don't your skills already have names, Edgar?" the professor asked.

"They do, but they're boring. This one is supposed to be called External Visualization. Bah."

"Are they real?" asked Jack. "Can they touch us?"

"Well, no... but maybe, in the future, they will-can!"

"They *will can*?"

"Yeah, what do you want? I'm a wizard, not a thesaurus."

A little blue monkey jumped next to Brock, who looked at it suspiciously. The blue monkey looked back with the same gaze. Brock punched it, making the illusion break apart, then snorted, raised his head, and proudly returned to his position beside Jack.

Harambe excitedly asked for his own copy, but unfortunately, he was too big. Edgar made him a palm-sized version, which completely horrified Harambe—its muscles were tiny!

He skulked the rest of the way.

Between banter and playing with illusions, they made it to Jack's cave—the ice pond cave. He stopped them before the entrance.

"It's down there. This is an E-Grade pond with extremely cold water. Its potential benefits are larger than all the other resources put together. You will see its description, but I have to warn you... This is completely unlike the F-Grade resources. It's painful, agonizing, even. Don't go too far or you'll be in danger of dying. And no matter what, *don't* touch the waterfall."

He was certain they couldn't make it that far with their stats, but you never know.

The professor's eyes hardened, as did Edgar's. They nodded. Jack looked at the professor; this was his mother, and to willingly put her through pain... It felt wrong. Absurd. But the apocalypse had come, and everybody had to make hard choices.

"You can go first, Edgar, Brock," he said. "Harambe will be there to save you if something goes wrong, but I think the rest of us should stay outside. You might want your privacy."

"Understood," was all Edgar said, while Brock pridefully stuck his chest out. Both walked inside, with Harambe squeezing through the crevice to follow. Jack took the professor away and sat on a pair of flat rocks.

Ten minutes passed in silence. When Edgar finally returned, he was pale and shivering from head to toe. His teeth were gritted so hard they might break, but his eyes held a victorious look. So did Brock's, despite the wet fur clinging to his body. Harambe's eyes were filled with pride.

Jack didn't need to be told anything else.

"Good job," he said. "Professor?" He turned to her, and his eyes softened for a moment. He almost blurted out that she didn't need to do this, but she did. They needed every edge they could get.

Reading his worries, she smiled. "Don't worry, Jack. I won't push myself too hard. Besides, a little bit of pain is nothing—I've been through childbirth twice."

He nodded, and she went inside, where Harambe waited.

Fifteen silent minutes passed. Jack almost went in thrice, but the thought of Harambe kept him steady. His bro was there. If anything went wrong, he would shout, and Jack would arrive instantly.

The professor deserved her dignity.

"How many steps did you take, man?" he said. He hadn't planned on asking, but he needed to get his mind off things.

"Five," Edgar replied, and Jack raised a brow. He expected way less.

"Have you invested in Physical?"

"Just two points. I'm at fifteen."

Jack tried to remember if he'd made it five steps in when he had 15 Physical. He wasn't sure, but it sounded like a lot. The pain must have been excruciating.

"Good job," he said.

Edgar smiled. "Thanks!"

Finally, after another fifteen minutes, the professor came out. Her eyes didn't seem victorious like Edgar's. She was haggard, shivering, sneezing, and coughing. She looked like she could barely stand.

Jack practically jumped up to support her. She was cold to the touch.

"What happened?" he asked. "Did you go too far?"

"My old bones are just unused to the cold," she replied with a forced smile, still shivering. "I'll be fine with some rest."

Jack forced himself to nod, then led her to the rock where he helped her sit. Harambe walked out of the cave as well, crossing eyes with Jack and giving a nod.

A moment later, when the professor stopped shivering as much, she said, "I think moving here is a great idea. We can have the protection of the primates, and these resources will help our faction members grow quickly. In this System world, the name of the game is getting ahead of the curve."

Jack found himself nodding.

Edgar added, "We could even let others use these resources for a price. Who will dare antagonize us then?"

The professor agreed. "Let's start the move the day after tomorrow. I will inform our faction members. We can also gather supplies, vehicles, and anything else we might need. The construction shouldn't take too long, given everyone's System enhancements—and we'll respect the forest in the process, of course. We should also bring some proper gym instruments for Harambe and his friends. We can't take their bananas and protection for free."

Harambe's eyes shone. He growled in thanks.

"Not a problem at all," she said. Her shivering had mostly passed now, and Jack heaved a sigh of relief. "I must admit, Jack, I thought you were our faction's single defining quality. However, with these resources, and the strength of the gymonkeys... The Bare Fist Brotherhood might truly become one of the strongest in this world."

Jack met her eyes, then smiled. "You betcha, Professor!"

CHAPTER FORTY-FIVE
SCIONS AND MAJOR FACTIONS

"There are three major factions on the planet right now," said Ar'Tazul, pacing back and forth before the fountain. Electricity had returned to Valville after they'd repaired the nearby power station, and the fountain's waters jumped high and glistened in the light of a setting sun. Jack and Edgar watched Ar'Tazul with rapt attention. They'd just bought the "Major Factions of Earth" information package.

"The first is called Flame River. It is a faction led by Vivi Eragorn on the native continent of Africa. They conquered the F-Grade dungeon Sunny Savannah.

"The second is called Ice Peak. It is led by Alexander Petrovic in northeastern Europe, and they conquered the F-Grade dungeon Iceberg Palace." Ar'Tazul turned to Jack and grinned. "The third, is the Bare Fist Brotherhood. Led by Jack Rust in North America, they conquered the F-Grade dungeon Forest of the Strong."

"Wait," Jack interrupted. "We're one of the major factions of Earth?"

"Only three factions have conquered an F-Grade dungeon so far, and you're one of them," Ar'Tazul replied with a smirk. "Of course, these major factions aren't the only ones you should keep an eye on. Not many people were lucky enough to have a dungeon nearby—there are only 1,111 on the entire planet, after all. Moreover, dungeons are usually accompanied by fierce infighting. There are plenty of factions strong enough to conquer dungeons in east Asia, for example, but they're busy fighting each other instead."

"I see," Edgar mumbled.

"Finally, though it pains me to say it, our information network isn't perfect yet. The System only gives information about factions. There were another four F-Grade dungeons conquered, but the ones responsible either weren't part of a faction or chose not to assimilate the dungeon into their territory."

"So, the Integration Tournament will be full of monsters?" Jack asked.

"Essentially, yes. I suggest finding a guide when you get there. They will know stuff that hasn't reached the official channels yet, and they can help you avoid all sorts of trouble."

"We'll keep that in mind, Tazul. I bet we'll find a cousin of yours waiting for us."

The little blue merchant smiled under his beard. "What a coincidence. I do have one, yes. His name is Ar'Karvahul. Tell him my name and he'll take good care of you."

Jack rolled his eyes.

"What about the five scions?" the professor asked. "We've heard rumors about them. Aren't they included in your 'major factions' information package?"

"Sadly, no." Tazul shook his head. "They are not a faction. I've only heard rumors myself... There could be some more specific information about them, but it will be costly. You know, supply and demand. Should I look it up?"

"Please do."

Ar'Tazul nodded and stared into space, fiddling with screens of his own, while the other three spoke between themselves.

"I can't believe we're such a big deal," Edgar said, all smiles. "Top three on Earth. Hehe."

"Jack's a big deal," the professor pointed out. "We are just riding his thunder."

"What big deal? I just punch stuff."

"But you punch them very well, dear."

"I was lucky."

She frowned. "Many people are lucky, Jack, but very few can turn that luck into something substantial. You did. And you know how things work. Don't get fake-modest on us."

"Sorry, sorry." He laughed. "In any case... Man. I really wonder what the Tournament is going to look like."

"So do I," Edgar said. "Think there will be more wizards there?"

"Of course. Everybody wants to be a wizard. The question is, will there be more pugilists or just me?"

"I hope it's just you," said the professor. "You're the face of our faction. The more spotlight on you, the better."

"Too much attention could be dangerous, though."

"It gives us something to work with. I'm confident I can turn publicity into good things."

"Marketing still rules the world, huh?" Jack mused. "I guess some things never change."

"Just don't die," she said. "Please."

"I don't plan to, Professor."

If I die after all that... It'd be such a waste. Jack clenched his fist.

Time left until Integration Tournament: 10 Earth-387 minutes.

It was finally arriving.

A few days ago, Jack had finished laying the faction's groundwork. He'd taken the professor and Edgar to the nature reserve, introduced them to Harambe and the other monkeys, as well as all the resources the reserve had to offer. The professor agreed to move there and had handled all the logistics, letting Jack free to do whatever he wanted.

They were currently building their headquarters in the previous goblin clearing.

After that, he'd spent the rest of his time between relaxing and training against the surrounding monster fauna. On the surface, he'd only gained a single level, bringing him to 35. In reality, not only did this time work wonders for his mental health, it also let him get accustomed to his new layer of awareness provided by the Fistfighting (III) skill.

He'd regained fine control over his body, even while fighting. His battle prowess had taken another leap forward. Moreover, he'd spent a big chunk of time Parkouring around until the movement became second nature, netting him a skill upgrade.

Parkour (II): A mix of finesse and bodily strength can allow you to navigate obstacles efficiently, have better control of your body, and move unpredictably. ***By seamlessly integrating the environment into your moves, the battlefield itself becomes your weapon.***

He'd also spent some time meditating in the ice waterfall—to little effect. His Dao Vision had reached a limit after he comprehended the Dao Root of the Fist and Meteor Punch. It wasn't that it didn't contain more insights. Jack felt them muddled, as if distorted just enough that they made no sense.

In the end, he'd just sighed and given up. He had to cultivate without external help to advance his Dao, and he could sense that what he lacked right now was battle experience, of which the Tournament should give him plenty. Therefore, he simply focused on being at the top of his game.

All in all, Jack was in great form. He'd even escaped his previous savage appearance, at least temporarily. His marble-chiseled chest was covered by a simple white shirt whose sleeves were ready to burst at the seams. He wore heavy boots, loose trousers, and carried a single backpack filled with utilities and the Dao Fruit he kept at hand for later.

He reviewed his status screen one more time.

Name: Jack Rust
Species: Human, Earth-387
Faction: Bare Fist Brotherhood (F-Grade)
Grade: F
Class: Pugilist (Elite)
Level: 35

Strength: 95
Dexterity: 95
Constitution: 95

Mental: 10
Will: 10

Skills: Fistfighting (III), Drill (II), Pugilist Body (II), Parkour (II)
Dao Skills: Meteor Punch (I)

Titles: Planetary Frontrunner (10)

So close... I wonder if something happens at 100.

Wait.

"Hey, Tazul, does anything special happen when you reach a hundred points in the physical stats?"

The merchant looked away from his screens. "I'll tell you for three hundred and fifty credits."

"Is that a price you just pulled out of your ass?"

"Maybe."

"Can you guarantee the answer won't be 'nothing?'"

"I cannot." He grinned.

Jack laughed. "Nevermind, then. I'll just find out in a few levels."

"As you wish." He turned to the professor. "There is some information on the five scions, but it's unverified. Only a hundred credits, so I'll just give it to you." His face went serious. "They're the favorites for the top five spots."

His seriousness went unanswered. Jack raised a brow. "But I beat one of them already."

Tazul shook his head. "You'll see."

"Oh? I thought you'd give us all information on them."

"I did." He crowded in a bit, his voice going hushed, like he was talking about a secret. "There are some things we aren't allowed to discuss... Just keep in mind that the scions are more than meets the eye. They're strong, and the Tournament is where they'll really shine."

Jack, Edgar, and the professor all looked at each other. "We'll be in touch as soon as telecommunications come back up," Jack said. He'd taken his trusty Samsung smartphone along. "Let's work together to keep an eye on everything."

"Absolutely. Don't forget about us, Jack."

"I won't."

Time left until Integration Tournament: 5 Earth-387 minutes. Do you consent to being teleported to the Tournament's location?

Jack and Edgar raised their brows and accepted.

"Only five minutes left," Edgar said. After training and honing his powers for a week, he'd finally used his Dao Fruit yesterday. He'd succeeded, and was now the proud owner of a Dao Root of Magic. In other words, he was also going to the Tournament—and his powers were impressive at the very least.

"Is there anything else you want to ask?" the professor said. "Any information from Ar'Tazul?"

"If you ask now, I'll give you a discount," the merchant said with a greasy smile.

"We're good." Jack laughed. He looked at Brock, who was cupping his chin and staring up at Tazul from his feet.

Though while he was content to let the final minutes tick by, the professor wasn't. "Wait!" she shouted. "You said the five scions are the favorites, and Jack's beaten one of them. That sounds like trouble."

"How so?" Jack asked.

"Tazul apparently can't say it, for some reason, but Gan Salin told you they're from the Animal Kingdom. They can certainly make things difficult for you in the Tournament."

"What should I do, then? I can't *unkick* his ass."

She rolled her eyes. "You can disguise yourself, Jack."

"But you said I should be flashy."

"Do that under a persona." Her eyes were filled with calculations. "Impress the world and try to find allies against the scions. You should keep your identity a secret for as long as possible, so they don't use their connections to sabotage you. Plus, if they don't see you at the Tournament, they will assume you are still here and won't send their subordinate factions to mess with us. We'll have time to move to the ape forest."

"I see. But how do I—"

"Tazul sells a disguise kit," she interrupted. "Quick! The clock is ticking. Buy it!"

It wasn't a matter of credits—he still had almost twenty thousand left, thanks to Gan Salin's generous donation. However, did he really want to disguise himself, like he was *ashamed* of what he'd done? Or, God forbid, afraid? That wasn't the path of the fist!

He crossed his arms and prepared his rebuttal, only for it to die on his tongue. The professor's eyes were strict. The kind she showed when he acted stupid as a child.

"This isn't about pride, Jack," she said sternly. "Don't become a puppet of your Dao. Be *smart*."

Strictness gave way to softness. Facing her pleading gaze, Jack's frown wavered. He took a deep breath.

"Fine," he said. "What do you have, Tazul?"

His Dao Root protested, but he ignored it. He defined his path, not the opposite, and the professor was right. Pride was one thing, idiocy was another. He'd still beat everyone up.

It occurred to him that Gan Salin might recognize his fighting style in the Tournament. He had to do something about that, too. He hoped there were many pugilists.

Time left until Integration Tournament: 2 Earth-387 minutes.

Ar'Tazul rummaged through his crate, then pulled out a vial filled with a grayish liquid. Jack squinted at it. "What's that?"

"Disguise potion. It can alter your form enough to make you unrecognizable and make you appear factionless and title-less to the System. Priced at a thousand credits," he replied.

"A thousand! Do you take me for a fool, Tazul?"

"It isn't easy to produce!" the merchant shouted. "Your mother's right. Hurry up, Jack. You only got a minute!"

He mulled it over.

"*Jack*!" the professor insisted.

Edgar watched on with worry. "I think you should do it."

"Fine," Jack consented. He whipped out his credit card and touched it to Tazul's, watching a thousand credits tick away. With a spark of curiosity, he wished the merchant's card showed its balance, too.

He grabbed the potion, popped its cork off with his thumb, and wolfed it all down. Brock made a low monkey sound and stared at him with worry.

Jack licked his lips, then looked at himself. "I don't—" He frowned and grabbed his belly. "Ohhh..." And promptly fell to his knees. He held his mouth and tried not to puke. His face twitched and then—to his horror—snapped into a different position. It was the most disturbing sensation he'd ever experienced.

By his side, Brock was going crazy with worry. He was leaning against Jack and shaking him with his little hands.

"It lasts until you choose to dispel it. Just channel your Dao as intensely as you can and it will go away," Ar'Tazul quickly explained. "D-Grades can see through it, but you should be fine otherwise."

The professor had stopped listening. "Jack? Are you oka—"

She didn't have time to finish her sentence. The timer hit zero. A blue flash appeared around Jack, Edgar, and Brock, blinding everyone. The next moment, they were gone, vanishing into thin air.

The Integration Tournament had started.

CHAPTER FORTY-SIX
THE INTEGRATION TOURNAMENT

Waves crashed in the Pacific Ocean. They always did. Tall and short, thick and thin, close together and farther apart. They traveled in groups of thousands, covering miles and miles of water before meeting another group and crashing together. Some waves—the stubborn ones—even crossed entire oceans.

On this day, their journey was interrupted. The surface frothed. Steam rose from below in tremendous quantities, scaring all sorts of marine wildlife for a dozen miles. Something appeared at the bottom of the sea. It was large, and rising.

Schools of fish darted away at top speed. Whales flapped their large tails to escape. Most managed—and the ones that didn't found themselves pushed away by an invisible dome.

A titanic structure rose for miles through dark waters. Dark shapes appeared under the ocean, growing larger as time passed. The top of a white tower broke the surface, and following it, an entire city emerged from the depths, with both squat and tall buildings, walls, shops, and even people watching in awe.

In its very center stood a massive arena larger than Rome's colosseum though similar in shape. Next to it, a tall tower cut into the sky, made of white marble, and reaching twice higher than the arena itself.

The protective dome started from the top of this tower, and a gray-caped form stood on its highest balcony. She was a middle-aged woman whose every breath could crush F-Grades. She was no human—her face was that of a lioness.

"Finally..." she murmured, gazing down upon the city edges, where confused people were already appearing out of thin air.

Integration City had successfully risen in the middle of the Pacific Ocean.

Teleportation was a disturbing experience.

Edgar felt his entire body wrap and distort, as if pulled in every direction at once. His vision was assaulted by blinding lights of infinite colors, forcing him to close his eyes even as he stifled a scream. He thought he was torn apart.

Then, everything returned to normal. He opened his eyes to find a wide plaza covered in people just as confused as he was, framed by serene white houses with blue windows. He'd seen buildings like these before, sprawled on the coasts of the Mediterranean islands. The ground was made of white marble—possibly polished stone—though the color was faded, soothing the eye. The houses were a true white, standing out from the ground, and rock-paved streets snaked into the town. Even farther back, he could see the towering walls of a stone colosseum, as well as a tall white tower that looked mystical against the clear blue sky.

White was the dominant color here, both in the buildings and the ground. Blue came second, in the sky and window shutters. It was like standing on clouds.

Surprisingly, this place didn't look as sci-fi as he expected. Advanced technology was undoubtedly a core part of everything, but it was subtle, lending itself to a city that looked more like a picturesque island resort than a high-tech arena. Edgar even thought he heard the sound of crashing waves.

No, wait.

He turned around and found the sea only a dozen feet behind him.

Waves splashed against a ten-foot-tall platform of white stone—the edges of the plaza—which stretched left and right to the ends of his vision and curved behind the buildings like the shore of an island.

The sea stretched unobstructed all the way to the horizon, where it merged with the cloudless afternoon sky. A salty sea breeze pressed against Edgar, making his messy hair fly back. His eyes widened behind his glasses as he took in the sight. It was beautiful.

Where are we? he couldn't help but wonder.

The next moment, he was assaulted by the strongest sense of nausea he'd ever experienced. He puked right then and there. Everyone did.

When he was done, Edgar looked to the side, where another man suffered from an even worse case of nausea. He was kneeling on the ground, heaving stomach acid on the pristine white stone. By his side, a little brown monkey watched anxiously.

When the man finally raised his head, Edgar was shocked to find him unrecognizable. His features were similar but distinctly different. Though his body shape remained the same, a host of minute differences threw Edgar completely off. It was difficult to put his finger on the change, but if he didn't know this was Jack, he would never recognize him.

With some quick thinking, Edgar left the Bare Fist Brotherhood faction. Otherwise, any scan he received would lead to suspicion, and he'd risk giving Jack's identity away.

Seeing his big bro recover, Brock widened his little eyes and looked around like an awestruck baby. Jack croaked out a laugh.

"Wow," Edgar whispered. "You look—"

"Handsome?"

"Different."

Jack felt his face going through a dozen expressions before settling on worry. "But still handsome?"

"As much as before."

"That's not a yes."

"Not my fault." Edgar smiled. "By the way, why is Brock here?"

Jack started and turned to the monkey, which stood there like a participant itself. "Yeah, what the hell. What are you doing here, Brock? Do you have a Dao Root?"

That would open up a whole new world of complications. However, neither of them could feel the aura of Dao from Brock.

"Maybe the System registered him as your pet?" Edgar ventured a guess. "I didn't know we had a plus one."

"I don't think we do," said Jack, looking around. "In any case, it doesn't matter much. Heh. Check this out. We did a number on their plaza. Serves them right."

Edgar found himself agreeing. The pristine white stones were now covered in tremendous quantities of filth, both from them and other people.

However, all filth started slowly absorbing into the stone like it was quicksand. They blinked in surprise. The next moment, the plaza was clean again.

"What the..." Jack muttered, turning around. "Did you see that, Edgar?"

"Yeah. That's magic alright. Can it eat us too?" Edgar wondered. He scratched his short, pointy beard—which was definitely sharpened on purpose—while sharp eyes shone behind his glasses. If he didn't look like a total nerd, he could have been a mysterious wizard.

Jack looked around again. There had to be a hundred people in this plaza, and all of them had an undeniable edge.

There were clean-shaven men in military robes who looked like action figures. A young girl grinned as she tossed a dagger up and down, a predatory gleam in her eye. There were men and women with silver hair, kind smiles, and piercing, well-intended eyes. Suited people who exuded commanding charm standing next to stern-looking men with the eyes of a killer—even before the System.

Everyone here was a master at something—a highly-skilled professional who stood head and shoulders above the masses—and it showed in their aura. It was a summit of the brightest, sharpest, strongest people on planet Earth. Nobody here was simple—so they seemed.

In comparison, Jack and Edgar were normal dudes. They felt like children in a room of grown-ups. The combined aura of everyone here pressed them down like a hydraulic press.

But it was an illusion. Jack clenched his fist, and his own aura erupted, formless but enough to turn heads. His gaze held that of masters until they looked away. He especially glared at those who eyed Brock—nobody else had a pet.

It finally occurred to Jack that Gan Salin might recognize Brock, until it occurred to him that the two of them had never met. Brock had stayed back to eat salami from the professor's cupboard when Jack ran into the scion.

He grinned.

"Don't fret, Edgar," he said. "We belong here. We're strong, too."

"I'm trying," Edgar squirmed. The poor guy was getting overwhelmed, but that was his problem to solve, not Jack's.

Jack felt more than one sharp glance land on him, and he stared back.

Human (Earth-387), Level 25
Faction: Dashing Meisters

Human (Earth-387), Level 31
Faction: Dragons of the West

He quickly scanned a few dozen people. Few were unaffiliated. Most belonged to factions with names ranging anywhere from grand to ridiculous, and their levels were mostly in the late twenties. There were exceptions, of course, and Jack even saw a little Asian boy at level 38.

He was close to the top of the pack, apparently, but not quite up there.

These people were all competition in the upcoming Integration Tournament, whatever that was, and every single one of them was stronger than Henry White. Jack grinned.

Behind him, Edgar had finally managed to recover. "Wait. Why's everyone a higher level than me?"

Blue screens flashed before Jack could reply.

This is a message from your assigned overseers, the Animal Kingdom faction:

Welcome to the Integration Tournament of Earth-387!

In the million-year history of our galaxy, the Integration Tournament has always been a major occurrence for any planet. Future C-Grade and even B-Grade powerhouses are born here. You are the elites of your species. Each and every one of you has gone through fire to reach this point, and your achievements are nothing to scoff at. In the future, you are destined to lead your planet, and this Tournament is your greatest chance to soar—so give it everything you have. There is no shortage of opportunity, only of talent.

The Tournament will start tomorrow an hour after dawn. You are expected to report to the Arena then. In the meantime, you are encouraged to explore everything Integration City has to offer for people of your status, as well as get to know others like you.

Remember: The strong get stronger, and the weak get weaker.

It was a long message. Jack took a moment to read it and another to comprehend it. Edgar was done in half the time, and he was already excitedly saying stuff.

Jack shook his head to clear it, then finally tuned in to Edgar.

"—should come first. Then lodging and socializing, in that order. Oh. We should also check what our credits can buy."

"What?"

It was the standard "I didn't hear anything" kind of what, and Edgar turned around in annoyance. "I *said*, we should first find Tazul's cousin. He'll point us in the right direction. Any idea where he's at?"

"Yes," Jack replied simply, pointing at a congregation of people that had just stepped into the plaza. They were completely alien.

There were short, blue people like Tazul. Some were tall, copper-skinned ones with large bellies and long beards, some resembled were-wolves, while others looked like spinning tops with four arms and one leg on which they bounced. How these guys made it through evolution, Jack had no idea, but he really wanted to find out.

"I can guide you through the city!" a creature that looked like a desert version of Santa Claus shouted in a deep voice, and the entire crowd of aliens erupted into similar shouts as they fanned out. Instantly, the situation resembled an open-air bazaar, with every merchant shouting to be heard over the others.

Some even waded into the crowd of humans, aggressively approaching their prospective victims and trying to sell themselves as a guide.

"Most people are first-timers, but I've been around." A little blue person shrugged, approaching two sharp-eyed girls. "I'm just trying to make ends meet and help people while getting rich myself. Truth is, customers are everything here. How about I give you a discount?"

Jack heard a spinning-top-like person proclaim themselves as friends of the Planetary Overseer, whatever that was, and a wolfman whispered—loudly—that the big, copper-skinned merchants weren't to be trusted.

"What the fuck?" Jack said in response to the chaos.

"Right!" Edgar replied. "Aliens shouldn't be like this. Where's the advanced technology? The System-driven, light-speed, streamlined market?"

"I expected to be thrown into an arena, not a bazaar..."

There were no fools here. Everyone was experienced and wouldn't fall for schemes, which might explain why these merchants were so forward. If anything, they knew their job, if the large number of successful transactions that Jack observed were anything to go by.

"Adapt to the market," he muttered, chuckling.

After all, an aggressive guide had better chances of getting good deals, as all these people loudly proclaimed. The ones that waited at the back had knowing smiles, placing their preconstructed stalls before them to entice customers.

Anyone that agreed to have a guide quickly transferred a number of credits—this price was actually whispered—and then instructed to wait somewhere while the merchant got more customers.

A wolfman approached Jack and Edgar, who were at the back of their group. "Are you guys—"

"We know someone," Jack cut him off, and the wolfman drifted away to another human.

"How do we find him, though?" Edgar asked, cupping his chin.

Jack barked a laugh, took a deep breath, then his voice boomed out, covering the entire plaza. "AR'KARVAHUL!"

Everyone fell quiet, turning to look at him. He took their stares in stride and smiled back.

A moment later, a blue person waded through the crowd to reach him. He resembled Ar'Tazul—as did all of them, if Jack was being honest. He barely reached Jack's chest, wore light, colorful garments, and carried what looked like a little shoebox, but it actually contained a wealth of merchandise. A turban was on his head, while his shoes were polished and pointy. He smelled like spices.

When he smiled, he seemed like the best person ever. His beard wiggled. "Did you call?"

"Yes," Jack replied suspiciously. "We're friends of your cousin."

"Ah, Tazul," said the merchant, and Jack instantly smiled.

"Ar'Tazul, not Ah'Tazul," Edgar pointed out, drawing Jack's empty stare and Karvahul's seemingly earnest laughter.

"You humans are always *spicy*," he said. "It's a pleasure to meet you both. We can leave this noisy place now, if you want."

"Already? Won't you gather more people?" Jack asked.

"That's for *new* customers. I know you guys—well, my cousin does, but he said I should take care of you. Could I get your names, by the way?"

"Mhm." Jack smiled, then spouted out the first name that came to mind. He was incognito, after all. "I'm John."

"I'm Edgar," said Edgar.

"And this is Brock," Jack completed, pointing at the monkey that was tilting its head at Karvahul, wondering if he was the same person as Tazul.

"The pleasure's all mine." The little blue person gave a curt bow. "I'm Ar'Karvahul, a djinn from planet Bing. For only five hundred credits —including a friendly discount—I'll show you everything Integration City has to offer. Shall we?"

Jack and Edgar looked at each other, then shrugged. The price sounded fair.

"Where are we going first, Karvahul?"

"Well, there's no rush. Don't mind the chaos here; it's only business. The market can wait, as can the arena—and the restaurants, of course. I was thinking of showing you your lodgings first. I'm sure they'll absorb you for the entire night."

"Oh? You already know the best hotel?"

Karvahul laughed. "Only visitors live in hotels. Participant lodgings are predetermined."

Edgar's eyes shone. "Are they free, too?"

"Of course!" Karvahul smiled widely. "Everyone loves Tournament participants."

CHAPTER FORTY-SEVEN
THE INTEGRATION CITY

INTEGRATION CITY WAS A GEM OF BEAUTY. THE BUILDINGS WERE MOSTLY WHITE with blue windows, making the town resemble a picturesque island. Ar'Karvahul took Jack and Edgar down the main street, where they saw restaurants, massage places, cafes, bars, as well as a large variety of shops selling anything from trinkets to weapons and armor.

Of course, everything looked expensive, and it was—even more so than it looked.

Edgar scanned the prices of a restaurant and exclaimed, "This is robbery!" Even the cheapest main dish cost twenty credits—in Valville's newbie market, one credit went for hundreds of dollars.

The nearby wolfman frowned. "I assure you, sir, that our prices are at the lower end of Integration City's market, and our products are more than worth it." Seeing Edgar's apologetic expression—he hadn't intended to offend anyone—the shopkeeper smiled and continued. "You can check it out yourself if you want to. I'll give you a 20 percent first-customer discount."

"Really?" His eyes widened.

"Are you hungry, Edgar?" Jack asked. They'd eaten dinner two hours ago—though it was late afternoon here, the sun had set when they left Valville.

"No, not really..."

"Then, let someone else have that discount. We can take a look at our rooms first."

"Yeah, alright." Edgar turned to the wolfman. "Thank you, but we'll return another time. I'm sure your food is delicious, though!"

"Of course it is. You're welcome anytime, friends. Enjoy yourselves!"

"You too!" Edgar replied, then cringed in awkwardness. The wolfman was just working here. He had nothing to enjoy.

"Real food is a delicacy that will blow your mind," Karvahul said after they'd gotten a bit farther away. "Not the native stuff you're used to. I'm talking Antesaurus rib and cockatrice thigh, phoenix omelet, and earth-Dao cabbage. Ah, that's the stuff."

Brock, walking by their side, was already salivating. He tugged at Jack's trousers and pointed at a stand with steaming meat skewers.

"Be patient, Brock. I'll get you some later," Jack said, then turned to the djinn. "Don't underestimate Earth, Karvahul. We have quite a culinary tradition."

"So does everyone, but you didn't have the Dao. It is *the* foundation of the universe, my friend, and I assure you that, when it melts in your mouth, you will never eat native food again."

"Wait, you can eat the Dao?" Edgar asked. "How is that possible?"

Karvahul laughed. "The Dao is infused into the body at the E-Grade. You'll see soon enough, I imagine. Give it a couple months, and your planet will have its first E-Grades to be proud of."

Jack smiled. There was no crowd around them, not yet, as most people lingered longer at the plaza than they had. Of the aliens he could see, almost all were manning various establishments, eyeing them curiously, and the few that were walking around were rushed.

Speaking of that, Jack took a wider look and noticed something off.

"Hey," he asked, "why is this place so big? We're only, like, a hundred. What are we going to do with all these shops?"

"There are another seven plazas like the one you appeared in," Karvahul replied, not breaking pace. It was fast enough to not be bored and slow enough they could take in the town's sights. "The Tournament's participants are 987, according to my primer, but that's not all. People from all areas of your planet will start flooding in soon. It isn't just an opportunity for you to network, but also for the powerful factions and native forces. Plus, they will get to watch their planet's most elite representatives go all-out against each other. This is the place to be!"

"Wow," Edgar drew a sharp breath. "Will the president be here?"

"If they have enough credits. But keep in mind that the distribution of spawned monsters is not uniform across your planet's surface—the challenge is. In other words, everyone faces roughly the same difficulty to survive, be it a farmer, an armed soldier, or the leader of a nation. What are the chances of your president becoming the one in ten million to make it here?"

"You sound well-informed, Karvahul," Jack said, his eyes gleaming. "Doesn't that mean armed soldiers will have higher levels, since they face stronger monsters?"

"Hehe." Karvahul chuckled. "No one can cheat the System. It takes *everything* into account. Don't worry."

"I see. Where are we, anyway? Is this place still Earth?"

"Of course! Inter-planet teleportation is expensive. According to my primer, we are somewhere in the middle of the Pacific Ocean."

"I'm pretty sure there weren't alien towns in the Pacific Ocean."

"Keep an open eye, John," Karvahul replied with a smirk, then stomped on the stone-paved street. "This is no town. It is a starship."

"A *starship*?"

"Of course! They teleport it to every newly-Integrated planet. Standard procedure."

"Wow..." Edgar looked at the ground and around him in shock, while Jack laughed.

"Do you come here often, Karvahul?"

"It's my first time, just like you! We're a good match!"

Laughing and talking, they made their way through the main street. It wasn't too large. The entire city only took up around ten square miles —though it was oblong in shape—Jack and Edgar had appeared in a plaza close to the participants' area.

"Tournament City is divided into sections," Karvahul explained. "There's the arena in the center, of course, along with the Overseer Tower. Then, towards the back of the ship—I think it's to the west—are the participants' lodgings, where Tournament participants can live for free and enjoy various amenities that are otherwise out of reach. You'll get kicked out of there the moment you're disqualified, so make sure to treasure the time. There are resources in your houses that even I am jealous of."

"Really?"

"Of course! That's why I suggested going there first. Anyway—then, in the opposite direction is the hotel district, where everybody else gets to stay. The space in between is for shops and, of course, the arena!"

"I see," Jack said.

"Of course you do."

"What's that?" Edgar asked, pointing at a building different from the rest. They'd just entered a large, empty plaza, similar to the one they'd appeared in but much closer to the center of the island—*starship*, Jack reminded himself.

The building that caught Edgar's eye was rectangular and resembled a mansion with walls made of heavy wood and a roof of red tiles. It was wide enough to cover an entire side of the plaza, while also towering over its surroundings. It must have been at least four, five stories tall, twice the height of most other buildings.

"Oh, that?" Karvahul pretended he'd just noticed the large building. "That's the Hand of God auction house. It won't open for a while, but when it does, it will be a sight for sore eyes... In any case, you can ignore it for now."

"Come on, Karvahul!" Edgar shouted out, almost pleadingly. "You're our guide! You can't just tell us to ignore stuff, you have to explain!"

Jack nodded. Karvahul, finding them in agreement, sighed. "Listen, my friends. You've just been shoved into a world of new information, and this city is filled to the brim with things you've never seen before. There's no rush. I'm taking things slow and focusing on the important parts so you have time to digest the information."

"Well, no need for that. We're smart. I have a PhD—almost—and Edgar—" He glanced at Edgar, realizing he actually didn't know much about the guy. "Well, he's smart."

Edgar nodded. "Well said, as expected from someone who has a PhD—almost."

Jack threw him an annoyed glare. Edgar looked the other way.

"As you wish." Karvahul shrugged. "After all, you pay. The auction house is set to run a single auction throughout the Tournament, but it will be filled with items of great value. Since only your planet's inhabitants are allowed to participate, you can get those items at pitifully low prices. It's a helping hand to your species."

"Oh!" The eyes of both humans widened. "Karvahul, that's important! Why wouldn't you tell us that?"

"Because it won't happen yet, and it's too early to even start saving up. The auction is the most important event here—besides the Tournament itself, of course—so it's set to happen just before the finals."

"The finals?" Jack asked, but Edgar burst with another question.

"Wait. Why is it called the Hand of God auction house?"

Karvahul smirked. "Good question. Unlike every other establishment in Integration City, the auction house is run not by the Merchant Union, but by a faction called the Hand of God. They generally focus on collecting and trading information, as well as various high-end products, but they are also interested in helping newly-Integrated species get up to speed. They will provide the auction's contents."

"I see. Rich people that also do charities." Jack nodded. "Sounds fishy to me."

"That's difficult to say. They don't show up much. Unlike the Merchant Union, they usually only participate in high-end trades, so most people never interact with them—and the ones that do, know to keep their mouths shut." Seeing Jack's darkened face, Karvahul hurried to add, "But they aren't known for bad deeds, either. Most people consider them a fair faction, if a bit heavy-handed at times."

"I see," Jack said, and cracked a smile. "You mentioned rare items, Karvahul... What were you talking about?"

"Oh, anything!" The merchant's mood did a one-eighty as the conversation turned to things he liked. "In previous Integrations, they've sold anything from enchanted Dao armor to D-Grade automatons and E-Grade Dao Fruits. The records also speak of elemental cores, purified Dao Seeds, hyper-condensed experience balls, spiritual pets, as well as all sorts of treasures. If the Tournament is a fate-turning experience for a planet's elites, so is the auction, but also for the richest factions."

"I see." Jack hummed. He looked at Brock, who was gazing incessantly at a nearby wolfman. "You mentioned spiritual pets. Tell me more about them."

"What more is there to say? They're pets. They're spiritual, which means they can cultivate. That's it."

"But they aren't included in a person's status screen?"

"It isn't really a System thing. However, it does seem to recognize the bond in some cases, like when the teleportation here brought your little monkey along."

"Hmm."

"Can we go in, Karvahul?" Edgar asked, pointing at the auction house.

"I'm afraid not. It's closed."

"Oh."

"Shall we get going, then? Night is already falling, and you probably want to be in top shape for your first battles tomorrow."

"Right." Jack's eyes went to the arena's tall, gray walls. He clenched his fist imperceptibly. "Let's go."

They exited the auction plaza and headed west, where the participant district was located. On the way, Karvahul kept talking about one thing or another, pointing at shops he liked or disliked, and telling stories about his home planet, Bing.

Bing was perpetually ravaged by the elements, which allowed it to develop several very different ecosystems. There were people who lived underwater and others who built on clouds. Some even inhabited inactive volcanos, taking them as shelter from endless snowstorms.

There were also several sapient species. The blue people, djinns, were ones who lived on clouds. The brown-skinned, big-bodied merchants in town also hailed from Bing—they were called efretis and lived in deserts or inactive volcanos.

The flora and fauna of Bing was endlessly diverse, according to Karvahul, who admitted he missed his home very much.

His stories kept Jack and Edgar entertained as they crossed the town—though it was officially called a city, it really wasn't one. There were a few wide, straight streets, but most were snaking alleys, making the place feel warm and homey.

They ran into other groups of humans, most following guides to different parts of the town or heading to the participant district. There were also some who, lacking funds or the willingness to spend them, chose to go alone. They seemed quite lost, as all nearby aliens gave polite yet vague instructions, but they'd eventually get the hang of things and be five hundred credits richer—or more, if Karvahul wasn't lying about his discount.

However, there was one exception.

As Karvahul was excitedly describing the spear-hunting methods of his people, an odd man exited an alley. Jack's eyes focused on him. He had a long, scraggly beard and wore old, torn clothes. Dirt was all over him as if he hadn't taken a shower in weeks.

Despite his shaggy appearance, there was spirit to his eyes, a slow, purposeful gait in his sandaled feet. He clasped his hands behind his back as he strolled through the town, sharing none of the others' wonder.

In all respects, he looked like a semi-crazy, harmless, homeless person.

Except Integration City had none of those. Jack scanned him. From the side, so did Edgar.

Human (Earth-387), Level 38
Faction: -

Jack had to resist frowning. 38 was the highest level he'd seen so far.

The strange man passed them, walking in the opposite direction. Karvahul kept talking as if not noticing him. Jack tensed. The odd man met Jack's gaze. He smiled, nodded politely, and kept walking. Just like that, he went past, and then he was gone.

Jack was left staring.

"Hmm?" Karvahul said, finally noticing something. "Is there a problem?"

"There was a weird guy..." Edgar replied.

"I noticed. Well, the crazy ones have an advantage in the early days of the System, but it will even out eventually. Don't worry about it. Violence is forbidden here, anyway."

"I could probably take him." Jack chuckled before turning to Karvahul. "What happens if someone tries to use violence?"

"The guards are sent after them."

"Huh… I mean, that makes sense, but I expected something like instant divine retribution. You know, the System smiting them or something like that."

Karvahul laughed. "You'll find that the System is a very aloof god. It doesn't care. Almost everything is run by people like you or me—much stronger and wiser, of course, but still people. If you want to stop violence, you station guards. That's how things work everywhere."

"I don't see any guards."

"Oh, they're here." Karvahul gave a toothy grin. "Pray that you never see them."

The rest of the trip was uneventful. The shops began to thin, and the four of them—including Brock, who was growing tired—reached an area filled with small houses. They sported the same color complex as the buildings outside—white and blue—and were squat, only one floor high. However, each covered an area of around a thousand square feet, enough to easily accommodate a family, and had a fenced-off garden complete with plants, tables, and chairs. Jack even saw a barbeque.

"The residences are fully furnished and operational. Additionally, you'll find many amenities that only the Dao can offer, like automated cleaning or self-sustained plants," Karvahul said.

"Really? Did the architect cultivate the Dao of Magical Brooms?" Jack asked.

"The Dao of Automation is a lucrative area of expertise. In any case, this is as far as I'll take you today. Find your assigned house—the number is on your identification token—and enjoy your night. Make sure to check the basement, too. I'm sure you'll find it interesting."

Jack raised a brow, but the djinn didn't comment further.

"Fine, then. See you around, Karvahul."

"See you, my friends. Let's meet here tomorrow at dawn."

With a nod, Jack waved goodbye to Edgar, too, and went off to find his house.

A djinn official had given them identification tokens as they left the plaza. They were small, round, and black, with a number etched in striking white color. They were also made of jade, like a human grandmother's most precious plates.

"425..." Jack muttered, looking between his token and the house numbers. "425..."

The arrangement of houses was pretty clear-cut. A few minutes later, Jack halted. "425!" he exclaimed, looking at the number carved over the entrance. He pushed the fence door, crossed the garden, then held his token against the lock—it seemed electronic, but who knows, it could also be magical.

With a click, the metal door slid open. Jack smiled. This was nice.

The house was nice too. No, not just nice, it was luxurious. There was everything from a mini-bar full of alcohol—both earthen and alien ones—to a hot tub in the bathroom. Even when he'd gone abroad for conferences, Jack had never experienced such luxury.

"Hehehe." He couldn't help but giggle, deciding to relax in his hot tub before going to sleep. He'd briefly considered fetching Edgar and going out to see the night life, if there was any, but hot water clearly took priority.

Oh, right, he remembered. Karvahul mentioned the basement. I wonder why...

After looking around, he found a door and, behind it, a flight of steps going down. He followed them to reach a dark space that felt spacious. After a moment of fumbling, he flipped the light switch, and...

Oh. My. God.

CHAPTER FORTY-EIGHT
TRAINING FACILITIES

A TRAINING ROOM STRETCHED BEFORE JACK AND BROCK.

The basement was large—almost as wide as the house above. Its walls held a blue metallic sheen, just subdued enough to force focus, and curved slightly outward, making the middle of the room wider than its top and bottom. When Jack touched a wall experimentally, it was soft, like the training mats people used for martial arts. The floor was made of the same material.

Moreover, the room had plenty of equipment: weights, dumbbells, wires, and training tapes. There was even a punching bag hanging from a hook in a corner!

Brock went bananas. He rushed to a small dumbbell and tried to lift it among cries of joy, only to be disappointed when it refused to budge. There was a "50kg" sign on its side.

While Brock was huffing and puffing at the dumbbell, Jack approached the punching bag, dropped his backpack, and drove a punch straight into it. There was a gong sound, and it barely budged. "Fu—" Jack clenched his hand in pain. That thing was solid metal!

"Fucking fuck..." he muttered under his breath as he walked away. "Who does that!"

Still shaking his hand, he then approached a heap of what looked like practice targets. When he touched one, it hummed and floated up.

"Woah!" he said, stepping back.

Practice Target
This target can repair itself after breaking, allowing for extended usage. Additionally, it is enchanted with floating powers. It can hover in place where the user indicates, making it suitable for complex training routines.
Enchanted by Horrificus Egen

"Woah," Jack repeated. The target was white and round, with a red ring drawn on it and a red dot dead-center. It was about the size of Jack's head. However, though the description mentioned enchanting, which sounded magical, the target's humming indicated mechanical components.

He'd never seen anything like it.

It can repair itself? he wondered, then punched the target.

It was hard like wood. A pre-System human would have broken their hand on it. Jack, however, wasn't a pre-System human, so his fist sailed smoothly through the wood, cleanly breaking the target into three parts that flew away.

There were no gears inside, only wood.

A moment later, the three parts floated toward each other and reconnected into a whole target. Jack blinked. He looked at the heap of practice targets. There were at least two dozen of them. He turned back to his target.

"So, you think you're tough."

He punched the repaired target again—this time even harder. The pieces flew off to different parts of the room then slowly reformed. Jack punched it again. The pieces were slightly slower this time. He grinned.

It took five minutes and about thirty breaks before the target gave up and stayed fragmented.

"Yay for science," he muttered. "Jack 1, targets 0." Bullying these targets was a great way to let off steam.

Leaving the poor wood aside for now, he explored the rest of the room. Most things were familiar, if completely out of whack compared to Earth. He spotted steel dumbbells weighing up to three hundred kilograms each. His waist hurt just looking at them.

However, what drew his attention the most was a mat placed in a corner. It wasn't eye-catching by itself, but the way it had been given space drew him in. Approaching to take a closer look, he noticed it was made of thin silk, like the most treasured carpet of a desert family. It was small, the size of a shower towel, and depicted psychedelic patterns that made little sense but prodded Jack's mind in especially peculiar ways. Just looking at the mat heightened his mind.

Meditation mat (F-Grade)
A meditation mat that can sharpen the focus of F-Grade cultivators. Its woven patterns resonate with the lesser Dao, making it more active around the mat and therefore easier to perceive. Moreover, gazing at these patterns is enough to put people in a meditative trance.

One part of Jack's mind noticed the differences between this mat and the practice targets. It had a Grade, and its creator wasn't mentioned. Moreover, it wasn't enchanted, but rather woven with patterns of mystical significance.

Another part was intrigued. He sat down on it, some hidden instinct urging him to sit cross-legged.

Immediately, his thoughts sharpened. His Dao Root became more active, and his mind started to wander by itself, daydreaming about the Dao of the Fist. It felt like a half-dreaming half-awake state, where he had the imagination of dreams but also conscious control over it. Ideas popped into his mind.

It was a wondrous state.

A moment later, Jack realized this sensation resembled the ice waterfall back in his cave, but with a few key differences. One, it wasn't torturous or dangerous to enter. Two, he was perfectly conscious, unlike the selfless state the waterfall thrust him into. And three... the mat was a bit weaker.

After all, for all its troubles, the ice pond was E-Grade.

The mat still remained wondrous, and Jack quickly forgot himself in this Dao-seeking stage. Images and thought fragments paraded his mind, appearing out of nowhere. It felt like someone was throwing ideas into his mind, but it was his subconscious speaking. He let it. His eyes got lost in the woven patterns and closed by themselves. His breath evened, and his body relaxed.

He hadn't had much progress in the Dao after escaping the dungeon. He didn't have a direction to go forward. The Dao Vision felt cloudy as if refusing to give him anything more.

Jack had realized the Dao of the Fist... but then what? Though he'd spent many hours pondering, he'd made virtually no progress. What he lacked wasn't meditation, but experience.

That was how the Dao worked. First, you had to go out and experience the world. Accumulate thoughts, questions, and realizations. Afterward, you meditated, reflecting on them and trying to pry them apart. If you were lucky, nuggets of wisdom relative to your Dao would appear.

These were the two components of understanding—experience and introspection—and that was the way to progress one's Dao.

Jack hadn't come up with these ideas himself, of course. They were written in the advanced information package they'd bought off Ar'Tazul.

So, he'd been stuck.

Until something happened.

After leaving the dungeon, Jack had experienced things. He'd dominated Henry's Fang, organized his faction, took control of Valville, and fought Gan Salin, who possessed two Dao Roots. There were hints there. Tiny realizations flickered in and out of his thoughts occasionally, like flies that got lost in the background. There was something there, some insight he was close to but kept missing.

Then, the Tournament came, and Jack appeared in a square filled with top elites from all ends of Earth. Something clicked in his mind, then. It was like his thoughts had reached an invisible threshold, and the insights that had constantly eluded him solidified.

He couldn't understand them yet, of course, but they were now an object he could touch at will. All he had to do was spend the time to unravel them.

And that's what he set to do.

On the meditation mat, his thoughts flowed smoothly. He reviewed the battle with Henry's Fang and contrasted it against the seed of realization he felt. Why had he dominated them? The answer came easy—because he was strong.

Why had he attacked them to begin with? Because he was confident. Because they were in a collision course already, and he wouldn't back down.

For the first time in a while, he was making real progress. These thoughts rang true but weren't the same ones he always had. This wasn't the Dao of the Fist. Rather, it wasn't *exactly* the Dao of the Fist.

He'd organized his faction and taken control of a town. What made that happen? It wasn't luck, not at all. It was a mixture of strength, skill, confidence, initiative... and yeah, a little bit of luck.

And how had he solved the Gan Salin situation? He'd just punched the guy.

Jack frowned. Something wasn't quite right. His thoughts had veered off the right path at some point, and the insight was tying itself into further knots instead of unraveling. Moreover, he felt tired. This wasn't right. The mat relaxed his thoughts. If he was tired, how long had he been sitting here for?

His eyes opened slowly. The lighting had lowered while he was meditating—was the simple light bulb above actually high-tech?

Jack stretched his legs and got up. He was a bit sore. His meditation felt quick, but it must have lasted at least half an hour, if not more.

Brock was lying next to the dumbbell, snoring with his belly up.

That long, huh? Well, no matter, Jack thought. He was finally making progress on his Dao. He was on a high.

With a final, appreciative look at the meditation mat, he walked away. Only one thing was left to check in this room—the unassuming door at its far end.

It was dark blue and made of metal. Jack turned the doorknob. The door swung open soundlessly, revealing a room similar to the previous one. It was the same size and had the same soft, metal walls, but there was no equipment here. Instead, the room was completely empty, save for a humanoid robot at the other end.

Jack's eyes widened. *A robot!*

It was made of gray steel. Various shades of the color decorated its body, painted to resemble martial arts clothing, and it stood with eyes closed, back straight, and hands clasped behind its back.

The moment Jack entered the room, its eyes snapped open, revealing white irises.

"Hello, master," it said in a smooth, un-robot-like, yet matter-of-fact voice. "I am your training partner. How can I be of assistance?"

Training Robot (E-Grade)
A robot made to be the perfect training partner. It is intelligent, obedient, can help with chores or exercise, and can spar at seven different levels of power.
Enchanted by Horrificus Egen

Jack stared at the robot, which stared back, probably expecting a response.

"Are you really a robot?" he asked.

"Yes, master."

"And what can you do?"

"I am only limited by the ends of my power and my core directives, which constrain my functionalities to training-related tasks."

"How do you work?"

"I have been enchanted by the Dao of Automation, Master. I do not know more details."

Jack was launching questions in rapid-fire mode, and the robot was responding simply and accurately. Befitting a robot, its patience appeared infinite.

Eventually, Jack calmed down. This robot was a training partner. What did its description say again?

"You have seven levels of powers," he said. "How strong are they?"

"They range from the early F-Grade to the middle E-Grade, master. Unfortunately, controlling my strength in finer detail is beyond me. I am obligated to inform you that by using me, you accept sole responsibility for any injuries."

"Injuries to me or you?"

"You, master. It is unlikely you will be able to damage me."

"Is that so? Okay. Wanna spar?"

"Of course, master. What level of power?"

"Which is closer to the early E-Grade?"

"The fifth."

"Then, that."

"Very well. You can begin whenever you want, master."

Jack cracked his knuckles, grinned, and charged.

He'd chosen the early E-Grade because, unlike what his bravado might indicate, he was careful. The F-Grade went up to level 50, and the black wolf Jack had beaten had been an Elite level 49. He'd gotten significantly stronger since then, too. The early E-Grade felt like a good challenge.

It wasn't.

The robot moved so fast it disappeared. The next moment, it was standing next to Jack, who was still mid-charge. He barely had time to lower his arm before a steel fist rammed into his elbow, planting it into his own ribs and sending him flying into a wall.

All air was knocked out of his chest. A rib must have cracked. Fortunately, the walls were soft, and they absorbed most of the momentum. The robot was still standing there, retracting its extended fist. At some point, a first aid kit had appeared in its other hand.

"Should I provide medical care, master?" it asked. Jack could swear its voice was mocking.

"I'm fine," he groaned, pulling himself off the ground. He glared at the robot, which wasn't the least bit intimidated. "Was that really the early E-Grade?" he asked. "How can the difference be that large? I've beaten an Elite level 49 monster."

"The transition from F to E-Grade is a large change, master," the robot explained. "The physical body is imbued with the Dao. All aspects rise, and the cultivator's Dao becomes much stronger and easier to use. I cannot use any Dao, but my physical prowess is enhanced to overall resemble an opponent at the early E-Grade level of power."

Jack grumbled.

At that point, a solid piece of poop flew through the door and smacked the robot in the chest. It seemed confused. Jack burst into laughter, then moaned as his cracked rib sent a jolt of pain through him.

Brock flew in after his poop with a war cry, ready to protect Jack. His little fists were clenched, and he didn't seem to care about the obvious size difference.

"Wait, Brock," Jack said with mirth. "It's okay. Don't hurt it."

Brock listened, stopping his charge, but he still said something threatening in monkey-talk. He pointed two fingers to his eyes, then to the robot.

"I am terrified," the robot said. "I will be careful, as you say."

Jack nodded. The robot pulled a set of napkins from inside its forearm, made sure there was no dirt left on it, then grabbed the poop from the floor and tossed it into a trash can in the corner.

"I recommend the fourth level, master," it continued, turning back to Jack with a hint of annoyance in its voice. "It will make me equivalent to the peak of the F-Grade. Then, you will probably be able to win."

"Probably my ass," Jack grumbled. "I will beat you at the fifth level. But not now. I have a cracked rib and a fight tomorrow."

The Tournament started in the morning, after all. As much as Jack wanted to play with this robot, he needed to be in top shape. Who knew how strong the opponents would be?

The medical kit, which had disappeared, was suddenly within the robot's hand again.

"I can provide medi—"

"I'm fine." Jack waved it away. Not that he held a grudge against it, but his natural regeneration would handle the injury if he just slept well.

Plus, what would a first aid kit do about a cracked rib? Bandage it?

"Very well, master." The robot returned to its original position after hiding the medical kit in a corner. "I wish you a speedy recovery. When your power is less lacking, I will be happy to fight you at my fifth level again."

"Wh—" Jack was caught off guard. "*Lacking*? Your mother is lacking!"

"I have no mother, master. I came out of an oven."

Jack glared. He could *swear* the robot was gloating. Was irritability built into it? Was it payback for before?

"Is there anything else, master?" it asked, weathering his stare like it was nothing.

"No. Rest well. I'm coming for you."

"Of course, master."

Ignoring the irritating robot, Jack put Brock on his shoulder, and closed the door behind him. Returning to the upstairs portion of his house, he spared a glance for the hot tub—as much as he would have liked to try, cracked ribs were painful.

Therefore, abandoning all thoughts of nightlife, Jack looked around until he found the bedroom, then fell on his king-sized bed with clothes still on and Brock beside him. He expected pain. Instead, the mattress was so soft and comfortable, he drifted away in seconds.

CHAPTER FORTY-NINE
ENTERING THE ARENA

JACK AWOKE CALMLY TO THE SOUND OF AN ALARM. HIS EYES OPENED, TAKING IN the foreign room.

"What?" he said before remembering where he was. "Right... The Integration Tournament. House 425."

He reached for his phone and turned off the alarm. There was still no signal—all satellites had been lost when the System arrived—but it was still useful for simple stuff like that. He stretched, fully healed, filled with energy, and pumped up. Then he looked down at his rumpled clothes. He'd fallen asleep with them on. *Well, it was a long day. And I got my ass kicked by a smug robot.*

Said robot had ignited his fighting spirit. He couldn't help grinning. The memory of his personal training room was fond. He'd pay that bastard back tenfold.

Look at that. I'm in a nice mood today. A good omen.

Whoever faced him in the arena today would be a very, very unlucky person. Jack might not have any idea how the Tournament worked, but that was fine. The mystery was intriguing.

His bedroom was spacious and decorated in light colors. There was an empty wardrobe, a king-sized bed, and two bed stands flanking it, each with its own lamp. There was also a set of shutters leading to the yard and a glass window on the roof, letting the morning sunlight stream in and fall on the wall opposite the bed.

He looked at his cellphone. Six o'clock.

Plenty of time.

With a light whistle, Jack got up and started his day. He visited the bathroom, which was disappointingly empty of high-tech Dao stuff. The only surprising thing was his face in the mirror, which he almost punched on reflex. He'd forgotten he was disguised and got spooked.

He then headed for the kitchen—which was very sunny!—and started opening cupboards at random. They were filled with every necessity, from salt to whiskey. He even had plenty of food ingredients, as well as pre-cooked steaks and breaded chicken fillets that only needed to be ovened.

He got sliced bread, honey, and a knife. He swept the honey on the bread, then practically inhaled the entire thing. Not only was he starving, but between hunting, meditating, and everything he did on a regular basis, good food had been pushed down the list.

Brock went for a block of ham and demolished it ravenously. He then grabbed his stomach and made upset monkey noises.

Jack laughed. "Eat slower, Brock. Everything good starts from a healthy and balanced diet."

Brock gave him the stink-eye.

"Let's go," Jack said.

He got up to leave, then thought better about it. He'd been to conferences abroad and knew just the thing to do. Opening the fridge, he took a bunch of cheese, salami, and chocolate, as well as a sharp knife and a bunch of napkins. He even put on his spare jacket to have extra pockets.

"Hehehe." He giggled at his own genius.

Jack placed his boots by the door and, after rummaging through cupboards for a bit, fished out a pair of soft, green flip-flops that were roughly his size. In the warmer weather, these would be much comfier than his boots. He fought barefoot, anyway. No shoe could handle his stats.

Finally done with preparations, Jack wiggled his toes, triple-patted his pockets—futuristic credit card, identification token, cellphone—told himself, "I'm ready," and opened his door.

"Oh, thank God," Edgar exclaimed from outside the gate. "I was afraid you'd oversleep!"

"Of course not. I'm a highly responsible person."

Edgar rolled his eyes. Jack smiled and headed for the gate, shaking Edgar's hand.

"I have a question," Edgar said, looking down at Jack's feet. "Why the flip-flops?"

Jack wiggled his toes. "Why not? They're comfy."

"You can't fight in those."

"I fight barefoot."

"We're in a large, planet-wide tournament. There will be thousands of people watching you."

"I don't care. Boots are stuffy, and the weather is nice. If they have a problem with my attire, they can let me know."

Edgar tried to retaliate but found himself unable to. Instead, he simply shrugged in acceptance. With his flip-flops, tank top, and muscular physique, Jack looked every bit like a seaside surf instructor.

"Shall we?" Jack asked, and Edgar, helpless, followed him into the participants' district.

"How are you feeling?" Edgar asked, hands shoved deep into his pockets and eyes flickering from side to side. "Nervous for the Tournament?"

"Not really. I'll just beat everyone up."

"Even me!"

"*Especially* you."

That got a chuckle out of Edgar, who loosened up a bit. There were people around them, too. Like yesterday, Jack noticed that each and every one of them had the aura of a top-tier expert. He even thought he recognized a few faces.

Acclaimed professors, international business people, sport champions, high-ranking military officers. All sorts of people had used their edge to claw through the System's arrival and come out on top.

Of course, these people were very few. Even if professional athletes had a hundred times higher chances to survive and thrive than a normal person, how many normal people were there to a professional athlete?

The vast majority were everyday dudes and gals, like Jack and Edgar, who'd discovered an edge they never knew they possessed. Regardless, that edge was present now. The air was suffocating around such people —and, at the same time, Jack couldn't help but feel proud for himself.

In this gathering of top elites, he was present. No, not just present—he was probably on the higher-end of strength. After all, he had the Planetary Frontrunner (10) title, along with only nine other people on the planet.

There was a steady stream of participants heading out of their designated area and toward the arena, but it wasn't a crowd, more like a trickle. They saw a blond couple, then four burly men walking side-by-side, and a short woman who Jack swore could have been a librarian pre-System.

Jack and Edgar walked by themselves, not speaking to anyone. They exchanged light banter until they reached the edge of the area.

"Hey!" A short blue person waved at them from the side of the participants' area's gate: Ar'Karvahul.

"Morning, Karvahul," Jack said with a smile. "Why did you wait here? The gate is open."

The djinn raised a brow at the flip-flops but didn't comment. "Good morning, John. Coming inside is forbidden for non-participants."

"But nobody's watching."

"There's *always* someone watching." Karvahul gave an enigmatic smile. "Good morning to you too, Edgar. I hope you had a good night's sleep."

"It was heavenly," the wizard said, reaching up to fix his glasses. "I haven't slept in such a good bed in my life."

"Hah. Integration City is no joke!"

There were more guides of all species waiting outside. Jack saw more wolfmen, spinning-top people, and a bunch of djinns.

"Do your people have a knack for merchant stuff, Karvahul?" he asked.

"More or less. But we have some very strong wizards, too! We aren't fully merchant-focused, like the kovans."

"Kovans?"

It finally occurred to Jack that he could scan these weird races to find out their names. He did so at once.

Kovan, Level ?? (E-Grade)
Faction: Merchant Union (C)

Lycan, Level ?? (E-Grade)
Faction: Merchant Union (C)

"How the heck did those guys evolve?" he asked, looking sideways at a kovan—the spinning-top-shaped people with four arms and a single leg on which they bounced.

"Their planet is odd," Karvahul said. "I think the air there is so dense they can fly. Only E-Grade and above kovans can handle the environment of more normal planets, like this one. That's why they're usually merchants, they have disadvantages in combat."

"Huh. Have you ever been there?"

"No. It lacks business opportunities."

"Makes sense."

Unlike Karvahul, Jack was very interested in knowing more, but he wasn't in a hurry. He'd just ask the first kovan he met. "Let's go."

The town was lively. There were lanterns and colorful lights hanging from the rooftops despite the bright daylight, and Jack thought the alien merchants all wore better clothes than yesterday—or maybe he just imagined it.

"The starting ceremony is a big occasion," Karvahul informed them as they walked through the festive town. "After all, it's not every day you get to see a C-Grade, let alone hear them speak."

"A C-Grade?" Jack stopped.

"Didn't you know? The Planetary Overseer is a C-Grade Sovereign!" Karvahul gestured animatedly. "That's why everyone is so excited! Normal people like us would never get to see a C-Grade in a million years if not for the Integration Tournaments."

"Why not?" Edgar asked curiously.

"What do you mean *why not*? They're Sovereigns! Don't you know how rare that is? We have more inhabitable planets than Sovereigns!"

"How many, then?" Jack asked calmly. On the surface, he was unaffected by Karvahul's enthusiasm. On the inside, however, he was burning. The bald man and the titanic beast had both been at the C-Grade. Now, he would see another person like that?

He couldn't wait.

"There are ten thousand inhabited, System-touchee planets in our galaxy," Karvahul replied, falling into Jack's pace. "Of course, there are billions more that are just floating rocks, and that's without mentioning that half the galaxy is still outside the System's reach."

"Really?" Edgar said.

"Of course. How else would Earth be Integrated if the System wasn't constantly expanding?" Karvahul explained. "Each B-Grade faction can offer the System energy to scan foreign space. In return, any discovered planet becomes a part of that B-Grade faction's territory. That's how the System expands."

"Scalable," Jack said.

"So, we belong to the territory of the Animal Kingdom?" Edgar asked.

"Obviously. The Animal Kingdom paid for the scanning of your astral area, so everything here belongs to them."

"I don't like the sound of that," Jack said. "We don't belong to anyone."

"Of course, of course. It's a figure of speech. Let's just call them your overseers."

A small crowd had formed around them. Other participants drawn in by Karvahul's words. As they had no guide of their own, they simply followed from close enough to overhear. Jack and Edgar didn't mind.

Conversation died down as they approached the arena. It loomed in the sky ahead of them like a stone giant.

The huge, round building—though colosseum really was a better fit—was made of stone, unlike everything else on this island-starship. It had an air of antique savagery that the pleasant town lacked.

However, knowing how large something is and seeing it for yourself are two entirely different matters. Jack watched a pair of birds fly toward the arena. They kept growing smaller until they became little more than dots that vanished behind the colossal structure.

He gulped.

"Don't go getting cold feet," Karvahul said. "I've bet good money on you. I want you to give it your best."

"There's betting?"

"Of course. How else do you think people make money around here?"

"By scamming us."

"You natives are piss-poor." Karvahul laughed heartily at that. "No offense meant, of course."

"None taken. At least we're tall."

Karvahul stared straight at Jack, who had a face of innocence.

"In any case," the merchant said, "I mean that *yes*, of course we're making some money off the natives, like in any market, but the Merchant Union limits our profit margins in accordance with the Star Pact. Nobody will make a fortune selling experience balls here. The real money is in betting. After all, we're experienced people, and the natives are nouveau-rich and clueless on System battles."

"I see. So information merchants have an advantage."

"Precisely."

They reached the arena. Hundred-foot-tall gates welcomed them, making them feel tiny. Stone arches decorated the outside, each housing giant stone sculptures of warriors, while columns thicker than rooms supported the entire building. The walls were made of stone, as were the stairs leading upward.

Of course, this was only one of the arena's two gates.

Entrance was free. However, there was also a little desk next to the stairs, where a djinn official hasted through paperwork, a small line of people waiting. They were all humans.

"This is the registration desk," Karvahul said. "Walk up, show your tokens, register, and let's go! We have to find good spots."

"Sure." Jack and Edgar shrugged as they approached the line. It wasn't that long. Only a woman with short black hair and an archer stood before them. Jack and Edgar obediently got in line.

"Next!" the djinn official shouted, and the woman stepped forth.

"Celin Sakula," she said in a Japanese accent. "Dao of Cold."

The djinn wrote down some stuff, then took her token and filled out a form. Meanwhile, Jack panicked. He turned and whispered to Edgar, "We need to say our Dao!"

"I know!" Edgar hissed back. "This is *terrible*!"

Jack was in disguise. If Gan Salin recognized him, it could spell trouble for both him and his faction back at home. However, this was already pushing it. The disguise potion had only changed his face, not his body shape. If his Dao was public, then Gan Salin could easily put two and two together.

"Robin Von Arginhold," the archer said. He looked like a forest hunter. "Dao of the Bow." The djinn started filling in the paperwork.

Jack was next in line. He looked around, but there were too many people watching. If he ran away now, they would know something was up, and suspicion would quickly blow his cover. Plus, even if he pretended to go to the toilet, it wouldn't help.

Could he lie about his Dao?

"Karvahul," Jack said, waving the merchant over, then whispered, "Can I lie about my Dao?"

Karvahul's eyes narrowed imperceptibly. If Jack wasn't paying attention, he would have missed it. "Of course," he replied, acting nonchalant. "How would they check?"

"Is the Dao of the Fist common?"

"It's quite rare."

"I see. Then I need to find a different one. What do you think would fit me?"

CHAPTER FIFTY
THE DAO OF WHAT!

Karvahul stepped closer. "Find a Dao adjacent to yours," he instructed.

"Edgar Allano. Dao of Magic," Edgar said, taking Jack's turn.

"Like what?" Jack whispered.

"I don't know... Battle? Power? No, you need a weapon. Gauntlets! No, that's too similar. Club? No, they'll know right away... We need something that can work with your skills but isn't *too* close to the fist. A small blunt weapon, maybe?"

There weren't many of those. Jack, at least, failed to come up with any on the fly.

"Next!" the djinn official barked, looking at Jack. A line had already formed behind him, but the next person—a Slavic, wide-necked man—didn't move to take his spot, only stared at Jack with a half-smile like he was onto him.

Jack looked around, searching for inspiration. By the side, Brock was squinting at him, trying to understand what was going on.

In truth, Jack didn't need anything too special. He was confident in beating people up no matter what weapon he used. His gaze wandered over nearby small items that could be used as blunt weapons. Credit cards, stones, pieces of wood, a brick, Karvahul...

The Dao of the Screaming Djinn, he thought with amusement.

The stones seemed to be the best candidate. They were everywhere, could be used as blunt weapons, and weren't too close to the Dao of the Fist, probably.

Problem was, that idea was terrible for publicity.

The professor had instructed him to make as big a wave as possible without blowing his cover. Besides winning the Tournament, their main goal was to gather allies in secret to defend against the eventual retaliation of Gan Salin and the other scions. To that end, who would trust a maniac that smashed other people's heads in with a rock? The rock bears sure wouldn't.

No. He needed something unrelated to the fist, but also something that would draw positive attention to himself. Something softer than a rock. Something that would make other humans want to work with him.

In other words, Jack needed something... *flashy*. He suddenly looked down, and his eyes shone.

"John Brown," he declared, stepping up to the official and handing over his token. "Dao of Spanking."

The crowd went silent. Even the people that were climbing the stairs to the spectator seats stopped and turned to look.

The official raised his eyes, then a brow. "Excuse me?"

"Dao of Spanking," Jack repeated with confidence, channeling his inner strict teacher. "Never heard of it? I'm not surprised. You look like a person that wasn't properly disciplined during their childhood."

The djinn's brows spasmed. "And do you have a weapon, Mr. Brown?"

"Of course I do."

"Interesting. But, I cannot see it..."

Jack stared at the merchant. His little blue eyes were narrowed and gloating. Undoubtedly, he was convinced Jack was lying, and that he'd caught him red-handed.

Unfortunately for the djinn, he was facing Jack Rust.

"If you insist." He shrugged, then stooped to grab one of his flip-flops. "There," he said, holding it like a weapon. "Happy now?"

The djinn's eyes narrowed further. "Sir, I have to warn you that lying in the presence of an Inte—"

He didn't have time to finish his words. Jack spanked the air above him. The world went monochrome. All color disappeared before erupting from the point where the flip-flop snapped, along with a tremendous *BOOM* and a blinding flash.

Some people protested, but the majority simply stared at Jack like he'd just proven the sky did not exist. Even the official was flustered, though he was completely unhurt.

"Is that enough?" Jack asked, holding the bottom half of a burnt flip-flop. The other half was plastered on the wall above the official's head. "Or should I strip myself naked so you can see I don't have any more weapons?"

Brock burst out laughing, pointing at the djinn's face.

The official looked like he wanted to say something, then thought better about it. His blue face turned a pale shade of red, and through clenched teeth said, "I apologize for my suspicions, sir. Everything is in order. Can I have your token, please?"

Jack handed him the token with a straight face, and the registration was completed. He then walked back to Edgar and Karvahul's side like it was the most normal thing in the world, ignoring all the odd gazes. After a while, people stopped paying attention to him, too. The Dao of Spanking was peculiar, but at the end of the day, nothing too important. There were many odd Daos in the Tournament.

"Your flip-flop is ruined," Karvahul said, pointing at the improvised weapon.

"Definitely unfortunate," Jack agreed, shaking his head in mock disappointment, speaking loudly enough that everyone could hear. He pointed at the official. "But prejudice must be disciplined. That is why I always carry a spare." In a broad show, he grabbed his other flip-flop. "Whoops. I'm out of spares. You'll help me find a replacement, right, Karvahul?"

Karvahul's face spasmed. "Of *course*. I will meet you in the arena above."

Thus, only three people ascended the stairs. Jack wielded a flip-flop and had a face of stone, Edgar was muttering to himself, and Brock wasn't really sure what was happening but was having fun.

Meanwhile, Karvahul was searching for flip-flops in Integration City's market, constantly lamenting his life choices.

The arena was a boiling pot of people. A population of many species filled the spectator stands, with humans accounting for the majority. The other four species were the djinns, lycans, kovans, and ifrits.

"Come on, Karvahul!" Jack said. "It's starting."

The merchant cast a stormy frown. "This is cheating. How can they sell corn that expensive and *still* make only 100 percent profit? They have to be lying."

"Should I spank them?" Jack asked. Both Edgar and Karvahul glared at him. "Okay, okay, no spanking..."

The inside of the arena was surrounded by spectator seats, separated from the arena itself by a ten-foot fall. Down that fall was a large oval expanse covered in sand. It sparkled from the sunlight that entered from the open air above. A white tower stretched from one end of the arena to the sky, and had to have been at least five hundred feet tall.

However, the most eye-catching thing was a large cube floating above the central point, even higher than the topmost spectator seats. Its sides were black and covered in a multitude of tiny lights that swirled around like the stars of the night sky, forming a kaleidoscope of constellations. One moment they depicted a deer, the other a fly, then a wolf, and a bunch of animals Jack couldn't recognize. Every few minutes, the stars would form into a roaring lion's head that was many times grander than any other constellation.

"That's the crest of the Leonines," Karvahul explained. "The leading family of the Animal Kingdom."

"Then it really is a kingdom of animals," Jack commented.

"Of course. After the Leonines come the Elefs, the Eaglers, the Sharkens, and the Canines. Those are the five noble families of the Animal Kingdom. There are many others that are less noble—like the Lycans."

"Their planet must have been chaos," Jack noted.

"I heard their evolutionary arms race was extremely intense before the System came. Most of their planet is covered in dense jungle, which led to many species developing opposable thumbs and, consequently, intelligence. The ensuing wars were beyond fierce. Legend says that's why the Animal Kingdom is so strong... but, of course, those could also be rumors. Not many would argue against the noble families in their territory."

"Fascinating..."

"Say that again..." Edgar agreed, though for a wholly different reason. He'd been staring at the magical cube for the past three hours, almost like he was meditating.

"Snap out of it, Edgar," Jack said. "It's starting."

"What?"

The entire audience quieted at the exact same time. Everyone shut up on instinct. There had been no sound, no horn to announce her coming. She was simply there, while the cube had disappeared.

Chills crawled down Jack's spine. His Dao Root shuddered and tried to worm deeper inside his soul. His hair stood on end, and his breath became shallow as he took in that majestic being. Her mere presence suffocated him.

There, hovering above the center of the arena, was the strongest creature Jack had ever seen, with the possible exception of the bald man in his vision. At first glance, she seemed like a cross between a human and a lioness. She stood on two light brown legs, had two arms and a head, and didn't seem to have much fur.

Most of her body was hidden under simple clothes, but so finely crafted they *screamed* power. They had the touch of the Dao on them.

Her most striking feature was her head. That of a lioness.

However, her appearance paled in comparison to the vast aura that roiled in waves from her body. Jack felt like he was staring at an entire ocean, a goddess, or an ancient tree that reached the skies. His every instinct screamed that she was an existence so far above him that even worshiping her would be his honor.

Without thinking about it, he stood and almost fell to his knees. He barely stopped himself at the last second, exerting every iota of willpower he possessed to remain at least somewhat standing. It wasn't a conscious reaction, but an instinctive one, and something that most others failed to do.

You could hear a pin drop the silence was so absolute.

"Rise," the lioness said in a strong voice, and Jack drew in a sharp breath, finally relieved from most of the pressure. He was covered in cold sweat and filled with fearsome awe. This lioness could end him with a thought, and there was nothing he could do about it.

That was nature.

And yet, deep in his soul, something resisted this feeling of absolute obedience. Something demanded freedom. Jack clenched his fists and used all the strength in his soul to ignore his instincts and scan her.

Leonine, Level ??? (C-Grade)
Faction: Animal Kingdom (B)
Title: Seventh Ring Conqueror

His will gave out. Simply summoning the courage to scan her had taken everything he had. He fell back onto his seat, shivering.

The next moment, her aura receded like it had never been there. Everyone regained their bearings. Even Brock was staring blankly at the lioness, his entire body trembling.

"What was that?" Edgar muttered.

Jack shook his head and stood back up just as the lioness started talking.

"Merchants of the Union and people of Earth-387," she began. "Welcome to the galaxy. I am Galicia Lonihor, the Overseer of your planet and a representative of the Animal Kingdom, your new supervisors."

She let the audience digest her words—perhaps carve her name into their minds.

She continued. "Your meaningless lives are over, for we have brought you the gift of the System. You can now participate in the War for Immortality, the System's ultimate directive, and help shape the New World as you see fit. You can grow stronger to degrees you've never imagined, comprehend the Dao and the world, and navigate the stars. Your species finally has a future, and it starts with you."

While she used grand words, Jack noticed her voice lacked color. It felt like giving out this speech was a chore she really didn't care about, and she wanted to be done with it as soon as possible.

"The Integration Tournament is your time to shine. The elites of your elites will fight each other for grand rewards. Some will secure a path to immortality, and others will prove themselves too weak.

"The rules are simple: Over the next days, the participants will be called to fight each other randomly in pairs until one resigns or becomes unable to fight. Death can occur if you are not careful, but keep in mind that willful harming of other participants will add a loss in your record. Whoever accumulates two losses is eliminated, and they lose all privileges of participation. Moreover, every battle will be transmitted through the System to all cultivators of your planet. When only sixteen remain, we will proceed to the final stage. Those sixteen will attain benefits beyond your wildest imagination, so try your hardest. That is the way of the System. The strong get stronger, and the weak get weaker.

"However, do not despair. To all who are watching us through the System transmission, and to all who made it here but will lose their rights to participate soon, this is an opportunity. Watch how strong you have the potential to be. Strive to reach the heights of these fledgling cultivators. Rush here, in the middle of your Pacific Ocean, to trade in premium rates or enjoy the spectacle.

"The future of your species will be determined by the people here. May they fight well. You have been Integrated, and so..." She raised a hand, and the entire arena shook from the ringing of ten massive bells hanging around it. "Let the Integration Tournament begin!"

CHAPTER FIFTY-ONE
THE TOURNAMENT BEGINS!

With the ringing of the ten massive bronze bells, the Tournament officially began.

People erupted into cheers louder than even the ringing. The C-Grade lioness disappeared, and three long energy walls split the arena.

They were transparent and shimmering blue. Two split the space into four equal parts, and the other was horizontal, stretching over the arena's lip and isolating the four mini-arenas that had been created.

A djinn jumped into the air. White wings spread from her back as she came to hover over the center of the arena, where the two criss-crossing walls met. She held a scroll in her hand.

Jack scanned her.

Djinn, Level ??? (E-Grade)
Faction: Merchant Union (C-Grade)

It was almost the same screen he saw every time he scanned a djinn. Though his sharp eyes noticed there was an extra question mark on this one. Ar'Tazul and Ar'Karvahul only had two question marks. Though the lioness also had three.

Does that mean her level is three digits? he wondered. Interesting... The E-Grade extends to the hundreds.

He then realized there was a much easier way to find out.

"Hey, Karvahul, up to what level does E-Grade go?"

"125," replied the djinn, shooting him a weird look. "Why are you asking this now?"

"Just curious."

He turned his attention back to the arena and the flying, three-digit-level djinn.

"Attention, participants," she read from her scroll. "The rules have already been announced to you by Her Nobility. I am Al'Marazith, the head judge for this Integration Tournament, and I will handle the more mundane parts. As Her Nobility said, you will fight a series of rounds, each lasting exactly one Earth-387 day. For every round, each participant will only fight once, at a maximum time limit of ten Earth-387 minutes.

"Before the beginning of each round, your fighting order and opponents will be randomized. Your identification tokens will buzz and glow an hour before your scheduled fight. To avoid no-shows, we encourage you all to be here each dawn, when the names are randomized. After all, you might have to fight first.

"Finally, the Animal Kingdom will graciously provide ten thousand credits to the winner of each fight. These will be transferred automatically to your identification token, from where you can draw it into your credit card."

Whispers erupted at the sound of such a large sum. A man with strong lungs, however, had another question. He stood and shouted, "What about ties?"

"Then, both opponents lose," she replied.

Jack found himself nodding. That made sense. *When is my fight?* he wondered, glancing at his token. It wasn't shining.

"I will randomize your names now," the flying djinn said, still staring at her scroll. It shone bright, then dimmed. Jack's token glowed silver. So did Edgar's.

"Dude!" Jack said, raising his hand for a high-five. "Nice! We're lucky."

"I'm scared," Edgar responded, matching Jack's high-five dispiritedly. "What if I lose on the first round?"

"You'll have another shot. Come on, Edgar! Live it up a little!"

"I guess you're right..."

"Here, have this. It will braven you up." Jack retrieved a pack of salami from his jacket pocket, and handed a slice to Edgar. They were already pre-cut, how convenient.

Edgar's eyes widened. "What's that?" he asked.

"Salami."

"No, I mean, where did you find it?"

"In my fridge. There's lots of them."

"No, I—" He was in utter disbelief for some reason. "Why do you have salami?"

"To eat it?" Jack raised a brow. "I have cheese too if you prefer."

Edgar groaned.

"Ooo, is that salami?" Karvahul asked. "Can I have some?"

"Sure." Jack let Karvahul have a slice, then took one himself. Two slices went to Brock, whose sneaky hand had already been reaching for them.

"Yummy, right?"

"Totally. Fuck those corn-selling cheating bastards."

The winged djinn's voice washed over them again. "First fights. Elijah Hogan and the Dao of the Chain versus Chloe Barnes and the Dao of the Axe. Billy Walsh and the Dao of Cold versus Lauren Foster and the Dao of the Dagger. Kane Vanderdecken and the Dao of Metal versus Xi Shin and the Dao of Beauty. Chad Morgan and the Dao of the Gun versus Kwau Okonjo and the Dao of Music."

The horizontal energy wall acting as the roof of the arena disappeared. A few moments later, eight forms jumped into the four mini-arenas, and the roof closed over them. The audience cheered. Jack opened his eyes wide, and even Brock leaned against the railing to have a better view.

Four djinns stepped on the arena lip, each overseeing one fight. "Start!" they declared at the same time, and a ton of magic went flying. Jack watched with rapt attention.

These people were good.

Of the eight down there, all were probably stronger than Henry White, and this was just the first round. Unfortunately, four fights at once were too much to take in. He glimpsed an axe-wielding woman getting tangled up in chains, while the dagger-wielder started shivering but bravely moving forth. The other two fights interested him more.

A long-haired young man with spiked wristbands and a leather jacket made a metal sign at his opponent. "Alright!" he shouted before starting to sing Chop Suey at the top of his lungs and head-bang. His opponent, a gorgeous young woman, covered her ears and screamed mutedly. Then, she powered through the pain to flash him a devastating smile.

The young man faltered, going off-tune. That was enough for the woman to approach him, hips swaying hypnotizingly. Jack had to shake his head to wake up—the young man wasn't so lucky. He stared at her with a stupid smile until she came within ten feet of him.

Suddenly, his long hair fell before his eyes, and he recovered. An electric guitar appeared in his hands out of thin air. Before the woman could respond, he struck a crescendo so hard it unleashed a visible shockwave, slamming her into the far wall. She fell on one knee, bleeding from the ears.

"I resign," she muttered.

The young man raised his pinky and index finger at her. "Begone, thot! I only play for the DEVIL!"

He strung his guitar once more, and the crowd erupted into cheers. Jack found himself cheering along. This was fun!

"Salami," Karvahul said, stretching out a hand without looking.

"I didn't hear a please."

"...Please."

"There you—Wait. Where's my salami!"

It was in Brock's rapidly-chewing mouth. He flashed guilty puppy eyes at Jack, who only laughed. "No problem. I have another."

The first battle was done—the axe woman got fully entangled in chains and resigned. In the second, the dagger-wielder reached the cold mage and made him resign. The fourth battle, however, was still going at full force.

A clean-shaven, military type man was shooting his rifle at a dark-skinned woman with a long wooden flute. Notes kept flying out of it, meeting the bullets midair and sending them off-course. Now that the metal guy had stopped screaming, Jack could hear her music. A sort of deep, calming tune that nullified the man's attacks.

At the next moment, finally uncreasing her brow—probably annoyed at the metal guy—she changed her tunes. Her flute now released deep, thudding sounds and crimson melodies like a song of war. Jack's blood boiled. Crimson notes flew out of her flute and rammed into the bullets, plowing through them in order to surround her opponent.

The gunman defended valiantly. He turned his rifle around so hard it seemed random, yet he hit each note accurately. He probably had a skill for infinite bullets, too.

The bard stepped forth as she reached a crescendo. Her music accelerated. A long row of notes flew out like an army. Half formed a shield before her, stopping the incoming bullets, and the other half darted at the gunman. He did his best, but he was overwhelmed.

A note smashed into him with a small explosion, making him grunt in pain, and another followed soon after, hitting his legs and dropping him to the ground.

"I resign," he said quickly, and a wave from the bard made all other notes disperse.

The crowd roared. Not only were these people extremely strong, but their powers were exciting, too!

"This is one of the allures of an Integration Tournament," Karvahul said with a smile. "On more developed planets, people know which Daos work and which don't. They are much more uniform. Here, you can see all sorts of fun stuff."

"I thought all Daos worked," Edgar said.

"Theoretically, yes, but some are more difficult than others. Take the gun person, for example. Even with his talent, he'll struggle to find suitable complementary Dao Roots, let alone step into the D-Grade."

"What?"

"I'll tell you later."

All fighters left the arena, either jumping back to their seats or taking the stairs and elbowing through the crowd. The head judge announced the next pairings. It still wasn't Jack or Edgar's turn. However, two of the pairings were very interesting.

One included a young man sitting right next to Jack. Jack had his eye on the guy. Though he looked like a kid, he was level 38. The previous fighters had all been under 30.

When he jumped into the stage, he seemed to fall faster than gravity would indicate. According to the announcer, he was Dorman Whistles, with the Dao of Speed. His opponent barely had time to draw her weapon—a metal pipe—before Dorman had his daggers at her throat.

"I resign..." she said breathlessly. The crowd didn't cheer as hard. Most were still reeling from this guy's speed, as was Jack.

He was fairly confident he could sweep the floor with any of the previous eight fighters. This Dorman, however... Jack looked at his flip-flop. *If I meet someone strong, this could be a struggle. Maybe I should have gone for the Dao of Spanking With My Fist.*

Dorman jumped back up, then flashed Jack a smile.

"Nice fight," Jack said. "Salami?"

"Sure," Dorman replied. He had Chinese features and commanded a nonchalant attitude and two daggers at his waist. He didn't even flinch when Jack pulled the salami out of his pockets—maybe he'd seen the previous one. "Nice monkey."

"Thanks. His name is Brock."

"Is he a good boy?"

"A strong one."

The other interesting pairing didn't end as fast. It was a battle between a dark-skinned man with the Dao of Fire and an eastern European woman with the Dao of Ice. These two were already polar opposites, so Jack expected a good fight. What he didn't expect was the tension in the spectator stands across from him, where two groups were facing off.

One was made up of dark-skinned people and led by a woman in fiery red athletic clothes. The other were pale-skinned, hard-faced Slavs, led by a big guy with hands as big as shovelheads. The two groups were a few stands apart, but they stared at each other while their leaders shouted something Jack couldn't catch.

"That's the Flame River and the Ice Peak," Karvahul explained.

"They're two of the three major factions of your planet, and they're expected to be at odds due to their opposite powers."

"Are factions supposed to be built around a power theme? Like fire or ice?" Edgar asked, inspecting the people across from them.

"Usually, yes. You'll see. When people get used to the System, your planet's factions will gravitate toward that model, too. Those ones are just ahead of the curve. They probably control fire-oriented and ice-oriented resources."

The Forest of the Strong had Physical-oriented resources. It was reasonable that Jack's faction would focus on melee combat.

The people in the stands shouted at each other for a bit, then focused on the battle below with heated eyes. Coming to blows was against the rules, but that didn't apply to the people in the arena.

The dark-skinned man with the power of fire and the Slavic woman with the power of ice clashed fiercely. Both were over level 30, unlike the vast majority of people, and their battle wasn't to be taken lightly. Incidentally, both also sported the Planetary Frontrunner (100) title, which probably meant they were one of the first hundred people on Earth to get a Dao Root.

They weren't the first people Jack saw with that title, but there were fewer of them than he would expect.

Torrents of fire smashed into chunks of ice. Sharp, frosty peaks rose from the ground under the fire man, who somehow used fire to propel himself through the air. His limbs were clad in flames.

The Slavic woman held a thick shield of ice. They appeared to be equally proficient in both ranged and melee combat because, when they clashed, it didn't end quickly. They kept striking and dancing around each other for a good minute before the Slavic woman snuck a fist in, sending the dark-skinned man flying to the far wall.

He fell to the ground and spat blood. He rose again.

"That's enough, Sadaka! Resign!" the dark-skinned woman—probably the leader of their faction—shouted from the stands. Her voice washed over the arena without need for magic amplification.

The dark-skinned man—Sadaka—glared at the Slavic woman, who made the "come at me" gesture with a smug smile. Sadaka almost charged before gritting his teeth so hard Jack was afraid they'd break.

"I resign," he forced out, shivering from the humiliation. The audience cheered for him—he was plenty strong—but that didn't make him feel better. At the same time, his opponent shook her head in disappointment.

Both fighters jumped back to their stands, where their factions were back to ignoring each other.

"Oh, wow," Jack said. "Those guys are really going at it."

"I told you, they're polar opposites." Karvahul shrugged. "They're heavily inclined to clash."

The announcer announced the next pairings. Among them, one stood out. "Edward Hole and the Dao of the Club versus John Brown and the Dao of... Spanking."

She hesitated for a split-second before announcing Jack's Dao, then looked at the arena curiously, waiting to see who showed up.

"Finally!" Jack said with a smile. "I'm up."

"Good luck!" Edgar and Karvahul said in one voice.

Beside them, Dorman quipped, "Careful," between bites.

Jack knew what he meant: *be careful not to ruin the salami in your pockets.*

He jumped down, floating through the air to land on the sand. The feeling was completely different here. The damp smell, the eyes on him, the big-bodied opponent staring him down with a large club on his shoulder.

This felt like the time he boxed Harambe, but so much grander. Jack grinned. The battle fever rose in him. He clutched his flip-flop.

It was time for a thorough spanking.

CHAPTER FIFTY-TWO
SPANKING THE LION

Jack's opponent was a large guy wielding an equally large metal pipe. His upper body was bare and scarred, his eyes were hard. Overall, quite badass.

Jack's physique was equally intimidating, except he wore a tank top and casually held a flip-flop.

"Dao of Spanking?" the large guy said, eyes twitching. "I will show you a world of pain, kid."

"Oh, yeah? It's clear your parents didn't spank you enough. Let me help."

The audience cheered at their trash-talking. Jack inspected his opponent.

Human, Level 28
Faction: -

There wasn't much to write home about. This guy was average for the Tournament.

Jack, however, wasn't. The large guy's eyes widened as he, too, fired off a scan. He dropped into a battle stance, not daring to take Jack lightly.

"So, you have some skill..." he muttered, watching Jack's every movement. "But I'm not weak either. Come!"

"Listen man, how about you just surrender and—"

"Shut up!"

Jack's eyes narrowed. "Fine. Have it your way."

The large man charged like a rhino, pipe held high. When it swung, the sand flew around him, and the sound was loud and sharp enough to make the nearby spectators frown.

Jack, of course, was no longer there. He'd appeared behind his opponent, shaking his head in mock disappointment. "What disrespect..."

Hearing the voice coming from behind, the brute panicked and tried to jump away, but it was too late.

The flip-flop landed on his buttocks with a crisp slap. Everyone recoiled, while the large guy flew and landed face-first into the sand, dragging through it for a few feet. When he stood up again, his face was red, and not just from blood.

"I will fucking kill you!" he roared, dashing in.

Jack sidestepped the pipe twice. He was already faster than his opponent. With such a large, unwieldy weapon, there was no chance of catching him.

Jack disappeared again. The giant of a man whipped around, only to find nothing. He turned back the other way in shock—Jack still wasn't there!

"Where are you!" he roared.

"Always behind you. You turn slower than a ship."

Another slap hit his buttocks and sent him into the sand again.

The audience erupted in laughter. Though there were three more fights going on, Jack had already become the star of the show. All eyes were on him—a fact that only increased his opponent's humiliation.

Jack felt a bit bad. He was lucky enough that the System didn't even consider the flip-flop a weapon, letting him use the Fistfighting skill. However, though he was easily faster than his opponent, he couldn't finish the fight quickly. If he attacked any harder, the flip-flop would break, and he might be exposed!

Even with Integration City's materials, it could barely handle this level of stress.

Jack took in his opponent's form, and his eyes softened. "Come on, man. Surrender already."

The large man glared daggers and clenched his teeth. He clearly wanted to tear Jack limb from limb. However, at the end of the day, he was someone with enough mental faculties to comprehend a Dao Root and join the Integration Tournament.

"I resign," he ground out, and the audience erupted yet again.

Jack extended a hand, but his opponent ignored it and jumped into the spectator stands, then departed the arena. Jack shook his head.

I'm sorry, friend, but you can only blame yourself for being weak—and your luck for pitting you against me. At least you have another shot at the Tournament.

It took two losses for disqualification.

Meanwhile, the audience was still buzzing with cheers for Jack. He'd already developed into a crowd favorite. When he climbed back to his spot, Karvahul welcomed him with open arms.

"I can already see it, my boy," he declared. "We'll make a fortune!"

"Sure thing, Karvahul."

"That was great, Jack!" Edgar showered him with excitement. "You beat that guy easily!"

"He wasn't too strong." Jack shrugged. He went to pet Brock, who was already extending an open palm and expecting a salami. "We'll see how long I can keep it up."

"Excellent victory," a woman from nearby came to congratulate Jack. Now that he'd shown his strength, people would clamor to meet him.

Not that he minded. They were all elites, and he needed as many connections as he could get.

"Thank you," he replied with a smile, shaking the woman's hand. "Would you like some cheese?"

"Excuse me?"

He removed a package of cheese from his pocket and gave her a slice. "They're excellent snacks, and cheap, too. The merchants here are killing it."

She nodded in appreciation before returning to her seat. Another man took her place.

Before long, a small crowd had gathered around Jack, basking in his glory and free snacks. Many had noticed Dorman Whistles—the one who'd displayed excellent speed—sitting next to Jack, but he outright ignored anyone who spoke to him.

Meanwhile, Edgar was getting more and more nervous.

"—Second fight, Edgar Allano and the Dao of Magic versus Robin von Arginhold and the Dao of the Bow."

"Shit!" Edgar paled. Jack got excited.

"Finally! Go, Edgar! And don't mind if you lose. Just do your best!"

"You got it, kid." Karvahul slapped his back, making Edgar stumble a step.

"Yeah..." Edgar gulped. "Fine. I'm going."

Despite Edgar's nervousness, his powers were flashy. Magic was no joke.

A blue cloud appeared under his feet and slowly delivered him to the arena, where a tall man with a bow and a green cap awaited. He was the one right before them in the registration line, and he stood at least a hundred feet away from Edgar.

Human, Level 27
Faction: Robin's Boys

Edgar nodded. The archer nodded back. Then, he nocked an arrow and loosed it.

Edgar was barely ready. He erected a hasty blue shield that stopped the arrow in its tracks, except he frowned in the process.

From the spectator stands, Jack also frowned. He didn't know exactly how Edgar's powers worked, but he assumed they used mana—the System's magical resource. Therefore, he could only imagine that stopping an arrow like that must have cost a lot.

Edgar seemed to agree. A second arrow was already on its way, and he curved his shield to change its course, not stopping it outright. This took significantly less mana.

The archer released two more arrows, which Edgar deflected with minimum effort. The archer countered by shooting straight into Edgar's center of mass, making deflections more difficult. Edgar countered the counter by running around, letting his deflections work with better angles.

Nobody got a Dao Root without putting in a lot of effort. For all of Edgar's squirming, he'd been the highest-level cultivator of Valville outside Henry's Fang. He hunted monsters alone, braved dangers, and danced with death. After Jack took over, Edgar continued hunting and reached level 24.

He was no weakling.

Even a quarter of the arena was enough for people to fight at long range. The archer kept firing from a hundred feet away, and Edgar was content to let that happen. After all, the opponent's quiver was emptying quickly, and his displeasure indicated he was out of ideas.

When the arrows became sparser, Edgar went on the offensive. He opened his arms and unleashed a flock of transparent blue hawks that flew at the archer from all directions. Seeing that, the archer charged right for Edgar, letting the birds surround him.

As he charged, he spun around and rapidly unleashed arrows. He no longer went for his quiver. Arrows made of mana materialized in his hands, letting him shoot faster and with no ammo considerations.

He was amazing to watch. He spun and worked the bow string at mind-boggling speeds, accurately taking down all birds that approached him. Edgar instructed them to maneuver, but his concentration was clearly stretched thin. The birds could only wobble, completely unable to dodge the onslaught or throw off the archer's aim.

Moreover, the archer was fast, way too fast. His left hand held the bow, and his right a machete that he'd drawn from under his cloak. He reached Edgar in a moment and slashed the machete at his shield at an angle that couldn't be deflected, only blocked head-on. The shield disappeared, giving way to a massive fireball that flew at the archer's face and torso—he'd seen it coming.

Instead of following through with his strike, the archer used the momentum to tilt his body heavily sideways, letting the fireball sail narrowly over his head. As his body was bent almost ninety degrees to the right, he resumed his slash, aiming at Edgar's armpit from below.

The change had occurred so fast Edgar had no hope of responding in time. And yet, the shield reappeared at the perfect spot to block.

Edgar had calculated exactly what the archer would do. Finding his attack blocked and himself completely off-balance, the archer had no time to move before Edgar's outstretched right hand—the one that had pushed the large fireball—slammed down into him, unleashing a new fireball equally massive as the first. It was like a fireplace. If it hit and pinned the archer to the ground, it would do more than second degree burns.

"I resign!" he rapidly croaked out.

Edgar's fireball winked out of existence. His hand slapped the chest of the other man, who fell on his back, already off-balance as he was.

The arena, that had been completely silent before, erupted into a new round of cheers. Jack cheered the hardest. Brock's triumphant monkey yells echoed throughout the stands—after all, he considered Edgar part of his pack!

Though Edgar and the archer's battle hadn't been at the highest level, it had undoubtedly been one of the most intense yet.

Edgar was sweating buckets, shivering, and breathing quickly. Despite that, he held out an arm for the other man, who grabbed it from the forearm and pulled himself up.

"Nice battle," the archer said. He had a thick blond mustache over his lips, and despite his face's sharp lines, he should have been around forty. "You got me there."

"It was just luck," Edgar said.

"What are you saying, boy? Open your ears. All those people are cheering for you!"

Edgar looked around, only now noticing he was showered in cheers. Hundreds, maybe thousands of people were clapping for him. He immediately felt flustered, proud, awkward, and simultaneously like he wanted to roar and hide in a hole. He had no idea what he felt.

"See you around," the archer said, waving and jumping back to his seat. As if dreaming, Edgar used his last dregs of mana to summon a blue cloud under his feet and fly next to Jack, where he collapsed in his seat.

"Well done." Jack smiled, patting his shoulder. "You were awesome down there!"

"I knew you had it in you, my boy!" Karvahul patted his other shoulder.

Edgar's thoughts moved so fast he couldn't form words. He almost spiraled into a panic attack before feeling a soft, warm feeling from his lap. Looking down, it was Brock, who was sitting on his lap and giving him a manly thumbs-up.

Edgar smiled.

"Thank you," he said.

"Are you okay?" Jack asked.

"No... but I'll be fine."

"Perfect. Want some salami?"

"God yes."

The nearby people erupted into laughter. Thanks to the performance of Jack and Edgar, as well as Jack's free snacks that served as easy invitations, a lively group had already formed around them, laughing and chatting. They couldn't see it, but many people were staring at them throughout the arena.

They stayed for a while longer, but not much was happening. Though some strong people appeared, their enemies were nothing special. No more interesting fights occurred. At some point, Jack was running out of snacks, and Edgar was feeling more and more stuffy thanks to all the people.

"Wanna go for a walk?" Jack asked. "We can't stay here all day. There will be fights for a long time, and they'll only get more interesting as time goes by."

It wasn't just him. Half the arena was empty now as people were trickling out. Edgar nodded quickly, and a beat later, so did Karvahul.

"See you, guys," Jack waved goodbye to their new friends. They didn't invite anyone else along. Though Jack had some social skills, he wasn't a particularly social man himself, and his networking efforts had a limit. A couple friends—and Karvahul—were enough.

However, as they were about to exit the spectator stands, the announcer's voice caught Jack's ear.

"Rufus Emberheart and the Dao of Supremacy versus Maylin Rubenstein and the Dao of the Fist."

Dao of the Fist?

It was the first time he heard his own Dao being called out. Karvahul had said it was really rare. He turned back to the arena, where two people faced off.

One was a barbaric-looking woman with clenched fists and teeth.

The other was a lion-man. A leonine, the same race as the C-Grade Overseer. One of the five scions. A blond mane framed his head, and his golden eyes seemed to see through everything.

"That's the Tournament favorite. He's almost certainly the winner," Karvahul said somberly. "Rufus Emberheart. The strongest of the scions."

"Is he really that strong?" Jack asked. He hadn't caught sight of Gan Salin or any of the other five scions in the arena—wherever they were hiding, they clearly didn't want to meddle with the common riffraff of this planet.

"You'll see."

Jack scanned both fighters.

Human, Level 31
Faction: -

Leonine, Level 49
Faction: -
Title: Planetary Frontrunner (1)

Forty-nine? Jack was shocked before realizing what his title said. His eyes widened. *One!*

The leonine stared at his opponent like she was a fly. Jack was intimately insulted. This girl had the same Dao as him—the Dao of the Fist—so there was kinship between them.

She charged, fists held at the ready. Rufus Emberheart raised his hand—a lion paw—and simply swiped it forward.

Jack didn't understand what happened. One moment, the woman was charging. The next, she was plastered on the far energy wall, the sound of her breaking bones echoing throughout the arena. She fell to the ground and didn't stand again.

The audience didn't cheer. They were too busy considering what just happened. A djinn healer approached the woman with glowing blue hands, kneeling beside her, only to frown deeply. A moment later, the blue glow faded. She looked at the head judge and shook her head.

The head judge glowered. She gave Rufus Emberheart a long stare. For his part, he simply remained motionless, then jumped all the way to a small, curtained-off section at the highest end of the spectator stands—probably where the scions rested. He parted the curtain and made to walk through it.

He'd murdered that woman of the Dao of the Fist. He'd clearly been significantly stronger and hadn't held back. Something that was clearly on purpose, and the rules indicated he should be punished.

However, the head judge remained silent, about to let this pass. Was it favoritism? Was it because Rufus was the Tournament favorite, one of the five scions, and a descendant of the Animal Kingdom—though nobody said that out loud?

Jack's gut said *fuck yes.*

Meanwhile, the other three fights had ended. The head judge announced, "Next fights, Mary—"

"Hey!" a voice interrupted her from somewhere on the stands, too loud to ignore. Everyone looked for its source.

Jack stood tall and proud. "He killed her on purpose. That's against the rules. He must be punished."

CHAPTER FIFTY-THREE
MAKING ENEMIES

JACK STARED THE LATE E-GRADE HEAD JUDGE DEAD IN THE EYE.

Next to Jack, Edgar's jaw was hanging, and Karvahul's face had gone through fifty shades of blue. The surrounding people took a few steps away, not wanting to be associated with Jack, as did most of the "friends" he'd made on the stands, who had followed them to the stairs to say goodbye.

Jack snorted at them.

Only Brock remained by Jack's side, staring at the leonine and flipping him off. Jack couldn't help cracking a smile.

Rufus Emberheart halted before crossing through the parted the curtain. He looked over, and the moment he did, Jack felt like he was back in his forest, hunting goblins and forced to kneel to an unbeatable black wolf, the king of the forest.

This Rufus was not someone he could beat. However, there was something important between them: rules. And Jack would be damned if he let this lion kill one of his comrades for free.

"It was an accident," Rufus replied. His voice was soft yet commanding, carrying an undeniable nobility. Jack didn't doubt that but rules were rules. Fuck cheaters.

"It clearly wasn't. Maybe the judges will let it go because of your status, but everyone saw what happened. You cheated."

Rufus bared his teeth. Jack could practically feel them wounding around his throat. He refused to back down. Violence was forbidden outside the Tournament, and Karvahul had made it clear there were guards ready to stop troublemakers. Even if Rufus Emberheart was so above the rules that he dared attack him openly, Jack was confident he could at least survive till the guards intervened.

"John," Karvahul whispered, "you must stop this before..."

Jack tuned him out.

The head judge remained frustratingly tight-lipped. Rufus gave Jack a long, hard stare, letting him stew.

"I have no status," he declared. "I am a wayward son of the Animal Kingdom, though my parents arrived on this planet centuries ago. I have no relation to any force in the galaxy. I may not be human, but I am a native."

Bullshit, Jack thought. He and the other scions were clearly sent here from the Animal Kingdom, forced to pretend to be natives to abide by the laws. It was a paper-thin lie, but it worked.

"I had no intention of harming that human. She was simply too weak," Rufus continued with a regal bearing, like a king giving his decree. "But if you *demand* I be punished"—he emphasized the word—"so be it. Count this as my loss, judge. It's fine. I won't have another. Let it be known that I am fair."

The head judge spoke before Jack could respond.

"Very well," she said. "Due to breaking the rules and harming a participant on purpose, Rufus Emberheart receives a loss."

The djinns responsible for record-keeping scribbled it down on their papers, and Rufus disappeared behind the curtain, not sparing Jack another glance.

"Let's go," Jack said, storming down the stairs with Brock close behind. The anger inside him warred with impotence. If there hadn't been rules he could levy, he wouldn't have been able to do jack shit about what happened.

I need to get stronger, he thought. No matter what.

"John!" Edgar called out. "Wait! I can't go down the stairs that fast!"

Jack stopped, letting Edgar catch up. Karvahul followed a moment later, panic written all over his face. "What have you done?" he asked. "That—You—You're a lunatic, that's what you are! Why did you do that?"

"Because he was cheating, and fuck cheaters," Jack replied. "And most importantly, fuck arrogant assholes who think they can get away with everything because their father is a big shot."

"Even if it kills you?"

"Even if it kills me." Jack stared Karvahul down until the djinn looked away. "If you don't like that, Karvahul, you're free to walk away. Same goes for you, Edgar."

"I'm staying," Edgar replied in a heartbeat.

Karvahul pondered it. "You know what? This will give you even more publicity, and as your manager—"

"You are not my manager."

"A figure of speech, John, a figure of speech. Anyway, I'm sure we can make money off this. Tons of money." His little eyes almost shone golden. "I'll have to jump planet afterward, but, hmm... Okay. Luck favors the bold. I'm in!"

Jack was suddenly unsure *he* was in.

"Don't look at me like that," Karvahul said. "If you're going high stakes, you need someone who knows the ropes. Experience balls, Dao Fruits, skills, information, wondrous treasures... For only a small cut, I can ensure all resources are at your fingertips. With that much wealth invested in you, you will grow stronger at a terrifying rate! Maybe even enough to fight that monster..." Karvahul didn't seem to believe that last part.

Jack thought about it, then sighed. He needed the money. "What kind of business are we talking about?"

"Anything! You're a famous person now. If you visit a restaurant, people will flock there. If you have a favorite shop, people will follow you! I can get those restaurants and shops to pay you a cut. Plus, since the scions wouldn't visit the town and interact with us common mortals, you're probably the biggest celebrity around, with only Vivi Eragorn, Alexander Petrovic, and Jack Rust—the leaders of the major factions—behind you." He winked. "But even they can't cause a ruckus like you did."

Jack scratched his head. At some point, his anger had melted away, giving way to wary confusion.

"Are you sure?" he asked.

"Very. Trust me. I'll make you golden."

"What do you think, Edgar?"

"I think you should agree," the wizard replied. "Think of all the stuff in the faction shop. Even if things go south here, our faction will stand strong with enough credits on their backs. We can protect them."

"Fine." Jack was a decisive man to begin with, and he trusted Edgar. If he said it was a good idea, then it was a good idea. "You work your magic, Karvahul. For now, I want to take a walk alone—well, just with Brock."

The djinn's smile was so wide it reached his ears. "Okay!" He dashed off like a kid going to play.

"I think I'll stay and watch a little longer," Edgar said. "Information is power. I'll keep notes on all strong people to study later."

Jack hadn't thought of that.

"Great. Thank you, Edgar. Here, have this." He fished his last block of cheese from his pocket and handed it to Edgar, who took it with amusement.

"This is cheese," he observed.

"Right. It's to help you if anything happens."

"Like angry mice trying to mug me."

"Exactly. And don't worry, I have other snacks."

"Of course you do."

Jack smiled. "See you, Edgar!"

"See you, John Brown!"

Jack laughed as he left, Brock following beside him. Now that he wasn't looking in the arena's direction, he could see a blue sky with little gray clouds. The sun was high, and the sea breeze still reached his nose through the town.

Almost like he was on vacation.

"Guess it's just you and me, buddy," he said, looking at Brock. "What do you want to do?"

Brock flexed his little biceps.

"Work out? Maybe later. Let's try something fun first."

Brock was confused—working out was fun—but eventually he rubbed his belly.

"Eat? Sure! I have some spare credits. Wanna go by the seaside, too?"

Brock rushed up to Jack's shoulders and they set out.

The town was still lively. The festivities may have died down, but Jack spotted many TV screens—mostly on shop walls—where the fights were displayed. That C-Grade had mentioned they were transmitted throughout the entire planet.

Is the Professor watching? he wondered. Ugh. She saw me spanking people and being corny.

Well, whatever. The die has been cast.

A pleasant smell hit his nostrils.

"Look, Brock!" he exclaimed, already salivating, as was Brock.

A small food cart waited by a corner, in the shade of a white building. It had a grill, where three meat skewers were sizzling in the heat. Their fat popped in bubbles, and the smell was so appetizing Jack found himself walking over before he knew it.

"Good afternoon," the ifrit who manned the cart greeted them politely. "A skewer for your thoughts?"

"These smell delicious!" Jack exclaimed. "What are they?"

"Earth pig. E-Grade meat. Best you've ever tasted, and only for five credits apiece."

"We'll have three."

"Sure thing!"

The ifrit turned up the heat and let them enjoy the fragrance for a little longer before the skewers were ready. He handed them over along with some napkins. Jack removed two pieces of meat and gave them to Brock, then chomped down on the second skewer.

It was heavenly.

The meat melted in his mouth, making his chest fuzzy and his legs weak. "Ohh," he groaned involuntarily. The ifrit laughed.

"Guess I avoided a spanking!"

"What?" Jack barely managed to recover. The ifrit pointed behind him, and Jack turned to look, finding a big screen embedded in a nearby wall. It currently showed two swordsmen clashing against each other.

"The Spanker," the ifrit said with a wide smile. "I saw your fight. You turned that big guy into a baby."

"Eh," Jack managed to grit out. Inwardly, he was cringing. He suddenly felt that claiming he had the Dao of Spanking would put him in so many awkward situations.

"Enjoy your stay, friends," the merchant said with a smile. "And remember to visit Estu's Cart often!"

"Wait. I didn't pay yet."

"You don't need to. These are on the house." The ifrit—presumably Estu—winked, and Jack realized that being a celebrity really did have its perks.

"Thanks, Estu. See you around!"

"I sure hope so!"

They kept walking. The delicious meat skewers and the smell that still wafted off them only made the sightseeing more pleasant.

There were no cars in Integration City, so there was very little noise, giving way to more beautiful scenery. Jack and Brock headed down stone-paved streets that snaked between white buildings. Clothes hung on lines above, going from one merchant's balcony to the other—most lived above or next to their shops. Every second house sold something, be it food, weapons, armor, or even souvenirs. Everything glistened behind glass.

The souvenir shops especially excited Jack. They sold stickers, magnets, postcards, shirts, hats, statuettes—anything, really—and all depicted starships, wizards, monsters, gladiators, or the large arena itself.

Jack didn't buy anything—to the disappointment of the spinning-top-shaped shopkeeper—but promised himself to get some before the end of the Tournament. For now, he was looking for more food.

They'd already run out of meat skewers, but he was still hungry, especially after Brock couldn't have enough of them. They'd ended up eating them half and half, though Jack initially planned to take two for himself—after all, he was buying, and Brock was so small!

At least they'd been cheap—can't get better than free.

"Wanna eat by the seaside, Brock?" he asked, and the monkey jumped up and down in joy. The street they were on opened into a wide area, where the starship's edge was visible. Waves crashed into it nine feet below. The stone-paved streets gave way to white metal when one approached the edge, and Jack noticed a small restaurant that had placed tables on said white metal. A wooden construction above protected them from the sun, with vines and all sorts of plants weaving a beautiful roof overhead.

He instantly liked the place. Without much thought, he took a seat on one of the wooden blue chairs, finding the straw pillow for a cushion rather comfortable. The moment he sat down, the strong sea breeze was accentuated. He leaned back, enjoying the moment while he waited for the waiter to come. The table was wooden, small, and square, and the tablecloth was white paper that occasionally depicted blue ships and seagulls, held down by four plastic pegs.

"Hello," a voice came from above him. When Jack turned to look, he didn't find a waiter. It was the homeless-looking person he'd seen once in the streets.

He still wore the torn old clothes Jack had last seen him in, and his grayish hair hid under a green cap. At least he was clean this time.

And he was level 38.

The homeless-looking person gave Jack a wide, yellow-toothed smile. "Hello," he repeated raspily. "Can I sit?"

CHAPTER FIFTY-FOUR
THE SAGE

JACK'S EYES FLICKERED UP, AND HE DIDN'T RESPOND TO THE HOMELESS-LOOKING man right away.

The other man's smile didn't falter. "Don't worry. Despite my appearance, I'm quite a pleasant person. They call me the Sage."

He extended a hand. Jack raised a brow.

"Appearances matter little here," he replied. "Is Sage your name?"

"My name means nothing. The Sage is who I am."

This person was quite enigmatic. Jack was intrigued. He grabbed the outstretched hand. It was steady and calloused, worn down by years of hardships. "John."

"A pleasure," the Sage replied. "So, may I? You might be interested in what I have to say."

Jack didn't need to be told thrice. He motioned at the chair. The Sage took a seat, then extended his hand to Brock.

"Hello, my muscular friend. I'm the Sage."

Brock had been wary so far. Suddenly, his face became filled with joy, and his mouth formed into an 'O'. Then, he pretended to be serious, grabbed the Sage's hand, and nodded in a manly way.

Jack cracked a smile. "Have you been following me?"

"Not at all. Coincidences are miraculous things."

"Good morning," a voice came from above. It was a smiling lycan waitress. "Would you like the menu?"

"Yes, please," Jack replied, and the waitress left two shiny leaflets on the table.

"Let me know if you have any questions," she said before taking her leave.

The Sage read through the menu as if forgetting Jack was there. Jack did the same, with Brock spying over his shoulder—though he couldn't read, there were pictures.

The restaurant offered all sorts of delicacies: meat skewers, steaks, as well as a variety of fish—both earthen and alien. There was also a plate that resembled pasta-pie, along with a slew of appetizers.

"I recommend the seafood," the Sage said. "The pasticcio is also good, but seafood is where this place shines." Pasticcio was the pasta-pie thing.

"How do you know?"

"I've been around."

Jack squinted, then dropped his menu. "Very well. Then, you can order for me as well."

The prices were in the tens at most, and he had thirty thousand credits to spare—twenty from Gan Salin and ten from his recent victory in the arena.

"Excellent choice!" The Sage gave a wide smile, motioning the waitress over. "How hungry are you?"

"Pretty hungry. So is Brock."

"Alright."

She arrived. "Yes?"

"We would like one grilled cheese, a Greek salad, a plate of fried squid, and fries, please."

"Very well." She wrote the order down on a white notebook. Watching someone use pen and paper in Integration City was disorienting. "Is that all?"

"Some white wine too, please. Three cups."

"Very well. Thank you very much."

She took their menus and disappeared in the building beside them.

"You're fast," Jack noted.

"I'm a Sage," the other man responded. "I knew what we would order before even sitting down."

"Ha! Am I that predictable?"

"Yes, but don't take it the wrong way. Everyone is."

"Being a Sage sounds boring."

"We have our days."

Jack laughed. This guy had come out of the blue, but he was turning out to be good company. "What's your story, man?" He leaned back on his chair, balancing it on the back legs.

"A simple one," the Sage responded, leaning back himself. "I was alone and forgotten, rotting between park benches, rehabilitation, and mental institutions. The world was lost for me. I had nowhere to go, no future, no escape from my destiny to die under a bridge. Then, the System came, and everything changed. I found power. I found purpose. I found myself."

"Mental institutions? So, you *are* crazy."

"I thought I was. As it turns out, I just didn't have the means to process what my mind detected." He shook his head. "I cannot tell you much more, unfortunately. There are secrets whose mere knowledge could destroy you."

"Come on. Now you're just bullshitting." Jack barked out a laugh.

"Maybe I am," the Sage said with a small smile. "In any case, I chanced upon the Dao of Divination, and here I am."

"Can you fight with that, though?"

"In certain ways. Though I am not built for single combat. I will make it to the final sixteen participants, but not any further."

"You're boasting again."

"I'm just speaking the truth."

"Then, how far will I make it?"

"Prophecies come at a cost. If I tell you, I risk changing fate and disrespecting the Dao."

Jack groaned.

However, he had to admit that he empathized with the Sage's story. Though he didn't have it nearly as bad, he'd felt equally trapped before the System came. His future wasn't a dead-end, but a compulsory, slow, dull ride to death.

In a way, both of them had been equally helpless. Now, they were free.

Jack already felt closer to the Sage.

"Thank you for waiting," the lycan said right as a tasty fragrance met Jack's nostrils. She placed three small, empty plates, three cups, and a tin wine jug on the table, along with a square block of fried, orange cheese and half a lemon. She also left them a bowl of salad filled with tomatoes, sliced cucumber, olives, green bell pepper, and red onion, with a wide block of feta cheese on top. Finally, there was a small woven basket of baked bread peppered with olive oil and oregano.

Jack gave Brock a piece of bread to stop him from tearing into the salad, then took a knife and cut the cheese into small square pieces. The Sage grabbed two big spoons and mixed the salad.

"Mmm," the Sage said, trying the cheese. "Delicious!"

"Damn." Jack agreed as the cheese melted on his tongue. Brock made monkey noises of incredible excitement. This was the best food he'd ever tried. Jack had to grab Brock's head to stop him from tearing into the salad.

"Easy," he said, laughing. "The food isn't going anywhere, Brock. Let's learn to eat like a proper person."

Brock pouted, but Jack was relentless. Eventually, the little monkey ceded and kept munching on his bread, pouting all the while. Jack filled a plate with salad, cheese, and bread, then gave it to Brock, who proceeded to annihilate it.

"Keep a piece of bread," the Sage advised. "You'll need it later."

Brock did not keep a piece of bread.

"These are very tasty," Jack said in approval, tasting his share of the salad. "Good choices."

"Of course."

Jack groaned again. The Sage laughed, a raspy, pleasant sound.

"You should be careful of Gan Salin, by the way," the Sage said, stabbing his fork into a piece of cheese. "The scions came here with enormous quantities of credits. They will destroy Integration City's market like Brock here would do to the salad, if you let him."

Jack pretended to be nonchalant. "Why Gan Salin specifically? It was Rufus Emberheart I antagonized."

"Yes, but you *beat* Gan Salin."

Jack tensed up. He didn't drop his fork, but he slowed down, and his stare became heavier.

"You shouldn't know that," he said, a vague hint of threat in his voice.

The Sage was nonplussed. "You don't need to worry, Jack. I won't tell anyone. I just happen to be a Sage."

Jack did a double take. Suddenly, he realized he couldn't read this man at all. "Carry on. You were talking about the scions."

"Hmm, yes. The scions. Not only are they talented prodigies of the noble families, but they're also equipped with knowledge and resources that a newly-Integrated planet like ours lacks. And, even amongst them, Rufus Emberheart is a monster. You should be careful."

"I'll try not to spank him too hard," Jack said, eliciting a chuckle from the Sage. Then, he leaned in. "The scions claim they are natives. Even the System said so when I scanned them, but I'm pretty sure that's not the case... What's up?"

"Workarounds. The noble families had scanned this astral space manually before having the System do it, so they were already aware of this planet's existence. Then, they secretly moved the top genius of each family here before the Integration, along with wiping all records of them. When the System came, it recognized them as natives."

"Isn't that illegal? My guide mentioned something about a Star Pact—a set of laws?"

"Highly illegal," the Sage agreed. "However, the Star Pact was made between the B-Grade factions of our galaxy, and it is also enforced by them. They allow some leeway for each other as long as it's done discreetly enough that the rest can claim ignorance."

Jack grumbled, stabbing at a piece of cheese. "Fucking cheaters."

"I echo that statement."

"But why do they need to pretend? If everyone wants to sneak people into newly-Integrated planets, they can just abolish the law that says they can't, right?"

"Ah, excellent question."

Jack waited, but nothing more came out of the Sage.

Does he mean that he doesn't know, or that he doesn't want to tell me? Or is he simply crazy? Jack wondered. He waited, eating in silence.

"In any case," the Sage finally said, "this is a rare phenomenon. The astral space outside the System's reach is tremendously wide and expensive to comb manually. The Animal Kingdom just got lucky with this one."

The waitress arrived again, placing a plate of fried squid on their table, along with one of salted fries. "Enjoy your meal," she told them. Jack and Brock fell on the squid before she even stepped away. It was cut into bite-sized pieces and rings, and the fragrance it emitted was heavenly.

Unlike the cheese and salad, this meal came from E-Grade creatures and was Dao-infused. When Jack bit on the squid, it cracked, releasing an aura that filled his mouth and reached all the way to his chest. His entire body was revitalized, and his Dao Root shivered in joy. The warm taste remained on his tongue even after he'd swallowed.

"This is incredible!" he exclaimed.

"Dao food is delicious. It's my first time trying it myself," the Sage replied with a nod. "This is cooked well, too."

"How do you know? I thought it was your first time."

"Yes, but I'm a Sage."

The squid practically evaporated from the plate. It was only then that Jack remembered the fries. He tried a few, and while they were tasty, they simply could not match up to Dao-infused food.

"Higher-end places will offer Dao-infused appetizers and salad, too," the Sage said. "Here, it's only the main courses. They stay low-cost to be affordable."

Suddenly, a ruckus drew his attention. Their tavern was placed close to a wide-open space by the island's edge, where two groups of people were currently facing off against each other. One was the Flame River, and the other the Ice Peak—the two major factions of Earth, beside Jack's Bare Fist Brotherhood.

They were led by a dark-skinned tall woman and a hard-faced, icy man respectively.

These two factions were polar opposites in everything. First came their Daos, of course, but they were also contrasted in terms of attitude and appearances. Each faction reflected their Dao. The Flame River was fiery, while the Ice Peak was cold.

Jack had seen them face off before. When two of their members fought in the arena. The two factions had exchanged heated words, but the rules against violence stopped things from escalating.

Now, however, though the rules remained, there were no spectator stands between them. The two groups stood in the square, staring each other down with the hardness of people who'd fought and killed to survive. At the same time, the leaders were jousting with words.

Jack couldn't hear what they were saying—many people were speaking at once—but he could see the tension brewing fast.

"Think they'll come to blows?" he asked.

"I already know what will happen, but it doesn't matter much."

"Oh yeah? Wanna make a bet?"

"What kind of bet?"

"Predict what will happen—*with* details. If you get it exactly right, you win, otherwise you lose. The loser pays for the food."

"Sure thing. However, to respect the Dao of Divination, I will write my prediction on a piece of paper and reveal it after everything is over. Is that fine with you?"

"Whatever."

The Sage smiled. He fished a pen from inside his tattered clothes, along with a very crumbled piece of paper, then scrambled down a few words. He folded the paper and gave it to Jack, who put it in his pocket.

"About our previous subject," the Sage said. "Most shops in Integration City tend to remain low-cost. The one who doesn't is the Hand of God. I believe you've heard about their upcoming auction."

"A bit."

Jack's gaze was still mostly focused on the two factions. He reached out with his fork to grab a fry but only met the plate. Looking down, it was completely empty.

He looked to the side. Brock's cheeks were inflated to their limits, but he shook his head and shrugged as if saying, "no idea where they went, Big Bro." Jack couldn't stop a chuckle. The little monkey had been sneaking his hand underneath Jack's gaze the whole time.

"The auction is a tremendously important occasion," the Sage continued. True to his foresight, he'd moved some fries to his plate before Brock's sneaky assault. "They will offer expensive items in a market that can barely match a fraction of their true value. The more credits you can save up by then, the better."

"Really?" Jack gave him a side glance. "My guide said it's too early to start saving up."

"Your guide wasn't lying. In most other cases, that would be the case, indeed. However, they simply don't know the truth, as the auction contents aren't public. The Hand of God will be very generous in this particular auction." His face turned serious, and he leaned in. "I will tell you this, Jack, and heed my words. You *must* gather two million credits by the time of the auction."

"What!" Jack exclaimed. "Two million? That's too much! Every victory in the arena gives me ten thousand. I'd need two hundred of them! No way the Tournament will last that long."

"There are other ways to make money. Bet. Trade. Borrow. Do everything in your power. It is extremely important that you gather two million by the time of the auction. That will be the tipping point for your fate and our entire planet's."

Jack narrowed his eyes. "Our entire planet? Nah, dude. You're just messing with me."

"Am I? I told you. Prophecies come at a cost, and this one..." He chuckled. "It's almost enough to bankrupt me. The decision is yours, of course, but remember my words well."

"Sure," Jack responded. He leaned toward believing this man was a Sage—he did know many things—but two million... That was a mind-boggling amount. A few moments ago, Jack considered himself rich with thirty thousand.

"Why would the auction be generous?" he asked curiously. "If what you say is true, they're losing money."

"There are various organizations in the galaxy, both big and small, and the higher-end ones don't care about credits. They have other directives. The Hand of God is trying to cultivate the galaxy's first A-Grade cultivator, so they're willing to invest in newly-Integrated planets, rising geniuses, and teleporting the most talented E-Grades to Trial Planet, the galaxy's greatest crucible—you should absolutely go there, by the way. On the other hand, the Black Hole Church wants to spread knowledge of the Old Ones and poach the galaxy's brightest geniuses for their own. Interestingly, those two organizations are at war. Funny, right?"

Jack had gotten too much information at once. "What?" was all he could get out. Before he could say anything further, the ruckus from the nearby square intensified. A dark-skinned man of the Flame River pushed a woman of the Ice Peak. A nearby man drew a white knife from his sleeve and plunged it into the dark-skinned man's chest.

Everyone's eyes widened. Shouts filled the square. Flames and ice rushed at each other from close distance.

Three large figures fell on the attackers out of nowhere, taking them head-on and extinguishing them. Five more appeared around the two groups, surrounding both. A final figure descended from the sky and landed right next to the knife-wielder. Before he could react, a set of large jaws bit around his head and crushed it, killing him on the spot.

Everyone froze—and not because of ice. Even Jack was lost for words.

The guards of Integration City had appeared, and they were massive, metallic dogs.

CHAPTER FIFTY-FIVE

MAKING MONEY

THE GUARDS OF INTEGRATION CITY WERE HUMANOID ROBOTS WITH DOG HEADS. And not just any breed. They were slick, dark, metallic Dobermans, with steel cords stretching over their bodies like muscles and iron plates bulging on their chests. As they stood on two legs, they resembled hard-core club bouncers. They even wore thin sunglasses.

However, they didn't need that. One of them had killed a member of the Ice Peak on the spot. That was intimidation enough.

Jack scanned them at once.

Guard Robot (E-Grade)
A humanoid robot with the head of a dog. Boasting heightened senses, budding intelligence, fast movement speed, and fighting power at the early E-Grade, these robots are ideal guards for low-Level occasions.
Enchanted by Horrificus Egen

Early E-Grade...

Each of these robots was equivalent to the fifth level of his robot training partner, the one that had beat him to the ground. Now, there were nine of them, and they weren't playing around. One had blood and brain matter flowing down its jaws and stood atop the headless corpse. The rest stared menacingly at the two factions.

Both the Flame River and the Ice Peak didn't move a muscle. Surrounded by unsurpassable opponents, they'd all but forgotten their previous quarrel and hoped to simply remain alive. Even the friends of the two murdered people—the stabbed one had too quickly bled out—didn't dare make a peep.

"We are terribly sorry," the leader of the Flame River—Vivi Eragorn—said. "We will not repeat this."

One of the guards spoke in a hard, calm voice. "Do not make us come again."

"Absolutely not, sir."

"The Ice Peak will obey," the other leader—Alexander Petrovic—said, bowing lightly.

The dog guards gave them a long, final stare, then retreated. Jack saw them jumping to nearby rooftops and hiding in their centers, where they weren't visible from below.

It was as Karvahul had said. There were guards, and he really hoped he didn't see them again.

The two factions were left in an awkward predicament. Both had lost one member, but they didn't dare continue. Exchanging hateful stares, they entered the town through different streets.

"Those dogs sure weren't playing around..." Jack said, keeping his voice low.

"No proper guard would," the Sage replied, smiling. "You can read the paper now."

"What?"

"My prediction. You can read it."

Jack reached into his pocket to remove the piece of paper. He unfolded it, took a glance, then looked at the Sage in disbelief.

"I told you. I'm a Sage."

He'd gotten the entire sequence of events right. From the pushing, to the stabbing, to the dog guards, to the *exact person* who would do the stabbing and consequently get his head crushed. It could be a coincidence, but what were the chances?

"Wait," Jack said, struggling to comprehend the consequences of this. "You're too powerful."

"I'm the Sage, my friend." He smiled, then stood. "Now, if you'll excuse me, I have other business to attend to. It was nice meeting you, Jack. You too, Brock. Thank you for the wonderful meal—and thank you for paying attention to someone like me. Keep being open-minded."

"Of course..."

Jack shook his hand in a daze, then the other man walked away. It was only when Brock punched him lightly in the shoulder that he recovered.

"What the hell happened?" he asked. "Did you see that, Brock? That guy really is a Sage. He's terrifying."

Brock shrugged, then punched his open palm.

"Strength above all? Well, yes, but..." Jack looked in the direction the Sage had disappeared in. "Imagine how heavily he can influence things." At the next moment, his eyes hardened. He'd decided to believe. "I *must* gather two million credits. There's no time to waste. Let's go, Brock."

After paying the bill—it had come to 69 credits—Jack put Brock on his shoulder and walked away. He wasn't gazing at the shops anymore. Instead, he was lost in thought. The Sage had shaken him in more than one way.

This place is filled with hidden monsters, he thought. I must get stronger fast. And two million credits... That's a lot of money. I'd never get that much by just fighting or doing odd work in the town. I must go all-out.

A plan was forming in Jack's mind. He didn't know if it would be enough, but it felt like his only shot.

But first, he needed to make an investment.

He visited a large shop filled with wondrous items. Its exterior was white and its interior light-green, giving a homey yet spacious impression. Unlike Ar'Tazul's crate that was larger on the inside, this place advertised its wares in glass cases. Jack assumed it would have what he needed.

"Hello," a spinning-top woman—a kovan—greeted him as he entered. Her smile was wide like a half-moon. "How can I help you?"

"I would like to buy an experience ball, please."

"Of course, sir. What size?"

"How many levels would the large one give me?"

Tazul had said the medium-sized experience ball would give Jack one level, maybe two. Since the large one was ten times as expensive, it ought to give him many more. Given the difficulty escalation of leveling, he estimated five.

"Around six," the kovan said, squinting at Jack.

It's close.

"Great. And the price?"

"Ten thousand credits, sir."

It was the same price Ar'Tazul had offered. In the meantime, the kovan had led him to a wall filled with glass cases, inside which shone a multitude of colorful balls.

Jack had never seen an experience ball before. They looked like glass spheres filled with rainbows and supernovas of color. The smaller ones had simple, bright strips flying around, while in the larger ones, the colors struggled to form primitive patterns, like some mystical force was guiding their rotations together.

The kovan noticed his wonder and explained, "The experience balls contain the essence harvested from a variety of monsters—the same energy we get from slaying them, which helps us level up. As a large portion of that energy is lost when directed at an experience ball, it takes a thousand F-Grade monsters for a single large ball."

Jack raised his brow. "Slaughter, then."

"The Star Pact limits the production of experience balls. Currently, the only legal way is during the suppression of monster breaks on smaller planets, or other necessary monster exterminations."

Jack held the kovan's gaze. "Can you fly, by the way?" he asked.

"I beg your pardon?"

"I've heard that you can fly on your planet. Is that true? Oh! Please let me know if this question is considered offensive. I had no such intent."

"It's fine." The kovan gave him a wide smile. "We originally evolved around the specific conditions of our home planet. That gives us a disadvantage everywhere else, as we must hop instead of walk. It is a serious problem, which is why we mainly gravitate toward auxiliary professions... Only those in the E-Grade venture outside our planet, as hopping everywhere is exhausting, and the thinner atmosphere of other planets can cause problems for F-Grade kovans. But, of course, all those problems are nullified if we can reach the D-Grade and fly."

"I see. Thank you."

"No problem. So, would you be interested in a large experience ball?"

"Yes. However, is it possible to buy it on credit?"

The kovan squinted at him. Jack braced himself.

This was the difficult part. After meeting the Sage and watching Dorman and Rufus Emberheart display their powers in the arena, he'd come to understand that there were strong opponents around. If he was unlucky and stumbled upon one of them, not only would he be forced to reveal his true Dao and endure the consequences of lying to the officials—whatever they were—but he'd also run the risk of losing.

And losing was unacceptable. Not only because of the Tournament itself, but mostly because of Jack's other plan: betting.

In short, he figured the ten thousand credit reward of every victory would never get him to two million in time. Therefore, he needed to take risks. The most obvious method was to bet everything he had on himself in every fight, since he was confident in winning, as well as bet on other fights based on his perception. He would also bet some money on the Sage, since he was convinced he could make the top sixteen.

Karvahul had said the betting rates were determined by those betting—the native humans—who clearly lacked the insight a djinn could have.

That's why, even though he had the ten thousand at hand, he wanted to pay on credit. This ten thousand might not seem like much right now, but it was a third of his budget. If he bet everything and won, this lost third would be deducted from all his future earnings.

"That could be possible..." the koval said. "However, you must be aware that it will incur a significant increase in the item's total value."

Jack's heart lightened with relief. "How much?"

"Fifty percent over the original price, and it *must* be paid before the Hand of God auction. Otherwise, a 5 percent fee is added for every day after that."

Jack considered it. If he played his cards right, this ten thousand would transform into hundreds of thousands by the time of the auction. Then, the extra five thousand would be a drop in the bucket, and he would have made a larger net profit.

However, he wouldn't just take the kovan's words at face value.

"Fifty percent is a bit much. Make it twenty-five and we have a deal."

"The lowest I can do is forty, sir—and that's only because of your performance in the first fight."

Jack smiled. Of course the merchants kept tabs.

"You have a deal," he said.

"Excellent!"

They shook hands. The kovan produced a paper contract with the terms they'd agreed on in very simple language—the System world hated legalese, apparently. No scam could hide in there. Jack even checked for invisible ink by holding it to the light, which provoked the kovan's grumbling.

In the end, both signed, and Jack was now the proud owner of a large experience ball.

It was around the size of his head and shining with every color in the observable spectrum—and even more, probably, but Jack couldn't see them. However, just as he was about to use it on the spot, he had another idea.

Wait. If I increase my level now, people will know, and my betting rates will fall. What if I keep it at hand until I get a strong enough opponent?

A sardonic grin split his face. *Hehehe.*

"Are you okay, sir?" the kovan asked, making Jack cough in his hand.

"Yes, all good. Can I have a bag, too?"

"Of course."

If the kovan realized something, she didn't show it—but Jack suspected this particular kovan would bet a lot on him in the next match.

Therefore, Jack left the shop with a simple bamboo bag containing an experience ball worth ten thousand credits. The bag was opaque, thankfully, and Jack even asked Brock to sit in it to hide the glow escaping from the bag's mouth.

Then, while whistling a happy tune, he crossed the town straight to his house. Once the door was closed behind him, he released a long, drawn-out sigh.

Things were going well. He had a plan, whose first phase he'd already carried out. The next task in line was to speak with Karvahul and have him bet everything on Jack in every single round. His opponents would be unknown until the last moment, but if he happened to run into Rufus Emberheart, that would just be bad luck.

To be sure, they could wait until a few moments before the fight and hold some credits back if Rufus hadn't already fought by then.

Jack nodded. He was proud of this plan.

They'd also need to lean into the business aspects Karvahul had described, where they used his influence to get sponsorships off shops. He'd make sure to be extra flashy, just for that.

All those things combined, along with his ten thousand credits from each victory, would hopefully be enough to catapult him to two million. If not, he'd borrow from the connections he'd make.

And if the Sage was speaking out of his ass... Well, then fuck that guy.

For now, it was still afternoon, and there was only one thing for Jack to do—er, two.

The first was to find a way to hide the experience ball and take it with him to the arena to use in a pinch, which would be easy.

The second... He grinned. The second was to kick the ass of a particularly smug robot. Or at least try.

CHAPTER FIFTY-SIX
WALKING THE ROAD TO MASTERY

A STEEL PALM SMASHED JACK INTO A WALL. HE LANDED WITH HIS BARE FEET against it and shot off again, turning to the right to avoid the robot's charge. It chased him, relentless, smashing hard into the walls and floor wherever he stopped even momentarily.

The training room's door was ajar, and Brock peeked from the opening. His eyes flashed as he scanned the battle, observing how they moved.

Jack landed and turned on the spot. A fist sailed over his head, barely missing him as he planted one of his own in the robot's chest. It did nothing. He jumped, kicked against a nearby wall, and spun to reposition himself. A palm met his side, but he was defending, and though the strike sent him flying, he was left unharmed.

The robot was after him again. It unleashed a barrage of attacks, forcing Jack to stay in place and frantically dodge. A punch clipped his shoulder. A kick found his knee, making him stagger. He leaned into the momentum to dodge the next attack, but he found himself airborne.

A hand grabbed his head and smashed him face-first into the floor. Even on the soft material, it hurt like hell.

The robot jumped back, giving Jack some space. "Much better than before, master," it quipped in joy. "Next time, you might even be able to attack me!"

"Yeah, fuck you too." Jack sat up, holding his broken nose.

"Would you like med—"

"For the last time, no, I don't need medical assistance. It'll heal."

"But it might soil your clothes, master."

Jack looked down and grumbled. "It's fine. I have more."

Brock fell on him right then, observing him tenderly before flexing his muscles. He pointed at Jack, then the robot, then pretended to have a broom and sweep the floor.

Jack laughed. Brock was still struggling with metaphors. "I will, bro, I will. Just give me a few days."

Brock pointed at the base of his tail as if asking, "Should I poop him, Big Bro?" Jack shook his head.

It was already the twentieth time he'd lost today. He refused to lower the difficulty, demanding to face the training robot's fifth level over and over. His greatest concession was asking it not to hit him too hard, as it might affect his performance in the Tournament.

At first, he was losing horribly. The robot moved at incredible speed, an entire league above the black wolf, and Jack's eyes struggled just to keep up. He could barely dodge one attack if he was fully focused, let alone two.

As time went by, he began to adapt. The robot's bodily gifts were fearsome, but they were all it had. Jack was smarter, more experienced, more skilled, and had his Dao to help. Plus, he had some skills sweating to keep him afloat.

Although, his stats hadn't moved in a long time. On the surface, even his skills remained stagnant. Though that was far from the truth.

Like Dao cultivation, combat training was also a cycle between two phases: expansion and stabilization.

Jack's life-and-death battles in the dungeon let him gain insights and progress his skills at tremendous rates. He'd already reached levels that most humans couldn't even dream about—according to the advanced information package, skills had five tiers, and even reaching the third was exceedingly rare. For Fistfighting, he'd achieved it within a week.

That was the expansion part.

However, after progressing, downtime was necessary. Simply fighting like mad would yield limited benefits. It was necessary to take your time, work with your skills, experiment, and discover their limits. After defeating Henry White and Gan Salin, Jack had taken the time to train seriously, unearthing more and more potential out of his skills.

That was the stabilization part.

It was odd, in a way. He originally thought skills were tools he could use to better control his weapons—his stats—but as it turned out, skills, too, were weapons, and the tools to using them properly were understanding and conscious effort. The only exception was his Dao skill, which Jack felt would increase with his Dao, not any sort of training.

For everything else, he had to take his time and work hard.

The road to mastery held no shortcuts. It was long and difficult. Every step a journey in itself. When he made it to the end, it would be the best feeling in the world.

After his week-long training before the Tournament, Jack had already improved his usage of skills and stats significantly. He'd dug out the potential of each skill, making himself stronger in ways the System didn't quantify.

If he fought the previous Jack, he would win eight times out of ten. He was nearing the point of complete stabilization, where he would have fine control over his powers and could progress again. Except he still lacked something. There were bottlenecks to cross, and little improvements he simply couldn't achieve.

Until he met the training robot.

What he lacked was strong opponents. Those that could push him to his limits constantly and consistently—helping him reach the highest power he could as his current self. Only when he truly reached those limits, when he could no longer progress by himself, would he be ready to advance through the System again.

This last part wasn't detailed in the information package. It was just something he understood deep inside, something that felt tedious, unpleasant, and deeply necessary. He was certain that was the way.

Now, after facing the robot for over an hour, he was exhausted but triumphant. He hadn't beaten it, but he'd gotten much better than before. His reflexes were sharpened, and his reactions streamlined. His thoughts were accelerated. His mental patterns had gotten more efficient. Where at first he couldn't even take two blows from the robot, he could now fight for a short time.

He could finally understand why Karvahul said the resources offered to the participants were very precious. Such a great sparring partner, who was always available and could control its strength perfectly, was rare indeed, and extremely helpful.

He shuddered to think how strong Rufus Emberheart, who had access to such resources since childhood, would be.

"Again," he said, dusting himself off.

"As you command, master." The robot adopted a stance. Brock widened his eyes and bolted toward the door. "Here I come!"

The robot became a flash of steel. It crossed the distance in an instant, but Jack was ready to meet it. He dodged a fist by a hair's breadth. Sidestepped into a feint, then jumped on the wall and used Parkour to rotate vertically. The robot didn't expect that. Its kick nailed into the wall.

Jack punched out. He had no thoughts because they'd only slow him down. He reacted on instinct and ingrained patterns. He flowed around the robot's hands before he could see them, jumped over its legs, then ducked under them. The robot flowed from one movement to the next, but though it was fast, Jack could read its tells.

It strained his perception and reaction to their very limits. Forced him to move in ways he hadn't considered before and keep developing his repertoire, because the robot was intelligent too.

His skills bled into each other.

Parkour and Fistfighting worked together. He jumped on walls while simultaneously twisting his body. He unleashed fearsome punches from midair and at any angle. He dodged by the narrowest of margins during complicated maneuvers.

Jack fell into the flow state. The world slowed down. The robot was manageable.

He ran, turned, and punched. His legs were wings. His arms, hammers.

He was close to something, he could feel it, but not quite there yet.

Jack went on the offensive. As he fell from a wall, he landed and pivoted, letting a fist sail over his head as he threw one himself. It met the robot's chest with a dull thud, doing little damage. A kick came at him, but he'd already jumped, aligning himself with the robot's head.

"Meteor Punch!" he shouted. The world turned monochrome. For the first time, the robot had to dodge, barely tilting to the side. Jack's fist came from above and exploded into its shoulder like a purple meteor, denting the metal and making it stumble.

At the same time, his knuckles cracked, and he had to suppress a groan.

Even his strongest strike wasn't enough to take down the robot. A slap met his head, catapulting him into a wall hard enough to bounce away.

The robot regained its footing. Jack was up a beat later. His knuckles hurt like hell, and he had a splitting headache, but he was victorious. He'd done it.

"How's this for touching, tin can?" he taunted.

"It was good, master." For the first time, the robot looked at him with something resembling emotion: it was surprise. "You are improving quickly."

"Of course! You just stay here and wait. By the time the Tournament is over, even your seventh level will surrender to me."

"I look forward to that, master. You should chase your dreams, even if they're impossible."

"Your mother is impossible."

"I came out of—"

"An oven, I know." He grinned. "Has anyone ever beaten you?"

"I have been to thousands of Tournaments, master. One person could fight against my seventh level briefly, but nobody could beat me."

"I'm glad. Remember my name, robot. I'm Jack Rust, and I will be the one to make you kneel."

"As in, a marriage proposal? That is also impossible."

Jack threw a surprised glance. He couldn't hold back a chuckle. "We should find you a name at some point. See you later, robot."

"See you, master."

Still smiling, Jack left the room. Brock had stopped watching at some point and was back to lifting the dumbbell—the same one he always failed at. However, like Jack, he refused to go lower.

Now, for the first time, the dumbbell moved. With a shout, Brock lifted it a foot off the ground, then let it drop with a heavy thud. He turned to Jack, and though he was sweating, tired, and probably in pain, he gave a manly thumbs-up.

Jack returned it.

"The world isn't ready for us, bro," he said.

Brock laughed.

Come dawn of the next day, Jack and Brock found themselves in the arena again. Edgar was there, as was Karvahul. However, the audience was significantly sparser than the previous day, giving them room to stretch.

Which made it even more surprising when a tall, slim, dark-skinned woman walked toward them and sat right next to Jack. Her hair was dark and long, while she donned a blue jacket, under which hid a red shirt. She held no weapon.

Human (Earth-387), Level 41
Faction: Flame River
Title: Planetary Frontrunner (10)

"Hello," she said in a friendly voice. "My name is Vivi Eragorn, and I'm the leader of Flame River. You must be John Brown, right? Would you like to watch the fights together?"

CHAPTER FIFTY-SEVEN

DAO OF MARTIAL ARTS

THE AMAZONIAN-LOOKING WOMAN CROSSED HER ARMS, GAZE ON THE ARENA. IN addition to her blue jacket and red shirt, she wore hard boots and long trousers. Her eyes were brown and her nose slim, as was her body.

Jack noticed she was only slightly shorter than him, and if they stood, her long legs would probably put them at the same height.

"Sure, we can watch together," he replied. "I'm John Brown, professional spanker."

"I know. I really hope I don't face you down there."

Jack held back a spicy reply.

"Where's your entourage?" he asked, looking around. "The rest of Flame River surrounds you every time I see you."

At this, she fidgeted a bit. "This is more relaxing. I just have to mind myself around them. I'm the leader, after all. No matter how close and friendly we are, they need to see my strong, confident side."

"But I can see other sides?"

"You're a stranger, and a strong one, too. We can speak as equals."

Jack took a better look at her. She was strong and vibrant like a river, but her eyes hid a playful spark.

"Fine by me," he said. He leaned back in his seat and crossed his arms. Sensing they weren't welcome, Edgar and Karvahul went to get some corn and sat back down a few seats away. Only Brock remained by Jack's side, cupping his chin while staring at the strange woman.

"And who's this little guy?" she said.

"That's Brock, my monkey bro. And he can understand most of what we're saying, so mind your words."

"Really?" she replied with interest. "I haven't seen intelligent pets before."

"You still haven't. Brock isn't a pet. He's my bro."

She stared hard at him. She almost told him off on reflex, like she would if one of her faction members spoke out of line. She held her tongue.

"You're right," she said. "I was quick to assume. Can I pet you, Brock?"

The monkey still stared at her. He'd walked right in front of her seat, inspecting her with interest. When she slowly stretched a hand, he leaned back a bit.

"Hmm," she said. "Those are some great muscles. Can I touch them?"

She'd obviously read his System description. At this, Brock perked up. From one moment to the next, he was flexing like a bodybuilder, exhibiting muscles that were lacking but still plainly visible.

Vivi touched his biceps and made a surprised face. "Oh my! You're so strong!"

Brock smiled so hard he got a chin cramp.

"If you think you can get close to me by befriending Brock, you're mistaken," Jack said, laughing while Brock rolled on the ground and held his cramped chin.

"It's not that. We have monkeys where I come from, along with plenty of animals. I always liked them."

"Where's that?"

"Burkina Faso. A small African gem."

"Hmm. I've never been there. They didn't hold conferences."

"Conferences?"

"I used to be a researcher. I've been to some."

"Interesting. I was a tour guide."

"Very nice."

Before they could say anything further, the arena went silent. The winged djinn flew over its center and announced, "The second day of the Tournament will commence. I will now randomize today's fights."

Her eyes shone, as did the scroll in her hands. A moment later, Jack's token glowed. So did Vivi's.

"Not again," he groaned.

Vivi laughed. "Cheer up. I had to fight at night yesterday, and I can tell you that the waiting was killing me. This is much better."

"Hmm. I guess you have a point."

"Do you think we'll fight each other?"

"I hope not."

She grinned. "I'd go easy on you."

"That's not the point. I'd just feel bad spanking you in public now that we know each other."

Her lips moved, unsure what expression to form. She settled on amusement.

"You speak big, John Brown. I hope your actions can match your tongue."

"Let's leave it to fate," he said, turning his gaze back to the arena.

"First fight. Ernest Bell and the Dao of..."

The head judge announced the fights, and people began streaming to the sand below. The arena was still split by energy walls, letting four fights occur concurrently.

Jack leaned in to watch. Brock, surprisingly, climbed on Vivi's lap and sat there, watching the fights too. After her initial surprise, she hugged and petted him.

The first few fights were nothing special. Eight people struggled against their opponents, with four eventually eking out a victory. Though the fights weren't particularly high-level, they were interesting to watch.

Jack noticed that many of these people held odd weapons. They weren't the normal, bland ones he was used to. Instead, these weapons sported various colors, and when the fighters used them, Jack's soul tugged from the hint of Dao.

He remembered the Dao weapons that Ar'Tazul sold. This had to be them. Everyone had clearly put their ten thousand credits from yesterday to good use.

Eventually, the fights were over, and eight new people took to the stage. They still weren't anything to write home about. In the *next* fights, however, someone caught Jack's eye.

It was an old Asian man wearing martial arts robes. His mustache was white, long, and thin, hanging from either side of his face, and he was so small that Jack almost felt pity for him.

However, scanning him...

Human (Earth-387), Level 31
Faction: -

He was clearly above average. According to the head judge, his name was Li Xiang, and he followed the Dao of Martial Arts. Jack was very interested in seeing how he would fight.

His opponent, a level 27 swordsman from America, charged first. His sword wasn't the fast kind Henry White had used—a katana—but rather a medieval greatsword as tall as its wielder. It was clearly a Dao weapon, too.

The old man adopted a stance—one open palm ahead of the other, and his legs slightly bent.

It seemed simple. However, the moment Jack saw the stance, something tingled inside his brain. It felt like the old man had just transformed from a human into an undeniable force of nature. His stance appeared perfect and unbreakable. Standing against it was futile.

The swordsman felt it, too. His steps slowed before his Dao Root of the Sword flared, imbuing itself into the blade and slashing forth with the intent to cut the world.

The sword flashed before Li Xiang, who seemed too slow to react to something so undodgeable. Then, at the last moment, Li Xiang tilted to the right and used two fingers to gently push the blade to the left mid-strike, making it miss. Sand flew under his feet, but Li Xiang was fine.

Then, Li Xiang's body uncoiled like a spring. He went on the offensive.

He held no weapon, but his palms were more than enough. Every strike was perfectly aimed. He took advantage of gaps so small Jack could only see them in hindsight. When the swordsman moved, he created tiny moments of vulnerability, and Li Xiang was already there, predicting them before they even happened.

Watching that old man fight was an experience. He controlled the flow of battle perfectly.

The sword fell like rain, but Li Xiang deflected or dodged effortlessly every time. Like an adult playing with a child. Not that the swordsman was unskilled. Jack could see no glaring flaws, but Li Xiang clearly could. He capitalized on every tiny imperfection, magnifying and exploiting it so that the attacks appeared widely off.

In hindsight, yes, of course that attack was flawed! But only a true master could reveal that to the audience.

The swordsman roared in impotence. He could sense he would lose, but he still tried his best. Li Xiang was threading the needle. One mistake would be enough.

But masters make no mistakes.

The moment the swordsman brought his sword back to attack, Li Xiang was already stepping in as if chasing the blade, smashing a palm into the other man's chest and knocking the air out of him. Then, while he was off-balance, Li Xiang stepped around him, grabbed his leg, and flung him through the air without much effort.

The swordsman didn't falter. Even midair, he ignored his fall and twisted, slashing his blade at Li Xiang. The old man was still recovering from the throw. Would he have time to dodge? Jack's heart reached his throat.

There was a ding and a flash. Sand flew, obscuring everyone's vision.

When the sand fell, the swordsman was on the ground, sword angled upward, where Li Xiang had caught the blade midair with three fingers.

"Hoho." He laughed gently. "Good move."

The swordsman didn't pull back his blade. "I resign," he said, and the crowd erupted into wild cheers. The old man was stunning!

"Wow," Jack said breathlessly. "Did you see that?"

"Yes..." Vivi replied. "Very impressive. I should speak to him. Maybe he can train my people."

Jack nodded. Li Xiang displayed a perfect balance of stats and skill. He perfectly controlled every second of the entire battle. If Jack could get skills like that...

"Wait," he said, realizing something. "He's so strong... How come he doesn't even have the Planetary Frontrunner (100) title?"

Vivi threw him an odd look. "What do you mean? Maybe he does."

"I scanned him. He's title-less."

Her odd look turned into a suspicious stare. Jack suspected he'd fucked up somehow. "He could be hiding it..." she said slowly. "Aren't you doing the same?"

Jack froze. Oh, you have got to be kidding me. I can hide *my titles?*

Displayed Title: Planetary Frontrunner (10)
Available Titles: Planetary Frontrunner (10)
Would you like to change the displayed title?

Now it appears! Jack cursed ten generations of the System. Why the hell did nobody tell me that?

"I don't have a title," he finally said. "I got my Dao a bit late. Spanking is tough to comprehend. Who could have guessed?"

"Hmm." Her expression said she was torn between believing him or not. He returned her gaze as innocently as he could. "Too bad, I guess. That 5 percent efficacy is a wonder to have... At least, you don't seem to need it for now."

"I can manage. Maybe I'll get another title later."

"Good luck with that." She laughed, regaining her previous mood.

Jack turned back to the arena. At least something had come out of this. He'd learned that the Planetary Frontrunner (100) title gave a 5 percent efficacy increase, as opposed to his own 10 percent.

The head judge continued announcing fighting pairs. Jack paid her little mind until she reached the final names. "John Brown and the Dao of Spanking versus Chen Zexi and the Dao of Beauty!"

CHAPTER FIFTY-EIGHT
THE SPANKING MACHINE

Before the announcer's voice had even finished ringing, Karvahul was already rolling on the floor a few seats away.

"What a pairing!" He laughed. "Go get her, John!"

Jack grimaced.

"Well?" Vivi asked, raising a brow with a smile. "Won't you go spank her?"

Stay in character, Jack. Stay in character.

"Of course I will. I merely hope she is disciplined enough..."

Grabbing one of his flip-flops and tucking the other in his belt, Jack jumped over the railings and into the fourth sub-arena, where the energy wall that served as the ceiling had opened to let him pass. He landed in a thin cloud of sand.

Opposite him stood a stunning woman. She seemed of Asian descent—like the majority of participants—with thin features and jade-like skin. She wore a thigh-long, flowing green dress that accentuated her perfect curves. From her face to the tip of her toes, she was a sight to behold.

She didn't reveal more skin than necessary, nor was she too erotic. That wasn't her goal. Instead, just a glance into her beautiful eyes was enough to make Jack's heart ripple with tenderness.

Human (Earth-387), Level 27
Faction: Chen Group

"Hello," she said, and her voice was like silk. She tugged a strand of hair behind her fair ear. "My name is Chen Zexi. Please take it easy on me."

She wasn't shy. Her countenance screamed of dynamism, and her playful smile lit a fire in Jack's heart.

"I'm John Brown, and if you could stop these games, I would appreciate it."

"Games?" She smirked, then laughed wholeheartedly. "Would that make me a naughty girl, John? Do I deserve a spanking?"

Jack had to try *really hard* not to visibly cringe. His face turned completely stony from the effort. "Yes."

She winked. "In public, too? That's rather bold."

The audience erupted into laughter, as did Chen Zexi. She was just messing with him.

"I'll start now," Jack said, unable to take this any longer. He groaned inwardly. These charm-related Daos rubbed him the wrong way. Then again, who was he to judge?

Jack clenched his flip-flop and rushed forward.

He'd seen the Dao of Beauty before. On the first day, another girl of that Dao had been pitted against the metal guy—the one with the guitar—and lost terribly. It was a Dao that, in System lingo, focused on soul warfare.

Of course, Jack had asked about this before, prompting Edgar into a full-blown explanation of how everything worked, starting from the three main stats and how they worked.

Physical was the easiest one. It was obvious. Physical was for bodily conflicts.

Mental made your mind stronger. It accelerated your calculations and made you better at visualization, faster to pick up patterns, and more efficient at categorizing them. It helped in all sorts of mental endeavors.

However, since most everyday conversation or decision-making didn't really demand superhuman mental abilities, the people of high

Mental shined best when excessive calculations were at play, when they were faced with complex social or emotional situations, or when they had to manage a large number of moving pieces—like an army, a faction, or convoluted magic.

While Mental made the mind stronger, it didn't insert knowledge or patterns into your head. It would never make you "street smart." The best it could do was help you become "street smart" faster when exposed to the right circumstances.

The caveat was that raising Mental didn't make you better at pursuing the Dao. None of the stats did, not really, because they all did in the exact same amount. Nobody had an advantage. The reason why was unknown, at least to Edgar.

Will was even more esoteric. It wasn't a measure of someone's willpower, but the power *of* their will, which wasn't the same. Willpower was forcing yourself to go to the dentist. Power of will was making your dentist come to you—the power to influence the world around you, mostly through magical means.

As different people progressed through the System, they emphasized different stats. Each of the three main directions focused on battles of different natures: Physical was for bodily conflicts, Mental was used for illusions and corporeal magic, while Will affected the so-called soul warfare, where people attempted to infiltrate each other's soul.

Through the Dao, all stats could be used for everything. With strong enough Dao, a warrior could punch illusions and mental invasions away. The Dao itself was a weapon that could dominate.

In other words, the System encouraged specialization, letting you cover your weaknesses with your strengths. Otherwise, every battle would be judged by who struck the first blow!

Jack arrived before Chen Zexi without a problem, then brought his flip-flop back to strike. She flashed him a smile, and he lost his mind.

His heart was in pain. She was so beautiful, so delicate, so passionate. From this close, her body exuded perfect harmony, and her face struck the deepest chords of his soul. Her wide blue eyes filled his world, and her sweet lips whispered promises of endless love. His flip-flop stopped, shuddering.

Hers wasn't the Dao of Seduction. Even her previous teasing had mostly been to have fun, not to turn him on. Jack didn't feel the urge to ravage her, but to protect her and hold her dear, to love her truly and wholly. In a way, it was more fearsome than any seductive Dao.

It was painful.

"Do me a favor, John," she whispered, leaning toward him. Her hot breath tickled his ear, lighting yet another fire inside him. "Resign this fight. Please... You are strong. You can win the next one, but I *need* this."

His brows spasmed.

"Come on, John," she continued, almost begging. From where he stood and how she was standing, he could see straight inside her dress, but it felt accidental—though it obviously wasn't. He had the urge to reach up and lift her dress to protect her from unwanted eyes. "I need your help. Don't leave me."

Jack's entire body trembled as his willpower warred against his instincts.

She flashed him the sweetest smile he'd ever seen and leaned in to hug him. "Thank you, Jo—Eek!"

The flip-flop met her left butt cheek with a crisp slap, sending her flying a few feet to the side. She tumbled, then quickly stood back up. Somehow, not a speck of sand was on her.

"Why did you do that?" she asked, pain in her eyes. "Am I not worth even that much, John? Will you abandon me like everyone else?"

It helped that his name wasn't John, so any mention of that broke his immersion.

"It's useless, girl." He channeled his inner manic spanker. "When I see bad girls like you, I do not feel aroused, only a need to spank."

"Then take me, rip my clothes off, and spank me on your bed!" she protested, changing tactics and going all-out. It had to be a skill of some sort. Jack felt red silk strands wrap around his soul.

His Dao Root awakened. It shuddered and rose, staring at the silk strands with the finality of a professional boxer staring down a random drunkard in a bar. The silk strands danced beautifully around Jack's soul, but the Dao Root of the Fist was relentless. It launched a rain of fist-shaped meteors that flew into the strands, destroying them without resistance.

Jack snorted, mentally grabbing the few strands that were left and ripping them apart.

When he was hesitating before, it hadn't been about resigning, as she wanted. It was between spanking her immediately to avoid the cringy humiliation or letting her carry on just a bit longer because his heart truly ached at the thought of fighting her. It felt like stomping on a beautiful flower.

However, Jack had forged himself on the razor-sharp edge between life and death. He'd crossed the ice pond. He'd fought to his very limit multiple times. He'd risked his life, thrived in danger, and faced off against the Dao itself. He'd even developed a Dao skill.

His heart could take the strain.

Plus, this particular girl was only level 27, and her powers weren't even suited for direct combat. If he lost here, it really would be a bad joke.

"Your tricks will never work on me," he said, shaking his head. The crowd was hollering from all around, but he tuned them out.

"Please, John!" Her eyes became wide and bright like a cartoon. By this point, it was clearly an illusion. "I'm begging you. I don't want to leave!"

This time, her despair must have been real because the power of her Dao was strong enough to almost make Jack question himself. Almost. He wouldn't risk everything for a random girl, no matter how beautiful she was.

"It's useless. Just be a good girl and resign. Don't make me spank you."

"Hell no!" she shouted back. "You'd like that, wouldn't you? You sick —Eek!"

Jack flashed to her side and spanked her again, this time on the other butt cheek. He could feel her skin rippling even through her dress and the flip-flop. She hopped a step forward, clenching her butt.

Her eyes held tears—maybe fake, maybe real. She bit her lip. "Please?"

"No."

"Okay. Then, I guess I can only—"

Her hand reached inside her dress, grabbing the hilt of something. She tried to be sneaky, but Jack saw it.

A third spank met her behind, this time going wide to get both halves. She yelped and fell to the ground. When she looked back, her face was red and teary, and though his heart felt on the verge of cracking, even that wasn't enough to sway him. His hard eyes told her everything she needed to know—and the crowd's reactions made her want to leave the stage on the spot.

"I resign," she spat, and with a final, complex look at Jack, she bolted away. The arena had doors leading directly to the outside—she used those.

Jack himself looked at her departing form, shook his head, then jumped up to his seat and sat cross-legged.

"That was quite a spectacle," Vivi said, still hugging Brock, whose face had gone completely red under his fur. He looked at Jack with a new kind of respect.

"Yes."

"Did you enjoy it?"

"No. The core of spanking lies in discipline, not pleasure. Her little tricks could have never broken my Dao Root."

"Hmm..." Vivi hummed, squinting at him.

Inwardly, Jack was both relieved and desperate. Relieved because the spanking bullshit now flowed naturally from his tongue, and he'd probably fooled Vivi. Desperate because, *oh my God, what am I* saying?

"Nice going, John!" Karvahul said. "You must be great with the ladies."

"Leave me alone, Karvahul."

"No, please continue," Vivi told him, laughing and extending a hand. "I'm Vivi."

"And I'm Karvahul," he replied, shaking it. "It's an honor to meet one of the planet's future leaders."

"There's a long way ahead. Who knows what could happen."

While the two exchanged pleasantries, Jack looked to Edgar, who remained in his seat, gazing at the arena with a red face. He grinned. "Hey, Edgar," he said, making the wizardling jump. "Why are you sitting there? Won't you join us?"

Edgar turned around. He glared at Jack helplessly, then said, "Nice spanking. You know this was transmitted around the planet, right? Including to the professor."

Jack's face fell. He leaned back and crossed his arms, regretting the fake Dao he'd chosen.

The crowd was still buzzing from Jack's fight when the other three finished. The announcer's voice filled the air again, and this time, she started with the hard match.

"Vivi Eragorn and the Dao of Flames versus Gan Salin and the Dao of Insanity."

Vivi's head snapped that way. Her features turned rocky, and her eyes stormy. "That's a scion... Crap."

"Crap," Karvahul repeated. "You sure are unlucky..."

"I know."

She stood, setting Brock on the chair. She then removed her coat, revealing the sleeveless shirt underneath. It was simple and red, with embroideries of blue flowers.

"This will be hard," Jack told her. He was very interested in this match-up. It would be the first truly high-level fight he saw in the arena.

"I know," she replied, flashing him a restrained smile. "Any tips?"

"Yes. He relies on speed but is physically weak. Pressure him from the start, overwhelm him, and don't let him get the initiative. Also, careful; he bites."

Vivi hadn't expected that. She stared deeply at him. "Okay," was all she said.

Then, she jumped. Warm air slowed her fall as flames licked the bottom of her hard leather boots, and she landed in the middle of her sub-arena with the grace of a feline.

"How unlucky..." Karvahul repeated, wistfully shaking his head.

"What do you mean?" Jack asked. "The strong people are bound to meet eventually. It just happened sooner for her."

"It isn't that. The pairings of each round *are* random, but weighted. Generally, the officials want to avoid pitting people with many victories against each other, as they risk eliminating future finalists early on. For the preliminary rounds—the ones we are going through now—the stronger you are, the weaker your opponents... But, in the end, there is always luck involved. Hers just ran out."

Jack didn't know that. "Are scions really that strong? Maybe she can take him."

"Maybe," Karvahul agreed half-heartedly. "We'll see."

Across them, a slim figure emerged from a high-up, curtained-off section of the spectator stands. Gan Salin wore the same relaxed smile Jack remembered, and even from this distance, his eyes carried the undeniable tint of insanity—maybe even stronger than last time.

However, he wasn't the only one to emerge from the curtains. Another figure followed after Gan Salin and leaned against the railings to watch the fight.

This man was humanoid, but that's where the similarities ended. He had gray skin, gills on the side of his throat, and webs between his four fingers. A large fin stretched from his back, sharp at the tip, and his eyes were elongated slits. Jack scanned him.

Sharken (Earth-387), Level 45
Faction: -
Title: Planetary Frontrunner (10)

Another scion... level 45, too.

The sharken didn't notice Jack's stare, so he turned toward the arena, too.

Gan Salin smashed into the sand like a rock, unhurt. "Hello," he said. "Sorry, but can you resign? I was in the middle of something up there."

Vivi stretched out a hand. Embers shone on her fingers. Flames flowed down her legs and licked the sand below. "Silence," she declared. "You have no place here. In the name of my people, I will stop you. I will show the world that scions aren't that strong."

"Sure," he replied, then squinted at her. "Oh, 41? This might be interesting."

Jack scanned Gan Salin, too.

Canine (Earth-387), Level 41

Faction: -
Title: Planetary Frontrunner (10)

Reaching inside his pockets, Gan Salin removed a pair of gauntlets and made to wear them. Vivi didn't let him. Flames gushed forth, covering the distance between them in the blink of an eye and swarming Gan Salin.

"Woah— Hey!" he shouted, jumping back. "Let me—"

She stepped forward, moving her arms in a circle. The flames she'd unleashed obeyed, rising from the ground and hurtling toward Gan Salin like an angry river. He struggled to put on a glove, but there were many latches, and the flames got there first. He was surrounded.

Luckily for him, his back met the energy wall, and pushing against it, he rushed through the flames as quickly as possible. His hair was partially charred, and the edges of his shirt were charred and still burning.

"You honorless bitch!" he roared. Froth bubbled in his mouth and ran down his chin. Veins popped all over his face, and his wide eyes turned bloodshot.

CHAPTER FIFTY-NINE
BREAKING THE MONSTERS

GAN SALIN ENTERED INSANE MODE.

He tried again to wear the gloves, but his hands were shaking, and the flames hot on his heels. "Fine! Canine Dash!" Letting the gloves drop, he fell on all fours and ran so fast he almost disappeared.

From the stands, Jack raised his brows, and the audience erupted into clamor.

A barrier of blue flames erupted around Vivi, flowing like water. At the same time, she kept moving, dashing backward and rotating her hands. Her previous river of flames followed Gan Salin and was lagging behind, but a new one appeared, stretching wide to block his path.

Gan Salin made a barking sound. Though his path was blocked, and though he was insane, he wasn't a simple character.

His second Dao Root—Resolve—flared, making him unwavering. He ran straight into the flames and cut through them like a dogfish, screaming but enduring the pain. A moment later, he was out, charred and tattered. His clothes were on fire at the edges, his red eyes staring right at Vivi.

She still wasn't done. Though her back had reached the wall, her hands still moved. The flames increased in volume, more rising from the ground every moment, and the nearby sand had turned into jagged glass. The first river was coming over as well. Gan Salin had to finish the fight or be drowned in fire.

He screamed and rushed forth.

The blue flames around Vivi formed into a glowing armor the color of hot iron. They were dancing and flowing around her, up and down, left and right, coming and going with the rhythmic movements of her hands like waves. That wasn't how flames were supposed to move.

Jack realized she had another Dao Root. *The Dao Root of Water? Of the River?*

Gan Salin reached her, and without stopping, fell onto her. His skin was charred, and his face twisted into a crazed visage, but he pushed through. Even through his madness, he knew this was do or die. Their battle had reached its climax in the blink of an eye!

The river of flames coiled harder around Vivi. Gan Salin opened his palm and stabbed it at her. "Five-Star Grasp!" he shouted. The tips of his nails—which were more like claws—glowed white.

His hand pierced the flames. The pain must have been excruciating because Gan Salin's screams rose to new levels. The closer he got to Vivi's body, the higher the temperature. His skin was melting, and his claws were about to drop. Still, he didn't stop.

With a final push, he dug into her chest, penetrating an inch. The flames prevented him from pushing deeper. He retracted his hand almost immediately, unable to take the scorching heat any longer, and fell back. His entire arm was black and smoking. Vivi was bleeding, but the flame rivers she'd unleashed had arrived to smother Gan Salin. He was surrounded and out of momentum.

"I resign!" he shouted fearfully, coiling around himself to protect against the flames. Some reached him, as Vivi was unable to stop in time, but they rapidly withdrew and vanished into red wisps, then nothingness.

Just like that, it was over.

The entire arena held their breaths. Then, all at once, they cheered like crazy, shouting so hard the rock shook. People stood in their seats and hollered, and first among them were the members of Flame River, who celebrated their leader's victory with joy rivaling hers.

This fight had been by far the most intense so far. Both opponents were at level 41 and possessed two Dao Roots. Where others fought with sticks and stones, Vivi had created multiple rivers of flame and unleashed them at her opponent, flooding her entire section of the arena.

Moreover, she'd fought against a scion and won. She had proven that humans could stand against these monsters. She brought hope.

Amidst the cheers, Vivi held her bleeding chest with one hand and extended the other toward Salin to help him stand. It was an offer of peace, and a way to further cement herself as a hero in the eyes of all who watched.

Gan Salin ignored it. Gritting his teeth in pain, he shot off the sand, then jumped again on some spectator stands and disappeared in the curtained-off section. Supposedly, there was a healer there.

Vivi used warm air to fly to the lip of the stands, then walked to her seat amidst the audience's cheers. However, when she got there, Jack wasn't looking at her. His gaze was aimed at the curtain separating the scions from common mortals, where the shark-man from before still leaned against the railing, following Vivi with his predatory eyes. He was clearly dissatisfied with the battle's result.

When she reached her seat next to Jack, the sharken caught Jack's stare and gave a wide, wide smile filled with rows of sharp teeth. He retreated inside the curtain, following after Gan Salin.

Jack turned to Vivi. "Well-fought! That was amazing!"

She gave him a tired smile. "I'm glad." She took deep breaths, calming herself.

"Do you need medical assistance?" he asked, motioning at her chest, where blood was still dampening her shirt.

She shook her head. "I'll be fine. I have regeneration. His strike wasn't too deep, anyway."

"Alright. Again... great fight. I really hope I never match against you."

"Because you admire me?"

"Because I'd have to spank a hero of humanity."

She groaned, but her smile couldn't be hidden.

"Whatever you say, big man."

"Excuse me," a voice came from the side. It was Edgar, who'd overpowered his antisocial tendencies and joined them. Jack noticed a glint in his eye. The excited glint he showed only when magic was on the table. “Can I ask you a question?”

Vivi hesitated, then said, “Sure.”

“How did you sustain all those flames? They looked tremendous, but they must have taken a lot of mana.”

She met his stare. Consumed in his fervor—he loved magic—Edgar stared back.

It then hit Edgar he was asking about her secrets. “It’s fine if you don’t want to answer! Sorry for asking!”

She still didn’t respond. A moment later, she lowered her voice and spoke slowly. “I was using the ambient energy. My flames were sustained by my mana, but they also fed on the oxygen in the air, significantly lowering my consumption. That’s one reason why I kept them moving around the arena.”

“Oh!” Edgar’s eyes widened in realization. “I see!”

“Magic in general should be used like that. The mana in our bodies is too little for meaningful applications. We should use the environment to our advantage, letting the world bear the burden of our powers. That’s how wizard classes become truly strong.”

Edgar’s eyes were practically glowing now. Vivi continued, “I saw your fight. Your magic is peculiar but lacks power. Birds made of pure mana are too wasteful. If your Dao Root and skills are compatible with any environmental forces, you should consider incorporating them into your arsenal. For example, you could make your birds fiery in nature, letting them consume oxygen instead of mana to a degree. Your shield could be watery, drawing in the air’s moisture, or earth-based, where you use your mana as the conduit to make the ground rise and form a stable shield, or where you use the sand specks of the arena to enhance its hardness without spending extra mana. In general, the more you can adapt to your environment, the stronger you’ll be.”

Edgar was starstruck now. If his expression was anything to go by, Vivi had become his favorite person in the world. “Thank you! That’s—Thank you! You’re amazing!”

She smiled back. “Of course I am.”

“I’ll go practice right away!” Edgar exclaimed, rushing back to his seat and conjuring a pair of birds to fly around him. A thousand calculations passed by his eyes.

"That was very generous of you," Jack said. "He could beat one of your faction members with the tips you gave him."

"I know. But the Flame River values our relationships. You gave me advice against Gan Salin—maybe I only won because of you. It was only fair I repaid the favor."

She still didn't ask how he knew, though she must have had her suspicions. Jack smiled.

"That's right."

"Are you familiar with the Ice Peak?" she asked, changing the subject. By her tone, this was something she intended to speak about from the very start. Karvahul wisely stepped away and found another seat—not next to Edgar, as he was still surrounded by blue birds.

"The ones that have been glaring at me ever since you sat here?" Jack replied, motioning at another part of the spectator stands.

"Yes."

"Then, yes."

"They're our enemies, as you might have noticed. We blend together like fire and ice. As we are two of the major factions, we will inevitably clash at some point, which is why we're looking for allies. The problem is..." She grimaced. "Alexander is allied with the scions."

"I see. That sounds pretty bad for you."

"It is. With the scions on the Ice Peak's camp, not only do they have the favor of the Animal Kingdom, but also a great fighting force. We desperately need strong allies."

"And you're telling me this because?"

"Don't play dumb, John. You know what I'm getting at. I don't mind what relationship you have with Gan Salin, but you helped me against him. You are opposed to the scions, who are allies of the Ice Peak."

"The enemy of my enemy is a friend."

"Exactly. Plus, you seem like an upstanding individual despite your... spanking... tendencies. I don't know how much you've heard about the Ice Peak and the Flame River, but even morally, you're much closer to us than them. We can help each other."

"You're offering an alliance."

"Precisely."

Jack pretended to think about it. He was already 100 percent in, as this was probably the best case scenario he could get, but it wouldn't do to agree too quickly.

Plus, this was a great chance to get information.

"What about the third major faction?" he asked. "The Fist Brotherhood?"

"The Bare Fist Brotherhood," she corrected. "They haven't shown themselves yet—at least, not openly. They could be hiding anywhere. There are disguise potions that could fool most of us."

She looked at Jack with meaning, but he played innocent. "It's not me. I'm John Brown."

"I believe you." She smiled. "Come on, John. Let's work together. If anyone can stop the scions, it's you."

Jack crossed his arms and grimaced. "Fine. What's the layout of alliances so far?"

"Not many have given a definitive response. I've approached Dorman Whistles, but he seems uninterested in our conflict. He's such a child." She pouted. "My members have talked to some promising fighters, too, but no one too important. Is there anyone you have in mind?"

"The martial arts master from before," Jack replied instantly.

"Already on my list. Anyone else?"

"Hmm." Jack did have someone in mind, but he first wanted to consider how all-in he should go on this thing. Vivi gave him time, turning to watch a couple of uninteresting fights.

Both him and his spanking persona were on the shitlist of two scions, including the strongest one, Rufus Emberheart. He was definitely an enemy of the scions, who were allied with the Ice Peak.

Therefore, he needed allies himself, and there wasn't a strong enough third party besides the Flame River, which was already opposed to both the scions and the Ice Peak. If he avoided their conflict altogether, he needed the Flame River to win, or he would be the next to fall.

And, if the Flame River could win without him, they sure as hell could win with him.

He was in.

"The Sage," he told her. She raised a brow.

"Who?"

"A guy who looks like a beggar. I haven't seen him fight, but his divination powers are scary. I'm still not 100 percent sure he's not a conman, but I tend to believe him."

"Divination powers?" Vivi's eyes widened. "As in, he can predict the future?"

"Kind of. I don't know exactly how it works, to be honest, but he seems like a pretty useful person to have at hand."

"I see." She nodded seriously. "Okay. I'll approach him."

"That's all from me. I don't know anyone else. Has the Ice Peak gotten anyone?"

"Nobody important. They aren't working as hard as we are, given that they already have the scions. They did approach the metal guy from yesterday—the one with the guitar—but I think he turned them away. He's also on my list."

Jack nodded.

"Good. I'm glad we got this out of the way, John," Vivi said, extending a hand. "To a pleasant cooperation."

"To a triumphant alliance." Jack shook her hand, perfectly aware of all the eyes on him.

"Then, I'll be going now," Vivi said. "I've already busied you enough for today."

"Sure thing. See you around, Vivi."

"See you, John."

With a final hug at Brock—who seemed oddly receptive of her affection, though he would have punched anyone else that tried to hug him—she took off, crossing the stands to get to where the rest of her faction waited. Most of those people—there were five in total, three men and two women—nodded at Jack, who nodded back.

"What was all that about?" Karvahul asked, approaching.

"We're in an alliance now, Karvahul. You too, Edgar. The Flame River is our friend, the Ice Peak and scions are the enemies."

Karvahul exclaimed, "The *scions?*"

"I was already enemies with those."

"Oh..." His blue face paled a little. "I see..."

"Don't worry. We got them."

With enough experience balls to reach level 49 and enough training, he might be able to stand against Rufus Emberheart. Maybe. His heart still clenched at the memory of that guy's attack, but it wasn't like he had a choice. It was do or die.

"What are you planning to do now, Jack?" Edgar asked.

"Watch the fights, I guess. I get the feeling that watching strong people fight will be good for my growth. Who knows—I might get some insight. I'll go train with my robot in the afternoon."

"Oh, the joys of being an Integration Tournament participant..." Karvahul lamented.

"Sounds like a good plan." Edgar returned to his birds.

However, the universe disagreed. It hadn't been a minute since Jack sat down to watch when a figure approached—a short, Asian teenager with two daggers strapped to his belt: Dorman Whistles.

"Hello," he said, speaking only to Jack.

"Hey."

"Spar with me."

CHAPTER SIXTY

BIG BRO BROCK

JACK RAISED A BROW. "SPAR WITH YOU?"

Dorman Whistles stared him in the eye. "Yes. Please?"

"Why do you ask?"

"Because you're strong. I can tell. I'm strong too. And these random weaklings aren't enough to make me stronger, but you are."

This was all a bit too sudden. He'd barely spoken to the guy before.

"I thought violence was forbidden."

"In the town, yes. But we have training basements."

Jack found something familiar in Dorman's eyes. The fire of a fighter burned there, the urge to test himself against worthy opponents and relish in battle.

"Okay."

Brock cheered and climbed on Jack's shoulder, eager to watch two strong people go at it.

"Are you sure, John?" Edgar said from the side. "What about the fights?"

Dorman glared at him. Jack raised a hand. "It's fine. The strong people will fight weak ones, mostly, so there won't be much to see. A spar will be better."

"So, wanna go?" Dorman asked. He looked like he couldn't wait. Jack shared the feeling.

"Sure. But come to my basement. Yours could be an ambush."

"Fine by me. Let's go."

The previous night...

Brock felt the wind on his fur, the night breeze on his face. He bared his fangs in a smile.

He jumped from the rooftop to a hanging rope, using it like a branch to launch himself farther. There were plenty of these ropes, and they made crossing the town fun.

Unfortunately, they weren't always empty. Brock fell face-first into a white shirt, unlatching it and taking it with him. He barely managed to stick his head out of a shoulder opening. Wrapped in white, he now resembled a ghost flying through the air. Thank the Monkey King there was no one on the streets to see him.

He paused on a rooftop to pull the shirt off and dropped it on the flat wood, then almost jumped away again. At the last moment, he realized this wasn't polite. He gently folded the shirt first, *then* left it on the rooftop and flew away.

Big Bro would be so proud.

Brock admired Big Bro. He was so strong, like a big brorilla! He could lift a lot of weight!

Brock himself wasn't that strong, and that made him sad. However, it also lit a fire in him. He would become strong. He would make everyone proud. Big Bro, Father, and Mother. He would be the strongest brorilla, and then the pack would never send him away again! Father said it was for his own good, but Brock knew the truth. He clenched his little fists, unleashing a monkey cry in the still night air.

Brock would become strong... He just had to figure out how.

He kept jumping, balancing between rooftops, hanging ropes, and lighting poles—he preferred the latter, as they resembled trees.

Bright shops and dark ones crossed under his feet. Bakers out to light their first oven of the day and barkeepers cleaning up. Locked carts of yummy food and heavily-clothed people pacing fast. Occasional speech wafted from below to disappear as Brock kept running.

The day was noisy and full of weird smells and sounds and people saying things he couldn't understand. Brock disliked the day. But the night... He liked the night. Even though he sometimes felt sad during it.

Now, only the faraway district was lit and noisy, the one where all the bros that looked similar to his Big Bro stayed, but he didn't need to go there.

He latched onto a lighting pole. He brought a hand over his eyes to shield from the bright light just above his head. His other hand kept him anchored to the pole.

A nearby alley looked inviting. A perfect place to think. Moreover, he could see the big-bro-with-big-stick statue of the arena right before him. That was pleasant.

A few moments later, Brock fell into a dark alley. The town's few sounds disappeared, cut off by the towering walls. The alley was strewn with empty boxes left over by the nearby shops, and its stone walls stank a bit of fish, but that was okay.

Brock found a crate that looked toward the end of the alley and sat on it, his fist supporting his chin. He was close to the arena, so he could also see the statue from before through the buildings. It was quiet, too.

Finally, Brock had found the perfect place to think. And so, he dived into his doubts, seeking to dissolve them.

Big Bro in the sky, he wondered, why Brock not strong? Dumbbell too heavy now, but dumbbell light at home. Is Brock weaker? Is Brock not working out enough?

He was distraught. Everyone around him was strong, but he was weak. No wonder Father kicked him out. He didn't even have impeccable pecs!

Brock sadly flexed a bicep. It only doubled his arm's girth. He scowled, a couple tears glistening in his eyes—being weak was shameful for a bro, but crying was not.

What am I doing wrong, Big Bro in the sky... he wondered sadly, not expecting an answer to his thoughts.

But he got one.

Rustling surrounded him. He looked around warily. Paper boxes and crates were pushed aside, and from behind them, five dogs appeared—one big black and four dirty brown.

He looked at the dogs deeply. They snarled and barked at him, eyes filled with hunger, but Brock's were only filled with pity.

These dog bros were so skinny. Their ribs showed, and their muscles seemed weaker than a newborn gymonkey's. How could they live like that!

And what were they even doing here? Brock didn't understand everything when Big Bro spoke with other tall bros, but he knew there weren't many small bros like himself here.

But, maybe, there were some. Maybe his Big Bro wasn't the only one who brought his pack. And, maybe, the other Big Bros weren't good bros. Maybe these dogs were only alone and starving here... because they'd been abandoned.

Rage clouded his eyes, quickly shifting back to worry.

He jumped up at once, staring at the dogs with a compassion they apparently did not share. They bared their fangs and jumped at him. Each reached at least his chest in height, but Brock wasn't afraid. With muscles that small, how could they beat him?

He ducked under the first dog and grabbed it by the leg, then spun it twice before dropping it on the second dog. A third tried to bite him, but Brock simply grabbed both sides of its mouth and forced it shut. He then wrapped a hand around its muzzle and put the other under the dog's belly, raising it and throwing it at the fourth dog like a big poop. Both tumbled away.

Only the fifth and last dog—the largest one—remained. It must have been the big bro of the dogs, and it eyed Brock warily. He didn't want to hurt it, so he jumped on its back and held on to its fur, butt bumping against its spine as the dog jumped and thrashed around, unable to throw him off.

Exhaustion came rapidly, and it collapsed, at which point Brock dismounted.

The rest of the dogs were staring at him now, eyes filled with fear. Brock had no intention of harming them. His heart hurt simply looking at them. These little dog bros desperately needed a big bro to guide them.

Suddenly, a thought struck Brock like a thunderbolt. Should *he* become their big bro? They were different species, but Big Bro had already shown Brock that different people could be bros.

But muscles are the most important, he thought with sadness. Two different desires warred inside him. On one side, he wanted to become the big bro of these dogs and help them. On the other, he wanted to spend all his time working out so he could become stronger and worthy of Big Bro's brohood.

He hesitated, but eventually chose the second path. He needed to become strong. He didn't want to be kicked out of the pack again.

Just as he was about to depart and leave the dog bros to their fate, a second thought struck him!

Wait! If muscles are the most important, why is Big Bro a big bro? Why is Father a big bro? They could be working out instead!

This was a predicament! Brock frowned and sat back down on his crate to consider the issue. There was something there, he just didn't know what. The dogs waited, unsure of what was happening.

I know! He slapped an open hand with the bottom of his fist. Father said all muscles are important. The heart has muscles too! Big Bros guide their little bros to work out their hearts!

His monkey mouth formed into a big 'O'. What a truth he discovered! "*Uu-ha-ha*!" he shouted.

He jumped up excitedly. He would become the big bro of these dog bros. They would be his pack!

Excited, he looked at the dogs and flexed his muscles to declare his decision. They didn't flex back, but that was okay. As a good big bro, he'd teach them how to properly communicate with other bros.

He'd also teach them to workout. But first came another thing. He just couldn't bear to see his little bros skinny like that.

Reaching into his pocket—Big Bro had asked him to wear a pair of red pants—Brock took out a pack of salami. He had been planning to use it as a snack for harder thoughts, but now, his little bros needed it.

The moment he took it out and opened it, the dogs jumped. Brock grabbed their muzzles and tossed them all away, then glared at them.

He was their big bro. They should show respect.

The dogs whimpered. Then, one by one, they looked down. Brock smiled warmly. He used his hands to cut the salami into five roughly equal pieces, then distributed it to his little bros. They practically tore into the poor salami.

They were so poor and weak... Luckily, they now had a strong big bro to help them. He was filled with pride, and his chest stuck out a bit —undoubtedly from his heart muscles getting stronger. He was working out already!

Big Bros were so wise.

Brock wondered something else. If he trained his heart, what else could he train?

Head muscles! he realized. Big Bro sometimes sits in silence. He works out his head muscles. Brock should do the same.

He nodded, resolved to try what his Big Bro called "cultivation" instead of fighting the dumbbell all the time.

Then, as his little bros had already finished eating, he started showing them how to workout. They normally shouldn't do it right after food, but... well, they needed it.

With his guidance and a lot of hard work, these dog bros would become buff in no time at all!

CHAPTER SIXTY-ONE

JACK RUST VERSUS DORMAN WHISTLES

Jack stood on one edge of the sparring room. Dorman Whistles stood on the other, twirling twin daggers. Brock peeked from the entrance door and was ready to pull his head back in case of rampaging shockwaves, while the training robot stood calmly in a corner, medical kit in hand.

"What say you we make a bet, Dorman?" Jack asked.

Dorman frowned. "A bet?"

"Yes. If I win, you join the Flame River alliance. If you win... Well, what would you want?"

Dorman had remained neutral so far. However, the alliances weren't just about Flame River versus Ice Peak. They also concerned Jack versus the scions. He still wasn't sure how exactly they'd stop the encroaching behemoth called Animal Kingdom in a year, when their grace period was over, but being in the strongest alliance now seemed like their best bet.

"Fine," Dorman said. "If I win, you'll give me one hundred thousand credits."

It was a tremendous amount.

"Okay," Jack agreed. "I don't have that much right now, but I'll give you what I have and owe the rest."

"Okay."

Jack gulped. The bet was a nice idea. He just had to not lose. How difficult could it be?

He grabbed up a flip-flop. "I apologize in advance. I would have preferred to use a more elegant weapon, but alas, we do not choose the Dao; the Dao chooses us."

"No problem. I also favor light weapons. It should be a good match," Dorman replied.

Jack felt proud. His disguise worked!

"Prepare yourself," Dorman said, then disappeared.

Jack barely caught a blur to his right before a dagger nicked his ribs, letting a thin line of blood drip down his waist.

"What's the matter?" Dorman appeared a few steps before him. "Can't you even handle that little bit of speed?"

Jack's brows twitched. "You little shit." He fell into a fighting stance. His eyes sharpened, his breath evened, and his chest inflated. His body was fire and his mind ice.

Dorman lunged. Jack barely caught a glimpse, but it was enough. He slapped his flip-flop in the air, barely missing Dorman, who'd jumped back.

He returned from another direction. Jack was there again, slapping before he knew it. Thanks to the training robot, he knew how to handle extreme speed. His reflexes worked directly from his senses to his limbs, without any sort of thinking required in between. He could react faster like that. Fast enough to catch dagger-wielding flies.

Dorman flitted in and out of reach, darting around the room like it was nothing. He moved at such speeds he befuddled the eye, but it wasn't just his speed itself, it was the ease with which he could completely change his momentum. One moment he was moving full speed to the right, then he instantly turned to the left at the same speed, and that change was so fast, the eye carried on to the right for a fraction of a second, making him seem to disappear.

It wasn't a hard tactic to grasp—Jack did the same thing on slower opponents—but to do that on *Jack* of all people spoke of his abilities. He was even faster than the robot!

Jack wasn't a pushover, either. Though he hadn't met an opponent like this before, he adapted mid-fight. Against his instincts, he stopped focusing on Dorman's body, widening his gaze so he could catch him even when he changed directions.

It worked.

A blur remained when Dorman tried to disappear. It flickered from side to side, getting behind Jack elusively fast, but he was there. He swung behind him, flip-flop slapping the air, but still received a shallow cut on his lower back.

"Your body's tough," Dorman said. "What's your Constitution?"

"95. What's your Dexterity?"

"It's not that simple. All stats matter... but it's almost 200!" Dorman laughed, then charged again. He seemed even faster than before. Jack stuck his back against the wall, but it felt like fighting the wind. Wherever his flip-flop was, there was always a dagger slipping in from somewhere else. He didn't catch Dorman even once. Laughter surrounded him from all directions like a jolly butcher.

Dorman's forte wasn't pure speed. It was a mix of skill, fine control, reaction, maneuverability, and *then* pure speed. Unfortunately, Jack didn't have time to care about the specifics.

In the blink of an eye, he'd received more than a dozen shallow cuts. His regeneration could handle them, but they stung like motherfuckers. He clenched his fist.

"Enough!" he roared. Dorman appeared opposite him.

"Enough? Do you resign already?" he said with disappointment.

Jack laughed hoarsely. "Can you keep a secret?"

Dorman's eyes narrowed. "I can."

"Good. Then, I'll fuck you up properly."

He let his flip-flop fall. Fighting spirit erupted out of him, along with an aura of suppression. His hair whipped in a non-existent wind as he clenched his fists.

He could barely use his Dao Root when wielding a flip-flop. It was like trying to fit a bucket's worth of water through a straw. Most got stuck.

Now, his Dao was unleashed, and it was fucking pissed. "Come at me!" Jack roared, adopting a boxing stance.

Dorman obliged. He struck again, his daggers closing the gap in the blink of an eye, but Jack was there. A fist smashed, and though it didn't hit Dorman, the air pressure itself was enough to make him wary. Another fist came immediately afterward, and Dorman had to jump away.

"You were holding back!" he exclaimed. The ends of his lips rose. "That's *awesome*!"

Jack lunged. He closed the distance in two steps and punched, making the air cave with every strike. Dorman fell on the defensive. Jack moved with slow confidence, and his fists were ready to jab at a moment's notice, waiting to sting when Dorman got close. Against Dorman's weak physical body, Jack didn't need to punch hard. Swift jabs would be most effective.

When Jack reverted to his original fighting style, he instantly knew how to fight better. After all, he was used to this, not a goddamn *flip-flop*!

He dashed and punched. His fists whistled through the air like bullets. Dorman's stance fell lower. His hair rose, and their tips flashed with lightning sparks, as did the tips of his daggers.

Jack instantly became wary. He stopped attacking and stepped back, barely saving himself. Dorman's daggers bit through the skin of his belly, so fast he didn't even register their motion. He only saw blood spurt out of him, a geyser that turned into a slow current. He ached with every beat of his heart.

"Heh," Dorman said, panting. "Nice dodge."

The robot took a step, holding the medical kit. "Master, should I—"

"No!" Jack cut it off. He stepped back into the fray, catching Dorman by surprise. His punches fell like a landslide, pushing the other man until his back met the wall. A fist connected cleanly. Dorman yelled as he was flung aside, crossing the room to smash into the far wall. Jack felt a rib crack under his hard knuckles.

Dorman tumbled to the ground and stood again. His daggers were steady, though his expression was pained.

"We keep going?" Jack asked.

"We keep going."

He dashed again. Daggers slashed the air into pieces as punches annihilated it altogether. Dorman danced around Jack, dodging cataclysmic strikes by the skin of his teeth as he unleashed a thousand cuts on Jack, who took them all and still stood. In contrast, one well-placed punch would be enough to end Dorman, and Jack defended his vitals well.

Their strikes were too fast to see. Brock's eyes had gotten hazy, and a moment later, he got dizzy, but he wouldn't let his bro's fight go unseen. He kept his eyes glued on the exchange even as he fought back the urge to puke.

Jack felt trapped in a ball of spikes. Daggers were everywhere. No matter where he moved, they waited to slice him. He couldn't get close like this. He couldn't last long enough. His regeneration closed the wounds, but it wasn't instant. Every slice was a nick at his perseverance.

Something needed to be done. And if Jack couldn't defend with his fists... he would defend with his body.

Awareness sparked in his mind. Something that had been bubbling right under the surface, brewing until it was mature. Jack gave in to it. He slowed, letting the rain of daggers carve his body. His hands defended his vitals, especially his face and throat.

The rest of his body defended itself. Jack felt transparent. He could see his entire layout of muscles, from the largest to the tiniest. He could even see many muscles he was sure weren't supposed to be there, yet there they were.

Dorman's dagger sliced at his ribs. Jack's skin tensed, a dozen tiny muscles working together to harden that particular spot. The dagger bounced off, barely breaking the skin. Another dagger came at his chest, but the same thing happened. Of his myriad muscles, the correct ones worked in perfect harmony to enhance the spot about to be hit.

Dorman's daggers kept falling, but their damage became minimal. Jack smiled. In slow motion, he met Dorman's eyes and realized that he, too, was smiling.

The rain of daggers turned into a flood. Dorman sped up, giving up precision for even more absurd speed. Jack's new defense mechanism rose in effectiveness in parallel to Dorman's speed; or, maybe, it was the opposite.

At some point, both plateaued.

Congratulations! Pugilist Body (II) → Pugilist Body (III)
Pugilist Body (III): Your body has adapted to your fighting style. You gain significant flexibility, reflexes, and durability, as well as increased hardness on your knuckles. You have heightened control over your body, including its natural limiters, and slight regenerative powers. *Additionally, you have the ability to harden every surface of your body at will, significantly increasing your defensive properties.*

Jack couldn't read the screen mid-fight, of course, but he didn't need it. He understood exactly what was happening.

However, even this upgrade wasn't enough to eke out a victory, because Dorman was getting better at the same pace. The battle raged on. No more breakthroughs came.

Some time later, Jack felt his edge slipping. It took the entirety of his concentration to keep up with Dorman, and he couldn't keep it up for long. Plus, he was bleeding from a hundred different places. He needed to end this.

He ducked in, extending both arms to the side. Dorman didn't expect that and ran into one of them, at the same time delivering a fierce cut in Jack's liver, but it wasn't enough to take him down. Suddenly, Dorman was trapped, and in the single moment that he stayed still, the world darkened. His every hair stood on end as a meteor exploded right next to his ear, rupturing his ear drum and showering the world in fiery purple. And yet still, he stood.

"I win," said Jack, who'd missed the Meteor Punch on purpose.

Dorman, though sweating, smiled. "Are you sure?"

Jack became intimately aware of a dagger—though he couldn't see it due to the angle—placed right before his left eye. Suddenly, he was sweating too.

"How did you do that?" he asked. "I was watching both your hands."

"A skill," was all Dorman replied, chuckling out a cough. "Thank you for not killing me."

"Same to you. I even got a skill upgrade mid-fight."

"I knew it. Me too!"

Then, their excitement wore off, and their weariness took over.

"Whew, man..." For a moment, Dorman seemed like a normal teenager as he took a step back and sat on the floor. He was exhausted and panting deeply. Now that he didn't take care to look serious, Jack noticed he was just a short, slim kid, the kind who'd get picked on in high school.

Now, his extreme elitism didn't seem all that off.

"What was the name of that skill?" Jack asked. "The lightning one."

"Twin Lightning Fang. But I can't control it well enough yet. Yours?"

"Meteor Punch."

"It sure felt like one." Dorman laughed. "At the end, I used a skill that makes me way faster. That's why you didn't see my dagger."

"Why didn't you use it earlier? You could have beaten me."

"I couldn't." Dorman didn't explain, and Jack didn't push further, either. Everyone had their secrets.

Jack stumbled. He wasn't as physically worn as Dorman, but he was mentally exhausted. Plus, he was still bleeding. "Hey, Sparman," he told the robot. "Can you bandage me?"

"That is not my name, master."

"Do you have one?"

"Yes."

"It doesn't matter. I'll call you Sparman."

"...As you wish."

It came closer, opening its medical kit for the first time and revealing rows of syringes, along with packs of bandages and other tools. It first stabbed a syringe filled with ice-blue liquid in Jack's abs, making him grimace, then expertly wrapped bandages around his largest wound, the one caused by Dorman's Twin Lightning Fang. The rest of the cuts would heal by themselves, so Jack let them be. His regeneration was growing with his stats, and it was plenty useful.

He extended a hand to Dorman, who grabbed it and used it to stand.

"Did you know the scions like to shout out the names of their attacks?" Jack asked.

"Really?"

"Yeah."

"Wow. That's so cringe."

"Ugh, don't use that word out loud. It's so..."

"Cringe?"

"Yeah, but don't use it."

Right then, Brock came running from the door and stopped in front of Jack, jumping excitedly on the spot and pointing at Jack's muscles.

"Of course I am, Brock," he replied. "I'm your father's bro, remember? He's strong, so I have to be strong, too!"

Brock protested.

"You're my little bro," Jack explained. "Since I'm the bro of your father, who is your big bro."

Another protest, more intense.

"Little in hierarchy, Brock. Your muscles are huuuge!"

That seemed to do the trick, and Brock, satisfied, turned to Dorman. He looked at the teenager's lanky arms, then did a "so-so" sign with his hand. Both men burst into laughter, and Brock followed a moment later, not really understanding but wanting to fit in.

"That's a cute monkey," Dorman said. "Where did you find it?"

"I'm friends with his father's pack. Brock here came along to experience the world and get strong."

"Hmm... He doesn't seem strong though..."

Brock reached behind his tail, armed, and threw a poop at Dorman, who dodged it hurriedly.

"What the—" he said. "That's disgusting!"

Jack laughed again, while Brock waved a fist in the air and called out Dorman in monkey-talk.

"By the way," Dorman said, "I know I didn't lose, but I'll join your alliance anyway."

"How so?"

"You're there, and you seem like an okay person. The Ice Peak... not so much."

"I see. That's great." Jack smiled, simultaneously narrowing his eyes at Dorman. "I'm not giving you the hundred thousand though. I need it for something."

"Of course." Dorman laughed. "It's okay. Money and equipment are inferior to skills, and you can't buy those."

"Sure you can," Jack replied in puzzlement.

"What do you mean?" Dorman asked back, puzzled himself. "Wait—we're talking about the real skills, right? The Dao ones."

"I was talking about all of them, actually. Why did you call Dao skills the real ones?"

"Because they are. Don't you know how skills *work*?"

CHAPTER SIXTY-TWO
CHASING THE DAO

"Dao skills are the true skills," Dorman explained.

"What does that mean?" Jack asked. Brock stood on the floor beside them, nodding as if following the conversation.

"It means that Dao skills are the way to go. Normal skills are useful, sure, but only at the start. As you rise in Grade, they lose their value. Imagine being a D-Grade immortal who can fly and destroy mountains. Would the ability to strike *slightly* harder with a hammer be helpful?"

"No," Jack replied easily.

"Exactly. At that level, simple skills are useless. Only the Dao matters."

"And that's where Dao skills come in."

"Dao skills are skills that have been adapted to your personal Dao. You can't just read an information crystal to learn them. You have to forge them yourself. Most people begin forming them when they choose their Dao Seed and break through to the E-Grade, and they're lucky to get *one* Dao skill in their entire lives. But if you want to become a true warrior, they're essential. They do with your Dao what normal skills do with your body."

"Use it better," Jack said, his mind wrapping around the difference.

"Exactly! The real use of normal skills is as the foundation on which to build your Dao skills. It saves us the trouble of learning mundane stuff so we can focus on imbuing the Dao into them."

"I see..." Jack had read the information packages on the Dao, of course, but they didn't give details on these skills. They mostly discussed the three first stages of the Dao—Dao Roots, Dao Seeds, and Dao Trees—and how to best advance from stage to stage. "You know a lot of stuff for a kid, Dorman."

"I am not a kid. I'm young. After the System, those two are not the same," he replied with a sad smile, dodging Jack's teasing.

Jack himself chuckled. He turned his gaze to the ceiling, trying to stare at the sky through it. "It's incredible that you managed to rise so far at such a young age," he finally said. "When I was sixteen, all I could think about was girls and video games—and not even in that order."

"I know what you mean. For me, it was just computer games. When the System arrived... I don't know what set me apart, to be honest. I was just lucky to be in the perfect circumstances to rise, along with the skills to capitalize on them. A ton of luck, too. Kobold nests are a nightmare."

Jack threw him a surprised glance.

"I guess," he replied. "Goblin tribes are easy. Just kill a bunch, avoid getting burned alive, then poof, levels."

Dorman chuckled. "Anyway. I'll go now. After this battle, I want to meditate on a few things. You should as well."

"Not losing any time, are you?"

"If I did, I would be dead."

Jack smiled as he waved his young friend goodbye. He watched him head for the stairs but didn't move to follow. As Dorman had said, they both had things to meditate on, and the sooner they did it, the better.

What a strange fellow... he mused, going to his meditation mat. Cold like ice, but opens up real quick if you're strong enough. And being so mature as a teenager... It's almost sad.

Jack hadn't forgotten about his Dao Fruit of the Fist, but he kept it in reserve. The description said it was better used to break through, and since he could only use one fruit in each Grade, there was no sense in wasting it now.

He reached the mat and took a seat, putting Dorman away from his mind. He took in the mystic patterns, which almost seemed to be moving. He closed his eyes, barely sensing Brock sitting beside him on the mat, which he hadn't done before.

Then, he was lost in meditation.

The Dao Root in his soul grew to encompass his whole being. His thoughts fell into order. He took a deep breath, relaxing his body to let his mind flow uninhibited. Unconsciously, he clenched his fist.

What was the Dao?

The Dao was the truth. It was everything, from the tiniest atom to the largest star. He was merely one of its infinite manifestations. But the Dao had a mind of its own—handles from which he could grab to shape it if his understanding was deep enough. Like the Dao of the Fist.

What was the fist?

The fist was a concept. A fantasy. It was five clenched fingers on a palm, but that was merely a physical shape, not the core of its Dao. The fist represented a person's intent to fight and win. Their willingness to strike hard and impose their will on others.

It wasn't a kind thing, the fist. It was hard. Entailing conflict and its resolution. It only appeared in war, during battle, and it wasn't generous. The fist was a tool of destruction.

In the end, the fist was something contained in every living being, regardless of whether they had a physical fist or not. In its deepest form, it was the desire to not step back. The bitter spite that appeared when someone tried to control you—at least, that was Jack's Dao.

But he'd been in many battles lately, and he realized that, while his Dao was that of the fist, it wasn't the *entire* fist. Because the fist wasn't one thing. It was many.

The fist of liberation was not the same as the fist of oppression. He clenched it to live, whereas others clenched it to dominate, to escape, to vent, or because that was all they knew.

Everyone had their own fist, and the Dao of the Fist encapsulated them all.

And while Jack's fist wasn't one with a singular purpose, at least not yet, he knew some things it wasn't. A mercenary clenched their fist because that was their job. Jack wouldn't do that. It didn't speak to his heart—to his Dao.

Jack clenched his fist for himself. He'd clenched it to fight for his life, as well as to fight in a packed stadium and hear the crowd chant his name. He clenched it because he enjoyed it, and to seek revenge for the faulting of his mother. He clenched it for justice *and* himself.

His fist had many purposes. He didn't have to pick a single path yet, though he would when the time came to reach the D-Grade. For now, all he had to do was pick a direction.

After meeting people who fought for their own reasons, Jack was clear that his Dao of the Fist was too wide. He needed to narrow it down. Eventually, it would become something that belonged solely to him, but for now, a single step would be enough.

He needed something to specify his Dao. What was the common factor in all his fists?

The answer sprang easily. It was desire. He fought because he wanted things: to live, triumph, and smile.

And as it was easy, it was also wrong.

Desire was indeed what drove him, but it wasn't what he sought. His desire was a general concept, not the right one to complete his fist.

He knew what the fist was. But what was the essence of *his* fist?

Desire... Freedom... Those were the values that drove him, and maybe they were directions he would pursue in the future, but they weren't what he needed now. They weren't what his clenched fist currently represented.

His fist was a direction. An intent. If a desire sprang up in his heart, he pursued it with his fist. Be it enemies, problems, or oppressors, he simply punched through them. His fist was unstoppable, and it broke through anything because it carried *his* Indomitable Will.

Something clicked. His Dao Root of the Fist shuddered in glee as something new appeared beside it, something that further defined it and made it more intimate to Jack. They didn't form a complete whole, but in his mind's eye, Jack saw them rotating around his soul, bound together forever and absolutely unshakable.

He opened his eyes with a calm smile. *So, this is what it feels like.*

Congratulations! You have developed the Dao Root of Indomitable Will.

To set a course and let nothing change it. To be the master of yourself. To have will indomitable. That is the one true path.

As Jack eased out of his meditative trance, his entire body was sore. Who knows how long he'd been sitting there. However, his mind felt at peace, like a calm lake filled with treasure. He was so much more than before.

His smile refused to budge. He turned to the side.

"What do you think, Brock? Am I—" His smile formed into a gape. Brock was sitting right beside him on the mat, eyes closed as he was in the middle of his own ruminations.

And he exuded the faint aura of the Dao. Brock had developed a Dao Root.

Jack tried to comprehend this. He did a double take. His little bro, a child monkey, had comprehended a Dao Root faster than billions of humans.

He almost forgot his own breakthrough as he scanned Brock.

Brorilla, Level 5 (Elite)

His description hadn't changed, and neither had his level—he was in his growing phase, so he'd already reached level 5 the previous day—but he was now considered an Elite! Did monsters with Dao Roots get the tag of Elite, or was that simply the case for the F-Grade?

Maybe Elite monsters had better insight into the Dao than most monsters of their level range. For the F-Grade, that meant having a Dao Root.

Jack still needed to confirm this theory with others, but it made sense.

However, he didn't bother Brock for now. He was still meditating, obviously, and to interrupt that would be sacrilege. Instead, Jack inspected his own status screen.

Name: Jack Rust: Species
Human, Earth-387
Faction: Bare Fist Brotherhood (F-Grade)

Grade: F
Class: Pugilist (Elite)
Level: 35

Strength: 95
Dexterity: 95
Constitution: 95
Mental: 10
Will: 10

Skills: Fistfighting (III), Drill (II), Pugilist Body (III), Parkour (II)
Dao Skills: Meteor Punch (I)
Daos: Dao Root of the Fist, Dao Root of Indomitable Will

Titles: Planetary Frontrunner (10)

A new row had appeared just above titles. Jack now had two Dao Roots, just like Vivi and Gan Salin. What else had changed?

He stood, scanning the space, taking everything in. His thoughts were steady and immovable, subject entirely to his conscious will. The constant noise his head was filled with, the one he'd never noticed before, was now absent. His entire being was an arrow he could point wherever he wanted.

His heart was light, and suddenly, everything seemed so very easy.

Jack grinned. He was in complete control, and he'd never felt better in his life. Moreover...

He clenched his fist, sensing waves of power course through his body. He didn't just have complete harmony of mind, he also had great strength, which he now possessed the full ability to wield.

The Dao Root of Indomitable Will wouldn't be directly applicable to combat, but it would be a great supportive ability, and it would help shore up Jack's weakness: mental and soul defenses.

It was perfect. He couldn't contain his smile.

Surprised monkey sounds from behind him drew his attention. He turned to find Brock staring at his own hands with wonder.

CHAPTER SIXTY-THREE
LIVING THE SYSTEM LIFE

"Come on, Brock, tell me. What Dao Root did you get?"

Brock looked at Jack with a smug smile, extending the wait.

"Come on, bro!" Jack insisted. With a laugh, Brock flexed his biceps—which were notably larger than last time. "Ohh, is it strength?"

Brock shook his head.

"Power? *Bromance*?"

Brock laughed.

"Hmm... Wait. Is it muscles?"

He nodded.

"That's great! You are now a strong brorilla, Brock! I mean, even stronger than before."

Brock was filled with pride. It was clear that joy flooded him. His little fangs wouldn't stop showing from all the smiles, he was full of energy, and his tail wagged like a dog's.

Amidst excited cries, Brock rushed over to the 50kg dumbbell that had become his mortal enemy ever since arriving to this place. He grabbed it, tightened his grip... and lifted it!

He did it so easily, in fact, that the dumbbell flew up a bit, and then he barely had time to draw his foot back before it was crushed. He made monkey sounds of fear as he jumped around on one leg before realizing he was fine.

"Woah, that's a serious upgrade," Jack said. "I'm sure your father will be proud."

Brock's smile widened so much Jack feared it would rip his cheeks. But what could be done? For all his mischievousness and tendency to throw poop around, Brock remained a child, and the approval of his elders was extremely important.

Watching his little bro's joy, Jack smiled warmly.

"What do you say, buddy? Wanna celebrate?"

Brock pumped a fist.

"Meat skewers? No, wait—What about *Dao-infused* meat skewers?"

Brock salivated. So did Jack. The thought excited him as much as the little monkey. *Then again, we are monkeys too*, he thought, and the two left to go get food.

The days passed and Integration City found its rhythm, and everyone entering the semblance of a routine.

Jack and Edgar would go to the arena every morning, just in case they were picked first. If not, they left and returned when their tokens shone. Karvahul joined them, but he usually stayed longer. He was now the manager of Jack's betting fund, for a generous commission of 10 percent—take it or leave it, Jack had said—and he was already making a fortune.

He stayed in the arena every day, watching the fights and keeping notes on many people. He then went to the betting desk and deposited a set amount for each promising participant. Of course, a large bet went to Jack every single day—since not many took his Dao seriously, and he had another Dao to rely on in a pinch, he was the ideal black horse.

Jack didn't know how exactly the calculations were made, and neither did he care. The important thing was that Karvahul was raking in the money. A lot of money. Enough that, if they kept at it, they might even reach the two million goal through betting alone.

Of course, they had other moneymaking avenues.

More humans were arriving at Integration City from all around the planet. They rode private jets, commercial ones, even fast ships. The Ice Peak was the only of the three factions to send representatives. As for the rest of the people, they were mostly from Asia, Australia, or the Americas, since Integration City was situated in the middle of the Pacific Ocean.

There was the occasional celebrity, but most people seemed like average joes that had just gotten stronger in a hurry, though not quickly enough to join the Tournament.

And, as people arrived, so were Karvahul's other schemes set in motion. Jack now ate out on a daily basis. His tabs were paid, of course, including Dao-infused food, and people streamed to the restaurants he endorsed just to hear him preach about the importance of spanking. He even gave interviews!

Though his income from those streams wasn't large, it was funneled into betting, where it had the opportunity to multiply—and it did. Karvahul was clearly gifted.

Of course, Jack wasn't the only one taking advantage of the situation. Many other minor celebrities had cropped up, and greatest among them was Kane Vanderdecken, the long-haired practitioner of the Dao of Metal. He organized small concerts in the wide plaza behind the arena, where aliens and humans alike streamed in to enjoy his Dao-infused music.

Alien performers weren't allowed, apparently—only merchants could enter an Integrated planet on its first year—so his competition was minimal. He even cooperated with other bards. He also kept up a winning streak. His performance on stage had led him to comprehending a second Dao Root, shooting him to the top echelon of participants.

Some merchants were already selling shirts saying "Dao of the Devil" over a hand wearing a black, spiky armband and extending its pinky and index fingers. If the System had gods, they obviously didn't take it as heresy, or they didn't care.

"Does the System have gods?" Jack asked one morning as he, Brock, Edgar, and Karvahul paced to the arena.

"Not really, no," Karvahul responded. "Though the B-Grades are quite godlike. I've heard they can destroy planets."

Jack and Edgar gaped.

Planets were much larger than most people thought. For reference, if Earth was shrunk to the size of a pool ball, it would be smoother than an actual pool ball, despite Mount Everest being almost five and a half miles tall and the Mariana Trench seven miles deep.

The planet's diameter was eight thousand miles. To destroy something that big was unthinkable.

"There are rumors of other galaxies and A-Grade cultivators of unfathomable power, as well as legends about godlike beings outside the System, but..." Karvahul shook his head. "Even if they exist, they're so far away from us little folk, they might as well not be there. The System is the only God we know."

"I see." Jack nodded, while Edgar fell in thought.

While Integration City was flourishing, the Tournament continued in full force. Three days after it began, the participant count had been halved. Jack could see people streaming out of the participant district every night, all bearing bitter, disappointed faces.

The resources offered by Integration City, especially the sparring robot and the meditation mat, were very precious. Unfortunately, these were the rules. Nothing could be done.

One day, Jack saw a man trying to sneak the meditation mat out in his backpack. The dog guards fell on him the moment he stepped past the gate, and they were not in the mood for jokes. The man didn't survive.

As time went on, Jack's fights became more difficult, but still within the sphere of easy. True to Karvahul's words, the randomizer always set him up against mediocre opponents at best. He understood the reason, but it still made him feel dirty, like an executioner. Every time someone faced him, horror was reflected in their eyes.

He just did his best to end the fights quickly, though nobody resigned easily. When his opponents were disrespectful, he would say a couple lines about the benefits of a good spanking, just to rile up the crowd. On the other hand, when they respected him, he would face them without the slightest hint of ridicule.

As more days passed, Jack had met plenty of colorful opponents. He'd spanked fierce young men and elegant young ladies. A fisherman from Greenland and a fakir from India. Even a famous British politician was spanked to oblivion by the infamous John Brown!

Edgar's fights had been far more exciting. Each and every one of them had been a struggle. However, since he'd gotten lucky and won in the first two days, he'd been seeded by the organizers, meaning he only got placed against weak or average opponents. Additionally, he'd bought enough experience balls to raise him to level 39, negating his largest disadvantage. Most people had done the same and were now around that level.

Any more than that and he would risk destabilizing himself. Skills and stats were supposed to be gained gradually, after all.

Edgar was also progressing rapidly. He often exchanged theories on magic and its implementations with Vivi and other members of the Flame River, leading to a steady increase in all their powers. Edgar improved the fastest of them all—though, to be fair, he was originally the weakest.

Now, Edgar could stand on his own even against strong opponents. He hoped to make it to the finals.

As for the scions, Gan Salin was the only one struggling. With a loss in his record, he was paired against strong opponents every day, though he was lucky—or favored—enough to dodge anyone too strong. When he used his Dao weapon—a pair of gloves that could extend sharp claws—he was a force to be reckoned.

Jack saw the other scions fight as well, though they never had to go all-out.

Rufus Emberheart was simply unfathomable. The sharken was impressive, too. He used the Dao Root of Momentum, giving him extreme physical abilities, and he fought using long gloves with two triangular blades sticking outside his forearms.

The other two scions were a massive bipedal elephant, at least nine feet tall, who possessed the Dao of Healing but could still cause major harm to her opponents, and an aloof humanoid eagle who darted around even faster than Dorman and absolutely destroyed anyone he met.

As it turned out, the scions weren't too united of a group. The eagle and the elephant were one team, while Rufus, the sharken, and Gan Salin were another—and clearly the stronger one.

On the ninth day, not many people were left. The Tournament would end in a few rounds. Now, all battles took place between dawn and noon, which made the people congregate back into the arena.

It was on this day that Vivi decided to take the people of her alliance out for a treat. It was both a show of force and a final outing before things got serious.

The large square on the back of the arena boasted the greatest luxury. On one side, it was framed by the arena itself and the base of the white Overseer Tower. On the other was a building that resembled a furnace, made of red bricks and with a sparkling antenna at its top. It was a teleporter, and according to the merchants, it could teleport people several astral areas away.

Jack and Edgar stepped into the restaurant with wonder in their eyes. Though they'd made plenty of money themselves, they still saved up for the auction, so luxuries like this were unfamiliar.

The walls were inlaid with gold, while red silk hung in ribbons. There were swirling columns supporting the ceiling, as well as a serene garden for tables. There were also isolated rooms for those who wanted privacy or extra luxury, and it was in one of those that the kovan waiter led them.

"What do you think, Sage?" Jack asked, nudging the other man. "How much will the total be?"

"To think I went from the streets to such a place..." The Sage shook his head, pretending not to hear the question. "Life has truly come full circle, hasn't it?"

Jack laughed. "Sure has, big guy."

"Were you really homeless before?" Dorman asked, walking beside them. Though he remained cold toward those whose strength he didn't acknowledge, he was oddly close to the Sage.

"Of course. Death wasn't too far away when the System came. I merely got lucky. In another sense, you could say the world gave me the just reward for everything it forced me to endure."

Jack nodded, asking no more. The Sage had been tight-lipped on the details of his first adventures, as he'd been tight-lipped on prophecies. After their initial meeting, Jack hadn't heard a single one.

However, nobody doubted the Sage. Everyone who made it to this stage were extremely special people. Of course, the Sage didn't win fights by prophesizing that he would—that would be an oxymoron. He simply pointed at his opponents, whose eyes went hazy, and they quickly resigned, then got super pissed that they lost so indignantly.

He had been paired against Dorman one time, but he resigned first. "I can't win. This is simply fate," he'd said with a shrug.

Come to think of it, that's when the two of them got close... Jack thought, but his attention was grabbed by the opulent room that appeared behind a set of closed doors.

A wide glass window overlooked Integration City and the ocean behind it—they were on the third floor. A heavy wooden table stood in the middle of the room, covered in a red tablecloth, and placed on it were sets of plates and cutlery.

This was high-society stuff. Jack counted three sets of cutlery, along with an equal number of napkins. A steaming soup bowl was placed before each chair, gray with golden lines, and the smell alone made all thoughts of conversation fly out the closed window.

Jack wasn't a stranger to luxury, but he'd never experienced it to this extent before—especially when even the soup was Dao-infused. Vivi was going all-out by inviting them here.

"Don't look like that," she said, laughing. "It's just food."

She sat at one end of the table and picked up the glass of wine before her—everyone had one.

"To a bright future," she said, raising her glass. Everyone followed suit, then they drank.

Sitting at the other end of the table, Jack almost choked. It was heavenly. Not only was the wine itself amazing, but the alcohol seemed to be augmented by the Dao, too, making his body crave it like a parched lake would crave the rain.

And it was strong. Maybe strong enough to make him tipsy for the first time since he got, like, a million Constitution.

"Guys, don't try the soup!" Edgar said, sipping it off his spoon. His eyes got red. "It's too hot to eat, but so delicious I can't stop now..."

Everyone shared a hearty laugh. Edgar choked a bit.

These were the core members of their alliance after all the recruiting: the Flame River—represented by Vivi—Jack, Edgar, Dorman Whistles, and the Sage. They weren't many, but on the bright side, the Ice Peak had fewer. Basically only the scions.

Besides them, the only strong people that hadn't yet picked a side were Li Xiang, the martials arts master, and Vanderdecken, the rock star. They both remained on the fence.

Light conversation flew around the table. The Sage, Jack, and Vivi were the most talkative ones, while Edgar and Dorman mostly listened. However, everyone went quiet when the next course arrived.

This would be a three-course dinner: soup, main course, dessert. Earth restaurants usually served appetizers instead of soup, but aliens had their own preferences. And when in alien-land...

Five lycan waiters arrived and surrounded the table, each holding a sealed disc. They revealed it theatrically at the same time, releasing the restrained fragrance all at once and threatening to short-circuit Jack's brain.

There, on his plate, now rested a large red steak surrounded by tufts of salad. Jack's eyes saw red. He tore into the steak, barely remembering to use cutlery. Next thing he knew, his plate was empty. So was everyone's.

"What the hell happened?" he asked.

"Antesaurus rib," Vivi replied weakly. "It's supposed to come from peak E-Grade beasts... and wow. Wow. I'm so glad I didn't splurge on the D-Grade main courses. I think I would die."

"Yeah. It's not even funny," Jack agreed. If he'd almost lost his mind for a peak E-Grade meal, what would a D-Grade meal do to him? Turn him insane?

Could this be weaponized? he wondered.

"Mmm, yes, it's very tasty," the Sage said, and everyone noticed he was nibbling on his steak, bite by small bite. Everybody else had devoured it. "What?" he asked innocently, receiving everyone's stares. "Can't a man eat at his own pace?"

The scent still wafted off the Sage's plate, but Jack held himself back. He promised himself to order one of those steaks in a package and give it to Brock. He'd been forced to leave the little monkey at home, as he didn't want to take advantage of Vivi's hospitality.

Not that Brock minded. He was probably having the time of his life working out and sparring against the first level of Sparman.

"*How* can you resist that?" Dorman asked, staring at the Sage like he was a ghost.

"Because I'm civilized," the Sage replied calmly. Jack realized that the only person on their table who ate properly was the one that looked like a beggar. He laughed.

"Nice going, Sage!"

"Thank you."

The dessert came soon after. It consisted of a small yellow thing that resembled jelly and shook like jelly but wasn't jelly. Jack didn't know what it was—though he practically inhaled it all the same. It was the most delicious thing he'd had in his life.

"Damn," he said, leaning back on his chair and crossing his fingers over his full belly. "I hate to admit it, but Karvahul was right. System food really is something else."

"Karvahul's your money maker, right?" Dorman asked.

"Yeah."

"How's that going, by the way?"

"Pretty—"

"Maybe we shouldn't reveal our budget," Vivi cut in. "The auction will come soon, and we might end up competing with each other—though, of course, it's best to avoid it."

"Naturally," the Sage agreed, and everyone nodded.

Jack's smile, however, couldn't be hidden. They'd already made close to the two million the Sage had warned him about. He was a rich man! And, in the auction... who knew what might appear for sale.

"I bet the scions are richer than all of us put together, anyway," Edgar said gloomily, but the Sage only smiled.

"We'll see," he replied, and refused to elaborate further.

More wine came after the dessert, and the rest of the night passed by in a fuzz. It was, indeed, strong enough to make Jack tipsy—which meant it was strong enough to make everyone else dead drunk if they didn't drink moderately.

Edgar didn't, and he ended up magicking an army of tiny Sages to fight against a single, palm-sized Edgar. The Edgar won, of course, partly due to using a fork as a weapon, and everyone had a laugh at the display.

They did have fights the next day, but it wasn't a problem. In all their infinite wisdom, the aliens had invented anti-hangover medicine. It would make a killing in the Earth market.

It was a peaceful night. One filled with friendship and laughter. They needed it before everything went to shit, as it unavoidably would, soon.

The night gave way to morning, and when everyone woke up, it was a new day. Jack walked to the arena at dawn, as usual, and it was a good thing, because he was in the very first round of fights for that day.

His opponent was a bald Tibetan monk with serene eyes, orange robes, and a thick metal pole. His entire body screamed hardness and discipline. And he had an unbroken win streak.

CHAPTER SIXTY-FOUR
FIGHTING A MONK

"JOHN BROWN AND THE DAO OF SPANKING VERSUS BROTHER TAO AND THE DAO of the Staff!"

Brother Tao wasn't his real full name. The Tournament rules required everyone to register with a first and last name, which lead to some interesting results when people wanted to be referred to in a certain way. Like Brother Tao. And also, amusingly, the Sage.

The announcer's voice had just finished ringing, but both fighters were already on the sand. There were three more pairs fighting, but few people paid them any mind.

"I have long yearned to face you in combat, Brother John," Tao said. He was a bald Tibetan monk with orange robes, clear eyes, and a black metal staff held steady in his hands. So far, he hadn't suffered a single defeat.

Human (Earth-387), Level 39
Faction: -
Title: Planetary Frontrunner (100)

Almost everyone remaining had that title.

"The pleasure is mine, Brother Tao," Jack replied with a nod. "My

Dao shines best not on mindless brutes or pretty girls, but on warriors such as yourself. Please do not be alarmed by its appearance. Spanking is as noble as every Dao, and not at all a disgrace."

"I would never think that. I understand that every weapon has a spirit, even those that on first glance seem dull or lacking." He spun his staff once, so fast it caused a gale. He then pointed it at Jack, one hand holding it from the front and the other from the back. He stood barefoot, steady like a tree and with eyes as clear as a mountain lake. He truly seemed every bit the fearsome opponent.

"I did not enjoy being the executioner in previous rounds, but alas, my monastery needs me," he continued. "Will you give me a good battle, Brother John?"

"Absolutely, Brother Tao. I feel the same."

Though he spanked people, Jack wasn't a mean person. When his opponents were respectful, like now, he returned that respect in full. He only mocked those who mocked him first.

"Then, here I come," Tao said, exploding into motion. He closed the distance in three steps and brought his staff down on Jack.

In Jack's eyes, this Tao was a true warrior. His entire body was riddled with hard, wiry muscles, and though he didn't seem muscular, he could have easily beaten most pre-System humans into submission. Tibetan monks spent most of their lives training their body and martial arts, and Tao was no exception.

The staff fell like a rock, then slithered like a snake. Its momentum spun as Tao turned his body, coming at Jack from the right. He had no choice but to block with the bottom of his flip-flop, absorbing the strike and sliding backward across the sand. His forearm hurt.

Jack grinned. *Finally.*

He then charged, slapping his flip-flop against the air. Tao stepped back, rotating his staff to defend. His skills were undeniable. As he turned the staff around his body, one end was always where the flip-flop would strike. Jack could only keep up because of his weapon's lightness. His strikes fell like the rain, but Tao blocked them all.

His defense was like a mountain, and he definitely had several body-augmenting and defense-augmenting skills. It would take more than brute force to overpower him.

Flip-flop and staff clashed a dozen times in the blink of an eye before Jack jumped back. He rushed to the left, planted his foot in the sand, and changed directions, trying to throw Tao off. He failed. The staff was already waiting, and Jack took a blow to the shoulder, throwing him backward. He somersaulted in the air and landed on his feet.

"Ouch," he said.

"I have trained for my entire life, Brother John," Tao said, still as clear-eyed as ever. "I hate to say it, but you are not my match in skill."

"Is that so?" Jack could feel the grin splitting his face and did nothing to stop it. His fighting spirit began to rise.

He echoed Tao's sentiments. The previous fights had been tiresome, unpleasant affairs. This time… Could the Dao of Spanking prevail against a strong opponent?

He couldn't wait to find out.

Jack gripped his flip-flop hard and charged. His strikes flew like eagles and fell like thunderbolts. The flip-flop danced through the air, weaving a pattern of green lines, and the staff danced with it, always a black blur. In the eyes of the audience, the two weapons and fighters moved together, stepping in and out in tandem like following a choreography.

In reality, their every clash was brutal, casting ripples throughout the arena.

Jack's narrowed eyes met Tao's. His flip-flop shot up, feinting a blow, then curving so hard that even its enhanced materials almost gave way. A slap fell on Tao's bare shoulder, echoing throughout the arena and pushing him back, but that was all.

Tao took the strike and stepped in. His staff wasn't meant for such close range, but he had the skills to compensate. He twirled it, striking Jack hard from above. One hand left the staff and formed a fist, digging into Jack's abdomen.

Jack barely had time to bring the flip-flop back. He put it between the fist and his abdomen, helping it cushion the blow, while raising his other hand over his head and meeting the staff with his palm. The dull thud reached the far ends of the arena. Only Jack's Fistfighting proficiency and strong body saved his hand from breaking.

He pushed out with both hands, pushing the staff into the air and the fist back where it came from. The staff needed time to recover. Jack stepped back and swung, aiming for Tao's face.

Tao halted the staff's ascent but didn't bring it back down. Instead, he let it go. Both his hands were available now. One blocked Jack's attacking wrist, while the other wrapped around Jack's hand, forcing him to let go of the flip-flop. Jack's elbow straightened under the force, and his feet left the ground as Tao threw him over his back.

Mid-throw, Tao also used a knee to kick one end of the falling staff, sending its other half smashing toward Jack's head.

Jack's thoughts accelerated. Though he'd been caught, he didn't give up. His other hand reached for his waist, grabbed the second flip-flop, then threw a vicious backhand blow at the staff, sending it spinning away.

His back met the ground hard, but in the process, he'd managed to pull his hand away. He grabbed the fallen flip-flop, too, and with two of them in hand, he spun from the ground and unleashed a barrage of crisp blows at Tao, who took them all with his thigh, dashing after his staff.

He grabbed it and turned to look at Jack, who now held two green flip-flops at the ready. One showed signs of tearing but was still whole.

"So, you can dual-wield," he said.

Jack smiled. "Looks like it."

The cheers of the audience reached his ears—they were deafening. How long had they been hollering like that? He didn't know. He was fighting. His Indomitable Will broke through the cheers like a fist of thought, clearing the way for him to concentrate fully on the battle.

Truthfully, everything was happening with extreme rapidness. If not for his new Dao Root allowing him unwavering concentration throughout the battle, Jack wouldn't be able to react accurately at this speed, and he might have had to use his true Dao.

As it was, though, he could manage. In fact, this battle was great training.

"Come!" Tao shouted, unleashing a loud cry. Jack obliged.

Bo watched the fight with bated breath, squeezed amongst others in the spectator stands. This was so cool!

Brother Tao was impressive in his own right, but this John Brown... He was a beast! The flip-flops flew faster than his eye could follow, bending from the wind resistance. They slapped the staff hard, somehow stopping its advance. Moreover, John Brown's entire body oozed an aura of hard violence that did not match his Dao. It sent shivers down Bo's spine. The flip-flops grew in his eyes until they were each the size of mountains, coming down with cataclysmic force. During all that, John Brown fought with a heated smile, like he loved what he was doing.

It made Bo's blood boil, and not just his. Everyone in the audience around him rose to their feet and cheered, unconsciously clenching their fists. Watching this fight released something inside him—his long-lost freedom, a striking image of how life should be. He felt like a boy again. It was awesome.

"GO, JOHN BROWN!" Bo shouted at the top of his lungs, one cheer among many.

Jack was deaf to the audience, too focused on the battle. He dashed forth with both flip-flops whistling through the air, unleashing a barrage of strikes far faster than before. Tao blocked everything. His defense was steady as a mountain and fluid as a river, and he could use one weapon to block two, but there was a limit to the mountain and the river.

Under Jack's barrage, Tao couldn't fight back. The most he could do was defend with all his might, but even that was a struggle. One flip-flop glanced his shoulder. Another met his chin. A third slapped his thigh.

Strikes seeped through. Slowly but surely, Tao's defense was crumbling like a faulty dam. After all, Jack's Fistfighting (III) skill made him an expert at martial arts, too, and his Pugilist Body skill made his body more malleable, more suited to fighting.

Tao knew he was losing. Between defending, he smiled. Jack saw it, knowing what that meant.

The staff reared back. All defense gave way, allowing one flip-flop to land clean against Tao's ribs, but the staff was now hurtling downward at extreme speed. This was a strike far slower than his previous attacks, but one surrounded by a deep red aura.

It had to have been a skill, and Jack had no time to escape. Moreover, he only had one flip-flop ready.

"Falling Mountain!" Tao shouted.

The world went black and white. All colors disappeared. A single flip-flop burst purple, drawing everyone's eyes like it was the only thing in existence. It flew upward, followed by a faint, starry purple tail. Everything went silent. Only Jack's voice was heard.

"Meteor Spank!"

The flip-flop met the staff, and all color and sound returned at once. The world exploded. The impact generated a shockwave so strong it shook the arena, burning a white flash that seared Tao's eyebrows clean off, making his head completely free of hair.

For a moment, the world went still, the two weapons locked in a heated clash surrounded by red and purple sparks. The staff gave way. It flew high, slamming into the energy wall that served as a ceiling before falling back down.

Tao let it hit the sand. He did not move.

Jack only had one flip-flop left—the other was a burned stump—and he pointed it at Tao's face with a bright, wide smile. Tao exhaled deeply, then opened his eyes and returned the smile.

"Congratulations, brother," he said. "That was very well-fought."

Jack's smile widened even further. "Same to you, Brother Tao. It was very close."

"Thank you for your kind words."

Jack lowered the flip-flop, then shook Tao's left hand—the right one lay broken at his side.

The audience erupted with cheers. They'd seen an amazing battle, and the two fighters had even reconciled at the end. What a sight! What a spectacle!

"You should get that looked at, Brother Tao," Jack said, motioning at the broken wrist.

"I will. You have my thanks."

"You too. I hope we meet again in the final phase."

"If fate wills it, we will."

Jack gave Tao a final smile before jumping to his seat, while the crowd still cheered at Tao's receding back.

"Great fight!" Edgar said.

"We did it!" Karvahul roared, red-faced from excitement. "We did it, my boy! We reached the goal!"

"The goal?" Jack asked.

"Oh, System dammit." Karvahul leaned closer, then did his best to whisper. "The two million. We just reached it!"

"*Really*?" Jack's eyes widened. "That fast?"

"That guy was strong. He had *a lot* of backers! Never mind the details, but the stronger your opponent, the more credits we get if you win. We earned four hundred thousand in this fight alone. We did it!"

"Yes!" Jack pumped a fist, unable to contain his excitement. That was one issue taken care of. Plus, there was only one round left in the Tournament.

Jack's qualification was guaranteed, and so were his credit goals for the auction. Moreover, he'd just gotten a second Dao Root, and his skills all felt on the cusp of evolving. He would need to be pushed to his limits to actually evolve them, but as the fights got tougher, it was bound to happen.

In other words, Jack was at an all-time high.

CHAPTER SIXTY-FIVE
THE PATH OF MAGIC

BROCK CROSSED THE NIGHT AGAIN. HE FLEW OVER ROOFTOPS, HUNG FROM ROPES like vines, and leaned on lighting poles to take a breather—their blue bodies were the perfect girth to grab, though the shiny yellow things on their tops were annoying.

Thankfully, he didn't need much rest. The Big Thought in his heart made him strong, and he could now reach the meeting spot easily, even with the big sack he carried. Besides, even that was a form of working out, and Brock wanted to be strong, so he'd decided to work out even while Big Bro slept.

Leaning against a lighting pole, Brock looked around. The surrounding streets were familiar. Moreover, he could see the big-bro-with-big-stick statue of the arena right before him. He was getting close.

Sometime later, he fell into a dark alley. The town's few sounds disappeared, cut off by the stone walls. The alley was strewn with empty boxes left over by the nearby shops, and it stank a bit of fish.

Brock waited.

The darkness moved. Rustling reached his ears as boxes were lifted and pushed aside. From under and behind them, five dogs appeared, looking at Brock with wide, expectant eyes.

Brock snorted. Dropping his big sack, he raised both arms and flexed them, turning his body to flex his legs as well, to the point where his red pants almost ripped. His new Big Thought was strong, and it made him stronger, too. His muscles shone like beacons of beauty.

He'd been looking forward to showing off, actually. Surely, his little dog bros would be impressed.

They were.

They stared at Brock, taking in his impeccable pecs. Then, one by one, they tried to flex too.

One jumped to its hind legs only to fall back down. Two others clenched their front legs, exhibiting the muscles under their chin. The big black one turned to the side and arced as it tensed its entire body, while the final dog barked—Brock assumed it was flexing its throat muscles.

Five dogs were trying to flex, each in their own way. Brock took them all in with a measured gaze. When they stopped and looked at him with hope, he simply gave a small nod, and five tails wagged.

Brock had honored his ancestors. Now, he had to honor his Big Bro, too. He approached each dog and grabbed their front right leg in a firm handshake, maintaining eye contact all the while. Soon, this ritual had been completed too, and Brock took a step back.

Satisfied, he grabbed the sack and started handing out presents to all the good bros.

These presents came in the form of food. Some were packs of cheese that the dogs ripped open. Others were ham or salami. A few more were fruit, as well as various pieces of meat that smelled odd but delicious.

Brock wasn't stingy. After all, Big Bro's nest was full with these things!

The dog bros ate while Brock watched over them. There was skin on their bones now, and after working out according to his instructions, they were finally developing some proper muscle. Soon, they would be bros worthy of attending a proper gym—even if Brock suspected the dumbbells here were fake.

But it wouldn't do for a big bro to stay idle.

"*Uu-aa-aa*!" he cried out, signifying that dinner was over. Though some food remained, they'd had enough.

All dogs obeyed, keeping their jaws shut despite the mouth-watering smells. It would help them try harder. Brock walked to an empty crate and raised it over his head three times, officially initiating their workout.

The dogs rushed to follow. Each found their own crate and, lacking arms with which to lift it, pushed it into the wall with their backs until it lifted off the ground. They then rubbed themselves against the wall with the crates on their backs, completing Brock's assigned exercise.

He nodded. This wasn't exactly what Father taught, but he lacked proper tools—he could have brought some gym instruments from Big Bro's nest, but those were Big Bro's, not Brock's.

Then, he fell to the ground and completed ten push-ups. His muscles glistened with sweat, roaring and growing as he pumped power from the Big Thought in his heart. The dogs followed suit, lowering and rising their bodies until Brock was satisfied. He nodded and petted them for good measure. All of them were very obedient.

Then, the next exercise...

Jack sat in the spectator stands, tossing his glowing token in the air and catching it. Today was the last day of fights, and the arena was packed.

"Who do you think I'll fight?" Edgar asked from the side. His leg was jumping nervously, and he clenched his crystal-topped staff to his chest. It was his shiny new Dao weapon.

"No idea, but it's fine," Jack replied. "You have no defeats. Even if you lose now, you'll still pass."

Edgar nodded. However, his leg kept jumping. His token glowed, too. "The anxiety is killing me," he said.

"Yeah. If my snacks weren't running out, I would have brought some."

"They wouldn't run out if you stopped devouring them."

"I'm not—"

The head judge's voice interrupted them, announcing the next fight. Since there were only a few participants remaining, each fight was now held over the entire arena. "Edgar Allano and the Dao of Magic versus Li Xiang and the Dao of Martial Arts."

"Hmm?" Jack's eyes narrowed. Beside him, Edgar jumped.

"Aah!" he cried out. "I'm fighting! Crap!"

"Dude, you're literally qualified already. Just go have fun."

"You're right." He took a deep breath. "Okay. I'm going now."

The crystal atop his staff shone as Edgar levitated into the field. He'd also gotten a blue cape somewhere, so he seemed every part the wizard he dreamed of being as a child. Edgar enjoyed the audience's cheers, feeling the familiar rush of blood to his head.

His shoes touched the sand.

Li Xiang already stood across from him. He was an old, Asian man of short and thin stature, yet his slightly narrowed, deep eyes spoke of a certain mastery that even Brother Tao, the monk Jack had fought before, couldn't match. He stood completely and utterly still.

"Magic," Li Xiang said pointedly, then nodded in approval. "You are not the first wizard I face, but you are the strongest. Come. Let us see if human ingenuity can trump the System's tricks."

"It's not tricks," Edgar replied, used to the weight of the arena by now. "It's magic."

His cloak fluttered. The sand flew. He waved his staff, and nature came to his aid.

The air swirled and formed birds of the gale. The sand gathered into waist-high hurricanes. Pure mana radiated out of Edgar's staff, coalescing into a formless cloud he used to fuel his magic.

Across from him, Li Xiang chuckled. He charged. Each of his steps was exactly three feet wide, and he moved with a grace that belied his age. His calloused hands, though they appeared lax, were ready to strike in any of a hundred different ways.

Edgar waved his staff again. It was four feet long and made of polished wood. Its entire body was carved with intricate red lines, and its head was a prism with twelve surfaces—a perfect dodecahedron that shone with all colors of the rainbow.

This wasn't a simple Dao weapon. Edgar had chosen not to save up for the auction and instead spend all his money on a high-grade magic staff. It was an investment that had already paid dividends, and a gift that kept on giving. It enhanced his visualization abilities, channeled his Dao nearly perfectly, and stored a large amount of mana to use in a pinch.

The gale birds, twelve in all, whistled as they rushed forth. They formed a swirling torrent, crossing each other's path to reach the old man. Some of the sand devils flanked them, while others followed close behind.

Li Xiang dove into the birds, moving his limbs and body at speeds that should have been impossible. His palms met the gales and pushed them away. His knees dove into sand devils and tore them apart. He dodged all attacks by the narrowest of margins, and every time he seemed cornered, he exploited the tiniest imperfections in Edgar's attack patterns to rush clean through.

Though the birds seemed unpredictable and chaotic to the untrained eye, they weren't.

The audience was shocked. They'd witnessed the power of Edgar's attacks in previous matches. Each bird could slice through a tree, and each sand devil could grind a rock into dust. Yet, Li Xiang faced them with his body alone like it was nothing.

Edgar wasn't discouraged. He still had plenty of spells to use.

Embers shone on his fingers. The air screamed as a rain of fireballs sliced through it, depriving it of all oxygen. The sand shifted under Li Xiang's feet, seeking to imbalance him. A blue glow surrounded his body as a transparent mana mantle formed out of thin air, closing around him and trying to compress his limbs.

Li Xiang laughed and took it all in stride. "Good!" he shouted.

His muscles strained as he tore the mantle apart. His palms met the fireballs, redirecting them into each other. His feet remained planted into the sand, merging perfectly with the ground's undulations to perform even stronger techniques. He'd adapted perfectly.

But Edgar *still* wasn't done.

His eyes shone blue, and his hair rose. The old man was closer now, letting Edgar use his strongest weapon with impunity: pure, raw magic. The core of his Dao Root.

A blue aura rose around Edgar, surrounding and enveloping him. The sand floated by itself. His shoulder-length hair turned directly upward, and only his brown eyes shone through the blue. He waved his staff a third time, and a stream of mana reached Li Xiang.

Even the greatest martial artist could do nothing against pure magic. He was blinded, but shook his head so hard he recovered.

Five Edgars surrounded him now, each wielding an intricate staff. Li Xiang's eyes flashed from side to side, taking in everything. The Edgars performed the same motion, sending three balls of highly condensed mana at Li Xiang.

He jumped. Three explosions came below him, but a swarm of gale birds was already falling on him from above. He rotated in midair, doing his best to defend. One tore through his robe and smashed into his shoulder, drawing a thin line of blood.

The audience gasped. It was the first time Li Xiang had ever been injured.

He fell back down, where fifteen more balls awaited. He observed their movements for a single second before diving into a group of them. When everything exploded, Li Xiang was unharmed—only three of the balls had been real.

He'd used echolocation to figure out who the real Edgar was from the explosions before, having memorized the positions and trajectories of all balls before jumping, and he'd inferred the launcher of each of the second wave of balls during the single moment when he watched their trajectories.

Li Xiang threw a punch at the real Edgar, but a blue shield appeared to block. It didn't matter. Li Xiang unleashed a chop and a kick, then an elbow and a knee. A river of martial blows flowed out of his body—several martial arts used interchangeably to maximum advantage.

Edgar had fallen into close combat with a martial artist, and that was never a good idea.

His shield held, but he couldn't tell where the next strike would come from, so he met them suboptimally. His mana dropped fast. He had to do something. Li Xiang turned into a maelstrom of violence, and the only things Edgar could make out through his swirling gray hair and body were his deeply smiling eyes.

The shield pounced, bending toward Li Xiang as if to wrap around him. This was nothing like the blue mantle from before. It was very much corporeal, but also very mana-consuming. If Li Xiang got caught, he would be a sitting duck for a couple of seconds. If not, Edgar would be out of steam. This strike was summoned from all the mana he stored in his staff.

The shield wrapped around Li Xiang, then burst apart under his overwhelming strength. He'd overpowered it with stats alone. A palm split the air and stopped an inch before Edgar's long nose; and he, shocked, took a step back, then froze.

The palm retreated, revealing Li Xiang's smiling face.

Edgar sighed. "I lost," he declared, and the crowd burst into an uproar again.

"You fought well," Li Xiang said in his sharp Asian accent. "Work on your fundamentals. Practice hard. And it will come."

"Thank you," Edgar replied, bowing lightly. Li Xiang nodded back and jumped away, retreating to his secluded spot in the arena stands, where he relaxed on his seat to watch the rest of the battles.

Edgar retreated, too, though he had to take the stairs—he was completely dry of mana. However, inwardly, he was very happy. Compared to when he arrived, he'd made tremendous strides. He used to be average at best. Now, he could put up a fight against one of the strongest contestants.

Before he could reach his seat, the announcer's voice rang again: "John Brown and the Dao of Spanking versus Shard Presht and the Dao of Momentum!"

Edgar almost missed the next step. He paled. Shard Presht was a scion.

CHAPTER SIXTY-SIX
THE MASK FALLS

JACK'S SHARP EYES STARED AT THE CURTAIN THAT SEPARATED SCIONS AND humans.

A light gray hand emerged, parting the curtain. Shard Presht stepped out. His skin was slick and slippery like a fish's. His mouth contained multiple rows of sharp teeth, and his back held a large fin. Gills adorned his thick throat, and thin webbing spread between his fingers.

He was the shark-man, the scion of the Sharken family of the Animal Kingdom. And the slits he had for eyes were staring directly at Jack. He licked his lips and clasped two long gloves around his forearms, each with a large, fin-shaped blade on its back.

Jack really considered resigning on the spot, just to make him having worn his blades in vain. He didn't need to fight. This was already the last day, and he hadn't lost once. He could just resign.

Plus, fighting a scion would absolutely force him to use his true Dao. Although he yearned to fight, he couldn't risk his people like that. He would resign.

On the one hand, he didn't need to do it immediately. All scions had made it to the finals, so Jack would eventually need to fight at least a few. He wanted to get a grip of their strength now, so he could prepare better. He wanted to see just how it felt to face a scion at their best.

However, before that...

Jack reached into the white bag he carried, ruffled around a bit, then removed a transparent ball glowing with multi-colored light. The people around him gasped.

He crushed it between his hands. The colors flew out, surrounding him before diving into his body. The notifications came instantly.

Level Up! You have reached Level 36.
Level Up! You have reached Level 37.
Level Up! You have reached Level 38.
Level Up! You have reached Level 39.
Level Up! You have reached Level 40.

5 levels. *Not bad.* Jack smirked. He'd almost forgotten the surge of power that accompanied level-ups. Now... Now, it was time to start climbing again.

5 levels also meant 10 stat points, and Jack quickly allocated them. He wouldn't ruin his nice, round numbers in Mental and Will, of course, so he poured them all into the Physical sub-stats. As he did, each point transformed into three subpoints he could allocate as he liked, which he spread evenly.

Jack took a second to glance over his status screen.

Name: Jack Rust
Species: Human, Earth-387
Faction: Bare Fist Brotherhood (F-Grade)
Grade: F
Class: Pugilist (Elite)
Level: 40

Strength: 105
Dexterity: 105
Constitution: 105
Mental: 10

Will: 10

Skills: Fistfighting (III), Drill (II), Pugilist Body (III), Parkour (II)
Dao Skills: Meteor Punch (I)
Daos: Dao Root of the Fist, Dao Root of Indomitable Will

Titles: Planetary Frontrunner (10)

It was beautiful.

The head judge had given him time to level up, but Jack didn't want to make everyone wait even longer.

He stepped on the railing and jumped into the arena, crossing the air and landing in a small cloud of dust. He stared the sharken down.

Sharken (Earth-387), Level 40
Faction: -
Title: Planetary Frontrunner (10)

When his Dao of Spanking proved inadequate, he would step down. Until then, he'd try to expose as many of his opponent's abilities as possible. After all, Shard Presht had yet to fight seriously.

The sharken smiled, revealing dozens and dozens of teeth in his long, narrow mouth. Then again, due to the shape of his mouth, he seemed to always be smiling. "John Brown," he said in a hissing voice. "You have amused me greatly. Is it time for you to finally be spanked back?"

"Dunno, man. Is it time for someone to toss you back into the sea?"

Some of the audience laughed. Jack was grateful—he'd made better trash talk.

"I am amphibious," the sharken replied, grinning like he'd said something ominous. Jack sighed in relief. He might not have been the best at trash-talking, but he was certainly the better of the two!

He didn't reply. Instead, he grabbed both flip-flops—he couldn't afford to go easy here.

Shard Presht readied himself. He crossed his forearms before his body, blades pointing outward. He ducked and leaned forward as if ready to sprint. Only his slit-eyes could be seen behind his blades, as well his bare belly—he only wore a pair of brown shorts.

Jack only had eyes for the blades themselves, which had wide, flat parts—like fins—but were razor-thin. They were undoubtedly Dao weapons, and sharp enough to cut him deeply.

He wondered if the weapons were fin-shaped to fit in with the whole shark theme this guy had going, or if the shape had some practical application. Then it occurred to him that if those things hit him, his only layer of defense would be his bare body.

Whoops.

The sharken charged. It wasn't a normal sprint. He didn't push off the ground and gradually accelerate. No, this guy used the Dao Root of Momentum to instantly reach full speed, creating a disorienting sight that threw Jack off-tempo just enough for the sharken to close the distance.

Jack cursed. *This is fucking unfair!*

Blades flashed. He barely dodged, letting one arm-blade sail over his head as the other came down from below. He slapped its flat side and pushed it off course, when he felt a strong impact on his shoulder.

He stumbled right as the other blade—the one he'd slapped away—altered its momentum in a flash, shooting at Jack again. The impact he'd felt was the previous blade doing the same thing. Defying physics to change direction sharply mid-strike without losing any speed.

Jack was in deep waters. He went all-out. He rotated, slapping the blade below him out of the air while letting the other strike his back at a different spot. Gritting his teeth through the pain, he dashed back, desperate to make some distance. Shard Presht let him, staring over with mockery.

Jack stopped halfway across the arena, panting and sweating. The sharken, who'd looked slightly ridiculous before, now loomed in his sight like death itself. Jack had tried not to underestimate his opponent, but the minute delay in going serious had almost cost him his life.

The audience erupted with incoherent shouts.

Jack met Shard's mocking gaze. His eyes narrowed to slits—just like the sharken's. Warm blood wet his back, and his shirt had a long tear running down its length. He'd endured the strike, thankfully. This sharken had a balanced Physical-oriented build, but he focused on speed, not strength.

Jack could have resigned—it was clear his fake Dao of Spanking could never beat this guy.

However, that mocking glint in his opponent's eye stopped him. He would resign, yes. But first, he wanted to share a true exchange with the guy. Not one where he was caught off guard. One where he used his poor flip-flops to their maximum.

Was it safe? Jack was convinced that, yes, Shard Presht couldn't injure him deeply in a short amount of time, even if he had somehow been holding back.

He wanted to feel what it was like to fight a scion at full strength. His blood was boiling, his skin was tingling, and the edges of his lips were dancing.

He clenched his flip-flops and charged. Besides not using his fists, he no longer held back. Shard Presht charged too, instantly accelerating. No, it wasn't instant—it was significantly faster than it should be, but there was still a build-up. That made sense. Otherwise, physics really would be broken.

As soon as the two came close, all color was sucked into Jack's flip-flop—his fist, actually, but they were indistinguishable. A purple meteor exploded hard into the flat part of an arm-blade, smashing it away, and a second meteor came right after, flying straight at Shard's chest.

The audience erupted into screams and cheers.

Shard fell sideways. His momentum shifted, pulling him out of the way as a meteor flew past, and then he shifted again into a spinning motion. A blade cut at Jack, who barely ducked in time. The blade stopped midair and fell at his head at high speed. Jack was ready, dodging again. His flip-flop met the sharken's arm from above, pushing it down even faster, burying the blade into the sand and stone below. The other blade met Jack's clenched shoulder, stopped in its tracks within a shallow cut.

For a short moment, Presht was stuck. Jack *spanked* him across the face.

The arena fell silent. The crisp slap echoed, over and over, as Jack's dirty flip-flop imprinted itself on the scion's noble face.

Then, the audience erupted again, showering the two with discordant cheers and open mockery. Presht's eyes narrowed further. His permanent smile was wiped off his face. Anger bubbled inside him so hard Jack could sense it, and he had no intention of staying to see what would happen. He'd made his point.

He jumped back, and to his horror, Presht followed him at exactly the same speed. Two blades slashed simultaneously, each aiming to bisect him. Jack had no room for errors.

He struck out with both flip-flops. One met a blade head-on and was cleanly cut in two. The top part of the flip-flop flew away as a deep gash was cut into Jack's ribs, easily penetrating his skin and only stopping when it reached the bone. He grunted.

The other flip-flop met a blade's flat part and threw it off-course. However, Presht turned his arm slightly, and the blade rotated with it. Its wide, flat side hit the air like a sail and came to an instant stop, letting it accelerate quickly again. Presht kept turning it midair, making it dance from side to side in unpredictability.

Jack dodged the sharp side, but the flat one smashed into his nose, sending him rolling into the sand. He jumped to his feet. His nose was broken, and the pain was great, though not something he couldn't handle. The deep gash on his ribs was worse, but thankfully, his regeneration could deal with that much.

The wound was gradually closing, and the blood was replenished.

Contrary to Jack's fears, Shard Presht didn't follow. He gave ample space, staring Jack down with mockery and taunting.

Jack wasn't an idiot. Though his face burned where his nose had been smashed, and though his pride and Dao cried out to fight, he was the master of himself. He opened his mouth.

"I resi—"

"Is Jack Rust a coward?" Presht spoke up, covering Jack's voice. Jack's attention was caught. That was his real name. The sharken's eyes held even more intense mockery.

Both fighters had come to a halt. The audience was only now realizing what Presht had said, and hushed whispers were already spreading like wildfire. Everyone knew who Jack Rust was. Now, they knew *who* he was, as well. Jack's secret identity had been exposed.

That was fine. It would never last through the finals, anyway. The time he'd earned had better be enough.

"What do you want?" Jack asked.

"A battle," Presht replied, staring with such intensity he seemed to see into Jack's soul. "For my cousin, I will destroy you."

Jack looked up. Gan Salin stood before the curtains, staring at the arena with an unreadable expression.

Jack cracked a grin. "I see how it is. The wild dog couldn't handle me himself, so he brought out his slightly bigger brother."

"Luck of the draw," the sharken replied. "Humans cannot defeat the scions."

"They already have. But fine. You just slapped and exposed me in public. Have it your way."

Jack had no reason not to fight anymore. His Dao and pride burst forth. Everyone saw his face squirm. People averted their eyes as John Brown disappeared, and Jack Rust regained his true face.

"You're ugly," Presht said.

"You're a fucking fish."

Jack let his flip-flop fall. He clenched his fists. The aura of a savage warrior erupted from his body, making the nearby sand hover by itself. His tattered shirt flew off, exposing his hard, bare chest. He cracked his knuckles. Everyone had goosebumps. Shard Presht smiled and crossed his blades.

The beast had awoken. Jack Rust was back. He laughed.

Then, he charged and smashed a Meteor Punch right into the sharken's face.

CHAPTER SIXTY-SEVEN
PUNCHING HARD

JACK'S NEXT MOVE SHOCKED THE ENTIRE ARENA.

This was completely different than when he used flip-flops. The shape of a true meteor appeared around his fist, and a purple starry tail followed it.

And it was fast. Too fast.

Shard Presht could barely raise his blades and block. The meteor smashed into him and sent him flying back at great speed. He used the Dao of Momentum to stop himself midair, but Jack had followed, and a towering fist smashed into his face in the next moment.

Shard Presht flew back again, and this time, he didn't stop until he crashed into the far wall.

Jack cracked his knuckles again while Presht stood. "Well? Is that all? I thought you were a tough fish."

"I'll show you what I am," Presht replied, simmering with anger. His face was slightly dented by Jack's fist.

"Be my guest."

The sharken adopted a sprinting position, then charged. Jack wouldn't make the same mistake twice. He adopted a battle stance long before his opponent was supposed to arrive, and it was a good thing, because Presht never stopped accelerating.

He reached his maximum speed and then kept going, accelerating at a tremendous rate. He reached Jack far sooner than anticipated, and at a speed that resembled an arrow's.

The audience was reeling. Jack punched out, and his knuckles met the blade head-on. Both fighters flew back.

Jack's body was beyond sturdy. He had 105 Constitution and the Pugilist Body skill, which augmented the hardness of his entire form, especially his knuckles. He also had the body-hardening technique brought forth by the third tier of Pugilist Body, the one he'd reached in his spar against Dorman, which allowed him to harden his knuckles even further.

All that still wasn't enough to completely block a sharp blade coming at high speed. A millimeter-deep gash was drawn on his knuckles, dripping with blood. It also limited the nimbleness of his fingers, but he didn't need those.

Blocking those blades was dangerous, but the real problem was that Shard Presht was fucking fast. If Jack couldn't block and had to dodge all the time, achieving victory would be ten times harder.

Worth a shot. Wasn't like he had a choice.

Shard Presht brought his bloodied blade in front of his face. He took a deep sniff of Jack's blood, then licked it. His smile returned and widened.

"Tasty," he said.

Some of the audience cheered, but most stayed quiet. The Ice Peak cheered especially intensely.

Jack snorted. "If you like my knuckles, shark, there's no need for blades. I will deliver them directly to your mouth. Just watch."

He jumped back into the fray. At the same time, his fighter's mind churned.

Against an opponent like Shard Presht, who could manipulate the momentum of his weapons at will, Jack should avoid extended clashes, as the Dao of Momentum would be too strong there. He needed rapid bursts of violence where he struck his hardest and hoped to outmaneuver Presht.

Presht took Jack's charge, blades held steady and ready to jump at any angle at full speed. Jack arrived, threw some quick jabs, then stepped back, narrowly avoiding a strike. Presht chased, and he was faster, but Jack could defend while retreating.

He dodged the blades or slapped them away. He struck out himself, forcing Presht to defend. Soon, their clashes turned into flashes of motion on the sand, where both fighters zoomed around the arena at great speed and met for only one or two exchanges before separating again.

Presht had the advantage in speed, though he couldn't afford to be careless. Nor did he need to. As Jack couldn't block, he was forced to fight awkwardly, and Presht held the upper hand—or fin—in the vast majority of exchanges.

Jack knew that. The problem was that he could do nothing about it. None of his skills could help here. He wasn't lacking in penetrating power, fighting skill, or even attacking potential. What he lacked was hardness on his knuckles. It was at times like these that he wondered whether he should buy iron knuckles, but he discarded the notion like all times before.

His Dao was that of the Fist. And, though the word *bare* wasn't there, he sensed that even the most discreet of weapons would only draw him away from the core of his Dao, even if it gave him temporary strength.

Yes, Jack was losing and had no idea how to turn this around. But did that mean he would resign? Of course not! He'd just keep punching!

Flashes kept exploding throughout the arena. Blades whistled and fists crashed through the air. Occasionally, blood flew from any of the two fighters—mostly Jack.

He was fighting measuredly, seeking openings, some weakness he could exploit. His will was indomitable. He had full control over his mind, which the sharken probably lacked. Jack could last long. Maybe Presht would tire first. He could only hope.

At least he knew the sharken didn't have a second Dao—he'd bought information on the scions. Still, he was losing.

Jack's only hope now was the Dao Root of Indomitable Will. He leaned hard into it, limiting all unnecessary thoughts and optimizing himself. His mind remained razor-sharp for a long time. More clashes ensued, where Jack ceased trying to take down Presht, now dragging him into a battle of attrition he could hopefully win.

Jack fell deep into the Dao Root of Indomitable Will.

He refused to bend; refused to retreat; refused to go down. His will could not be stopped.

Why, then, could his fists?

The thought struck him like thunder, disrupting him so abruptly he almost lost a hand. He retreated again; his mind was only half on the fight.

My will is indomitable. My body is the carrier of my will. Why do I have to let him break my fists? Why can't they *be indomitable as well?*

He clenched them again, and this time, something was different. As the Dao Root of the Fist was revving inside him like a steam engine, so did the Dao Root of Indomitable Will. Jack guided it into his fists.

The next time he clashed with Presht, he did not dodge. He did not run. He punched straight into the blade, refusing to lose. It wasn't only his will that was indomitable. His Dao was, too. And so were his fists.

Knuckle met blade and both flew back. Not a drop of blood appeared on Jack's hand. He grinned savagely. Presht's slit-eyes widened in surprise, revealing deep blue irises.

Got you, fucker.

Jack had a new weapon. His punches were imbued with both the Dao of the Fist and the Dao of Indomitable Will. He struck out again and again, and Presht could do little to stop him. He was like a storm of fists that only accelerated the more they fought.

"You're *combining* two Dao Roots!" Presht hissed as he retreated. "You're only F-Grade! This is impossible!"

Jack's grin widened. "Look better," he said, then smashed his *impossible* fist into Presht's face, sending him reeling.

In the F-Grade, cultivators developed Dao Roots, but those Dao Roots weren't part of a whole. They were each a different weapon. It was only when a cultivator transformed one of their Dao Roots into a Dao Seed that fusion was achieved, allowing them to channel all their Dao Roots through the Seed.

Jack wasn't truly fusing his two Dao Roots. He was simply using them at the same time, and he could only achieve that because both were passive in nature and fit well. If he really could combine them, the strength increase from that would have been exponential.

Fortunately, it looked like concurrent use was enough here.

Jack chased after Shard Presht, not giving him time to rest. The sharken could attack, but he didn't dare. The price was high. Jack could just block, and as his strength was higher, he would win every exchange!

Presht stepped back, and Jack was there. One fist smashed at his abdomen and was blocked by a blade. Presht flew sideways from the impact, then channeled that into his blade, spinning at great speed to lop Jack's head off. Jack had seen that coming and leaned back, dodging at an impossible angle.

He then used both hands to directly grab Presht's blades, enduring the pain to push them both aside. For a moment, Presht was wide open. His slit-eyes widened again as they met Jack's predatory gaze.

"I re—" he started saying. Before he could finish his words, the world turned monochrome. Everything became black and white, and only a single purple meteor shone in Presht's vision, taking it over completely. He quit speaking and tried to dodge, but it was too late.

A full-force meteor smashed hard into his mouth. All color returned in one, massive explosion, a blinding flash, and an ear-rupturing bang. Dozens of sharp teeth flew away half-broken as Presht himself was catapulted backward with tremendous force, smashing into the wall.

He tried to stand. Therefore, the battle wasn't over, and Jack rushed in again. He didn't intend to kill a scion—that might have invited more trouble than he could bear—but he sure could roughen him up a bit.

"Enough!"

A massive aura crashed onto Jack from the sky. He screeched to a halt, then looked up to find the head judge flying over him.

"What is the meaning of this?" he asked. Though the aura was heavy, it was something he could handle. After all, this judge was only a merchant class, as was every alien here, with the exception of the C-Grade Planetary Overseer.

"Stop immediately," the judge said. "Your opponent has resigned."

"He has not!"

Jack felt the blood rush to his head. Shard Presht clearly hadn't resigned. And he knew this because he'd seen many people try to resign in the Tournament but get hit before they could finish their words.

True, this rule had never been officially stated. It was technically in the officiating judge's discretion. However, of the djinn judges who oversaw the fights when four were happening at the same time, there was only one who accepted clear resignation attempts—like Shard's—as resignation. All others only accepted the full utterance of "I resign," and even for this more merciful one, he only acted when the losing party just couldn't speak properly mid-battle.

After Shard Presht went flying just now, he could have resigned ten times over before the judge intervened if he still wanted to, but he'd clearly changed his mind and intended to keep fighting. That was why Jack attacked, only to be stopped midway.

Technically, the decision was proper. But for someone who watched the Tournament carefully, it was clear that the judge was partial.

Fucking cheaters. Jack was boiling. A purple glow flashed on his fists, coming and going like a wave. He itched to plant it into the judge's righteous-looking face. He held himself back.

He clenched his fist harder. *Will indomitable.* The purple color was extinguished. He closed his eyes and took a deep breath.

When he reopened them, Presht was staring with a bitter gaze, and the judge acted as if nothing was happening.

"John Brown wins," she declared. "However, for breaking the rules of the Tournament and attacking a resigned opponent, he receives one loss in his record."

Jack glared at her. They hadn't done this when Rufus Emberheart openly murdered that girl, and they didn't mind all the previous occasions when someone tried to resign but couldn't.

Fucking cheaters, he said inwardly.

"Hey!" a guy with strong lungs shouted from the audience. "This is unfair."

Several agreeing voices rose to meet his.

"It is my ruling, and it is final," the judge replied, cutting them off.

She clearly didn't give a shit about their opinions. "That was the final match for today. The sixteen finalists have been determined. All finalists please gather in the arena and await Her Nobility."

Jack hadn't heard anything about a closing ceremony for the first stage. Nobody had.

CHAPTER SIXTY-EIGHT
THE IMMORTALS DESCEND

Suddenly, there was confusion in the arena. Jack shot a last, angry glance at the head judge before looking around, finding everyone puzzled. Even the alien merchants in the stands were whispering, wondering what was going on.

His anger gave way to curiosity.

That's odd.

These merchants knew how things worked. Was something different this time?

"Gather on that side," the head judge said, pointing at one side of the arena, the one farthest away from the Overseer Tower. Jack complied. Shard Presht did, too, though he kept his distance from Jack.

Gradually, more finalists jumped down from the stands. Vivi was the first. She landed next to Jack and said, "I saw what happened. They suck."

"I know," he replied.

Edgar, Dorman Whistles, and even the Sage jumped down from the stands to land on the sand beside Jack. Another member of Flame River, the man named Sadaka who'd lost on the first day, joined them—he was level 49 now and had barely clinched his way through.

Up on the stands, another member of Flame River kept Brock company.

Alexander Petrovic—the leader of Ice Peak—landed close to Shard Presht, followed by a woman of his faction—Elena Richter.

Vanderdecken—the metal guy—landed between the two groups. Soon after, Li Xiang and Brother Tao landed beside him.

The crowd's confusion was mounting, but so was their excitement. All finalists were coming on stage. Whatever happened would be big, and doubly so since it apparently hadn't happened before.

The finalists themselves were confused too, as well as wary. Only Presht appeared calmer, though still shooting malicious glances at Jack, who only snorted. Both were still bleeding, but djinn healers at the peak of the E-Grade arrived and made them good as new, then departed again.

The curtain at the top of the stands parted. Rufus Emberheart walked out, followed by Gan Salin, and regally floated his way down to the sands, taking position in front of Shard Presht. The eagler and elef—the eagle-like man and the elephant-like woman—appeared a few seconds later and landed close to the Ice Peak and the other scions, though not too close. Even within the noble families of the Animal Kingdom, there were different groups.

Jack, Edgar, Vivi, Dorman, the Sage, and Sadaka.

Vanderdecken, Li Xiang, and Brother Tao.

The five scions, Alexander Petrovic, and Elena Richter.

Sixteen people. Sixteen finalists. And all stood on one half of the sandy arena. The crowd could barely contain their excitement. This was the absolute peak of Earth!

A rough breeze descended from the arena's roof. The sand swirled; their clothes fluttered. Jack felt the sand specks land on his bare skin like bitter kisses, while his bare feet could feel the hard, jagged rock under them. Presumably, there was hard metal below that—the hull of the Integration City starship.

"What's happening?" he whispered.

"No idea." Vivi shook her head.

"Karvahul didn't know either," Edgar said.

Everyone turned to look at the Sage, who turned his head the other way and observed the swirling sands.

Even the scions seemed confused, with only Rufus Emberheart's maned head staring ahead like everything was under control.

This was the first time Jack got close to him. He could feel the raw power emanating from his body, and the aura of a supreme Dao leaking from his skin. His paws were clasped behind his back, and he stood straight like a ramrod, not staring at anyone in particular, but nobody could deny the threat that oozed off him.

Even Jack was apprehensive, and his Dao Root trembled.

A heavy aura blanketed the arena, and the crowd quieted at once like all sound had been cut with a knife. Galicia Lonihor, the C-Grade Leonine, the Planetary Overseer, was in the air, hovering high above the center of the arena, over the level of the crowd, yet everyone could see her clearly.

Nobody saw her arriving. From one moment to the next, she was simply there.

"People of Earth-387 and Integration Tournament finalists," she addressed everyone in a voice loud enough to shake the arena all the way to its foundation. Despite that, she maintained a rushed, bored tone as if simply completing a chore. "The twentieth assembly of the Galactic Alliance has introduced a new element to Integration Tournaments to foster even stronger cultivators. You will have the honor of experiencing it first."

"Like beta testers," Dorman whispered, eliciting a chuckle from Jack and Edgar. They shut up immediately afterward as a sense of danger washed over them.

"In a moment, the astral projections of sixteen D-Grade immortals from around the constellation will appear before you. They have volunteered to be the mentors for this Tournament and sent over a part of their consciousness. Each mentor can select up to one disciple. If you are chosen, it will be a fate-changing point for both you and your planet... so act accordingly."

Without waiting for the crowd to digest her words, the lioness pulled out a token and crushed it. Nothing happened for a moment. Then, the space below her began to ripple. One by one, ethereal forms appeared in midair, transparent like ghosts but unable to hide the towering aura of their Dao.

The weakest humans present shivered. Some had to leave, unable to take the pressure, while a rare few fainted and had to be carried outside by their friends.

The merchants were all reeling, unable to believe their luck. Such a collection of D-Grade beings and the C-Grade lioness was something they would never get to experience otherwise! As for the finalists themselves, they could only stare.

Jack heard a voice in his head: *"Do you see now why the auction will be bountiful?"* He turned to the side. It was the Sage, who was smiling as if uncaring about the mentors. He'd somehow developed telepathy.

Soon, sixteen forms floated under the lioness. A few resembled humans. Some were animal-based humanoids, like the scions, while the five noble families had each sent one representative as well. There were also weird creatures that Jack couldn't quite understand, like a long worm and a moving blob of... jelly?

Is that a slime!

Each and every one of them practically shone with the power of the Dao. Jack felt invisible flames immolating him and the cold of the north seeping into his bones. He thought he saw a heaven-towering warrior and a massive cloud sitting right above the arena.

The experience was very disorienting, and he only got used to it after a few moments.

The sixteen forms remained where they appeared, not uttering a sound. Neither did the lioness.

They were inspecting the finalists. Jack felt naked as several all-powerful glances saw through to his very soul, and he held his breath. Here he was, bare-chested and barefoot in front of seventeen gods and the entire population of Earth.

"None," a person said, then winked away, disappearing into the air.

"None," came a second voice.

"None."

"None."

Four people disappeared just like that. Jack frowned slightly.

Getting a D-Grade mentor sounded great, and it would likely let him shoot for the stars, but it didn't look easy.

"*Him.*" It wasn't a voice, more like a thought that spread throughout the entire arena. The worm disappeared and reappeared beside Dorman. Its thought-voice sounded oddly feminine.

Dorman's face shone like the sun. "Thank you!" he exclaimed. The worm didn't respond—or, if it did, it only spoke mentally to Dorman.

"Him." "Him." "Her." "Him." "Him."

The five representatives of the noble families each raised a finger and pointed at the respective scion. What a coincidence.

The scions nodded with grateful looks on their faces, while everyone else became slightly awkward. The Animal Kingdom wasn't even pretending anymore.

The blob of jelly disappeared without a word. A bearded old lizardman wearing blue robes pointed at Edgar and smiled. "You," he said. Jack could swear he heard Edgar squealing in joy.

A slim, bare-chested person who looked like an ascetic, smiled and pointed at the Sage.

"I am most honored," the Sage replied, bowing deeply. For once, his voice was incredibly serious, and it didn't carry its usual aloof tint.

Only three mentors remained: a short, pudgy woman, a bear-man, and a bald, bearded, muscular man in orange monk attire.

On the other hand, there were plenty of mentor-less people: Jack, Vivi, Sadaka, Alexander Petrovic, Elena Richter, Vanderdecken, Li Xiang, and Brother Tao. Brother Tao, especially, looked at the mentor in monk attire with hope.

"Him," all mentors said at the same time, raising a finger. And they all pointed at Jack.

The silence that descended could have been cut with a blade. Then everyone erupted into whispers that weren't even hushed. The remaining finalists looked at Jack in disbelief. The lioness raised a brow. The three mentors glanced at each other, while every other mentor that hadn't disappeared looked on with mild amusement.

The Sage, for the first time ever, looked surprised. His ascetic mentor only nodded with a small smile.

And Jack was just lost.

"What?" he said. Why would all three of them choose him? Was this even supposed to happen?

"He carries a strong soul," the pudgy woman said.

The bear-man snorted. "He clearly belongs to my people."

"I ask my fellow cultivators to give me face," the monk said. Under his beard and hard eyes, his voice was steady. "This child has the Dao of my faction's ancestor. Honor *demands* I take him in."

"He doesn't even use the fire arts," the bear-man snorted.

"My faction focuses on raw power, too."

"This is not even your constellation," the pudgy woman retorted with a frown. "You are stealing from another's plate."

"This planet is near the border, and we have received a formal invitation," the monk replied evenly. "I want this boy as my disciple."

The bear-man and pudgy woman frowned. They clearly had more things to say, but in the end, publicly arguing over a disciple didn't fit their statures. There were a million other planets to choose from.

"Very well. The Ursus Mountain will do you this favor," the bear-man said, disappearing immediately after.

"So will the Belarian Outpost," the pudgy woman said, disappearing too. Even if there were more people below they fancied, they couldn't possibly go to their second choices now.

Of the three, only the monk remained, and he looked at Jack with a deep smile. For the first time, Jack dared to inspect him.

Human (Earth-44), Level ??? (D-Grade)
Faction: Exploding Sun (B-Grade)
Title: Fifth Ring Conqueror

"You are—" the monk started saying, but this time, it was the C-Grade lioness that cut him off.

"Wait. I was just informed that there was a mistake," she said, looking straight at the monk, then turning her heavy stare at Jack. He almost buckled. "This participant received a loss for attempting to harm another participant after they had surrendered. He received another loss for submitting false information to the Tournament officials. Therefore, with two losses, he is disqualified. Please depart the arena."

CHAPTER SIXTY-NINE
TOURNAMENT REWARDS

As she hovered high above the arena, carrying the might of a God, who would dare disobey?

Jack paled. "Wha—"

Several heavy auras fell on him. Dog robots—the guards—stared at him from every arena entrance. He might have been able to handle one of those, but not that many!

Plus, only an idiot would fight here.

However, his heart was on fire. His face was going red. This was so unfair! Yes, he'd lied, but he hadn't broken the rules to attack Shard Presht! He only had one loss! This was blatant cheating! Bias!

Yet, what choice did he have? He *had* lied to the officials, though he'd never expected it to be such a big deal. The fault was half his. And, most importantly, he was powerless.

At least he'd protected his people for many days. Hopefully, they would be better prepared to face any blowbacks.

Right as he stood there conflicted, ready to walk away in shame and helplessness, the monk above frowned. "Stay there for now," he said, then turned to the lioness. "Your Nobility, I have watched some battles of this Tournament, including the last one. The boy lied, but he did not cheat."

"Are you saying I am mistaken?" the lioness responded calmly. Her Dao flared, enveloping the entire arena in a blanket of supremacy.

"I wouldn't dare," the monk replied, bowing slightly. "Though I believe a person of your grand stature would never lower themselves to watch the first phase of an Integration Tournament. Perhaps your subordinates made a miscalculation?"

"My subordinates know the rules well enough. They do not miscalculate."

The lioness took a hard stance, cutting off all paths to retreat. She was dead set on eliminating Jack from the Tournament.

The monk stayed silent, deliberating his next words. However, another immortal, the ascetic mentor of the Sage, spoke first. "The boy should remain," he said in a quiet voice, yet everyone heard him.

This person was skinny as a stick. His ribs showed over a pair of dirty brown pants—he wore nothing else. He hovered cross-legged, and milky eyes could be seen under messy gray hair.

Jack shot him a grateful stare. The lioness turned to him. "Your Holiness," she said, addressing him respectfully despite being a higher grade. "The rules are clear. He committed two acts worthy of a penalty, and two losses lead to direct disqualification. If that is disharmonious, we can replace him with the last person to be disqualified before him."

"The Barren High speak wisely," Jack's mentor hurried to agree. "Let us keep the boy, Your Nobility. I can sense his frustration, as can you. He clearly feels this is an injustice. Why would he lie to himself?"

The ascetic did not respond, only nodded.

"I concur," the worm's thought-voice spread over the arena.

Jack looked at it in surprise. The mentors of the Sage and Dorman had helped him... Even if he ended up disqualified, he would remember that.

The C-Grade lioness clearly didn't want to give ground, but there was a limit to how many immortals she could publicly ignore—even if they were of lower rank. "Very well," she agreed. "The Animal Kingdom will grant the Exploding Sun this wish. The boy remains."

The monk's face tightened.

"As per the Star Pact," the lioness continued, addressing all mentors, "please visit the participant district, where you will remain for the duration of your stay."

The monk turned to Jack. "When you are done here, come to me," he instructed, then flew away so fast he practically disappeared. All other mentors said similar things and followed suit.

Everyone was left gaping, unable to process what just happened, and most confused of all was Jack.

What the hell was that? But hell, I remained!

"Congratulations to those of you who were chosen," the lioness continued. She completely ignored everyone's confusion, not giving them any time to process things, while also maintaining that arrogant tone as if she were reading a script to ants. "For the rest, do not despair. The road to immortality is fraught with opportunities for those who deserve them. I will now announce the rewards of this Tournament."

Rewards! Who cared about mentors? Everyone refocused at once.

"Every finalist will receive one hundred thousand credits, effective immediately. Additionally, every victory from now on will be rewarded with an additional hundred thousand instead of ten."

Most people's eyes widened. Even to Jack, who now possessed more than two million credits, this number was no joke.

"More rewards will be given to those who place in the top four," she continued. "Fourth and third place will receive a Trial Planet Token. Second place will receive a Trial Planet Token and an Immortality Serum. First place will receive a Trial Planet Token, an Immortality Serum, a Dao Soul, and a D-Grade automaton bodyguard. Additionally, the Tournament winner—"

For the first time, the crowd's clamor rose so high it interrupted her. The merchants on the stands were discussing so animatedly they'd forgotten to lower their tones. The collective noise was annoying even to Jack.

"Silence," the lioness commanded. Her godly aura, which had previously been suppressed, was released, enveloping everyone and making them unable to even breathe too loudly. From one moment to the next, the arena was so silent you could hear a pin drop.

The lioness continued like nothing had happened. "Finally, the Tournament winner will be granted entry into the Animal Kingdom and apprenticeship by a C-Grade immortal. The final phase of the Tournament will begin in three days at dawn. Good luck."

The crowd remained quiet, but the eyes of the merchants were about to pop out of their sockets. The lioness disappeared, and they erupted into an even more chaotic collection of voices.

"Are the rewards that good?" Jack asked, looking at the members of his alliance.

"They're unheard of!" Vivi hurried to respond. "I've looked at the rewards for previous Tournaments, and the Animal Kingdom has never invested so much in a newly-Integrated planet."

"Maybe it's because we're very strong?"

She gave him a straight look. "I'm more inclined to believe they ramped up the rewards because they're confident their scions will get them all. For example, Rufus Emberheart is almost guaranteed to get first place. They would have already given him all that, but now they can also cultivate a reputation as generous overseers."

Jack glanced at the lion-man. He was ramrod straight and surrounded by the other scions, gaze lost in thought. He didn't seem surprised by the rewards.

"But what are those things?" he asked.

"The Trial Planet Token is something that only the most elite of E-Grades can obtain. It allows entry into a hollow planet, where potential is given an extra set of wings," Vivi explained. Everyone gathered around her to listen, except for the Sage, who only nodded as if he already knew these things. Jack knew this too—he already had a token—but pretended not to.

"The Immortality Serum is a very coveted elixir which is said to unlock the potential of all those below the D-Grade. It is essentially a breakthrough in a bottle. It can increase your attributes and your resonance with the Dao. It's priceless!"

"Sounds nice," Jack said.

"As for the Dao Soul, it greatly amplifies a person's connection to the Dao. According to rumors, it can double the speed of one's cultivation... of course, those are only rumors. These things are so rare, only the most promising youths of the galaxy get them, and they keep their mouth shut.

"Finally, the D-Grade robot is priceless, too. The galaxy is a dangerous place, and such a strong bodyguard basically guarantees you can adventure in relative safety. Plus, D-Grade automatons are extremely expensive to manufacture. We're talking about dozens of millions of credits."

"Dozens of millions!" Dorman raised his voice. "That's a lot!"

"Yeah, and that's just the material cost." Vivi shook her head. "Anyway, it seems that Rufus Emberheart is a very promising scion of the Animal Kingdom. No wonder he's so strong."

Everyone nodded. Even Jack had to acknowledge that Rufus Emberheart was the absolute favorite. After all, his every battle so far had ended in a single, effortless strike.

"Immortality Serums are not that rare," the Sage said, drawing everyone's glances, but only smiling and not elaborating further. He often said stuff like this.

From the stands, Karvahul was waving at them to head over, but Jack ignored him. "I think I'll go see my mentor," he said. "Karvahul can wait."

"Of course." Vivi grinned. "Mr. Golden Boy needs to get his benefits."

Jack felt a bit bashful. After all, everyone hoped for a mentor, and he'd hogged three of them.

"I—"

"It's okay, Jack. I was just kidding. But you still need to make up for giving us a fake name, okay? Treat us to something later."

He smiled. "Will do. Anyone else heading home?"

Edgar, Dorman, and the Sage nodded instantly. All of them had a D-Grade mentor now, and they looked forward to talking with them—except for the Sage, maybe, who remained as unreadable as ever.

"I'll speak with Karvahul," Vivi said. "Just go."

"Thanks, Vivi."

The four of them headed away. However, right after they approached the arena's exit, so did all five of the scions. Jack came to a pause. Each of those people was a planet-class powerhouse, and seeing all five of them together was quite a sight.

He looked to Gan Salin. "Sup, dog."

He was already an enemy of the scions. So what if he offended them even more?

Gan Salin bared his fangs. Beside him, Shard Presht did the same. Rufus Emberheart, who walked in front of them, completely ignored Jack—however, the latter happened to stand between the scions and the arena exit. If he didn't step away, they would have to step around him, and Rufus clearly wasn't willing to do that. He stopped, chest pointed directly at the exit through Jack.

"You are blocking the way," he said matter-of-factly.

"I am not. It's a big arena. Walk around me."

"You stopped in front of me."

"I needed to tie my shoelaces," Jack replied, all too aware that he was barefoot.

CHAPTER SEVENTY

TRAINING WITH A GHOST

Rufus raised his eyes to meet Jack's. He felt the pressure. This lion-man was strong, way too strong. His Dao Root even felt on the cusp of something greater, as if ready to reach the next level. Moreover, the aura of supremacy that surrounded him was palpable, and it made Jack feel like a child standing up to his father.

His soul punched through the illusion. Rufus raised a brow. The pressure mounted.

"Those are handsome rewards," Jack said. "The Animal Kingdom believes in you a lot."

"A coincidence. I will be the winner regardless of the rewards."

"Come on, Rufus. Nobody's listening. Tell me the truth. We both know those rewards are meant for you."

The eagler and elef looked over. Gan Salin and Shard Presht stared. Even the people on the stands began to notice there was tension mounting.

Rufus was still expressionless, as if Jack's witty tongue were but a chore to him.

"You should watch your baseless slander," he said evenly. "I remember your attachment to integrity. How amusing that the one who complained about cheating got disqualified for cheating *twice*, then cheated his way into the finals anyway."

Jack smiled. "Not everyone who breaks the rules is cheating, and not everyone who cheats gets caught." He stepped aside. "I look forward to meeting you in the finals."

"You really shouldn't."

Rufus walked by. Jack found himself holding his breath. Unconsciously, his fists tightened. Then, Rufus was past, and Gan Salin with Shard Presht followed a moment later. The other two scions lagged behind.

"You have a talent for antagonizing people," the Sage said with amusement. "It's as though you wish to be bullied."

Jack shrugged. "Both his followers had a grudge against me already. Rufus would strike out even if I said nothing. This way, I can at least embrace my Dao. Mental Fistfighting is also a form of cultivation."

"Of course."

"Can we go?" Dorman asked. "I want to see my mentor."

"Always in a hurry, aren't you?" Edgar laughed.

The four of them walked out of the arena, then crossed the now-bustling Integration City. People discussed spiritedly in every corner, and Jack caught several glancing their way. They were celebrities, now.

They exchanged merry banter all the way. Brock found Jack outside the arena, and Jack bought him five meat skewers to celebrate his qualification. Brock's appetite grew by the day, as did his muscles. He already looked as buff as a gymonkey.

Eventually, they reached the participant district and split up to head to their respective houses.

The ghost monk stood outside Jack's gate, arms crossed, his gaze thunderous. His skin was bronze, his face stern and marred by slight wrinkles, while a dark, triangular beard stretched from his cheeks to the base of his throat. He was also bald, though his status as a projection made him immune to reflecting the sunrays.

He waited for Jack to greet him first.

"Good afternoon, mentor," he said cautiously. This was a projection of a D-Grade being. Who knew what the proper etiquette was?

"Hello, my new disciple," the monk replied. Though he looked harsh, his voice was friendly, and a small smile was on his lips. His narrowed eyes seemed to take in everything about Jack with mild disapproval. "It is time for proper introductions. My name is Shol Pesna, an immortal of the Exploding Sun faction."

"It is my honor. I'm Jack Rust, the leader of the Bare Fist Brotherhood. This is Brock," he pointed at the brorilla, "my little bro."

Brock stared at the ghost. Shol's eyes narrowed. "Do you refer to each other as "bro" in your faction?"

"No, but that's actually a good idea."

Shol chuckled. "Very well. Come. We only have three days until the final rounds begin, so there is no time to waste."

"Yes, mentor."

"And call me master."

Jack resisted the urge to raise a brow. "How about *teacher*?"

"I am an immortal, boy. Do not talk back to me. You will call me master. When you reach the D-Grade yourself, then you can call me whatever you want."

Jack rolled his eyes. Then again, who was he to retort against a D-Grade demigod? "Fine. This way, master."

He passed his identification token over the gate, then the front door, unlocking both. The sound of his door sliding open rang loudly in the lonely participant district, which only had sixteen occupied houses out of a thousand now.

"To the training facilities," Master Shol instructed, and Jack complied. He was expectant about receiving an immortal's—whatever that meant—training, but also slightly apprehensive. This person didn't have the air of a god like the lioness. It was more like a next-door ghost.

"I can see the doubt in your eye, boy," Master Shol said.

"But I was looking at the front."

"You should know that mortals outnumber immortals one hundred thousand to one. In other words, there are roughly 99,999 other newbie cultivators that do not have the opportunity to receive my teachings. Appreciate what you get."

"Yes, Master Shol. Immortals are D-Grade cultivators, right?"

The ghost gave him a look, then nodded slowly. "D-Grade and above. When we form our Dao Tree, not only do we gain abilities like flight or absorbing the natural energies to strengthen ourselves, our lifespan also increases greatly. Hence, we are called immortals."

Jack glanced back with surprise. "How greatly?"

"By a factor of ten. But focus on yourself, boy. You have a long way to go till then."

Jack turned back ahead. He flicked the light switch just beyond the door to his training room.

"This place is fine," Master Shol said. "You should have a training robot too."

"I do. It's in the next room."

"Excellent. That will make things a lot easier."

He walked to the center of the room and turned to look at Jack. He crossed his arms. "Narrate your status screen to me."

"Narrate it?"

"I need to know what we're working with. Don't worry, you have nothing I would covet, and even if I did, I cannot harm you in this form. I am incorporeal, and my Dao is only a hollow illusion."

Jack hesitated, then opened his status screen, reading off everything it listed. Shol waited patiently, nodding in approval occasionally and frowning at times.

"You said your Mental and Will are both at ten?" he asked. "Why is that?"

"I thought it was a nice, round number."

"Nice, round numbers won't save your life. *Efficient* numbers will, and yours are too low."

Master Shol considered it for a moment, then added, "I suppose I shouldn't fault you. Playing to your strengths is the best way to survive the Integration. However, now that you're out of danger, at least temporarily, I advise you to split your attribute points in an 8-1-1 distribution: eight out of ten go to your main attribute, and one tenth goes to either of the other two. That's what most people do around the galaxy."

"I see. So my Mental and Will are actually decent."

"Yes, but the attitude that got them there was not."

Again, Jack found himself without retort. *Nice, round numbers* wasn't easy to argue for.

"That said, the equal distribution between your three Physical sub-stats is fine. Given your fighting style, all three are equally important, so you might as well keep them like that."

"I see," Jack replied.

"You haven't used a Dao Fruit yet, right?"

A person could only use one Dao Fruit in each Grade. That was part of the reason why Jack hadn't used his despite the price being so low—and also the reason *why* the price was so low.

"No, sir."

"Good. Save it for your breakthrough. Is there anything else I should know?"

Jack considered it, and decided to trust this person.

"I also have this," he said, reaching into his pants and retrieving a golden coin. The professor had someone sew him a hidden pocket behind his left thigh.

"A Trial Planet Token!" Master Shol's eyes shone. "That's excellent! You are going to need that."

"Thank you, Master... but what exactly is Trial Planet?"

Master Shol smirked. "Oh, to be newly-Integrated... The Trial Planet, otherwise called the Hollow Planet, is one of the most important and mysterious places in the galaxy. It is packed with Elite monsters, even King ones! The brightest E-Grade disciples of all B-Grade factions meet there, and they combine their forces to push as deep into the planet as they can. There is great danger, but also unbelievable opportunities. In fact, the fortunes of Trial Planet are so extraordinary that a cultivator's future achievements can be accurately predicted by how many rings of the planet they conquer."

"What? Rings?"

"Yes. Like my title, Fifth Ring Conqueror. But let's not focus there. You still have a long way to go."

Jack wanted to ask more things, but he nodded reluctantly. He secured the golden coin back inside his hidden pocket.

Master Shol continued. "Now, your Dao Roots are fine. The fist is a strong weapon if you wield it well, and Indomitable Will is a great supportive Dao—just don't accidentally make it your Dao Seed. In fact, you don't need more Dao Roots for now, save them for the E-Grade."

To advance from the F to the E-Grade, one had to understand one of their Dao Roots deeply enough to transform it into a Dao Seed, then connect it to all the other Dao Roots. When meditating freely, it wasn't unheard of to accidentally turn the wrong Dao Root into a Dao Seed—after all, insight was quite a random thing.

"What you really need to work on," Master Shol said, "is your Dao skills. You only have one! Where do you think you are, a backwater village's elementary school?"

"Most people in the Tournament don't even have one."

"Don't hold yourself to their standards." Shol shook his head. "You are gifted and carry tremendous momentum. You should aim to be leagues ahead of your peers—otherwise, your momentum will quickly run dry, and you will stagnate. Listen. Dao skills are crucial both to battle and to cultivation."

"I see."

"By the time you reach the D-Grade and crystallize your path, you should have at least four: one for attack, one for defense, one for the mind and soul, and one for movement. And they should be as close to your path as possible. Do you understand?"

"By my path, you mean the Dao of the Fist, right, master? Path and Dao are the same thing?"

"The fist is the core of your path, but one Dao by itself is nothing. Your path is the fist and all your complementary Dao Roots together. That is your true Dao."

"I see, Master," Jack said, this time more wholeheartedly. He felt like a lost man finally finding his way. Having a teacher was great!

Master Shol nodded in approval. "Of course, you don't have to get the four Dao skills I mentioned. Every person forges their own combinations. There aren't many Tournament finalists here using mind or soul attacks—which is natural, as your planet just got Integrated—so you can leave those aside for now. What other aspect do you feel you are lacking in?"

It definitely wasn't attack—Meteor Punch had yet to meet its match. When it came to defense, he was adequate. His new application of the Dao Root of Indomitable Will, along with his skills, could resist Shard Presht's blades head-on.

He was fairly well-rounded, though if he lacked anything, it was movement. Parkour was nice, but not too useful in open combat.

"Speed, I guess," he finally replied.

Shol nodded. "Correct. However, unlike what you might imagine, the best option for you isn't speed itself, or even a movement skill. It's a fighting style."

"A fighting style, Master?"

"Exactly. So far, you have been using the Fistfighting skill as your base. However, as your Dao advances, a normal skill will soon meet its limit. It is time to dive deep into it, understand it, conquer it, and make it truly yours. Then, it will be your true fighting style—a Dao skill that will follow you for millennia!"

Jack's eyes lit up. He set his jaw. "I understand."

"We will also incorporate some of your other skills into it," Shol continued. "Parkour can be one—I don't know what it is, but it doesn't matter—any movement skill will do if you're proficient. Drill should be included, too. It is not a flashy skill, but it is essential to your path of the fist.

"Therefore, we should set that as our target: to develop you a *proper* Dao fighting style," Master Shol declared. "Before that, we should bring Parkour and Drill up to a standard. You should reach the third tier in both. That is the hallmark of proficiency."

"I understand."

"I will craft you a proper training routine—I know Drill, and I can craft some exercises for this Parkour skill, too. I believe I grasp its general concept. Can you narrate its description to be sure?"

Jack complied.

Parkour (II): A mix of finesse and bodily strength can allow you to navigate obstacles efficiently, have better control of your body, and move unpredictably. By seamlessly integrating the environment into your moves, the battlefield itself becomes your weapon.

"I believe I've got it. Let's start by—"

"Um, Master," Jack interrupted. "Can I ask some things first?"

Master Shol exhaled, drawn out of his rhythm. "Yes."

"Brock here is my little bro. He is quite talented himself. Already a child and he developed a Dao Root. Would it be possible to train him as well?"

Jack held Brock from his armpits and raised him high, presenting him to the ghost. He hoped he wasn't crossing any limits, but he'd promised Harambe to make Brock a strong brorilla.

Brock himself didn't expect this, but he didn't dare react harshly. He understood this ghost was the Big Bro of his Big Bro. That made him... a Very Big Bro.

"Your monkey?" Master Shol asked with slight derision. "My time is precious, disciple."

"Please, Master. Brock is an important friend of mine."

Master Shol didn't reply right away, he almost seemed to study the dangling monkey. "I will give him a few pointers, but I will not train your monkey. You will have to train him yourself. The only reason I am even training *you* is because you share a Dao with one of my ancestors."

"I understand, Master. This is already kind of you," Jack replied earnestly. Though his Dao made him a headstrong person, he wasn't an idiot. A D-Grade cultivator taking time to train him one-on-one was already beyond what he could reasonably expect.

He placed Brock on the floor, who then turned and extended a hand at the ghost with a serious face. Master Shol smirked and said, "I am a projection, little Brock. I cannot touch your hand."

Brock was upset at this, but he settled for a deep, manly nod. Master Shol turned to Jack.

"Your next question?" he asked.

"Only one more, Master... You mentioned I share a Dao with your ancestor. Could you tell me more about that person? Was he a bald man dressed in yellow?"

He'd had this suspicion from the moment he read the name of Master Shol's faction: Exploding Sun. It wasn't the first time he saw that name. The bald man in his Dao Vision was of the same faction.

Master Shol's eyes widened. "You have had a Dao Vision of my ancestor?" he asked in disbelief.

"Yes, Master."

The ghost's face went from disbelief to joy, practically lighting up.

"That is wonderful! I knew I was right to insist on you. We are bound by fate, boy. I must definitely bring you back to the faction!"

"Bring me back?" Jack suddenly had a bad feeling. "I have my own faction here on Earth, Master..."

"Of course, of course, do not worry. I won't force you into anything. However, in the galaxy, seeing a Dao Vision of someone makes you half their disciple. The Exploding Sun would love to assist you on behalf of our ancestor! Again, I will not force you into anything. When the time comes, you can choose for yourself."

Master Shol's smile relaxed. "Now, is there anything else?"

"No, Master."

"Very well. Then, let's begin training, there is no time to waste. We will start with Drill."

He paced to one end of the room and, after some silent calculations, pointed at the floor. "Get some dumbbells and form a line here. Then, place a practice target on the wall. I want you to stand behind the line and try to punch the target. You cannot reach it physically, so you'll have to use Drill to send your fist through the air."

CHAPTER SEVENTY-ONE

THE SYSTEM WORLD

JACK STOOD BEHIND THE LINE AND GLARED AT THE PRACTICE TARGET. ITS WHITE and red wood stared at him mockingly, just out of reach.

"You can start," Master Shol said.

Jack fell into a stance, took a deep breath, and punched out. His outstretched hand met the air. The wind of his punch met the target, shaking it but not breaking it.

"Good," the ghost said. "Now keep doing that until it works."

Jack looked back with half-doubt. He wasn't sure how to do that, but he could try. His punches shot out, sending gust after gust at the target. It shook in the wind but held steady.

"You are too focused on your fist," Master Shol said. "Look at the target, not your hand. Imagine that your fist is a projectile."

Jack obliged. He struck out, picturing his fist as a missile. He remembered the bald man's strike in the vision—it'd traveled through the air for a large distance and still drilled straight through the massive, skyscraper-like beast. He tried to imitate that feeling.

His punch shot out a tad straighter. Its force dissipated the moment he finished swinging, sending errant wind gusts around.

"You are targeting the air. Your punch must only cross through it, not explode on it. The air is a delicate friend. The target is the enemy."

Jack's fist straightened. He didn't whip it to its final location, but shot it out more purposely and slightly slower, letting it ride its own wind. This time, when his arm could stretch no longer, he didn't feel the recoil. A shimmer in the air was the only indication his punch was still there. Then, the target shook violently and cracked down the middle.

"Much better." Master Shol nodded. "That is the way. You have been content with using the Drill skill to penetrate only a superficial layer of armor, so it didn't matter if your energy dissipated. However, if you want to become truly proficient, you must send the fist deeper, like a straight bullet that explodes only when and where you want it. At the later stages, this skill will allow you to send strikes through the vacuum of space, or from the earth to the sky. You will be able to punch clouds from the ground."

Jack's eyes widened. "Really?"

"Yes. But to do that, you must first learn to punch a target from a foot away. Again."

Jack refocused. He had the feeling, now all he had to was practice, keep practicing, and master it to such a degree that it would come by itself in the heat of battle. The target became his whole world. His bare upper body glistened with sweat as he punched over and over, letting the hours pass uninhibited.

He was making progress. The skill was there, and the System was helping him. He only had to learn to harness that power. Jack entered a trance where he kept punching, retrieving his hand, then punching again. The wind gusts became his breath. Every jolt of the target sent a ray of joy through his brain. Every crack was his pride.

His Dao Root of Indomitable Will sank him deeper.

He kept punching. One fist turned into a hundred, which turned into a thousand. Every time the target cracked, it would repair itself as if mocking Jack's efforts.

Until one moment, when everything clicked. It came without warning. Jack punched like every other time, but something was different. His arm was straight. His entire being was aligned. The air parted in the wake of his fist's shockwave, carrying it forward. It smashed into the wooden target so hard it broke into three, then the shockwave erupted, sending wooden shrapnel around the room.

Jack exhaled deeply, blinking rapidly as he returned to reality. A piece of sharp wood had shot at his chest and then fallen to the floor, unable to penetrate.

"I did it!" he shouted, pumping a fist.

"Good job," Master Shol's disgruntled voice came from somewhere behind him. Turning to look, Jack found him overseeing Brock's workout. They seemed to be in some sort of disagreement as Brock insisted on Master Shol spotting him to lift some weights over his chest. Master Shol repeated that he was incorporeal.

Taking the opportunity, he left Brock alone and headed over to Jack, who looked into the void puzzledly.

"I didn't get an upgrade?" he asked.

"Of course not. It's not that easy. Now that you can hit the target from a foot away, repeat until you can do it reliably, then move to two feet, then three. When you can consistently send your fist three feet through the air, we will move on to the next part."

"Oh."

Master Shol smiled. "The road to mastery is long and difficult, Jack. While it seems like an ordeal now, one day you will look back, and all these little steps will form a beautiful path in hindsight."

Jack raised his gaze. "I understand, Master. I'm not afraid to work hard."

"Of course not. You are an indomitable fist. If even you slacked off, everyone would." He snickered. "Good job. Rest for a bit. Then, we'll move to Parkour training. I have finished devising it."

Jack hadn't noticed before, but at the mention of *rest* he became highly aware of how tired he was. He plopped down on the floor. Brock left his weights and came over, giving Jack a big thumbs-up. "Work hard, Brock," Jack said. "There are so many things we don't know yet... and if we want to explore the world and protect our pack, we'll need to be strong."

Brock's determination redoubled on his face and he took off to lift more weights.

"But rest is important too!" Jack hurriedly added, but it was too late. He'd already set the young ape's heart on fire. At this point, he could only chuckle.

As Jack rested, Master Shol remained by his side, each thinking about their own thing.

"Can I ask you something, Master?" Jack asked.

"Go ahead."

"When I scanned you before, I saw that your faction was B-Grade, but I thought the Animal Kingdom was the only B-Grade faction in this constellation."

Under his thick beard and hard eyes, Master Shol's lips played a small smile. "That is true. My Exploding Sun rules the nearby constellation. However, this planet is very close to the border, and the Galactic Alliance instructed that mentors should be invited also based on proximity. That is why I am here, though the Animal Kingdom would love to kick me out."

"Why would they?"

"Because our factions are enemies."

Jack raised both brows. "Really?"

"Of course. We contest for the astral space between us and various resources. Me poaching disciples from them is the last thing they want. That is partially why they tried to disqualify you when they saw that I chose you."

"Oh. Good thing you stopped them, then. But, wait, why did those other immortals back you up instead of the lion bitch? Are they from your constellation, too?"

Master Shol failed to hold back a grin at Jack having called the C-Grade Planetary Overseer a *lion bitch*. "No, though they'd love to be. The Animal Kingdom is not beloved by their subordinate forces. Their powers are based on lineage, which means they don't take outside disciples, which in turn means they oppress the factions below them freely. They are tyrants."

"Oh..." Jack thought back to how the scions acted, then how quick the judges were to favor them. *Makes sense.*

"Why don't they revolt, then?" he asked.

"Because the Animal Kingdom is far stronger than all of them put together."

"You could help them. You're enemies of the Animal Kingdom, right? If you waltzed in with the full force of your constellation and half of this constellation joined you, I doubt the Animal Kingdom could resist."

"That is correct." Master Shol's face was now colored with amusement. "Unfortunately, these things are not so simple. The Star Pact forbids treason. If we attacked, the entire constellation would have to fight against us."

Jack scrunched his brows. "The Star Pact again. That name keeps coming up..."

"Naturally. It is the only true law in the galaxy."

"Well, what does it say?"

"Too many things to mention now. Just take it as a set of laws that let B-Grade factions coexist peacefully, as well as ensure that newly-Integrated planets can grow into their power. The one galactic year grace period and the Integration Tournament, for example, are enforced by the Star Pact."

"Hmm..." Jack's current knowledge had many gaps, and Master Shol seemed capable and willing to fill them in. "Ensure that newly-Integrated people can grow into their power... Doesn't the Hand of God do something similar? With the auction?"

"They don't do something similar. It is the exact same thing. The Hand of God is an elite force sponsored by all B-Grade factions and dedicated to cultivating the galaxy's first A-Grade. They are also the enforcers of the Star Pact."

"Really? I thought they were just high-end merchants."

"They are a bit of everything, from merchants to peacekeepers. Unfortunately, they have had their hands full with suppressing the Black Hole Church recently, leading to many monster outbreaks, planet poachings, and pirate invasions around the galaxy."

Hearing that, Jack's eyes shone. He was practically brimming with questions.

"And what about this Black Hole Church?" was the one he chose to ask. He'd heard about them before. *Who was it that mentioned them? The Sage? Or Karvahul?*

"Do you never run out of questions?" Master Shol threw Jack a side glance. "You jump from subject to subject like a rabbit. Are you not dizzy?"

Jack took his words in stride and laughed. Brock, on the other hand, came to his assistance instantly, angrily waving a fist at Master Shol and preparing to launch a poop. Jack stopped him.

"Show respect, Brock," he said before turning to Master Shol. "I'm sorry, Master. I'll stop now."

He'd already gotten a ton of new information, anyway. This Master Shol really was a treasure trove—if a bit uppity.

Master Shol, however, was of a different mind. "No, boy. It is fine. I approve of your thirst for knowledge, just care not to overwhelm yourself. The higher the volume, the greater the loss."

Jack nodded thoughtfully.

Master Shol rubbed his beard. "The Black Hole Church is... complicated. They're also an elite force like the Hand of God, but they operate outside the established frame. Nobody knows who leads them or what their goals are. By decree of the Galactic Alliance, they're terrorists."

"And also a cult, I assume."

"In a way. What do you know about the Old Ones, Jack?"

"What? You mean like Cthulhu?"

"I have no idea what that is. I am talking about the Old Ones. The Gods of the universe."

"Oh..." Jack hesitated. "Well... nothing, I guess?"

Master Shol sighed tiredly. "Then work as we speak. You have already rested enough. Grab the instruments I show and spread them around the other room."

Jack grabbed a bench press that Master Shol indicated and somehow managed to fit it through the door to the training room. Sparman watched with silent amusement. "Help me," Jack told him, and the robot got to work.

"The Old Ones are legends," Master Shol spoke as he directed Jack and Sparman around. Brock wanted to help, so he carried some dumbbells one by one. "It is unknown whether they actually exist or not. If they do, they have never appeared in our galaxy."

"This one can't fit through the door," Jack said, then dropped the instrument and went to grab another.

"According to our current knowledge, the System came from a distant part of the universe," Master Shol continued, his voice taking a slow, reverent tint. "We can glimpse some things through the text of System notifications and the Dao Visions. There are almost certainly other galaxies, though it's unknown why they don't contact us. As legend has it, the System was created by a race called immortals for the purpose of fighting the Old Ones, who sought to dominate all existence with their godly powers.

"There was a war, once. A crusade—though we only have fragmented knowledge about it. The immortals and all the System races against the Old Ones."

Jack was still carrying instruments to the other room, but his attention was fully on Master Shol's words—so much that he almost tripped, then whispered a curse.

"We do not know who won," Master Shol continued, shaking his head. "In fact, we know almost nothing about those things. However, the ones who claim to know are the Black Hole Church. They worship Enas, an Old One presumably trapped in a black hole in the center of a far-off galaxy by its own kind. It is unknown why they worship a being so terrible that even its godly companions would imprison it forever. But worship it they do, so the claim stands.

"And they are collecting power. They are gaining ground in the galaxy. There have been uprisings recently. Entire planets have disappeared off the astral map. The Galactic Alliance and the Hand of God are worried, and have sent entire armies of immortals after them. The problem is that the Black Hole Church operates in secret. Its members hide among us. Things are complicated."

He shook his head. "But I over spoke. You don't need to bother with those things. What you should focus on is winning the Integration Tournament, accumulating power, then finding a way to save yourself and your people from impending doom. And the best way to do that is to Parkour better."

Jack's brain short-circuited. "What?"

"Parkour better. Look, you already moved everything. The training room is ready. Here's what you're going to do."

The Forest of the Strong burst with activity. Builders came and went, carrying materials in abundance. Their enhanced bodies made everything faster.

Gymonkeys and brorillas swung through the trees, watching the humans below, while Harambe lounged at the roots of the bananarm tree, absent-mindedly lifting a 100kg dumbbell. A human arrived beside him—a member of the Bare Fist Brotherhood. Harambe didn't know her name, but he was used to her presence.

With a small bow, the young woman reached up to the tree and plucked three bananarms. She then bowed again and took off, where three red-dressed men waited in the distance. Only a moment after she left, the bananarms regrew.

The situation around the Clear Pond and the High Speed Bush was much more hectic. People arrived occasionally, transferring a set amount of credits to a Bare Fist Brotherhood clerk before either picking a leaf off the bush or stripping to their underwear and entering the pond, which was packed full with no regard for gender.

The professor had been industrious.

After all their members had benefited from the resources, she'd contacted the nearby towns and offered the resources for a price. They were magically renewed every time, so they could be distributed freely.

They wouldn't last forever, of course—that would make no sense. The Brotherhood had someone watching over the resources at all times. If they showed the slightest hint of decay, the business would end—but so far, everything was going great. The professor estimated that, in the short-term, the credits they made off this business were more useful than keeping the resources intact. After all, the faction shop offered many great things, including a goblin battle simulator she'd already purchased.

For a hundred credits, anyone could access one of the resources. Three hundred would be enough to access all three, and that was a great price for the lifesaving +10 in all Physical stats. Only the ice pond was kept a secret, as it was the true core of the Brotherhood's strength.

Cultivators streamed in from the nearby towns, slowly at first. Then, news began to spread, and people arrived from farther and farther away to partake in the Brotherhood's resources. Credits were flowing in at a tremendous rate, more than ten thousand a day, and the brorillas took care of any troublemakers. Thanks to the influx of people, the nearby Valville was flourishing, too.

The Brotherhood was still relocating its headquarters from the town to the forest, and the main building was almost built, as were the training grounds and gyms. Due to the nature of their resources, most members chose Physical-oriented paths.

On the surface, everything was going great. But in reality... the professor was worried sick. Both for Jack, whose every battle she watched with bated breath, and for the future. Their faction's leader had just defeated the sharken scion, revealing his true identity, and the Animal Kingdom wasn't above playing dirty. They had to gather power fast.

For that reason, she let some nearby factions use the resources for free in exchange for a sworn alliance. She also kept their massive profits at hand, ready to buy whatever defensive items were necessary at a moment's notice.

All in all, things seemed to be going great, but the professor didn't allow herself to relax. The clock was ticking. When the brewing storm arrived, it would be her job to protect everyone.

And to do that, the Bare Fist Brotherhood had to grow fast.

CHAPTER SEVENTY-TWO
SUIT-UP!

Alexander both loved and hated the Integration.

On one hand, it gave him power. He'd risen in status and in the chain of command. His former bosses would have to serve him, if he hadn't killed them already.

On the other... he now had to deal with idiots. Those people would have never achieved success in the pre-Integration world. They were stubborn, naive, short-sighted, and idealistic. Qualities that should put them as far away from power as possible, dooming them to remain cogs in the machine for the remainder of their lives.

And yet, here they were.

Just because they could punch or whatever each of them did, they'd suddenly climbed to the top of the world. And they thought they *deserved* it. Dealing with them was so tiring for Alexander... At least this situation was only temporary. The elites would seize back control, cultivation resources would be tightly moderated, and society would return to relative order.

And he would be the king of Earth.

He knocked on the door—a number 1 was painted on it in gold—and waited. Somebody pulled it open from the other side. "Alex!" an excited voice reached him, further souring his mood, but he showed a smile.

"Sir Salin. Thank you for your patience."

"Don't be like that! Come on, loosen up a little." The canine slung an arm over his shoulder, grabbing him like a friend and pulling him inside. Alexander resisted the urge to freeze him, or even better, pull out his gun and shoot him. He still carried one of those. They did wonders for intimidation. Integrated memory was wonderful.

Plus, it gave him confidence.

Still with an arm over his broad shoulders, Gan Salin led Alexander inside. Two more people waited. Shard Presht—the sharken—leaned against a counter. Rufus Emberheart faced the window, only showing Alexander his back.

This leonine was the only person Alexander acknowledged. He knew how to behave. Serving under him was a good decision—which was handy because there was no other choice. In this new world, the only way to survive and prosper was to hug the legs of the strong, and anyone who didn't see that was a fool.

"Alexander," Rufus's deep voice rumbled.

"Sir," Alexander replied, lowering his head in subservience. "I have the information you requested."

"Good. Let's hear it."

Alexander didn't dare dally. "The Flame River has recruited Jack Rust, Dorman Whistles, Edgar Allano, and the Sage. They also approached Li Xiang and Kane Vanderdecken, who both remain neutral. No important factions have sided with them."

"Of course they haven't," Rufus Emberheart replied softly. By the side, the sharken chuckled darkly.

At this point, Alexander could have waited, prodding Rufus to ask him to continue. That would subconsciously raise Alexander's standing. Unfortunately, he didn't dare. The leonine was frighteningly sharp, and he permitted no tricks. Alexander had already lost an agent like that.

"On our side," Alexander continued unprompted, "we have five smaller factions whose leaders participated in the Tournament, as well as sixteen independent fighters. We are awaiting the response of nine more, but most will probably join us as well. Additionally, we have established contact with every major government that is still standing. All of them have pledged allegiance to you and the Animal Kingdom."

"How long would we need to squash any resistance?"

"One to three days, sir. Nuclear weapons are forbidden by the Star Pact, but we can use starships to send elite teams into their bases—provided the Tournament has ended, of course. Only Dorman Whistles and the Sage have no known base of operations, but with our connections, we'll discover them within two days even if they try to hide."

"Very well. Is there anything else?"

"No, sir."

"Then, you may go."

Alexander turned to leave, politely shaking off Gan Salin's arm, which had remained on his shoulders all this time.

"And, Alexander?" Rufus's voice came again. Alexander turned, bowed, and waited. "You don't need to bow that low in my presence. I can see your respect, and that is enough."

Alexander took the cue and raised his head, meeting Rufus's gaze. He was stern without being threatening, while his eyes and smile carried the charm of a friendly yet skilled commander. He practically oozed confidence.

He was a born king.

"Thank you, sir," he replied.

"I am pleased with you, Alexander. Do not disappoint me, and this planet will soon fall to your feet."

Alexander waited for a moment. When no further words came, he replied, "Thank you, sir," and departed.

As the door slid closed behind him, he tilted his face toward the afternoon sky. The gambles of his entire life were paying off. He would finally rise.

Jack jumped over an elliptical, turned atop a rowing machine, then launched himself forward. A mechanical hand missed his back by the tiniest margin, close enough that Jack could feel the breeze.

Shit!

He ran around with Sparman hot on his heels. He landed on the treadmill and activated it just as Sparman stepped forth, ruining its balance. That was enough to pass between the bench press and the elliptical, dashing the other way again.

To train in Parkour, Jack had to play tag.

They'd moved most of the gym equipment from the other room to the sparring room, filling it until it felt neither empty nor full. Now, Jack rushed to escape from the sparring robot operating at its fourth level. The room was small, roughly like a round tennis court, so they were like blurs as they ricocheted from wall to wall, passing under, above, and through instruments.

Jack had no hope of escaping without Parkour. His only chance was to use the terrain to his advantage, somehow outsmarting and outmaneuvering the robot to last a second longer.

It was quite stressful, and his Dao Root of Indomitable Will shone again.

He parkoured around the rowing machine and—

Sparman's palm slapped his back, sending him tumbling into a wall.

"Dammit!" he said, jumping up. "How long was that, Sparman?"

"Six seconds and eleven hundredths, master. This was the longest you've ever lasted!"

"That's what she said," Jack mumbled under his breath as he stretched his arms. He'd been going at this for hours, and even his Dao Root was struggling to keep him focused. "I think that's enough. We can try again tomorrow."

"Don't forget about the auction, master."

"I won't. Thank you for the hard work, Sparman. See you around."

"I am always available, master, and I look forward to spending another six wonderful seconds with you."

Jack glared but couldn't help laughing.

It was the second day after the first phase of the Tournament concluded, and the auction would be held that night. Jack had spent both days training, of course—but to no skill upgrades.

"Are you ready, Brock?" he asked, exiting the room. He shouldn't have. Brock lay on his back on the soft floor, arms spread wide and snoring loudly. Jack smirked. "Wake up, bro." He squatted and nudged his friend. "We have an auction to attend. Don't want to leave the others waiting."

The moment his finger touched Brock, he jumped up and flexed instantly. He then looked around in confusion before his gaze locked onto Jack. He smiled, blinking the bleariness away, then made happy monkey sounds.

"Good evening to you too, Brock." Jack smiled. "You worked hard."

Brock flexed his biceps. He really had worked hard. While Jack was training in Parkour and Drill, Brock had been following an intense workout routine focused on maximum gains.

Jack inspected him.

Brorilla, Level 7 (Elite)

A gorilla variant from planet Green. Brorillas usually live with Gymonkeys and train them in the ways of working out. It is due to the Brorillas' unmatched pecs that Gymonkeys use poop to fight—they consider themselves too weak for anything else.

Brorillas are usually calm, measured animals. However, if anyone harms their little cousins or invades their territory, they go bananas.

This particular Brorilla is a variant that visually resembles a Gymonkey. Though not weaker than other Brorillas, the members of this variant are often shunned due to their lack of bulging muscles.

Though he hadn't grown much in size—he could still stand on Jack's shoulder—Brock now had muscles so condensed, he could easily rip a pre-System human to pieces. He wouldn't do that, of course, because he was a friendly brorilla.

"Come on, Brock!" Jack said, growing excited.

It was time to see if the extravagant claims people spoke of really held water—and if they did, Jack was prepared. He gazed at his credit card, where yellow digits glowed.

2,137,469

A nice number of credits.

He took a quick shower upstairs. The setting sunlight streamed in through the window as Jack opened his wardrobe. It was filled with suits of all sizes, and he reached toward the right end to pick out one that fit him.

The shirt was white with a low collar. He buttoned it up, feeling the smooth fabric hug his wide shoulders. The sleeves stretched around his arms, completed with a black tie. He put on a pair of black pants and clean, brown shoes.

His final piece of attire was a dark suit jacket. With slick dark hair, brown eyes, and a slightly larger than average build, Jack looked sharp.

He smiled at the full-body mirror. He felt like a businessman.

Brock didn't have anything else to wear, unfortunately, so he simply stuck with his red pair of shorts.

"Ready?"

"*Uu-uu-aah*!"

Jack and Brock left the house in style, crossing the empty participant's district. Edgar, Vivi, Dorman, the Sage, and five members of Flame River waited for him at the entrance, each dressed as well as him —with the exception of the Sage, who apparently enjoyed looking homeless.

"You're late," Dorman said.

"Sorry. I was busy."

"You look good," Vivi said. She wore a simple red dress that contrasted her dark skin, and her hair was caught in an intricate braid.

"You too," Jack said. "Are we waiting for anyone else?"

"Of course not. You're the last one."

He scoffed. "Then let's go."

They were an outstanding group. As they crossed Integration City, people turned to look, and eyes followed them all the way until they went out of sight. Alien merchants and humans alike eyed their group with interest. Though they were few, they were one of the two major alliances in town, and they were dressed well.

"How is your training going, Edgar?" Jack asked.

"My master is amazing!" Edgar replied. He looked like he'd been dying to talk about this. "He knows so much stuff and has so many ideas about everything. Did you know there are *twelve types* of magic? And that my pure arcane mana can resonate with *all of them*? Just in two days, I've learned six new spells, and that's only because master wants me to get used to them first before teaching me more. I can craft better illusions and sound attacks, and—"

He went on, detailing so many things that Jack lost track, but that was okay. He got the gist. Edgar would be strong.

"Unfortunately, master said that wizards are weak in duels," Edgar finished with a sad expression. "But I can do so many things now!"

"Yeah. I'm really happy for you."

"What about you? What did you learn?"

"I can punch a target from slightly farther away, and I played a lot of tag," Jack replied. Then, seeing Edgar's frozen face, he laughed. "It's good training—probably. Master Shol seems reliable."

"Of course! I didn't mean to imply anything. I'm sure you'll be a beast at the finals."

"That, I will. And not just me."

Dorman was walking with new vigor in his steps. Even Vivi, despite having no mentor. And the Sage... Well, the Sage looked the same as ever.

The auction house was visible from afar. It had opened its gates for the first and last time in this Integration, and it wouldn't spare expenses. Every window was lit, and the entrance was guarded by two robo-dog guards with sharp red eyes behind their slick sunglasses.

A crowd of people waited outside, but most of those who wanted to participate had already entered. A dog guard stopped them at the entrance. "Ten thousand credits a head," it commanded in a rough, mechanical voice.

They complied. Jack had to pay twice, for Brock as well. Then, they were in.

There weren't many rooms in the large building that served as the auction house. Most of the interior was taken up by a single large space extending from side to side and with balconies on the second floor that overlooked the main stage.

It reminded Jack of a big theater.

An upraised platform stood at the very front, where all the velvet seats pointed. Only an empty wooden table stood on it, covered in a red tablecloth, with passages leading behind the stage.

The place was packed. The ground floor could seat at least a hundred people, and each of the sixteen balconies that surrounded it had a round table with three chairs. Jack and the rest were about to enter the main room when a dog guard stopped them.

"Finalists have balconies," it said, then pointed them to a set of stairs. They smiled.

"We can't all fit in one," Vivi said. "Let's split up. And let's be kind to each other, yes?"

"Of course," Jack replied. The Sage nodded.

They climbed the stairs and arranged themselves into balconies. Jack sat with Edgar and Brock. Vivi took two members of her faction to her balcony, while Sadaka, the other finalist from Flame River, took the other two. The Sage and Dorman sat together.

Jack removed his dark suit jacket and hung it on the back of his chair. He then rolled up his white sleeves—it was hot in there—and took a seat, enjoying the feel of the luxurious cushion on his suited butt.

"This is nice," he said, grinning.

"But everyone's looking at us..." Edgar muttered. Brock sat on the edge of the balcony to have a better view, letting his feet dangle over the people below.

"No pooping, you hear me?" Jack said, and Brock made an insulted face. Jack took it to mean, "Me, poop? Never!"

From where they sat, they had a clear view of the stage as well as all the other balconies—the venue was circular in shape.

Brother Tao sat in a balcony by himself, as did Li Xiang. Vanderdecken—the metal guy—had a red-haired girl with him.

Alexander Petrovic and Elena Richter each had two Ice Peak members in their balcony. The scions were split in two: the elef and eagler sat together—with the elef not fitting in a chair, so she had to remain standing—while Rufus Emberheart, Shard Presht, and Gan Salin sat together.

Coincidentally, Jack managed to feud with all three members of the last group. How nice.

Of course, many balconies remained empty, but nobody dared claim them. They couldn't come up the stairs.

Jack scanned every other balcony. Some didn't notice him; some ignored him; a few—his allies—nodded back. Only Shard Presht and Gan Salin met his gaze and held it. Both had been defeated by Jack, and both held a grudge. Rufus Emberheart didn't put him in his sights. He seemed to be resting—or meditating. Jack really couldn't tell.

The auction house was noisy as people spoke amongst themselves. Those below were either defeated Tournament participants or representatives of other factions who had traveled here by their own means. No aliens were allowed to attend.

All whispers were interrupted as an alien stepped on the stage. They weren't from any race Jack had seen before. They were humanoid with pale skin and black eyes, and they carried an innate regality that even Jack found himself acknowledging.

Jack scanned him.

Vampire, Level ??? (E-Grade)
Faction: Hand of God (B-Grade)

"You have got to be kidding me," Jack and Edgar said at the same time. Many people in the audience had similar reactions, but the vampire's clear voice cut through their clamor like a blade.

He didn't seem evil, as Earth tradition would have him. Just noble.

"Welcome to the Integration Auction, people of Earth-387," he declared. His charm was evident. "My name is Vocrich Eretor, a vampire lord of Kotsiya, and I will be your host for tonight."

CHAPTER SEVENTY-THREE
THE INTEGRATION AUCTION

VOCRICH ERETOR, THE VAMPIRE LORD THAT WOULD LEAD THE AUCTION, STEPPED off the stage center. Another vampire, a woman, walked out and placed a shiny cube on the table.

"The first item," Vocrich declared, "is a high-grade starship. Forged by an apprentice of the famous Horrificus Egen, this ship can cross space at a speed approaching a thousand miles a minute. It operates on the user's Dao, meaning it's cost-free, and can accommodate up to five people—or more if you pack light."

Scattered laughs came from the audience. Vocrich smiled. "The starting price is 500,000 credits!"

Silence.

"How the hell is that a starship?" Jack whispered to Edgar. The item was a cube that could fit in one's palm.

"No idea," the wizard whispered back, shrugging. "Magic, I guess."

Jack shook his head as he ran the math.

One thousand miles a minute was sixty thousand an hour. That ship—if it really was a starship—was faster than anything Earth had developed, could reach the moon in four hours, and didn't cost massive amounts of resources to operate.

However, five hundred thousand credits...

Jack was aware that most auctions started with a heavy-hitter item to rile up the crowds. Though the starship intrigued him, he couldn't spare the expense.

Unless this is the item the Sage wanted me to get, he thought.

The Sage's voice rang inside his mind. "Your item will come last." Then out loud he said, "I offer five hundred thousand."

Many heads turned to the Sage, who smiled jovially. Sitting across from him, Dorman didn't bat an eye.

"Six hundred thousand," a suited-up man from below offered, standing up. He was bald and muscular, and he oozed an aura of authority. He must have been someone important in the pre-System world. Now, he was only qualified to sit among the crowd.

"Seven hundred," the Sage retorted.

"Seven fifty."

"Eight hundred."

The bald man frowned deeply, then sat back down. Nobody else spoke.

"Eight hundred thousand credits, offered by the mysterious Sage," Vocrich announced. "Is there anyone willing to trump that? Starships of this caliber don't appear often in underdeveloped worlds!"

He waited a moment, but nobody spoke up. "Very well. Then, this high-grade starship has been sold to the Sage for eight hundred thousand credits. Congratulations!"

"Thank you," the Sage replied with a smile.

"An assistant will bring the item to you at once. You can deposit the sum in her credit card," Vocrich said. "The next item is a set of seven F-Grade servant robots, so you never have to do housework again. The starting price is one hundred thousand credits."

Seven white robots with smooth curves walked onto the stage. Several people bid at low increments, but the item finally went to Li Xiang, the martial arts master, for two hundred thousand.

"Next is an E-Grade Dao Fruit of the Blade! Ideal for anyone wanting to sharpen their Dao Seed!" Vocrich announced as a vampire assistant brought a Dao Fruit on stage. It resembled the one Jack had taken from Henry White, except it radiated an aura of sharpness so strong it was almost corporeal. It was like staring down a gun barrel.

"The starting price is—"

"Five hundred thousand," Dorman interrupted. The announcer smiled and didn't say anything. Neither did the crowd.

"Six hundred," Gan Salin called out.

"One million," Dorman replied calmly.

Jack's eyes widened. One million credits, gone like that...

F-Grade Dao Fruits were only sold for ten thousand. Of course, E-Grade fruits were much, much rarer—otherwise this fruit would have never appeared in such a prestigious auction—but a million was definitely over the market price. Dorman must have wanted it deeply.

Then again, everyone could only use one Dao Fruit of each Grade. Investing in the right fruit for you was worth it.

Jack's eyes glimmered as he considered the F-Grade Dao Fruit of the Fist he kept hidden in his house. It was perfect for him, and he'd been saving it for when he attempted to breakthrough into the E-Grade. However, if an E-Grade Dao Fruit of the Fist showed up, how much would he be willing to spend to get it?

Hmm.

Nobody dared bid against Dorman, so the fruit was sold for a million credits. Vocrich had a wide smile—then again, that was always the case.

As time passed, more items were brought out. There was an E-Grade bodyguard robot similar to the dog guards—bought by someone in the crowd—a meditation mat similar to the ones in the participant lodgings—also bought by Dorman—as well as several high-grade Dao weapons.

Dao weapons were split in tiers. The cheapest ones could go for as low as ten thousand credits, but if you wanted something good, you had to spend upwards of a hundred thousand. Edgar had bought his staff for three hundred thousand credits.

High-grade weapons had several advantages over weaker ones. They were sharper, lighter, harder, more durable, and most importantly, could channel the user's Dao with less resistance.

The weapons presented in the auction were all of the highest caliber. They weren't suited for everyone—after all, they were already made and so aligned with a single Dao—but to those who used that Dao, they were priceless treasures. Fierce bidding wars occurred for each and every one, with the winning prices ranging from two hundred thousand for a long-barreled handgun to five hundred thousand for a pitch-black wooden staff that, according to Vocrich, weighed a thousand pounds.

Brother Tao got that one, and though it seemed to strain him, he could lift it. With some practice—and some strength-oriented level-ups—that staff would aid him well in battle.

Vanderdecken also got a Dao weapon. It was a simple chain attuned to the Dao of Metal and it only cost him three hundred thousand. "Alright!" he shouted.

The rest were bought by those in the audience.

So far, Jack hadn't bid once, and he wasn't the only one. Of the scions, only Gan Salin had made a bid, and he hadn't even won. The Ice Peak and Flame River also hadn't participated yet.

"The next item is an ancient spear containing hints of the Dao of Space," Vocrich said, voice getting serious. "Though it cannot be used as a weapon, meditating on it and examining its properties could give a cultivator great insight into space. The starting price is five hundred thousand credits."

Whispers spread across the audience.

"Five hundred thousand!" someone called out from below, only to be quickly rebuffed.

"Six hundred!"

"Seven hundred!"

"Eight hundred thousand!" Elena Richter, the second finalist of Ice Peak, called out.

"One million!" the eagle-like scion called out. His name was Fesh Wui, and he used the Dao of the Wind.

"One million two hundred!" Vivi called out, drawing surprised glances. Jack thought she was trying to make the scions pay higher, but it was unnecessary. They could do that themselves.

"One million five hundred!" Shard Presht announced, staring at the eagler, who only snorted.

"You cannot outbid me, Presht," he said in a high-pitched, sharp voice. "One million six hundred."

"One million seven hundred," the shark-man retorted.

"One million eight hundred."

Shard Presht frowned. He looked at Rufus Emberheart, who still had his eyes closed and paid him no heed. Finally, Presht snorted. "Fine. If you want to go crazy, I won't join you. You can have it."

Vocrich didn't push much. This was already a high price. "One million eight hundred by the fascinating Fesh Wui. Anyone else?" he said, then a beat later, "Congratulations, Fesh Wui!"

"Was it really worth that much?" Jack asked Edgar.

"Probably," Edgar replied. "The Dao of Space is very strong. If your Dao is compatible, a Dao Root of Space could increase your battle prowess tremendously. I don't know how helpful this spear can be, but I wager it would have been ten times more expensive in the wider market."

"Hmm... Why would the Hand of God invest so much in this auction? They're clearly taking a loss."

"How am I supposed to know? Maybe these things are gifts to the scions of the Animal Kingdom, like the Tournament rewards, or maybe everyone's performance in the Tournament has been great. Or, you know, maybe they just have tremendous budget. Integrations don't happen often."

"Man, I want to bid for something too..." Jack said. The auction was exciting.

After selling the spear, Vocrich didn't slow down. He kept the bangers coming.

"The next item is extremely precious," he said, drawing everyone's attention. "It was discovered in the desolate wastes of Poltergeist, a planet that follows a highly elliptical trajectory. Most of its rotation is in the outer reaches of its solar system, but for fifty-one galactic days every year, it passes very close to its star. As a result, the planet's surface alternates between extreme cold and extreme heat, and anything that grows on that planet is a treasure for both Daos."

Vivi and Alexander Petrovic stared at each other. A vampire assistant walked on stage, carrying what looked like a cabbage from afar, except its base was made of white leaves and the rest of fiery red ones. The vampire wore thick gloves, and she carried the item on a black plate. She didn't leave it on the table, holding onto it instead.

"The lotus of fire and ice!" Vocrich declared. "Holding both extremes at once, this lotus flower can greatly help the users of both Daos. The starting price is one million credits."

Jack raised both his brows. This was a sky-high price.

"I offer one million two hundred," Alexander Petrovic said.

"One million five hundred," Vivi replied quickly.

"One million seven hundred."

"Two million."

The price instantly climbed to incredible heights. Except for the two major factions, nobody dared bid. Of the people on the balconies, nobody else used suitable Daos, either—but Vivi and Alexander both understood that this fruit might well be the turning point in their future clash.

Alexander glanced at Elena Richter. "Two million two hundred," he declared.

"Two million four hundred."

"Two million five hundred."

Vivi frowned. She looked at Sadaka, who nodded. "Two million seven hundred!" she announced.

By now, Jack was beginning to feel poor. He'd tried his best to gather credits and thought himself rich, but these guys were all richer than him.

It makes sense, he skulked. They had more people, so more chances to gather credits... but still...

I hope the Sage didn't get the number wrong... He only told me to gather two million.

Alexander Petrovic lowered his brows and didn't bid immediately. It looked like two million seven hundred was already his ceiling, even when utilizing the funds of the entire Ice Peak.

Vivi adopted a victorious look.

Out of options, Alexander turned to Rufus Emberheart, who still sat there calmly with his eyes closed.

"Sir..." Alexander said. Rufus opened his eyes. His supreme gaze stared deep into Alexander's soul as if conquering it.

"Very well. I will assist. Three million," Rufus declared. The auction fell silent.

Vivi's face darkened. She looked at Jack, who raised both brows. *Shit! We're doing this too?*

Her stare remained. A moment later, he gritted his teeth and nodded. They were in an alliance. He couldn't just let Vivi get her ass handed to her. He just hoped she wouldn't go too far.

Her eyes showed her gratitude. She looked at Rufus.

"Three million two hundred," she said.

"Four million," Rufus said calmly as if it meant nothing.

He didn't have to raise the price that high. He just did it because he *could*, and because he followed the Dao of Supremacy.

Jack held his breath. Assuming Vivi only had close to three million herself, if she announced a higher price, she would be cutting deep into his budget. He needed that.

However, she knew the limit. She wouldn't go too far on her allies' money. She gazed at the Sage, who only shook his head.

She retreated back into her chair.

"Four million by the unfathomable Rufus Emberheart," Vocrich said. "Is there a higher price?"

Nobody spoke. Probably, nobody else had that much, either.

"Sold! Congratulations, Rufus Emberheart."

The lion-man nodded. Alexander disappeared into the corridor, soon arriving at Rufus's balcony, standing there obediently—there were no more chairs. He took out his credit card and passed his money to the lion-man. When the vampire assistant showed up, Rufus paid her, received the lotus, then gave it to Alexander.

"Do not disappoint me," he said.

"I swear I won't, sir," Alexander replied, bowing deeply.

They'd just made a point to the entire human race of Earth-387. Rufus had shown he treated his underlings well. And Alexander had shown that the best of humanity was inferior to the scions of the Animal Kingdom.

Alexander Petrovic returned to his seat under many heavy glares. The auction continued. It had been going on for an hour already, and the final items were rapidly approaching. As they did, the quality shot up, too.

The other scions were participating now. Two Dao armors came on stage, one after the other. They were human-shaped, elastic pieces of knight-like metal armor that could hug tightly the wearer's body, providing excellent protection even against the E-Grade. Against attacks in the F-Grade, they were almost impenetrable.

Both sets of armor included everything from helmets to boots, and they incited fierce bidding wars. Gan Salin and Shard Presht were the ones who won, each paying slightly over a million credits.

Then came a green orb glowing with soothing light.

CHAPTER SEVENTY-FOUR
THE RAINBOW DAO PILL

"This is the heart of a D-Grade manatee of the Evergreen planet," Vocrich said, motioning at the green, glowing orb. "It carries healing properties so strong that it can heal even the user's Dao and bring people back from the very precipice of death. Moreover, meditating on it can give insights into the Dao of Life. It is a priceless item for large sects or life-attuned cultivators under the D-Grade. The starting price is one million credits."

There must have been word of this thing beforehand because many people rushed to bid. Several factions in the crowd pooled their resources and called out prices, climbing to two million before the shouting stopped. The winner so far was the suited bald man from before.

However, as it wasn't the last item, Jack didn't bid.

"Two million five hundred," the elephant scion called out. She was humanoid with thick, gray, wrinkled skin, standing at nine feet tall and bearing a physique somewhere between a human's and an elephant's. She also had wide ears and a trunk in place of her nose, while her fingers were short and stubby.

And she won the Manatee Heart. Everyone else that might have been interested in betting was already out of money.

Vocrich took the stage again, carrying a covered item in his palm and smiling from ear-to-ear. It was a bittersweet smile, too, almost making Jack feel sentimental before he mentally punched through the charm.

"Our auction is coming to an end, ladies and gentlemen," he declared sadly, which quickly turned into enthusiasm. "However, the last item is also the crown of this auction. An item that has never appeared in Integration Auctions before. The legendary pill to help form a Dao Seed and breakthrough to the E-Grade faster, saving months or years of effort without harming your foundation. If you're talented enough, it could even let you break through before the end of the Integration Tournament!"

He paused for dramatic effect, then theatrically pulled the fabric covering the item. Jack's eyes widened. People shouted. A rainbow-colored light shone out, along with an aura of serenity that made everyone want to cultivate on the spot. Jack felt one with himself, the world, and his Dao. It was a truly wondrous feeling.

"The Rainbow Dao Pill!" Vocrich shouted over the clamor. "Produced by a C-Grade alchemist of the Hand of God, this pill can greatly accelerate the process of forming a Dao Seed for anyone who swallows it. You can't find this on the market! And the starting price is only a million credits! Who can offer more?"

This was the item he'd been waiting for. Winning the Tournament was unlikely because Rufus Emberheart stood at the peak, unshakable and unfathomable. But if he could break through to the E-Grade...

And everyone else had spent a lot of credits already. Once again, Jack felt he owed the Sage a favor.

"One million credits," he called out.

"Two million credits," Rufus Emberheart announced calmly. Jack met his gaze. The leonine's eyes hid absolute certainty of victory, mocking Jack for daring to stand against him.

But Jack wouldn't go down without a fight. After all, this was the last item in the auction; if he didn't get it, what was he supposed to do with all his money?

"Do you have any spare credits, Edgar?" he asked, to which Edgar nodded.

"Less than a hundred thousand."

"Okay," Jack replied before raising his voice. "Two million two hundred!"

"Three million credits."

Rufus's voice fell like a guillotine. Jack was speechless. *Two million credits would be enough? Bullshit!* He glared at the Sage, who only smiled back.

Suddenly, Vivi's voice cut through the clamor.

"The Flame River will assist our allies," she said. A member of her faction appeared from the corridor, stepping into Jack's balcony and whispering something to his ear. "We can lend you three million," was all the man said. "But we hope you can pay it back."

Jack grinned. That's right, he had allies! And they hadn't managed to buy the lotus, so they still had most of their credits!

"Four million," he shot back.

"Five million," Rufus replied calmly. However, Jack could sense that the leonine was getting slightly flustered. There had to be a limit to his budget. He'd already spent over a million to help Alexander Petrovic get his lotus.

"Five million two hundred!" he declared. This was actually his full budget, including Edgar's and Vivi's money.

"Six million," Rufus said. Both Gan Salin and Shard Presht looked at him oddly. Shard's gaze, specifically, carried a hint of accusation. After all, Rufus hadn't helped him get the spear with the Dao of Space.

Jack gritted his teeth. Suddenly, the weight of money pressed hard on him. Ten thousand credits were already a lot anywhere on the planet, and here he was, betting in the millions. Moreover, borrowing that money.

He couldn't deny the feeling of relief that flushed over him when Rufus declared a price he couldn't beat. However, in the next moment, both his Dao Roots flared and shot down that feeling. It was weakness and he was strong. He was indomitable.

Indomitable and, apparently, poor. He gritted his teeth harder.

"*I happen to have a spare million,*" the Sage's voice rang in his mind. "*I could give it to you for free.*"

Jack glared at him, half-accusing and half-calculating. His two million credits prediction had been wildly off the mark. Moreover, the million credits he offered were most definitely not for free. They came with a string attached—and, in this case, it meant Jack would owe him a favor. A favor that his Daos wouldn't easily let him forget about.

Wait, his mind shouted at him. *What if the two million prediction wasn't off? Did he calculate things would reach this point? Did he trick me and did all this to earn a favor?*

He stared into the Sage's eyes, but they were too deep, and he could not see the other man's soul. He gritted his teeth.

"Six million two hundred!" he shouted out. The silence could be cut with a knife at this point. These sums were just ridiculous.

"Six million five hundred," Rufus said with a stony face. Jack regarded him with surprise. This bid wasn't supreme and wild like all the previous ones. It was a minor increase that didn't fit the Dao of Supremacy.

Moreover, both Gan Salin and Shard Presht looked at Rufus in shock. He just looked at them and said something in a low voice, then both reclined in their seat, very much unhappy. He'd just used their money as well.

Rufus had run out of money.

Jack's eyes glowed as he caught on. Unfortunately, he needed just a few more credits to match it. Just four hundred thousand, and he could win.

But he had no more allies. He looked at Dorman, who shook his head helplessly. He'd already spent everything.

Jack's gaze scanned the rest of the balconies and the crowd below. Suddenly, he felt like a beggar. Could his pride really stand asking to borrow from people? He knew they'd give it to him, and that Rufus would never have the stomach to do the same, but...

As Jack's thoughts warred, Brother Tao spoke up.

"Brother Jack is an honorable fighter. I have five hundred thousand credits remaining, and I am willing to sow good karma with you."

Gratitude washed over Jack. "Thank you, Brother Tao," he responded. "I am sure your monastery will flourish soon. Six million seven hundred credits."

Money could be heavy. At this moment, Jack felt so many expectations on him. He'd borrowed from many people and made many promises, both implicit and explicit. Would his future strength be enough to keep them? Would he betray their expectations?

His heart steeled. That was the future, and this was the present. He would just do his best.

He stared at Rufus Emberheart, who, for the first time, stared straight back. His arms remained crossed, but there was tension in them now. His eyes held deep dissatisfaction.

Unlike Jack, he wouldn't borrow money. His Dao was the express opposite of receiving outside help. What he could do was commandeer the money of his underlings, but unfortunately, he'd run out of underlings.

He had already used the funds of Gan Salin and Shard Presht. The Ice Peak had used everything they had to buy the lotus—they'd even borrowed from him.

Actually, Rufus must have been regretting that decision. If he hadn't helped Alexander win over Vivi, he could have won the Rainbow Dao Pill. Unfortunately for him, what was done was done.

"This Rainbow Dao Pill is very important to me," he said. "Rescind your bid."

"Is this a threat?" Jack asked. Rufus Emberheart did not respond. He simply maintained his glare. The Dao of Supremacy was above asking for favors, but it wasn't above securing supremacy in any way possible.

Surprisingly, Vocrich stepped up. "I have to ask all guests to maintain decorum," he said steadily. "The Hand of God will not tolerate injustice from anyone. Bids are not rescindable. The Rainbow Dao Pill is sold to Jack Rust for six million and seven hundred thousand credits. Congratulations."

Not only did he speak up against Rufus, but he also ended the bidding war on the spot.

Jack threw him a grateful stare, which Vocrich shrugged off. Unlike the Tournament officials, it seemed the Hand of God wasn't going to favor anyone.

However, Rufus Emberheart didn't relent. "Well?" he insisted, looking at Jack. In truth, there was no need to directly rescind the bid. There were a thousand ways to do this if Jack wanted to. But he didn't. He refused to bow to anyone's threats. He'd already chosen the road of not submitting to the scions.

He would win this Tournament and use his strength to cement himself and his faction in the volatile System world—and when the Animal Kingdom came, he would be so strong that they'd rather befriend than kill him.

"Are threats all you can do? Where is your supremacy?" Jack asked mockingly.

Rufus took a moment to reply, but when he did, his voice was bitter. No matter what he said, he had already been humiliated by making a threat and Jack refusing to yield. "Supremacy is in the heart. A clown like you could never understand it."

"A clown with the Rainbow Dao Pill," Jack retorted, then laughed. "I hope your minion enjoys his lotus, Rufus."

Rufus Emberheart was simmering as his last name indicated. He took a deep breath. The aura of the Dao exited his body, remaining constrained around him and helping calm his mind. His air of supremacy, that had faltered before, regained its splendor.

"You will regret these words," he said, threatening Jack yet again, then closed his eyes and leaned back in his chair as if none of this concerned him.

Everyone else didn't dare butt into the fight. Things could have ended there.

But they didn't. A single piece of poop tumbled through the air. Everyone who saw it widened their eyes and opened their mouths as if in slow motion. Nobody stopped it. The piece of poop crossed the venue to land gracefully on Rufus Emberheart's chest.

Plop.

Brock laughed. Gan Salin and Shard Presht gaped, then took a step back. Everyone gasped. The leonine opened his eyes and looked down. His aura exploded. His Dao roiled. Several dog guards streamed into the room. Vocrich shouted something.

Rufus Emberheart jumped to his feet and waved a paw toward Jack's balcony. The giant phantom of a lion's paw coalesced in midair and flew forward, carrying irresistible momentum. It was stronger than anything he'd shown in the Tournament. Before anyone could even blink, the paw crashed down on Brock, seeking to squash him like a bug.

Jack flashed before Brock and smashed out a Meteor Punch. The two strikes collided. The world exploded.

CHAPTER SEVENTY-FIVE
BREAKING THE AUCTION

Jack's Meteor Punch clashed against Rufus's attack in front of his balcony, releasing a ring-shaped shockwave. Both attacks carried a hint of unyieldingness—supremacy and indomitable will—and both refused to give an inch. Therefore, the shockwave had no choice but to escape sideways, forming a ring of pure force that slammed into the unfortunate people below.

Chairs were crushed, screams pierced the venue, hats went flying. From one moment to the next, the auction was turned on its head. People ran left and right as the two attacks extinguished each other, leaving the air glittering with force.

Rufus Emberheart was boiling. His golden mane danced in the gale of his Dao, which had pushed the tables and chairs on his balcony aside. A brown stain was clear on his silken chest piece, though Brock's poop itself had evaporated. His eyes burned with yellow light as his gaze crossed the venue to land on Jack.

Jack stood tall on the edge of his balcony, shielding Brock, who'd fallen back from fear. His white shirt was taut as his muscles bulged, and his eyes were filled with fury. His fists were clenched.

He was boiling too.

If he'd acted just a moment later, Brock would have died. Brock. His little bro. Harambe's son, whom he had sworn to protect with his life.

"How dare you?" Jack thundered.

His Dao erupted. The air moved away from him, creating a gale that raised cups and chairs. Behind him, Edgar grabbed Brock and moved back.

The gazes of Jack and Rufus collided in midair, and so did their Daos. Sparks flew. None would budge. Everyone on the balconies were ready to battle. The scions and the Ice Peak stared down the Flame River, the Sage, and Dorman, who only had a smirk as he twirled a dagger. The people below almost stampeded each other to get away faster.

Robotic dog guards streamed into the venue. Three of them jumped at each balcony, landing next to Jack and Rufus with heavy bangs that shook the wood.

The ones on Rufus's balcony stood straight and stared coldly, chests puffed out as they met his gaze. Red dots of light shone behind their slick sunglasses, and they bared their fangs. Rufus stood at the same height as them—six and a half feet—and looked straight ahead, his gaze boring through them to reach Jack.

Two dog guards flanked Jack from where he stood on the balcony's railing, a third directly behind him. His stare intensified. He wouldn't do anything stupid, but he would be damned if he looked away first.

"**Enough**."

The sound ruptured Jack's eardrums. It bore into his head and sought to crush his brain, making him grimace. He fell back, landing on the table and breaking it.

"Jack!" Edgar shouted, but Jack couldn't hear him. He blinked furiously to clear his static-filled vision. When he refocused, the three dog guards loomed above him with fangs bared. He stayed still.

"Easy," he said. "I'm subdued."

They did not cease their posturing. Jack tried to stand, and they let him.

On the opposite balcony, Rufus was still standing, though he'd retreated until his back met the wall. He was barely visible between the three dog guards who were ready to gang up on him.

Jack looked down.

Vocrich stood in the middle of the stage. His black suit and cape were flowing in a non-existent wind, and his still body hid a threat that made even Jack think twice. When he looked into the vampire's eyes, they were so dark and sinister, it was like facing twin black holes. All nearby light seemed to be sucked into them, creating a red and black torrent around his pale face.

His Dao was rolling out in great waves, reminding Jack of the second black wolf he'd killed, the one with the Dao Root of Darkness. However, Vocrich's was on a completely different level.

His aura washed over Jack, who felt like he was facing the open maw of a gargantuan beast. The darkness pierced inside his head, stealing all of his senses. His Dao Root attempted to resist, to punch through the darkness, but it was as ineffective as someone punching the night. It was easily swept away and made to bow like hay in a storm.

Only a single sound remained in Jack's perception, and it was an irresistible voice that commanded, "Enough."

Though he couldn't feel it, Jack was sure he was drenched in sweat. His world disappeared for a few moments. He even lost his perception of time, alone in a cold, boundless night.

When the darkness receded, Jack found himself on the floor of his balcony, looking up at Edgar and Brock's worried faces.

"The Hand of God will not tolerate this disrespect," Vocrich's voice commanded. It wasn't infused with the Dao this time, but nobody dared take it lightly. "Jack Rust and Rufus Emberheart, you are both held responsible. All your further monetary winnings in this Tournament will be confiscated by the Hand of God. Additionally, you will each owe us an additional one million credits in compensation, and you will be blacklisted from all our events for one galactic year. Am I clear?"

Jack raised his upper body. The auction was calmer now. Those who'd run away earlier were returning to watch the show, gloating in the misfortune of the Tournament's top dogs. The dog guards had disappeared. With Vocrich here, they were completely unnecessary.

Jack looked at the vampire and shivered. He'd hid his aura again and resembled just a man in a suit, but the power he displayed was the greatest Jack had felt so far. He had never before received an E-Grade cultivator's attack, and Vocrich wasn't even a normal E-Grade. He scanned the man.

Vampire, Level ??? (E-Grade)
Faction: Hand of God (B-Grade)

Three question marks... They aren't just for show, he thought, shivering again. Merchant my ass.

On the opposite balcony, Rufus Emberheart was shaking. Who knew what he was feeling. Wordlessly, he disappeared into the corridor that connected the balconies, then appeared briefly in the venue's entrance before walking out into the night. He did not forget to shoot Jack a hateful glare. He would not forget this. Shard Presht and Gan Salin followed him, though the latter threw an amused glance at Jack. It didn't hide animosity, this time. It was like Gan Salin welcomed this insane turn of events.

"I understand, sir," Jack said, bowing his head toward the vampire. "I apologize. It will not happen again."

"Of course. Now get out. You do not get to hear the auction's closing words."

Jack nodded, scooping his rumpled suit jacket out of the debris of their broken table, and turned around, only to find a vampire assistant at the entrance of his balcony. She held a palm-sized dark cube. "The Rainbow Dao Pill, sir," she said evenly. "Could you pay the six million seven hundred?"

Jack went beet-red. "One moment, please," he muttered, then quickly looked around the balconies. He didn't dare meet Vocrich's persistent stare.

Thankfully, the Sage and Brother Tao arrived by themselves, and the Flame River had already transferred their funds to Jack. He received all the credits, thanked everyone, paid the assistant, and put the dark cube in his suit jacket's inner pocket.

"An impressive stunt," the Sage said with a smile. "You should be careful, though. Our flame girl did not enjoy this."

Jack raised his brows, then looked across the venue, where Vivi stood. Her glare told him everything he needed to know.

"I'll be careful," he promised. "Let's go, Brock. We have some things to talk about."

The ape shrunk back, then walked beside Jack with small steps. He knew he'd messed up. Jack bid goodbye to everyone and exited the venue, heading toward his home.

"What the hell was that?" he asked, glaring at Brock. "Do you understand how much trouble you created?"

Brock looked down.

"Don't think you can get away with this," Jack said strictly. The passersby looked at them with curiosity, but he ignored them. "If I was just a moment slower, or if Rufus was slightly stronger, you would be dead, Brock. *Dead*. What would I tell your father, then? Who would lift dumbbells with me all day long?" His voice mellowed slightly. "You're my little bro, Brock, but I can't always protect you. You must learn to protect yourself. You cannot afford to act like a kid anymore."

Jack's words were strict and spoken harshly. Brock had thick tears in his eyes, but he was clenching his little face as hard as he could to keep them from falling. Jack's heart almost wavered, but he maintained a stony expression. This was important. Brock was still a child, and he had to learn.

"You cannot do stupid shit like that, Brock," Jack said. "You are a *bro* now. Would a bro throw poop for fun? Would a bro put himself in danger for no reason and hope that his other bros would save him? Would a bro create trouble for his big bro? What you did was incredibly stupid. Never do it again."

Brock's face spasmed as the salty tears fell. He pretended not to feel them. He sniffed and wiped his nose, then used both hands to wipe his eyes. Finally, he sat on the ground and looked away from Jack. A girl who was passing by almost cried too.

Jack's heart melted a little.

"Tsk. Come here, you," he said, lifting Brock and hugging him to his chest. "I know you're a good boy, alright? A good bro. You just have to be careful, okay? Don't do that shit again."

Brock looked up at Jack and nodded tearfully, then hid his face into Jack's chest and cried a little more, wiping tears and snot on the pristine white shirt.

"It's alright, Brock, it's okay," Jack said, patting Brock's little head. "We all make mistakes. Now you know, right?"

Brock looked up again and nodded. By this point, he was too cute for Jack to resist. With a big smile, he rubbed Brock's head and said, "You were very brave for trying to protect me, Brock. I'm proud of you. Now, who wants some meat skewers?"

Brock raised a shaky hand. Jack laughed, then placed him on the ground. "Well then, let's go. The meat won't eat itself."

"*Uu-uu-aah*!"

Brock responded hesitantly, raising a fist despite his tears. His nose twitched and he pointed in a direction.

"That way? Okay!"

And so, while all the surrounding pedestrians watched, Jack grabbed Brock by the hand and led him away toward very delicious food.

CHAPTER SEVENTY-SIX
DOOMED

THE MOON HUNG HIGH. JACK SAT ON HIS ROOFTOP, ENJOYING THE NIGHT BREEZE. He was alone. Not even Brock was there. His brows were deeply furrowed.

He needed to think.

I'm an enemy of Gan Salin, Shard Presht, and most importantly, Rufus Emberheart.

What happened in the auction was different than every other time. Gan Salin and Shard Presht envied Jack's strength and were bitter that they'd lost to him. Gan Salin bore the heavier grudge, obviously, due to what happened in Valville, but he wasn't someone to worry about.

Both scions felt relatively unimportant in the grand scheme of things, and their enmity wasn't too deep. They were enemies, yes, but only in the context of Earth. The Animal Kingdom would probably ignore these frictions if they had something to gain from it.

Now, however, Jack had deeply offended the strongest of the scions. The one who channeled supremacy in everything he did. The one who was far stronger than everyone else, and hence more important.

Even after Brock's reckless actions, he could have diffused the situation in the auction. He could have apologized. Instead, he'd embraced his Dao and stood up to Rufus Emberheart. He didn't regret it. Only now, he had to face the consequences.

Jack's plan had been to form an alliance on Earth to protect himself and his faction until the planet's grace period ended. By that time, he would have become so strong that the overpowered aliens would rather befriend and recruit him than fuss over small disputes. It was a bet on himself.

But what happened with Rufus Emberheart didn't feel like a small dispute. Rufus's Dao of Supremacy now demanded that he step on Jack like a bug, the same way Jack's Dao demanded he punch Rufus hard into the ground. Their conflict couldn't be resolved unless someone died or accepted a large crack in their Dao.

Could Jack's plan still work? Or had he shoved himself into a dead end?

Even if he beat Rufus now, would the Animal Kingdom still choose to befriend Jack and ignore one of their brilliant youth? If he killed Rufus, would his family—the strongest noble family—drop the matter? If he did nothing, would the Animal Kingdom let him go, and would Rufus Emberheart forget about him?

The Animal Kingdom acted in an overbearing manner, paying little to no heed to their subordinate factions. They were rampant tyrants—Master Shol had said as much.

Suddenly, every path led to the Animal Kingdom squashing Jack and his faction as an example to all would-be defiers. Maybe it wouldn't happen. But could he guarantee it?

I only intended to banter a bit... Jack sighed, then shook his head. *What's done is done. I just have to find the best way forward. Like a fist.*

While the fist had its strengths, it also hid flaws. Jack couldn't even take a step back and submit to Rufus, as their enmity was such that his Dao demanded to fight. If he bowed now, he would be ruined. His Dao Root would be crippled, he could sense that much in the deepest recesses of his soul.

He was trapped between a cliff and a wildfire, and only one option was left.

Will we really have to flee Earth... he asked himself, looking to the sky. *Fuck. I really don't want to...*

That had always been his last resort. There were teleporters and space travel. If push came to shove, he would take his entire faction and the gym apes and travel somewhere far, far away, where his enemies wouldn't find them.

That was such an ugly solution. He would have to leave behind so many people—Valville was huge, and he considered it under his protection. He would also have to uproot the gym apes from their home and take everyone on a desperate escape between the stars so harsh, that chances were they were all going to die. Jack himself might be strong on Earth, but in the wider galaxy, he was just a slightly larger ant.

But what else can I do?

The stars did not reply. Hints of pink already colored the horizon. Jack had been up there the entire night and still hadn't found a solution. The final round of the Tournament would start in just a few hours.

To be precise, he did know one other thing he could try, but it was improbable and came at great cost. Unfortunately, he was left with no other choice. He couldn't drag his people to their highly probable deaths without exhausting all other avenues.

Jack resolved himself to try.

He hopped off the roof, landing before his door and stepping inside. The warmth hit him like a pleasant wave and reached all the way to his bones. He would have sighed in pleasure if he wasn't so downcast.

Master Shol was there. He was gazing east through the large kitchen window, enjoying the rising sun. His ethereal form glowed with light, and his face had an unreadable expression. Jack hardened his heart.

"Master..." he said, stepping closer to the ghost.

"Hmm?" Master Shol turned around. "What is it? Did you enjoy your rooftop?"

Despite his heavy heart, Jack chuckled, only to turn serious again. "I have something to ask you, Master."

"Again? Fine. Ask away."

Jack looked into his master's eyes, though he couldn't read them. His face, marred by strict lines, was still hidden behind a hard beard. He looked harsher than he really was. He had already helped Jack a lot without asking for anything in return... and Jack was about to ask for more.

He gulped.

"I am enemies with the scions, Master," he began. "They come from the Animal Kingdom, and in the auction... I offended the strongest one, Rufus Emberheart, the leonine."

Master Shol raised a brow. "Offended how?"

"Brock threw a piece of poop at his chest. It left a stain. He was furious and struck out at me, but I blocked his strike in public. The Hand of God representative then kicked us out."

"I see. That is not good." Cogs were already turning in his mind. He probably suspected what Jack was going to ask.

"I feel that our enmity is now too deep to resolve peacefully. I have also defeated Gan Salin and Shard Presht, two other scions, who also hate my guts. I'm worried that, no matter what happens in the Tournament, they will attack me and my faction afterward."

"They will," Master Shol replied without hesitation. "And even if they don't, or if you somehow survive, the Animal Kingdom will come in a year. I already told you they are tyrants. They won't even bother with an excuse. They will just wipe your faction off the map."

A knot caught in Jack's throat. He'd suspected as much himself, but it had only been a hunch. Hearing his doom stated with such certainty ground his heart to dust. "They will?" he asked in a trembling voice. "What if I'm strong enough that they choose to let me live instead? That they forget about this enmity?"

Master Shol chuckled hoarsely. "The Animal Kingdom's power is hereditary. They are organized around lineages. In their eyes, a human like you could never compare to one of their star disciples, no matter how promising you are. In fact, given your enmity with them, you are more of a threat to eliminate than a disciple to nurture. Your entire faction will be culled as a show of force. It wouldn't be the first or second time they have done such an act."

"I see... But could they really just show up and slaughter us? Aren't there laws in the galaxy? What about the Star Pact?"

"The Star Pact deals with higher things, and it is not infallible. A titan like the Animal Kingdom can easily bend the rules against a small F-Grade faction." Master Shol turned back toward the window to admire the rising sun.

"The galaxy is a violent place where death is commonplace, and the Animal Kingdom especially is infamous for its brutality. Perhaps they wouldn't have acted over just the minor frictions against the canine and the sharken, but Rufus Emberheart is a different story altogether. He is a true noble and a rare genius, even to them. Make no mistake. They will slaughter you or suppress and herd you like cattle until he gains the strength to slaughter you himself."

Jack's heart practically tumbled out of his chest. This was the worst-case scenario.

"So, there's no way out," he managed to say.

"It depends. Unless you do something about it, you and all your allies are a lost cause. Do you have a plan?" Master Shol still looked at the window. Jack could only see his straight back and clasped hands.

"We can flee from the planet," Jack replied. "Except that would be so painful... Our primate allies would be uprooted from their homes, and I would have to drag my people through a perilous path. We might all die."

"Would you prefer to die at home?"

"No. It's just..." Jack gritted his teeth. "I apologize in advance, Master, but the Exploding Sun is enemies with the Animal Kingdom. You said it yourself that we are close to the border. If you could protect us, my people wouldn't have to die. Maybe..."

His words trailed off. He didn't have to say anything else. His master clearly got the point.

"No," Master Shol said, his voice even. "What you ask is impossible."

Jack's heart descended further. "But you're enemies, Master. If—"

"No, Jack." Master Shol turned around. His face was truly stern this time. "You do not understand what you are asking. There are rules in the galaxy, give-and-takes. You are telling me to make my faction pay a high price to save yours."

"The Animal Kingdom can break the rules. Why can't you?"

"Enough. You are speaking out of line." Master Shol's frown deepened as he scolded Jack. "Not another word. You are my disciple, and I will help you if I can, but this is too much. You receive my guidance and ask for even more in return? You ask me to sacrifice my faction to benefit yours?" He sneered. "Shameful.

"You have to shoulder the consequences of your decisions. I will help you get stronger and win the Tournament. After that, your people will have to run, and you can join them if you want, but it won't change a thing. Most of them will die, if not all. The galaxy is not a place for mortals, and you won't have the strength to protect them even in a year's time. F-Grade cultivators can't even teleport, Jack... Most of them won't even be able to run away."

This knowledge struck Jack like a sledgehammer. "They can't teleport!"

"Only E-Grade and above."

"But I teleported to the Tournament!"

"That was intra-planetary. If someone without a Dao-infused body tried to travel many star systems away, they would only arrive as a puddle of blood."

Jack stepped back. "No..."

"Yes, Jack." Master Shol's strict gaze held a hint of pity. "If you want to escape the scions, I can take you to the Exploding Sun as my disciple... but only you. The rest of your faction and allies will have to find their own way through the galaxy. Some might survive."

Jack gritted his teeth. "Master, I am begg—"

Master Shol had had enough. His eyes widened to the extreme. "Enough!" he roared, much like Vocrich had. Jack's vision was filled with a massive explosion greater than a mountain. He took a step back, cupping his ringing ears.

"I will not help you. I couldn't even if I wanted to. Only Elders have the right to invite subordinate factions, and I am a Deacon." Master Shol's intense voice cut through the ringing.

Jack opened his mouth to say something, but his master beat him to the punch. His hard eyes cranked as he barked out a harsh rebuttal. "Still you dare speak? Are you completely shameless? This is not how a disciple of mine behaves! Shameful! Shameful!"

The sound filled Jack's house, ringing in every brick and piece of furniture. Brock appeared from the basement stairs, looking around in fear and rushing to climb on Jack's shoulder. He narrowed his eyes at Master Shol and almost moved a hand to the base of his tail but stopped himself immediately.

"I—"

"Don't you *dare*!" Master Shol interrupted. "You have disgraced yourself enough. The sun is up. Go fight. And if you win, I will keep training you as honor demands."

Jack clenched his fists so hard his nails dug into his palms, and he lowered his head. "Yes, Master..." he said bitterly.

Master Shol didn't reply. Without another word, Jack took Brock and headed for the arena. His head was lowered the entire way, and his mind was submerged in dark thoughts.

I killed my people... he thought. *And I disgraced myself so fucking hard. Master Shol is right. I asked for too much, but what choice did I have? Fuck. Fuck!*

"Jack—" Edgar tried to greet him at the gates, but Jack just waved him away.

Do I really need to bow? Do I need to break my Dao to save them?

His heart burned as he crossed the town. Everyone got out of his way. And in his frustration, he did not notice that, from a window in the participant district, a pair of old eyes followed him the entire way.

CHAPTER SEVENTY-SEVEN

DAY ONE OF THE FINALS

JACK REACHED THE ARENA IN A HAZE. HIS MIND WAS FILLED WITH DARK thoughts, and he was torn.

Images of the professor's house on fire sprang uninvited. Valville being razed to the ground, five dark forms darting through the streets and massacring everyone in sight. He saw Harambe and the brorillas valiantly stepping up to protect themselves, only to get easily butchered. The light leaving their wide-open eyes as their blood stained the ground.

There has to be a way. He boiled inwardly. There has to be a way! Why do they have to be so cruel?

It made no sense. Why would they slaughter hundreds of people over a small disagreement? Were they *animals*?

He chuckled darkly. They were. It didn't matter. He refused to escape by himself while leaving everyone else to die. He would find a way or die trying. Worst-case, he would just beg for forgiveness and damned be the Dao.

Before he knew it, Jack found a random seat and sat down. He was surrounded by strangers who gave him a wide berth. Belatedly, he realized Brock was still on his shoulder, and he looked over with sadness. "I'm sorry, little bro... Though this is partially your fault."

Brock replied in monkey, but Jack didn't understand. He wished Brock could talk. At least he seemed appropriately sad.

While Jack was lost in thought, he didn't notice the crowd calming. It was only when the head judge's voice pierced the arena that he raised his cloudy gaze.

"People of Earth-387 and honored arena spectators, the final round of the Tournament is starting!" she declared excitedly, riling up the crowd. Jack only heard mockery and fakeness in her voice. "Starting today, the sixteen finalists will fight each other in elimination matches. There will be four rounds until the winner is decided. Four days of the best fighting this newly-Integrated planet has to offer."

The people cheered. Jack chuckled grimly. *Four days until the real war starts.*

"Without further ado, I will now announce the first round's pairings as produced by our randomizer. The first fight is Dorman Whistles and the Dao of Speed versus Brother Tao and the Dao of the Staff!"

The crowd cheered as the two fighters jumped into the arena.

"Amithaba, Brother Dorman," Brother Tao said, cupping his hands before his chest. "This will be my final day in the Tournament, but I am thankful to have reached this far. I have made my monastery proud. Let us make this a fight to remember."

"If you're strong enough, sure," Dorman said dismissively, settling into a fighting stance, ready to sprint in any direction. His daggers were poised as mandibles.

Brother Tao didn't take Dorman's disrespect to heart. He smiled—Dorman only respected the strong.

"Very well. Let's fight!"

The crowd cheered. He removed his weapon from his back and held it in both hands, clearly straining a bit. This was the black metal staff he'd bought in the auction, the one that weighed a thousand pounds. "I have to warn you, Brother Dorman," he shouted. "My staff is very heavy. If you let it hit you, you might die on the spot!"

"There is no way you'll hit me," Dorman replied with a smirk. Then, he charged.

Jack's eyes widened. This wasn't the movement Dorman had used in their fights. He sailed over the sand at times, then jagged randomly in every direction. He was fast for a bit, then slow, then fast again, like a worm stretching and compacting as it crawled. This must have been a skill taught by his master, the D-Grade worm.

Brother Tao spun his staff above his head, creating gusts that rose the nearby sand into a sandstorm that obstructed everyone's vision. Dorman dived right in. The staff fell like a mountain, but he dodged it easily as he delivered cut upon cut on Brother Tao's body.

Surprisingly, Brother Tao could wield the staff at decent speed despite its weight. He used its momentum to flow from one stance to the next, striking with both ends in a single uninterrupted movement. Unfortunately, this also made him predictable, and Dorman wove around the strikes with great ease.

In the blink of an eye, Brother Tao was bleeding from a dozen different shallow wounds. He had hard skin, as well as a regeneration skill, but Dorman was faster.

He couldn't deliver deep wounds, as that would require more time and might get him struck by the staff, but he didn't need to. He would inflict death by a thousand cuts.

It only took a few seconds for Brother Tao's regeneration to be overwhelmed. It reminded Jack of when he fought the earth bears, except Dorman's strikes were far more deadly. At least he avoided his opponent's vitals—probably on purpose.

"Falling Mountaintop!" Brother Tao shouted. His staff took on a dark red hue as it collapsed downward at great speed. Dorman jumped out of the way, reaching ten feet back before the staff even hit the ground, and that was a good thing because the strike was *heavy*.

The entire arena shook from the impact. Sand flew everywhere, the sound was deafening, and a large crack was formed on the hard rock underneath the sand.

Brother Tao slowly raised his staff. He cupped his hands. "Thank you for the pointers, Brother Dorman. This monk resigns."

Dorman smiled and nodded. "That final strike was dangerous."

The crowd cheered wildly. Even Jack found his mood lifted a bit at the sight of this battle. Both fighters retreated, and the head judge, who'd been hovering over the arena the entire time, announced the next pairing. "Fesh Wui and the Dao of Wind versus Vanderdecken and the Dao of Metal!"

The crowd cheered as both fighters took the stage. Vanderdecken raised his electric guitar and shouted, "Alright!" The crowd roared even harder. He stuck out his tongue and headbanged, playing a couple of grating notes on his guitar.

He was the crowd favorite for a reason.

Opposite him, the eagler landed gracefully on the sand. His humanoid body was covered in dark brown feathers, while his head was white, and his beak shone a radiant yellow, as did his eyes. Sharp talons adorned his feet, and unlike eagles, he had a pair of arms under his wings. There was something regal about him, though it was lacking compared to Rufus's majesty.

Fesh Wui spread his wings to a full ten feet. "I am coming," he said, then took to the air. He was the only Tournament participant who could fly.

"You are strong, but I fight for the DEVIL!" Vanderdecken shouted, playing a raging solo on his electric guitar. Though it wasn't plugged in anywhere, the notes physically jumped out, forming jagged black shapes that flew into the air to hunt down the eagle.

Vanderdecken's fingers danced on the strings as more and more notes appeared, and for a moment, he sounded like multiple musicians playing at once. "Six centuries ago..." he started singing. Jack couldn't stop a smirk from forming—he knew the song.

The eagler halted in midair and spread his wings. A strong gust blew out, distorting the notes and shattering them on impact. Vanderdecken created more.

"Gate One!" he shouted, powering up as he went.

Fesh Wui wouldn't let him. He dived down from the skies, talons extended to strike.

Suddenly, Vanderdecken's singing accelerated. His fingers blurred on the guitar, and the lyrics flowed out of his mouth faster than seemed possible. It was like someone put him on fast-forward.

"Fight! Fight!" He spat out half the song in a second. His guitar pulsed with green light, becoming a blur as a torrent of notes barreled for the eagler. Fesh Wui folded his wings and turned to dodge, flying around for another strike as a black gate appeared above Vanderdecken's head. It was transparent and barely visible but clearly there. It opened a tiny bit, letting darkness flow out.

With his current strength, that was the most he could open it, but it would hopefully be enough.

"AND DANCE WITH THE DEVIL!" Vanderdecken peaked his solo with a crescendo and a scream as the darkness formed into notes that flew after Fesh Wui, faster and stronger than all the rest. They chased him through the skies as Vanderdecken embarked on an epic guitar solo, supporting the high-power notes that crossed the air.

The crowd went crazy.

Fesh Wui reached so high that the head judge had to rush out of the way. He turned and cawed at the rapidly ascending notes. He flapped his wings thrice, forming strong gales that impacted the notes and weakened them. Moreover, the gales circled back to him, growing stronger with each flap of his wings until they became a visible force that descended like the apocalypse.

They reached the jagged black notes and broke them apart, twisting Vanderdecken's song into a discordant melody that made everyone plug their ears. Vanderdecken tried to play faster and recover, but Fesh Wui dived through the gap and reached him in an instant. His claws raked a deep gash across Vanderdecken's chest and broke his guitar in two, tossing him back with a cry of agony.

"Resign," Fesh Wui said as he hovered over the broken guitar. The audience booed so abruptly and intensely that even Jack was impacted. The eagler looked around in surprise.

"Why are you booing me?" he shouted. "It wasn't even nice music!"

"My guitar!" Vanderdecken cried out, ignoring the deep wound in his chest. He waved his hands. "Get off it, get off it. Shoo, shoo!"

"You dare treat me like a pest?" Fesh Wui's eyes narrowed.

"Resign!" Shouts rose from the audience, first one person and then a hundred. "Resign! Resign!"

Vanderdecken looked around as if lost, then his eyes flashed. "Right. I resign! Now get off my guitar, you beast!"

Fesh Wui snorted and flew away, retreating back behind the curtain that hid the scions from the rest of the spectators. Vanderdecken rushed to hug his guitar even as djinn healers showered him in green energy. Unfortunately, they could only fix him, not his instrument.

"How could he? How could he?" he shouted at the sky. "I swear revenge!"

"Yeah!" the crowd cheered again, wholly swept in Vanderdecken's tragedy. So what if half of them were E-Grade alien merchants and the other half were Earth's top dogs? A good show was a good show!

Man, this guy will become Earth's greatest superstar from now on, Jack thought, especially since the Tournament was televised across the planet. *Unless the scions kill him, of course.* He grimaced, his fists tightening. The nearby people glanced at him warily as a hint of his Dao aura escaped his body.

"The next fight!" the head judge announced when Vanderdecken left the stage and the crowd calmed down a bit. "Elena Richter and the Dao of Ice versus Rufus Emberheart and the Dao of Supremacy!"

Jack's eyes snapped to focus.

The leonine landed on the stage, gazing at the woman opposite him with apathy. She was a member of Ice Peak, one of his underlings. Jack hadn't seen her fight, but he knew she was an ice mage.

"I resign," she said immediately. The crowd showered her with booing. She didn't even look their way. Rufus nodded slightly and jumped back to his section of the arena. So did Elena.

Jack was disappointed. That was so anticlimactic.

The head judge announced the next fight: "Shard Presht and the Dao of Momentum versus Jack Rust and the Dao of the Fist!"

Jack looked up. He stared at the curtain that parted as the sharkman walked out and gave him a wary look.

Jack grinned. He smashed his fists together. This guy again... He just wouldn't stand down, but that was fine. He and the scions were already irreconcilable.

This was the perfect target to vent on.

CHAPTER SEVENTY-EIGHT

A BRUTAL BEATDOWN

THE IMPENDING FIGHT DREW JACK TO THE PRESENT. HE WAS FULL OF DARK thoughts, and the best way to get rid of them was to punch something hard and repeatedly. His Dao agreed.

Jack grinned as the shark-man landed in the arena. The nearby crowd cheered for him.

However, before jumping in himself, Jack had something to do. Reaching inside the white bag he carried, he removed a head-sized glass sphere shining with all colors of the rainbow. After the first one he'd purchased, he'd gone back and secured himself an edge. He crushed it between his hands—it wasn't really glass—and inhaled the colors. They smelled like lit tinder.

Level Up! You have reached Level 41.
Level Up! You have reached Level 42.
Level Up! You have reached Level 43.

The audience wasn't surprised by this, but they gasped as he took out another ball. Grinning, he inhaled that one, too.

Level Up! You have reached Level 44.

Level Up! You have reached Level 45.
Level Up! You have reached Level 46.

Another.

Level Up! You have reached Level 47.
Level Up! You have reached Level 48.

The last one.

Level Up! You have reached Level 49.

That was it. Jack closed his eyes and took a deep breath, then let his face split into a grin. There was no point in holding back the levels anymore. Every other finalist was at 49 already, and Jack sure didn't lack the fighting experience. He didn't need to bet anymore, either.

Forty-nine was the peak of the F-Grade. To level further, he would need to advance one of his Dao Roots into a Dao Seed.

Grinning, he surveyed his available free points and quickly allocated them. He followed Master Shol's advice on an 8-1-1 distribution between Physical-Mental-Will, but since none of the other finalists used mind attacks or anything like that, he leaned toward Physical a little more.

Name: Jack Rust
Species: Human, Earth-387
Faction: Bare Fist Brotherhood (F-Grade)
Grade: F
Class: Pugilist (Elite)
Level: 49

Strength: 119
Dexterity: 119
Constitution: 119
Mental: 12
Will: 12

Skills: Fistfighting (III), Drill (II), Pugilist Body (III), Parkour (II)
Dao Skills: Meteor Punch (I)
Daos: Dao Root of the Fist, Dao Root of Indomitable Will

Titles: Planetary Frontrunner (10)

One extra point would have made the numbers prettier, but it was what it was.

For the first time, Jack had increased all his stats at the same time. The ensuing euphoria overwhelmed him. His body burst with power at the seams, muscles tightening. His mind expanded and sank into a deeper level of worldly awareness as his willpower sharpened, ready to impose itself on the world and force it to obey.

Jack felt like he was ascending.

A moment later, the feeling was gone, but the power remained. His entire body buzzed and hummed with power. He clenched his fist. He was *strong*.

"Jack Rust, please proceed to the arena," the head judge instructed.

He only glanced at her then jumped. He landed with a hard thud against the rock-bedded sand, but his knees didn't even budge.

He raised a closed fist high in the air, and the audience cheered like crazy. Jack, too, was a crowd favorite.

He grinned, lowering his fist and staring down Shard Presht. "You again. You never learn, do you?"

"This battle will be different from last time," the shark-man hissed, crossing his arms before his face. He already wore his forearm-blade gauntlets. "Master has helped me a lot. My strength has increased tremendously."

"Too bad. So has mine. And I got more levels than you."

"I—"

Jack wasted no more time talking. His heels dug against the sand and he launched himself forward. The wind screamed in his ears, the crowd was a blur, their screams empowering him. His bare feet smashed against the ground with every step, taking him over the sand like an arrow.

He closed the distance almost instantly and smashed out a punch.

"Fin Sail Dance!" Shard Presht cried out, moving his hands so fast before his chest they were like a curtain of blades. If Jack tried to reach through it, his arm could be severed. "Touch me now, human!" Presht laughed.

Jack was unfazed. He planted a foot firmly into the ground before the shark-man, reared a fist back, rotated his body, and struck with all his strength. Shard's surety turned to disbelief.

Jack's fist came to a booming stop right in front of the curtain of blades as if hitting a wall. A *whoosh* filled the arena as the shockwave of his fist traveled through the air to explode in front of Shard's face, sending him flying backward with a yelp.

"Not enough," Jack tsked. He'd tried to make the shockwave *touch* Shard's face, but he still wasn't skilled enough with Drill. It didn't matter. It was good enough.

As he was flying back, Shard spread his fin-like forearm-blades and stopped his flight instantly. However, the moment he did, Jack's fist was there. It smashed hard into his face, sending him flying back again until he met a wall with a bang.

"You made the same mistake last time," Jack said, shaking his head. "You really never learn."

Scattered laughter came from the audience as Shard stood. A thin line of blood flowed down his chin, and one of his many needle-like teeth had been broken. His face was a visage of fury. He glanced momentarily at the curtain before turning his gaze at Jack.

"You will pay for this, human," he hissed.

"Less talking, more fighting. Come on."

Shard burst forth with instant acceleration, even faster than last time. His right blade cut out at Jack's chest, expecting a block or a dodge. Jack grabbed his arm mid-strike and leaped over it, then leaned back to avoid the other blade and spun in midair. Shard struck again, and though his Dao could give his attacks great speed, the same didn't go for his reflexes.

Not expecting Jack's abrupt Parkouring, he missed—and, as a result, left himself wide open.

In Shard's eyes, the world turned black. Only a purple meteor still held color, crashing down from the highest orbit and directly into his face. His slit-eyes widened. He tried to duck, but it was too late.

Meteor Punch.

Jack's fist smashed hard into Shard's face, sending a dozen teeth in the air and the shark-man himself flying like a broken kite. He slammed into the wall even harder than before, and all spectators cheered at Jack's display of strength—after all, Meteor Punch was a very flashy skill!

Jack landed on his feet. His hand was bruised but fine.

"I'm in a really bad mood today, sharky," he said, cracking his knuckles. "Please don't resign too soon."

Shard Presht looked up from the ground. His face was warped and even slightly indented where Meteor Punch had hit him. He gritted what remained of his teeth.

He was completely outmatched so far... but he still had tricks to show.

"Wind Swim!" he shouted.

He shot up, not rising to his feet, but taking to the air! His fin-blades spread like wings and he flew around at high speed, changing directions randomly. Jack's narrowed eyes followed him the entire time.

"Would you look at that," he said. "A flying fish."

Shard rose high and then fell on Jack, aiming for his head. At the last moment, his momentum disappeared, leaving him still above Jack's head to pummel him with slashes. His forearm-blades became a blur as he struck from above, an angle that Jack couldn't really defend against, and one that was especially close to his vitals.

Shard Presht held nothing back. His blades aimed for the throat, the face, anywhere they could reach. Jack slapped two strikes away before taking a slash to the shoulder, making him buckle and grunt in pain. Another came from his blind spot and headed for the exposed side of his throat—he ducked.

He kept going lower until he was squatting, and as Shard followed, Jack shot back up as fast as he could. A blade raked his entire back as he passed, drawing a line of blood, but he was sturdy enough to take the hit. He didn't even try to defend. Instead, he grabbed Shard's other wrist as he shot up, dragging him along in the air.

Shard's eyes widened. He tried to change his momentum, but his momentum was relative to his weight, and Jack could easily handle that.

Still holding Shard's wrist, Jack somersaulted twice in the air and spun Shard like a rag before smashing him face-first into the ground with all his strength. The shark-man gasped as all air was pushed out of his lungs.

Jack wasn't done yet.

Having never let go of Shard's wrist, he spun him around once more and smashed him into the ground again, then raised him and started smashing him to the left and right alternatively.

It was like a cartoon fight in real life, and that shit was brutal. Every smash rocked the arena and sent teeth flying. Stones and sand tore into Shard's body.

Shard gathered the last of his strength to resist, but grappled by a stronger opponent, it was hopeless. The most he could do was use his Dao to slow himself down and soften the blows.

"How does it feel to be bullied for once, fucker?" Jack yelled in rage. When he pulled Shard up again, he clenched his free hand into a fist and smashed it into the shark-man's face directly against his momentum, slamming his head into the ground so hard it bounced. He then punched him again on the way up, driving him down once more.

Jack released Shard's wrist and stepped back.

"Had enough?" he asked. "Surrender, or I might accidentally kill you."

He'd already vented. Now, this was just bullying.

Shard spat blood, struggling to stand. His arms shook under the weight of his upper body. "I... am... not..." he muttered, barely managing to get on his wobbling feet. He was clearly in no shape to continue.

"Come on, man," Jack said, extending a hand and stepping closer. "Don't do this."

Just as Jack approached, a sharp glint shone in Shard's eyes. He instantly shot forward, blade cutting directly at Jack's throat. From this distance, dodging would be very difficult if Jack didn't expect the attack—but he wasn't an idiot.

He ducked, letting the blade sail over him. His eyes hardened. He found himself crouched under Shard's extended arm, poised to strike. He clenched his fist.

The colors disappeared again. Shard's eyes opened wide in terror. "I—"

A purple meteor smashed into his chest from below with terrible force. Bones broke and blood flew as Shard Presht was launched upward like a missile, flying diagonally over the arena to crash into the curtain that separated the scions from everyone else.

The curtain collapsed from the impact, revealing a section the size of a tennis court with only five chairs occupied, as well as a screen that displayed the Tournament. Shard slammed into a wall and collapsed on a seat. Three djinn healers were already rushing to save him.

Rufus Emberheart was sitting with his arms crossed. His stormy gaze met Jack's as the curtain fell, exposing the scions to the world, and Jack stared right back.

Jack turned to the head judge, who was glaring at him. "What? I didn't kill him, and he clearly refused to resign. He even attacked me with intent to kill."

The judge's eyes were hard, but she did not speak.

"I win, right?" Jack asked, just to drive it in.

She nodded. He smiled.

"Thanks!"

His frustration vented, at least for now, he jumped back to his seat in the stands and high-fived Brock. Who knew punching fish was such a great way to let off steam! The healers were already working on Shard, so he would live. Jack hadn't hit him too hard.

However, the fight served to prove one point: humanity wasn't powerless. Jack had easily beaten one scion. If he could do that to Shard Presht… Could he dethrone Rufus Emberheart?

Whispers spread like wildfire as everyone wondered the same thing.

Jack was drawn out of his thoughts by a familiar form. The Sage sat beside him, his calm gaze taking in the arena. "We have all done well thus far. Don't you think, Jack?"

"Yea, I supp—"

"Next fight," the head judge declared, demanding their attention. "Edgar Allano and the Dao of Magic versus The Sage and the Dao of Divination!"

CHAPTER SEVENTY-NINE
A GRANDMASTER IN ACTION

JACK LAUGHED, TURNING TO THE SAGE. "I STILL CAN'T BELIEVE YOU REGISTERED *The* as your first name."

"Blame them for insisting." The Sage joined in his laughter. "Now, if you'll excuse me, I have a duel to attend to."

Jack nodded. "Good luck, may the best man win."

Edgar jumped off the stands and rode a blue cloud to the arena stage. The crowd cheered.

The Sage excused himself through the audience and reached the stairs. A few moments later, he appeared in the arena amidst kind laughter. Everyone knew him by now, he was just like that.

"Are you ready?" Edgar asked.

Jack could see the resolve in his friend's eyes, the tightening of his grip on the crystal-topped staff. He was handling the pressure well. The Sage, on the other hand, seemed nonplussed. His clothes were as ragged as ever, his teeth remained yellow, but his eyes were deeper than the ocean. As he stood there, under the cheers of thousands of people and the eyes of billions, he acted like this was another day in the park.

"No need, my friend," the Sage said, laughter still on his lips. "I resign."

The audience descended into silence before hushed whispers and less-hushed shouts erupted.

"What?" Edgar blurted out, surprised.

"I know the limits of my power. I cannot defeat you," the Sage replied. "In fact, I cannot even fight you. You would resist my charm, and then what? I am just a weak old man. I can't survive your magic. It's fine, it's fine. I simply resign."

The crowd booed a bit as Edgar shot the Sage a suspicious glance. Even Jack was surprised.

In fact, throughout the Tournament, nobody had seen the Sage fight. All he did was arrive at the arena and point at his opponent, and they would resign. When asked later, none remembered what happened. They described it as an incredibly frustrating experience.

The one time the Sage lost in the first phase of the Tournament—against Dorman—he'd resigned immediately as well.

"The winner is Edgar Allano," the head judge announced to a confused round of half-hearted cheers. Edgar reddened a bit as he flew back to his seat, while the Sage climbed up the stairs and again excused himself through the crowd.

Jack was sitting by himself—and Brock, of course—so he couldn't talk to Edgar, but he could imagine his thoughts.

At least he won, Jack told himself. That's an extra hundred thousand credits, plus the fame of reaching the top eight. He'll get his fight in the next round.

He refocused on the arena.

The next two fights were as impressive as the first ones. Besides the Sage, there were no duds in the finalists.

In one fight, Alexander Petrovic, the leader of Ice Peak, faced Sadaka, the second-in-command of Flame River. One was a hard-faced Russian man wearing a trench coat and gloves despite the pleasant weather. The other was a dark-skinned man wearing a red T-shirt and yellow pants in classic Flame River style.

The fight was impressive but short. Flames rose around Sadaka, shaping themselves as serpents. His hair and fingers caught on fire. He unleashed his full might at Alexander, who simply smacked his palms together. Alexander's movements were jagged, sharp, with no fluidity in them—like icebergs rubbing against each other.

A large wall of ice materialized before Alexander, at least a foot thick. The fire serpents tried to crawl around it, but the temperature was so low they shrunk and gradually disappeared. The audience felt the cold and hastened to put on their jackets.

Alexander then waved a hand and collapsed the wall on Sadaka's head. Sadaka burned like a torch, roaring as he melted his way through the ice, but Alexander was there. A massive ice pick hovered over Sadaka's head, falling and stopping inches before impaling him.

Sadaka met the Russian's glacial gaze, gritted his teeth, and resigned. The audience cheered.

The next fight was Vivi versus Dana Fray, the elef scion who used the Dao of Healing. She stood at nine feet tall and was surrounded by vivid green light that carried such power it made those who looked at it uncomfortable.

Vivi conjured two flame rivers and sent them rolling toward the elephant-shaped humanoid. She also summoned a third one, which she folded in the space between them to limit the elef's visibility. Unfortunately, the elef's spells weren't based solely on eyesight. Vivi screamed as she almost doubled over, her skin squirming as it tried to grow beyond its bounds. Doubtlessly, her insides were ravaged, too.

Jack's eyes took in Vivi's agonizing form, her tightly gritted teeth and clenched fists. He watched her wide eyes shake with pain and resolve, fighting back against the urge to resign. It was a grotesque, stomach-turning sight that made him wish the Tournament's televised version had some sort of gore filter.

Despite the pain, Vivi held. Her rivers of flame drowned the elef only a moment later, submerging her in blue fire, and a rough bellow left her trunk as her healing powers worked in overdrive to keep her alive. Her skin flailed and regrew, while the green aura struggled to keep the flames at bay.

Both women screamed. In the end, though Vivi's pain had started earlier, it was more manageable. The elef cried out her resignation, focusing all her power on defense as Vivi let the flame rivers dissipate. The djinn healers rushed in to help them both. Jack noticed that the green auras on their hands were fainter than the elef's. She was undoubtedly a top-notch healer that just wasn't suitable for one-on-one fighting.

The fight had been short but deeply disturbing, and Jack noticed Vivi shiver as she flew back to the stands, then collapsed in her seat. Sadaka and the rest of Flame River showered her with worry and praise, as did Edgar, who was sitting with them.

That said, seven of the eight battles had already been carried out, and only one remained. The audience buzzed.

"The final fight for today," the head judge declared. "Gan Salin and the Dao of Insanity versus Li Xiang and the Dao of Martial Arts!"

The crowd cheered. Jack's eyes narrowed. He was wary of old man Li Xiang. Throughout all his fights so far, only Edgar had been able to injure him a bit, and even then, Jack had a feeling that the old man hadn't gone all-out.

The two fighters stepped on the sands. Li Xiang took in Gan Salin with narrowed eyes. "Disgraceful," he scolded in a sharp Chinese accent. "Your kind belongs outside. This is our battle. You have no place here."

"Shut up, old man. I was born here, too. Can't you see my species?" Gan Salin replied, pointing at himself. He already wore his battle gauntlets that had a blade extending behind each finger like a cross between Wolverine and Scissorhands. He scratched his steel blades together.

Li Xiang took a deep breath, then adopted a battle stance. At that moment, he seemed like a force of nature. The lines of his body hid perfection, and his every muscle was exactly where it needed to be. His stance had no holes. Even Jack would be wary of approaching him. The audience grew quiet.

Gan Salin was the exact opposite of wary. He laughed, fell on all fours, and dashed.

"Canine Dash!" he cried out. "Five-Star Grasp!"

Xi Liang's eyes focused so hard it was visible. A small smile appeared under his long and thin mustache. He rapidly adjusted himself into what resembled the crane stance of kung-fu.

Gan Salin reached him. Attacks fell like rain. Blades slashed and fingers cried. Jack's eyes widened so hard they were about to pop out, as did everyone's.

Li Xiang was a grandmaster of martial arts.

His speed was inferior. So were his strength and durability. He was unarmed. His body was old and frail.

Despite all those, he held his ground through sheer technique. His hands moved slower than Gan Salin's, but they were always at the perfect spot. Every parry flowed into the next one. His feet moved in perfect tandem with the battle, his balance impeccable, and he shifted his body weight around effortlessly.

Gan Salin attacked frenziedly, his arms nothing but twin blurs, and somehow, Li Xiang held him back. It was like the old man was dancing alone or performing a solitary kata, while Gan Salin just happened to attack exactly where Li Xiang was poised to defend. The attacks flowed around the old man.

One fighter was playing whack-a-mole; the other, chess. And chess was holding its ground.

Gan Salin had charged, but Li Xiang hadn't taken a single step back. In fact, as the battle raged on, hundreds of strikes exchanged already, he was steadily taking steps forward. He was sneaking attacks as if his hand just happened to be where Gan Salin's torso rushed.

Most people hadn't even noticed these sharp jabs, but Jack had. And, of course, so had Gan Salin.

As much as the canine itched to dive into his opponent's guard and take two hits to deliver one, it was impossible. Not only did Li Xiang defend seamlessly, he was also perfectly placed to stop an infiltration at all times. If Gan Salin tried to force his way in at any point, he would just receive a barrage of attacks and have to retreat with nothing to show for it.

Gan Salin was no slouch himself. He had trained his martial arts under veritable masters. Moreover, his fighting style meshed flawlessly with the Dao of Insanity, a style designed to be unpredictable.

How could this old human counter everything so perfectly?

How is this possible! Gan Salin panicked. He had never felt more helpless in his entire life. He tried to accelerate, to focus on offense and ignore defense completely, to mix in double and triple feints with his attacks, but it was meaningless. Every single time he feinted, Li Xiang saw through it and sneaked in his own attack.

This is impossible!

"AAAAH!" Gan Salin screamed as he attacked even harder. *He has to make a mistake! He has to!* Foam splattered everywhere from his mouth. His eyes were red like tomatoes, and his body was spasming from the effort.

Li Xiang was simply watching, responding to everything with impossible precision, while simultaneously setting up his next moves. Gan Salin was trying to be as unpredictable as possible, but Li Xiang knew what he'd do next even before Gan Salin himself!

The strongest counter to insanity was consistency. Gan Salin stumbled. His body wasn't used to attacking frenziedly for this long with nothing connecting. He was almost cramping. His attacks weakened and slowed, leaving more gaps for Li Xiang to exploit. More jabs snuck in, some as fists, some as chops, and others like hard finger stabs. No attack was heavy, but they added up.

Gan Salin found his entire body sore and in pain. His limbs weren't responding properly.

"This is unfair!" he screamed in impotence. "You're cheating, old man!"

"This is the spirit of the world you seek to conquer," Li Xiang replied calmly, merging his words into his breathing. "Earth is great. Humans are strong. Next time, think twice."

Jack couldn't take his eyes off the fight. He was shivering.

The old man's advance had been slow but unerring, stretched over entire minutes without a single mistake or flaw. He merged multiple martial arts at once, leaping from one stance to the other like they were all parts of the same whole, and even inventing new martial arts on the fly like it was trivial. He always had the perfect answer for every situation. It was like playing rock-paper-scissors against someone who showed their hand after seeing yours.

He had no fancy moves, no active skills, no sky-high stats. His title was only the Planetary Frontrunner (100) version. He was just a grandmaster of martial arts.

"I want to fight, old man!" Gan Salin screamed again. "At least let me show off my new moves! I didn't posture like that for noth—"

Suddenly, Gan Salin's wrists passed by Li Xiang's hands at the same time. Li Xiang grabbed them both, turning the blades away from him, then used Gan Salin's momentum to pull both arms to the side, bringing their bodies close. In the same movement, he raised a knee.

"Uh oh," was all Gan Salin could say before Li Xiang's knee hit his chin hard, shaking his head and making his eyes fuzzy. He instantly lost consciousness.

Li Xiang didn't push the attack. He released Gan Salin's wrists and let him land on his back, then took two quick steps back.

Gan Salin recovered in the next moment.

"Huh?" he said, eyes blinking as they took in the blue, spotless sky through the arena ceiling. "Oh! The fight!"

He jumped up and looked around wildly, only to meet the old man's calm stare. "You lost," Li Xiang declared.

"What? I—"

"Gan Salin has been rendered incapable of fighting. Li Xiang wins!" the announcer's voice cut him off, and the audience cheered as Gan Salin looked up in incomprehension.

Jack smiled wryly. Gan Salin had been knocked out. Even if it was only for a second, the rules were clear. It wouldn't even matter if the judges cheated again and let them keep fighting—Li Xiang was clearly the stronger fighter.

Gan Salin's face soured. "I couldn't even show off my new moves," he said, pointing at Li Xiang. "Fuck you, old man. You should have died of old age mid-fight. Why does everyone keep bullying me in this Tournament?"

"Show respect to seniors," Li Xiang responded strictly as Gan Salin stormed away and back to the scions' section of the arena stands, where the curtain had been restored to its previous position by a djinn craftsman.

"With this, the first day of the finals is over," the head judge announced, drawing the crowd's attention. "The remaining finalists are: Dorman Whistles, Fesh Wui, Rufus Emberheart, Jack Rust, Edgar

Allano, Alexander Petrovic, Vivi Eragorn, and Li Xiang. The next round will be held tomorrow, an hour after dawn. We expect you all here!"

The audience roared with cheers and shouts of various nonsensical things. A merchant called for people to buy corn. Jack ignored those around him as he stood.

The remaining fighters were no joke. A few of them even brought him deep apprehension. He would especially hate to fight Rufus Emberheart and Li Xiang. Rufus Emberheart's strength was so deep it was unfathomable, and as for Li Xiang... Jack wasn't sure how he stacked up against the old man. Fighting him would be such a humbling experience that he'd rather not go there. It would make his own martial arts seem completely childish in comparison.

Then again, maybe that was exactly what he needed to advance his Fistfighting skill into a Dao skill, as Master Shol had instructed. Before that, he also had to advance his Parkour and Drill skills to the third tier. He was close.

And that meant...

Jack's eyes narrowed. Training. A ton of it. I can't fucking lose. And I must find a way to escape my impending doom, too.

CHAPTER EIGHTY
CRAWLING OUT OF THE ABYSS

DESPITE HIS RESOLVE TO TRAIN, JACK TOOK BROCK TO VISIT A SEASIDE CAFE—and not because he liked the coffee. A guillotine was hanging over his head, and if Master Shol refused to help, he needed to do something. With the light of day and his frustration vented, his thoughts would hopefully flow smoother.

An hour later, when Jack was nearing his house, he saw Vivi leaned against his gate. He grimaced. "Hey, Vivi. How are—"

"You understand how stupid that was, right?" she interrupted. "When I lent you most of my faction's credits, I bet our future on you. My reputation hangs on your actions. Don't be an idiot."

Jack sighed. Truth be told, he'd caught her eye more than once during the battles earlier, but he couldn't bring himself to speak with her. She was bold coming here like this—a trait he found endearing.

Brock stepped forward to take the claim, but Jack stretched out a hand, silencing him. "Can I make it up to you? Drinks tonight—they're on me." The invitation just rolled out of his mouth.

"After that shit show, they better be." She pushed off the fence, her hard stare softening a hair. "Nine o'clock."

"It's a date."

He watched her go, his thoughts now swimming between doom and intrigue. Entering his house, doom tipped the scales. He let Brock snack in the kitchen and headed directly to the basement.

"Good afternoon, master," he said. The old ghost was meditating on the treadmill, and he opened his eyes as Jack walked in.

"Welcome, disciple," he replied. "You won again."

"I did."

"And you are here to train."

"Mostly."

Their interaction was a bit awkward after the morning's altercation, but Jack felt glad for Master Shol's good heart. Though they disagreed on some things, and though Jack had shown great disrespect in Master Shol's eyes, he still continued to train him.

"I thought hard about my problem, Master," Jack began. Master Shol frowned in warning but didn't interrupt. Of course, Jack didn't intend to ask for his help again. "I have a few ideas on how to deal with things, but I would like your advice, if you don't mind."

Master Shol nodded. "Go on."

"We cannot escape, and we cannot find someone to defend us, nor can we convince the Animal Kingdom to let us be. Therefore, I only see three options. The first is for me to leave the planet and the faction, and for my faction to denounce me. Do you think that could work?"

"It might, but there is no guarantee. They could still be culled as an example. They'd have to leave your base and scatter around the planet to ensure they are not a target."

"Yes, that's what I had in mind."

Master Shol nodded. "Two more things. The first is a technicality. A faction leader cannot leave or disband their faction, except by death. Forming a faction binds you for life. You would have to kick all your members out instead."

Jack raised a brow. He hadn't known this information, but that was okay. It was just a technicality for now.

"The other thing is that you can't do that directly after the Tournament, or even now, before it's over. Your enemies are not idiots. They intend to wage war against you after the Tournament is over to prove they don't need the Animal Kingdom to fight their battles for them. Moreover, they certainly have people keeping an eye on your faction. If you try to scatter them now, they will be hunted down. Some will escape, but many will die. Unless you want to take that risk, you should first wage war against the scions, defeat them, and *then* leave the planet and scatter your faction before the grace period is over."

"I see," Jack replied, nodding. He had his alliance, and so did the scions. Fighting the third world war was dangerous, but it didn't sound like he had a choice. He just had to hope his allies were in for it. "That sounds complicated."

"Only if you can't kill them."

Jack looked up in surprise. The casual look of his master, like he'd said nothing special, shook Jack to the core. It really drove home just how brutally violent this new world was.

"I see," he replied, weaker than before. "The next option I had in mind was similar. I leave the planet after the Tournament—and after defending my faction, as you said—but this time, I return with a big-ass starship, shove all my people in there, and travel to far-off lands. But I don't know how space travel works. Do you think it's feasible?"

"Unlikely," Master Shol said. "You probably refer to starships similar to what your cryptic friend bought at the auction. Those aren't meant for space travel. Reaching even the closest star system would take centuries. These ships are just meant to travel around a planet faster, as well as access the satellite bases that some high-grade factions build. At most, you can use them to explore neighboring planets."

"Oh," Jack deflated. "So, the only way to meaningfully cross space is teleportation?"

"There are other ships, too. If you can reach the D-Grade, you can use space-warping starships that can cross great distances in the blink of an eye. In theory, you could use one of them to transport your entire faction to the Exploding Sun constellation, but reaching the D-Grade in a year is... highly unlikely. Not to mention buying a ship like that. Their prices are astronomical."

"Hmm." Jack frowned in thought. "What if I found a D-Grade immortal with a space-warping starship to ferry us?"

"Also highly unlikely. Not impossible, mind you, merely improbable, and it includes the risk of being at that immortal's mercy. Most D-Grade immortals don't even have ships like that. I don't. Do you really think you can win a world war and become close friends with a high-level immortal in less than a year?"

Jack grumbled. Highly unlikely my ass.

"You could maybe buy a service like that," Master Shol continued. "However, it would include selling your soul and body to the lowest bidder, and you'd probably get cheated anyway."

"Okay."

"Is there a third option?"

Jack couldn't tell whether Master Shol found this amusing or heartbreaking. He clenched his fist. "Yes. After the Tournament is over, we go to war and exterminate the scions, the Ice Peak, and all their allies. We make the entire planet our accomplices. What's the Animal Kingdom going to do then? Nuke the planet?"

Master Shol's gaze told him everything he needed to know.

"No way," Jack said breathlessly. "They would actually nuke the planet!"

"There are always bigger fish, Jack. And where there's bigger fish, there's a need for examples. The Animal Kingdom never takes losses."

"Fuck me..."

"Exactly." Master Shol finally stood, dusting off his phantasmal orange robes—needlessly, of course. "Take heart, disciple. As you said, there are ways, and I'm proud that you thought of them yourself. They might be ugly, but in the end, everything depends on your own strength. If you can reach the right heights, you will protect your people. If not, they will die. So train hard and win this Tournament. You can consider your next steps after that."

Jack clenched his fists harder. That's right. In the end, I just have to get stronger. I'll figure out the rest when the time comes.

"Thank you, master. Your advice has helped me extremely."

"It's a good thing you understand gratitude a bit better now," Master Shol replied, making Jack grimace. He hadn't forgotten about that. "Then, let's get started. Your skills won't advance by themselves. Go Drill."

At least he was a good person.

"Yes, Master," Jack replied. He grabbed a practice target from the steadily dwindling heap, anchored it to the wall, took position where his punching arm came two feet short, and started punching.

He went at the task with a single-mindedness that surprised even himself. Despair and helplessness drove people to their limits, and Jack wasn't an exception. Under the pressure of the scions and the Animal Kingdom, he was forged like a sword, and his potential was violently drawn out.

Master Shol watched wordlessly from the side.

An hour later, Jack managed to break the target twelve times in a row. His fist crossed the air, and the punch traveled beyond where his fist stopped, exploding directly on the target and blasting it to smithereens.

"That's good enough," Master Shol said. "Move another foot back. When you can reliably break the target from that distance, we will move on."

Jack complied, taking a step back. His fist crossed the air, shooting out shockwaves that came up short. He only used his good hand for now, as getting used to the feeling was the important part. Once he had it down, learning to use the other hand as well would be a walk in the park.

Over the next three hours, he managed to break the target a few times, but he was far from 100 percent accurate. His punch fizzled out or exploded midway most of the time. Jack kept trying, despair infiltrating his psyche. After all, he might face Rufus in any round. He had to advance as fast as possible.

"Enough, enough," Master Shol said. "You have already practiced this enough for today. You are now mindless like a toad. Let's move to Parkour."

"Yes, Master," Jack replied obediently, suppressing his urge to keep punching. "Say, Master," Jack asked as they walked to the other room, "how strong do you think I am, compared to the other fighters?"

His master thought for a moment. "The remaining eight of you are all roughly at the same level. Only the leonine scion is a cut above the rest, and your friend Edgar is a cut below."

Jack grimaced at the sound of Rufus's strength. Even his own master praised him. "Edgar is trying really hard," he said to defend his friend.

Master Shol gave him an odd look. "I know. His strength might be slightly lacking right now, but haven't you noticed?"

"Noticed what?"

"His talent is exceptional! Reaching this level was a given for *you*, but that Edgar fellow had to fight for every inch he walked. When he arrived at this Tournament, he was so weak I didn't even take notice of him. Suddenly, he's in the top eight. Maybe luck played a part, but it doesn't change the fact that nobody has improved more than he has, and he doesn't even have the benefit of the Frontrunner titles like the rest of you little monsters.

"He had nothing special compared to any other participant at the start, no unique advantage to give him an edge, yet he stood out brilliantly. That is the very definition of talent. Moreover, his state of mind is wonderful too, and his Dao is rare and powerful. His future potential is no less than yours. No wonder that lizard took him in as a disciple."

Jack was surprised by this torrent of compliments for Edgar. He knew these things, of course, but hearing Master Shol praise someone so excessively was a new experience.

Jack felt proud for his friend. "Yeah, Edgar is like that," he said with a genuine smile. Not a hint of jealousy was in his heart.

Master Shol gave Jack a deep glance, then nodded. His face, that had been hard and expressionless since their morning fight, softened imperceptibly.

"Many of you are talented, actually," he said after a moment. "It is rare for scions to participate in an Integration, as discovering an inhabited planet before the System is like looking for a needle in a haystack. However, when it does happen, they usually blow the rest of the competition out of the water. That is not the case here. You, Dorman Whistles, Xi Liang... You are outliers. Dorman Whistles is from the same paste as you, and Li Xiang is extremely gifted at martial arts. If he wasn't so old, half the immortals would have fought over him. A shame, really."

"It's the scions' fault for messing with Earth," Jack said with pride.

"I guess it is... And then, there's that Sage fellow. Even I can't see through him."

Jack stopped and turned to look. "You can't?"

"I can't. Something is off about him, though I can't put my finger on it. I guess he's perfectly suited for the Barren High—almost too perfectly. That's the faction his master is from. A remote group of ascetics that are famous for their prophecies. People come to consult them from across the galaxy, even the illustrious B-Grades, and they hold great sway in this constellation. They're also very secretive and mysterious."

"Oh yeah, he fits like a pea in a pod." Jack nodded. "He strikes me as a good guy, though."

"I didn't say the opposite. He's just... more than meets the eye." Master Shol looked down for a moment. "Anyway. Parkour."

Jack opened the door to let his master pass, revealing the sparring room filled with gym equipment. On the other side, Sparman opened his eyes.

"Welcome, master and master's master," he said. "I am ready for another six breathtaking seconds with you, master."

Jack had disliked this robot at the start, but now, he was growing to like it. Compared to the desperate struggle that permeated this Tournament, Sparman's casual smugness was a breath of fresh air.

"One day, Sparman. One day..." he said, then settled into a running stance. "Catch me if you can."

"With pleasure."

They darted around the room, playing tag. They zoomed from end-to-end, one moving up, down, around, or through gym instruments, and the other just dashing with little technique but great speed. Jack maneuvered at the edge of his skills, only narrowly dodging Sparman's open hands every time.

Whenever he was caught, they took some distance from each other and restarted. Master Shol watched for some time, then got bored and walked back to the other room to keep meditating.

Hours passed.

Sparman's open hand slapped Jack's back, sending him rolling into a wall. Despite that, Jack had a big smile on his face. "Thirty seconds!" he yelled with pride. "That's a new record!"

"That's what she said," Sparman replied in a deadpan manner. "Congratulations, master."

Jack gave him a weird look. “How are your jokes getting even worse?”

“I’m adapting to you, master.”

Silence stretched. Jack was the one to break it. “Well, I got to thirty seconds, anyway. My skill upgrade should be just around the corner. By the way, Sparman, what time is it?”

“Eight thirty, master.”

“Eight thirty? Shit! Thanks, Sparman. See you!”

Jack waved goodbye to Master Shol—who was still cold at him, if endlessly helpful—and rushed upstairs. He had a very important appointment at nine o’clock, and he really shouldn’t be late.

After all, he owed Vivi a drink.

CHAPTER EIGHTY-ONE

DATE NIGHT

Jack rested at the entrance of the participant district, leaning against the side of the open gate. He wore a dark blue buttoned shirt—taut over his wide shoulders and bulging muscles—and light brown pants, while his hair was tidy, and his shoes polished. Not by him. He'd just found them in a cupboard.

He stood there with his arms crossed, gazing at the setting sun and letting his mind wander.

I don't have a cellphone, he realized, having at some point left it tucked away. Wow. I can just... stand here and do nothing. What a wondrous feeling. It's so much better than being buried in a screen.

Idle time was necessary for the mind to relax and think. If a person was constantly busying themselves with one thing or another, and if their downtime was occupied by mindless scrolling, when would they think about their lives, realize what they were missing, and set a direction for themselves? They would just be drones.

"Hey," a gentle voice distracted him from his thoughts. "Hope you didn't wait long."

"Only fifteen minutes," Jack replied with a smile. "Barely a blink."

Vivi smiled. She was radiant. A red dress hugged her body and reached to her flat shoes, while her hair was done in a ponytail that fell between her shoulders. She wore no makeup that Jack could see.

"You look good," he said.

"Thanks. You too. Thank God neither of us has to carry a weapon. It would ruin the look."

Jack chuckled, leaning off the gate. "Shall we?"

"We shall."

They walked into the city side-by-side, drawing many looks. Merchants stared, and the humans of the city gave them side-glances. Whispers spread where they passed.

"Who do you think they're looking at?" Vivi asked. "You, or me?"

"Both, probably. You're beautiful, and I'm a superstar." He cursed inwardly the moment he finished speaking, understanding what he'd said. Vivi gave him a slightly disappointed look.

"I don't think that's the only reason they're staring at me..."

"I know. I didn't mean it that way... Sorry. I just wanted to pay a compliment."

She took the comment in stride.

"You *are* a superstar," she said, her expression unreadable. "First, you spank Earth's best, then you punch a scion, dominate the auction, and openly antagonize the baddest person around. And *then* you punch the same scion again, only harder." Her eyes smiled a bit at the last part. "I didn't expect you to be the brutal type, by the way."

"You know I follow the Dao of the Fist, right? What else could I be?"

"I thought you were a big, kind softie under your macho look. You know, the type that would show mercy and only use his fists to protect himself and others. Guess I was wrong."

Jack considered her words, then shrugged. "This is no place for games. The world is hard, and so is my fist."

She gave him an amused look, unable to hide the smirk on her lips. Jack smiled back, raising a brow. "It's too early to reply to that, Jack Rust," she said. "However, I have to admit that your understanding of the world is a relief. As odd as it may sound, many people here don't understand the gravity of the situation. We have been plunged into an eat-or-be eaten world. If we don't eat others, we will be eaten ourselves."

"Tell me about it... To be honest, I was a bit harsh on that fish because I had frustration to vent. Do you know that the Animal Kingdom are tyrants who will oppress and exploit us to no end? At least, so I've heard. After my stunt in the auction, they will probably massacre my faction as an example."

"I've heard the same from multiple reliable sources," Vivi replied casually. "It's not the end of the world. You can run away before the grace period ends. The teleporter is open."

"But many of my people will have to stay behind."

"You said it yourself, Jack, the world is harsh. And unfortunately, we are too weak to do anything about it right now. Maybe your people will be spared."

He looked at her. Her lips were clenched, and her large brown eyes stared right ahead.

"What's your plan?" he asked.

"What choice do I have? I must protect my people. I will do my best in this Tournament, then submit fully to the scions. Anything else would be a death sentence."

"And what if there was another way?" he asked seriously.

She met his stare. "I would fight to my last breath... but you'll need to convince me it's doable, Jack Rust. I won't risk my people's lives for nothing."

"Yeah. I understand." Now wasn't the time to talk about this. First, he'd decide on his path, then ask others to join him.

They lapsed into silence for a while. The colorful town passed them by, with its white walls and blue window shutters. The night breeze was chilly, though their high stats kept them warm, and the stars overhead were beautiful, only slightly obscured by Integration City's night lights.

Many people walked around them. Some were alien merchants: djinns, lycans, ifrits, and kovans. It still amazed Jack that he walked past people with four arms and hopping on one leg like it was normal.

Most of the passersby were human. They walked in small groups, all dressed sharply and talking excitedly. The novelty of an alien town hadn't worn off even after two weeks, giving everyone the energy to explore it fully. The only thing holding them back were the exorbitant prices of the nightlife here, where a simple drink could go for ten credits, but that was only a constraint for the relatively poor.

"What do you think about this place?" Jack asked, motioning with his head at a seaside bar. It was placed directly on the edge of the island, where the platform dropped nine feet into the sea, and wooden walls shielded it from the town's noise and lights.

It was simply called "Night Sea."

"You buy, mister. You can choose any place you want," Vivi replied coyly, and Jack nodded, walking into the bar with her behind him.

Inside the Night Sea, the illumination was discreet—mostly candles—and the music was low and calm. One entire wall was missing, giving way to the sea, and only one in every five tables were occupied. Jack surveyed the place, taking in the slightly crowded bar before spotting a small round table right by the open water. He headed over, then waited for Vivi to take a seat before he did.

"Charming," she commented.

"Always."

A candle was lit in the center of their table, with the sound of its whooshing flame only matched by the gentle crashing of the waves below. The low, soul music came from speakers on the walls, adorned with the logo of Philips on the side. The aliens were either embracing Earth tech, or didn't want to pay the fee to bring their own.

"I like this place," Vivi said. "I like the sea."

"Is there a seaside in Burkina Faso?" Jack asked.

"Your geographical knowledge amazes me," she responded dryly. "We're a continental country. Only rainforests and desert winds as far as meets the eye. I didn't see the ocean until I was eighteen."

"Hmm... How was life back there? If I'm not intruding."

"Why? Because I'm African and you'd expect me to be a starving, uneducated farmer?"

"No."

She waited, but Jack didn't add anything, only looked at her leadingly. She chuckled, then her eyes darkened. "Unfortunately, most people *are* starving, uneducated farmers. Things are shit. I was lucky to have well-off parents, which allowed me to study in Egypt."

"Really? What did you study?"

"English literature... but you know, in the end, it wasn't my calling. I love my country. After I graduated, I came back and became a tour guide for any poor tourist who found their way to the jungle."

"Sounds interesting."

"It wasn't. Most people expected me to sleep with them for ten dollars." She shrugged. "Which wasn't a bad offer given my country's financial situation, to be honest, but I luckily didn't have to worry about money. Can you believe they would spend more to buy a random stone from the jungle than to sleep with a woman? Tourists can be so dumb and disgusting at the same time. At least they bring money."

"This sounds even more interesting, but I take it you didn't like your job."

"It was decent... but I prefer the System. The apocalypse found me in the jungle, which became a dungeon, which quickly caught on fire because some fucking tourist had seen a documentary on how to rub stones. And you'd think a rainforest would be safe, but no, because: fucking magic.

"I buried myself in the soil and covered myself with a wet towel to avoid the flames. I was the only survivor. That's how I got my first Dao Root. Then I worked hard to clear the remaining dungeon, leveled up, returned to civilization, gathered a large group of fighters, and led them to destroy the country's dictators. I am effectively the leader of a nation now."

She took a deep breath. "And that's my life story in a nutshell. What about you?"

Jack took a moment to respond. That was a lot of information to digest. "So, I've gone out with the equivalent of a president?"

"We are more important than presidents now, Jack. The world's changed."

"I see. No wonder you seem so assertive. You're badass."

She smiled.

"Well, my story is much drier," Jack began. "I lived in an orphanage with a lunatic director until I was seven. Was adopted by a couple of professors, grew up, studied biology, then got a PhD—almost. I still have to finalize a couple details, which probably isn't happening anytime soon, given that the world has changed."

Vivi chuckled. A lycan waiter arrived then, well-dressed and discreet.

"I would like a whiskey, please," Jack ordered. "Double, no ice."

"Make that two," Vivi said. Jack glanced at her. She shrugged. "What? A girl can drink."

He laughed. The waiter thanked them and walked away, then Jack continued his story.

"But all the studying and working, all that life, it never filled me, you know? Not the way that punching stuff does. I love the thrill of a battle. The System tore away my shell and revealed my true self, and for that I will be ever grateful. It took a fucking dungeon spawning in my face for me to find my true self."

"Have you ever considered the possibility of all this being mind control?" Vivi asked. "Maybe you didn't discover your true self—you were changed by a god that speaks in nerd."

"I've thought about it, but I don't think so. Why me, of all people?"

"Because you were in a dungeon?"

He shrugged. "I've always been an adrenaline junkie. I never acted on it, but I remember that nothing made me feel alive like danger. When I was fifteen, I fell down some stairs, and I still remember how the world slowed down and I angled my descent perfectly to bounce down as harmlessly as possible. It was fucking amazing. That's the only memory that comes close to the thrill I feel when I battle."

"Why?" Vivi asked curiously. "If you knew you loved that feeling, why didn't you pursue it?"

"Because I was stupid. I was always busy with one thing or another, or I just couldn't be bothered to lift my ass off my chair and go to the boxing gym."

"At least it all worked out in the end."

"That was luck. What if the apocalypse hadn't come? I would have wasted my life away. The thought keeps me up at night sometimes, and I cannot believe how fucking lucky I got." He paused at that. Something about Vivi made him open up. "I'm not sure I deserve this."

"You deserve this on the basis of your strength," she replied calmly. "The apocalypse did come, and you exploded with such momentum and potential that you put everyone else *on the planet* to shame."

"But why me? I was a fucking loser."

"Don't beat yourself up, Jack. Just because you didn't make all the best decisions in the past doesn't mean you can't become someone great in the future."

The waiter returned, placing two drinks before them. They thanked him. Jack thought about Vivi's words, rotating his whiskey and taking the first sip. "I guess you're right. It's just hard to compare myself, an average joe, to people like you, who ran an entire revolution the second they had the power to do it. The most I did was befriend monkeys."

"You're biased, Jack. I am not the person you think I am," Vivi replied. Jack looked outside his own head and saw her gazing at the horizon beyond the sea. "Don't think I'm someone great. I am just like you; everyone is just like you. I just did my best to survive, then happened to get powerful and find myself in a community of hardened warriors who looked at me as a leader.

"And if you must know, I made so many mistakes during my revolution. We lost dozens of proud men for no reason, as well as thousands of civilian lives. People were tortured. I made wrong call after wrong call, I showed weakness time and time again, I hesitated, and we nearly got obliterated. We won not because of my leadership, but because we were strong to begin with. The only reason I still lead is because I respect everyone and everyone respects me, but I sure as hell didn't deserve it at the start, nor could I manage it."

She was still lost in the distance, the light sea breeze pushing a strand of hair away from her face.

"Don't beat yourself up," he said. "Just because you didn't make all the best decisions in the past doesn't mean you can't become someone great in the future."

She glanced sideways at him, smirking. "Wise words."

"Always. But really, the world is a mess, and nobody is perfect. We just improvise all the time and do our best. Everyone makes mistakes. You just don't see it from the outside."

"Do you think they will ever forgive me?" she asked, her voice softening. "All those people who died because I messed up... All the warriors who fought under me and watched me fail... Do you think they will ever see past that? Or do they all pity me in silence and wish I would just leave? Are they simply settling for me until a real leader comes along?"

"You *are* a real leader, Vivi," Jack said, grabbing her hand on the table. "One of the best on the planet. You are brilliant, and you did great. You won the war. And if anyone judges you, know they would have fucked up ten times as hard."

She looked up at him with surprise, then smiled playfully. "Hard this, hard that... Does everything have to be hard with you, Jack Rust?"

"We'll see." He laughed, squeezing her hand softly before pulling back.

"Thank you," she said. "I needed to hear that."

"Yeah... Me too."

They smiled at each other, locking eyes. The night passed far too quickly. Their conversation lightened, exchanging stories from their childhoods and anecdotes about their System days—they had more of the latter than the former.

The moon rose. Their drinks were emptied and refilled as conversation flowed freely. They laughed a lot, teased each other at every opportunity, and their legs kept accidentally brushing under the table.

"You are a fascinating man, Jack Rust," Vivi said, crossing her arms and leaning forward. The waning candlelight danced on her dark copper skin, her wide smile was carefree, and her cleavage supported on her forearms gave him a run for his money to keep his eyes above her neckline.

Jack noticed that the music had gotten slightly louder as most people had left the bar. "Wanna dance?" he asked.

"Sure!"

They left their drinks aside and stood next to their table, slowly moving left and right. Jack wrapped his arms around her waist. Vivi wrapped hers around his neck, touching the back of his hair. Their fiery gazes interlocked.

The minutes bled together.

"Do you kiss as well as you dance?" he finally asked.

"Even better."

Jack pulled her closer and locked his lips with hers.

He hadn't kissed someone in half a year. It was far better than he remembered. Was the System amplifying his senses, or did he and Vivi have chemistry?

He didn't know and didn't care. He let himself sink into the kiss, savoring every moment. They lost track of time. When they recovered, the bar was empty, and only the kovan bartender was left, wiping clean glasses behind the counter.

Vivi chuckled. Jack said, "Sorry man, time flew. We'll get going."

"Not a problem," the kovan replied. "Take your time."

"You know... You do kiss pretty well," Vivi said, leaning on his arm as he paid the tab.

"Heh. So do you."

"So. Your house or mine?"

He looked into her playful eyes. "You do know I'm an expert spanker, right?"

"Oh, trust me, I do. That's how you got me in the first place." She winked.

Jack laughed. Guess all that practice won't go to waste after all!

"My house is difficult. I have a monkey and a ghost," he said.

"I have three nosy war veterans."

"Well... I guess the monkey and ghost can have an overnight workout in the basement. I'm sure they'll love it."

She smiled sweetly. "I'm so glad we don't need sleep anymore."

"Let's just hope we don't fight each other tomorrow," he replied, planting a soft kiss on her lips.

She giggled. "I'd kick your ass," she taunted.

"You wish. I'd spank yours."

"A spanking won't take me down, mister."

"Clarification: I'd Meteor Punch the shit out of your pretty face."

She feigned shock. "You'd punch a frail, little woman?"

"I'd punch anyone. I'm an equal-opportunity ass-whooper, and you're neither frail nor little. You're the most Amazonian-looking woman I have ever seen."

She giggled again, leaning closer to his ear and whispered, "Wait until you see me without clothes."

Jack grinned. "I can't wait."

CHAPTER EIGHTY-TWO

BIG PACK, BIG BRO

THE MIDDLE OF THE NIGHT FOUND BROCK RUSHING OVER ROOFTOPS AND jumping from house to house. He landed a long leap, then did a tippity dance in celebration before continuing. The big dog bros who hid on the rooftops looked at him with disinterest, so he ignored them back.

Brock was happy because he had food!

Big Bro had arrived with a Big Sis and told him to go elsewhere. Brock didn't understand that. They would just mate, right? What was the big deal?

But Brock was a good bro, so he listened. He wouldn't betray his Big Bro's trust again like the time he threw poop at the Big Bad Evil Bro. That was the previous Brock, the child. He was now a new Brock. A true brorilla.

He smashed against a lighting pole and kept his body close to it, easily weathering the impact. The Big Thought made his muscles strong. He then slid down the pole and walked into the darkness between two buildings, where the stink of fish and rotten food was invasive.

His little bros came out of hiding. They were five dogs, with one black and larger than the others. When he'd first met them, they'd been starving, and weak. Their ribs showed, and they attacked without restraint.

Now, they were bros.

The five dogs surrounded Brock, each leveling him an even stare and nodding. Brock nodded back. The dogs then flexed their muscles. Two rose on their hind legs to show off their chests, two others clenched their front legs and neck, and the last dog flexed her neck muscles and barked so hard that a human from a nearby house yelled at them to reproduce.

Brock didn't understand humans sometimes.

Regardless, he dropped his bag of food and flexed back. His bulging muscles were now clearly visible through his brown fur. Thick veins crisscrossed his skin, which was hard like stone.

The dog bros made faces of astonishment at his impeccable pecs—as they should. Brock then proceeded to give all of them a firm handshake, accompanied by a gaze and nod they bravely returned.

He unloaded his bag of many foods and let them feast. Salami was torn to pieces, cheese flew left and right, sausages were cracked down the middle, and roast chickens were eaten to the bone. The largest of the dogs carefully picked up the juiciest steak and deposited it at Brock's feet.

Good, he thought, grabbing the steak and devouring it in three large bites. *My little dog bros have learned respect.*

All the meat was raw, but that was fine. It simply helped them workout their stomachs. As his Big Thought dictated, all muscles were important, even the invisible ones.

Their meal finished, Brock gathered his dogs around him and inspected them. They were strong now. Not as strong as he was, obviously, and they didn't have Big Thoughts, but it would be enough.

Brock had a plan.

He couldn't keep feeding these dogs from Big Bro's food. He now realized this was disrespectful. If he wanted to have little bros, he ought to take care of them himself. Even better, teach them to take care of themselves.

They couldn't steal food, as that might create more trouble for his

Big Bro, and Brock refused to shame himself again like that. No, they couldn't steal. But there were more avenues to food.

Namely, garbage.

The dogs had already been feeding on trash before he met them, but they weren't too good at it. That was why they were so weak and skinny. Brock would now teach them the way.

He banged his chest and screamed at the sky to encourage his bros, who barked loudly themselves. It worked, of course. More humans shouted weird things at them, and one even threw a shoe from a window. Brock plucked it out of the air, sniffed it, then made a face as he pinched his nose and threw the shoe right back at its owner.

There came a crashing sound.

"What the—" A head poked out of the window, gazing with wonder at Brock and his little bros, who were already exiting the alley.

"Damn aliens..." the man said, shaking his head and returning to bed.

Brock led his little brotherhood through the streets, searching for a suitable target. He found it three alleys down. A large, green garbage bin twice his height and many times as long.

The dogs looked at him in confusion. They could smell the food inside, but they had long learned they couldn't get it. The lid was closed!

Brock gave them a monkey smile, reached up to grab the edge of the lid, then lifted it. The little bros looked at him like he'd just turned the sky pink.

He repeated the motion a few times to be sure they got it. They would have to figure out a way for the dog bros to do this themselves, but Brock was confident they'd manage. They were working out, after all.

Brock was aware that disturbing the town like this might bring complaints to his Big Bro, but he also understood that his little bros needed to eat, and there was no other food around. If anything happened, Brock would handle it, and Big Bro would understand. Bros shouldn't expose their bros, but they also shouldn't shy away from the correct course of action.

Brock knew that because he had strong brain muscles.

"What's all the—"

Two men rounded the corner, both stumbling as if exhausted from too much working out despite their large bellies. Brock could respect that. Therefore, the moment he noticed them, he turned sideways, grabbed his wrist with his other hand, and flexed his biceps to greet them as fellow bros.

The two men—both humans—froze.

"What the hell is that?" one stuttered out.

The second man had eyes bulging wide. "Well, I'll be damned. Are those strays? I didn't know Integration City had strays."

"Strays? That's a bloody monkey!"

The two men were shocked, undoubtedly by Brock's large muscles. He grinned smugly. He had a rough sense—one of those invisible muscles—for how strong a human was compared to him, and he could tell that, despite these two humans being larger than him, they were on the same level of strength.

Compared to Big Bro, Metal Bro, Very Big Bro, Father, and now Big Sis, it was a welcome breath of fresh air.

"They're eating the rubbish... Should we shoo them away?" one of the men wondered.

That was a big mistake. Brock's gaze instantly switched from respectful to challenging as he turned his head to stare straight into the man's eyes. He cracked his knuckles and started beating his chest to intimidate them.

If they wanted to harm his little bros, they would have to go through him.

"That thing's level 10 and Elite!" one of the men spoke in gibberish. "I ain't bloody going."

"Me neither! Let's go, mate."

The two men scampered away, no doubt scared shitless by Brock's stare. His eye muscles were pretty strong, after all. He trained them on what Big Bro called a mirror.

Brock turned around with a proud smile, but stopped midway. His eyes, properly worked-out as they were, had caught a glimpse of something. He squinted at the entrance of an alley and could barely make out a tiny white cat staring at his feasting little bros. Its little eyes held a mixture of fear and intense desire. Brock noticed that the cat was also skinny to the point its ribs showed.

That will not do. No cat bro shall hunger.

He grabbed a piece of meat from the spilled garbage—the non-humans threw away a lot of food—and waved it at the tiny white cat. Hesitantly at first, then boldly, the little animal darted out of the shadows and came to nibble on the meat. Brock caressed its dirty fur, though the cat tensed, it let him.

He nodded. This bro was tiny, but it had good manners. It would make a good addition to his little pack.

Wait! Brock realized. He must have had bright muscles inside his head because he could have sworn his eyes shone. *If there is one cat bro... are there more? And other dog bros, too?*

He thought back to the town's size, and how all his five dog bros had been huddled together into a tiny corner. He jumped on a rooftop and inspected the layout of the town, all the way to the sea, where the sun was about to rise.

He grinned. Big pack, big bro.

Jack awoke to a naked Amazonian sprawled on his bed. The sun had barely glimpsed over the horizon, but his alarm clock was unerring.

"Mm? Good morning," Vivi said. She rubbed her eyes, lifting her upper body from the white sheets. "What time is it?"

"Six."

"What!" She jumped up like a cat. Jack admired her form as she hastily grabbed her clothes from where he'd dumped them on the floor. "Are you serious? We're late!"

"What are you talking about? There's still over an hour before the fights start."

She struck him with a glare. "I envy your life, Jack Rust."

"What?"

Vivi got dressed quickly while he continued to watch her from the bed. Her previous glare turned into playful exasperation. "Like what you see?"

"Duh."

"Well, enjoy it while you can. Who knows when the next time will be."

"Hey, I have to train too, but there's always time to let off steam."

"For you, maybe... but I'm so busy. You can't imagine how hard it is to run a faction AND a country—even if I've dumped most duties to a representative."

"Amateur move. Just find a skilled person to handle everything and you can be carefree like me. Management is the devil."

"I *am* the skilled person, Jack." She rolled her eyes, plopping back on the bed to plant a kiss on his lips. "I'd love to go another round, but I have to go. It really was great last night. I hadn't had such fun in... God. I don't even know how long. And I don't mean just"—she motioned at the bed— "this. I hope you understand I don't have the time or energy for a boyfriend right now, but... let's do this again, okay? I like you."

"As long as we don't die," Jack replied cheerfully, then winked at her. "I like you too."

"Great. See you in an hour, Jack. Good luck today!"

"Same to you."

And with a final kiss, she was gone. Jack stayed in bed for a little longer, going over last night in his head. "What a nice girl..."

His adopted father had once said that the best girls kept things simple. Thinking back, he was probably right. Jack's story with Maria had been long, difficult, and complicated, and it still didn't go anywhere. With Vivi, it just... happened.

Simple is good, complicated probably isn't worth the hassle. Unless it is. Damn. And here I thought I'd got it.

He jumped up, got dressed, and left the bedroom. He didn't see Brock anywhere, but Master Shol was there, gazing at the rising sun through the wide kitchen window like he did every day.

"Good morning, Master," Jack said respectfully.

"Morning, disciple. Good luck today."

"Thank you."

With that, Jack proceeded to the kitchen to have breakfast.

Their relationship had chilled significantly after yesterday's altercation. Perhaps they would get over it eventually. But for now, though it saddened Jack, he also felt a hint of satisfaction deep inside. Master Shol had his reasons, but in the end, he'd chosen to let Jack's faction die. Jack couldn't easily get past that, the same way that Master Shol apparently couldn't get past Jack's disrespect.

Both had their own views, and that was fine.

At least Master Shol taught Jack as heartily as before. He was a man who devoted himself wholeheartedly to teaching a stranger even when their views differed on some things, and Jack respected that deeply.

He opened a cupboard to find food—meat had become his go-to—and couldn't hold in his surprise. "Just how much does Brock eat?" he exclaimed. "I swear, the equivalent of a week's meals disappear every night."

"Little Brock is growing quickly. The food goes to a good cause," Master Shol replied with a small, rare smile.

"I guess. If he already eats as much as a grown brorilla, I'm looking forward to his growth spurt."

"The girl is kind, by the way," Master Shol commented, looking back at the rising sun. "It's a shame no immortal chose her. If you find the chance, tell her that her two Dao Roots are enough for now. She should focus on developing a full set of Dao skills while meditating only on the Dao Root of the Flame. She should make that one into her Dao Seed, not the Dao Root of the River."

Jack threw him an appreciative look. "I will, Master. Thank you. When should *I* start working on my Dao Seed, by the way?"

"When you have enough insight. You know the cycle of experience and introspection. You are in the experience phase. When you gather enough wisps of wisdom, you will know, and that will be the time to start meditative introspection. For now, focus on Drill and Parkour. You are approaching a breakthrough."

"Yes, Master." Jack bowed in thanks. Master Shol nodded. "Have you seen Brock? We should get going now."

"He is rushing over as we speak. You will meet him at the district's gate."

"Great. Thank you, Master."

Jack grabbed a loaf of bread—he had no time to eat or he'd miss his daily appointment with Edgar—and rushed out. As Master Shol had said, he saw Brock the moment he arrived at the gate of the participant's district. The little ape was rushing from the opposite way, toward Jack's house, and slid to a halt when he saw Jack.

"Hey there, buddy," Jack said, noticing the empty sack that Brock dragged along. It still smelled of food. "Where did you go? To eat by the sea?"

"Jack!" Edgar called out, approaching. His face had a big smile. "Right on time."

"You too, man." Jack smiled back. "Why so happy?"

"I developed a Dao skill just an hour ago!" Edgar replied excitedly. "It's—Oh, wait. I shouldn't tell you. Maybe we'll have to fight each other."

Jack laughed. "Good call. I'm looking forward to seeing you in action. Let's go."

With Brock in tow, they crossed Integration City along the familiar route to the arena. Jack also whispered his nightly adventures to Edgar, who said, "Dude, nice!" and high-fived him.

They were adults, and these things were not taboo. Sharing the information with their friends was natural.

Together, the three of them reached the arena and climbed to their usual spots. Jack and Edgar were the first ones there, as they were half an hour early—it wasn't common for both of them to be on time. They watched the arena fill up with a background of light chatter, and their allies arrived too.

Jack greeted Vivi with a bright smile, which she returned. He also relayed his master's advice to her. The other members of Flame River gave him a smile and a nod, which he also returned.

Soon, the arena was packed full again, and the head judge took to the sky.

"Today marks the second day of the final phase," she declared in a loud, magically-enhanced voice. "We will see four brilliant duels that will reduce the participants from eight to four. As always, the pairings will be randomized. I shall now announce the first fights."

The scroll she held glowed blue as the randomizer—whatever it was—got to work. Jack watched with rapt attention. Honestly, almost everyone remaining was a beast. He was more confident against some people compared to others, but there was one person he really didn't want to meet: Rufus Emberheart.

Jack had matched the leonine's strike in the auction, but Rufus's attack had been hasty and from a distance, while Jack had used a full-power blow. Truthfully, if they met now, Jack had little confidence in winning. Even more truthfully, Rufus would probably annihilate anyone he met. The other seven participants were playing Russian roulette.

The scroll finished glowing, and the head judge announced the day's first fight. It was Jack, and he wasn't fighting Rufus.

"Jack Rust and the Dao of the Fist versus Edgar Allano and the Dao of Magic!"

CHAPTER EIGHTY-THREE
MAKING MAGIC

EDGAR STEPPED INTO THE ARENA UNDER THE DEAFENING CHEERS OF THOUSANDS of people. System-enhanced lungs thundered with roars, feet stomped on the wooden stands, and the constant din of conversation flowed underneath the rest of the noise, difficult to perceive but always there.

The cheers hit Edgar like a warm wall of humidity entering a marsh. The sun came immediately afterward, shining on his eyes and making him shield them, while the sweat-filled breeze of the arena blew into him along with grains of sand.

Two weeks ago, Edgar would have been overwhelmed. Now, he just gulped.

This pressure wasn't something you could get used to this quickly. You either had it in you or you didn't, and Edgar didn't, but he tried his hardest anyway. By now, he could stand it.

He walked deeper into the sands, approaching the center of the arena. The cheers intensified as he conjured two mana birds and sent them spinning through the air in recognition of the crowd's fondness.

Jack Rust stood opposite him. His bare chest glinted in the sun, his wild eyes stared Edgar down like a beast of prey, and his nonchalant hands were ready to smash Edgar's face apart. Under the cheers of thousands of people and the eyes of billions, Jack seemed nonplussed, like this was another day in the park.

He smiled and nodded. Edgar did the same.

"We finally meet on the sand," Jack said. "Are you nervous, Edgar?"

His voice shouldn't have reached through the clamor, but the arena had some magical sound enhancement going on. Not only could Edgar hear him, but so could everyone in the audience.

"A bit," Edgar admitted, chuckling. His glasses shone under the rays of light, and his messy dark hair was ruffled by the breeze, as were the cyan wizard's robes he wore. He tightened his grip on the crystal-topped staff. "But don't let your guard down, Jack. I'm here to win."

That was meant more to himself than Jack, but the crowd didn't know it. They cheered in response to his taunting—though it wasn't anything spectacular.

Edgar waved his staff around and summoned three balls of condensed mana around him. At the same time, he let his inner mana spread out of his body and into his surroundings, imbuing the air and sand to make it easier to manipulate later. His master, the lizardman archmage, had taught him many tricks. Edgar's strength had risen meteorically.

And yet, Jack remained as tall as ever. He simply cracked his knuckles. Suddenly, Edgar felt an aura of brutality blanketing the entire arena and suffocating him. He'd seen Jack fight. He was a beast in man form, a relentless, unstoppable machine of pain, a towering, invincible behemoth.

There was a mental component to Jack's fighting style. Anyone who saw him fight shivered at the thought of facing him. His last battle against Shard Presht, that brutal, merciless beatdown, had especially driven the point home.

Edgar's knees went weak and his breath quickened. His concentration faltered momentarily.

Jack Rust was a monster.

A monster that Edgar would tame.

"Come, Jack!" he shouted to embolden himself. His entire body flared with blue light. The air around him warped from power as reality bent to his will. His eyes and mouth spilled magic.

Opposite him, Jack grinned. "Oh, I will." Then dashed forth. His legs hammered at the sand. Edgar suppressed a pang of fear as he sent an opening salvo Jack's way. A flock of two dozen birds materialized—pigeons with sharp talons, made of blue wind. Each of these was equivalent to a level 15 beast.

They fell into formation to face Jack. Their flight patterns interweaved, making them unpredictable.

Jack grinned as he stopped and adopted a boxing stance. His left fist darted out faster than Edgar's eyes could perceive, unleashing a series of jabs that blew birds apart like they were made of foam. His punches reached beyond the physical length of his arms, shooting down birds from a couple feet away.

Edgar gritted his teeth. He knew about Drill, but he didn't expect that Jack could use it so well. His birds had attempted to surround Jack, but only half remained. He sent them into a kamikaze attack, diving at Jack with talons extended. Both his arms blurred into strong punches, annihilating the swarm with ease.

Two birds managed to reach him, but their talons only left superficial scratches that closed before Edgar's eyes.

His opening salvo had been destroyed, but he never intended to defeat Jack with it, anyway. Its role was to gather information and scout out his opponent's current capabilities.

This was how a wizard battled. Efficient utilization of resources backed by higher intellect. Scouting, feints, defense, analysis, attacks, and killing blow. To a wizard, a battle was a highly intellectual affair. Much like chess.

Edgar's flock had completed its assignment. His mind took in the skills Jack revealed, analyzed his movements, and formed a simulation. A dozen different scenarios played out in the blink of an eye for how Jack would fare against a combination of different attacks.

The solution was clear: he had to limit Jack's mobility and attack from below, where his fists would struggle most to reach.

Fortunately, Edgar had many weapons in his arsenal, including the perfect one for this situation.

As Jack charged again, his face still brimming with confidence,

Edgar's mana flowed into the sand. In the blink of an eye, fifty small sandstorms—sand devils—danced around Jack's feet.

Jack's eyes narrowed. Edgar saw the calculations running within his mind. Stepping hard into the sand, Jack jumped, only to smash head-first into a blue wall Edgar had already conjured over his head. It'd been small enough that it was outside the range of Jack's eyesight.

Jack collapsed to the ground as the sand devils swarmed him. The arena's sand was already harder than normal, and Edgar's magic enhanced this property. The sandstorms rotated at high speed, grating their caltrop-like grains against Jack's exposed skin.

Jack shouted in pain and fury. His arms blurred as he punched down faster than the eye could see, but the sandstorms were resistant to blunt damage by nature. They were a great counter for his skills.

Jack's body tightened. A renewed aura of violence erupted, sensed only by the Dao. His two Dao Roots pulsed together, revving harder, like train engines, as Jack embraced the deadly juggernaut that he was.

Edgar buckled down. The real fight was starting.

Jack ignored the sandstorms and rushed forward. He wisely didn't leap through the air, as that would make him an easy target. His legs were bleeding as the skin was flayed off them, revealing red muscle tissue underneath. His speed was noticeably impacted, but he was nowhere near falling.

Edgar felt a shot of guilt at the pain he was inflicting on his friend, but it was part of the battle.

He tried to conjure energy walls before Jack, but they took time to form, and a well-placed punch was enough to rip through them. This tactic could only work in Jack's blind spot.

The sandstorms were slower than Jack, but they were many, and Edgar had placed them between himself and his opponent. Jack had to wade through a field of pain. Hopefully, his muscles would be injured enough to overwhelm his regeneration. If that happened, Edgar would win.

Unfortunately, Jack's skin was beyond tough. It was like trying to cut a tree with a razor.

Jack fell into a full-on sprint. He was a bull. Red eyes, manic fury, and the promise of excessive violence once he caught up. Edgar retreated as fast as his legs could carry him, but he was nowhere near fast enough.

Thankfully, he never planned to rely on his speed. Blue light reflected off his glasses, and his dark hair rose as a torrent of mana left his body—he was already down to 50 percent, but this could be the end.

The arena's rock floor rose vertically before Jack, forming a thick wall and tossing a few sand devils on his upper body. The wall blocked Edgar's sight. At the same time, a tightly-packed formation of wind-birds appeared in front of the wall, ready to ambush Jack the moment he broke through.

Edgar couldn't see it, but he felt a meteor appear on the other side of his wall. The colors and sounds disappeared, like the final moments of life before a natural disaster strikes you head-on. Purple flared around the wall's edges.

An explosion rocked the arena. The rock wall shattered on impact, sending fist-sized stones flying everywhere. Edgar cursed and hastily conjured a shield to block, but his birds weren't so lucky. The stone fragments tore them apart. All sand devils near the point of impact were blown away.

Jack flew through the destruction, his legs deeply wounded but healing. Edgar's killing blow had been utterly annihilated.

Seeing Meteor Punch used on someone else was a grave underestimation of its power. When Edgar faced it directly, even by proxy of his magic, it was a true natural disaster. A meteor crashed down from orbit. What was he supposed to do against that!

Before Edgar could fully understand what happened, Jack was already closing in. One Edgar instantly became nine—eight were illusions—and they scattered in all directions. Rock rose, sand flew, the wind formed into birds. Fireballs flew out of every Edgar in rapid succession as glimmering dots of multi-colored light brewed in their hands.

Edgar threw a menagerie of attacks at his friend. Jack roared and crashed into them like a freight train. He was going all-out now. Birds disintegrated, sand scattered, rock shattered. Jack was a flurry of blows tearing through a flood of magical attacks like an unstoppable, invincible fist.

Jack was a monster, and Edgar could only delay the inevitable. Terror clawed at his chest, but he pushed it down.

Fireballs smashed into Jack and burned his skin, they entered his lungs and blistered his insides, but even that wasn't enough to stop him. He stampeded forward with his fists held high and his eyes staring straight at Edgar. Two fists tore through the faces of two mirror images, a sign of what would soon happen to the real one, amplifying his terror.

For the first time, Edgar realized that Jack might not be wholly conscious of the mental warfare he was waging.

However, Edgar hadn't reached this point by being a coward. He'd entered the Tournament as one of the weakest participants. His every battle had been an uphill struggle. He worked harder and more efficiently than others, he spent the entire day watching fights and taking notes to form counter strategies against every opponent.

He pushed on through the Tournament, capitalizing on every advantage he could get. He refined his magic again and again, maximizing his power. He surpassed others every day, clawing his way up the ladder of power. Every bit of his soul had been devoted to this task since the System's arrival, and he only barely made it through every choke point.

Meanwhile, Jack steamrolled through without a care in the world.

Why couldn't it be me?

The thought had been bouncing around in Edgar's head since the very start. Jack deserved what he had, but so did Edgar. He just hadn't been as lucky. Everything he had came from sheer hard work.

Bitterness gripped his heart.

However, Edgar was the master of himself. The world was unfair. He wouldn't envy his friend.

But he sure as hell would try his hardest to win, no matter how invincible or terrifying Jack was. Fate was in his hands. He would just beat the odds again.

Jack plowed through Edgar's attacks. He was unstoppable. Attacking like this was a waste of Edgar's mana, so he stopped. Jack tore through two more mirror images in an instant.

The remaining five Edgars tossed their dots of condensed, multicolored mana that had just finished forming. He thought Jack would dodge. The madman just grinned and punched one of them—the right one. Edgar hurried to jump back, but it was too late.

An explosion rocked his world, breaking his glasses and making his ears ring. He was plastered against the ground, all mirror images broken. Without his glasses, he could just barely make out Jack's mangled hand and blackened wrist. Jack roared through the pain, but his eyes remained clear. He still had another hand, and Edgar was out of options.

"Game over," Jack said. Edgar noticed that his opponent's hand wasn't regenerating—was it because he'd used a skill containing his Dao? Did the Dao skill interfere with anything?

If only he knew sooner...

Edgar crawled backward and to the side as Jack approached and loomed over him. "Resign. You fought bravely, but this is over."

"I—" Edgar gritted his teeth. His remaining 20 percent of mana evaporated. His fake despair receded, revealing triumphant eyes. "Quintus Convergius."

Jack's shock revealed he understood that he'd fallen into a trap. His entire body tensed. Mana filled the air. The dispersed wind and sand glowed, the hints of fire shimmered, the broken rock rumbled, and the large bottles of water Edgar carried under his robes trembled.

Elemental mana traveled all over.

The crystal atop his fallen staff shone with ethereal light and launched a beam at Jack. It was fire, water, earth, wind, and sand, all at once. It carried the strengths of all five elements simultaneously, combined into a beam of elemental power that could blast through steel walls.

The laws of physics protested. You couldn't just combine different things like that. It was illogical. It made no sense.

It was Magic.

Jack had been caught unprepared. There was no time to dodge. His good hand was ruined. The cyan beam flew over the fallen Edgar and reached him in an instant.

All colors disappeared, but the beam remained cyan. A purple meteor fell from orbit and met it head-on.

A blinding explosion rocked Edgar harder than before. His vision swam. His ears bled. The shockwave pushed him into the ground until his bones cracked. The elemental particles in the air danced in disarray.

Jack had been sent flying. He skipped off the ground twice, then smashed into the back wall. From where he lay, Edgar could only hope it had been enough. That Jack was unconscious.

Such just wasn't meant to be.

Through the dust and sand, Jack rose. He wobbled a bit. Both his hands were mangled now—he couldn't punch if he wanted to. But he was standing, and Edgar was not.

"Fuck," Edgar whispered, letting his upper body fall again. He faced the bright blue sky. He had lost, but he'd challenged and held his ground against Jack Rust. The strongest human of Earth.

A grin formed on his lips. He proved himself worthy. He wasn't just another loser. He had done his best, and that was enough.

"I resign," he croaked out.

The crowd erupted into the loudest cheers he'd ever heard, and Edgar lost consciousness with a smile.

CHAPTER EIGHTY-FOUR
A CONTEST OF SPEED

As Jack watched the healers pour green energy over an unconscious Edgar, he marveled at how close the battle had been.

Truthfully, he'd walked in expecting it to be a walk in the park. He walked away with two broken hands, several cracked ribs, many superficial wounds, first degree burns, and entire chunks of skin missing on his legs. Plus, the pain of all those combined.

You little fucker, he thought, watching Edgar regain consciousness. He grinned. *Well fucking fought.*

Granted, things would have been a lot easier if he hadn't underestimated Edgar, but that sort of mental warfare was also part of a battle. All in all, this fight had been the closest he'd come to losing.

The djinn healing Jack stopped, having completed her duties. He was now good as new.

Note one, I must befriend a good healer, he thought, admiring how all his injuries had disappeared. He flexed his fingers. And note two, my regeneration struggles against wounds produced by Dao skills.

Edgar stood, thanked the healers, and approached Jack. "Shit, man," he said with a smile, "you kicked my ass there."

"You did a number on me, too. Sorry for the glasses."

"No worries, I have spares." He extended a hand. "Win this thing, Jack."

Jack gripped his hand. "I damn will."

The crowd's cheers reignited—they were still amidst the arena, after all.

Both healed, Jack and Edgar took the stairs and squeezed through a congratulatory crowd to reach their seats—Edgar was too exhausted to fly. They were greeted by a wave of congratulations for a battle well-fought.

"I was very impressed, Edgar," Vivi said. "To think you were asking me for advice only two weeks ago. Now, you could give me a run for my money."

"I'm not there yet," Edgar replied, blushing. "My final attack only worked because Jack didn't expect it."

"But it did work. Mental warfare and the element of surprise are crucial in every battle. Don't undersell yourself."

Surprisingly, even the usually silent Dorman approached Edgar. "I underestimated you," he said with a bright smile and an extended hand. "You are not a weakling. I respect that."

"Thanks," Edgar replied awkwardly, shaking his hand.

Jack had been congratulated by everyone, too, but discreetly. He took his seat between Edgar and the Sage and accepted Brock's firm handshake.

"That was a nice battle," the Sage said.

"Thanks, Sage. Any unsolicited words of wisdom?" Jack asked.

The Sage chuckled. "Your faction is very lucky to have you two. Did you notice? You were strong from the moment you arrived at the Tournament, but Edgar had to fight for every inch of ground. He has advanced tremendously. I really wish I could see him grow into his potential."

"Hmm?" Jack frowned. "Why? Are you planning to leave the planet?"

"Maybe, maybe not. Only the future will show."

"Ah, of course. The future."

Jack reclined back in his seat, content to watch the rest of the battles. Since he'd already advanced, he wasn't worried anymore, so he could enjoy them.

"The next fight," the head judge announced. Dorman and Vivi tensed. "Dorman Whistles and the Dao of Speed versus Fesh Wui and the Dao of Wind."

Dorman grinned. "Finally!" he exclaimed, jumping into the arena.

Jack leaned forward. This would be the highest-level battle of the Tournament so far. Both fighters were roughly on his level of power.

Dorman landed without raising a single grain of sand, his daggers already out. Fesh Wui flew down from the curtained-off section of the arena. He was unarmed, but the talons he sported on both hands and legs were more than sharp enough.

"I've wanted to face you for a while," Dorman said, brimming with fighting spirit. "Speed versus wind. Let's see who's faster."

"You're an intriguing opponent," the eagle-man admitted with amusement. "I do not believe I'll lose against a human, but it will be a worthy fight. You might even give me the final flash of insight I'm missing. Do your best, smoothskin."

"Back at you, duckface."

Dorman charged. At the same time, Fesh Wui flapped his wings and shot up. Dorman screeched to a halt, then tsked. "That's annoying." He couldn't fly.

"Dance of the Gales!" Fesh Wui shouted from above. Winds picked up around the arena. The sand rose and flew in low-altitude streams, while many spectators held on to their hats to keep them from flying.

The sounds of crashing winds filled the arena. Gusts and gales zigzagged in random directions over the sand, crashing into each other. They followed profound patterns and natural laws that seemed completely random to laymen. It was a chaos that only Fesh Wui could navigate.

And navigate it he did.

As the winds tossed and turned, a hundred gales that never stayed constant, the eagle-man merged into them. He flew left and right, up and down. He was always at the right place at the right time for errant winds to guide him.

On the sand below, Dorman narrowed his eyes and adopted a fighting stance with both daggers raised.

Fesh Wui cut circles, constantly coming lower. Most people could only see a blur. He was threatening to attack at any moment.

Until he did.

He came crashing down, talons poised to strike. Dorman reacted instantaneously, redirecting the blow and striking back. In the blink of an eye, both fighters had received light cuts, and Fesh Wui was back in the air.

"Interesting!" he cawed. "Let's see how long you can last! Storm of Talons!"

The winds intensified. Fesh Wui's speed increased. He circled over Dorman's still form like a lightning bolt without pattern or warning. The strikes were near-instantaneous and terribly dangerous, and it took all of Dorman's concentration to react in time.

The winds kept picking up. Fesh Wui's strikes became sharper. Though he sported several cuts and ripped feathers himself, Dorman was in worse shape. Blood drenched his tight clothes in places, and more flowed from a deep cut on his forehead, blinding his left eye. Without it, Dorman lacked depth perception, and that only made the situation uglier. However, he wasn't discouraged.

"Oh yeah?" he shouted in rage. "I can run, too!"

Suddenly, Dorman became a blur himself. He couldn't fly, but he moved around the arena floor at blinding speed, zigzagging at random. He was a flash that moved from one end of the arena to the other without rhyme or reason. Moreover, he used the worm-like movement that alternated between being slow and fast without a set pattern, and he even occasionally darted sideways as if leaping at prey.

It would be more difficult for Fesh Wui to hit a moving target.

But it was a challenge he welcomed. The two fighters disappeared between the winds and sands, becoming two streaks that occasionally clashed in flashes of steel. They exchanged dozens of strikes in a few seconds. The spectators cheered, even though most couldn't tell what was happening or who was winning. Even some E-Grade merchants couldn't tell.

Jack could. His high stats helped him keep track of the fighters. They were roughly equally matched. However, as the seconds passed, Dorman found himself on the back foot more and more. His left eye inhibited his depth perception, disorienting him just enough that Fesh Wui could seize the upper hand.

Of course, Jack knew that Dorman still hadn't revealed all his abilities, but it wasn't difficult for Fesh Wui to infer that, too. Almost everyone had an active skill.

The critical clash came unannounced. It was one strike amongst many. Jack barely caught the signs. As the two of them were about to collide, his gut whispered that something was different.

A spark of electricity flashed between Dorman's daggers. They snapped forward like an insect's mandibles, accelerating more than should be possible and aiming to cut off Fesh Wui's extended legs. They were wreathed in lightning and boomed like thunder.

Fesh Wui reacted just in time. Two blades of wind shot out of his legs, from just behind the talons, so highly condensed they could be seen by the naked eye. They headed for Dorman's daggers. If the blades of wind blocked the daggers, as Fesh Wui clearly intended to do, Dorman wouldn't have time to reposition, and he would be pierced clean by the talons.

But Dorman had another ace in his sleeve.

Mid-skill, he activated another. His speed shot up tremendously as Fesh Wui slowed in his eyes. He went on overdrive, putting the rest of the world in slow motion. He jumped and rotated. The talons only scratched his side, inflicting deep but manageable wounds. The wind blades missed his daggers, which turned vertically instead of horizontally.

The lightning snap carried on, and the daggers crossed each other in the base of Fesh Wui's left wing, cutting it clean off without slowing in the slightest. Fesh Wui's momentum carried him forward, but missing a wing, he could only drag against the sand until he came to a halt.

These all take time to describe, but they happened so quickly, if Jack had blinked, he would have missed the entire exchange. Most people didn't understand what transpired. They only saw them clashing like every other time, a momentary flash of lightning, and then Dorman was standing with his arms straight out and crossed at the wrists, while Fesh Wui screamed on the ground.

"I resign!" he cried out in blind panic. "Heal me! My wing! My wing!"

The despair in his voice was such that even Jack felt a hint of pity. The djinn healers practically flew into the arena to help him, ignoring Dorman, who'd fallen to the ground and panted hard with obvious injuries.

A healer grabbed the wing off the ground and pushed it against the stub, while the head healer—a djinn with three question marks in place of a level—chanted as she pressed her hands to the wound. Three more healers touched her on the shoulder, transferring green energy from their bodies to hers.

Muscle and sinew tied together. The process was slow. Then the lead healer was left kneeling on the ground, panting, while Fesh Wui shone with joy. "My wing!" he cried out. "My wing is back! Thank you! Thank you!"

Jack didn't know what to feel. He'd seen people lose limbs in the first phase of the Tournament, and almost all of them had ended up crippled. Only healers at the D-Grade could reattach or regrow severed limbs. The only way for a high E-Grade healer to do so was to act immediately after the dismembering, and even then, it was a tall task.

Their urgency to treat Fesh Wui and ignore Dorman wasn't unjustified. However, it still left a bitter taste in Jack's mouth.

Fesh Wui flew away, cradling his reattached wing with extreme love, completely ignoring Dorman. The healers finally turned to him, quickly fixing his wounds. Dorman jumped up to the stands and was congratulated by everyone. He sported a big, wide grin.

"Were those both Dao skills?" Jack couldn't help asking.

"Yes. One from the Dao of Speed and one from the Dao of Lightning."

"Shit, man. Well done."

"Thank you!"

I must get more Dao skills. After seeing the synergy between Dorman's Dao skills, Jack's resolve was renewed.

"But if you have the Dao Roots of Speed and Lightning, what is that worm teaching you?" he wondered aloud, only to get a strange look by Dorman.

"My master is a cloud worm," he replied, like it was self-explanatory.

Jack nodded. "Oh yes, my bad. A cloud worm. Of course."

Dorman nodded back, either not getting or ignoring Jack's sarcasm, but the announcer's voice cut them off.

"Next fight," she shouted, then announced the duelists. Jack turned to look at the sands with deep interest.

CHAPTER EIGHTY-FIVE

F YOU, RUFUS EMBERHEART!

Rufus Emberheart stood at one end of the arena. He wore a set of chainmail armor that glistened in the morning sun, with armored pants underneath. There was no helmet, leaving his majestic mane free to sway with the breeze. He was unarmed and supremely confident, though his piercing eyes left no doubt that under the arrogant nonchalance slumbered a mighty titan.

Li Xiang faced him. The old man wore traditional kung-fu attire, was equally unarmed as his opponent, and his hands rested calmly at his sides. His long white mustache was still pristinely thin, hanging down the sides of his chin. Under his bushy eyebrows, however, his eyes were clear as day and sharp as a knife. He met Rufus's calm stare with challenge.

He had met many practitioners in his day. Had toured the world to experience different martial arts, and practiced from infancy to old age. That was supposed to be the end.

However, the System revitalized Li Xiang. It wasn't enough to make him young again, but it stroked the fire in his heart, the unyielding tenacity that pushed him to pursue martial arts with complete devotion. The same tenacity that made him challenge the world's most accomplished martial artists.

And this lion alien was the strongest of them all.

Simply standing against him gave Li Xiang pressure, but his heart was strong. For honor and pride, he would win. His disciples were heavy on his shoulders. He couldn't let them down.

And if there was one thing that Li Xiang hated, it was cheating.

"You cheat," he declared in a sharp Chinese accent. "You do not belong here. You show no respect. Your victory is our dishonor."

"I do possess respect," Rufus replied steadily. "Please resign. My strength is undeniably greater than yours, and it would pain me to harm an elder."

"Never." Li Xiang adopted a kung-fu stance, fine-tuned as his Dao Root indicated. A host of minute alterations perfectly suited to countering the lion's fighting style.

"Very well," Rufus casually said. "You can have the first move." He did not assume a stance. He simply stood there, paws resting at his sides and eyes piercing his opponent.

Li Xiang spoke no more. He charged and arrived beside Rufus in a heartbeat. The sand still hadn't settled where he'd originally stood as his punch flew out.

Rufus welcomed it. He crossed his arms and blocked. There was little power behind the strike, but Li Xiang kept going. His arms and feet became a tornado as he unleashed blow after blow on the leonine, incredibly fast and impossibly precise.

Every attack was meaningful. His moves bled into each other, becoming a constant rain of blows that neither paused nor ceased. Li Xiang was poking for holes, feinting, and striking at Rufus's vitals. Being shorter, he focused around his opponent's torso.

It was the same flawless technique that had rendered the previous scion, the canine, helpless.

Rufus blocked everything. He used his own martial art, one Li Xiang didn't recognize, and which was aggressive in nature. His wide arms moved abruptly as he shielded everything, parrying and catching each strike. He also had claws, which made Li Xiang's job harder, as well as thick fur that weakened any glancing blow. His physiology was different than a human's, forcing Li Xiang to adjust his martial arts on the fly.

Li Xiang dived into the flow state. He'd long developed the ability to do so at will. The battle became a dance of power. Scenarios spread out like flowers in his mind. His mastery was so great that even the tiniest hints unfolded into clear patterns. He did not have the speed to match his opponent, but he did have the efficiency. It was an uphill battle.

But Li Xiang was a master. His Martial Arts (IV) skill wasn't for show.

The audience had gone silent. Only the sound of smacks and shouts filled the arena as Rufus and Li Xiang kept exchanging strikes for close to a full minute. Unlike Gan Salin, Rufus didn't seem flustered. He took no steps back, matching Li Xiang's efficiency with ferocity. His face was calm and focused.

Li Xiang was on full alert. The leonine would break the tempo soon, but how? The attacks came so densely he had no time to strike back.

Rufus opened his lion's mouth and roared.

The sound was deafening. It was deep and booming, as well as regal. It struck out like thunder. The audience reeled as their minds were filled with awe, and only the staunchest ones escaped.

Li Xiang received the roar at point-blank like a physical blow. He stopped mid-strike and jumped back twice, shaking his head to clear it.

"Your martial arts are impressive," Rufus said. "I don't know how much of that is due to your Dao Root, but you undoubtedly have great talent. If the Integration had met you at your youth, you could have roamed the galaxy as a member of the Animal Kingdom's Foreign Guard... Unfortunately, you are long past your prime."

Li Xiang did not reply. He just kept staring at Rufus, watching for sneak attacks and devising battle plans. After all, their close-quarters bout had been roughly equal. He had hope.

"I will attack now," Rufus warned. He swiped a paw through the air. The winds picked up and the air came alive with glinting light. Though they were separated by more than ten feet, the gigantic phantom of a paw materialized and closed the distance.

Li Xiang jumped out of the way with reflexes that belied his age, dodging by a hair's breadth and letting the attack fly on. It met the back wall with a loud bang—less than half of its power dissipating on the way.

Rufus wasn't done. He swiped paw after paw, sending out multiple projections. Each was larger than his entire body, and they crashed into the back wall with resounding bangs. Li Xiang dodged them all. His face darkened. He'd seen this strike before, when Jack Rust blocked it at the auction house. He had assumed it was a full-force attack... As it turns out, he'd underestimated the leonine.

He can shoot them at will. Fine.

Rufus charged. One moment, he was far away, the next, he stood right in front of Li Xiang, and he swiped down with a paw. The old man hadn't even seen the movement. It was like Rufus had teleported. He didn't have time to dodge. He raised his arms to block the overhead strike.

The phantom of a paw superimposed itself on Rufus's. The entire sky practically came crashing down on Li Xiang. His arms buckled near-instantly under the pressure. He was helplessly weaker.

The attack smashed his forearms into his face and flung him back like a ragdoll, nailing him to the far wall that remained pristine despite receiving all those previous attacks. Li Xiang stood, but he was hurt. One of his arms hung limply at the side, bent oddly at the elbow. His forehead was bleeding, as was his nose, and his robes were torn in places. His short hair was disheveled.

Only his long mustache remained unharmed—he'd protected it during his crash. It was the symbol of his pride, and it had taken him decades to grow.

"Had enough?" Rufus asked. Li Xiang grabbed his dislocated elbow and set it in place with a loud snap. He didn't even flinch. He then flexed the fingers on his just-relocated arm, frowned, and nodded to himself. It hurt, but he could still use them.

He charged.

He had no ranged attacks. His only chance at victory lay at close combat.

Rufus could have tried to keep him at a distance, but he welcomed the challenge. The underestimation burned like a flaming rod in his guts. Li Xiang vowed to win.

"Come," the leonine said. "Let me prove my fists superior."

His hands were closer to a human's than a lion's. Twin phantoms formed over his closed fists. He struck out the moment Li Xiang approached.

There was finality in those strikes. Li Xiang instinctively felt they were unstoppable. To dare block would be suicide. He would be effortlessly blown away.

He tilted to the side. The air screamed as Rufus's strike shot past, and there were more close behind. Rufus's hands blurred as he launched into a fierce offensive, pummeling Li Xiang, who struggled to survive under the onslaught. He dodged as well as he could. When left with no choice, he even redirected a few strikes, though they were so heavy his balance was affected.

This was the first time Rufus truly showcased his fighting style. He was a melee fighter. His technique was refined, his defense solid, and he struck hard.

Li Xiang weathered the assault, but he constantly backpedaled. Rufus opened his mouth again and roared. Li Xiang expected it and did not flinch, but the disturbance was enough for him to finally reveal an opening.

Rufus got a punch in. Li Xiang flew away, spitting out blood and stomach fluids, and once again rammed into a wall. The audience gasped. That strike wasn't deadly, but it was enough to put almost everyone out of commission.

Not Li Xiang. The old man stood again, unable to suppress a frown. He had several broken and cracked bones around his chest. His elbow was dislocated again, and this time broken, a bone jutting out. His mustache once again remained safe.

Despite all that, Li Xiang tried to settle into a fighting stance. He even extended his broken elbow, intending to use the bone as a weapon. He would rather die than lose to a dishonorable child.

"I will not yield," he said with blazing eyes. "You are an enemy. Kill me if you must."

He longed for a warrior's death. If he had to endure that to save his honor, he would be happy.

Rufus frowned. "Why do you insist, old man?"

"Because I have honor. Something you lack. Alien."

At this, Rufus *really* frowned. "How many times must I repeat this?" he growled. "I am a native of this planet. My ancestors were running away from misfortune and ended up here, and we have been living quietly ever since."

"Those are lies. You claim to be supreme, but your actions are those of a thief. You bully us, who are like children to you and your people. Where is the king in you? Where is your supremacy? Where is your honor?"

"You have a mouth, but it can only spout nonsense," Rufus declared regally. "Fine. Have it your way. Let me punish you."

Rufus wasn't angry. He was simply condescending, like a god striking down an arrogant mortal. Li Xiang prepared to defend—though he couldn't walk without trembling, his fighting potential wasn't completely snuffed out yet.

Rufus took a deep breath, then opened his mouth. It wasn't just a roar, it was a storm. The winds rose from their slumber and cut like blades as they flew at Li Xiang. The sound reached him first, booming across the entire stadium and making everyone cover their ears. Then came the wind, and it shredded him.

Li Xiang crossed his arms to defend, unable to dodge, and the winds struck him like razors. They tore through his clothes and into his skin. It lasted but an instant, reducing Li Xiang's robes to tatters, barely hiding his privates anymore. His exposed, pale, wrinkly skin was covered in deep red lines, one of his eyes was shut and injured, and even his mustache had been severed on both sides.

Li Xiang had gone to great lengths to protect that mustache throughout the fight. Now, it was just white hair on the bloody arena sands.

For the first time in decades, Li Xiang lost to his emotions. He was frozen in rage and indignation. He'd been defeated and stripped bare. His pride had been severed. His honor had been dragged through the mud.

This wasn't a warrior's death. And he was forced to stay conscious, experiencing every agonizing moment. His aged face warped into the bitterest scowl. His disciples and family were watching. So was the entire world. He was living a nightmare.

Li Xiang opened his mouth and screamed.

"I showed you respect, but you only returned insults and hypocrisy," Rufus declared. His voice reached Li Xiang's ears, but he was too lost to comprehend the words. "You spoke of honor, so I severed your pride. This is a fitting punishment for your blasphemy at my face. Now, let me put you to sleep."

He swiped a paw.

Li Xiang was still frozen in utter rage and indignation, unable to even muster a response. Rufus's attack reached him in an instant, crushing his body against the wall and breaking most of his bones. He had absolutely no hope of resisting. His scream cut off sharply when he lost consciousness, and the djinn healers rushed in to save him.

He wasn't granted death. Instead, he'd been condemned to spend his final years in shame.

The audience was only now comprehending what just happened. Dozens of voices rose from across the stands, cursing at Rufus and crying out in outrage for what he'd done to the old man. Jack shouted too, as did everyone around him. Even the Sage broke his calm facade, and Dorman erupted with the temper of the teenager he really was.

Rufus stood in the center of the arena and took it all in stride.

"Silence," he roared, and the magical nature of his voice helped him overpower the audience. "Open your eyes and see. What action of mine was unjust? I showed respect, but he replied with insults. He attempted to slander me publicly and humiliate me, so I paid him with the same coin. His humiliation was deserved. What action of mine was unjust?"

The audience was not silenced. Rufus's words did contain a twisted logic, but only a lunatic would agree.

Li Xiang was an old martial artist who valued honor above all. In previous matches, he had always been polite and respectful to his opponents, with the exception of Gan Salin, whom he also accused of cheating. Everyone knew that was true, anyway. Li Xiang just voiced the obvious and despised it exactly *because* it was dishonorable.

Now, he'd been humiliated in front of the entire planet. Stripped almost naked, beaten to an inch of his life, and having his proud mustache severed. The healers saved his life, but his honor was unsalvageable.

The outrage was simply maddening.

"Hey, Rufus Emberheart!" a voice louder than most cut through the clamor. It wasn't Jack's. It belonged to a nondescript man with particularly strong lungs and a tendency to meddle everywhere. He was the same person who asked the C-Grade lioness to clarify a rule on the first day.

The people quieted as they looked to this man. He took a deep breath, then shouted, "Fuck you!"

"Remember your insolence," Rufus replied. "Because when the Tournament is over and the Animal Kingdom is no longer protecting you, I will come to collect my dues."

"You'll come to suck my *dick*!" the same man shouted, prompting the entire arena to laugh.

Rufus's eyes darkened. With a leap, he flew over the stands and landed in front of the curtain that separated the scions' seats, then hid himself behind it.

Jack cracked a grin. He'd been about to shout something himself, but that random dude beat him to the punch, and he'd vocalized what everyone thought: "Fuck you, Rufus Emberheart!"

Jack clapped, both for Li Xiang and the man too brave for his own good. The entire arena followed.

Then, he had an idea.

"Fuck you, Rufus Emberheart!" Jack started chanting. "Fuck you, Rufus Emberheart!"

People caught on. They roared the same words, over and over. Not everyone chanted with him, but many did, and their System-enhanced voices filled the arena and rocked it to its core. Most alien merchants looked at the surrounding humans in horror, but the humans themselves couldn't give a flying fuck.

Who would dare mock a scion like that? Who would dare antagonize the B-Grade overlords? Who would bring the attitude of hooligans into the planet's most prestigious event?

Earth-387 would! And the prick deserved it.

The entire arena thundered with the people's cursed shout, filling all of Integration City, echoing out into the surrounding ocean. They went at it for a long time, until the entire planet knew.

It was glorious. Nothing brings humanity together like cursing out loud.

CHAPTER EIGHTY-SIX
THE PHOENIX AND THE DRAGON

THE HEAD JUDGE JUMPED TO THE AIR, TRYING TO ANNOUNCE THE NEXT FIGHT, but she was swarmed by the audience's shouts. "Fuck you, Rufus Emberheart!" still echoed across Integration City.

She didn't stop trying to calm the crowd, probably too afraid of what would happen to her if she let this continue, but she was helpless.

It took a few minutes for things to calm down.

The Sage turned to Jack with an amused smile, panting slightly. He'd been shouting as fervently as everyone else. "That was unwise."

"But fucking deserved."

"But deserved, indeed. It is beautiful to see the entire planet unite against injustice—even if it's just to curse."

"Nothing brings people together like common enemies." Jack laughed. "Man, I really hope I can kick that guy's ass."

"It's not impossible. Just highly improbable," the Sage replied, smiling with yellow teeth, and Jack laughed again. He then turned to Vivi.

"Good luck," he said. "Show that ass-kisser how hot you are."

She rolled her eyes with a smile. "Thanks." All four other members of Flame River shot him dark looks.

Jeez, those guys are like her little brothers, he thought. They'll become good friends with Brock.

The brorilla had participated in the chanting, unable to form words but joining in the fun nonetheless. After all, what Rufus had done was very un-bro-like.

He must have been steaming like mad behind his curtain.

"If you find the opportunity, can you toss the Russian into the curtain?" Jack asked Vivi. "I want to see Rufus's face after this fiasco."

"Me too... But you know, Jack, I don't toss people around." She winked, a flame flashing in her open palm. "I burn them."

She then closed her hand and jumped into the arena, landing in a thin cloud of sand. Alexander Petrovic was already there, waiting.

"Took you long enough," he said in his thick Russian accent. "I saw you chanting. It was deeply disgraceful."

"Heh. I see you know where you stand, Petrovic. No wonder you couldn't find allies here. Your tongue was too busy between that guy's hairy butt cheeks."

"Such a vulgar mouth... It doesn't matter. The Ice Peak bows to no one. Prepare to die."

He really would kill her if given the chance. They were enemies. His only punishment would be disqualification, and with Rufus Emberheart here, he never intended to win the Tournament, anyway.

The temperature dropped sharply. Alexander Petrovic unleashed his power, conjuring ice around his hands. Vivi's entire body caught on fire like a torch. The temperature around her climbed, and hot air clashed with cold in the middle of the arena, forming strong winds and making the air wave.

The people sitting behind Alexander hurried to put on coats. Those behind Vivi hurried to take them off.

They attacked simultaneously.

Embers appeared around Vivi, flourishing into a million tiny flames that combined into a torrential river. The air froze where Alexander's ice gauntlets touched it, spreading like a giant snowflake or a spider's net that shone with radiant white and blue light.

Vivi pushed her hands forward. The river frothed as it flowed, expanding. She wasn't making three rivers this time, just a large one.

From the spectator stands, it looked like the floodgates of Hell had opened wide, letting flame-water pour out like a broken dam.

The flames burned and the river flowed, but there was no antithesis between them. To be fluid and ever-moving, while maintaining a strong, burning heart: that was the path of the Flame River.

Suddenly, the arena seemed cramped. Vivi and Alexander were two dots in a raging sea as the flames expanded to cover the sand, splashing against the arena walls like waves. Alexander crossed his arms. The ice retreated and formed a sphere around him, shielding him in a transparent, clear dome.

Vivi's flames struck the dome and parted. They reached the far wall and freely splattered about, filling up the entire sand-covered arena like a bathtub. The temperature rose greatly, and only the protective energy wall that capped the stage protected the audience, cutting off some of the heat.

Alexander's ice was a lone island in a sea of fire, but it held. No matter how fiercely the flames circled, no matter how much the ice steamed and evaporated, he created more. In fact, where the ice and flames met, the flames were doused more than the ice melted. And at some point, the dome had become opaque.

His Dao is stronger, Jack realized with a grimace. It's that fire ice lotus, whatever it was called. Fuck.

Rufus helped Alexander outbid Vivi in the auction. With the lotus of fire and ice, Alexander's Dao was able to progress faster, surpassing Vivi's.

Which brought up some questions in Jack's mind. He'd been under the impression that Dao Roots were all at the same level. Was that not the case?

"Hey, Edgar," he asked, leaning toward the mage. "Can Dao Roots become stronger without advancing to a Dao Seed?"

"Hmm?" Edgar glanced over before turning his gaze back to the arena. "They can, but not by much. Dao Seeds are the ones that have multiple stages of advancement. Dao Roots can grow, too, but not enough to warrant distinction. Alexander's Dao Root is just closer to evolving, that's all."

"I see," Jack replied. Their faces were illuminated by red light as the flames struggled to suffocate the ice in their midst. "Who do you think will win?" he whispered.

Edgar bit his lip. "I don't know, man... I really hope it's Vivi, but the Ice Peak is no joke. I've heard they were some secret service that went rogue during the Integration. They tore through a dungeon by pure skill."

Jack turned his gaze back to the arena. He watched closely. This battle wasn't just about the Tournament. The power dynamic between these two factions would define the future of the entire planet.

Alexander's dome glistened with melted ice, while the sea of flames was abating. Vivi couldn't keep it up forever. Suddenly, Alexander struck out. The dome shone, repairing and enhancing itself as thick spears of ice extended in every direction, infiltrating the flames. They were constantly melting, but their growth speed was greater, and more spears jutted out from the existing ones, jumping in every direction.

The flames fought them at every step, but the ice spears were rapidly forming into what resembled a giant snowflake, its every stroke a foot thick. Alexander was reclaiming territory.

Vivi must have judged the exchange to be losing, because the flames retreated. No, they didn't just retreat, they swirled around her like she was the exit of a giant, water-filled bathtub. For a few moments, she was completely shrouded in flame. It merged into her form, disappearing down some bottomless pit as Vivi was gradually revealed again.

She was on fire. Flames danced up and down her body, covering her head like an open helmet and her clothes like a suit of living armor. Moreover, two large, fiery wings spread from her back, and she held a whip of blue flames in one hand.

Vivi had become a fire Valkyrie.

The audience erupted in cheers. Jack could only stare wide-eyed.

"That's a Dao skill!" Edgar cried out. "And that's my Fierus Whipus!"

Beside them, Sadaka stuck out his chest. "That's Vivi's newest skill: Flame Form! That Alexander is toast now."

"That's unfair!" Jack shouted. "Why does she get to be so cool but I can only punch harder?"

"Your Dao skill is pretty cool, too... unlike mine." Edgar scratched the back of his head, then shrugged. "But I like it anyway."

Vivi's wings flapped and she took to the air. A piercing snap echoed as her whip crashed into the dome, carving a deep, molten line on it. The strike had penetrated at least a foot deep, but it seemed that below was only solid ice, like Alexander was encased in a glacier.

Vivi's whip screamed through the air as she rained blows on the dome. The defense was solid. Digging through would take time. She stopped attacking with a frown.

"Alexander Petrovic!" she shouted. "For how long will you keep hiding in your egg? Come out and face me!"

"Huh?" Jack wondered. "Egg?"

"Egg!" Edgar's eyes shone. "She's right! That's not a dome, it's an egg! I mean, it's dome-shaped, and it's more like a cocoon—"

"Get to the point, Edgar!"

Before he could reply, the sound of roaring laughter filled the arena.

"How perceptive of you, Miss Eragorn. Very well. I will entertain you."

Cracks spread over the ice until, with a violent snap, the entire dome exploded. Shrapnel rained everywhere. Vivi whipped them out of the air —she was proficient with her weapon.

When the white dust cleared, Alexander could be seen in full. Two massive, dragon-like ice wings spread from his back, though smaller than Vivi's. He didn't wear armor. Instead, the ice covered both his arms from hand to shoulder, and each held a sharp, freezing sword. His legs were covered in ice too, up to the knee.

More importantly, a long, sharp-tipped tail stretched behind him.

"Why are they similar?" Jack asked, looking between the two fighters. "Is it a coincidence?"

"I think so," Edgar replied. "Man, what luck."

Vivi laughed warmly. "Hah. Great minds think alike."

"Not quite," Alexander replied frigidly. "I know what I'm doing. You are just a girl out of your depth."

"We'll see about that." She grinned with battle lust, snapping her whip in the air. "Come, Petrovic. Let me rid the world of your ass-kissing blight."

She, too, would kill him if given the chance. Neither were playing around.

Alexander's wings flapped, pulling him into the air, darting at her with great speed. Though made of ice, his wings moved dexterously, like real ones. Then again, Vivi's were made of fire, and they worked just fine.

The whip struck out, its tip carving shiny blue lines in the sky. Alexander's swords danced impossibly fast as he blocked and redirected the strikes, showcasing extreme skill. Using swords against a whip wasn't easy, but he made it work.

Their wings flapped as they embarked on an aerial battle. Vivi was darting around and Alexander chased her, defending all the while. Their speed made the arena seem small again.

Unfortunately, space was limited. Alexander caught up. His swords shone with cold light. Every swing froze the air, and his wings left ice where they passed. Vivi's whip was less effective at this range. It melted and formed into large talons that covered her forearms and extended a foot beyond her fingers. She met Alexander in a frontal collision.

Both used twin weapons. Every clash sent sparks flying, and the air came alive with ice and blue flames. Small explosions sounded out of nowhere from the wide and rapid temperature shifts.

Vivi was forced to retreat. Her Dao was slightly weaker, she was less optimized for close combat, and she was less proficient with her weapons than Alexander was with his. She could hold her own, but not for long. She reached the ground.

Jack sensed the conclusion looming closer. He didn't dare blink. Everything was happening so fast that most people only saw flashes of light.

Alexander lunged into an attack, and Vivi's entire body flared. The hyper-condensed flames erupted with their full power for a single moment. She opened her mouth, and all that heat was condensed into a single, sun-like point between her teeth. Orange flames poured out of her throat, merging with singularity, and shot out of her mouth with the full force of a raging river. Her entire body shook from the pushback.

It all happened in the blink of an eye. Alexander resumed his attack despite her flames coalescing, stabbing one of his swords deep into her side and leaving it there before flying back at top speed. Seeing the torrent of flames coming at his face, he crossed his wings before himself like a shield.

Vivi's dragon breath fell on Alexander at full force. His wings sizzled, burning away. A scream filled the air as he struggled to repair them, hoping he could endure the onslaught. He was like a rock splitting a river, and an orange glow came from where his wings met the flames.

Vivi ran out of steam first. Her dragon breath lessened, then dried up, and she was left panting and weak. Her wings and armor had disappeared as all the flames she could muster had gone into the breath attack. The sword at her side had evaporated, but the grisly wound was still there, and she was bleeding profusely. It'd struck a lung.

Opposite her, Alexander still stood. His once-majestic wings now only a skeleton, and their membranes were paper-thin and transparent, but he'd pulled through. Though his exposed back had received deep burns from the sheer temperature, and his tail had evaporated into a small stump, these weren't enough to stop him.

Vivi took in the sight of her opponent still standing. Heavy disappointment clouded her eyes, then she opened her mouth to resign... and only incoherent sounds came out.

After all, one of her lungs had been pierced!

CHAPTER EIGHTY-SEVEN
COLD MURDER

VIVI HAD LOST, BUT SHE COULDN'T RESIGN!

Through his pain, Alexander took that in with grim pleasure. He'd attacked her lung on purpose.

His tail reformed and snapped out like a lance, aiming to penetrate her head and kill her on the spot. He was sluggish, exhausted, and injured, but still moving faster than any pre-System human.

Vivi barely managed to veer out of the way. Completely out of mana, she tilted her head to the side and fell on her back. The tail carved a deep wound on her left cheek, exposing the mouth and bone underneath. It then reared back for another strike. Vivi was on the ground now. She couldn't dodge, and she couldn't resign.

She gritted her teeth. An explosion went off inside her head. Her eyes lost all light as she slumped, losing consciousness. She'd fried random things inside her head hoping the healers could save her, because she had no other choice.

Since she lost consciousness, the battle was over.

However, Alexander's tail pierced at her head again. He didn't care about the Tournament. His goal was to murder her. The judges and healers were too far away to react in time.

Nobody could save her.

A man-shaped meteor tore through the protective energy wall and crashed into the stage, shattering Alexander's tail just before it pierced through Vivi's eye. Jack Rust stood there, tall and proud. The air around him fluctuated with palpable violence. His eyes shone like fire as he glared Alexander down right in front of his face.

"She lost consciousness. Fuck off," he said with barely restrained fury.

"Hmph. I didn't notice. What do you care, American?"

"I told you to fuck off."

Not only had they slept together, Vivi was Jack's friend and a close ally. He would be damned if he just stood by and watched her get murdered like this.

In fact, he'd already been flying over before Vivi lost consciousness. It was only the brief delay brought by her action that allowed him to reach in time. Three healers arrived just after him and were already pouring their power on Vivi.

Alexander snorted again but did not move back. His cold eyes met Jack's.

It was the first time Jack saw Alexander from up-close. He was a stout man, big and stocky. His clean-shaven face was wide with heavy features, and as his ice disappeared, it revealed a loose shirt underneath. He reminded Jack a bit of Hugo, the Slavic man who'd been keeping watch on his mother. The first person he'd ever killed.

However, Alexander's most striking feature were his eyes. They were a cold, icy blue, and they stared in a way Jack had never witnessed before. He was staring down a machine—a cold-blooded, highly-trained killer. These eyes chilled him to the bone.

Of course, Jack had never lost a stare-off since the System arrived. His glare punched through Alexander's brain, promising violence. Jack, too, was a highly-skilled killer. Maybe he wasn't cold-blooded, but in this case, that made him even more dangerous.

"Stop!" a commanding voice came from above as the head judge swooped in between them. A gust of wind pushed them both back, forcing them to look at her. "The fight is over. Retreat."

"He interfered. That is against the rules," Alexander said. "He should be disqualified."

"He tried to kill a downed opponent. *That* is against the rules," Jack echoed. "He should be disqualified."

"That was an accident. We cannot demand that our fighters have perfect awareness in every possible scenario. There is a margin of error," the head judge said, turning to Alexander. "Jack Rust intervened after the battle was over. That is also punishable, but not by disqualification. You get one strike. However!" She rounded on Jack. "Since you already have more strikes from the first phase of the Tournament, I have to—"

"I say we let him stay," another voice came from the top of the stands. It was Rufus Emberheart. Everyone turned their gazes on him. "He did invade the arena, but since his actions led to better adherence of the rules, I would argue that it is excusable. I believe nobody disagrees."

Jack frowned before realizing what was happening. Rufus wanted to fight and destroy him publicly in the Tournament. He wanted to truly cement his position as number one, and if Jack got disqualified now, some wouldn't be convinced of Rufus's supremacy.

The head judge looked around, and indeed, nobody questioned Rufus's judgment. Why would they? It was to everyone's benefit.

"Very well," she agreed. "Jack Rust, you are let off with a warning. Alexander Petrovic, you too. Please return to your seats."

Jack met Rufus's stare. He only found arrogance there. Certainty of victory.

"Also, Jack Rust," the head judge said, drawing his attention, "why is it that every time something happens, it is always *you*?"

Her exasperation seemed genuine, but Jack didn't care much. He disliked her already.

"Guess I'm a troublemaker, chief," he responded, shrugging. He jumped back to his seat. Sadaka and the other members of Flame River thanked him profusely, their words filled with guilt. When he faced Alexander, they'd been ready to jump into the arena if the Ice Peak joined, but that hadn't come to pass.

"Don't worry about it," Jack said. "As I said, I'm just a troublemaker."

His attention wasn't on them. He was eagerly watching Vivi. The healers kept pumping magic into her. Only when her eyelids fluttered, and her eyes opened did his shoulders un-bunch. She had a hushed conversation with the head healer, probably asking if she was okay, then the healer nodded and let her go.

Vivi wobbled to the stairs. She reached the others between a crowd that parted to let her pass. She might have lost, but her resolve at the end had garnered everyone's respect.

The people of Flame River fell on her the moment she arrived. A few moments later, she pushed past them to collapse in her seat.

"Are you okay?" Jack asked. After all, who knew what brain injuries were treatable by magic.

"Physically? Yes," she replied tiredly. "Mentally? Not at all. I lost, Jack. Flame River lost."

"Nothing is over yet."

"I know. But it fucking hurts."

"Yeah... I know it's hard, but you're strong. I believe you can recover."

She clenched her fists. Jack could understand what she was going through, more or less. It sucked, but in the end, it was her battle to fight. She would either pull through or wouldn't. He couldn't help.

The Sage and Dorman didn't offer any words of comfort either, besides the polite ones. Surprisingly, neither did Edgar.

"What are you guys planning to do now?" Jack asked. "The fights are over."

"I think I'll relax a bit," Edgar replied, leaning back in his seat. He seemed over his defeat already, and his eyes were already twinkling with new ideas. "Now that I don't have to fight anymore, I don't have to train all the time... Not to mention that my master is off-limits, like my house. Oh, I have to pack up, too. Where are you staying?" he asked Sadaka.

"The Jade Skin hotel," the man replied. "We can get you a room."

"Yeah, that would be great."

"I will relax as well," the Sage said. "Maybe go watch the waves until nightfall... Yes, that would be nice."

"You would watch the waves for hours?" Edgar raised a brow. "They're just waves."

"They hide very interesting patterns, young wizard. Predicting them is difficult. Perhaps you would benefit from the practice, too."

"Ah no. As I said, no training today."

"Same for me," Vivi added, letting out a sigh. "I must find a way to deal with the public relations mess of my defeat."

"It's not that bad, Vivi," Sadaka told her. "Everyone saw how hard you fought and how strong you are. Maybe you lost, but you honored the Flame River's reputation."

"Hmm, true," she replied, already deep in thought. "Maybe we could twist this into us being the underdogs? Everyone loves the underdogs."

"That's the spirit!"

Jack raised a brow at her scheming, then glanced at Dorman, who was staring right back at him. They were two of the four remaining finalists. They had a one in three chance of fighting tomorrow.

"I'll go train," Jack said. "You should do the same, Dorman. I don't want to kick your ass too easily."

"You wouldn't even be able to touch me," the Asian teen shot back.

"Heh. We'll see about that. If you get matched against Rufus, I really won't have the opportunity to touch you."

"I will win the Tournament. It doesn't matter who my opponent is."

Jack smiled as he stood. "Anyway, see you guys. I have to go now."

"Oh, really?" Vivi said, raising a brow. She was clearly still distraught, but she kept it for herself. "Do you have a date?"

Jack laughed. "Well, technically, yes."

CHAPTER EIGHTY-EIGHT
A PEEK BEHIND THE CURTAIN

Jack walked down the streets of Integration City. On his right was Brock. On his left, Karvahul. The streets were mostly empty since the fights had just finished, so if they kept their voices low, nobody would overhear.

"It isn't looking good, Jack," the djinn said, shaking his head. "You spent everything we had at the auction. I want to bet, but our funds are just minuscule now. So are our profits."

"Mhm."

"Plus, the fights are easier to predict now. There are no black horses anymore. I can't earn much each fight, at least not without risking big."

"I see. But we got the hundred thousand from Edgar's victory, right?"

Karvahul nodded. "That helped," he admitted.

Every fighter got a hundred thousand credits for every victory in the final phase of the Tournament. The only exceptions were Jack and Rufus, whose monetary earnings were confiscated by the Hand of God.

Edgar had entrusted Jack with his wealth, who in turn, entrusted everything to Karvahul.

Jack stopped and took an earnest look at his manager. "Give it to me straight, Karvahul. How much do we have?"

The djinn took a deep breath. "Two hundred fifty thousand, give or take."

"Okay."

"What are you planning to do with it?"

Jack considered the issue. "I have something in mind... but it requires I ask you a favor."

"Me?" Karvahul was surprised. "Listen, Jack, if it's about borrowing, I can only—"

"Not that," Jack cut him off. "I plan to send some credits to my faction. They might need it to protect themselves, but I don't have a way to send it over a large distance."

"Oh. Okay. I could send some to Ar'Tazul, who's still in your town, but then we'd get taxed."

"Taxed?"

"Yeah. The Animal Kingdom levies heavy tax on all transactions in the constellation. You are still protected by the one-year grace period, but we aren't. If I send money to Tazul, 50 percent will be taken away."

"Fifty percent!" Jack almost jumped. Even Brock protested, though he didn't know the numbers.

"I know," Karvahul replied bitterly. "It's the maximum tax allowed by the Star Pact. They're bleeding us poor merchants dry..."

"Well, fuck the Animal Kingdom. Isn't there a way to cheat them?"

"Of course. If we send the money through a native, it should fall under the grace period term... But we'd need someone we can trust. Someone who can reach that place in a reasonable period of time. It's half an ocean away! Any ideas?"

"I might have one... The Flame River doesn't have a jet, unfortunately, but I know someone with a starship. Does that count?"

"Only if they can ride it. It's not easy."

"I suspect my person can ride it just fine," Jack replied enigmatically. "And he's trustworthy, I think. Problem is, I already owe him multiple favors... but this is important. I guess one more won't hurt."

"Lots of people have jets here," Karvahul suggested. "You could ask one of them. With your status, I don't think anyone would refuse."

Of the people who'd arrived after the Tournament started, most had come in private jets. There were landing strips at the back of Integration

City, and Jack had even seen a US airplane carrier docked in the distance.

"I don't want to owe favors to strangers," he said, shaking his head. "And I want to keep this a secret. People might be out for my faction."

"Okay, then. I suppose the person you're talking about is the Sage?"

"Yes."

"I'll contact him discreetly on your behalf."

"Thank you, Karvahul."

"No problem. How much should I give him?"

"All of it."

"*All of it*?" Karvahul almost embraced the Dao of Heart Attack.

Jack nodded seriously. "I'm afraid for the safety of my people, Karvahul... I have friends and relatives there. I want them to be as protected as possible, and there are many defensive mechanisms that credits can buy. With two hundred and fifty thousand and their own strength, they should be safe against anything short of a scion."

"Are you sure, Jack? With this kind of money, you—"

"I'm sure."

The djinn struggled, then squeaked, "But what will I bet?"

"You have your own money, right? Use that."

Karvahul's feet dragged against the ground. His eyes alternated between gold and sadness. Since he was short, too, he reminded Jack of a disappointed child.

"It's all those scions' fault..." he muttered. "Damn the System and its stupid blind spots!"

Jack raised a brow in interest. "Blind spots? Does it really have those?"

"Of course it does. When the Ancients created it, they neglected many things, and now the immortals lack the skills to patch it up—so the legends say." Karvahul turned to him. "The System may seem like a god to you now, but in truth, it's neither omnipotent nor omniscient. It's just a very complex, gigantic machine, and it has many limitations."

"Really?"

Karvahul shook his head. They'd reached the edge of the participant district, but being an alien, he couldn't enter, not even as a guest. Therefore, he leaned against the fence and motioned for Jack to do the same. Nobody else was nearby.

"Listen, Jack," he began, taking a deep breath. "The System operates based on the Dao, but its functions consume energy voraciously. For that reason, they are limited. It barely keeps tabs on the classless, for example, and it stops tracking them when they exit System space. They just aren't worth it."

"System space?"

"The part of the galaxy that has been terraformed into a System-friendly state. If you ever go outside it, you will notice that your powers decrease, and many System functions fail. Anyway, that's how the scions arrive at a planet. If their home force can discover an inhabited planet manually, they can use a space-warping starship to transport some of their talented youths over. Then, they conduct a System expansion in the nearby space. When the planet is Integrated, these scions are assumed to be natives, since they weren't tracked outside System space."

"Oh, so that's how it's done!" Jack replied. "Does that mean they revert to level 1, too? Can they level up to 14, move outside System space, then re-enter and re-level to gather more stat bonuses?"

"Yes and no. Not everyone starts at level 1. The System makes adjustments based on your species and personal power. The method you describe could grant them an extra three, maybe four levels at the most, and it would only work once."

"I see." Jack mulled it over in his mind. Something felt off. "Oh! Wait. You said they were transported here in a space-warping starship, right? Only immortals can use those, if I remember correctly, and I bet the System tracks immortals even outside its space. Therefore, when the immortal arrived on Earth with the scions, didn't the System see the inhabited planet? Why wouldn't it Integrate on the spot?"

"It doesn't work like that." Karvahul shook his head. "The System doesn't have eyes. It can only perceive certain kinds of signals from you, like when you scan or kill something, or when you have an insight into the Dao. If the immortal didn't scan anything here, the System would be none the wiser... and even if they did, it couldn't just expand by itself. The System can't teleport, nor is it bubbles around planets. It would need to advance slowly by terraforming all the space in between, which is very energy intensive. It wouldn't do so without a B-Grade faction's assistance."

This was interesting information, but Jack still felt something was off, even if he was unable to pinpoint it.

"I don't know, man," he said. "I understand that the System is trying to save its energy, but... that seems like a pretty big hole to me. If everyone sends scions to new planets, doesn't that kinda ruin the entire Integration thing you have going on?"

"Oh, no. First of all, the System's Integration only involves spawning monsters and dungeons. The Tournament isn't a System thing." Karvahul wagged a finger. "It is run entirely by the B-Grade factions, according to rules detailed in the Star Pact. The System's *only* involvement is when the faction in charge uses some of its high-Grade functions to teleport the participants here and broadcast messages."

"Really?" Jack's eyes bulged. "I thought—"

"I know how it seems. But really, the System is very hands-off. Almost everything is run by people. However, even if scions were a System problem, it wouldn't matter, because they are very rare. Manually scouting space takes time. Even with space-warping starships, and even knowing which planets are inhabitable and which are not ahead of time—we have that technology—you would need months to travel from one planet to the next, and only a tiny percentage of them are inhabited. It would take decades or even centuries to find one.

"Moreover, just one immortal isn't enough. Not only could they get lost, they would also be attacked by space beasts. You would need at least a full crew, preferably with a C-Grade in charge. Do you think a B-Grade faction can afford to send C-Grades out on such missions for decades? Or do you think any C-Grade would be willing?"

Karvahul shook his head, then continued. "No, they would only do so when they have already identified an inhabited planet. There are ways—divination, mostly—although it's a rare case. You were just unlucky."

Jack had stopped listening at one particular point. "Did you say space beasts?"

As a biologist, the subject intrigued him. The only animal he knew that could survive in space was a kind of micro-organism called sea bear.

"Yeah?" Karvahul raised a brow. "What? The sea has fish. Why wouldn't space have its own beasts?"

"Because it's a frozen void where nothing can survive."

"Immortals can survive, at least for a bit. And it isn't really empty. Where there is space and time, there is the Dao. And where there is the Dao, it can get spontaneously warped into a semi-sentient existence that instinctively hunts down bright sources of the Dao—for example, cultivators."

"Wow," Jack replied breathlessly. "Can they attack planets?"

"Not often, no. They don't approach celestial bodies without reason."

"Wow..." he repeated. "Space beasts, space pirates, immortals who can survive in space, the Dao, civilizations stretching over the stars... What a wondrous world this is, Karvahul. I had no idea!"

"Space is filled with wonders, my friend," the djinn replied with a sad smile. "But also with danger. I pray that you never discover the latter."

Jack opened his mouth to reply, then smiled with gratitude. Those were the kind words of someone who'd experienced pain. "You said you *pray*, Karvahul. Who do you pray to?"

"The System, the Immortals, the Old Ones, the Universe..." He shrugged, then laughed. "Where there is a will, there is a deity."

Jack laughed, too. "Wise words, Karvahul. Say, what do you do in this town all the time? You don't hang out with us often, and you don't have a shop to run."

"Oh, I own a wholesale business. I've recruited some amazing workhands west of here, and I provide all the souvenirs you see in shops. Why did you think there are so many action figurines of you?"

Jack looked over with surprise, then both men laughed. "Do you pay them justly, though?" Jack asked. Karvahul had mentioned workhands west of Integration City, which was in the middle of the Pacific Ocean. That meant Asia, where people were regularly exploited before the Integration.

"Of course," the merchant replied immediately. "Generous to

employees, kind to partners, ruthless to customers. That's the djinn way!"

"Wait, am I a partner?"

"Of course, Jack. My favorite on the entire planet."

"And also the only one, I presume?"

"Of course not. I have dozens, though not as famous as you."

"Oh. Well, you're my favorite partner too!"

"And also the only one, I presume?"

Jack looked down. "Maybe."

They laughed again. Karvahul was great company—just like Ar'Tazul, actually, the djinn merchant in Valville. No wonder they were cousins.

"Anyway," Jack said. "I have some training to do. Will you handle the credit movement we talked about before?"

"Of course. We'll pretend the Sage sold and bought products worth 250,000 credits... If he agrees, of course."

"I think he will. That guy loves favors."

"Then, good. If he doesn't, I'll find another way."

"You rock, Karvahul. Good luck!"

"See you around, Jack! You too, Brock!"

The merchant took off, and Jack headed for his house. He'd learned a lot of interesting information, but now wasn't the time to focus on that.

There was a one in three chance he'd fight Rufus next morning, and a two out of three chance he'd fight another very strong opponent. Even if he made it through tomorrow, the final would be the next day after that, which meant Jack had at most two days to reach his peak.

He would let no time go to waste.

It's time to finally advance some skills.

CHAPTER EIGHTY-NINE
SKILL TRAINING

JACK SCRAMBLED TO REACH. HE FLEW OVER THE TREADMILL AND PUNCHED THE air, sending the shockwave of his punch to meet an airborne wooden target. The moment he punched, he was already turning the other way, shooting another punch at a different target.

His jabs flew like arrows as they shot down targets, yet many snuck through. He tried to punch again, but he failed to hold on to the feeling, and the shockwave exploded way too early, letting the target sail harmlessly past.

"Ugh!" he yelled in frustration.

"Again!" Master Shol shouted. Sparman darted across the room, gathering the whole and reformed targets into a big pile on his left hand.

"This is so frustrating!" Jack protested. "Are you sure it's necessary? Can't I just fight Sparman?"

"How will you advance Drill or Parkour while fighting a real opponent, idiot disciple? When would you even use them? I've seen your usage of Parkour in the arena, and it was disgraceful at best!"

"Here I go, master," Sparman, the training robot, declared happily. "Try to fail less this time."

"You don't have to phrase it like—"

Jack jumped into motion as Sparman flung the targets haphazardly left and right. Some went for the floor, some for walls, some for the ceiling. All of them flew in Jack's general direction like frisbees, but they were too many and too fast. He had to break them all mid-flight, and to achieve that, he had to use Parkour and Drill efficiently and concurrently.

This was the training regime Master Shol had devised. Jack had already reached a level of proficiency in the two skills. If he could use them freely in the heat of the moment, it would be enough to earn him the third tier.

The annoying gym instruments got in Jack's way as he scrambled to reach the targets, barely managing to shoot out a punch before having to turn around and dash in the opposite direction. He also sent out a string of curses. Not only did he have to do all that, but he also had to aim his punches properly!

As he Parkoured over an elliptical machine, Jack let go of the instrument to punch in three directions at once. He then tried to grab it again and keep going, but missed. His forehead slammed against the bar, and he stayed there as another two targets flew past. One smacked against his butt.

He was certain that one was on purpose.

"Damn you, Sparman!" he shouted, but his anger was eclipsed by Brock's laughter. The little brorilla had fallen to the ground and was holding his belly.

Those two are in cahoots!

"Again!" Master Shol declared mercilessly.

They'd been going at it for five hours already, to little benefit. There were forty-eight targets. When Jack had started training, he could only get about seventeen of them per round. Now, he could get twenty-two.

Which was extremely frustrating because he *knew* he was getting better. The damn robot just kept ramping up the difficulty, shooting faster and farther away from him the better he got.

And, as if that wasn't enough, it *mocked* him.

"Master, you are supposed to *hit* the targets, not *miss* them. Did you forget the rules?"

"Ah, you could have gotten two more if you pivoted harder there. Shame."

"Watch out. To your left."

Jack turned and the target whooshed past behind him. "THAT WASN'T THE FUCKING LEFT!"

"I meant my left."

"I'LL MAKE YOU INTO A TIN CA—" Jack yelled but was forced to run mid-sentence as Sparman started throwing again.

Brock was having the time of his life. He'd even gone up to fetch some corn while he enjoyed the spectacle. He mimed that he was working out his laughter muscles.

Master Shol, on the other hand, watched impassively. Whether he hid his amusement or didn't feel any, Jack didn't know. He didn't care, either. All he cared about was blasting those damn targets.

"Twenty-three, master!" Sparman mocked again. "Wow, you got almost half of them!"

You think you're better than me, Sparman? Jack thought, boiling on the inside. He wasn't threatening and joking around anymore. He was just really fucking pissed. *You think you can mock me? Fuck you.*

He didn't even care about beating Rufus anymore. He just wanted to beat this fucking robot. Nothing else mattered. He had to succeed.

Unfortunately, he was now too skilled for blind anger to be helpful.

Focus, Jack. Burning body, ice mind.

His eyes sharpened. He glared at Sparman and imagined it speechless. Both his Dao Roots demanded retribution.

The targets flew again. Jack forced his body to operate at its very limits. He observed every movement of the robot, trying to predict where it would throw the next target. His mind dropping everything else except his focus. He saw a trajectory through the gym instruments strewn about the room. He saw a pattern. He followed it.

He jumped everywhere like a monkey. He was in complete control. His anger gave him the power to tame the deepest recesses of his mind, bend them to his will. He flew through the room, his every movement multi-purposed. His Drills were precise. His Parkouring efficient.

He unleashed his own storm against the flock of flying targets, picking them out of the air with mastery. He was succeeding.

He felt so damn cool.

When the targets stopped coming, he was confused before realizing there were no more. "Again!" he shouted. "I will pulverize your iron ass, robot!"

"It is over, disciple," Master Shol said with pride, approaching. "Check your notifications."

Jack frowned, then remembered the point of all this. He willed the exclamation mark open. As always, the System was kind enough to present the changes in italics.

Congratulations! Drill (II) → Drill (III)

Drill (III): Passive/*Active* Skill. By punching straight and true, you carry significant drilling power, letting your strikes penetrate hard defenses. You can bypass most kinds of armor, including thick ones.
Additionally, you can now shoot the shockwave of your punch as a short-range projectile.

Congratulations! Parkour (II) → Parkour (III)

Parkour (III): A mix of finesse and bodily strength can allow you to navigate obstacles efficiently, have better control of your body, and move unpredictably. By seamlessly integrating the environment into your moves, the battlefield itself becomes your weapon.
Your control over this Skill is enough to grant you conscious mastery.

"Conscious mastery?" he muttered, looking at the last line of the new Parkour skill. Something about that change felt different compared to all his other skills.

"It means you have mastered the skill," Master Shol explained. "You said Parkour was an experimental skill forged off this planet's culture, correct? Well, it was faulty. It reached its apex in the third tier, unlike the fifth as it should."

"Is that bad?" Jack asked worriedly.

"It could be, but not in this case. The skill will disappear when you use it as the basis of a Dao skill. It has served its purpose."

"I see..."

Ar'Tazul had warned him the skill might present problems later on, but that it would last him through the F-Grade. This must be what he meant.

Jack allowed himself a moment to admire his status screen before proceeding.

Finally! After all this effort, I've finally achieved symmetry.

His physical and mental stats were perfectly balanced, as all things should be. His skills were all in the third tier. Jack was proud of a job well done.

"Oh, right." He turned to point a finger at Sparman. "You..." he said, voice brimming with endless fury.

"I was just joking, master," Sparman replied, raising his hands defensively. "Please don't turn me into a tin can. Oh, I forgot. You can't."

Jack's eyes narrowed dangerously.

"Look on the bright side, Jack," Master Shol said, clapping his shoulder—turns out he wasn't actually corporeal, but he still stopped his hand where Jack's shoulder began. "Now that you have your skills at the proper level, it is time for you to form a Dao skill. The Dao skill of your fighting style, to be exact—the cornerstone of your E-Grade class. And how do you think that will happen?"

Jack looked at his master. The cogs in his mind snapped into place. His face was filled with elation, then split into a massive, evil grin. He turned back to Sparman.

"I will fucking smash you."

"Unfortunately, master, our physiologies are incompatible."

"Oh, I'll make your face incompatible."

"That is illog—"

Jack shouted and lunged, not even removing the gym instruments that littered the place.

"The fifth level, Sparman!" Master Shol shouted, while Brock ran for the door—as he was still relatively weak, he had to watch from there for safety reasons. It was his workout for the muscles of foresight.

Jack slammed into the robot and nailed it with punches. Sparman tried to defend, but it had been ambushed, and it was on the back foot. Jack saw the robot block and smashed a fist right into it, then another. He jumped to the side and threw a right hook, then ducked and unleashed a fearsome uppercut.

When Sparman blocked and was tossed to the ceiling, Jack kept punching, using Drill to send his punches straight at the robot. He kept it on the ceiling by sheer momentum. Sparman was defending, and struggling.

Jack let it fall, then a purple meteor sprang into existence and smashed into the falling Sparman from the side, shooting it into the wall with a heavy impact. There wasn't a scratch on the robot's metal—its actual durability didn't change, even if he decreased his power—but Jack had grabbed the initiative with both hands and refused to let go.

He arrived at Sparman a moment later, smashing out a hail of punches before it could even escape the wall. Sparman tried to punch back, but the improved version of Parkour let Jack dodge with perfect control of his body.

Sparman's punches became sparse as it focused entirely on defense. Jack was relentless. He occasionally threw a Meteor Punch, shaking the entire building, though he couldn't chain those attacks yet. They took a moment to charge, and they were tiring.

Jack punched away, venting all his previous frustration. "Die, die, die!" he shouted, laughing between punches.

Master Shol sighed and shook his head, while Brock looked on in great admiration. After all, his Big Bro was working out his revenge muscles!

CHAPTER NINETY
THE INVINCIBLE RUFUS EMBERHEART

THE ARENA WAS AS BUSY AS EVER.

Merchants wandered the stands and hollered for people to buy snacks; spectators gathered in groups and discussed excitedly with each other; and the crowd continued to trickle in through the two entrances.

"I can't believe it's the semi-finals already," Edgar said, taking in the excitement around them. "It feels like yesterday when everything began."

"I can't believe this will all be over tomorrow," Vivi added, crossing her arms. "And then, the real fight will start..."

Jack arrived next to them with a large smile. "Come on, guys, cheer up. Want some salami?"

"How can you not be nervous?"

"I am. But I also have salami. Want some?"

Just this morning, he'd discovered a forgotten pack in a cupboard. It was a bit too salty for his taste, but it would do. He'd also brought a water bottle.

"Dorman," he turned to the man, waving his pack in the air. "This can make you stronger."

Dorman grabbed a slice. "It *is* tasty," he admitted, chomping down on it. "You should have brought some cheese, too."

"I'm out. Why didn't you bring your cheese?"

"I'm not the food master."

"You're fast. Can't you just... go get some?"

"It doesn't work like that."

These were two of the four strongest people on Earth. As was proper, they could resist the tension. After all, they'd already trained as hard as they could. Now, they just had to fight.

"Look, it's starting!" Edgar pointed at the sky, where the winged djinn now hovered. Everyone grew quiet.

"Welcome, everyone, to the semi-finals," she announced. Her voice boomed into the spectator stands. "There will only be two battles today, and they will be the grandest yet. Four fighters remain: Rufus Emberheart, Alexander Petrovic, Dorman Whistles, and Jack Rust. The brightest geniuses of Earth-387."

The crowd cheered. She let them calm down before continuing. "Now, without further ado, let the semi-finals commence!"

More cheers.

"First fight: Dorman Whistles and the Dao of Speed—" Dorman held his breath, as did Jack "—versus Rufus Emberheart and the Dao of Supremacy!"

Some people cheered. Dorman's face grew stern. Jack threw him a conflicted glance.

Of the four of them, Rufus was probably the strongest. Realistically, any of the other three had a chance to get to the finals as long as they didn't run into him.

In fact, Jack had been half-certain that he'd be called to fight the leonine today. In the end, that didn't come to pass.

"Good luck," he told Dorman. "I look forward to meeting you in the finals."

Dorman nodded in reply. Clenching his jaw, he leaped to the stage, landing amidst claps and cheers. Rufus Emberheart dropped opposite him in a cloud of sand. When it cleared, his eyes were full of confidence.

"You are one of the few worthy humans," he declared in a booming voice, like a man speaking to a child. "You are unlucky to face me but try your best. With a good enough performance, the Foreign Guard might be interested in you."

"The Foreign Guard and the entire Animal Kingdom can take a hike," Dorman replied, holding his twin daggers in a fighting stance. "I have no interest in allying with you. I will beat you today, then win the final."

Many people gaped at these words. Not only were they bold, they were reckless. There was no need to antagonize Rufus so hard at this point.

The leonine himself raised an annoyed brow. "Are all humans this idiotically disrespectful?"

"Only the best of us," Dorman responded, then lunged. His daggers left afterimages as he reached Rufus near-instantly and fell into an attacking pattern. He moved jaggedly to the left and right, striking out in a flurry of blows that resembled a storm.

Dorman's attacks were difficult to predict because they aimed at random places, not the opponent's vitals. He wanted to inflict death by a thousand cuts.

Facing him, Rufus growled. A transparent, spherical blue shield materialized around him. When the daggers plunged into it, they slowed tremendously, making them easy to deflect.

It was the first time he'd used that skill.

Dorman's brows rose. Rufus smacked out a punch, and the blue phantom of a lion's paw flew unimpeded through the shield. The teenager jumped and twisted around it, using his daggers to block another strike head-on, but his momentum had been stilted. He rode the impact of blocking Rufus's attack to make some distance.

The leonine smiled.

"Inferiority is weakness. So long as your Dao is inferior to mine, you cannot touch me."

Dorman frowned deeply in thought. The blue shield still surrounded Rufus, stretching about a foot away from him. He hadn't used this skill in his fight against Li Xiang. Was it because he wanted to meet the old man's martial arts head-on, or had he just developed it in the last day?

Maybe Li Xiang's Dao was so strong that it wouldn't have been stopped by the shield?

Dorman had absolute confidence in his skills, but his cultivation was split in two directions. He was cultivating speed and lightning. Each of these Dao Roots were far from advancing to a Dao Seed, but he was sacrificing time now for stability later on.

Could Rufus's skill block those with inferior Daos? That was ridiculous.

"Why are you surprised?" the leonine asked. "Since I am obviously superior to you, is it not natural that my Dao of Supremacy will be at its strongest?"

Dorman's frown deepened further. If Rufus could just stand there leisurely and talk, it meant his shield didn't have a short time limit. Dorman would have to find a way through it.

That was fine. If the shield made him slower, he would just have to become even faster.

"I didn't expect to use this so early in our fight," Dorman said. His short hair stood on end. Sparks flew between them, transforming each hair into a lightning rod, and electricity raced from his toes to his face. His every movement was full of static, and his daggers were wreathed in lightning.

The crowd made noises of surprise.

"A third Dao skill," Rufus acknowledged, nodding in approval. "You do have potential. If you can just curb that arrogance of yours, you will have a future."

"Fuck you."

Dorman charged, but this time, he was way faster than before. He left lightning in his wake, reaching Rufus in an instant. His right dagger plunged into the shield. The moment it did, Dorman felt his strength waning. His muscles went limp, his control of the Dao fluctuated. He experienced the effects of awe and terror without actually feeling those emotions. His Dao Roots tried to resist, but a heavy blanket of inferiority muffled them.

It was like his Dao and body were subdued facing a greater power. He simply couldn't muster his strength. Inside the shield, his dagger slowed down tremendously. Rufus slapped it away with a paw.

"It is impressive that you beat Fesh Wui while holding back," he commented. "Or did you just develop this Dao skill yesterday?"

Dorman wasn't in the mood for idle chit-chatting. He withdrew from the shield's range and ran circles around the leonine so fast, he left afterimages. A ring of lightning appeared to surround Rufus, shooting streaks of electricity in random directions.

"Your naivete warms my heart," Rufus said, laughing. He didn't try to defend. When the lightning bolts entered the shield's radius, they lost all power. They couldn't even burn Rufus's clothes.

Dorman kept running circles, but he was slowly descending into panic. The Lightning Form Dao skill drew his mana like a hungry eel. He couldn't keep it up for long... and it was utterly useless! That shield countered everything he did.

How was he supposed to fight against that!

Dorman set his jaw, refusing to give up. He'd trained hard for this. Had developed new skills. He was confident that, besides Rufus, only Jack Rust could match him in combat.

How could he be so *helpless*? Ridiculed like a child? He refused!

He was supposed to be the main character!

As he ran, Dorman pointed a dagger in Rufus's direction from afar. Most of the lightning running through his body was absorbed into the dagger, then exploded forth in a rumbling spike that struck Rufus. The moment it entered the shield, its power decreased by more than half. It blackened a few rings in Rufus's chainmail armor, but all it could elicit of the leonine was a frown.

"It is a pity," he said relaxedly. "If my power didn't counter yours, you could have forced me to go all-out... but there is no medicine for regret, nor can the weak seek justice. If you want to complain about anything, complain about your own luck."

Dorman gritted his teeth so hard they were about to break. Rufus hadn't even attacked yet, and he'd been rendered hopeless.

Not like this! he screamed inwardly.

He had come on stage prepared to lose against a fierce struggle. He wanted to demonstrate his powers to the whole world, and if he wasn't enough, then yes, he could lose.

But what kind of joke was this? He couldn't even use his movement technique or show off his speed. After everything he achieved, he was treated like a pathetic weakling. And why? Just because his powers didn't *match well* against Rufus? He didn't deserve this!

Dorman screamed at the top of his lungs. The lightning running around his body intensified, new sparks and bolts conjured out of nothing. His body spasmed as he cranked up the electricity to its limit.

The daggers glowed like molten iron. The world slowed to a crawl, even Rufus. The leonine's mocking smile still hung on his face. Dorman's arms became coiled springs, which then erupted with force. He unleashed everything he had in an instant.

Fast Mode! Lightning Fangs!

His daggers flew forward at a speed his muscles could not support, pulled by the power of the Dao. The electricity running over his body accelerated everything further.

This was the fastest, strongest attack Dorman had unleashed. All three of his Dao skills were used in tandem. A boom came from the tips of his daggers as they broke the sound barrier.

They plunged into the blue shield. Panic snared Dorman when they slowed. The wisps of electricity died out, his muscles cramped, and the daggers wobbled. They remained fast, but it was nowhere near the speed they should have.

Even in slow motion, Rufus's paws shot up. He grabbed both daggers by the blade, freezing them mid-slash. Thick, regal blood flowed from his palms, but the mocking, triumphant smile on his face widened.

This was all Dorman's ultimate attack could amount to: scratches on Rufus's palms.

"You drew blood," the leonine said, his voice equal measures impressed and disappointed. "I did not expect that. Very well. Carry this achievement as your badge of honor, little human. You, an ant, drew the blood of a king."

He let go of the blades, and Dorman collapsed to his knees. He panted heavily, and it took everything he had not to puke on the spot. He was completely out of power.

Rufus watched him from above. "I would advise you to reconsider. The Animal Kingdom can offer you much more than a tiny planet in the fringes of the constellation... but if you want to waste away here, that is your choice to make."

The crowd had gone silent. Even Jack and the rest couldn't form words. They'd expected Rufus to win, but this... This was a travesty! From start to end, he hadn't even attacked once, and Dorman was already on his knees. Where was the heroic struggle, the valiant battle? Where was the fierce clash that befitted a semi-final?

Dorman, who revered power above all, had been humiliated!

"Dorman Whistles is unable to stand and is at the mercy of his opponent," the head judge declared from the sky. "Therefore, Rufus Emberheart is the winner. Congratulations!"

Only scattered claps came from the audience, as most were still too shocked to react.

Jack, too, had his eyes glued on Rufus in utter shock. The leonine was his enemy, but suddenly, he seemed as tall as a mountain. Jack hated his guts but was forced to admit that Rufus truly embodied the supremacy he preached.

In the first phase of the Tournament, he had annihilated every opponent in one strike. In the second phase, one battle had ended by his opponent resigning immediately. He challenged Li Xiang in the latter's area of expertise and won, and he even returned the shame that the old man tried to inflict on him tenfold in an overbearing manner. He treated Dorman, one of the strongest people around, like a toy.

With the exception of the auction and the chanting of "Fuck you, Rufus Emberheart," the leonine had absolutely dominated the Tournament.

And Jack was mortal enemies with that guy.

He gulped. In the next moment, the spirit of the indomitable fist inside him flared. Dorman had only lost so decisively because he was countered. Jack wouldn't be. He focused on one Dao, and it couldn't be that much weaker than Rufus's. He was strong, too. He had a chance.

For now, he just had to make it to the finals, then spend the remaining day creating a new Dao skill.

His gaze crossed the arena to land on Alexander Petrovic, who regarded him coldly.

Jack didn't even wait for the head judge to speak. The moment Dorman leaped off the sands and landed beside them, Jack jumped away, falling to the sands and standing straight. Rufus was already gone, too.

Alexander arrived a moment later. He seemed ready to trash talk, but Jack wasn't in the mood. If he wanted to face Rufus as an equal, then he had to treat Alexander as a small fry.

"Bring out your strongest form, Alexander Petrovic," he declared, cracking his knuckles. His fighting spirit surged out and blanketed the stage. "This will be over quickly."

CHAPTER NINETY-ONE
THE UNSTOPPABLE JACK RUST

JACK STOOD OPPOSITE ALEXANDER PETROVIC, GLARING INTO HIS EYES.

He hadn't forgotten how Alexander tried to murder Vivi, his friend and ally. He also hadn't forgotten how the Ice Peak shamed humanity by prostrating like cowards. And most importantly, he hadn't forgotten that Alexander was only a stepping-stone. The real enemy was Rufus Emberheart.

The other man's short blond hair glistened in the morning sun, and his piercing blue eyes tried to see all the way to Jack's soul.

"You underestimate me," Alexander said.

"You do not know your place. You're just a big dog. How could you possibly stop me?"

"What would that make your ally, then? Worse than a dog?"

"Wild dogs can eat humans. But when the hunter arrives, there is only one path: death. Unless you plan to submit to me, too, as you did to the slightly larger dog you serve."

Gasps ran through the spectator stands. Insulting Rufus while hidden in a large crowd was one thing. Doing it openly was another. Then again, it wouldn't be the first time for Jack. As he had told the head judge, he was a troublemaker, and he wouldn't have it any other way.

"Your tongue runs, American. Let's see it freeze."

The temperature dropped sharply throughout the arena. Jack felt it up-close for the first time, unprotected by the energy ceiling of the stage. It was cold, yes—perhaps dozens of degrees below freezing point. To his highly-strengthened body, it was merely a chill.

Contrary to his boasts, Alexander did assume his ice form immediately. The glacial egg appeared around him, and half a minute later, it cracked open, revealing a man clad in ice. He had ice wings, an ice tail, two ice swords, and his arms were covered in ice up to the shoulder. Even his feet were encased in ice, such that they resembled talons.

Alexander's body itself now exuded a deep cold.

Jack let that all happen. He did not strike the egg, only watched with arms crossed.

"You sure took your time," he said when Alexander emerged. "I was getting bored out here. Thought I'd eat an ice cream."

"You are arrogant, American."

"No. I am strong."

Jack clenched his fists and assumed a fighting stance.

He hadn't developed a fighting style yet. He'd fought against Sparman for several hours last night, all the way until the moon reached its peak, but he got nowhere. Unfortunately, his current strength was enough to overpower Sparman's fifth level but lose catastrophically to the sixth, and neither option was suitable for developing a fighting style.

He could feel that he was close. All he lacked was fighting experience with his current level of skills. He hoped Alexander could give him that.

The ice man flew forth. He left traces of snow behind him as the air froze over, and anything his feet touched became ice. His twin swords cried and whistled as they came crashing down on Jack.

One would argue that fighting bare-chested wasn't the best way to go about this. Jack had his reasons. Anything between himself and the heat of the battle limited his connection to the Dao and hampered his progress—or, at least, so he felt.

He stepped back, anticipating Alexander's attack. Though he was durable, he was reluctant to block those blades with his hands. Jack shot out a hail of jabs.

His hand moved back and forth so quickly it left afterimages. His closed fist punched the air, letting its shockwave travel forward and explode on Alexander's body. Thanks to Drill's advancement, he could now shoot his fists up to nine feet away.

Alexander hadn't expected that. The moment he approached Jack, shockwaves flew at him like ghost fists. They arrived a dime a dozen and crashed hard into him, halting his momentum and sending him flying back. Alexander rolled across the ground, and Jack was already there, having closed the distance.

He punched repeatedly. Every strike was hard and fast, barely kept at bay by Alexander's defenses. Alexander tried to block, parry, and redirect, but always found himself on the back foot. He tried to counter-strike, but Jack possessed perfect balance and control of his body, and he could dodge while still shooting out punches.

A fist landed clean on Alexander's face, two more in his sternum, and a fourth on his left wing, shattering it in the process. The audience watched in silent shock before cheering.

Compared to Rufus's absolute demonstrations of power, it was easy to forget that Jack had never come close to losing in the Tournament so far. Some battles had been more difficult than others, but he always emerged the clear, undisputed victor. In this Tournament, he was undoubtedly one of the top contenders.

But Dorman had been the same until he ran into Rufus. Jack had to get even stronger.

His fists crashed mercilessly, pushing his opponent into a corner. Alexander managed to escape and create some space, bruised and battered as he was, but he couldn't fly with only one wing. He was forced to remain on the sand, where Jack gave him no time to rest.

They clashed again. Alexander brandished his swords and even his stalactite-tipped tail, but it was useless. Thanks to Drill, Jack had the longer reach. And thanks to his high Physical, he won frontal collisions, too!

Moreover, he'd discovered a neat trick. He didn't have to use his fist to clash against the blade. He could send out a Drill punch just before the moment of impact. The reduction in strength wasn't too large.

That goes to say, Alexander was completely cornered. His attacks didn't land once. His defense was unable to stand up to Jack's strength. He couldn't even fly. What else was he supposed to do?

He opened his mouth and unleashed a cone-shaped blizzard. A meteor crashed into it, stopping it thoroughly and exploding it back into Alexander's face. He barely stepped back in time to avoid a second meteor, but the shockwave alone was enough to blast him screaming into the far wall.

"Had enough?" Jack laughed, standing in the middle of the arena.

Alexander flew out of the debris. He changed tactics. The ice on his person melted away, becoming pure white mana that flowed into the ground. The ground under Jack's feet became slick ice. Towering glacial walls rose around him and sought to crush him.

Jack only laughed. He didn't even try to dodge. In the end, no matter how hard Alexander tried, it was only ice.

And Jack's fists were harder.

Purple light blazed in the arena as the ice walls exploded, revealing large, circular holes the size of doors. Jack easily darted through before the other walls smashed him into paste.

Ice statues rose from the ground. There were white-capped dwarves wielding pickaxes, barbarian lumberjacks hoisting large axes, thin people with long limbs, as well as two polar bears. They all moved to fight him as if alive. At the same time, Alexander opened his arms wide. Finger-sized ice pikes materialized out of thin air and flew at Jack.

Jack laughed again. Alexander was grasping at straws, throwing every attack he could think of.

His punches fell like rain. All statues were shattered. The slick ice under Jack's heels was broken by strong stomps, and the small ice pikes couldn't penetrate his indomitable skin. The larger ones, he met with his knuckles, shattering them.

A wall of ice larger than any other appeared to block Jack's way. He couldn't see through it. It must have been extremely thick. While he was fighting the statues, Alexander had spent the entire time conjuring it.

The wall stretched dozens of feet high, possibly a hundred. Jack had to tilt his head to see the top—it was even taller than the energy wall, which rose and formed a large dome around the stage, as it did for flying fighters.

Jack wasn't really sure what Alexander intended to do with this wall, but it was pretty damn big. Then, slowly but surely, it began to fall.

Jack could have tried to dodge it, but that was too easy. It smelled like a trap. So instead, he shot off the ground, rearing back his fist. It shone like a purple star. Colors and sounds were absorbed by it, leaving only a man faced with a gigantic, thick sheet of ice. He took his time, pouring his entire body and mind into the strike.

This was the strongest attack Jack had ever unleashed.

It crashed into the ice with a tremendous boom, shaking everyone's ears and making their vision waver. The intense light and searing heat were blocked by the energy wall, so the audience was safe, but the wall wasn't.

A large, bowl-shaped crater was carved into it, stretching ten feet into the ice but hadn't reached the other end—it'd barely crossed the halfway point.

The wall's fall had been momentarily halted by Jack's attack, but it resumed, and Jack was still airborne. For all his power, he couldn't fly, and the momentum of his Meteor Punch had been absorbed into forming the crater.

"Shit," he said. The giant wall of ice fell on him and smashed against the ground. Its weight was such that the entire arena shook greatly, making the standing spectators lose their balance.

The wall must have weighed tens of tons, and it had all crashed on Jack's head.

Everyone held their breath. Then, laughter resounded from somewhere, seeping through the ice. With a deafening boom, part of the ice wall exploded outward in a circular hole, out of which leaped Jack.

"You fool," he said, charging Alexander at full tilt. "I made a crater!"

The audience cheered. Jack was still pristine, not having suffered a single hit. As for Alexander, his brows were furrowed. Seeing Jack charge him, he raised an open palm. Thick sheets of ice materialized in front of him, acting as shields. At the same time, he prepared to shoot ice spikes at the sides or above, in case Jack dodged the sheets.

Ice was a predominantly defensive Dao. However, the fist was predominantly offensive—and Jack was stronger than Alexander.

He clenched a purple fist, stealing the world's colors. The sound of his footsteps faded as the ice turned paler. He drove his fist through the ice sheets, piercing and shattering them all like glass. His punch met Alexander's face straight-on, exploding like a meteor and sending him flying back head-first into a wall.

The people cheered.

Jack stopped his advance, panting a bit. His forearm now sported shallow red cuts from the ice, but other than that, he was unhurt. He stared at Alexander, who was struggling to stand. His nose was broken, his entire face bloodied, but his most wounded part was his pride.

Jack didn't pursue the attack. He simply stared at Alexander with the gaze of a conqueror. His point was clear, as was the battle's winner. He didn't intend to kill his opponent and be disqualified here, anyway.

"Had enough?" he asked, and this time, Alexander had no retort.

After a moment's hesitation, he uttered, "I resign." The crowd erupted in cheers. Jack raised a fist into the air, and the cheers intensified.

He'd struck back against Rufus's mental warfare. He, too, had obliterated his opponent—though he, too, was a clear counter.

Most importantly, he'd proven himself as Earth's strongest human.

"Remember this the next time you bully my allies, dickhead," he roared at Alexander, pointing a finger at him. A loser had no right to retort. This last provocation was for Vivi, though he kept himself discreet. This was her battle to fight, not his. His real opponent was still waiting. "Now run to your master like the good dog you are and tell him to sleep in fear. Jack Rust is coming."

They were already irreconcilable enemies—what did he have to lose?

Alexander conjured a staircase of ice and walked back to his seat in the stands, where his people welcomed him with a deep nod. He only sat on his chair and closed his eyes.

The Ice Peak was not the Flame River. Even if he lost, Alexander Petrovic would never show weakness, or he'd be backstabbed in the blink of an eye. He had reserved enough mana to return to his seat gracefully.

The crowd still cheered as Jack jumped on top of the giant mountain of crushed ice and raised his fist in triumph. A moment later, magic flashed from the djinns responsible for cleaning up, and the wall disappeared. Jack returned to his seat with a wide smile.

"Hey," Vivi was the first to speak. "That was pretty tame. I expected you to yell about taking revenge for me."

"Well, I kinda did, but I kept it low-key. Why? Do you need me to take revenge for you?" he asked, a brow raised.

A grin crept on Vivi's face. "No. I will take it myself. I just didn't know you were so... thoughtful."

"I know you're not a damsel in distress, Vivi. You can handle your own battles. It's part of your charm," he said with a wink, and Vivi couldn't help but smile.

"Thank you, Jack."

"No problem. It's what allies do, right?" She rolled her eyes but couldn't hide a smile.

"Jack," Dorman said, walking up to him. "Good luck in the finals."

"Thanks. Actually, I have something to ask of you, Dorman," Jack said. "I need a training partner for today. Are you up for it?"

Dorman raised a brow, then grinned widely. "Of course."

Edgar and the Flame River fell on Jack to congratulate him, and the Sage nodded wisely. The head judge's voice came again.

"Tomorrow at dawn, we will watch the final battle of the Integration Tournament. Rufus Emberheart and the Dao of Supremacy versus Jack Rust and the Dao of the Fist. The greatest genius of Earth-387 will be declared tomorrow!"

The crowd cheered and stomped their feet on the wooden stands, raising a thunderous sound that echoed throughout Integration City. Behind the curtain, Rufus nodded. Atop the white tower, the C-Grade lioness turned her head.

And in one particular estate of the participant district, a bald monk with a sharp beard had his brows furrowed as he desperately argued against an invincible opponent.

Finally, his brow relaxed. A wide smile appeared on his face. "Thank you, master!" he roared, laughing.

CHAPTER NINETY-TWO

TOO GOOD?

JACK AND DORMAN WALKED SIDE-BY-SIDE, BROCK BETWEEN THEM.

They entered the participant district and reached Jack's house. Jack swiped his identification token to let them in, and the door slid open soundlessly.

"Isn't it odd to see such high-tech next to swords and sandals?" Jack asked, walking in.

"It is. But the magic is odder."

"I guess."

Both were ready to kick each other's asses. They loved battle, and they couldn't wait.

"Jack."

Master Shol waited by the kitchen, staring out the window. The moment Jack saw him, he raised a brow. Something was different. Was he... smiling?

"I suppose you are here to spar," Master Shol said.

"Yes, Master."

"Excellent."

Dorman nodded deeply at Shol. "Greetings, venerable immortal."

"You may rise," Master Shol replied off-handedly. Jack raised a brow at the exchange. "You are called Dorman, correct? Could you wait outside for a moment? I must discuss something with my disciple."

"Of course," Dorman replied immediately, the very image of respect. He moved backward, not turning the other way until the door slid closed in front of him.

"What was that?" Jack asked, turning to his master.

"Manners, kid. You should try it sometime."

Master Shol was clearly more relaxed now that they were alone. A small smile played on his lips. "I have great news for you, Jack."

Jack's heart skipped a beat, but he tried to appear composed. "Oh?"

"Your previous request to seek shelter under the Exploding Sun was too excessive. Where I come from, such disrespect could get you severely punished." He paused to let his words sink in. "However, a master-disciple relationship is sacred. As I have authority over you, I also have a duty to protect you."

Jack raised a brow.

"I do not have the power to extend the Exploding Sun's protection to your faction," his master continued. "As I've said, I am only a Deacon of the faction, one amongst many. However, my master does have that power."

Jack's eyes shone. "Your master, Master?"

Master Shol nodded. "My master is Elder Huali of the Exploding Sun faction, a high C-Grade immortal. She possesses great authority, including the right to accept subordinate factions. I spoke to her and negotiated on your behalf." He took a breath. "Under certain conditions, she is willing to take the Bare Fist Brotherhood under her wing."

Jack took a moment to digest this. Hope rose in his chest, but he didn't dare believe it. This was too sudden.

"Does that mean we will be protected?" he asked in disbelief.

Master Shol's smile was all the answer he needed. "Congratulations, my boy. You have a way out."

Jack's emotions burst through the floodgate. He felt relief, joy, exhilaration. His people weren't doomed. The professor, the brorillas and gymonkeys, the people of Valville... He could save them all!

However, he didn't let himself get swept by those emotions. He'd been cornered at the edge of a cliff before, and now, Master Shol could solve all his problems, just like that?

This was a bit too easy.

"Wait," Jack said. "Did you say you negotiated on my behalf?"

"My master is a risk-averse person. She requested a few things in return for shielding your faction. There is nothing to worry about, though," he added quickly, noticing Jack's frown. "What she asked will benefit you, as well."

"Okay. So, what is it?"

"The first is that you must become her disciple and enter the Exploding Sun. Many would kill their family for such a fortune. A B-Grade faction can offer incredible benefits to its members, and a high C-Grade master is the fortune of seven lifetimes. Since your faction will be protected, I went ahead and agreed on your behalf. Is that fine with you?"

"But, you're already my master," he replied reflexively.

"Cultivators can have multiple masters throughout their life," Master Shol explained, shrugging. "No shame in that, as long as those masters aren't enemies with each other."

"Oh."

Joining a high-Grade faction hadn't been in his immediate plans, but it sounded way easier than wandering the hostile galaxy by himself. Plus, his faction would be safe, so he had nothing to worry about. He could pursue the Dao at his leisure.

"That sounds great," he replied honestly. "And I can enter another faction without disbanding mine, right?"

"You couldn't disband yours even if you wanted to. The System lets you join up to two factions at the same time, granted you're the leader of one of them."

"I see. Okay, that's good. You mentioned that she asked for other things?"

Master Shol nodded.

"The second is that your faction will only be our subordinate in name. The Animal Kingdom won't touch you lightly, but you also won't receive any other benefits from the Exploding Sun until you prove yourself worthy of our favor. Additionally, the scions are considered part of your planet now, and the Exploding Sun won't interfere in your planet's matters. You are expected to pull your weight."

"Okay," Jack agreed. Just saving them from the Animal Kingdom was a blessing. He and his allies could handle the scions—but if they couldn't, that was just their fault for being weak. Even Rufus could be taken down by superior numbers.

"Then, there are a few constraints." Master Shol frowned. "This is the difficult part. As I said, my master is a risk-averse person, as well as one of extremely high status. My personal recommendation isn't enough for her to take a disciple. For this to be worth her while, she requests that you win the Integration Tournament."

Jack blinked. "What?"

"Trust me, this is the lowest requirement she has ever offered. In the Exploding Sun, her prospective disciples must complete harder tasks to earn her tutelage."

"So if I don't beat Rufus Emberheart, none of this matters?"

"Unfortunately, yes... but you can't ask for more, Jack. This is already an incredible concession on her part. If you want the Exploding Sun to have your back, you need to show at least that much potential. This isn't charity."

Jack frowned deeply. He was aware that his strength was probably inferior to Rufus's. In the Tournament's final battle, the odds would be stacked against him, and that's only if he managed to develop the fighting style Dao skill. Otherwise, his chances of victory would be very, very slim.

"You could have started with that," Jack said, scratching his head. "You got my hopes up."

"My disciple should have the presence of mind to handle it. This is training, too."

Jack sighed. "Tell me honestly, master. Do you think I can beat him?"

"It is possible," Master Shol replied. "It won't be easy, but if you can develop a fighting style today, your strengths should be close. Anything can happen in battle."

"I see... Then if I beat Rufus Emberheart tomorrow, the Exploding Sun will protect my faction from the Animal Kingdom, and a C-Grade immortal will take me in as a disciple. And this is something you negotiated for me." He threw a side glance at his master. "Pardon me, master, but this sounds a bit too good to be true. Is there a catch?"

And then, for the first time ever, Jack saw his master smile. Not the small rising of his lips that usually happened, or the faint smirk that was occasionally drawn on his face. This was the wide, ear-to-ear grin of a happy person.

"The galaxy is full of greedy, unreliable thieves who will try to cheat you at the first opportunity, but there are also good people, Jack. I try my best to be one of them. There is no catch. I am simply taking care of my disciple as my master took care of me."

Jack was caught off guard. He never expected such a radiant smile from his stern master. Could his words be true? Could he just be... a good person?

What were the chances? Master Shol had appeared out of nowhere, insisted on choosing Jack, and even helped him not be disqualified from the Tournament. Now, he was dropping a massive pie from the sky. This man was an enigma. He sounded too good to be true.

Could Jack have been that lucky?

His reason told him the chances were low. This looked like a scam whose punchline had yet to be delivered.

On the other hand, Jack's instinct told him that Master Shol wasn't that kind of person. His heart told him to have trust—which was exactly how skilled conmen made their victims feel.

However, Jack had to admit that his master had done nothing wrong so far. He offered training and knowledge abundantly, even when they were at odds. He was a strict man, but had proven at every opportunity that his heart was in the right place.

Jack still suspected that something was off—again, this seemed too good to be true—but he decided to trust his master, at least for now. It wasn't like he had a choice. And when the other shoe dropped, when and if Master Shol actually requested things from Jack, he could reconsider.

And if, by any turn of luck, this was real... He had hope!

"Okay!" he replied, letting himself be filled with excitement. That was the path of the fist: all-in. "So I just need to train hard and beat Rufus."

"Exactly!"

Brock joined in their joy, jumping around and hollering. He pumped a fist in the air. Jack laughed.

"Then, there's no time to lose," he said. "Should I get Dorman?"

"Of course! Let's get started. We have a lot of work to do."

Jack rushed for the door. He finally had a real solution to his problems, one that didn't involve heavy casualties. It was a difficult solution, yes, but this was nothing new. Just like when he was level 1 and asked to kill two level 49 Elite wolves, Jack just had to bulldoze his way forward like a fist.

It was do or die. So long as the problem was punchable and in his weight class, Jack just had to succeed.

The sparring room had been cleaned. Sparman had moved all gym instruments back to their original positions and now waited in a corner with a medical kit at hand. Master Shol stood beside him, ready to give out pointers, while Brock peered from behind the ajar door.

Jack and Dorman clashed in the middle of the room. Dorman was wreathed in lightning, moving at speeds that befuddled the eye, while Jack waved his fists with enough strength to break brick walls.

Shockwaves flew around the room, smashing into the walls, ceiling, and floor. Sparman was too durable to be affected, while Master Shol was only a spiritual projection, and their Dao wasn't deep enough to injure him.

Jack roared as he charged. He smashed out a rain of fists, each indomitable, demanding to hit Dorman. Some were physical, others were spectral phantoms made by Drill.

Dorman danced between the fists. Sparks flew everywhere as he dodged, his speed way beyond anything Jack could achieve. He slipped through the onslaught like a leaf and even struck out occasionally, but his daggers were too weak to leave meaningful injuries.

Jack's bare chest was covered in slowly regenerating scratches, as were his limbs. He'd only managed to get one attack in, but the damage it inflicted had been equivalent to all of Dorman's attacks put together. The one time he smashed a fist on Dorman's abdomen, the smaller fighter had gone flying, crashing into the soft walls with a strong thud.

He'd stood again and kept on fighting, but lacking a regeneration skill, the injury persisted. He was slower now.

They were both going all-out from the start, and they knew each other's powers, so there were no secrets to uncover or aces in their sleeves. Their fight transitioned into a battle of attrition. Would Jack succumb first, his regeneration and stamina unable to keep up with all the injuries, or would Dorman mess up even once more, allowing Jack to strike a devastating blow?

Once again, Jack was reminded of his battle with the rock bear. Only he was the rock bear now.

Dorman also had his finishing blows, but Jack was confident he would see them coming and dodge in time. Then, it would be game over. Dorman would be out of energy.

Every clash sent sparks flying as Dorman used his daggers to redirect fists. He jumped back, reaching the far wall in an instant and pointing his dagger at Jack. A lightning bolt the size of his hand shot out. Jack roared and punched it head-on.

The lightning bolt dissipated, but part of it entered his body, making him convulse for a split-second. Like Dorman's other attacks, it wasn't enough to overpower Jack's defenses, but it was enough to hurt him slightly.

He charged again.

Throughout the battle, Jack had been trying to use all his skills. Fist-fighting, Drill, Parkour, Pugilist Body... At least some of those could be combined into the fighting style Dao skill he sought.

However, as time passed, he realized with growing horror that nothing was happening. The skills flew out in sync, but he couldn't see how to combine them into something greater. They didn't grow deeper or more effective.

It was useless. He was running but staying in the same place.

Dorman had the skill to challenge Jack, but this whack-a-mole they were playing wasn't the kind of battle he needed.

Master Shol reached the same conclusion. "That's enough," he said, putting an end to their battle. Both fighters looked at him, panting and sweaty. Jack was bloodied, while Dorman sported a cracked rib.

"This is going nowhere," Master Shol shook his head, echoing Jack's thoughts. "We need someone with the strength to challenge Jack's limits and a head-on fighting style. Your speed works great, but it is not what we need now, Dorman."

"This one understands." Dorman nodded deeply, leading to another raised eyebrow from Jack. Since when was he so well-behaved? And why did he call himself "this one?"

Regardless, now wasn't the time to care about that. Tomorrow's battle was approaching fast—it was already noon—and Jack had to win, no matter what. The future of himself and everyone he cared about hinged on it.

"Can't I use the Rainbow Dao Pill, Master?" he asked. "Or the Dao Fruit of the Fist? I've had them for a while now."

"Those are breakthrough treasures," Master Shol said. "Their effects now would be minuscule. There is no sense in wasting them."

Dorman shot him an odd look but said nothing.

"What about dungeon resources?" Jack said, an idea flashing through his eyes. He'd thought about it before, but it was never a priority. "We could take the Sage's starship and tour the dungeons of our alliance, getting a lot more stat points. That would help, right?"

"If that was possible, everyone would be a genius," Master Shol shot down the idea. "The System won't let you. Dungeon resources give you fewer and fewer benefits the more of them you get. Even if you're lucky enough to find an F-Grade dungeon with an E-Grade resource, the time expenditure just isn't worth it right now. A few attribute points won't save you. A Dao skill will."

Jack gritted his teeth. He was running out of ideas. He had to somehow develop a fighting style, and for that, he needed the right opponent. But whom?

Then his eyes flashed.

"I know the right person," he said, drawing the eyes of both Dorman and Master Shol. "We need Li Xiang."

CHAPTER NINETY-THREE
THE PEAK OF MARTIAL ARTS

JACK ONCE AGAIN STOOD IN HIS HOUSE'S SPARRING ROOM, CRACKING HIS knuckles. It had taken him two hours to find Li Xiang and bring him here. That made it afternoon, but the wasted time was more than worth it. Jack could feel it.

The old Chinese master stood calmly. He wore new robes, though his face was still warped from his previous humiliation. Anger and hatred burned in his eyes. Unfortunately, he knew he was too weak for revenge. The next best thing he could do was help Jack.

Two days ago, he might have refused sparring. Today, he jumped at the opportunity.

"Thank you again for the assistance, senior Xiang," Jack said, nodding deeply.

"Not a problem. You must beat that person, no matter what. He deserves no honor." Li Xiang turned to bow at Master Shol. "And a thousand gratitudes to Master Shol. This young man appreciates your pointers."

A smirk played on Master Shol's lips. He brought down a hand. "Start!"

Jack charged.

Li Xiang adopted a fighting stance. There were no gaps or flaws, his stance was as absolute as the looming mountain. Suddenly, Jack felt hesitant, foolish, like a child about to attack an adult.

Thankfully, he was a very, very strong child.

His fist came crashing down. Li Xiang's hands blurred, slapping Jack's wrist out of the air and sending the strike wide. Jack persisted, shooting punch after punch. These were light jabs, not carrying much of his body weight, so he could easily recover even if they missed.

Li Xiang wasn't fast, nor was he strong. However, his hands and body moved with such uninterrupted harmony, that he was almost dancing, and Jack merely followed a choreography that ended with him losing. Whenever Li Xiang redirected one of his strikes, Jack felt like a stray gust of wind had touched his wrist and moved it gently to the side. Whenever his jabs were dodged, it felt like he'd missed. He couldn't harness his own strength.

It was incredible. Even while fighting, Jack could barely hold back his awe.

He had fought hobgoblins and skilled human warriors, even scions, and he didn't always beat them by virtue of higher stats. His skill in fighting was way better than most. He dodged minimally and struck hard. He manipulated his momentum to cycle between attacks. He read patterns in his opponents, mixed up his attacks, and capitalized on their weaknesses. His fists were his weapons, and he was damn good at wielding them. He even had his Fistfighting skill in the third tier.

So why did Li Xiang make him feel inadequate?

None of his tricks worked! Every plan he made fell right into one of Li Xiang's traps. The old man was always a step ahead, no matter how Jack tried to feint or break the cycle.

Now he understood why Gan Salin had been so angry after fighting Li Xiang. This was frustrating!

A foot came straight up and smashed into Jack's jaw. He hadn't seen it coming. Li Xiang's body hadn't betrayed the movement in the slightest. It was like a third leg had sprouted out of thin air.

Jack flew up, somersaulted backward and landed on his feet. He touched his chin. "Nice one," he said, fighting spirit welling up inside him.

He wanted to develop a Dao skill fighting style, and this little old man was proving his current fighting style completely insufficient. He was the perfect anvil. Jack would break himself against it until something happened.

"Less talking, more fighting," Li Xiang ordered.

Jack didn't need to be told twice.

He dashed forth, practically flying over the floor. He lashed out in a flurry of punches. This wasn't the restrained testing he had done before. He was now going all-out.

Punches alternated between fast and slow. Sometimes, he threw out projectiles with Drill—other times, he used his physical fist. He employed the perfect control over his body—granted by Parkour and Pugilist Body—to bend his punches oddly, sending them into angles that a pre-System human would struggle to achieve, or striking with force from odd positions. He even mixed in a kick or two. Though his path was that of the fist, he had legs, so why not use them?

The only skill he didn't use was Meteor Punch, as it wouldn't help him develop a fighting style.

Li Xiang took everything in stride. His hands and feet blurred as they slapped the air. His dance had become a martial art, fast and fierce. His momentum was perfectly conserved, and not a tiny bit of strength was wasted. He was using inferior stats to hold Jack at bay.

Jack felt like he was trying to punch the rain. From the side, Dorman watched with interest, while Brock's eyes had gone wide. Sparman simply waited with the medical kit.

Jack accelerated. His strikes deepened. For the first time in a while, he felt his skills strained. It wasn't a problem of stats or the Dao, He had the power to beat this opponent, he just couldn't use it properly.

No. Thinking back, it hadn't been a while. It was the first time he felt like this since the System arrived. Not once had he fought an opponent so superior in pure skill.

It set him on fire. His frustration grabbed something at the deepest recesses of his soul and squeezed.

Jack dove deeper.

His strikes flew off the mark. His feints were read. His perfect control over his body was insufficient because his body wasn't the problem. Li Xiang faced him sternly, his hands a hurricane of flowing water. Every single strike missed. A palm met Jack's gut, painless but infuriating.

Jack's flames were fanned further. Irritation rose inside him, and he channeled it all into striking faster. He used his Dao of Indomitable Will to clamp down on his mind, forcing himself to operate at the very limit of his abilities.

His strikes got slightly straighter, faster, more accurate. He began to see the inkling of patterns behind Li Xiang's movements.

It wasn't enough.

Li Xiang weaved patterns inside patterns. Every time Jack thought he had something, he just fell into another trap. Every time he committed slightly more to an attack, thinking it would land, all he received was a palm to his face or his chest.

Jack was getting better, but it wasn't enough. He was getting tossed around like a toddler. Li Xiang's occasional attacks couldn't harm him —the old man was too weak—but they were an affront in the face of his unstoppable, indomitable Dao.

Jack was getting angry now. His fists had an edge to them. He forgot about the spar, truly aiming to hit Li Xiang with every fiber of his being. A ferocity was born within his fists. Wild, unrestrained violence. He got even faster.

It still wasn't enough.

Li Xiang met Jack's ferocity with the coldness of a stone wall. He ignored it, dealing with it as easily as he had with everything else. Jack's attacks were imbued with all his power, the full force of his mind, and every bit of resolve he could muster. They were also useless.

He roared like a beast as he cut off everything else. Only the battle remained. He hadn't lost control—his Dao of Indomitable Will would never let that happen—but he willingly gave in to his instincts, hoping they would carry him to the breakthrough he desperately needed.

From the outside, Jack and Li Xiang's fight was beyond impressive. The old man was facing a tiger with his bare hands. He stood calm in the face of wild, unrestrained ferocity displayed by a man bigger, stronger, and faster than he was.

And yet, he defended.

Martial arts were a wonderful thing. No matter how Jack struck, it was useless. He employed every trick he knew, mustered his full force, utilized every weapon he possessed to the extreme. The floor and walls around them had been ravaged by stray Drills. Ten minutes had already passed, and exhaustion was beginning to settle in on Jack.

And the breakthrough wasn't coming.

He could feel it. He was so close, but something was always missing. Every time he thought he had it, every time he felt his skills becoming an integral part of himself and working in tandem with his Dao, it just wasn't enough.

Li Xiang still stood, a wall that Jack couldn't cross. All this time, he hadn't landed a single strike, though he had received dozens himself. He just couldn't find a way to progress against such an overwhelming opponent. Anything he tried failed. How could he discover a path like that?

Even Rufus Emberheart had only matched Li Xiang in a frontal brawl, not beaten him.

Brock was still watching starry-eyed, but Dorman and Master Shol were both frowning. It had already been too long. This wasn't working well.

"Maybe Master is just not good enough," Sparman ventured a guess.

"The best sharpening stone is neither too soft nor too hard," Master Shol replied thoughtfully. "Perhaps this is futile. What Jack needs is an opponent slightly stronger than himself, and with slightly better martial arts. Li Xiang is too weak to pull out Jack's potential and too skilled for Jack to adapt to."

"But then, who can make it happen? Who should we get?" Dorman wondered.

"I know what you are thinking, but only a fool would rely on real-battle breakthroughs," Master Shol said. "No, if not Li Xiang, there is nobody. There is still time. We just have to hope."

Jack wasn't listening to their conversation—he already understood the truth in their words. Li Xiang was just an impassionate mirror. Nothing worked against him, and he remained exactly the same no matter what Jack did. He couldn't improve like that. It was like playing tennis against a wall.

Dammit!

Jack's energy reserves were running low and his concentration faltered. Even the Dao of Indomitable Will had its limits. He couldn't keep this up forever, and the more tired he became, the smaller his chances of a breakthrough.

He was pulling away from success, and if he failed now, he likely wouldn't succeed the next time, either. He would have to face Rufus as he was, and he wasn't ready. He had to succeed.

Jack's mind sparked with ideas.

This isn't working. He's too strong, he thought. *I must provoke some weakness.*

Suddenly, purple light flared on his fist. In the moment it took to activate Meteor Punch, nobody spoke out to stop Jack. This spar had to work. He should try anything.

Li Xiang's eyes widened as he jumped back. He understood, too. He was a master himself. He knew why Jack was failing, but even he couldn't control himself enough to lower his skills. That would only be a fake fight, and it would never end well.

A meteor exploded before Li Xiang, who'd retreated by two steps. Sound and light filled the small sparring room, making everyone's ears ring. Brock yelped. To his honor, he did not rush to escape. He cupped his ears, resolved to watch his big bro's fight to the end.

Li Xiang advanced again. The light and sound had certainly impacted him, but he seemed unaffected. He returned to the fight with renewed vigor, trying his best to pressure Jack so he couldn't use Meteor Punch again. By pushing him as hard as he could, maybe something would happen.

Unfortunately, some gaps could not be bridged by skill alone.

Five exchanges later, Jack had a moment. Purple flared. The colors washed away from the world. Brock gritted his teeth.

The explosion was even stronger this time, shooting out a shockwave that ruffled Dorman's robes and Brock's fur. Li Xiang was unharmed. He perfectly predicted when Jack would smash his fist forward and jumped back, escaping the blast radius. The explosion's aftereffects were clearly getting to him, if his slight frown was any indication, yet even Jack's strongest attack failed to harm him.

Jack felt his stomach drop. Rufus had manhandled Li Xiang with ease. If he couldn't do the same even when he went all-out, what would that mean?

He didn't want to think about that, and he struggled to stop himself. Suddenly, a new goal flared in his mind. Maybe he wouldn't develop a Dao skill. That was fine. But he had to beat Li Xiang quickly, or his confidence would crumble, and that could be a threat worse than any skill.

He rushed in, this time going for blood. His fire had been renewed. He used every trick in his arsenal, preparing the ground for his Meteor Punches. Li Xiang always got the timing perfect and jumped back. He defended perfectly against everything else, too. Maybe he couldn't harm Jack, but Jack couldn't harm him, either.

And the breakthrough still wasn't coming. Jack was trapped. He was already panting. This battle reminded him of the time he fought the rock bear until he fainted, but he was winning back then. He'd been the one in control. This time, it wasn't pleasant. He was useless. How could he win like this? How could he save anything?

Break through, dammit!

He screamed, digging deeper inside himself and dragging out everything he could find. He tried to activate every skill he had at once, completely surrendering himself to his instincts. The skills came out and flew haphazardly, dissolving into the wind. They refused to combine.

He sank into the Dao of the Fist, the core of his would-be Dao skill, activating and embracing it to its fullest extent. It was like trying to touch two similar magnets. *Useless.*

He roared out in fury and smashed out a Meteor Punch.

And something happened.

His Dao, that had refused to combine with the other skills, was pulled into the familiar home of Meteor Punch. That always happened, every time he used the skill. But this time, he'd galvanized the Dao harder than ever. As he watched Li Xiang jump away, escaping the blast radius, his Dao Root screamed that this was unacceptable. His fist should be unstoppable, unavoidable.

He embraced the Dao. Li Xiang could never escape.

Colors disappeared. Sounds were dampened. Jack's hand smashed into nothing but air… and the colors didn't return. The meteor didn't explode. It left his punch and flew out like a true meteor, tiny purple stars trailing behind it as it reached Li Xiang, who only had time to widen his eyes.

And *then* it exploded.

The old man flew back like a broken kite and smashed against the far wall. It was soft, thankfully, limiting the impact, but he still slumped down with multiple bones broken. His hand gripped his chest, and he gritted his teeth so as not to shout.

"Li Xiang!" Jack shouted, appearing next to him in a flash. Dorman was already there.

"What do we do?" he asked frantically.

Sparman arrived a beat later. He opened his medical kit and retrieved a thick needle filled with a shiny green liquid. It resembled the magic of the healers, except trapped in a bottle. In one fluid motion, Sparman jammed the needle into Li Xiang's shoulder and pressed the tip. The green liquid flowed out.

Magic surrounded Li Xiang. His bones were repaired and set in place with a loud *crack*. He took a deep, stunned breath, magically forced into perfect health again. He grabbed at his chest in wonder. Besides the front of his robes getting blackened a bit, he had no injuries.

"You always had that!" Jack exclaimed, staring at Sparman's medical kit. Taking a closer look, there were no bandages inside, it was simply filled with similar syringes of various sizes.

"The road to mastery is long and difficult, Jack," a voice said from behind him, and as he turned to look, he found a half-smiling Master Shol. "Every step is a journey in itself. Maybe this wasn't the one you wanted, but congratulations are in order, anyway."

Jack blinked in confusion. Then, he realized there was an exclamation mark blinking in the corner of his vision. He willed it open, and a grin split his face. This felt right.

Congratulations! Meteor Punch (I) → Meteor Punch (II)

CHAPTER NINETY-FOUR
THE LAST NIGHT

Meteor Punch (II): When meteors fall from space, they cause exponentially more damage than their size would indicate. Your punches can carry the same effect. Overdraw your body's potential and combine it with your Dao of the Fist to unleash a devastating attack. *Shoot out your punch like a meteor.*

THE SKILL DESCRIPTION HADN'T CHANGED MUCH. JUST A SINGLE SENTENCE AT the end. However, Jack could now shoot out his punches like meteors. He looked at his fist, lost in thought.

He didn't feel like fighting from range. As useful as this new ability would be, he would rather save it for when needed, and dive head-first into the action when he could.

He had to experiment, but first...

"Sorry, Li Xiang," he said, bowing slightly to the old martial artist. "I lost control of my strength for a moment."

He expected a fierce rebuttal. After all, Li Xiang valued honor above all. He did not expect the light-hearted laughter that emerged from the old man's throat.

"There is no problem. Losing is no dishonor. You are stronger. I cannot complain."

Jack smiled. He reached out a hand, and Li Xiang grabbed it to stand.

"Was this the breakthrough you wanted?" he asked curiously.

Jack shook his head. "No. But it is a breakthrough."

"Go on, disciple," Master Shol chimed in. "Test it."

Jack smiled, turned, and punched. He poured his Dao into his fist, imbuing it with the purest essence of the Fist he could distill. It was unstoppable, undodgeable, inviolable. Whatever obstacle stood in his way, whatever he turned his fist at, was bound to be eradicated.

The world darkened, uncontested by other Daos. The movement of Jack's hand was imprinted on everyone's mind. They only saw a purple meteor shuttling through space in a graceful arc, carrying a purple tail of stars. It was beautiful.

It shot out, dislodging from Jack's hand and following a straight line. Though the movement looked slow, it was fast like an arrow. It crashed into a wall with a massive explosion that rocked the room.

The wall itself wasn't harmed—it was built to withstand E-Grade battles—but the explosion itself had been deafening in this narrow space. Thankfully, Brock managed to cup his ears in time. He wouldn't be caught off guard twice.

"That is not the same skill my ancestor had," Master Shol said, rubbing his beard. "But it is decent."

"Did the breakthrough make it stronger, too?" Dorman wondered.

Jack nodded.

It was hard to pinpoint the difference between the new version and the old one. It was similar to Drill, but only superficially. Where Drill was more of a technical skill, Meteor Punch had evolved with the Dao.

Jack felt that his Dao was deeper, somehow, as if he'd uncovered aspects of it that were previously hidden, and he was now pouring those into the Meteor Punch as well.

He had thought the fist was meant to be merely unstoppable. That he selected a target and punched out, and the target could only get out of his way or be destroyed.

But that was a shallow interpretation. The fist was the carrier of his will. His punches were meant to land, not as a show of force. If he attacked someone but let them dodge, it was the same as being blocked. His fist had lost. And that could not be allowed to happen.

So what if someone ran away? Could something as silly as distance stop Jack's will, mounted on his fist? Was he really so constrained in his power, to only affect the world within two feet of himself?

Of course not!

And as his will to destroy had seeped deeper into his fist, it also exploded harder. Before, the explosion had just been the Dao of the Fist venting angrily. Now, it was purposeful. The difference was spiritual in nature, but so was the Dao. The power of Meteor Punch had increased significantly.

Wait.

"You knew this," Jack turned to his master. "You said your faction teaches the Dao of the Fist, among others. There's no way you didn't see this coming. To you, my faults must have been clear as day. Why didn't you tell me earlier? I need every advantage I can get against Rufus."

"Because the Dao is a path that must be walked by each person alone," Master Shol replied. "If I had guided you too much, I would have influenced your path, and that would risk your future prospects."

Jack felt exploited.

"I don't need future prospects," he protested. "I need to defeat Rufus Emberheart and save my people."

"Both are equally important," Master Shol replied.

"Not to me. I would return myself to level 1 if it meant winning tomorrow."

"Hmph! You are young and foolish. I don't need to explain my actions to you."

"We're talking about my friends and family here! I won't risk them to increase my future chances, and you have no right to make that decision for me."

"I have every right, as well as the *responsibility* to do it. You don't even see beyond your nose. I can't let you run off a cliff for a lost cause."

Master Shol was quick to anger, as was Jack. The previous celebratory mood had shattered in a moment, leaving high tension between master and disciple.

Jack held a fiery stare. The battle fever still hadn't left him. "I have repeatedly told you what I want: to save my people. And you would sacrifice them to cultivate me as a talent for your sect," he accused his master. "You don't care about me. You only care about my potential. I know our relationship is one of mutual benefit, but for me, this means everything. I *need* all the help I can get. I'm not telling you to risk yourself or your sect; I'm asking you to risk *me*. Teach me everything at once. Let me choose my own path and fuck up if I have to. I am not a child, goddammit! I'm desperate!"

Everyone held their breaths. Li Xiang shook his head. Master Shol exploded.

"Ungrateful disciple!" he barked. "Do you think I'm an unfeeling beast? That you know better than me how to progress faster? You are a desperate man, and I will *not* give you the tools to destroy yourself for little benefit. I *know* what I am doing. You, on the other hand, are naive beyond belief. I have already overstepped the boundaries of kindness for you. I have honored my status as your master. Why can you not do the same and show me even the most basic of respect?"

Jack's temper flared. His Dao of Indomitable Will shot out, an extension of himself, and brought him back down to the ground. *Am I speaking out of turn?* he wondered. *Is he right?*

He wasn't sure. He knew his side, but not the other. That, by itself, was a bad sign.

Master Shol took his silence as admittance. "I will forgive you this once because your reaction is natural," he said, more calmly this time. "You are still a child, and I do not expect this to make sense for you. However, this is already the second time you disrespect me. There will not be a third. Am I understood?"

Jack gritted his teeth. His mind told him he had every right to be angry, but his instinct warned him he was wrong, that things weren't quite so simple. He would think on it.

"Understood, Master," he replied, only half-meaning it.

"Good. Then heed my instructions. You cannot make any further breakthroughs tonight. Sit here and meditate until night falls. Then, go find your friends, and let them calm your mind. Sleep for precisely six hours. And tomorrow... fight like your life depends on it. Because it does."

Jack was relaxed. His entire body felt soft, his mind fleeting. He was deep in the moment, not letting erroneous thoughts pull him away. He was at peace.

"Can you believe how lucky we are?" Edgar said, savoring the moment. Soft music reached their ears from above, along with the splashing of waves on the platform below. Candles lit their faces.

They were in the same bar Jack and Vivi had gone on a date. They were more, this time; Edgar was there, as were Dorman and the Sage. They were gathered around a small, round table, each with a drink at hand—except for Dorman, who leisurely held a lemon juice.

"I used to be a nobody before the Integration," Edgar continued, melancholically staring at his glass. "I was nothing. An emotionally incomplete young man stuck in a hamster wheel with no way out. And look at me now." He magicked a bird into existence, directing it to sit on his shoulder. "I'm a wizard. A *real* wizard."

"It's been a month, Edgar." Jack laughed. "How are you still not used to this?"

"I don't think I ever will be," the wizardling said. He gestured widely around them. There was a kovan bartender, a lycan waiter, and a group of djinns drinking loudly at a nearby table. A month ago, this bar would have made the news in every part of the world. Now, it was almost mundane. "This is all so... magical."

"Many people died," the Sage reminded them with a small smile.

"Oh, come on, don't ruin the fun," Vivi scolded. "We pulled through. So did you. And you still haven't told us your story, by the way."

"It was nothing interesting." He waved the subject away. "Let's just say I found my calling."

Dorman chuckled like he got some inside joke. Jack raised a brow.

"We did reach high," Jack said. "I mean, look at us. The scions come from a B-Grade faction. They had every resource they ever wanted at their disposal, immortal masters, a paved road to the Dao, and martial arts to complement it. Moreover, they came to Earth with a leg up on us, ready to form a Dao Root. They had every possible advantage... and we're matching them."

"Not every advantage," the Sage corrected. "The Integration is an advantage in itself. It is a giant meat grinder that takes a billion people and produces only a handful at our level of strength. It forced us into desperate situations without giving us any tools to survive. Whoever made it through got an edge and experience that even a B-Grade faction cannot instill in their disciples."

"Really?"

"Of course. Do you think they can afford to risk their most talented disciples? Of course not. No matter what kind of training they put them through or how closely it resembles life-or-death situations, it just isn't the same. That is our edge over them, and it is a gap they will probably never bridge, because to try means almost certain death."

"That doesn't make sense," Edgar said. "The Animal Kingdom constellation has thousands of planets. If they wanted to simulate an Integration, couldn't they just throw monsters at a planet, enforce lawlessness, and wait for a handful of strong people to emerge from a billion corpses?"

"They can and they do. They have even developed their preferred monsters for that very thing. Where do you think goblins came from? But, it isn't the same. First of all, their powers are mostly based on bloodlines, so those of random planets are not as useful to them. Even if they were, the Planetary Frontrunner titles would be unavailable. There would be no dungeons. And finally, an Integration is not random. The System uses a large amount of power to scan the planet and organize everything to maximize the chances of talented people to rise. Even a B-Grade faction cannot achieve that."

"Wait a moment," Jack said. "Do you mean the dungeon was spawned on me on purpose? I was singled out?"

"Maybe, maybe not. Who could know?"

"A Sage."

The Sage laughed. "I cannot see through the System, Jack. There are people out there who can, but compared to them, I am only a charlatan at the side of the street."

"Can we drop the serious stuff?" Edgar asked. "This is probably our last night of freedom. Starting tomorrow, all of us might be at war. Can we relax? Please?"

Everyone's spines stiffened, and then, they let go.

"To survival," Vivi said, raising her glass.

"To lifting the System's oppression," the Sage replied as enigmatically as always, raising his glass.

"To strength," Dorman added.

"To magic," Edgar said, laughing.

"To victory," Jack finished, raising his glass and tipping it over. Everyone else followed. He wasn't drinking Dao-infused alcohol, so it wouldn't affect him at all. He had to remain in top shape.

The night flowed lazily. They exchanged stories about their past. Dorman entertained them with stories of his school life, finally peeking out of his shell a little, and Edgar performed a magic lightshow. The Sage gossiped about other people in the bar—he hadn't overheard anything, but he knew—and told them funny trivia about the galaxy.

Vivi described scenes from her revolution—the pleasant ones. She told them all about the great banquet they'd hosted to celebrate their victory, about the piss-drunk soldiers playing stupid pranks on each other. She had a sharp edge to her that sometimes caught Jack off guard, but one he didn't dislike.

He didn't speak much that night. He mostly let the others talk, occasionally interceding with witty comments. It was a fun evening. They laughed a lot, and his heart, that had been tied into a knot, could finally let loose. For a few hours, he forgot the burdens on his shoulders and was simply a guy living his best life.

When midnight struck, Jack stood. "I have to go now. You keep having fun—just don't be late tomorrow. I'll need your cheers."

"You bet!" Edgar replied, smiling.

"I'll go too," Vivi said, standing up. Her strapless white shirt fit her nicely.

They left together, meandering toward the participants' district.

"This isn't the way to your hotel," Jack said with a smile.

"I know," she replied. "But if this is your last night in this world, I can't let you spend it alone, can I?"

He laughed. "There's no way this will be my last night here."

"You never know." She winked, and they laughed again.

The arena was packed tighter than ever. Jack stood center stage, preparing himself for what was to come. He was at his peak. He was ready. His Dao Roots were both flaring. Whether he won or lost, he knew he would have done his best.

Looking around, it felt like every single person in Integration City had come. Many stood, unable to find a seat, and the wandering merchants had disappeared as they couldn't cross the crowd.

As this was the final, even the C-Grade Planetary Overseer was attending. She sat on a solitary throne close to the front of the arena, everyone was pushed sixty feet around her. The only ones who were allowed close were Vocrich, the vampire of the Hand of God, and the ghost-like immortals. They all sat three rows below the Overseer.

Every immortal who'd taken a disciple was still here, even if their disciple had been eliminated from the Tournament. They'd been allowed to leave the participants district, where they were normally confined, just for this fight.

Jack saw his master watching sternly from a seat under the lioness. Alongside the lizard archmage, the cloud worm, the ascetic, and the five immortals of the Animal Kingdom, one for each scion. The leonine immortal sat proudly near the Planetary Overseer, only one step below her.

Jack spotted the Flame River, the Ice Peak, the scions, all of Jack's allies, Karvahul, as well as every important person of Earth. Most of the Tournament participants had remained, and Jack recognized a few faces he'd spanked in the first pairings.

He smiled fondly at the memory—it was a welcome break from the tension that threatened to break him. He hadn't forgotten that every single person on Earth was probably watching. The pressure was insane. Standing there without shivering was so difficult he had to use his Dao Roots to steady himself.

The head judge flew over the arena. She seemed straighter today, more formal.

"Honored Planetary Overseer, distinguished immortals, brave merchants, and people of planet Earth-387," she declared. "Today is the last day of this planet's Integration Tournament. 987 fighters emerged from the planet's population of eight billion, and of those, only the strongest two remain. The winner of today's final will be the face of the planet, a badge of its honor, and proof of its strength."

The crowd cheered loudly. Of course, she was only saying those things to raise up the Animal Kingdom, since Rufus Emberheart was expected to win, but everyone loved a good show.

Jack didn't mind. The odds may be against him, but he was confident that he at least had a chance. He would either win or go down swinging. He was ready. He looked for Rufus in the stands but didn't find him, even though the scion curtain was open.

"Then, let the final battle begin!" the head judge raised her voice. "Rufus Emberheart and the Dao of Supremacy versus Jack Rust and the Dao of the Fist!"

The crowd cheered hard.

Jack raised his fist and the people cheered even harder. Almost everyone present wanted him to win. He savored this knowledge.

Then, he settled down, waiting for his opponent to arrive.

And waited. And waited. And half a minute later, Rufus was still nowhere to be seen.

CHAPTER NINETY-FIVE

DEFYING A GOD

The previous night...

Rufus Emberheart sat alone in his house.

There weren't many moments when he could think freely. Around others, he had to show the face of a king. Only now, in his privacy, could he let his mind roam free.

And he needed that, because his Dao was struggling.

Settle down, he commanded it, furrowing his brows, but it was difficult. Supremacy was fleeting.

His Dao was already strained by coming to this planet. It whispered that a truly supreme person wouldn't need to lie or cheat. That was the way of the world, he'd remind it. The rules only applied to the weak, which he was not. It was power guiding him, not fear.

He could control that doubt.

But now, his vest had been stained by a *monkey*. Moreover, he'd been unable to avenge that insult on the spot, even though he tried.

"Argh!" Rufus roared, freely releasing his frustration. He raised a paw and smashed one of the mundane instruments to pieces.

Additionally, the owner of that monkey had *defeated* him in a bidding war. That was the hardest to stomach. Rufus had miscalculated, played his cards wrong, and because of that, he'd lost.

All those incidents combined into a heavy pressure on his soul. Cultivating the Dao of Supremacy was like walking on a sword's edge. It gave the cultivator tremendous power, but its requirements were overwhelming. Every step had to be perfect, or you would tumble into the abyss. Missteps could not be tolerated. It was a Dao that would either take you to the heavens or nowhere at all.

Thankfully, he was still low in Grade. The Dao Tree of Supremacy would never stand for these insults. It would crumble like a tower of cards.

I need to regain my momentum, Rufus thought, narrowing his eyes. *I must turn adversity into opportunity and triumph with the majesty of a king.*

There was nothing he could do about his Dao's protests to cheating, but as for the other two... They both converged on one enemy.

Jack Rust.

Rufus Emberheart would never lower himself to antagonize a monkey. The real culprit was Jack Rust, who'd taken away his Rainbow Dao Pill and dared meet his blow without shattering.

There were many paths to regaining the upper hand, but only one of them was truly supreme.

I will break through to the E-Grade right now, proving I do not need the pill. I will make it in time. Then, I will destroy him in fair battle, I will slay his monkey before his face and dominate his allies. In one fell swoop, my Dao will be justified.

He needed that resolve. If not, his Dao would become unstable, and his breakthrough to the E-Grade would not be perfect.

The pill was only an extra assurance. He was confident in succeeding regardless. His master—who was also his grandfather—advised against it, but to follow that advice was cowardice, and Rufus could no longer afford it.

For his path to be perfect, he had to follow it with all his heart.

As this resolve filled him, it resonated with his Dao. The crown in his soul invited him, as it had been doing for the last few months. This time, Rufus obliged. The world faded away until only the supreme crown and himself remained. He had unshakable confidence in himself.

He would reign supreme.

A minute passed with Jack waiting, scanning the stands and arena entrances, confused. Rufus never appeared. He even suspected the leonine was hidden under the sand to launch a sneak attack, but if so, he had ample time to attack already.

Where was he?

The audience shared the same question. Everyone whispered, filling the arena with noise. Edgar spoke to the people around him, then looked at Jack and shrugged.

"Hey!" the guy with strong lungs and a tendency to meddle shouted. "How long does he have to arrive?"

The head judge took a moment to respond. Even she seemed to be doubting her own words. "For the final battle, the waiting time is one hour. If Rufus Emberheart fails to show up by then, he will automatically forfeit the fight..."

More whispers spread through the audience.

Even the ghosts and Vocrich appeared confused. The C-Grade lioness showed no reaction. The ghosts and Vocrich turned to look at her, all at once. Jack felt something brush against his soul so softly that he would have missed it if he wasn't battle-ready.

Is she scanning us? Is she scanning the town to look for Rufus?

He stared at the lioness, then remembered she was a literal goddess and cast his eyes away.

Then a voice rang in his mind, carrying the majesty and authority of a queen. "*Resign.*"

Jack flashed another look at the lioness. He recognized her voice. Why was she speaking to him?

"*Rufus got delayed. He will come in a few minutes, but my time is too precious to waste here. You cannot win. Resign.*"

Jack was so shocked he couldn't think straight. She wanted him to resign the most important battle of his life... just because she couldn't wait *two minutes*!

There was no pressure in her words, but he could feel it looming right behind them. The threat wasn't even veiled. To disobey a C-Grade's words, especially a hostile C-Grade's, was blatant suicide.

Jack gritted his teeth. What was happening? This wasn't part of the plan, but when a god asked...

He didn't want to resign. Could he survive making his position even worse? Offending the scions was one thing, but a C-Grade immortal was infinitely greater.

However, if he resigned now, the C-Grade master of his master wouldn't take him as a disciple. There really wasn't a choice.

He didn't know how to reply through his thoughts, nor did he dare look any longer at the lioness. Jack simply clenched his jaw and remained silent. In that moment, he became more aware of the pressure. He was standing alone in the middle of a vast arena, bearing the honor of his planet and watched by everyone on Earth. Eight billion sets of eyes watched him simply stand there, including several immortals and a godlike being.

He'd never been more aware of his breath, his blinking, or the way he stood.

"*Do you dare disobey my words?*" the voice rang in his mind again, and this time, it wasn't alone. A heavy pressure descended on him, covering him from head to toe, so strong it made him sweat. If the threat had been implicit before, it was now clear as day.

Jack gritted his teeth. He dared look at her, and found the lioness leaning back with her eyes closed, as if nothing here was worth watching. She was hiding the fact that she spoke to him. Why?

He maintained his silence.

Something foreign infiltrated his mind and soul. His Dao Roots shivered and crumbled, squeezed into tiny dots on the verge of shattering like glass beads. Suddenly, he was in the presence of something greater than he could comprehend. A giant was bearing down on him, a mountain-sized beast. He lacked the means to comprehend the sensation or put it into words, but it was similar awe as you watched a gigantic tsunami crashing on your face, except lasting more than an instant.

More accurately, like being completely tied up and shoved between the jaws of a hungry lion just before it devoured you.

Primal fear welled up from everywhere inside him. His soul screamed at him to surrender, and his Dao Roots couldn't make a peep in the presence of something so superior.

The world disappeared around Jack. His senses were cut off as if his mind didn't dare perceive anything in the face of this beast.

"*Resign*," the voice exploded inside his mind, shaking him to the very core like he'd swallowed an industrial-strength speaker.

But Jack retained control of his mind, and hidden behind his fear, his thoughts still worked. Why was the lioness threatening him? Why did she care so much? And, most importantly, why was she pretending that nothing was happening?

Jack's mind raced. Vocrich, a representative of the Hand of God, was right beside her. The Hand of God were the enforcers of the Star Pact, the galactic law, and interfering with the Integration Tournament went directly against that law. If she went to the trouble of hiding, then it meant Vocrich could and would punish her if he knew.

Which meant she couldn't be too obvious. He was between the jaws of a lion, but it wouldn't dare chew.

He also considered speaking up to expose her, but only an idiot would pit his word against a C-Grade's. She was bullying him, and all he could do was endure.

No, he replied weakly, speaking in his thoughts. He didn't even know if she could hear him. It was a wild gamble, but it was the only thing he could do. To save his people, he had to beat Rufus Emberheart. In any other case, most if not all of them would die, and Jack didn't mind dying with them. It would be his fault, anyway.

The Dao brimmed with rage in his mind. The lioness could end him with a thought, but she didn't. She considered her next move in silence, and Jack knew his prediction had been right.

She couldn't harm him. Her next words, still spoken in his mind, served as confirmation.

"I will not lower myself to kill a mortal. Know that your insult will be repaid tenfold. Every second you disobey me, you will regret it enough for a lifetime."

Jack didn't care about her threat. The only thing he minded was, *Why the hell does she care so much?*

Was it a matter of pride? Because she'd given an order and he refused, she would go all the way to threatening him? Just to save a few minutes of her time? And where the hell was Rufus?

Something was fishy here.

Jack's eyes swiveled to meet his master's, who was looking straight at him.

"*I don't know either,*" Master Shol's voice rang in Jack's mind. He shrugged, not seeming to have noticed the lioness's actions.

A third voice reached his mind, then. The Sage. "*He is not coming.*"

Jack had to try not to raise his brows. *Why is* everyone *suddenly telepathic?* he wondered. *Is my mind so much fun?*

The Sage continued, "*Rufus Emberheart made a mistake. He was cultivating before the match, and he accidentally reached the final insight he needed to break into the E-Grade. The process cannot be stopped, and if it is interrupted, it would harm his Dao so severely he might never recover. It will probably not finish within the hour.*"

Jack was filled with astonishment.

Wow, he thought.

"*Wow, indeed. Not even I expected that.*"

Wait. You can hear me?

"*We are conversing. Of course I can, as long as you will your thoughts to be transmitted.*"

Jack's astonishment transformed into elation. The lioness is trying to make me surrender. She knows Rufus is not coming. If I just persist, will I win the fight?

"*Who is speaking to you, mortal?*" the lioness's voice rang again. Jack's eyes widened, and he felt a need to swear, but he resisted even do it in his thoughts.

"*You cannot hide communication from a C-Grade. Everything you say to me, she hears too,*" the Sage's voice rang again, sounding flustered. "*But she cannot hear my voice. She doesn't know who I am. Don't even look at me.*"

Jack kept his gaze on the ground. What was he even supposed to do? If he spoke to the Sage, the lioness could hear, too. At least he had the privacy of his own thoughts.

"*Resign,*" she commanded within his thoughts again. "*It doesn't matter if Rufus is coming or not. I can guarantee you that disobeying me here is far worse than losing the Tournament.*"

Jack hesitated.

"*What is happening, disciple?*" Master Shol's mental voice rang again. "*Why is Galicia Lonihor telling me nonsense?*"

I can't fucking reply! Jack thought to himself. *And also, stop speaking to me all at once. Ugh!* After speaking with the Sage, he could instinctively understand which thoughts he was sharing and which he wasn't. It was pretty easy, actually, though not something he consciously understood yet.

He didn't reply to his master. That was response enough. On the stands, Master Shol narrowed his eyes but didn't communicate further.

Jack couldn't pay him much mind right now. What should he do? He doubted the lioness's threat was empty. Should he really resign? But he couldn't! Should he speak up and tell Vocrich what was happening? And then what? She would refute it, and if it were his words against hers, only one of them was a literal god.

"*Listen to me, Jack,*" the Sage's voice came again. "*No matter what she says, you must not resign this fight. My master can protect you. Just persevere. And don't reveal what is happening. The Hand of God will not side with you without proof.*"

Can everyone stop using my head as a telephone pole? Jack lamented—not sharing the thought, of course. Nobody else contacted him for some time, waiting to see what he would do.

What was he supposed to do?

Suddenly, Master Shol spoke again. "*I know what is going on. I was contacted by your friend. That bitch sure has balls to interfere like this. If her cub accidentally broke through, that's his problem. Do not resign.*"

Why? Will you protect me? Jack wanted to respond, though he didn't dare.

The crowd was only getting louder as time passed, but Jack had no mind to pay to them. He took stock of his situation.

Rufus Emberheart wasn't coming. If he just waited an hour, he would win the Tournament, then Master Shol's master would protect him. And the Sage's master, unless he was lying. Even if Jack faced the lioness's wrath, it would be fine... right?

If he did resign, nothing would change, and he would still be doomed. Especially since Rufus Emberheart was now breaking through to the E-Grade. That was a tremendous leap in power. If Jack had a chance before, he would now be completely helpless. He would be slaughtered the moment Rufus finished his breakthrough.

It didn't sound like he had much choice. He was still between the lion's jaws, but they didn't dare close on him. Let the lioness shout all she wanted. All he could do was wait.

Moreover... he would win!

Decision made, he was again open to perceiving all the attention on him. He was conscious of the lioness's intense pressure, of every eye on the planet glued on him, of the many lives he carried on his shoulders. Sweat dripped down his brows. Was he just supposed to stand in front of everyone for an hour without doing anything?

His Dao Roots couldn't help, suppressed as they were by the lioness, and only now did he understand how much they helped him withstand the insane social pressure. This really was quite a feeling. No wonder most of his opponents seemed so nervous.

Five minutes passed. Jack felt like invisible hands were poking at his brain. Not only was everyone staring at him, but the lioness was still pressuring him from the inside, and the feeling had now escalated to severe discomfort. He would never resign for that, but it was difficult to bear. His body itched to move, and without his Daos, only his strong will kept him from awkwardly shuffling.

He was not having fun.

It reminded him of the time he fought Harambe, actually. Back then, the crowd of brorillas and gymonkeys had also pressured him in a similar way, though nowhere near in intensity. He focused on the memory to lessen the pressure. It was only a minor distraction, but as he thought about it, an idea flashed in his mind.

Back then, this pressure had given him some insight on the Dao of the Fist. He'd broken through the pressure exactly like that, a fist. Could he do the same now?

Now that Jack thought about it, this pressure was rather inviting. Something in his soul resonated with his desire to withstand it, something that wasn't yet part of his Dao, but that could be.

Wordlessly, Jack sat cross-legged and began to meditate.

CHAPTER NINETY-SIX

FACING THE FIST

THE MOMENT JACK SAT DOWN, EVERYONE KNEW THEY WERE IN FOR A WAIT. Some complained, but most simply settled down. Before the most exciting battle on the planet, one hour was nothing.

The C-Grade lioness was furious. She sent wave after wave of mental pressure at Jack, whose only reaction was a set of furrowed brows. Even she couldn't hurt him like that, at least not covertly. The soul was inviolable.

His eyes were closed, but he remained acutely aware of his situation. Every eye on Earth was directed at him, including several immortals, a representative of the Hand of God, and even the C-Grade Planetary Overseer. Of course, the professor was also watching, as were Jack's friends and every single person he'd ever met—except for the ones who died. And he was still shirtless.

Overnight, he had become Earth's greatest superstar. That kind of attention was hard to bear. Moreover, his decisions now, made in the spur of the moment, impacted the fates of thousands.

He focused on his senses, preparing to enter meditation. He could sense the slow breeze on his face, the fluctuations of *his* crowd's noise as it reached his ears, the sand shuffling under his bottom. The C-Grade Dao loomed over him, breathing in his face. His Dao Roots remained suppressed, forcing him to rely only on himself. For the first time in a while, he was struggling to concentrate.

Jack was in a crucible, squeezed from every side. It should have been torture. And yet, something inside him whispered that this was exactly what he needed. His mind and will were energetic, like muscles during a workout. Despite himself, he smiled.

The mental pressure of the lioness, combined with the social pressure of the crowd and the looming threat of death, forced Jack into a corner. They were pressing down on his mind, and he refused to bend.

The forces formed a kind of tense equilibrium, where Jack endured significant but not back-breaking amounts of pressure for a long time. As he was forced to sit there and withstand it, he recognized it was sharpening his resolve, and by extension, his Dao.

For a person of the fist, this was the perfect training to forge their mind!

Though Jack had been struggling to concentrate, he slid into a trance without even realizing it. This meditation was even deeper than when he used the meditation mat. He was hanging in an empty, endless void. Darkness surrounded him from every direction except the front, which was occupied by a massive fist pointed at him.

He couldn't tell how big it was. Maybe it was the size of a boulder, or maybe it was as big as the sun and infinitely far away. It was surrounded by wild purple light, dancing and flickering, highlighting every line and corner, every tense muscle.

That was a fist about to punch, but it simply hovered in the void, unmoving. It wouldn't punch anyone. It was simply clenched because that was its nature. To possess strength even when there was no need, to radiate its intention without fear. To be proud and unyielding.

This resembled a Dao Vision, but not exactly. It also resembled the giant fist Jack had briefly glimpsed when comprehending the Dao Root of the Fist, only infinitely lesser.

It was his Dao Root. And as it was isolated from the rest of his body, as he was pressed into himself by terrible weights, they met midway. For the first time, he could really see it for what it was, and it filled him with such awe that he lost himself in worship.

Jack was captivated. It tugged at the strings of his soul. Inspired him. As he observed it intently, filled with a desire to understand and embrace it, he lost track of time. The edges of his mind remained tense from the pressure, allowing him to maintain this state.

As he sank ever deeper, he forgot where he was. Only the fist remained.

Thirty minutes after the start of the fight, Rufus had yet to show up, and the crowd had gotten noisier. They were talking amongst themselves, half in annoyance and half in excitement. This was such a monumental event, and they could watch it with their own eyes.

What was going to happen? Nobody knew!

Even the immortals had abandoned their aloof facade and were quietly conversing. Only the lioness and Vocrich remained silent, each for their own reasons.

"What is your disciple doing, Shol?" the lizard archmage asked. "Is he really cultivating under these circumstances?"

"He's an odd boy." Master Shol shrugged, but his voice contained hidden pride. "With such resolve to train, he will go far."

"The most difficult step to take is the first one," a third voice came, and everyone turned to regard the ascetic immortal from Barren High. He was thin as a stick and dressed in rags. However, when he spoke, every other immortal paid attention.

"Are you referring to his battle against Rufus Emberheart, honored seer?" Shol asked carefully. The seers of Barren High always spoke cryptically, but with the right questions, it was possible to squeeze out more information.

This time, either Shol had asked the right question, or the seer felt like talking. "Yes, and also no. Your disciple's path stretches far, but it is rife with danger. Such is his fate. He will always be faced with insurmountable odds. Should he survive time and again, he will never stop advancing."

Shol turned the words around in his mind. "Thank you," he replied, nodding in respect. The ascetic smiled.

"If I may," the lizard archmage cut in, "you mentioned the first step being the most difficult one."

Nobody expected the seer to respond. Getting so much out of him was already great. Except, he spoke again.

"If Jack Rust can survive until tonight, he will truly embark on his path, and the sky will be his limit. But surviving until then..." He shook his head. "It will be difficult. Layers of threats will stand in his path, and he cannot make it alone. I suggest, Immortal Shol," he turned to look at Shol, his milky eyes filled with depth, "that you bet on him."

Shol raised both brows. The seer had advised him directly. This wasn't common. Did the Barren High have a horse in this race? Did they care about Jack? But how? *Why?*

It didn't matter. Shol didn't quite understand, but only a fool would ignore the advice of Barren High.

"I understand, honored seer. I will do my best."

The seer nodded and spoke no more. Shol settled down in his seat, but he was secretly rushing to contact his master.

In another place of the stands, the Sage leaned to Vivi and whispered, "I know the Tournament's rules prohibit all violence until tomorrow, but I suggest you prepare your people for battle. Gather our allies."

She shot him a glance, then turned and whispered something to Sadaka, who nodded and discreetly departed. Across the arena from them, Elena Richter was also nowhere to be seen. The four scions sat side-by-side, visible for the first time, and each had crossed arms and sharp gazes.

While most were enjoying the show and having fun, all powers were moving. An hour was neither short nor long. Many things could happen.

Suddenly, a sharp, metallic note cut through the clamor. Everyone looked around, searching for the source of the noise, only for their eyes to land on a long-haired young man dressed in black leather.

"Excuse me," Kane Vanderdecken shouted at the head judge. "Can I entertain the crowd while we wait? They do it for Superbowl."

She frowned and shouted something at him, but he happened to scratch his guitar loudly right then, covering up her voice. He smiled and replied nonetheless.

"I can? Thank you, head judge! I knew the Animal Kingdom took care of its people!"

With a somersault, Vanderdecken landed on the stage close to Jack. "Alright!" he shouted, filled with genuine excitement. He'd just secured a performance in front of the entire planet. He was set for life. "Are you ready to metal, Jack Rust!"

Jack ignored his shouts, remaining cross-legged with his eyes closed. Vanderdecken wasn't discouraged.

"The power of the *strong*!" he yelled at the audience. "What a man! What brutal arrogance! Everyone, let's give it up for Jack Rust, the man of the *fist*!"

The crowd cheered, and Vanderdecken struck a chord. He launched into a short guitar solo, then abruptly stopped and started singing, "Wake up! Grab a brush..."

The crowd went wild at his performance. The head judge glanced at the Planetary Overseer.

The Planetary Overseer herself didn't give a shit about a singing mortal or the crowd's approval. She had other problems. If Rufus lost, and if they were forced to give the Tournament rewards to a human... She would have to take responsibility. Those things weren't cheap.

She frowned, intensifying her Dao pressure to the limit of what she estimated Jack Rust could bear. She couldn't see inside his soul, but even if he tried to meditate, he could only last for so long. The level of pressure she exerted was torturous.

Jack couldn't hear, see, or feel anything from the outside world.

His entire being was focused on the larger-than-life fist inside his soul. He inspected every nook and cranny with fanatical devotion. Everything about this fist spoke to him, be it the strength that clenched it, the intent it signified, or the towering, meteor-like purple aura surrounding it.

There was something here, but what?

After a while, he noticed the fist wasn't alone in the void. A second existence stood beside it, though it seemed far less real.

It was an amalgamation of stars that shone with metallic light—a barbed, iron wire wrapped orderly around itself. There was profoundness there. It was the Dao Root of Indomitable Will, but Jack didn't look much at it now. He focused on the fist. *That* was what really spoke to him, the core of his existence.

So why did it stand beside the wire like they were equals?

And why was *he* so far away?

Jack felt on the precipice of some big discovery, and he let instinct guide him. This was his soul. He was in control. The distance he perceived was only true in his imagination.

The next instant, he was standing right before the fist, and it towered over him. He only reached a third of the way up its curled fingers. He reached out and touched it. The feeling was unlike anything he'd ever experienced before.

Like home. Like his perfect destination.

He let that feeling expand in his mind until it swallowed him whole. He dropped all defenses, all doubts, all hesitation. Nothing remained except the fist. Every fiber of his being yearned for it. He inhaled, and the purple aura that danced around the fist was sucked into his body, little by little, filling him up.

It tasted like stars.

But it was heavy. Demanding. To fill himself with the aura, Jack had to forgo everything else. As it entered his body, he himself was washing away. Gradually, bits and pieces of himself dove into the aura, into the power of the fist, disappearing forever. Jack didn't even remember what he'd lost.

This wasn't right.

The fist sought to *claim* him. Proving to be unyielding and proud. It demanded his total submission, pressing down on his soul harder than the lioness ever could. It was wiping him away.

But every drop of aura that entered his body made him stronger. He didn't want it to stop.

CHAPTER NINETY-SEVEN
BREAKING THROUGH

"*I'm begging you, master.*" Shol gritted his teeth, conversing mentally with his master. "*The boy is worth it. Even the Barren High advised that we take him in.*"

"*His reputation is stained, Shol,*" a woman's voice echoed into his mind, filled with age and majesty. Her will was absolute. "*I cannot provoke the Animal Kingdom for a mere baby. The risk is too big, the cost too high. I requested a victory, and this is no victory.*"

"*But, master, he...*"

Shol's words trailed off as something odd brushed against his perception. His head snapped up. His eyes went wide and he shot to his feet. So did the rest of the surrounding immortals, all at once.

"Is he breaking through to the E-Grade?" the lizard archmage asked in disbelief.

"*How bold,*" a female-sounding voice rang out in their minds. It was the cloud worm, who'd raised her head to stare at Jack, despite the lack of any face whatsoever. Her words sounded like a compliment, but they really weren't. Shol agreed.

"*Idiot* disciple!" he muttered in panic, gritting his teeth. The next moment, he flashed to the center of the stage, right next to Jack.

The mortal called Vanderdecken was still playing, riling up the crowds without paying attention to Jack.

"SHUT UP!" Shol barked, unleashing the full power of his Dao. Everyone in the audience fell dead silent. So did Vanderdecken, who jumped and turned to look with horror in his eyes.

"I'm sorry..." he started saying, but Shol wasn't paying attention. His hand was on Jack's shoulder, and his soul was scanning inside his disciple. Jack's body was getting infused by the Dao, bit by bit, filling up like a drop-fed bottle.

This was far too fast. The breakthrough to the E-Grade wasn't supposed to go like this. There were security procedures to follow, but Jack didn't know them. Shol had never told him.

He really is breaking through... He shuddered. This is my fault. I didn't warn him. I never thought it would come this fast! How?

But the how and why didn't matter. The process had already started. Jack would either succeed or fail—and if he failed, Shol would have failed as a master, as he hadn't warned Jack about the dangers of breaking through too early.

In truth, any of the scions could try to break through anytime they wanted. It just wasn't worth it without certainty of success.

However, Shol had his reasons for withholding this information. Jack had asked once, but he'd brushed the question away, saying it wasn't the time for him to know yet.

He didn't expect Jack to accumulate insight this quickly. He was also afraid that, had he said anything, Jack would have been tempted to make a hasty breakthrough just to beat Rufus, crippling his future. It would have certainly increased his chances.

But Jack didn't understand anything. He was a *child*. He couldn't understand the weight of immortality like Shol did.

After Shol reached the D-Grade, he'd bared witness to his entire family withering and dying while he remained young. That was why immortals rarely took disciples, and why nobody bonded with people of a different Grade. Anyone below you was simply wasted effort, and to anyone above, *you* were wasted effort.

If Jack had the means, he would cripple himself to beat Rufus and extend his faction's survival. Shol had toured the galaxy for six centuries now. Compared to Jack's potential, his faction was nothing but sand in the wind, a handful of mortals in an endless cycle of death.

Crippling himself for them was a decision that Shol, as his master, couldn't let him make. Such was the crushing weight of immortality.

But what was done, was done.

Shol's soul focused intently on his disciple's body. The breakthrough to the E-Grade was all about infusing the body with the Dao Root that you planned to advance. When the infusion was complete, the breakthrough was a success, and the Dao Root became a Dao Seed, taking root deep inside your soul.

But if you couldn't infuse your *entire* body, your foundation would be cracked, and you would be stuck between the peak of the F-Grade and the start of the E-Grade for your entire life. That was why everyone only attempted the breakthrough when they had certainty of success.

The System and the Dao never offered second chances.

Jack simply went at it the moment he found the opportunity. To Shol's mounting horror, he probably didn't even realize *what* he was doing. He also didn't know how to stop the process when he reached his limit. After all, the Dao Root wasn't meant to be absorbed in full. He just had to absorb as much as he could, hope it was enough to infuse his entire body, then forcefully stop the process and let the rest of the Dao Root dissipate.

Shol had never heard of someone going into the breakthrough without this knowledge, but he hoped it would come instinctively. If not...

His eyes narrowed. This wasn't his real body, just a spiritual projection, but since push came to shove, he would do everything in his power to help.

He looked up, where the metal mortal had already scrambled off the stage, leaving the audience in a stunned, expectant silence. The sharpest among them were realizing what was happening and couldn't contain their shock. Shol's eyes scanned the stands, finding Jack's friends.

"Edgar!" he barked out. "Grab Jack's bag and come over."

The wizardling jumped and panicked. He grabbed Jack's backpack. A blue cloud appeared under his feet as he shot to the stage, approaching Shol.

"Retrieve the fruit," Shol said before Edgar had even landed, his tone brooking no disobedience. The wizard dropped everything to hurry. He quickly riffled through the backpack and retrieved a pear-shaped fruit that seemed wrapped around itself like a clenched fist.

"Mighty immortal," he said quickly, "what is happ—"

"No time. Feed him the fruit."

"Feed him?" Edgar asked. "But he's not moving."

"Just shove it into his mouth! It's crystallized Dao. He doesn't need to chew."

Edgar complied. He opened Jack's mouth and pushed the fruit inside, hesitantly at first and then harder. When it touched his tongue, the fruit dissolved into orange streams that quickly turned to purple and vanished down Jack's throat.

Edgar looked around, all too aware that he'd just force-fed a fruit to an unconscious man in front of the entire planet and multiple immortals. His stomach turned from nervousness.

Shol didn't care. He wasn't done yet.

"Dig into that bag again and retrieve the Rainbow Dao Pill," he commanded. Thankfully, Jack carried everything with him. He said it felt safer that way.

Edgar's shaky hands went through the backpack and retrieved a sphere wrapped in white fabric. He pulled the cover away to reveal a knuckle-sized pill shining brilliantly with all colors of the rainbow.

"Feed him," Shol commanded, and Edgar complied. Unlike the fruit, it was perfectly corporeal, and it didn't melt when it touched his tongue. Edgar wasn't sure what to do. "Shove it down his throat if you have to," Shol barked. "He must swallow it no matter what. Hurry!"

Edgar panicked. Shol wished he had a body to do it himself. Left without options, the wizardling pushed the pill down Jack's throat with a finger, eliciting a few cries from the audience. Jack almost gagged, his eyelids shaking a bit before instinct took over and he swallowed.

"Good," Shol exhaled in relief. There was a chance they would interrupt Jack's breakthrough by force-feeding him the pill so brutally, but he would certainly fail without it.

"What... what's happening?" Edgar asked again, panic tinging his voice. "I-Is Jack breaking through?"

"Yes."

"Can he make it?"

"I do not know." Shol's eyes darkened. "He has the perfect fruit and an excellent pill. He is also highly compatible with his Dao from everything I have observed of him. There are chances. Now, it's up to him." He then raised his voice. "Listen up, mortals! Anyone who approaches the stage or even *looks* at my disciple the wrong way will immediately become the enemy of I, Deacon Shol Pesna of the Exploding Sun faction! Moreover, you will be infringing on the dignity of the Animal Kingdom, who safeguards this Tournament!"

This last sentence would hopefully stop the scions and agents of the Kingdom, who would be dying to interrupt Jack's breakthrough. At least, they wouldn't attempt anything *openly*.

His voice echoed over the arena. Almost instantly, a blur flew down from the stands. Shol cursed inwardly and prepared to blast the intruder with the full force of his Dao—even in this weak form, he could incapacitate most F-Grades.

He held himself back at the last moment. The blur landed on the sand and rushed beside Jack. It was Brock, who stood before his big bro, spread his hands, and glared unflinchingly at the audience. Even the immortals present didn't escape his threat.

Nobody would touch his big bro.

Shol nodded. This little brorilla was much to his liking. *Jack has found a good partner. If only he can survive...*

"Immortal, please give us permission to come over and guard Jack as well," Vivi Eragorn stood up from the audience and cupped her fists.

"Denied." He'd seen too many backstabbers in his day. Even calling Edgar here had been a gamble, but he was fairly certain the wizardling was loyal.

The only one he truly trusted was Brock.

Edgar stepped behind Jack, ready to protect him against anything. He conjured a transparent blue shield around the four of them.

Vivi obeyed Shol's command, but she didn't back down completely. On her orders, the members of Flame River fanned around the arena, each glaring at a section of the crowd. Dorman, the Sage, Li Xiang, Brother Tao, and even Vanderdecken also stood on the arena lip, gazing toward the crowd.

Shol narrowed his eyes. His threats wouldn't be enough to stop the Animal Kingdom's agents from interfering, but he was ready to blast the first unlucky attacker with the full power of his Dao, killing them on the spot. That should be enough to intimidate most into inaction. These humans would hopefully be able to deal with the rest, because Shol would be out of juice after that first strike.

He could already spot various people in the audience exchanging shady looks. The scions were whispering between themselves.

Before anything could happen, a new voice cut through the clamor.

"*Anyone* who interrupts that man's breakthrough will answer to the Hand of God."

It was Vocrich, whose faction didn't care about the Animal Kingdom. They just wanted to raise strong cultivators.

The vampire was only at the peak of the E-Grade, but his one sentence was enough to stop all in attendance. Not even the Planetary Overseer would dare act wildly now.

Nobody opposed the Hand of God. Anyone who tried didn't live long enough to regret it.

This calmed Shol somewhat, though he still maintained full vigilance. He glanced at Jack, who remained cross-legged and unaware of his surroundings. The Dao was seeping into his body, but it still had a way to go. Hopefully, the pill and fruit would pull him through the most difficult parts, and he could handle the rest. If not...

If not, then that was fate.

In the meantime, Shol had something very important to do. "Sorry for interrupting my words, master," he once more spoke mentally. "I must tell you something that will surely change your mind!"

Jack was lost in an ocean of purple. The aura of the giant fist was seeping into his body bit by bit. Wherever it passed, he disappeared. The fist was the master, and he was only a tool to wield it.

Jack didn't want this. It was *his* fist. *He* was the one in charge. He didn't want to sacrifice himself to it.

He tried to stop the aura, but it was like trying to hold back a river with your bare hands. He tried to close the floodgates, but there weren't any. The giant fist was an emptying container. It would all flood into him, and whatever happened, happened.

Jack panicked.

And warmth filled his entire body, starting from his tongue. In the next moment, it was like his eyes opened for the first time. He was in touch with the Dao of the Fist. Revelations came to him, from simple to complicated things. A series of visions flashed through his mind, presenting the core aspects of the fist.

Some, he knew. Some, he did not, but they became clear from the visions. His understanding of the Dao of the Fist shot up.

He could see now. The purple aura wasn't drowning him. It was *challenging* him. It represented the Dao Root's understanding into the fist, the understanding *he* had originally created. Now, he was called to contend with it.

There were two simultaneous challenges to overcome. The first was to prove that he and this Dao Root were compatible. This challenge came from within. The second was to prove that he had mastered it. This challenge came from without. From the Dao of the Fist in the universe beyond, whose acknowledgment he sought.

Jack's inner eyes opened as he saw what he had to do. The purple aura was made up of exactly nine hundred and ninety-nine tiny drops—he was sure of this—and each drop carried a riddle. If he beat the riddle, the drop would submit. If he didn't, the speck would drop him to the death.

Visions filled his mind. He was thrust into a gladiator's fight, a school room, a back-alley brawl, a knife fight, a gunfight, the trenches of a war, shouting arguments against all sorts of people. Each vision came at once, and all asked him the same question: "What would you do? How would you feel?"

It wasn't as tangible as that. The visions all occurred inside his soul simultaneously. Jack didn't really find himself in those situations. Instead, they were forced into his soul, and then the answer flowed out by itself, uninhibited. Everything coalesced into a phantom deep inside him which slowly took the form of a fist borne of his very soul.

Unfortunately, he was just a watcher. This battle of visions didn't seem to be his, yet it was. Maybe not now, but to answer the riddles, his soul just used everything he'd fed it over his entire life. He'd shaped himself. That was his part in the battle, and it was over. Now, all he could do was watch and hope.

Instinct told him that the more similar this phantom got to the giant fist, the more perfect his union with the Dao Root he was internalizing.

Only now did he understand he was breaking through to the E-Grade. He was confused and worried, but the ball was rolling. He buckled down and prepared for a fight.

Hope turned to despair. The phantom was still vague, but he could see it wasn't exactly like the giant fist before. There were differences—malformities. The shape wasn't quite right. The fist in his soul wasn't as clear as it should have been. Slowly but surely, it was drifting into a travesty of a fist, and he was powerless to stop it.

Suddenly, warmth filled his stomach, and colors invaded his world. The black void was painted in rainbows. Jack drew a deep breath as his spirit expanded. All at once, his mind was clearer than it had ever been. Way, *way* clearer.

It was like a meditation within a meditation. A trance in a trance. Every complex thought dissolved into simple parts, and all that was difficult became easy.

Jack wanted to laugh. Why had he even struggled?

A watcher? Your mother's a watcher!

He dove into his soul, brimming with confidence. The Dao of the Fist was strewn wide before him. He now floated between dozens of visions, each resolving at the same time, but he understood the truth.

The visions were illusions. Only one thing was real—the fist—and as long as he kept the fist in his soul unpolluted, he would always prevail.

The visions unraveled. They were foundational questions, nothing more than child's play. And in that understanding, Jack recognized that his compatibility with the fist was perfect. From his toes to the deepest recesses of his soul, he was willing to embrace the path of the fist until the very end.

After that, the visions truly were simple. All he had to do was project his soul—the fist—and they would have their answer.

They melted like snow in the oven. The purple aura vanished as it entered his body, gathering obediently in his soul and becoming one with him. The shape of a fist became clearer and clearer in the very core of his being, and the deformities were lessening.

Jack was disgusted by them. He grabbed the phantom and twisted it into shape, using his strength to force it to obey. He ironed it out. The giant fist outside wasn't giant anymore—it shrank as he took its aura, from a hill, to a tree, to a boulder. Finally, it reached the size of his own fist. They were indistinguishable.

The Dao asked him one question: "Will you give me everything?"

"Yes," Jack replied. "But *you* will serve *me*."

It was the right answer.

His soul hugged the phantom of a fist inside it and they became one. The Dao coursed through his body, empowering and transforming it. This was only a tiny part of the true Dao of the Fist and all its transformations, but it was a part Jack had thoroughly conquered. It belonged to him.

His turmoil was over. His soul and the Dao Root of the Fist had seamlessly fused, becoming one thing: the Dao Seed of the Fist.

At least, so Jack hoped.

He looked at the rainbow-colored void around him. The Dao Root of Indomitable Will now orbited around him like a satellite, admitting its inferiority to the fist inside him. From now on, Indomitable Will was a weapon, but the fist was *himself*.

He felt perfect. Whole. For the first time in his life, even more than when the Integration happened, he was certain he was exactly where he belonged. This was his world.

Jack roared in laughter, venting all the pent-up frustration of his life, and punched out. The void cracked and shattered like glass. Jack opened his eyes, finding himself in a blue bubble, surrounded by Edgar, Brock, and Master Shol, whose eyes were wide as saucers.

Around him, thousands of people watched his every move, but so what?

"Thank you for waiting, everyone," he said, slowly standing. The power that coursed through his veins was euphoric, and the notifications blazed in his vision, begging to be opened. He'd practically ascended... and this was only the E-Grade. He grinned. "I'm back."

CHAPTER NINETY-EIGHT
CLASS SELECTION

THE ARENA HAD FALLEN SILENT. MOST HUMANS DIDN'T UNDERSTAND WHY, BUT they could tell something was wrong.

All the aliens were gaping at Jack like he was a monster. So were the most knowledgeable of humans, and even the immortals. The C-Grade lioness was gripping her throne's armrest tightly, though no one noticed. Vocrich's dark eyes blazed. Only the ascetic of Barren High maintained his cool, though even he was surprised.

"A perfect Seed..." Barren High muttered, sighing. "Why this planet?"

"Planetary Overseer—" Vocrich began saying.

"No," she cut him off. "This man is a possible *threat* to my faction. He *must* be ended here and now."

Vocrich's upper lip twitched. "The Hand of God wants him."

"This is our territory."

"You would refuse our request?"

"We can pay the price." She tore her eyes off Jack to stare at Vocrich. "This boy will die *today*. If you interfere and break the Star Pact, so will I."

Vocrich hesitated, then slicked back his dark hair, flashed her a charming smile, and said, "Let's not argue. There are other perfect Seeds. We could forget about him, but..." he trailed.

"I have no time for games. Name your price."

"A hundred spots into Trial Planet, and a hundred promising recruits over the next ten galactic years," he offered confidently. "New generation for new generation."

"I will add another hundred of both, but you must guarantee that the Exploding Sun will stay out of this."

Vocrich smiled. "Deal."

Both satisfied, they turned back to the arena. In the blink of an eye, Jack's fate had been sold and bought.

Meanwhile, right next to Jack, Master Shol was about to have an aneurysm. "My boy," he said with a tremble. "You..."

"Thank you for your protection, Master," Jack responded, bowing deeply. "You fed me the Rainbow Dao Pill and the Dao Fruit of the Fist, right? You saved me."

"Nonsense, nonsense." Shol quickly waved it away. "Quick! Check your notifications and tell me what they say."

Jack was rather taken aback at the enthusiasm, but he complied regardless. He, too, was extremely curious to see what the System had to say. The lioness's soul influence had disappeared, for whatever reason, making him breathe a sigh of relief.

Congratulations! Dao Root of the Fist → Perfect Dao Seed of the Fist (early)

Congratulations! F-Grade → E-Grade

Congratulations! Your body has been infused with your Dao, taking on its attributes.

All stats +10
Free stat points per Level up: 2 → 5
Level Up! You have reached Level 50.

Congratulations! The Bare Fist Brotherhood faction has reached the E-Grade. New functions unlocked in the faction screen.
Congratulations! For being the first cultivator on your planet to develop a Dao Seed, you are awarded the Title: Planetary Torchbearer (1).
Planetary Torchbearer (1): A Title awarded to the first cultivator to develop a Dao Seed on an Integrated planet. A sign of great potential, marking the owner as a person worthy of the Immortal System's assistance.

Efficacy of all stats +15%

Class Upgrade available. Please choose your new Class:

There was a long blue screen after that, detailing his class choices, but he put it aside for now. As much as he couldn't wait to choose, it sounded like something that would take time, and he didn't know if he had time.

He was already plenty excited, anyway. All other benefits aside, the Planetary Torchbearer (1) title... It was humongous! Coupled with the Planetary Frontrunner (10), he now had a 25 percent increase in the efficacy of all his stats—assuming the effects was additive. That would put him head and shoulders above everyone else at his level.

The truly strong people in the galaxy would doubtlessly have some titles of their own, like Rufus, but Jack could get more in the future, too. For now, he was definitely way ahead of the curve.

Finally, he opened his status screen.

Name: Jack Rust
Species: Human, Earth-387
Faction: Bare Fist Brotherhood (E)
Grade: E
Class: Pugilist (Elite) (Upgrade pending)
Level: 50

Strength: 129 (+)

Dexterity: 129 (+)
Constitution: 129 (+)
Mental: 22
Will: 22
Free points: 5

Skills: Fistfighting (III), Drill (III), Pugilist Body (III), Parkour (III)

Dao Skills: Meteor Punch (II): Daos: Perfect Dao Seed of the Fist (early), Dao Root of Indomitable Will

Titles: Planetary Frontrunner (10), Planetary Torchbearer (1)

It was glorious.

"It says a lot of things, Master," he replied.

"Your *Dao Seed*, boy. Tell me what that says!"

Master Shol was really flustered, which worried Jack. Had he done something wrong? He felt that everything had gone smoothly. Maybe breaking through now was a mistake?

"It says I got the Perfect Dao Seed of the Fist, and then the word early in parentheses."

Just when he thought Master Shol's eyes couldn't widen further, they did. His mouth trembled as he spoke. "Perfect? Are you sure?"

"Yes, Master. I *can* read."

"This is... This is wonderful! Excellent! Good job, my boy! Incredible job! And you were so fast, too—that's *marvelous*!"

Jack hadn't seen his master express joy like that before, though he had no context. He hadn't even known Dao Seeds were split into tiers.

"Is a perfect Seed so rare, Master?" he asked.

"Extremely! Even in the Exploding Sun, we only get a handful of those per generation!"

"Oh!" Jack's eyes brightened. That sounded pretty good.

"With this, I'm sure my master will take you in. You will be safe!" Master Shol continued excitedly. He'd completely forgotten they were watched by billions of people and several other immortals. At the very least, Edgar's bubble blocked sound.

“Mhm, that’s great,” Jack said, nodding. In one fell swoop, he’d advanced to the E-Grade, gotten a perfect Dao Seed—which apparently was very rare—and secured the protection of the Exploding Sun, which meant the Animal Kingdom couldn’t touch his faction. Once he took care of Rufus Emberheart, who now counted as a native, all his problems would be solved. “How long do we have until the Tournament is over?” he asked.

“Five minutes,” Master Shol said. “Go on and choose your class. No need to consult me. I trust you will make a good selection. I will speak to my master.”

Jack raised a brow. He didn’t know it was possible to communicate in real time over such distances—they were in different constellations—then again, Master Shol was an immortal. He had his tricks.

Jack turned to the side, smiling at Edgar and Brock. The little monkey took this as its cue and flexed at Jack, then reached out for a congratulatory handshake. He was brimming with joy for his big bro. Jack felt so glad to have him.

Edgar was wide-eyed, too, and he let out a soft whistle. “Shit, man. I can’t see your level.”

“I’m fifty,” Jack replied. “Thank you for protecting me. Did people try anything weird while I was out of it?”

“No. Your master and that Hand of God vampire scared everyone away.” He looked like he wanted to say something more but didn’t know what. He scratched his head. In the end, he simply said, “You’re amazing.”

“Hey now, don’t undersell yourself. You haven’t broken through yet, have you? What do you know? Maybe you’ll get a perfect Dao Seed, too!”

“You never know,” Edgar replied with a small smile. “Well, what are you waiting for? Don’t you want a new class?”

“Right.” Jack immediately opened his screens again. He was dying to choose.

The very first class didn’t disappoint.

Bare-Knuckled Berserker (Elite)

Berserkers are warriors who draw energy from rage. They lose

themselves in battle, gaining extraordinary power in return. Additionally, the more damage they receive, the stronger they become. Bare-Knuckled Berserkers are rare variants, usually appearing in barbaric tribes of desolate planets. They plow through enemies with their bare fists, standing tall and proud on a mountain of corpses.
"Punch until there is nothing left."

This class sounded cool, though with a major drawback. Losing himself in battle didn't sound practical. He could understand why the System offered that class—more than once, Jack had let fury drive him mid-fight.

But the fist included control. It wasn't just a weapon.

Juggernaut (Elite)
A warrior who does not falter. Juggernauts dive into the thick of battle, using their extraordinary resilience to trade blows with anyone in their path. Their offensive capabilities are only adequate, but they will be the last ones standing.
A juggernaut is a one-man army: "Never fall."

This also sounded intriguing, if a bit simple. It focused on defense rather than offense, which wasn't Jack's preference, but it would do. After all, defense was the foundation of a good offense.

His only doubt was that the fist wasn't specifically mentioned anywhere, as it was in his Pugilist class and the Bare-Knuckled Berserker one. Did that mean anything?

Regardless, Jack filed this class away as a good option and proceeded to the next.

Lightning Fist (Elite)
A martial artist that uses superior speed to whittle down their opponents. They can use lightning to strike from a distance, as well as imbue their bodies with it.
Lightning Fists slip through the battlefield like fish in water, striking precisely when and where they should.
"Strike like lightning, hit like thunder."

This reminded Jack of Dorman. It sounded practical, but it wasn't the path he wanted. His Dao had just formed, and it was based on power, not speed. After all, fist meant power.

The bald man in his first Dao Vision hadn't needed speed to destroy the titanic beast.

So far, he was torn between the previous two options. Being a one-man army suited him, though he would prefer to focus on offense rather than defense. The other option was the berserker variant, which he was wary of. Losing himself in battle was dangerous, and not the way of his fist.

Both were good, but neither was perfect.

There was one final class to inspect, and Jack hoped it would be something better.

Fiend of the Iron Fist (Elite): A solitary, unstoppable warrior. A conqueror who crushes all opposition with an iron fist.
A Fiend of the Iron Fist is a balanced fighter who focuses on delivering devastating punches. While this Class contains no inherent morality, most previous wielders went down in history as heavy-handed tyrants, hence its name.
This Class hails from the Iron Fist Empire.
"Power rules the world."

This was... intriguing, but it was nowhere near the clean choice Jack hoped for.

This last class raised quite a few red flags. It had the word *fiend* in its name, which sounded ominous. Most previous Fiends were tyrants—that couldn't be a coincidence, right?

On the other hand, the class was about "a balanced fighter who focuses on delivering devastating strikes." That was Jack's current fighting style, and he liked it. It suited him and his path perfectly.

Then again, so did the bare-knuckled barbarian. One had the clear drawback of losing his mind in battle, and the other was... ominous?

Let's see, he considered, narrowing his eyes. Time was running out, but they still had a few minutes, and if there was anything worth considering, that was his class selection. He decided to dissect the issue.

While this class contains no inherent morality, most previous wielders went down in history as heavy-handed tyrants, hence its name. That was the core sentence. If Jack read it correctly, it seemed like a coincidence, or maybe a result of the class originating in the Iron Fist Empire—which didn't sound like the happiest place.

At the very least, the "no inherent morality" part was an explicit assurance that the System wouldn't mess with his mind, right? If anything, it implied that either brain-washing or stupid skills like "this skill automatically kills the people who enrage you" were possible, and Jack wanted none of that. His mind was his final bastion, and he would defend it no matter what.

On second thought, the barbarian class also implied mind control. He'd assumed that "lose himself in battle" was a mild side-effect, but what if it wasn't? *Fuck that.* He bid the class goodbye on the spot.

Nobody would control him. He was the master of himself.

Back to the Fiend of the Iron Fist. If one got past the *Fiend* part, it sounded perfect. A solitary, unstoppable warrior: that was him. Crush all opposition with an iron fist: that was his Dao—fist meant power. A balanced fighter who focuses on delivering devastating punches: that was his exact fighting style, as well as the direction he wanted to take going forward.

Suddenly, Jack realized that, of all his class choices, the Fiend was by far the most specific one, and it was perfect for him—too perfect to let go.

If anything went wrong down the line, he would deal with it then. Besides, how hard could it be? If he remained himself, things would work out.

He braced himself and locked in the selection, already giddy with excitement.

Congratulations! You are now a Fiend of the Iron Fist (Elite).
Congratulations! Pugilist Body (III) upgraded into Iron Fiend Body (II).

Class Skill unlocked: Ghost Step (I).

CHAPTER NINETY-NINE
ABANDONED

MOLTEN IRON FLOWED THROUGH JACK'S VEINS. NO, THAT WASN'T IRON, IT WAS his blood. He screamed and seized as his entire body tensed at once. From his skin to his intestines, even the muscles he couldn't control cramped, tightening to their hardest.

They didn't relax again. Over the following seconds, Jack gradually felt the rigidity leaving his body. Then, he was fine. His body was flooded with more strength than he'd ever dared hope for. His muscles were veritable steel cords, and his entire body had gotten at least twice as durable.

He clenched a hand in wonder. The movement of his fingers felt unstoppable. He stomped on the ground, and the rock below shook like he'd dropped a piano on it. Moreover, he could sense that his reflexes and kinetic vision had evolved with his strength.

He was frozen for a few moments, unable to believe it. He was drunk, euphoric with power. He felt like a god.

He'd never experienced such a leap in power before. Even when he got 9 levels at once, or when his skills all rose a tier after the fight against the black wolf, it hadn't been such a total, overwhelming upgrade as this.

He estimated that he was now fast enough to give Dorman a run for his money, even with the teen's Lightning Form activated. And speed was traditionally his weakest aspect. His current strength... Even he didn't know how strong he was.

Just what would a Meteor Punch look like if fired with this body?

Jack quickly opened the blue screens and kept reading, eager to see where all these changes came from. After all, his new class hadn't given him any stat points! He opened the Iron Fiend Body skill first.

Iron Fiend Body (II): You have iron knuckles. Your muscles resemble iron cords, possessing explosive strength and great tenacity. You have significant durability, slight regenerative powers, and heightened control over your body, including its natural limiters. Additionally, your mind is fast enough to keep up.

The massive strengthening of my body must have been due to this skill... Jack thought. *But, boy, the description doesn't do it justice. This skill is incredible!*

He willed the description of Pugilist Body III to appear. Iron Fiend Body was the upgraded version, and it read pretty similar.

Pugilist Body (III): Your body has adapted to your fighting style. You gain significant flexibility, reflexes, and durability, as well as increased hardness on your knuckles. You have heightened control over your body, including its natural limiters, and slight regenerative powers. Additionally, you have the ability to harden every surface of your body at will, significantly increasing your defensive properties.

Basically, Jack had gone from a Pugilist's Body to one made of iron. It was certainly an upgrade, even though the skill had lost a proficiency tier. And it wasn't even a Dao skill!

Of course, there were many reasons working in tandem for his massive strengthening. Reaching the E-Grade was a big one—that, by itself, was a tremendous change. His body had been imbued with his Dao. Since he had the Dao Seed of the Fist, that made him stronger and harder than before. Add the Iron Body to that, and he was at least twice as durable as he used to be.

He'd also gotten ten points in all stats, and if his math was correct, he had also leveled up once, netting him another five points—meaning the level-up bonus had increased massively. He invested them in Physical. At this rate, his stats would rise exponentially as he climbed through the grades. The seventy-five levels in the E-Grade alone would give him... almost four hundred stat points.

Dear mother of God... How strong is an immortal? he asked himself, glancing at his master, who still seemed intently focused on his thoughts. *Five hundred?*

He wanted to test his new power properly, but before that, he read through his other new skill, Ghost Step.

Ghost Step (I): Active skill. Step like a ghost, moving quickly and silently to anywhere within nine feet of you.

The description was deceptively simple, but the skill itself sounded useful. A movement skill had been exactly what Jack missed. He did have Parkour, but it was... insufficient.

Neither of these two new skills were Dao skills, but that was okay. With time, they would be.

Jack inspected his status screen, and when he closed it, he was filled with pride. The first E-Grade of his planet, and a perfect one, too... How far he'd come.

But now, it was time for the truly fun stuff. "Hey, Edgar," he said, turning to the wizard a few feet away. "Check this out."

"Wha—"

Before Edgar could reply, Jack took a step. His form blurred like a ghost as he soundlessly hurtled through space, appearing right in front of Edgar almost instantly. "Ah!" Edgar shouted, jumping back. The shield flickered. "Jesus, Jack! You scared the crap out of me."

"Heh." Jack chuckled, panting a bit. Ghost Step had practically teleported him, but it was tiring. It'd felt like wading through mud.

But it was extremely fast. Jack was no longer slow. He was... well, he didn't know the E-Grade's standards, but he was at least decent.

"Check out how fast I am," he told Edgar, then sidestepped in circles around the wizard. His movement was so rapid it raised a cloud of sand.

"Hey, stop that!" Edgar complained, forming a second blue barrier around his face. "No need to—"

Jack punched the ground. His hard-as-iron knuckles slid through the sand like it wasn't even there and rammed into the stone. The entire arena shook. Some people on the stands lost their footing. When Jack pulled his hand back, the stone had a bowl-sized crater—and his knuckles were completely unhurt.

"I think I'm going to like this," he said. He couldn't test his durability right now, but surely some random scion would help him soon.

"Holy shit. What's your new class?" Edgar asked. "You chose already, right?"

"Yep. Fiend of the Iron Fist."

"Fiend of the Iron Fist..." Edgar mouthed the name, testing it. "Why *fiend*?"

"Because I'm suppo—"

The world fell away. Jack found himself in an overcast world, hovering high over a field of broken bodies. Blood and weapons littered the barren dirt. Jack himself was only a ghost, lacking a material form.

He grimaced. He'd forgotten about this part, but he had to admit that he really looked forward to it. His eyes swiveled, looking for the caped bald man of his first Dao Vision, but he was nowhere to be found. Instead, a new person had taken his place.

It was a big-bodied human. He was bare-chested, with wide shoulders and bulging muscles. His hands were clasped behind his back, and he stood straight like a ramrod. Three long, gray lines were tattooed on the right side of his chest, like a wound left over by an animal's claws.

He did not look like a kind person. His long gray hair fluttered in the bloody breeze, while his gray eyes were harsh and narrowed into slits. His skin was bronze. His face was hard. In Jack's eyes, this man resembled a merciless, brutal master.

Gedritch, Level ??? (C-Grade)
Faction: Iron Fist Empire (C-Grade)
Title: Leviathan Slayer

Facing him was a fortress. Colossal dark walls stretched three hundred feet into the air and many miles on either side. Squinting at their top, Jack could make out a host of people preparing to defend. They sported all sorts of weapons and magic. With a few random scans, he discovered they were also gedritch, the same human-like species as the bare-chested man, and they were all in the E-Grade.

He also spotted dozens of figures assembled into battle formations, flying over the walls—immortals.

A single woman stood on the wall ledge. She was clad in golden plate armor from head to toe, and she radiated bright power. When Jack scanned her, she was also at the C-Grade—though the fact that she stood on the town walls indicated she was at a lower level than the bare-chested man.

In contrast, the man stood completely alone, facing down a fortress of immortals.

"We are willing to pledge our allegiance, Baron Longform," the woman shouted. Her voice echoed to the nearby mountains, easily reaching everyone's ears. "Promise the safety of our descendants and disciples, and we will serve the empire without a word of protest."

The bare-chested man shook his head. "Once a traitor, always a traitor." His voice was deep and harsh, sharp enough to cut through stone, and that wasn't a metaphor. The walls and ground shook. The E-Grade defenders atop the walls screamed, when a wide curtain of golden light spread over the entire length of the wall, shielding them. Jack was glad he had no body in this vision.

The woman's eyes were hard now.

"Very well," she responded commandingly. Her entire body erupted with a column of golden light that reached all the way to the sky, splitting the dense clouds, and ethereal wings spread from her back. "Then let the emperor's dog die here."

Thundering shouts came from the immortals in the sky, joined by the still-reeling E-Grade defenders on the walls. Jack couldn't see behind them, but he thought he heard many more voices rising from inside the fortress—either civilians or back-up forces.

The bare-chested man smiled grimly. He did not move a muscle. Suddenly, a wave rolled out of him.

It was invisible and formless. Jack only sensed it when it washed over him, and he was flooded with unease. The man's form had changed, but not visibly. He'd gotten sharper, stronger, more intimidating, twisting him into a bomb of violence ready to explode. Like a killer, a tyrant, a monster, a devil...

Or a fiend.

An aura of palpable violence spread in all directions, drowning the town in fear. Screams rose from all directions. The immortals in the air dropped like flies. Only a few were able to resist, but even they were unable to advance on the man.

True terror gripped Jack's heart. This man could tear him limb from limb, bringing unimaginable pain. There was nothing he could do to resist, only despair.

He lost all power. His Dao Roots were suppressed, his soul shivered, and he couldn't stop shaking. If not for the protection of the System letting him experience this vision, he was sure he would have crumbled on the spot.

Jack couldn't see beyond the wall, but he sensed that people were dying in droves, their souls and wills crushed beyond redemption, overwhelmed by terror.

And the more people that fell, the stronger the bare-chested man grew. He fed on their terror until his body overflowed with power, and the black-and-red aura around him grew so thick that it seemed to form horns over his head and leathery black wings on his back.

This all happened in an instant. The woman's golden light did nothing to stop this aura. A second later, her face contorted in fury and despair. She charged forward. "Have you no honor? No *shame*?" she screamed at the top of her lungs so hard it tore her throat.

A lance of pure light materialized in her hand, filling the entire world with heat. The man clenched his fist and stepped forward. Then, abruptly, the vision cut off. It had shown what it wanted. The rest of the battle did not concern it.

Jack was back in the arena, reeling and losing his footing. Only a moment had passed in the real world, but he was shaken, like the terror of the bare-chested man had seeped deep into his bones.

It receded, like it had all been a bad dream, leaving Jack stunned.

That Dao Vision had been... alarming. Perhaps the new class would come with some complications after all... but a weapon was a weapon. Even if the aura targeted his allies as well, which he doubted, he would just have to use it carefully.

Even better, twist it to his path. His Meteor Punch had also deviated from what the bald man used, according to Master Shol. He could do the same with this aura. And then, it would be an incredible weapon. Feeding on the enemies' fear... How cool was that?

"Jack?" Edgar's voice snapped him out of his thoughts. "Are you okay? You were saying something, and you just cut off."

"Sorry, the Dao Vision came. It was..." He trailed. As soon as he had the chance, he would meditate on that Dao Vision intensely. He looked forward to what he would learn.

"Promising?"

"Terrifying. But yeah, very promising. I think I made a great choice."

"I'm glad to hear that." Edgar smiled widely. "Now, you were saying something about your class name. The reason it included the word 'fiend.'"

"Oh, yeah. Well, it's mostly a historical thing, as the previous wielders of this class were tyrannical, and I suspect that some skills will be pretty fiend-like. I'm supposed to oppress others with an iron fist."

"And you'll do that?"

"Only if they deserve it. I'm a pretty good guy," Jack replied with a sardonic smile that wasn't at all reassuring.

Brock was hopping in place in front of Jack. He seemed as excited as his big bro, which made Jack even *more* excited. Finally, someone he could brag to.

"Check this out, Brock!" he said, flexing a bicep. Brock raised a hand to grab it, but no matter how he pushed, the bicep didn't budge. His monkey mouth formed into an 'O', and then he started yelling congratulations in monkey.

Jack wished he had a bananarm to give him.

"Disciple," Master Shol's voice came from behind him, and Jack turned excitedly, eager to share everything.

"Master, I—"

"Please wait."

Master Shol's voice was raspy, tired. His eyes were sunken and helpless. He seemed like a man who'd lost a battle.

"What's the matter, Master? What happened?" Jack asked.

"I don't fucking know." It was the first time he heard Master Shol curse like this. "Listen, boy. There are only a few minutes remaining until the one-hour deadline, and we must come up with a plan, quickly. My master abandoned you. She will not take you in."

"What?" Jack's eyes opened wide. "But I—"

"I know." Master Shol was visibly furious. "She *promised* that she'd accept you if you won, but she claims this is not a proper victory. However, you broke through so quickly, and with a perfect Dao Seed, too! This marks you as a talent worth nurturing! Even C-Grades should take you seriously now."

"So, what happened?"

"That's the problem: I don't know! My master just told me she received a direct order from the faction's Grand Elder. And do you know what it said? Leave Jack Rust and Earth-387 alone."

"I—What?"

"How would the Grand Elder know about Jack?" Edgar asked, stepping up beside them.

"There is only one explanation: the Animal Kingdom." Master Shol's eyes were dark. "Do you understand what this means, Jack?"

His heart sank. "Of course I do..." he muttered. Right when he thought everything was going great, he was once again plunged into despair, deeper than ever.

If the Animal Kingdom went so far as to ask the Exploding Sun to stay out of this, doubtlessly paying some sort of compensation, that could only mean one thing: they considered him too large of a threat to let live. He was already their enemy. If they believed he had the potential to grow into a threat to their faction, they would nip this problem in the bud.

"But why would they go so far?" he asked. "I'm only at the E-Grade!"

"You formed a *perfect* Dao Seed, Jack." Master Shol shook his head. "You should know that over half of those who have a perfect Dao Seed become immortals, provided they can survive until then. They even have a chance at reaching the C-Grade! Moreover, you have repeatedly insulted their scions and targeted the entire faction, and you are part of an alliance against them on this planet. Most importantly, you defied the Planetary Overseer just now, too."

Jack gritted his teeth. His master was right.

"Even the Animal Kingdom has a bottom line, Jack. And it appears you just crossed it." Master Shol's eyes were tinged with sadness. "You are marked for death, my boy... and nobody will help you. Only I can try, but my power is very limited in this state."

"Doesn't the Grand Elder's order extend to you, master?"

"It does, but fuck the orders. I'm here already, and you're my disciple. If it doesn't expose my faction to trouble, I will help you."

"Master..." Jack's eyes went wide.

CHAPTER ONE HUNDRED
CARVING A WAY OUT

"There is no time for sentimentality!" Master Shol regained himself. "We must find a way out of this or you'll die at the stake. The Tournament will be over shortly, and the Animal Kingdom will surely find an excuse to attack you as soon as possible."

"I see."

"Luckily, it seems you are going to win the Tournament. One of the rewards for first place is a D-Grade robot bodyguard. That should be enough to protect you, unless the Planetary Overseer acts herself, and if that comes to pass, nobody can save you, anyway."

"Do you think she will?" Jack asked hesitantly.

"No. Regardless, there is no point in worrying about that. If she acts, you're dead. If she doesn't, every scion and agent of the Animal Kingdom will be after you soon after you walk out of this arena. They won't be able to touch you or your people while you have the robot bodyguard, but that will only delay the inevitable. In one year, the Animal Kingdom's true forces will arrive, and the very first thing they will do on this planet is execute you and anyone you care about."

"I see." Jack didn't let fear cloud his judgment. Now was the time for action, not worry. "We return to the plan where I must take my people and flee." It pained his heart to say it. He would take a bunch of mortals into shark-filled waters. Even if he found some way for them to escape without teleportation, the chances of them surviving were slim.

"There is no other choice." Master Shol sighed.

Jack refused to accept this. He put his mind to work. Simple and direct solutions had worked for him so far—or they hadn't—but the time had come to use the intelligence that almost netted him a PhD pre-apocalypse—a PhD that now seemed as far away as a distant dream. He would never complete those few missing details.

At the same time, anger and stubbornness boiled up inside Jack. These aliens made rules and broke them. Rules were nothing to the strong.

But that was fine. If rules meant nothing, then Jack would make his own. If power was all that mattered, then Jack would reach for power.

If he wanted things to go his way, he had to take charge. Suddenly, he felt like his eyes had been half-closed and were now finally open. *This* was how things worked in the galaxy.

So what if there was no way out? He would find one.

Jack grinned.

He poured through every bit of knowledge he had. Even if Master Shol appeared resigned, Jack refused to give up. That was *not* the way of the fist. He would find a path to survival, to victory. No matter how difficult, if there was a path, he would walk it, and if there wasn't, he would make one.

And as he thought of that, an idea sprung to mind. An undoubtedly insane idea, and one which might be his only chance.

"Master, what are the chances of me reaching the C-Grade in a year?"

"What?" Master Shol gave him an odd look. "None. Why do you ask?"

"Is it really impossible? Or is it just highly improbable?"

"Don't use my words against me, kid." The ghost forced himself to smile. "Highly improbable is an underestimation. You have the same chances as randomly choosing the correct grain of sand out of an entire beach."

"But it's a chance."

"What's in your mind, boy? The things you are saying are impossible."

"Nothing is impossible," Jack replied. He was aware that his abrupt increase in power was skewing his perception, but he was also confident that he made at least some sense. "How about this? I leave the D-Grade robot bodyguard to guard my faction, and I leave the planet right away. Today. As *soon* as the Tournament ends, before they can make a move on me."

Master Shol could hide his disbelief.

"Think about it," Jack insisted. "Everyone will be protected here. Even the Flame River, Dorman, and all of them can hide in my faction if they want. They'll be safe for a year. Nobody will reach the D-Grade by then."

"Rufus Emberheart might, but that too is highly improbable," Master Shol muttered. He didn't agree with Jack's plan, but his enthusiasm was clearly getting to him.

"Exactly," Jack said. "At the same time, I will be alone in the galaxy. It will be tough out there, but you said it yourself: the greatest growth comes with the greatest danger. I will hunt opportunities with everything I have, and if I survive, my power should rise meteorically. It's the same principle as the Integration: a large meat grinder that heavily rewards the survivors."

"That is suicide," Master Shol said. "With your potential, risking your life like that is idiotic. There is no need."

"Do you have a better suggestion?"

"Jack, even if you do that, there is no way you will reach the C-Grade in a year. I suppose you mean to fight the Planetary Overseer?"

"Exactly. The Animal Kingdom can't send reinforcements. If I can beat her and destroy their teleporters before the grace period is up, we'll be cut off from their network. They will need to reach us physically, which will take at least several months. And if I can beat the Planetary Overseer, who exactly will they send against us? A B-Grade? The galaxy's strongest for one planet out of millions?"

Master Shol muttered something to himself. "That is incorrect. If you insult their honor like that, a dozen C-Grades will be on the planet within a week. There are ways to accelerate space travel, they're just expensive." He watched Jack's tight frown. "However..."

At this, Jack perked up.

"What you describe has a name," Master Shol continued. "Planet poaching. It has happened before, though not by a planet's natives. It is a method used between B-Grade factions during silent war. If you defeat the Planetary Overseer, you can claim the entire planet for your faction. Then, if you are close to the border, you can choose to join another constellation, provided the other B-Grade faction allows it."

Jack's eyes lit up. "I could join your constellation?"

"Theoretically, yes. If you really manage to defeat a C-Grade in a year, there is no way my faction will ignore you. But as I said, that's simply impossible."

"You said it's not impossible."

"Almost impossible."

"All I hear is that it's doable." Jack smiled. "And even if not, there might be other opportunities for me out there. Maybe I can find another C-Grade willing to help me take over this planet, or maybe I can find some way to transport all my people out of here. In any case, all answers lie in one place: the galaxy."

Master Shol pursed his lips. "And you would leave the D-Grade bodyguard here? You must know that an early E-Grade is nothing out there. Barely an ant. Half the people you meet will be able to crush you under their boots."

"That's fine. I'll find a way to survive. I'm no coward."

"Protection isn't cowardice."

"It is, if it means sacrificing others."

Master Shol fell silent at this. Jack could tell his master mulled over the information, trying to convince himself to believe it.

"I agree with Jack," Edgar spoke up. Sweat shone on his forehead from holding up the shield all this time, but he couldn't let it go now. "We're *all* marked for death. As difficult as it sounds, what he proposes is our only chance at survival—I mean, obviously defeating the C-Grade is impossible, but he can find some other way. He's strong enough to garner attention."

Brock beat his chest and released a battle cry. Jack smiled sadly at him. "I'm sorry, buddy, but... you cannot join me. Teleportation doesn't work on F-Grades."

Brock's eyes went wide as saucers. Tears welled up in their depths.

"He could, actually," Master Shol intervened. "The System obviously recognizes your spiritual bond, since it teleported him to the Tournament with you. It will let you bear the pressure for him. It will be tough, but given your strength, I think you can handle it."

"Really?" Jack's face showed a massive, bright smile. He'd been prepared to part ways with Brock. His spirit soared. Brock, too, jumped up and down in joy. Jack turned to him. "What do you say, little bro? Will you join me?"

Brock nodded instantly.

"Are you sure? It means you won't see your family for a while—and, to be honest, we'll probably both die."

This time, Brock considered it, but he nodded in the end. What kind of bro would say no?

Jack's eyes moistened, and he blinked it away. For the first time, he noticed that Brock had grown rather big. Where he used to sit on Jack's shoulder, he now reached above his knees.

Brorilla, Level 21 (Elite)

"Oh, wow. You're growing so fast, Brock!"

The brorilla cheered.

"Fine," Master Shol's voice came from the side. "Fine, you crazy disciple, *fine*. You have the mind of a true cultivator; if you perish, that will only be fate."

"Thank you, Master!"

"Can we hurry, please?" Edgar said, his voice strained. "We're running out of time."

"Yes. Listen closely." Master Shol leaned in. "The teleporter is right behind the arena. You've seen it, haven't you? The big, furnace-like building. As soon as you receive your Tournament rewards, rush there and teleport to a random place so they can't follow you. As a newly-Integrated native, the first teleportation will be free for you. After that, don't slack on your training —find strong opponents to hone yourself against. Maybe strong masters to guide you, too. Don't rely too much on experience balls. They will get you through the E-Grade fast, but they will stump your growth later on."

Master Shol's advice was rapid-fire, but it was also golden. Jack kept every word in mind. "Understood, Master."

"And most importantly, find a way to reach the Trial Planet. It's the single most important place for you right now. There is no shortage of opportunity there, only of strength. You'll either make it big or be torn apart by King monsters—the next step after Elites. The easiest way to reach the Trial Planet is through the Belarian Outpost, the trade center of this constellation, but any place with advanced teleporters will do. You have a token, so you've already cleared the tallest hurdle. Also, while you're out there, look for a beast master. Brock is a brave young brorilla, and he will be of great help to you if trained properly."

Jack nodded, as did Brock.

"As for you, Edgar," Master Shol turned to the wizard, "you must let your allies know about the situation. The safest option for them would be to move in with you under the protection of the D-Grade bodyguard. It will protect you from the most important threats until Jack returns, but a large number of other problems will undoubtedly arise, and someone needs to take charge and deal with them. When you unlock the faction's long-distance communication function, you will be able to contact Jack and plan ahead. Am I clear?"

"Yes, sir!" Edgar responded.

"Thank you, Master," Jack said from his heart.

He had understood some things in the post-breakthrough clarity. Master Shol had obviously withheld some information, mostly that he could have accelerated his breakthrough in return for an inferior Seed, as well as the Dao Fruit's usefulness outside breakthroughs, which Master Shol had severely outstated. After experiencing the process himself, these realizations came easy.

He could have been angry. Maybe he should. Master Shol's teachings had been partial, even intentionally skewed.

However, after all was said and done, his master had been right. If he knew he could accelerate his breakthrough, he would have done it, and the results would have been much worse than now. If he knew the

Dao Fruit would be effective even earlier on, he would have used it and wasted most of its potential.

He was angry that the decision had been taken from his hands, but that didn't lessen the fact Master Shol had been right.

Moreover, their relationship was one of mutual benefits, as he'd made clear multiple times. Master Shol never pretended to be a saint. He wasn't made of kindness and selflessness, but he was a pretty damn good man.

In the end, though Jack begrudged his master for some things, he had to admit that he owed him way, way more. Master Shol was the best master he could ask for.

Jack reached out a hand. "I don't know if this is considered rude in your faction... but on my planet, this is how we express respect. And gratitude."

Master Shol stared at the hand for a long moment. Then, he grabbed it, spending some of his power to make his hand corporeal and flashing Jack a big smile. "Give them hell, kid. I believe in you. And I'm sorry for being unable to help you more."

"It's alright, Master." Jack smiled. "The next time we meet, I might even be stronger than you."

"Heh. I'd like to see that."

"Sorry to interrupt, but it's almost time," Edgar cut in.

He had long made the sphere opaque so people couldn't see what was happening, and sound was blocked, but they were keeping track of time. They wouldn't want to remain isolated after the Tournament was over.

"Yes." Jack let go of his master's hand, nodding. "Any last words, anyone?"

Master Shol stayed silent.

Edgar stayed silent.

Brock said, "B."

"What?" Jack looked at the brorilla by his feet.

"B," Brock repeated. His face was strained from the effort. "B."

Jack's eyes went wide. "Brock?" he asked. "Are you... trying to speak?"

"He picked the goddamn worst time to say his first word," Edgar cursed. "The deadline is over already!"

Jack didn't reply. His eyes were glued on Brock.

"B—B—" the little brorilla tried to say, furrowing his brows in deep concentration. His throat wasn't made to speak, but he was flexing his voice muscles. "B—Br—Bro!"

He looked up in pride, flashing a monkey-ish grin.

"Woah!" Jack cried out, throwing his hands in the air. "Brock! You said your first word!"

"Bro!" Brock repeated, then laughed in monkey, full of glee. His voice was rough and his pronunciation terrible, but it was clearly a word. He threw his hands in the air, jumping from side to side. "Bro! Bro!"

"Well done, Brock! I didn't even know you could speak!" Jack celebrated.

"Guys, please get serious. Everybody's waiting for us," Edgar pleaded. Master Shol coughed in his palm.

Jack recovered. He coughed once, too, then said, "Right. I believe we have said everything. I got massively stronger. We have a plan. Brock said his first word. Everything will work out." He took a deep breath. "Lower the shield, Edgar."

At his command, the blue dome disappeared, exposing Jack to the pressure of immortals and a billion set of eyes. This time, however, *he* pressured *them*. In danger, he smiled. Walking the razor's edge, he thrived.

Facing impossible odds and the threat of imminent death, this was Jack Rust at his best. The tension sharpened his gaze until it could stab through stone.

The arena went silent as if people could sense that something was different. All four scions that were present narrowed their eyes. The immortals and Vocrich leaned forward in their chairs with interest. Even the C-Grade lioness glanced at Jack, but this time, she didn't invade his mind.

As if on cue, the head judge landed in front of them the moment the shield went down. Her white feathered wings were like an angel's, and her blue skin glistened in the morning sun. She had dark hair fashioned into a braid and was dressed in white silken robes.

Jack scanned her.

Djinn, Level 101
Faction: Merchant Union (C-Grade)

He grinned widely. He could finally see her level. He also glanced at the stands, where Vocrich stood.

Vampire, Level 124
Faction: Hand of God (B-Grade)

Peak of the E-Grade... Yeah, I saw that coming.

"The one hour is up," the head judge said. "Rufus Emberheart failed to appear. If you have nothing to say, I will announce this battle as your victory."

She let the silence drag for a long moment, obviously waiting for Jack to resign. He flashed her his brightest smile. His bare chest puffed out, proud and strong.

Eventually, boos came from the crowd, and the head judge was helpless. With a heavy heart, she announced, "Rufus Emberheart failed to show up, forfeiting the fight. As a result... *Jack Rust* wins the final. He is the winner of Earth-387's Integration Tournament."

Her voice was impassionate, and so were the crowd's cheers. Only Jack's allies cheered hard. The rest of the people were expectedly half-hearted about it. After all, they came to see a spectacle, and they waited an hour for nothing to happen.

However, success isn't measured in claps. Jack had won. He raised a fist into the air, filled with glee.

"There is supposed to be a closing ceremony, but since the second place isn't here, I will distribute your rewards now," the head judge announced. She was clearly bending the rules again, but Jack didn't care. The faster this went, the better for him. "Dorman Whistles, Alexander Petrovic, please come to the stage. Everyone unrelated, please leave."

CHAPTER ONE HUNDRED ONE

CHALLENGE

MASTER SHOL HAD ALREADY FLASHED BACK TO HIS SEAT, HIDING HIS EXCITEMENT and nervousness as well as he could, and Edgar hurried to pick up Brock and fly back to his seat. The moment he landed, he began conversing with their allies in hushed tones.

Dorman and Alexander Petrovic landed next to Jack. He gave Dorman a smile and a nod, which the young man returned.

"Fourth and third place receive a Trial Planet Token," the head judge declared, fishing out two golden coins from her robes. They were the size of Jack's palm and looked old and faded; exact replicas of the one he had. "Congratulations!"

Dorman and Alexander Petrovic received their coins, thanked her, then jumped back to their seats. Only Jack was left in the arena now, facing the head judge directly. He glanced at the stands and saw many people whispering darkly, including the scions, the Ice Peak, his own allies...

Everyone important was mobilizing. He had no idea what the Animal Kingdom would try to do, but it was coming.

Hurry up... he urged her mentally.

Fortunately, the head judge showed no intention to delay things.

"The first-place winner receives several rewards," she announced.

"The first is a Trial Planet Token." She handed him the coin, which he quickly slid into his front right pocket. He now had two of those—the other was safely kept in a secret pocket on the inside of his pants. After the fruit and the Rainbow Dao Pill had been used up, it was his only important possession.

"The second reward is an Immortality Serum," the head judge announced, revealing a teardrop-shaped bottle filled with sparking green liquid. The bottle itself was only the size of two fingers, and it could barely hold a few drops. Everyone still gasped. "The Immortality Serum can rejuvenate the body, granting an extra hundred years of longevity. Moreover, it greatly enhances the Physical attributes of whomever drinks it, and the process is quick and painless."

While the audience gasped in admiration, Jack accepted the bottle, popped off the intricate cork, and gulped the liquid down. No sense in waiting.

He felt its effects instantly. It was like he'd had the best night's sleep of his life ten times in a row. He'd never felt fresher.

Immortality Serum bonus acquired! Physical +50

Plus what!

Jack almost shouted before his body convulsed. He dropped to a knee, unable to control himself. His muscles were twisting and expanding, threatening to rip out of his skin. His heart pumped blood with such force it made him dizzy, and his body was filled with such vitality that he felt like running a marathon every day for the rest of his life. His reflexes and dexterity spiked so hard it took him a few moments to regain control of his body, and even then, his movements were jagged and clumsy.

He groaned. This was so strange, but at least he would get used to it in a few minutes, unlike the changes brought by skills.

Still, 50 Physical... Wow. That's like... tons. Wow.

When he came to, the judge was glaring at him in annoyance, while some people in the audience were laughing. *Let them,* Jack thought with a smile. *I'm in danger. Why would I delay?*

He'd considered saving it for the professor after hearing about the hundred years of longevity, but surviving the first year was more important.

"The third reward," the head judge said, raising her voice over the crowd's, "is a Dao Soul."

She pulled an item out of her robes. It was a purple gem that could easily fit in Jack's hand. It seemed normal at first glance. At the second, it was anything but. Two thick lines swam inside it like eels, one black and the other white, cutting circles around each other. It reminded him of the yin-yang sign.

"The Dao Soul is a mystical item said to split one's soul into two," the head judge explained, raising the gem high. "It can help a cultivator practice their Dao against themselves, rising their cultivation speed tremendously."

Many people gasped again. She handed it to Jack, who looked at it oddly.

"And how does one use this, oh great judge?" he asked.

"Ingesting it takes time," she answered with a tight smile.

Jack nodded, then stuck it inside his secret pocket, which he no longer cared about keeping secret. It was on the inside of his left thigh, a place that would both protect his major artery and shield the item from would-be thieves.

"Finally, there is a D-Grade automaton," she exclaimed, turning behind her. Two djinns carried a robot onto the stage through the back entrance. It was humanoid, with bulky limbs and squarish proportions. It was entirely made of a shiny gray metal Jack didn't recognize, but even he could sense that it was extremely hard. Enough that he could *sense* it.

Even as he was, he doubted he could dent that metal. It was only a feeling, but he trusted it.

"This robot was forged by the famous Horrificus Egen as a bodyguard for one of his disciples," the head judge explained. "When that disciple passed away, the Animal Kingdom bought the robot, and now, it will be used to protect one of this generation's shining stars. The Animal Kingdom takes care of its geniuses."

Even she didn't believe her words, but she said them nonetheless.

The weird thing about the robot was that it seemed deactivated. The two djinns had carried it over like an unconscious human, one holding it from the armpits and the other from the legs, both clearly straining from the effort despite their E-Grade bodies. They arrived next to Jack and the head judge, then struggled to lift the robot upright.

Robot Bodyguard (D-Grade)
A robot designed to guard and fight for its user. This particular specimen has been tempered with the Dao of Fire and forged by a master blacksmith, achieving extreme hardiness. It can fight even an early D-Grade cultivator to a standstill. What is lacks in mobility, it makes up with sapience-level intelligence.
Manufactured by Horrificus Egen

"We also offer three personality capsules to choose from," the head judge said, fishing three small gems out of her robe. They were only the size of Jack's thumbnail; one was white, the other black, and the third blue. "The first is—"

"Excuse me, honored judge," Jack cut her off. He hadn't known that robot personalities came in capsules. Now that he did, he had an idea—perhaps he could fix his only regret from this Tournament. "If I may ask, do all robot personalities come in capsules?"

"Where else?" she replied, looking at him like he was an idiot. Jack didn't mind.

"In that case, I have a small request. I'm sure you wouldn't mind, since the Animal Kingdom takes such good care of its geniuses." Her face stayed perfectly still. "During the Tournament, I came to like the training robot in my house. Would it be possible to use that personality capsule, and you can keep these three in return?"

The head judge looked at him like he'd said something stupid. "You came to like a robot?" she asked.

"It's pleasant. We became good friends," he replied, nonplussed.

After glancing toward the Planetary Overseer, who hadn't even looked at them once while the rewards were handed out, she said, "We can arrange for that. However, be warned that an already calibrated capsule will need a short period of adjustment in a new body. The bodyguard won't be usable for approximately one hour."

Jack frowned. *That's a bummer.* He'd been planning to have the bodyguard protect him while he made a run for the teleporter, just in case the Animal Kingdom tried anything, but he was confident he could make it, anyway. Especially after that monstrous +50.

He liked Sparman. After training together for weeks, he just couldn't bear to leave the poor robot behind.

Even if it was annoying at times.

"That's fine," he said. "Please make the swap."

The head judge looked at him like he was stupid—again—but nodded. Then, she made him wait.

A few moments later, a djinn raced into the arena, then walked the last few steps slowly. He carried a slimy green capsule in his hand, a little gem that Jack *knew* was the color of sarcasm.

The head judge grabbed the gem, thanked the runner, and inserted it into a small opening in the back of the robot's skull. A metal plate rose from below immediately after, covering the opening and making it indistinguishable from the rest of its metal skin.

Slowly, the robot opened its eyes. The two djinn handlers let it go. The robot wobbled.

"Ohhh," it said in a metallic voice before collapsing to the floor like a sack of potatoes. Its legs and arms jutted around, but it was unable to stand. The audience burst out laughing. The head judge's face was a frozen mask of irritation. She clearly hadn't intended for the award ceremony to be funny.

The robot flailed helplessly, rotating in place, when it caught sight of Jack. "Oh, master! I sense bodyguard functions in my wiring. Very well. I suppose that serving you for the rest of my life is a fitting punishment for my poor performance earlier. It is my fault for reminding you that you had to *hit* the targets, not *miss* them."

The audience remained silent, and even the head judge was visibly confused.

"It's okay, everyone, he's just kidding," Jack said, raising a hand. "This guy has a *special* sense of humor."

"Handlers, please move the robot outside the arena," the head judge said, finally unable to take this any longer. The two djinns grabbed it by the arms and legs again, and heaving, picked it up.

"One moment, please," Jack said. He approached the robot and whispered a few commands in its ears: To guard the Bare Fist Brotherhood with all its strength.

Sparman nodded. For once, its voice didn't sound mocking. "Rest assured, master. I will follow your order to my last breath—metaphorically speaking, since I do not breathe."

"I believe in you, Sparman. Good luck."

Jack then rose, muttered a quick apology to the two handlers—who had held the robot high while Jack whispered at it—then turned back to the head judge.

"The final reward," she said, "is entry into the Animal Kingdom faction and apprenticeship by a C-Grade Elder. Unfortunately..." She stood a touch straighter. "Due to the nature of your final victory, no elder was willing to accept you as a disciple. As a result, this final reward will have to be rescinded, but a person of your talents will certainly find a worthy destination."

"That's okay. I'm sure some wise person will eventually accept me as their disciple," Jack replied, smiling. That was a jab toward the Animal Kingdom, half-implying they weren't wise, but the head judge showed no signs of picking it up—though she probably did.

"Therefore, the reward ceremony and the Tournament are over. Congratulations to everyone who participated, especially the winners, and we wish your planet prosperity for the rest of the Integration Year. May your days in the New World be bright!"

The crowd cheered. However, before anyone could relax, a sharp voice broke though.

"One moment, please."

Everyone craned their heads to look. Fesh Wui stood on the railing before his seat, on the highest end of the stands. His arms were crossed, his wings were spread wide, and his eyes were as sharp as his voice.

"The four of us have grown on this planet together with brother Rufus," he declared proudly, gesturing at the other three scions. "All evidence pointed at him being stronger than Jack Rust. However, when an accident happened and brother Rufus was unable to attend, Jack Rust did not resign. He grasped this dishonorable victory that belonged to our brother."

Whispers spread through the crowd. The smartest ones were already streaming outside the arena, and many others noticed them and followed suit. Before long, the arena was quickly emptying.

Only a few people stayed in their seats: The Flame River, Edgar, Brock, Dorman Whistles, the Sage, Li Xiang, Brother Tao, the scions, the Ice Peak, as well as around thirty other people scattered throughout the audience. Some of those were in groups, while others were alone, and all of them glared at Jack.

"As a result," Fesh Wui raised his voice, "we wish to take revenge for our brother and challenge Jack Rust. Esteemed Planetary Overseer—" he turned to the lioness, bowing deeply "—we know the rules forbid violence until tomorrow, but would it be possible to let us defend our honor against this vile thief?"

The immortals had also stayed in place, of course, as had Vocrich and the Planetary Overseer. She rose, adopting a face of righteousness. "Honor is a cultivator's most important possession," she declared in a voice that left no doubt. Jack resisted the urge to roll his eyes. Master Shol sighed in his seat.

"Indeed, Jack Rust not resigning was a cowardice action," she continued. "Your words are proper, Fesh Wui. Very well. By my order—" Her voice boomed out extremely loudly, spreading over the entirety of Integration City. "The rule forbidding violence is lifted immediately. Additionally, the planet-wide transmission will remain active, so that the world can see honor trample villainy."

"We thank you for granting our request, esteemed Overseer." All four scions fell on their knees. The Planetary Overseer nodded. Then, a white cloud appeared under her feet as if oozing out of the arena below, carrying her, Vocrich, and the immortals high in the sky. The head judge had already flown out of the arena, and all other djinn officials were retreating.

Every other alien had already left.

Jack bumped his fists together, unleashing a metallic sound that echoed in the now-empty arena. He was done waiting. Their theatrics had taken long enough, but now, they could advance to the main course.

It didn't matter what tricks the Animal Kingdom used. Even if Rufus

Emberheart arrived in time, nothing would change. With his new stats, Jack didn't believe he would lose to anyone.

And, since they served him this opportunity on a silver platter, he might as well clean house before teleporting away.

He inspected his status screen one last time, eager to see all the changes.

Name: Jack Rust
Species: Human, Earth-387
Faction: Bare Fist Brotherhood I
Grade: E
Class: Fiend of the Iron Fist (Elite)
Level: 50

Strength: 184
Dexterity: 184
Constitution: 184
Mental: 22
Will: 22

Skills: Fistfighting (III), Drill (III), Parkour (III), Iron Fiend Body (II), Ghost Step (I)

Dao Skills: Meteor Punch (II): Daos: Perfect Dao Seed of the Fist (early), Dao Root of Indomitable Will

Titles: Planetary Frontrunner (10), Planetary Torchbearer (1)

"Very well," he said, turning to glare at all four scions at once. He grinned wildly, and the full force of his perfect Dao Seed rolled out. "Come at me, losers."

CHAPTER ONE HUNDRED TWO

EARTH VS. SCIONS

"WHAT!" Professor Margaret Rust grabbed both armrests of her chair and squeezed, making them creak.

Her assistants ceased celebrating and looked mutedly at a television screen, where the arena was displayed. Just a moment ago, they'd seen Jack Rust, the leader of their faction, become the strongest person on Earth and receive tremendous rewards. Everything had been going perfect.

Now, things had suddenly gone wildly off the rails. The scions wanted to fight Jack? And the Planetary Overseer let them?

"What is happening?" the professor cried out. All sorts of scenarios went through her head, filtering themselves until she was left with only one possibility: the Animal Kingdom, those impossibly strong alien overlords, wanted Jack dead. "No..." she muttered breathlessly.

A heavy hand steadied her shoulder. It was Harambe. They were currently gathered at their new headquarters in the Forest of the Strong, and the brorillas had joined the faction's top brass to watch the finals.

"Are you worried too, Harambe?" the professor asked, looking behind her. The brorilla nodded slowly. He could see his son right there, standing next to the strongest person of this world, their ultimate Big Bro.

He'd never been prouder.

"What do you think, Professor?" her assistant, Emily, called out in worry. "Can Jack escape?"

"I don't know. Even if he's reached the E-Grade now, how strong can he—"

Jack disappeared from the screen. A moment later, he appeared before the four scions. Before they could react, a massive meteor was hurtling at their faces, and it crashed with a great explosion. Smoke and debris filled the screen.

The professor was left staring, and then she laughed. "You know what? I think he's going to be fine."

Jack was *not* fine. He'd expended some energy to Ghost Step successively, reaching the four scions in the blink of an eye, and smashed out his strongest attack. He wanted to nip the problem in the bud. He thought he had them.

Unfortunately, he didn't. A massive steel shield appeared at the last second to block his strike, denting heavily but remaining solid.

A humanoid robot stood before the scions, having appeared out of nowhere. It was jet-black, wielding a sword and a shield which had barely managed to block Jack's strike.

Robot Bodyguard (E-Grade)
A robot designed to guard and fight for its user. This particular specimen has been enchanted with the Dao of Hardness, resulting in a defense that can resist even the middle of the E-Grade. It also sports high mobility, allowing it to cover its user from all attacks.
Manufactured by Horrificus Egen

This Horrificus Egen was getting on Jack's nerves.

Black light flashed, and three more robots appeared, similar to the first. Each stood before a scion.

The fuckers have back-up, Jack thought, gritting his teeth. No wonder they dared attack him despite his breakthrough.

Each of these robots were roughly equivalent to Sparman's sixth level, though focused on defense. Before today, he couldn't beat that level. Now, he had to fight four of those at the same time, plus the four scions.

Jack welcomed the challenge.

"Bring it on!" he shouted. Iron ran in his veins, firing him up. He settled into a fighting stance atop the railing, and his form blurred as he moved behind Gan Salin.

The canine froze. "Hey, chill, it was just a jok—" he tried to say. Jack's fist smashed out, but a robot stood between them, stopping the attack with its large tower-shield. It slashed out at Jack, who was already gone.

This time, he feinted moving at Shard Presht before using Ghost Step again and appearing above the elef. She was their healer, and Jack knew the golden rule: always attack the healer.

Unfortunately, the scions also knew the golden rule. A robot intercepted him the moment he appeared, pushing him to the side and forcing him to retreat. The other three tried to surround him, each brandishing a one-handed sword. Their metallic heads, which had no hint of a face, were all turned toward him.

Jack was irritated. He could easily beat one of these robots, but he couldn't afford to try. The moment one of them locked him down, the other three would be upon him in an instant, and he doubted that even his new durability could fully block those razor-sharp blades.

At least he had Ghost Step now. It was a bit tiring to use, but it greatly broadened his spectrum of options. Feinting to the right, he Ghost Stepped twice in a zig-zag to escape the robots. Thankfully, though they were fast, they weren't particularly agile.

The rest of the people in the arena had been waiting for the result of this clash. Seeing Jack back off and the scions unharmed, the morale of the scions' allies shot up.

"Listen up!" Fesh Wui raised his voice, spreading it even outside the arena. "One million credits to anyone who injures Jack Rust, and ten million to whoever brings me his head!"

Jack cursed. There is no way the scions had that kind of money by themselves.

Regardless, it was enough motivation. Those who'd remained on the stands had avarice in their eyes, and others started trickling in through the entrances. They weren't many, only around twenty, but that was twenty more than Jack had. Including the ones who never left the arena, there were now fifty people ready to lunge at him, most of whom had participated in the Tournament themselves.

Jack had powered up significantly, but even he couldn't survive these numbers.

"Flank him!" a rough voice came from behind. Jack felt the cold before he saw it. A large spike of ice flew over. He raised a hand to block, but it was unnecessary.

A flame whip hit the spike mid-flight and changed its course, sending it veering off Jack.

Thankfully, he had allies.

Vivi stood behind him, her form clad in flames, wielding a burning blue whip. "Attack the traitors. For Earth!" she cried out. Her voice filled the arena. The members of Flame River roared and charged, each turning into a human torch.

The Ice Peak moved to meet them. They spread into a rhombus and moved with perfect coordination, each covering the other's weakness, and shot out ice bullets from their fingers.

The Flame River also showed excellent coordination. They combined their flames into walls, meshing them perfectly to stop the bullets.

The Ice Peak was made up of highly-trained special agents. The Flame River had the elite soldiers of an entire country, and they'd successfully staged a revolution just weeks prior. Four on four, these two squads of professional killers clashed, demanding a part of the arena stands for themselves.

The Animal Kingdom didn't care for its arena's fate.

Wood burned, seats froze, all of it became a weapon. Fire mixed with ice into a chaotic battle that only they could navigate. In the air above, Vivi clashed against Alexander, each brandishing their element to the maximum.

Jack was attacked by the four robots, rendering him unable to help. They couldn't touch him, but they didn't let him go, either. They matched his speed, shielding the scions from his attacks.

Said scions didn't attack Jack. They knew they would achieve nothing. Instead, they turned their gazes at his allies and charged at them, with only the elef remaining behind to heal whoever got injured. Two figures flashed before them.

Dorman and Li Xiang stood side-by-side, one wielding daggers and the other straight palms. On the stair-shaped arena stands, these two stood a few steps below the three attacking scions, showing no intentions of letting them pass.

"We are enemies. You will die," Li Xiang said.

Beside him, Dorman chuckled. "We already beat you once. We can do it again."

"I'd like to see you try," Fesh Wui replied with narrowed eyes. His voice was filled with rage. "You almost took my wing, the pride of an eagler. I will pay you back or die trying."

"Sure."

They clashed, three against two. Blades and wings flew as everyone used their Dao to the maximum. Li Xiang moved faster than ever before, blocking attacks from all directions. Shard Presht focused on him, but all his momentum-changing attacks could achieve was delay the old man. Gan Salin circled behind him, but Dorman fell on the canine, buzzing with electricity, and it took only two exchanges for Salin to be covered in deep red lines.

Fesh Wui arrived then to block Dorman, and the two clashed at a speed nobody else could follow. They weren't trying to overpower or outmaneuver the other. They simply clashed again and again, and whoever could strike more times would win.

"Nice!" Gan Salin raised a thumb. Green energy washed over him from higher in the stands, closing his wounds. He turned his thumb at the elef, too. "Thanks! You rock!"

"Focus on the fight, Salin," she instructed in a low voice, her brows furrowed. Green light shone from her eyes and the end of her trunk, and she was slightly crouched as if ready to jump in any direction. Her robot returned to her side and remained there, making sure it could stop any surprise attack from Jack so she could focus on healing.

"Kane, Tao, Sage!" Edgar called out, having jumped to the middle of the arena. "Take the crowd!"

The three people he'd named were already positioned between Jack and the fifty who wanted his head. They were strong, but so were their opponents, and one side had seventeen times more people than the other.

"I will defend my monastery's honor to the last breath," Brother Tao said calmly, raising his thousand-pound black staff. "Come. I will not allow you to defile my planet. If I am to die, I will take some of you with me."

"This is not ALRIGHT!" Vanderdecken shouted, stringing his guitar—he'd gotten a new one after Fesh Wui broke his previous one. "Those assholes broke my guitar, man. Don't help them. Credits are temporary. Metal is forever!"

Their opponents weren't impressed. There were archers, swordsmen, gunmen—from small arms and sniper rifles to machine guns, as well as people holding all sorts of melee weapons. They took a step forward together, like a well-oiled army squad.

"Hey, Sage," Kane said, lowering his voice, "are you sure this is a good idea?"

"Oh, yes," the Sage replied calmly, as if this all didn't concern him. "Hey, you guys!" he shouted at the approaching enemies. "This is really not a good idea. I suggest you turn back right now, or you will be killed!"

"You can't even touch us, fuckface," a burly man holding a thick iron pipe called out.

"But he can."

A form crashed between the two parties. When the crowd saw who it was, they went limp. It was Jack Rust.

The robots were always placed between him and the scions. Since the crowd was in the opposite direction, he had a moment before the robots caught up. And a moment was enough.

The truth was, Jack could escape the robots temporarily and help in these battles if he really wanted to. He didn't choose to do so for two reasons.

One, it would exhaust him. Rufus might appear at any moment, and if that happened, only he could stop him.

Two, this was a great opportunity for their allied forces to show off their might. They needed the world to side with them. And if they seemed to be losing, Jack could step in before the losses got too heavy. It was harsh, but then again, so was war.

But fifty against three was hardly fair.

"Sto—" a man tried to say, but he didn't make it in time.

Jack's eyes narrowed. These people wanted to kill him for money. He had no reason to show mercy. He was too strong to be stupid.

A Meteor Punch flew into the middle of the crowd and exploded. The first two men it met were annihilated, flying off in pieces. The crowd below was thrown back, many sporting broken limbs or deep burns. People screamed. Jack didn't care.

"Fuck off," he said. His perfect Dao Seed unleashed its pressure, blanketing them in thick, bloody violence. They knew what he was capable of, and that he wouldn't hesitate to do it.

Most turned their backs and ran. Three robots descended on Jack. He had to dash out of the way. As he did, he took one more glance around the arena, but he still couldn't find Brock.

Where the hell did he go! He wondered, sick with worry, but there wasn't much he could do about it right now. *I hope he hid somewhere.*

When everything was said and done, only seven people remained against Brother Tao, Vanderdecken, and the Sage. These seven were content to make it big or die trying.

"See? Not *alright*!" Vanderdecken cried out, raising his hand with the index finger and pinky extended. "But *alright*! Let's form a pit! Fight, fight, fight... *and dance with the devil!*"

They roared and charged. Black, jagged notes erupted from the guitar, which shone with red light—it was a Dao weapon. The faint outline of a blood-stained brown gate appeared above his head. It opened a crack and released small quantities of black mist that seethed toward the fight.

Brother Tao roared as he spun his heavy staff, then crashed it down. It got a man in the leg, breaking it completely, and also cracked the wood and stone beneath. The once-pristine arena was gradually being torn down.

As for the Sage, he simply pointed at people every once in a while, making them dazed for the fraction of a second that Brother Tao needed to smack them. He also called out instructions to Vanderdecken, who moved his mist and notes to the right place *before* the enemies even got there.

The seven bounty hunters didn't back down easily. Each were strong in their own right, and lights flashed as all sorts of abilities were activated. An iron pipe met the staff and broke in two, but that only gave its wielder two new weapons to use. Arrows flew from a crossbow, meeting each note midair and breaking it apart.

Edgar watched their fight from the center of the arena and nodded. He would assist whoever needed him, but they seemed fine for now. He turned his gaze to Dorman and Li Xiang, who were embroiled in fierce combat against two scions—

Wait. Two? Where is Gan Salin?

"Excuse me, do you have a moment to talk about our lord and savior Dogod?"

Edgar barely had time to conjure a shield behind him and jump away. Gan Salin's wolverine-like steel claws clashed against it, breaking it apart in two strikes. He grinned. "I guess not. Oh, well."

"What the hell are you on?" Edgar asked. Sandstorms rose before him, and birds of wind flew around him. This was a scion. And Edgar was alone.

He no longer had time to help others. Now, someone needed to help *him* or he'd become dog food!

Gan Salin's eyes grew bloodshot, and foam bubbled at the edges of his mouth. "Here I come!" he screamed and shot forward. Edgar flooded him with sandstorms. It was the same technique he'd used against Jack —hopefully, it would work better this time.

CHAPTER ONE HUNDRED THREE

FOR THE ALLIANCE!

Vivi and Alexander clashed, each flying around the other as they exchanged attacks. "You got better," Alexander noted.

"I practiced!" she shouted back between strikes. Her whip was sharp and unpredictable, rapping the air with a series of fiery booms. A ring of liquid fire surrounded her, blocking Alexander every time he approached.

"So what? You are just a girl, a child. You are useless. Your achievements are due to luck, and your subordinates all doubt you," he berated her, his attacks never-ending. "You are a fake leader, an imposter. You are bound to crash eventually, as the world realizes your fake status. You were nothing before, and the apocalypse cannot change that."

"Silence! I am not a fool, Alexander. I will not fall for such blatant mental warfare!"

But she did. Being aware of what was happening didn't change much. Alexander had struck her most painful chords, and a portion of her attention was snapped away. It was enough for him to gain the upper hand.

She screamed and unleashed a torrent of flame, but he easily dodged out of the way.

"You're weak!" he shouted.

"No," Vivi replied, smiling. "You're just stupid."

His eyes narrowed, then widened. He didn't look behind him, but he knew. The torrent of fire flew through the air and landed on the arena stands, exploding like a water bomb.

Coincidentally, the moment it landed, the seven bounty hunters happened to move right in front of the explosion. They screamed as the fire burned through their clothes and clung to their backs. Brother Tao's staff broke one's chest, and a note slashed another's throat.

The Sage smiled. "Whoops. How lucky." He'd messaged Vivi mentally and told her exactly where to aim.

The other bounty hunters recovered, but only four remained—one had fallen during the battle—and their opponents stood strong, though Tao and Vanderdecken were injured.

Their eyes filled with hesitation. Right then, green energy showered them, filling them with energy. They were brand-new men and women. Even the one whose chest had been broken stood up, ready to fight again, bringing their number back up to five.

Vanderdecken cursed. "Not *alright*!" he shouted, then dropped out of his persona. "Somebody needs to handle the fucking healer!"

Edgar was floating on a blue cloud and flying back as fast as he could. His sandstorms clung to Gan Salin's legs, flaying the skin off them, but the canine didn't seem to care. He'd gone so insane that he probably didn't even feel the pain.

"Come back here!" he shouted, slicing through wind-birds like they were nothing. "I just wanna talk!"

"Hell no!" Edgar screamed back, rushing to escape. The distance between them was shortening, and his mana was running out fast. Would he last more than the maniac who felt neither pain nor exhaustion? Probably not. He had to do something.

Unfortunately, nobody seemed about to help him. Dorman and Li Xiang were locked down by Fesh Wui and Shard Presht, Vivi was fighting Alexander, the Flame River was busy with the Ice Peak, the other three were fighting a bunch of greedy assholes, and Jack was trying to punch through three E-Grade robots.

Edgar was alone.

At least, he wasn't doomed to lose. He was strong. If he played his cards right, he could win. Gan Salin's legs were already close to crippled.

Green light washed over the canine, restoring the flayed skin and torn muscles. Edgar cursed. "Someone get the fucking healer!" he screamed, accelerating his retreat. The difficulty of healing rose exponentially when people reached the E-Grade and got Dao-infused bodies, but in the F-Grade, healers were kings!

Jack was punching robots. His body was durable, easily shaking off any glancing hits. His new skill, Ghost Step, was enough to outmaneuver them, and he was smarter. His knuckles were hard and his muscles strong, sending the robots flying with every strike.

The problem was that they never stayed down. The most he'd achieved was denting them a bit!

"Fuck me," he muttered. All he could do was wait for his allies to win—hopefully.

"Somebody get the fucking healer!" Edgar's voice reached him. Looking down at the sand—he was on the top of the spectator stands—he saw Edgar locked in combat with Gan Salin.

"Fuck me," Jack muttered again, but this time, it was decisive. They couldn't win like this. The sky went dark and all sounds disappeared. A purple meteor formed around his fist, carrying tremendous power—even he didn't know how much.

The disappearance of colors and sounds was an effect that was usually countered by other Daos. Now that he had a Dao Seed, however, his Dao eclipsed the Dao Roots of everyone present, making the effect persist.

He smashed a robot. It raised a shield to defend, but Jack didn't care. He struck so hard that the explosion rocked everyone else, disturbing their fights, and the robot smashed into the stands hard enough to crack the stone. Jack struck again. After getting strengthened so much, he could now throw a few Meteor Punches in quick succession.

A second Meteor Punch struck the stands where the robot was embedded. The arena exploded under his fist. Chairs and broken wood flew everywhere, and a large crack appeared in the stone as the arena split. He'd cracked it open like an eggshell, a thin line exposing the city beyond.

Idly, he wondered if breaking the arena was customary for Integration Tournaments.

The robot was still there, but it was so deeply embedded in stone that it would need some time to extricate itself. That left Jack with only two robots, which wasn't enough to stop him.

He Ghost Stepped multiple times in succession, out-maneuvering and escaping them. He rushed for the elef. Her personal robot flashed before him, but Jack expected this and unleashed another Meteor Punch without stopping. This one came from below and to the side, smashing into the robot's shield and sending it flying away, over the top of the arena. It wasn't hurt, but neither could it fly.

Until it returned, the healer was exposed. Jack hadn't stopped running, taking a deep cut in his outer thigh for the trouble, but this was more important. The elef didn't hesitate in the slightest. She took out a wooden-looking badge with weird lines on it. Jack recognized the device—it was the same thing Gan Salin had used to escape him back in Valville.

He prepared a Meteor Punch, but it wouldn't reach in time.

She squeezed it. Light gathered around her.

In that instant, Jack Ghost Stepped mid-strike. His Meteor Punch left a long purple tail as it was dragged alongside him, appearing before the elef in an instant. The explosion happened at the same moment she teleported away. Jack only managed to see her expression of pain before she disappeared.

He looked around but didn't see her anywhere. However, he did spot her robot landing atop the arena and then jumping away, heading for the town at full speed. Either it was a risky bluff, or the elef wasn't here anymore.

Jack chose to believe the latter.

The other two robots fell on him, soon joined by the third, and he returned to conserving energy and watching how the others persisted. After all, there was no telling when Rufus would emerge from his breakthrough. He had to remain at his best.

The Flame River and Ice Peak clashed furiously, each faction employing their own team tactics. Sadaka led the effort on the Flame River's side, and Elena Richter did the same for the Ice Peak. Flames danced and melted ice, which froze again on the spot. Complex geometrical shapes were formed on the stone where the spectator stands used to be, the wood long sheared off.

Eventually, training outdid experience. Elena drove an arm-sized ice spike through Sadaka's chest. His eyes grew wide. Then, their light faded, and Sadaka was gone. The surrounding flames destabilized, letting the Ice Peak advance.

Li Xiang and Dorman were a fearsome duo. The old man played around the teenager's moves, covering every hole. After Gan Salin had left, this dual battle was slowly tipping in their favor. The only thing keeping the scions in the game had been the elef's healing powers.

"Damn!" Fesh Wui cried out. "We lost our healer! Shard, we must retreat!"

He backed away, but Shard Presht was a beat too late to follow. Dorman and Li Xiang fell on him at the same time. He was unable to defend. They tore him to pieces.

Vivi clashed repeatedly against Alexander, but she was pushed back. They used to be equals until he won the lotus of fire and ice. His Dao was slightly more advanced, and that small advantage was enough to secure his victory.

She more felt than saw the flames wavering far under her feet, where her faction fought. They were unstable, which meant they'd lost their core. That could only mean one thing.

"No!" she screamed, launching out her defensive rings of flame as a jet heading directly downward. She had to at least secure her people some time to escape.

Unfortunately, that took away her greatest defense. Alexander flashed inside her guard instantly, striking with his twin swords without leaving her a moment to reorient herself. Her whip was slashed in half, a wing was shorn off. Vivi's throat bulged as it prepared to unleash fire, but Alexander had seen this trick before.

He flashed behind her. "Nobody will save you this time," he said, then stabbed.

Without disturbances, Brother Tao, Vanderdecken, and the Sage tore into the five remaining bounty hunters, who were already trying to retreat. This battle wasn't going their way.

"Scatter!" one of them said.

They did. Vanderdecken's notes rushed after the one with the crossbow, catching up to her and cutting her to pieces. Brother Tao hunted another, but he was too slow. Suddenly, the running bounty hunter missed a step, his eyes going blank for a moment.

It was the Sage's interference.

Brother Tao's heavy staff smashed into the fallen man's body and pulverized it. Before he had time to rejoice, the Sage's warning out in his mind: "*Careful!*"

He barely turned in time. A sharp machete came from behind, shining with the power of an active skill aimed at his neck. He took the hit to his left arm. It was lopped clean off.

Brother Tao screamed as his staff took the offending woman's head off.

Edgar was cornered. Healing energy had stopped streaming into Gan Salin, but he remained insane and resolute, shrugging away all damage. He was bleeding from many places, his clothes were torn, one arm hung limp, and he sported heavy burns, but he remained as wild as ever.

"Got you," he said, pouncing at Edgar. "DIE!"

Gan Salin's Dao Roots gave him the power to run through Edgar's magical salvos. They also made him stupid. If not, he would have recognized the pattern.

"Quintus Convergius!" Edgar shouted, siphoning out the final bits of his mana. His staff lay broken at his feet, but the gem at its top still worked. The elements nearby shook as the gem unleashed a white light of pure magic at Gan Salin, who took it right in the chest.

He was catapulted backward, leaving a trail of blood from his mouth. He landed hard against the back wall and stayed down. Edgar chuckled. *I beat a scion*, he thought. *Who's the loser now, Mom?*

He didn't dare let himself lose consciousness, but he was completely spent. Any random attack could end him. Slowly, he used his last bits of strength to crawl under some nearby debris, hiding himself as best as he could, and only then did he let himself faint.

"Nobody will save you this time," Alexander said, stabbing at Vivi's back. Suddenly, all color disappeared around him. He folded his wings without the slightest hesitation, letting himself fall, and the meteor that exploded above his head sent him flying diagonally toward the stands below, where Dorman and Li Xiang had just killed Shard Presht, and were now pursuing Fesh Wui. The eagler didn't even have time to pull out his escape talisman. He was covered in wounds and only barely surviving by running away at top speed.

The moment Presht died, his robot had gone stiff, then turned away and flown toward the town. Gan Salin's robot had also retreated beside its unconscious owner, guarding his body. That left Jack with only one robot, which gave him the room to interfere in other battles more easily. Alexander and Vivi's fight was climaxing, and he shot a meteor at them, trying to stop Alexander. He succeeded, albeit barely.

Alexander's one wing was broken by the meteor, so he couldn't right himself, but he knew an opportunity when he saw it. As he rotated in midair, he launched two successive ice spikes at Dorman, who was too busy hunting Fesh to notice the attack. It came for his head.

Li Xiang jumped in between. He smashed one ice spike aside with his palm but didn't have time to stop the second one. Left without a choice, he took it with his body. The ice spike pierced clean through his belly, nailing him to the stands—he'd slowed it for an instant, and that was enough for Dorman and Fesh Wui's fight to move a step away.

As the old master was nailed into the stone, Dorman looked at him with wide eyes. Fesh Wui grabbed the opportunity to crush his escape talisman, disappearing, but Dorman didn't care.

"No," he muttered, then screamed, "NO!"

Li Xiang smiled. "Be brave," he said, coughing out blood. "Strong. Honorable."

And then, without another word, he passed away. Blood oozed from his belly like a fountain and painted the stone red under his feet.

Dorman turned to Alexander, face warped in rage. Jack beat him to the punch. He appeared next to the falling Alexander like a ghost.

Jack had expected people to die. He had seen many suffer that fate since the Integration, and he'd even killed people himself. But they'd all been strangers. When Li Xiang passed away, someone who was just an acquaintance, the flood of emotions hit Jack like a solid wall. They frothed up from somewhere deep inside him with an intensity he never expected, tinging his vision red and filling his heart with mute despair.

If he felt like this on an acquaintance's death, what would happen if someone truly important to him died? The professor's smiling face flashed in his mind, and the fear that overtook him fueled his rage.

"Fuck you," he spat out, readying a full-force Meteor Punch. Alexander wrapped his remaining wing around himself, but there was no way he could take the strike head-on. He braced himself for death.

The attack never arrived.

"*Careful!*" the Sage's voice rang in Jack's mind. It was too late. A tremendous power landed on his back, shooting him into the stands so hard he dug into the stone. He spat out a mouthful of blood as he looked up.

Rufus Emberheart landed across from him. His mane fluttered in the wind, and his face was a begrudging scowl. The aura of a perfect Dao Seed spread outside his body, contesting Jack's, and everyone who looked at them felt like they were looking at two mountains crashing into each other.

Leonine, Level 50
Faction: -
Title: Planetary Torchbearer (10)

Rufus clenched his paws, then said, "You owe me a battle, Jack Rust. Stand up."

CHAPTER ONE HUNDRED FOUR

BOSS FIGHT

THOUGH JACK HAD BEEN SMACKED HARD, IT WAS NOTHING BUT A SCRATCH TO HIS new, iron-like body. The true loss was the energy he'd expended so far. Going into the boss fight weakened was a terrible idea, but what could he do?

"Sure," he replied, dusting himself off. "Are you sure you're ready, though? I can wait another hour."

"Silence, weakling," Rufus sneered. "I admit I miscalculated. I thought I could finish the breakthrough in time, even without the Rainbow Dao Pill... but in the end, I underestimated my own superiority. Something truly perfect takes time."

"Is that what you tell yourself to feel better? I don't know, man. I started my breakthrough after you and still finished first."

"That has nothing to do with your *strength*. You simply ignored all security guidelines. You went at it like a monkey, heedless of failure's consequences."

"I didn't intend to fail. If you needed fail-safes, maybe you just aren't as superior as you like to think."

"We will see about that." Rufus's eyes sharpened at every word that left Jack's mouth. His heavy aura circled his body, striking Jack with its majesty. Perhaps taunting an angry lion wasn't a good idea.

"Our battle will prove who is superior," the leonine declared loudly, speaking to the world. "We have both just broken through to the E-Grade. We are at the same level, both with perfect Dao Seeds. Our titles give us the exact same benefits. We have both drunk the Immortality Serum. The victor between us will be decided by pure skill."

Jack counted the +50 from the Immortality Serum as a huge advantage. He'd forgotten that, as the second-place winner of the Tournament, Rufus also got one of those.

Who am I kidding? He would have gotten it anyway. Who knows what else he has.

"Enough talking, Rufus. Let's fight," he said, bumping his fists together. Over the last month, this had developed into his pre-fight ritual.

He couldn't deny his excitement. Despite all the stakes riding on his back, he had been really looking forward to this battle ever since the Tournament began. Rufus Emberheart was the biggest, baddest guy around... and Jack was about to punch his face in.

"Of course," Rufus replied. "Shall we give our battle the attention it deserves by moving to the main stage?"

Jack gazed at the sands. The stage was filled with debris, as well as Gan Salin's unconscious body and his guardian robot. He also spotted Edgar's legs peeking out from under a bunch of fallen seats. Worry gripped his heart, but he didn't have that luxury right now.

"No need," he said, turning back to Rufus. "Here is good enough."

The leonine frowned. "Then prepare yourself. I shall let the whole world see the consequences of challenging a king."

"The only king here is your mo—"

Before Jack could finish his words, Rufus appeared before him. There was no warning, no sound, no time to respond. One moment, he stood twenty feet away, and the next he was right up Jack's nose, an open paw already hurtling at his chest. Jack clenched on reflex.

The paw smacked him head-on, sending him flying into the stage. He smashed hard into the sand and the rock below, skipping over the ground twice before rolling to a stop. His head was wobbly as he stood, and he had trouble breathing for a moment.

"What's the matter?" Rufus asked, landing softly. "I thought you wanted to stay in the stands."

"You didn't give me a choice, dipshit."

That wasn't the right response, apparently. Rufus disappeared again. This time, Jack saw how he did it. He caught a glimpse of his foot tapping the ground right before he teleported. It was a movement skill, like Jack's, except he wasn't used to the speed of E-Grade fighting. It was simply on a whole new level.

Unfortunately, glimpsing something and stopping it were two entirely different concepts. Jack ducked by pure instinct, but the paw still smashed the top of his head and sent him flying. He crashed into the wall, forming a web of cracks behind him, then landed on his feet and stumbled.

"Perhaps all that waiting got you rusty," Rufus said, laughing. "Let me bring you up to speed."

The guy was a sucker for posturing. Be it against Li Xiang, Dorman, or Jack, he always tried to win in the most overbearing fashion.

That made Jack angry. Rufus could be as fast as he wanted, but Jack would be damned if he just stood there and let himself take a beating.

He had a movement skill, too.

He shot out. His fists clenched. Rufus disappeared, moving with that incredible speed again, but Jack activated Ghost Step to the side. When Rufus appeared, he was facing empty air. When Jack appeared, he was facing Rufus.

"Think again, dickhead," he said, smashing out a punch. A blue shield appeared around Rufus, but it didn't affect Jack much. It was like punching through slightly denser air. Their Daos were on the same level.

His fist landed clean on Rufus's cheek, sending the leonine tumbling away. He shot back to his feet. Eyes filled with indignation as if Jack touching him was some sort of blasphemy.

Jack, meanwhile, just stood there and looked at Rufus in incomprehension.

I... got him? he wondered, glancing at his own fist. *It was that easy?*

Throughout the Tournament and during their fight so far, Rufus had been an untouchable existence. He'd asserted his dominance so many times that, unconsciously, Jack regarded him very highly. He intended to fight, he even yearned for it, but his heart was always clenched by deep fear.

And now... he'd just struck Rufus.

Jack looked between his fist and the leonine. He saw the truth. Rufus wasn't invincible nor always ten moves ahead. He was just a dude with a knack for posturing. A dude who could mess up like everyone else, who could get hit and feel anger or pain.

The only difference between Rufus and all of Jack's previous opponents, was that Rufus was slightly stronger. That's it. He just played it cool.

Jack met the leonine's eyes which burst with confidence and arrogance, a confidence that was nothing more than a prop. Rufus was just a guy.

He grinned. Once again, he smashed his fists together, and this time, he was full of spirit.

"You fucking liar," he said. "What king? You're just a dude—a dude who's about to get his face caved in."

Rufus's eyes flickered. He roared and charged.

The sand flew under his feet. The distance evaporated. He stood before Jack in the next instant, but Jack was ready. He Ghost Stepped to the side, dodging a blow and striking his own. Rufus turned and met it.

Fist and paw clashed, one carrying brutal violence and the other unyielding supremacy. The air exploded around them. Sand flew away from the point of impact. Jack and Rufus withdrew their hands at the same time—neither had been pushed back—and struck again.

They fell into a melee. Blue phantom paws disintegrated into hard fists. Meteors smashed into a golden mane. Jack roared and Rufus growled as they tore into each other, neither giving up. Blood drops splattered everywhere, dying the sand red.

Jack clenched his fist. A purple aura surrounded it, transforming it into a falling meteor. Rufus drew his paw back. A blue phantom of itself superimposed the paw, cladding it in undeniable supremacy. The air shook as both blows flew forward, and they collided frontally at full force.

Jack and Rufus were both pushed back, tumbling and rising to their feet. Jack's fist was trembling. Even with the Iron Fiend Body and all his new stats, that had fucking hurt.

Rufus's paw didn't tremble.

"Inevitable Charge!" Rufus roared. His feet kicked against the hard ground, and he flickered to a new position—not close to Jack. He did it again, and again, and again, and Jack's surroundings were filled with afterimages of a pissed off super-warrior.

Jack wasn't an idiot to put himself on the back foot. He used Ghost Step, flickering unpredictably along the sand. He no longer cared about conserving energy. His eyes caught a glimpse of Rufus's.

At the next moment, both stopped simultaneously and punched at each other. A phantom paw flew out of Rufus, and a meteor was launched by Jack, impacting between them with an explosion that neutralized both attacks. Rufus charged again, and Jack met him fist-first, once again moving into a brawl.

However, Jack's mind wasn't entirely there. He kept an eye on their positioning, making sure they wouldn't accidentally throw an attack where Edgar lay. At this point, a stray punch could kill the wizard.

His worries left him open. Attempting to face Rufus without his full attention was a fool's errand.

A paw snuck past his guard, smashing into his abdomen. Jack bent, and a phantom tore up into his nose, sending him flying. Jack opened his eyes and saw Rufus disappeared. Reflexively, he shot a Meteor Punch to the right, using the momentum to push himself out of the way as Rufus fell from above and landed with enough force to crack the arena.

Jack somersaulted and landed on his feet. He still struggled to breathe, and his nose was broken. His regeneration had slowed to a snail's pace. That was expected. Starting at the E-Grade, when the body was infused with the Dao, all sorts of healing got exponentially harder. Before that, it was easy as pie. That was why the djinn healers had been able to heal practically anything the F-Grade Tournament participants suffered.

"You surprise me," Rufus declared. Though Jack had gotten a couple hits in, Rufus looked no worse for wear. His back was straight, his chain mail armor unblemished, and his eyes still held that arrogant spark inside them. Only his nose was bloodied. "If you hadn't picked the wrong side, you would have made a fine ally. It is a shame."

Jack, on the contrary, sported several shallow cuts, as well as an equally broken nose. "Is it too late?" he asked. He was trying to buy some time so he could think of a way to draw the battle outside the arena. Could he run?

However, Rufus only smiled sadly. "Yes."

Jack barely managed to react to Rufus's attack in time. He took a punch and flew back, then landed, turned, and charged back in. All the while, his mind whirled. What was the best way to disengage?

Dorman roared like an animal; daggers held at the ready. "*Right,*" a voice rang in his mind, and he sidestepped just as an ice spike flew past.

He, the Sage, Brother Tao, Vanderdecken, along with Vivi and what remained of the Flame River—only half their original number—were clashing against Alexander Petrovic and his four Ice Peak members. Jack Rust was battling Rufus Emberheart in the arena below, but that wasn't their battle. This was.

Lightning flew over Dorman's skin as he tore through the Ice Peak defenses, but a new wall of ice appeared to block his path. He cursed as he jumped backward.

Though they were more, the fighters of Ice Peak could work together to block them. Especially Dorman—for the second time, he found himself countered by his opponents. It was even more infuriating now because he was sure he could beat Alexander if they fought one-on-one.

Vivi was injured, but she stood behind the front line and did what she could to help.

The battle was balanced. Dorman was confident they would win eventually... And only if Jack didn't lose to Rufus.

Lightning crawled over his skin again. He charged.

"Ooh..." Gan Salin grabbed his head. "What happened?"

His ears were filled with explosions. His eyes snapped open, taking in a field of destruction. Two forms flickered in and out of his sight, fiercely tearing into each other: Rufus Emberheart and Jack Rust.

Gan Salin had lost to both of them before, but now, they weren't even on the same level as him. Their arms moved so fast he couldn't track them. Their forms blurred in his eyes. They exchanged more than one hit at the same time, and every punch or paw landed with a colossal impact that could easily blast Gan Salin apart. And these madmen were throwing dozens of these hits like it was nothing.

Like berserk immortals.

I must be dreaming, Gan Salin concluded. He closed his eyes, counted to four, then opened them again. *Crap. I'm not dreaming.*

A stray meteor flew his way. Before Gan could even consider fleeing, his robot bodyguard got in the way, bracing its shield. It was instantly sent flying, darting past Salin to land on the wall behind him. It recovered, but its shield was now dented.

Gan Salin couldn't dent that shield if he struck it for a day and a night.

Alrighty, he thought, standing and dusting himself off. *Time to go.*

His entire body was in pain, his clothes were so tattered they barely protected his dignity, and he bled from several places, including a shallow, bloody hole in his chest where at least one bone was broken. Thankfully, he had a regeneration skill.

He was lucky to be alive.

The pain was terrible, but he'd gone through worse. The Dao of Insanity was a bitch to cultivate.

While Rufus and Jack went at it, trying to smash each other into paste, Gan Salin tiptoed to the arena exit and passed through, his robot in tow.

He then climbed the stairs and reached the stands, from where he could watch the fight in relative safety. There was another fight going on, but he didn't care about it; only Rufus's was important. He was very curious to see who would win. No, that wasn't entirely true. He knew Rufus would win. He hadn't even used his King Form yet.

The question was, how far would Jack Rust push him?

If Gan Salin was being honest, he kinda liked Jack. He made fun things happen. Too bad he'll die today, but oh well. Enemies get stitches. No, wait—was it graves? Frenemies?

He laughed. It didn't really matter. Most things didn't.

CHAPTER ONE HUNDRED FIVE

OVERPOWERED

JACK SMASHED HIS FIST INTO RUFUS'S PAW, THEN FLICKERED TO THE SIDE AND ducked under a backhand swipe. The leonine stood in place, tall and proud, unleashing hits like an avalanche. He was a force of nature.

Jack met him hit for hit, but he was being pushed back. He was losing.

And he still had to get out of this fucking arena. But he didn't want to *run*. That would be like retreating. And what kind of fist would retreat from a frontal, winnable fight?

Maybe he should go all-in, instead. Crush Rufus with an iron fist.

No, he stopped himself. This was the Dao talking, but *he* was in control. *I must get out of here. I must protect Edgar.*

When their fists clashed again and Jack was pushed back, he turned a set of angry eyes at Rufus. "Fine! Have it your way. Fist Radiance!"

He crossed his arms while jumping backward, landing on the arena lip. Rufus snorted with amusement and prepared himself. "Are we finally going all-out? Perfect! I will block your ultimate attack with my —Hmm?"

Jack had jumped backward on the arena lip as if about to unleash a long-range attack, but he just kept jumping. Before Rufus had finished his words, Jack had reached the top of the stands. He then turned around and leaped atop the arena. The tall white tower framed his retreating back.

Rufus's eyes widened with anger. "Get back here!" he ordered. Jack flipped him off, then jumped outside the arena.

He fell through the air. Free-falling seemed slow, but there wasn't much he could do about it now. Stone statues three times his height passed by him, each intricately carved and carrying a wide array of weapons. Some held spears, others hammers, sickles, knives, glaives, bows, whips... Practically everything could be found on these statues.

They were all kinds of species, too. Some were animal-shaped warriors, like the scions of the Animal Kingdom, but many were humans, and there were also a bunch he hadn't seen before. There were also many empty grooves, where statues had yet to be added.

These were the previous winners of the Animal Kingdom's Integration Tournaments. Now, Jack would get his statue as well—unless the arena crumbled, of course. Or unless they simply didn't make him one. It was a tribute of honor, and he was an enemy.

He landed on the street, ignored the panicking crowd, and jumped on a rooftop. He landed an inch before a dog guardian. He froze. He'd forgotten that they hid on rooftops. The guardian looked straight into his eyes, red dots flaring behind its sunglasses, but it didn't move.

Jack got over his surprise and moved on. He was now stronger than one of these guardians, anyway. He jumped from rooftop to rooftop, heading deeper into the town.

He wasn't just trying to draw Rufus away from Edgar. He had to escape through the teleporter as quickly as he could, or there was no telling what weapons the Animal Kingdom would unleash. He had to take care of Rufus first, of course, or he would turn back and massacre everyone.

He caught sight of the plaza he was heading for. It was large and empty, usually saved for a bazaar that was now getting packed up as fast as the E-Grade merchants could manage. Jack caught himself on the television screens that lined the streets. His fight was still being broadcasted, and the invisible cameras followed him even here, outside the arena.

For most people, it was their first time seeing Integration City.

He landed in the plaza. It was square with a length of at least a hundred feet in every direction, all lined with tiles of white marble. At the back of the plaza stood a windowless building shaped like a chimney-topped furnace, with a closed wooden door blocking its entrance.

It was the teleporter leading out of here. To the galaxy. Having it operate was part of the Star Pact, so even the Planetary Overseer couldn't deactivate it without reason.

The last of the merchants were packing up and running away, none sparing Jack a glance. The dog guardians, however, did. They arranged themselves around the plaza, not stepping in, but ready to intervene if anyone overstepped a line. They were allowed to fight each other, but not to attack the merchants or damage the buildings beyond a reasonable degree.

The moment Jack landed, he turned to look backward. He didn't see Rufus. Even when he looked at the arena's top, he still failed to spot anyone.

The arena was a third of a mile away. No matter how fast Jack was, Rufus should have at least scaled the arena by now. Where was he?

Jack felt like an idiot. He assumed Rufus would follow because of his pride, his need to act in the most supreme way... but what if he didn't? What if he wasn't as prideful as Jack imagined. Perhaps his pride worked in a different way, and he chose to slaughter everyone in the arena instead.

Jack looked at the screens around the plaza, seeing himself alone and lost, surrounded by dog guardians in the distance. The screens cut to Rufus, who thankfully didn't appear to be in the arena. The camera looked at him from below, with the blue sky as a backdrop. He had his hands in the air, his legs bent, his face hardened, and he seemed to be fall—

Jack Ghost Stepped away right as Rufus landed on his previous location. The marble under their feet was much harder than the arena's stone, but even it cracked under the impact. Rufus looked unhurt.

He unraveled himself, standing straight. Jack frowned. Something was different.

The leonine's golden mane was raised like he'd been electrocuted.

He carried an air of power around him. Most importantly, he was surrounded by a faint blue and yellow aura.

Jack gaped. He'd seen something similar before, but it couldn't possibly be...

"Disgraceful," Rufus spat. "You cannot escape, Jack Rust. You have insulted a king, and you will pay for it. However, in recognition of your strength, and to honor the people of Integration City, I will fight you at my strongest. Prepare to face my King Form."

The winds picked up. His aura towered to the sky. Rufus lowered his head and growled, a fierce, drawn-out lion roar that echoed throughout Integration City and gradually picked up in volume. He was filled with absolute rage as he shouted at the top of his lungs. The surrounding merchants hurried to scramble away, while Jack could only watch as Rufus's power climbed unendingly. His aura was so strong that it tore a nearby piece of paper with the number nine thousand on it—probably the price of something in the bazaar.

His golden mane had somehow gotten longer. Sparks flew inside the blue and yellow aura around him. When he stopped shouting, he raised his head, and even his blue eyes had turned yellow.

Jack couldn't believe what he was seeing. "What King Form?" he shouted. "That's a Super Sai—"

Rufus's knee met his abdomen. He flew back like a rocket and crashed into a building, demolishing it in the blink of an eye. The dog guards around the square grew restless, but they did not move.

"Stand up," Rufus said. "I know that wasn't enough to kill you."

Jack crawled out of the debris, then forced himself to stand. He was hurt. That knee had come with tremendous force. Most importantly, Rufus had just powered up, and Jack... Jack had nothing of the sort.

"What's the matter?" Rufus asked, raising his chin. "Didn't you want to fight me? I'm right here. Waiting for you."

Jack spat on the ground. This was unfair. He'd done everything correctly. Gotten stronger than anyone ever expected. Been able to face Rufus, even if slightly on the back foot... but Rufus had *more* cards up his sleeve.

How the hell am I supposed to win! Jack asked himself, heart burning with rage. He clenched his fists. This was clearly impossible.

He looked around. The dog guardians, the merchants, the screens where this fight was televised, the teleporter...

If he escaped, he would be fine, and so would his faction... but all his allies here would die. Rufus would slaughter them.

Edgar, the Flame River, Dorman, the Sage, even Vanderdecken and Brother Tao.

But there were ways. If he gave them enough time, maybe they could use the Sage's starship to escape and hide within the Forest of the Strong, where Sparman would protect them. He was a D-Grade bodyguard now, and Rufus had just broken through to the E-Grade. They would earn some time. Maybe they could break through themselves, or maybe Jack would return stronger...

No. Those were empty hopes.

The war would end before it even started, overwhelmed by Rufus's impossible strength. They would be trapped like mice, simply delaying the inevitable. The Animal Kingdom would have achieved its goal, televising their scions' victory over the entire planet while the strongest human turned tail and ran for his life, leaving them all to die.

And Rufus would be the king.

Jack didn't want that. He desperately yearned to raise his fists and fight to the death, like a true fist.

Except he had a responsibility to his people. He was shacked. If he fell, they would all inevitably die. If he escaped... then, though his Dao would inevitably be damaged, there would still be hope. Perhaps he could find a way to save them in the future.

His Dao Seed screamed in protest. It had become one with his body, one with his *soul*, and this was not what he'd promised it. He felt its pain deep inside him. He shared it.

But he was in control. *He* wielded his fist, and *he* chose how to use it.

Jack eyed the teleporter, then turned back to Rufus, who stood between them. If he wanted to escape, he had to be smart about it. He raised his fists.

"Fine," he said bravely. "Let's see if your paws or my face will break first."

Rufus laughed. "Who are you trying to trick, human? I can sense the turmoil in your Dao. You are planning to *run*." Jack's face darkened.

"Unfortunately, that is impossible. I stand in your way, and I am inevitable. You can try to escape, if you want. I'll show you the futility of your efforts."

Jack believed him, but what choice did he have? He charged, Ghost Stepped into Rufus's guard, then shot out a Meteor Punch. Rufus blocked it with his forearm. The impact rolled around him, split like a river by a rock. Rufus grinned. Jack despaired.

His fists flew out. He used all his skills in tandem to rain blows on Rufus, who blocked and dodged everything. Eventually, Rufus struck back, sending Jack flying into the rubble of the same building he'd crashed into before.

Jack stood again, bleeding from his forehead.

This is unfair.

He roared his defiance. Punches fell like hail, but Rufus took them all in stride, laughing.

In truth, his King Form skill hadn't increased his powers by too much. It was a noticeable increase, but not a world-shaking one. The problem was that Rufus had already been slightly stronger than Jack before. Now, he was clearly superior—just as his Dao indicated.

Jack roared as he tore into the fight. His bitterness fueled him. The world had set him up with an impossible fight. He'd surpassed all expectations, and he still couldn't win.

He resolved to give Rufus at least one good hit. Maybe then, he could escape.

This time, there was no Edgar to distract him. He embraced his Dao and gave everything to the fight. He got sharper. His Dao Root of Indomitable Will squeezed his brain dry, pouring everything into this moment. This was Jack at his absolute best.

Rufus punched, and Jack dodged out of the way.

Now, he could barely match Rufus. Winning remained impossible, but at least he could stand his ground for a bit. Rufus wasn't even fighting seriously. He was smiling, treating Jack like an exhibition target.

Which was exactly what he was. This was a battle to demonstrate the Animal Kingdom's and Rufus's superiority, and Jack was just a prop.

He refused to go down like that. His bare chest stuck out. He struck at Rufus with everything he had. His brain worked at maximum capacity, analyzing Rufus's patterns and desperately trying to adjust.

Rufus was a frontal fighter, just like Jack, only stronger. He fought at a speed and strength that was just above what Jack could manage. Jack was forced to pull out everything he had. He couldn't make his body faster, but he could make his moves sharper, his transitions more refined, his dodges smoother.

He mixed in feints, using his perfect control over his body granted by Parkour to make them realistic. He dodged by a hair's breadth, sometimes taking glancing blows, but always improving. He calculated his Drills precisely, making them explode just before or behind Rufus's guard to spread at least some of the shockwave around his body.

Jack forgot himself. The world faded away. He was simply fighting with everything he had, pouring out the entirety of himself. His skills mixed better. Slowly, he was getting better at fighting.

Rufus hadn't hit him in a while. The leonine noticed at the same time Jack did, and he struck out a real blow, faster than before. Jack didn't see the move coming. His body dodged on pure instinct, surprising even him, then struck out with a vicious counter.

His fist met Rufus's regal face, making him take a step back.

It all happened so fast, so instinctively, that Jack felt like there was someone else fighting in his body. Someone with the power to match even Rufus. Someone invincible and unstoppable. Someone terrifying. A fiend with iron fists.

And finally, everything clicked.

Congratulations! Skills Fistfighting (III), Parkour (III), and Drill (III) combined into Dao Skill Iron Fist Style (I).

Iron Fist Style (I): You have mastered the mortal forms of combat, but that is only the beginning. Your body is infused with the Dao of the Fist, and you can use that to reach realms previously unfathomable. Reality bends before the Dao.

Jack blinked in disbelief, then grinned.

"Fuck you, Rufus Emberheart," he whispered.

Rufus roared and charged. His blue and yellow aura flared. He could sense that something was different. He was no longer going easy.

And Jack could meet him. They clashed strike for strike, like back in the arena. Jack channeled every scrap of power he possessed. His fists came down hard and true. His moves were unpredictable and infused with the Dao.

A mortal body fought with mortal martial arts. A Dao-infused body had its own weapons, even if the skill description itself was vague and cryptic.

Jack's Dao was an active participant in the battle. It enhanced his movements. Whether he sought to strike or dodge, he was unstoppable, like a fist. When he defended, he was immovable, like a fist.

Magic dove into his muscles. His will gave them strength, pulling and pushing his body in unnatural ways. He missed on purpose sometimes, knowing that his Dao would help him hit anyway. He redirected strikes he shouldn't because his Dao wouldn't allow him to be defied.

Causality itself bended to let his fist strike Rufus's face.

It was a kind of battle he'd never experienced before. It looked simple from the outside, but from the inside, it was anything but.

Now that Jack had a Dao skill fighting style, he could tell that Rufus's King Form was something similar. That was why he'd gotten so much stronger. His stats hadn't gone up. He simply channeled supremacy with every movement, making them inviolable.

Now that Jack's own Dao had joined the mix, he could match the leonine. The Daos were of similar strength and canceled each other out.

The fight returned to a brawl, and in a brawl, the fist was king.

Jack roared as he took a punch to the gut, making him keel over, but his Dao enhanced his body to prevent further damage. His fist struck out at once as if pulled by an invisible cord, meeting Rufus's face, which stayed still and refused to jump by the recoil.

Rufus snarled. Jack growled.

They tore into each other at the apex of their power. Rufus was no longer a king. He was a man locked in heated combat, fighting for every scrap of victory he could get. Jack matched him in power and ferocity. Suddenly, the battle wasn't so doomed after all.

CHAPTER ONE HUNDRED SIX

A CRESCENDO OF VIOLENCE

JACK DUCKED UNDER A STRIKE, THEN PIVOTED AND SMASHED OUT HIS OWN. Rufus took it to the chest and whimpered, then his elbow came crashing down on Jack's head, whose hair was now wet with blood. Jack barely pulled himself aside to evade the strike, right into a knee that further crunched his nose. He endured the pain to plant his iron knuckles in Rufus's eyes.

Every hit was brutal and meant to kill. They fought like rabid beasts, neither backing down an inch.

The remaining merchants had fallen silent. More people had shown up around the plaza, and even the immortals had arrived, riding on their cloud. They watched as two supreme geniuses engaged in a battle that only one could win. The other would be broken forever.

Jack and Rufus traded blow for blow. They no longer bothered with defense. Both bled from many places and sported various injuries. Jack's bare chest was covered in cuts and bruises, while Rufus's chain mail had been broken. His once-pristine golden mane was now marred with blood.

The only part of Jack that remained unhurt were his knuckles, which he rammed into Rufus with every opportunity. Rufus snarled and growled, sending phantom paws into Jack's body, each with the power to destroy buildings.

Jack's mind was in a state of serenity. He was wholly invested in the battle. Nothing else existed. This was the strongest he could get. His soul simply had nothing else to give.

And yet, it wasn't enough. Rufus was stronger and more durable, just by a tiny bit, but enough to reign supreme. Despite Jack's advancements over and over again, it *still* wasn't enough.

He fought regardless. Fleeing was no longer in his mind. It was no longer strategic, just cowardly. In this battle, he would triumph or die trying.

His limbs were losing strength. His arms were heavy, laden with lead. His breath was shallow, his lungs cramping up. His legs buckled, barely keeping him upright.

He hadn't felt like this in a long time. Ever since he beat the black wolf, no battle had truly pushed him to the limit, scraped him dry of potential. He felt ready to quit.

But Jack had been forged in that dungeon. Back then, this state was normal, an everyday occurrence, and he regularly pushed past his limits. Now, everything returned at once. The man retreated to let the beast out. Jack was back in the dungeon.

He faced the first goblin. He remembered how he walked through fire to destroy the goblin shaman. How he fought the rock bear to the point where he fainted mid-swing. How he challenged Harambe, how the ice pond made him want to die wreathed in pain, and how everything in him screamed not to touch the waterfall, but he did it anyway.

Those memories weren't gone. They were inside him, hiding just below the surface. They were his past, his true birth.

This was the true Jack Rust.

And once again, he was there. He was trapped and desperate with no way out. And no matter how death loomed, he refused to give up. No matter how heavy his limbs got, Jack kept punching, over and over again. It didn't matter that his attacks no longer connected, that his Dao was running dry, that Rufus clearly had more to give. He refused to slow or cower. He would go down swinging.

And then, as if a miracle, his fist landed on Rufus's face.

To the people watching, Jack had lost all sanity. He was bleeding from head to toe. Bones cracked with every hit he received. He should have fallen long ago.

But he still stood. His fists were iron, his form planting terror in the minds of everyone present. He wasn't a man, but a beast—a *fiend*. People scrambled to get away, intimidated by Jack's visage. Others held their mouths open, unable to believe what they saw. Beyond terror, some had eyes filled with respect.

This man was the hero of Earth. His shoulders carried their honor, and though he was weaker than his opponent, he simply refused to fall. This image, where Jack was covered in blood, riddled with pain but still fighting, would forever remain engraved in everyone's memories.

On the other hand, Rufus's eyes were filled with horror. "Just *die* already!" he shouted, though Jack couldn't hear him. His paws landed cleanly. He could feel the bones cracking under Jack's skin, he could feel the impact he delivered.

But Jack simply refused to fall. To Rufus, it was like facing a monster —and he was running out of power. His limbs were heavy from striking. His Dao was running dry. He was close to the end of the line.

And, for the first time in this fight, he wondered, *What if I fall first?*

He'd never considered the possibility of defeat before. Of death. Rufus hadn't been forged in a dungeon, never been forced to pit his life against another. He hadn't experienced the things that made Jack a monster. He'd been raised as a prince, and had only been sent here to squash some backward natives who could never stand up to him.

Rufus had never truly fought for his life before. Even if some battles seemed dangerous, he knew they never were. There was always an immortal waiting to save him if things went wrong. Except now, there wasn't. His aunt might not openly violate the Star Pact for him.

And as the possibility of death loomed over him... he flinched. He felt fear. His Dao weakened like chalk in the rain, shivering in doubt.

Jack's fist met his face, sending him flying back. Rufus was stronger, but he was not a true warrior.

Jack was.

Rufus turned to land on his feet, but Jack was already there. A meteor smashed into his abdomen, making him buckle. Another hit his face, bending him backward, and then Jack jumped and planted a third meteor into his chest, nailing Rufus's back against the ground.

Rufus spat blood.

This was too fast, too sudden. He only gave Jack one opening, but Jack grabbed it and didn't let go.

When Rufus had the upper hand, he'd stood and gloated. When Jack got it, he simply never stopped. He showed no mercy, no hesitation. He didn't give Rufus the slightest opportunity to recover. He was a hardened warrior, and this was a fight to the death. This truth dawned on Rufus for the first time. It was his fault.

His Dao cracked down the middle.

Jack hovered two feet above Rufus, who'd just been nailed to the floor. He sensed something in his opponent give in, something in his soul break. He didn't pause. This was battle, and there was only victory or death.

Though Rufus had dropped his defenses, Jack prepared a meteor and struck. It met Rufus's chest, digging him deeper into the ground. White marble chips whipped up. Jack struck again, hitting Rufus in the head, the chest, the abdomen, the legs.

One meteor followed another until they became a fierce rain. Jack could no longer feel his arms, but he had to keep punching. He screamed until he tore his throat, his arms never stopping. Purple lit up the white plaza, and it kept going, faster and faster.

The impacts of his Meteor Punches kept him afloat over his opponent, counteracting gravity. Rufus had stopped defending, but the meteors kept falling. A dozen blows, two dozen. They shoved him deep into the marble, burying him under a rain of violence.

Jack realized Rufus had lost consciousness. He could stop attacking.

He'd won. But if he stopped, Rufus would recover. He would return to kill Jack, his people, and his allies. Jack couldn't let that happen.

He would kill Rufus Emberheart. Right here, right now.

He accelerated, screaming out his soul. The people around them only saw a flurry of meteors slam down, shaking the entire island. Slowly, they realized what was happening. Their faces went pale as they ran away.

"Stop!" a shout came from the skies. The Planetary Overseer understood Jack's resolve a beat too late, but she still had time to save Rufus. Her Dao came crashing down.

"Wait!" a second voice thundered. Master Shol appeared in the sky above Jack, arms spread apart. His Dao poured out until his form was so transparent it was barely visible.

The lioness's Dao tore through his. It drowned his spectral body, ripping it apart in an instant.

"Hold!" a third voice came as another figure appeared to block her Dao. It was the ascetic of Barren High, and though he didn't release his Dao, his gaze was aimed deep into her eyes. "In the name of Barren High, stop!"

The lioness gritted her teeth. Her Dao screeched to a halt just before his face like a storm of daggers—every second was precious.

"What are you *doing*?" she roared, unleashing her full majesty. "This wasn't part of the deal! Get out of the way!"

"I cannot do that," the ascetic replied, not moving an inch. The lioness's eyes widened like saucers. She had to save Rufus. But no matter what, she could not afford to offend the Barren High.

She was forced to watch helplessly as Jack pulverized her nephew before her very eyes. She engraved this memory deep into her heart. In her long life, she'd never been so humiliated.

Jack smashed down Meteor Punch after Meteor Punch. He could sense Rufus's body giving in, his bones breaking, his skull caving, his organs puncturing and breaking apart.

He kept going, using everything he had to make sure Rufus never stood up again. The meteors kept falling. This was the strongest attack he'd ever unleashed.

"Meteor Shower!" he screamed. It wasn't a skill, merely a name that bubbled out of him. He screamed again, this time incoherently.

There was beauty in his violence. Each meteor had a purple tail filled with tiny stars, making his meteor shower a lightshow second to none. They were fireworks aimed at the ground and filling the sky with their splendor, almost making the watchers forget that there was someone buried under those meteors.

Even Dao-infused bodies had their limits.

Jack ran out of steam. Rufus was an unrecognizable puddle of blood and grime buried deep into the marble. Even his chain mail had been ground to nothing.

Jack had obliterated a favored scion of the Animal Kingdom. Publicly. In front of the entire planet. This was a slap to the face unlike any other, and even the Planetary Overseer had been forced to watch.

He collapsed next to the large crater he'd made, completely spent. Maintaining consciousness was the most he could do, laying face-up on the marble.

For a moment, everyone watched mutedly. Then, a lone figure pushed its way through the crowd. It was bleeding and panting, heavily injured, but its hand was topped by four wolverine-like claws.

"Hey, bud," Gan Salin said, approaching Jack. "Nice fight. I wish I didn't have to kill you. But, I do. So, yeah, goodbye."

He was so hurt that his movements were slow and weak, but Jack couldn't even move. All he could do was watch as the claws came for his throat—

And a brown shape flew in out of nowhere, slapping them off-course.

"What?" Gan Salin exclaimed, looking to the side. Coincidentally, that was where Jack's eyes were directed, too.

A pack of dogs emerged from the alleys, running full tilt. There were dozens of them. And at the very front, riding a black dog larger than any other, was Brock, hurtling another piece of poop at Gan Salin.

"Wha—" Salin jumped back to defend, but by then, the dogs had reached him. They growled and snarled as they jumped on him. Ordinarily, he could have easily cut this pack apart, but he was heavily injured.

"Whaaa!" he shouted, raising his hands and struggling to defend against the dogs. One jumped and chomped down on his forearm. Another got his leg. The teeth of dogs shouldn't have been able to pierce his body, but somehow, they managed.

The dogs ignored Jack, who simply watched from the ground. He noticed they all seemed... muscular, for lack of a better word.

I must be dreaming, he concluded.

Brock arrived then. He jumped off his dog, flew over the pack, and punched Gan Salin in the cheek with all his power, sending the canine to the floor, where the dogs piled on him.

"Shoo, shoo!" The smarter merchants were already rushing over, trying to kick the dogs away. They could never have saved Rufus Emberheart, but if they simply watched a heavily injured scion get torn apart by a pack of wild dogs, they would be summarily executed!

Jack didn't watch that little fight. Two strong arms grabbed him under the shoulders. Brock slinged him on his back like a sack of potatoes and ran through the plaza. Jack wanted to tell him to go to the teleporter, but he couldn't even open his mouth.

Through the crowd, he thought he saw the Sage winking.

"Happy travels, my friend," the Sage's voice rang inside his head. "We will meet again soon."

Jack tried to respond. He already owed the Sage so much. *Thank you...* he thought back.

"No need!" the Sage's voice rang again, oddly cheery. "If you want to thank anyone, thank the Black Hole Church! And remember your favors!"

Before Jack could consider the implications of those words, Brock slammed a door open, and they were inside a building. The walls were dark and painted with stars like the night sky. Brock carried him inside a column of cyan light.

Jack could barely think anymore. *System, hide my titles...* he managed to order, taking a final precaution.

He then watched as Brock squinted, probably at a System screen detailing several destinations. The brorilla made an annoyed face and jammed a finger into the air, picking a choice at random.

*That's not how you—*Jack thought. In the next moment, the room around him disappeared, and he was hurtling through space. Rivers of stars filled his vision. It was the most beautiful thing he'd ever seen—and it was filled with the promise of adventure.

He was in the galaxy.

The story will continue in Road to Mastery, Book 2!

THANK YOU FOR READING ROAD TO MASTERY

We hope you enjoyed it as much as we enjoyed bringing it to you. We just wanted to take a moment to encourage you to review the book. Follow this link: Road to Mastery to be directed to the book's Amazon product page to leave your review.

Every review helps further the author's reach and, ultimately, helps them continue writing fantastic books for us all to enjoy.

Also in Series:

Road to Mastery
Road to Mastery 2
Road to Mastery 3
Road to Mastery 4

Want to discuss our books with other readers and even the authors? Join our Discord server today and be a part of the Aethon community.

Facebook | Instagram | Twitter | Website

You can also join our non-spam mailing list by visiting www.subscribepage.com/AethonReadersGroup and never miss out on future releases. You'll also receive three full books completely Free as our thanks to you.

Looking for more great LitRPG?

What happens when cultivation meets mad science? *Lu Jie woke up in a world filled with scheming sects, arrogant young masters, and the mad chase for the immortal heavens. He wanted none of it, and soon finds himself beaten bloody in a spar he didn't remember and treated as less than worthless. But his plan to escape the sect is interrupted by an old Alchemist's pills that heal him within moments—a magical cure. These medicines ignite the flame of curiosity to learn true magic in him, rekindling his love of discovery. Lu Jie sets out to study the immutable truths hidden within the world, and soon finds an all new path of cultivation that could take him to the very top. Time to make some drugs... err... "alchemy pills".* ***Don't miss the start of an epic Xianxia Cultivation Series perfect for fans of Beware of Chicken and Cradle. The series features weak-to-strong power progression, a light scientific approach to magic, tons of alchemy, spirit beast companions, and so much more.***

Get The First Law of Cultivation Now!

The surface is frozen. The depths filled with monsters. Can anything survive? *Extreme sub-zero temperatures suffocate the surface. Frozen structures of bygone eras span across massive ice-wastes. And the survivors closely guard any technology rediscovered within them. The only escape from the deadly climate is beneath the surface, but that doesn't mean it's safe... Monstrous machines lurk in the depths. Unhinged demigods war against them, dying over and over, treating it all like a game. The depths themselves shift over time, more contraption than rock. When an expedition into the far uncharted north goes terribly wrong, Keith Winterscar and his father get trapped together in a desperate fight for survival. Stumbling upon an ancient war of titanic scale, the two will need to set their differences aside while they struggle against Gods, legends, and the secrets of the realm that lies below.* ***Don't miss the start of this Progression Fantasy Epic set around a pseudo-medieval society clinging to existence on frozen post-apocalyptic Earth. Impossible odds, weak-to-strong progression, epic battles, scavenged tech, prophecy, magic, and mystery—12 Miles Below has something for everyone. Grab your copy today!***

Get 12 Miles Below Now!